PENGUIN BOOKS

THE PORTABLE KIPLING

Each volume in The Viking Portable Library either presents a representative selection from the works of a single outstanding writer or offers a comprehensive anthology on a special subject. Averaging 700 pages in length and designed for compactness and readability, these books fill a need not met by other compilations. All are edited by distinguished authorities, who have written introductory essays and included much other helpful material.

"The Viking Portables have done more for good reading and good writers than anything that has come along since I can remember."

— Arthur Mizener

Irving Howe was born in New York City and graduated from the City College of New York. He is the author of numerous works of literary criticism and social history, including *Politics and the Novel* (1963), *The Decline of the New* (1969), and *World of Our Fathers* (1976), which won the National Book Award. Among his prizes and awards are the National Institute for Arts and Letters Award and Bollingen, Guggenheim, and MacArthur fellowships. A Distinguished Professor at the City University of New York, Mr. Howe is also the editor of *Dissent* magazine.

THE PORTABLE

KIPLING

*Edited and with an Introduction
by Irving Howe*

PENGUIN BOOKS

PENGUIN BOOKS
Viking Penguin Inc., 40 West 23rd Street,
New York, New York 10010, U.S.A.
Penguin Books Ltd, 27 Wrights Lane, London W8 5TZ
(Publishing & Editorial), and Harmondsworth,
Middlesex, England (Distribution & Warehouse)
Penguin Books Australia Ltd, Ringwood,
Victoria, Australia
Penguin Books Canada Limited, 2801 John Street,
Markham, Ontario, Canada L3R 1B4
Penguin Books (N.Z.) Ltd, 182–190 Wairau Road,
Auckland 10, New Zealand

First published in the United States of America
in simultaneous hardcover and paperback editions by
The Viking Press and Penguin Books 1982
This paperback edition reprinted 1983, 1985, 1986, 1987

LIBRARY OF CONGRESS CATALOGING IN PUBLICATION DATA
Kipling, Rudyard, 1865–1936.
  The portable Kipling.
  (The Viking portable library)
  I. Howe, Irving. II. Title.
PR4851.5.H68   1982b   828'.809   81-15402
ISBN 0 14 015.097 8   AACR2

Printed in the United States of America by
Kingsport Press, Inc., Kingsport, Tennessee
Set in CRT Janson

The Introduction to this book appeared originally in *The New Republic*.

Grateful acknowledgment is made to Doubleday & Company, Inc., for permission to reprint the following selections. From *Rewards and Fairies:* "Brother Square-Toes" and "'A Priest in Spite of Himself'"; copyright 1910 by Rudyard Kipling. From *A Diversity of Creatures:* "As Easy as A.B.C.," "Friendly Brook," "Mary Postgate," and "The Village That Voted the Earth Was Flat"; copyright 1912, 1914, 1915, 1917, by Rudyard Kipling. From *Debits and Credits:* "The Wish House," "The Eye of Allah," and "The Gardener"; copyright 1924, 1926, by Rudyard Kipling. From *Limits and Renewals:* "Dayspring Mishandled" and "The Church That Was at Antioch"; copyright 1928, 1929, by Rudyard Kipling. From *Rudyard Kipling's Verse: Definitive Edition:* "The Veterans," "Cold Iron," "The Recall," "A Charm," "A St. Helena Lullaby," "The Way Through the Woods," "Dane-geld," "The Dutch in the Medway," "Edgehill Fight," "Norman and Saxon," "France," "'For All We Have and Are,'" "My Boy Jack," "The Fabulists," "The Holy War," "MacDonough's Song," "Mesopotamia," "The Benefactors," "The Craftsman," "Epitaphs of the War," and "The Roman Centurion's Song"; copyright 1907, 1909, 1910, 1911, 1913, 1914, 1916, 1917, 1919, 1924, by Rudyard Kipling; and "The Waster"; copyright 1939 by Caroline Kipling.

CONTENTS

~~~~~~~~~~~~~~~~~~~~~~~~~~~~~~~~~~

III. ESSAYS

EDITOR'S INTRODUCTION

"Life as we find it is far too hard for us; it entails too much pain, too many disappointments, impossible tasks. We cannot do without palliative remedies. We cannot dispense with auxiliary constructions. . . ."

Whatever its timeless truth, this passage from *Civilization and Its Discontents* marks Freud as a writer whose vision of things was formed in Europe during the late nineteenth century, a time when men's claims for dominion and hope were shrinking to a hard skepticism. The world, said Max Weber, was starting to grow cold, starting to seem a place indifferent and engulfing, without transcendent options. Beneath the surface of society, violent forces were in motion. Bourgeois optimism was coming to its end. Imperialism was showing signs of inner weakness—"all our pomp of yesterday / Is one with Nineveh and Tyre." The idea of historical twilight was finding its way into the work of writers holding almost every opinion.

We know by now that these apprehensions of terrible things to come were justified. Life had indeed become too hard, with too much pain and too many impossible tasks; a predicament for which the twentieth century would soon find its inimitable remedies.

These were not, of course, the images and feelings that were first evoked by Kipling's work when he started publishing in the 1880s. Encountering his stories of Indian life, with their high, even garish coloring, Kipling's early readers delighted in his crude energy, his air of manly assertion, his ration of exotica, his touches of "barbarism"

which seemed so bracing to a culture suspecting itself of
decadence. It was precisely his "difference" that brought
Kipling a quick and enormous popularity, enchanting
even such unlikely admirers as Henry James and Oscar
Wilde. Later generations, with the presumed advantages
of historical distance, have been much more inclined to
place Kipling in the moral setting of his time, as a writer
who shared with Freud, as with many others, a deepening
anxiety over the fate of civilization.

These two quite different men, starting from quite different premises of belief, shared—together with many of
their contemporaries—a growing skepticism about the life
of Europe, the durability of civilization, the future of the
human enterprise. They shared a persuasion that civilization, if it was to survive at all, would require strict modes
of discipline. Freud spoke gloomily of "repression" and its
costs; Kipling wrote that "for the pain of the soul there is,
outside God's Grace, but one drug; and that is a man's
craft, learning, or other helpful motions of his mind." And
perhaps because they did take so uncompromising a view
of the cost in repression that we pay for every advantage
of civilization, both men appreciated—Kipling drew his
best work out of—those yearnings we all have to cast
away the commands of authority and somehow return to
the freedom and comeliness of childhood.

Both Freud and Kipling were inclined to see religion
primarily as a mode of social discipline, an order and sol-
ace for the chafings of self-denial. Kipling did not theorize
about this, but his feelings come through in a number of
stories. "The Church That Was at Antioch," a late story,
is a sophisticated, occasionally biting account of primitive
Christianity, with Peter and Paul not saintly presences
but decidedly human figures not yet able to contain the
enthusiasms of their coarse followers. Civilization rests
here largely with the hard, skeptical Romans. In "The
Eye of Allah," a charming story, Kipling shows religion
in its disciplinary narrowness, holding back the sci-

entific enthusiasms of Roger Bacon, checking the spirit of inquiry on behalf of social peace. Civilization requires here an acceptance of irksome constraints.

Both Freud and Kipling placed a heavy emphasis on the role of aggression in the human economy. For Kipling it was a theme so urgent it sometimes escaped his control. And both Freud and Kipling could not suppress a recurrent shudder before the final emptiness of things, a pang of dismay before the helplessness of man and the feebleness of his comforts. "When a man has come to the turnstiles of Night, all the creeds in the world seem to him wonderfully alike and colorless." The words are Kipling's, but they could stand as an epigraph for *Civilization and Its Discontents.*

Kipling is a writer with an astonishing variety of voices, some of them livelier and others more shallow than Freud's stoical gravity. Nor is Kipling the sort of writer who envelops one with a large, harmonious vision of life which, if only in the experience of reading, seems sufficient as a reading of experience. He often breaks, or breaks down, into a multiplicity of selves, and one of the problems critics have faced with him has been to align these selves with one another. Still, to notice the anxiety at the center of his work is to make possible a singling out of that portion of his work which remains valuable. It is to rescue him a little from his reputation as bullyboy of empire, declaimer of manliness, preening toughie of combat.

For it is the second-rate Kipling who has survived best in common memory, partly because of the pugnacity with which he broadcast his opinions, partly because the literary public has cherished its antipathy to his ideas. That antipathy I largely share. Kipling the tub-thumper for imperialism; Kipling the trumpeter for what Edmund Wilson has called "the Anglo-Spartan code of conduct"; Kipling the celebrant of brutality as an education in manliness; Kipling the authoritarian scoffer at democracy (in

this respect far from alone among the writers of his time);
Kipling the baiter of "brittle intellectuals / Who crack beneath a strain"; Kipling the little chap with thick spectacles who loves to cozy up to strong men as if to show the
world how readily they accept him—all of these dominate
the inferior work and sometimes blemish the superior.

Kipling did not have a supple or reflective mind. He had
only a small gift for self-doubt and not much more for
contemplativeness. Only occasionally could he show that
largeness of spirit we like to associate with the greatest
writers. His work keeps dropping to a display of values
likely to repel civilized readers.

And yet ... He was blessed with a rare abundance of
natural talent. As early as 1891 Henry James was calling
him a genius and Oscar Wilde slyly modifying that ver-
dict to "a genius who drops his aspirates." Leave aside for
the moment the later and more difficult Kipling, sufficiently aspirated, a brilliant if unacknowledged fellow
traveler of literary modernism. It is the early Kipling, the
one people think they know, who solicits astonishment,
not only in his own day but among such later writers as
Brecht and Hemingway, Babel and Borges.

The early Kipling glows with gifts of a primary bright-
ness. He gathers up details of Indian life that are completely fresh to English literature. He knows intuitively
how to prod and halt a narrative so that it will pulse with
tension—as in the wonderful "The Man Who Would Be
King," written in his early twenties. His language is
strong but not yet sufficiently modulated, perhaps because
at his age literary intelligence cannot keep pace with such
exceptional gifts. Anyone opening himself to these early
Indian stories—"The Strange Ride of Morrowbie Jukes,"
"The Story of Muhammad Din," "Lispeth," "Without
Benefit of Clergy"—must be struck by the sheer energy of
rendering. Kipling's gifts break past an evident crudeness
of mind and many falsities of taste. Sometimes—and here
criticism must retire baffled—they are gifts that reveal

themselves *through* Kipling's crudeness of mind and falsities of taste. For Kipling is one of the great performers of English literature, in this respect, at least, a successor to Dickens. These brightly colored early stories must always raise in one's mind uneasy questions about the relation between literature as spectacle and literature as vision, questions about how to value works in which the spectacle is far more striking than the vision is steady.

The matter is more complicated still. There is not a single one of Kipling's deplorable values that is not balanced in his work by a countervalue. The Blimpish authoritarianism of a story like "The Head of the District" is subtly controverted by the savoring of free personality in "The Miracle of Purun Bhagat." The schoolboy coarseness of *Stalky & Co.* is matched by delicacy of feeling in the treatment of such diverse characters as English soldiers in "Black Jack," ailing old ladies in "The Wish House," and a wide assortment of Indians, both Hindu and Muslim, in *Kim* and the stories. The brutality of some war poems is overshadowed by the compassion of a story like "The Gardener," as well as by a number of poems that speak unaffectedly about the suffering of soldiers. And the sidling up to established power is complicated by solidarity with plebeian victims, as in the stories from the underrated *Soldiers Three* and such poems as "Harp Song of the Dane Women" and "The Last of the Light Brigade."

Throughout his lifetime Kipling was savaged by liberals who could see only his faults and praised by jingoes who found comfort in his posturings. It has taken time to sort things out, and the job is by no means finished—for there are stories and poems in which the detestable values and undeniable talents interweave so completely that one is at a loss for a secure response. By and large, however, Kipling's career seems to confirm the truth of Yeats's observation that "we make out of the quarrel with others rhetoric, but of the quarrel with ourselves poetry." Kipling's best work—I take it to be *Kim*, parts of *Soldiers Three* and *The Jungle Books*, perhaps a dozen stories and two dozen poems—constitute a quarrel of inner self with outer mind, of precarious sensibility with blunt opinions. His enduring work was written apart from—it was written despite and sometimes against—his asserted beliefs.

A specter haunted Kipling's imagination, the specter of a breakdown of authority: at first the authority of public life, but in his later work that of private life as well. His fear showed itself in, or hid behind, a persistent brooding over the *problem* of authority, what it could legitimately signify, how it might be justified in the world, and through which devices one might learn to bear it as a weight upon one's nerves. This brooding, given Kipling's childhood and adolescent quaverings before adult commands, was frequently inseparable from a readiness to prostrate himself before authority or to crouch beside it— a desire to be "in" with the powers of this world.

The problem of authority is of course another name for the problem of civilization: what we make of the structure of relationships and institutions, values and traditions, by which we live. Kipling's idea of civilization was largely a Roman one: discipline, command, and upon need, sacrifice. Whenever Kipling felt reasonably at peace with this idea, he wrote well—though not at his very best. Whenever he felt threatened by the barbarians without and intellectuals within, he wrote badly. Except perhaps in fictions meant simply as entertainments, such as "Brugglesmith" and "Brother Square-Toes," Kipling would struggle with the problem of authority throughout his career. In his early stories, where precisely his confused responses as an Anglo-Indian proved to be extremely fruitful, there is often a barely overheard rumination or questioning: By what rationale do we yield power to others? How is it that others hold legitimate power over us? What if the long-silent and lowly were now to rise up in anger? Such questions cast their shadow over stories about Indian life so brilliant on the surface as "The Man Who Would Be King," "The Strange Ride of Morrowbie Jukes," and "The Miracle of Purun Bhagat."

This troubling shadow has been felt by a number of Kipling's critics, and by no one more brilliantly—though, still, not with complete justice—than W. H. Auden. In a 1943 review Auden asked himself, "What is it that makes Kipling so extraordinary?" and he answered:

> ... while virtually every other European writer since the fall of the Roman empire has felt that the dangers threatening civilization came from *inside* that civilization ... Kipling is obsessed by a sense of danger threatening from *outside*.
>
> Others have been concerned with the corruption of the big city, the *ennui* of the cultured mind; some sought a remedy in a return to Nature, to childhood, to Classical Antiquity.... In Kipling there is none of this, no nostalgia for a Golden Age, no belief in Progress. For him civilization (and consciousness) is a little citadel of light surrounded by a great darkness full of malignant forces and only maintained through the centuries by everlasting vigilance, will-power and self-sacrifice.

Keen as this surely is, it suggests that Auden knew mostly the young Kipling, since later the idea is strongly present that the dangers threatening civilization also come from within. In any case, Kipling is a writer intensely conscious of how thin is the crust of civilization, how easily that crust can be broken, and how unrelenting are the pressures, both social and psychic, that would break through.

Authority for Kipling means the proper use of command. It is rendered proper by selflessness, the wish to serve and the readiness to work. It gains support from the accumulated traditions that form the very soil of civilization:

> Dear-bought and clear, a thousand year,
> Our fathers' title runs.
> Make we likewise their sacrifice,
> Defrauding not our sons.

These lines may not set hearts beating wildly, especially in America today; but they merit respect. They body forth whatever strength Kipling can give to his case for authority, an earned and measured conservatism that has reckoned the costs of civilization and takes them to be worth paying.

It is out of this moderate conservatism—the best Kipling's mind (though not his imagination) could do—that he built his notion of "the Law" in *The Jungle Books*. As declaimed, sometimes with an amusing pedanticism, by Baloo the Bear and Bagheera the Panther, this code does at times approach the simplicities of the Boy Scout Pledge. But when realized in conduct by these stately creatures of the jungle, it lays down guidelines for civilized life making possible social fairness, restraint of appetite, respect for others. "The Law," so to say, is the oversoul of the fallible laws that human beings enact—this notion comes to us from the measured, the bearable Kipling. His greatest work is something else again.

What I'll call here the "official" Kipling seems always driven by some need to overstress; some urge to demonstrate his loyalty, even submissiveness, before authority; some wish to show, probably to himself most of all, that he is "in solid" with the commanders of the world, a friend of lords and admirals, a pal of all those experts, professionals, and Englishmen (three categories that melt into one) to whom authority belongs by right. Overassertive and clubbily eager, this Kipling can be quite ugly. The question of what authority means slides too readily into a celebration of those who happen to possess it.

Some of Kipling's critics, notably Edmund Wilson, have argued that this aspect of his work forms a compensation for a traumatic childhood and unhappy adolescence, in both of which—as a nearsighted, fragile, and bookish boy—he was made to feel that he belonged to the ill-fated, the hopelessly clumsy. That Kipling suffered a great deal in childhood seems indisputable. When his parents shipped him at the age of six from India to England, there to board at "the House of Desolation" (as he later called it) with a mean-hearted "Auntie," the results were damaging. When he went off later to a second-rate school for the sons of impoverished army officers, he was made into a butt of jokes. But to what extent these early troubles account for his later need to ingratiate himself with figures of authority, becoming thereby a psychic source of his mature opinions, there is no way of determining with certainty.

It's only fair to add that in his fascination with authority Kipling shows no interest whatever in profit or power, those motives that a later, disenchanted age would see as the underlying design of imperialism. He is touchingly innocent of debunking theories. It is the *claims* of imperialism that grip him, the claims of service and construction. And because he takes these claims with much seriousness, he can show—what at times must have been true—that there were numerous English administrators in India who also took seriously the code of service. (Indeed, in Kipling's devotion to the technocrats and soldiers who "get things done" he can be quite savage with the idle rich, "flanneled fools at the wicket and muddied oafs at the goal.") When Kipling describes the readiness of a certain kind of Anglo-Indian to work and sacrifice, often under conditions of hardship, we can respond with at least partial assent. We think, Well, there's more to it than *that*;

but still, that's how it must have felt to them. When Kipling exploits his innocence about the economic grounds and moral wrongs of imperialism, then we can no longer suspend disbelief and find ourselves doing what sophisticated readers have been told not to do: we find ourselves "arguing" with works of fiction.

But how hard, in truth, do we now "argue"? Not quite with the heat, I think, that his work would have aroused several decades ago. Perhaps time does have some healing powers. Perhaps, as W. H. Auden wrote, because it "Worships language and forgives / Everyone by whom it lives," "Time . . . with this strange excuse / Pardon[s] Kipling and his views." The gradual fading of the British Empire into history has made those views seem less urgent than they were forty or fifty years ago. The political issues raised by Kipling's Indian stories, though still troubling, are slowly fading into the historical background, and the way is now clearer for the vibrancy of Kipling's language, the richness of his imaginings. And there is still another way in which history has come to Kipling's rescue. What has replaced imperialism has often been something much worse, the totalitarian blight of fascism or Communism—though it's worth adding that this blight has one of its sources in imperialism. Our sense of social disaster has been "cultivated" in these recent decades to an extent that not even the most stringent of Kipling's contemporary critics could have foreseen; so that the nastiness, a real nastiness, of "The Head of the District" seems almost mild by comparison with what our century has finally shown of mankind's capacities.

Kipling is not always an apologist for authority; far from it. He often depicts authority—the powers that make laws which must fall short of "the Law"—as harsh, brutal, unseeing, stupid. In one part of himself Kipling is a realist who does not draw back from the ugliness of the world. Authority can damage vulnerable clerks; authority can bully damaged soldiers; authority can torment helpless children. Authority can be blind and gross and cruel. Nobody knows or shows this better than Kipling.

There is still, however, another Kipling whom his writings ask us to imagine—shy, gentle, an enchanting figure, closely in touch with his childhood self, the little Ruddy who grew up speaking Hindustani, language of his "inferiors," until he was six. What stirs Kipling's imagination is a fantasy of the happy suspension, even evasion, of authority. He seems a cousin to a number of nineteenth-century American writers, notably Twain and the young Melville, who also find their creative powers stimulated by visions of a harmonious life, friendly and fraternal, in which no one can, or need, hold power over anyone else.

And this I take to be the great Kipling: a poet of odd sublimities and patches of transcendence, who yields himself to the voices of the helpless. He appears fully in *Kim*,* but is also visible in some of the stories and poems. By the time he reaches his last writings Kipling can no more sustain his visions of bliss than Twain or Melville could sustain theirs; but like Melville, if not Twain, he settles on a stubbled plain of compassion, writing stories like "The Wish House" and "The Gardener," which indicate, if not a resolution of, then a human resignation before the problem of authority, the quandary of civilization.

That sense of evil which for cultivated people has become a mark of wisdom and source of pride—indeed, the very sun of their sunless world—is not a frequent presence in the pages of *Kim*; and when it does appear, it can rarely trouble us with either its violence or its grasp. We

---

* Which, unfortunately, could not be included in this volume, simply because there was not enough space. To have included *Kim* would have meant to reduce sharply the number of Kipling stories, many of which, unlike *Kim*, are by no means readily available. But I have written a few words about *Kim*, since otherwise there would be no possibility of understanding Kipling's place and achievement as a writer.

are inclined these days to exalt the awareness of evil into a kind of appreciation. We find it hard to suppose that a serious writer could turn his back upon the malignity at the heart of things. But *Kim* is unsubdued by the malignity at the heart of things. Whatever evil it does encompass tends to be passed off onto a troop of bumbling Russian spies who muddle along on the northern borders of India, stage-comic Russians about as alarming as Laurel and Hardy. *Kim* is at ease with the world, that unregenerate place which is the only one most of us know, and because at ease, it can allow itself to slide toward another possible world.

Kim evokes and keeps returning to sensations of pleasure, a pleasure regarded as easy, natural, and merited. The pleasure of *Kim* is of a traditional and unproblematic kind, a pleasure in the apprehension of things as they are, in embracing a world as enchanting as it is flawed. Kipling's book accepts the world's body, undeterred by odors, bulges, wrinkles, scars. *Kim*, though far from an innocent book, takes delight in each step of the journey bringing us closer to the absurd: delight in our clamor, our foolishness, our vanity, our senses, and—through the lumbering radiance of the lama who comes from and goes back to the hills of Tibet—delight in an ultimate joy of being which beckons from the other side of sensuous pleasure but which, implies Kipling, all who are not lamas would be advised to seek through pleasure.

Part of the pleasure that *Kim* engages is that of accepting, even venerating sainthood, without at all proposing to surrender the world, or even worldliness, to saints. *Kim* embraces both worlds, that of the boy and that of the lama, the senses and beyond, recognizing that anyone who would keep a foot, or even a finger, in both of these worlds must have some discipline in adjustment and poise—otherwise, what need would there be for the lama's or any other serious education? But never for a moment does the book propose to smudge the difference between the senses and beyond, or worse still, to contrive some facile synthesis. The "Wheel of Things," to which we are all bound in this world, and the "Search," by which we may penetrate another, have each its claim and dignity. The two speed along in parallel, but what they signify cannot readily be merged. There is earth, there is spirit, both are real. In any case, a writer open to the allurements of pleasure is more likely to explore the Many than strain toward the One.

When Kim first meets the lama, an ungainly rhapsodist who makes transcendence seem a familiar option, the two of them quickly find common ground. They share a meal; they bound their territory; they match prospects for the future. To the boy, the old man represents a new experience, a guru such as the mainland does not yield; for the old man, the boy is a guide through the bewilderments of India and a friend ripening into a *chela*, or disciple. Kim is possessed by the evidence of his senses, the lama knows only what lies beyond them, and the book will make as its central matter an unfolding of the love between the two, that grace of friendship which in nineteenth-century literature comes to replace the grace of God.

Kim and the lama move through a world that is like a vast, disorderly bazaar. People are quick to embrace and to anger. They speak suddenly from the heart, as if any traveler may be a friend. They curse with the expertness of centuries. ("Father of all the daughters of shame and husband of ten thousand virtueless ones, thy mother was devoted to a devil, being led thereto by her mother. . . .") Running errands for Mahbub Ali, the freethinking Afghan horse trader who initiates him into the British secret service, Kim charms a fierce-tongued old Indian lady into helping him and the lama. (The old lady is straight in the line of Chaucer, from one pilgrimage to another.) Kim trades stories with retired soldiers, jests with travelers, even pokes a little tender fun at his lama—for this is Kim's world, a stage for his multiple roles as urchin, beggar, raconteur, flirt, apprentice spy, and apprentice *chela*, who is always eager, as Kipling shrewdly notes, for "the visible effect of action." Picked up by some British soldiers who propose to educate him ("sivilize," says Huck), Kim tells the lama: "Remember, I can change swiftly." It is the motto of every youth trying to evade the clamp of civilization.

And the world's evil? The poverty, injustice, caste rigidities which must have been so grinding in the India of eighty or ninety years ago? The book has no assured answers. All the wrongs and evils of India are there, steeped in the life of the people; yet these do not keep them from grasping the sensations of their moment, or from experiencing the appetites and ceremonies they rightly take to be their due. What so wonderfully distinguishes Kipling's characters is their capacity for shifting from treble to bass, from pure spirit to gross earth, from "the Search" to "the Game." It is as if their culture actually enables them to hold two ideas in their heads at once. They make life for themselves, and it has its substance.

Though in much of his work Kipling shows a quite sufficient awareness of evil, even at some points an obsessive concern, he seems really to want to persuade us through *Kim,* his most serious book, that in the freshness of a boy's discoveries and the penetration of an old man's vision, evil can become ultimately insignificant, almost as nothing before the unsubdued elation of existence, almost as nothing before the idea of moral beauty. Others, long before Kipling, have said as much, though few have embodied it with the plastic vividness that Kipling has. We may not entirely grasp the import of this vision of ultimate goodness or harmony; it can seem a kind of moral slope, very slippery, very attractive. Yet in reading *Kim* one yields to its vision, just as upon meeting a saint one might for a moment come to accept beatitude. Nor should we try to get round the problem by remarking that *Kim* is a children's book. For it seems intolerable that the best things in life should be supposed available only to children. Old bones have their rights, too.

The India of the late nineteenth century is the richest presence in Kipling's work. He approaches India as a stepson, but scrutinizes it from the distance of a stranger. He is the kind of stranger who yields his heart, forever, and then must leave. He makes his India one of the enduring "places" of the literary imagination.

India for Kipling is at once the cradle of remembered happiness and the site of the Other, dark and unknown. Kipling loves the overlapping amiability of traditional Indian life, its talkativeness, its casual friendliness and noise. He loves the sudden shifts from metaphysics to gossip, from timeless reflection to sharp trading. He loves the range of figures, warrior and beggar, saint and picaro. Life in India seems to run more thickly, clotting into habits that can be relished insofar as they are simply assumed. The traditional and the day-to-day, the religious and the commonplace, the temple and the market—all entrance the young Kipling, this stranger who makes himself at home. By comparison the ways of the English seem thin, nervous, lacking in blood. And the mind of this Kipling has not yet turned hard, or his voice shrill; even his prejudices—after all, he is still an Anglo-Indian—have a speckle of charm.

Being a newspaperman in his youth teaches Kipling to write incisively, if sometimes also glibly. It teaches him to find an interest in small doings, intrigues at distant hill stations, the eruptions of modest lives. Toward his fellow Anglo-Indians he is respectful, knowing, critical. They don't really like him, or know what to make of him, since they sense that no matter how often he runs up the flag, his very enterprise carries a touch of the subversive. Toward the people of India he is affectionate, sometimes condescending, at best prayerfully loving. Sketches such as "Lispeth," "Jews in Shushan," and "The Story of Muhammad Din" fill out his picture of India. Historically accurate? A literary refraction? Suffice it to say that no one before or after has done it so well, with such ambivalent kinship.

There are deeper Indian stories, such as "Without Benefit of Clergy," wistful in its treatment of a destroyed love between an English official and an Indian girl. Here Kipling writes with a lyrical quaver, honoring the readiness of his lovers to cross the barriers between the two peoples while never calling into question the rightness of the barriers themselves—oddly like some Faulkner stories in *Go Down, Moses*.

Very strange is the story, "The Strange Ride of Morrowbie Jukes," of an English engineer who stumbles into a frightful crater in which there live starved natives, hardly human anymore, feeding off crows. Jukes finds a companion in an old Brahmin, Gunga Dass, who mocks the Englishman with lines more telling than Kipling may have known: "We are now a Republic, Mr. Jukes." Angus Wilson, in his fine biography of Kipling, is surely right to say that this expressionist fiction is "one of the most powerful nightmares of the precariousness of a ruling group, in this case of a group haunted by memories of the [Indian] mutiny not yet twenty years old." So, too, if in a somewhat different way, is "The Man Who Would Be King" haunted by images of dispossession, the perils awaiting those who are too presumptuous in their grasping of power.

As imaginative renderings of an unfamiliar world, the early Indian stories still keep their vitality and charm. It is in the sense of history that they are weak, at the point where Kipling's fear for the survival of authority gets in his way. Intuitively he foresees the end of empire, but intellectually he will not let himself foresee another India. The step he cannot finally take is the one that E. M. For-

ster does take in *Passage to India*, when Aziz tells Field-
ing, "We shall drive every blasted Englishman into the
sea, and then . . . you and I shall be friends."

I propose now to glance at just a few of Kipling's short
fictions in order to see how he develops in them his char-
acteristic themes and concerns.

The Jungle Books present a sedate conservative idyll in
the form of animal fables. We encounter the mild pleasures of a reasonable order of hierarchy, spoiled only by
the occasional misbehavior of the tiger, Shere Khan.
(Someone has to misbehave.) The wild child Mowgli is
apprenticed to the schoolmasterish Baloo the Bear and
Bagheera the Panther—they teach him civilization as a
norm of nature. In turn, Mowgli will go back to the
human fold and reassert man's dominion.

The best of these stories move both "above" and "beneath" the conservative idyll. "Toomai of the Elephants"
is a lively Indian boy who works with his father as an elephant tender, and the story has for its spine an affectionate
rendering of pleasure in work:

> What Little Toomai liked was to scramble up bridle-
> paths that only an elephant could take; the dip into
> the valley below; the glimpses of the wild elephants
> browsing miles away; the rush of the frightened pig
> and peacock under Kala Nag's [the elephant's] feet
> . . . the steady, cautious drive of the wild elephants,
> and the mad rush and blaze and hullaballoo of the
> last night's drive. . . .

The story then moves past the lyricism of work, toward
a transcendent moment which stirs the deepest layers of
Kipling's imagination. Because he has not yet been defiled
by adult judgments, Little Toomai is privileged to witness
one night the great elephant dance, a hidden ceremony at
which the tamed elephants slip away, meet secretly in the

jungle, and plunge into a joyous stamping dance, a ceremony of return. The boy's nocturnal visit becomes an initiation, as the men in the camp salute his experience:

> And the big brown elephant-catchers, the trackers and drivers and ropers, and the men who know all the secrets of breaking the wildest elephants, passed him from one to the other, and they marked his forehead with blood from the breast of a newly killed jungle-cock, to show that he was a forester. . . .

The boy's vision of the dance points to everything beyond order, beyond hierarchy, beyond "the Law."

As if in direct brooding contrast, "The King's Ankus," one of Kipling's masterpieces, moves into the darkness where greed and folly rule. As with "Toomai," the story begins on a note of sedate contentment, Mowgli playing in mock-battle with his friend Kaa the Rock Python. "What more can I wish?" Mowgli asks himself. "I have the Jungle, and the favor of the Jungle! Is there more anywhere between sunrise and sunset?"

The answer comes when Kaa takes Mowgli to the Cold Lairs, where an ancient cobra guards a mass of glittering objects. It is the treasure of old kings who have long turned to dust, "the sifted pickings of centuries of war, plunder, trade and taxation" which the cobra faithfully, mindlessly guards. Mowgli does not even trouble to take the gold or jewels; he wants only the golden ankus, or elephant goad, that has attracted his eye. The story ends with the death of several men inflamed to greed by the golden ankus and Mowgli's glad return of it to the cave. Saved by Kaa and Bagheera, his wise jungle friends, Mowgli has had his first taste of evil, in the glittering murderousness of the Cold Lairs.

The animal fable is one of Kipling's happiest genres, since his flaws of brashness and smartness are largely absent here and the balance between skill and moral judgment is all but perfect. Here, too, the problem of authority is handled with ease, as a hurdle to be overcome in behalf of ecstasy, in "Toomai of the Elephants," and as a discipline against the "bestiality" of men, in "The King's Ankus."

There is a similar ease—the writer at ease with his own feelings—in the lovely story called "The Miracle of Purun Bhagat." We meet Purun Dass, minister of a semi-independent native state, who seems entirely capable of managing responsibility; but overnight he takes up "the begging-bowl and ochre-colored dress of a Sunnyasi or holy man," to become Purun Bhagat. Toward his old life of authority "he bore . . . no more ill-will or good-will than a man bears to a colorless dream of the night." He wanders to the foothills of the Himalayas, where he settles into a rock cell:

> He had come to the place appointed for him—the silence and the space. After this, time stopped, and he, sitting at the mouth of the shrine, could not tell whether he were alive or dead; a man with control of his limbs, or a part of the hills. . . . He would repeat a Name softly to himself a hundred hundred times, till, at each repetition, he seemed to move more and more out of his body, sweeping up to the doors of some tremendous discovery. . . .

The spell does not last. Purun Bhagat must leave his cell to warn nearby villagers of an impending avalanche, thereby reverting to his old posture of authority, "no longer a holy man, but . . . a man accustomed to command, going out to save life." When he dies from this effort, the villagers see him again as a holy man, building a temple in his honor but never knowing that "the saint of their worship is the late Sir Purun Dass." A momentary balance is struck here between the way of the world and the way of contemplation, so that authority takes on an almost "natural" character, to be discarded at the edge of bliss and reassumed at the edge of peril.

Finally, let us turn to a story very different in kind, "As Easy as A.B.C.," Kipling's venture into utopian and/or antiutopian fiction, a tour de force at once brilliant and malignant, but creating out of itself a countercharm to its malignancy. The story is set in the year 2065; the world is ruled peacefully by the benevolent "Aerial Board of Control," with representatives from all the leading countries.

There is peace, but also, in the benighted province of Chicago, upheaval. A tiny group of malcontent intellectuals, "the Serviles," refuses adjustment to the new order and tries to return to the old ways of holding meetings and raising slogans about "popular government." The people of Chicago, incensed at this "crowd-making and invasion of privacy," threaten to exterminate the Serviles. To restore peace the Aerial Board flies to Chicago, uses a ray to paralyze briefly protesters and antiprotesters, and decides—for Kipling *is* clever—to transport the archaic democrats to the London music halls, where they can amuse civilized people with their rantings about votes and participation.

That Kipling feels a considerable sympathy with the authoritarian thrust of this story, seems beyond dispute. Yet what must also strike any careful reader, lending the story an undertow of despair, is the fact, as Angus Wilson remarks, that the narrative "contradicts the proposition of the technological paradise it purports to portray. For it is only in this moment of breakdown, in this unexpected visit of the pestilence of disagreement and conflict in this perfect world that Kipling's imagination can work upon it."

The members of the Aerial Board, decent enough technocrats, are beset by self-doubt, even nostalgia for the days when "the Planet [had] ... Crowds and the Plague. . . ." They yearn for a time when there were still "heroes." One of them, cowering before the (harmless) rays, makes the telling admission: "Pardon! I have never seen Death." The poor Serviles at least "raged, they stormed, they palpitated, flushed and exhausted their poor, torn nerves, panted themselves into silence, and renewed the senseless, shameless attacks." These are the misfits of tomorrow—and who is to say that simply in his prediction Kipling is wrong? But the Serviles "weep aloud, shamelessly—always without shame." So sly and insidious is this story, one has to remind oneself that these wretches are human beings, by our lights the only ones in the world of 2065 as projected by Kipling. They have feelings, they believe in personal voices, even if at the cost of the gentlemanly tyranny, the silky authority, that has come to rule the world.

Kipling's later stories—which means roughly those written after about 1905—have in recent years won an increasing critical reputation; some of these stories are indeed masterpieces, though it is by no means a settled judgment that they are superior to the fiction set in India.

The later stories are, in Henry James's phrase, elaborately "done." They are full of complicated observation and ingenious plotting. Kipling's themes now become veiled, diffused, mixed. The theme of authority, for example, is largely shifted from public to private relationships, and as it comes to be treated in more subtle ways, in a voice no longer ringing with assurance, it also acquires unexpected emotional resonance, strange breakthroughs of feeling. Anger, hatred, and revenge manifest themselves in devious, sometimes unpleasant ways. The later Kipling often seems an uncentered writer, without that obsessive relation to subject or place which can be a writer's blessing. He seems also a deracinated figure, despite his enormous prestige in English society and his association with the political leaders of the "radical right." Yet his craft, already formidable, grows still finer; he becomes a master of one of the purest English prose styles—incisive, flexible, a model of what might be called the demotic middle-style. Curiously, he also picks up many of the devices, and fragments of the sensibility, we associate with literary modernism. Though without sympathy for its declared ends, he comes intuitively to share the modernist stress upon doubt, division, anxiety, and depression—in short, upon the problematic. The First World War has a shattering impact on Kipling, not only because he loses a son in battle but also because it becomes clear to him, as to many others of his generation, that the world he has known and loved is rapidly disappearing. There are times when he still yields to his smoldering rancors and aggressions, but other times when—in an effort at self-transcendence that seems genuinely admirable—he breaks into a moment of peace, a phrase of forgiveness. A remarkable virtuoso, he emerges at the end as a writer fractured but enlarged.

These later stories are sometimes marred by a tremulous spirituality, a hovering over otherworldly emanations, which Kipling makes more of than he can do with. They are also marred by an excess of "technique," beyond any visible need in the material at hand. It's as if Kipling were struggling to grasp perceptions beyond his usual reach, or his virtuosity were spinning off freely on its own. The much-admired "Mrs. Bathurst," for example, tends to reduce its matter to a puzzle; for while it is easy enough to discern Kipling's intended theme—the destructiveness of overreaching love—few readers are likely to be clear in their minds about the way the story's conclusion realizes this theme.

But a handful of Kipling's late stories rank with the great short fictions of our century, if not quite with those of Joyce and Lawrence, then certainly with those of Hemingway and Flannery O'Connor. Both "The Wish House" and "The Gardener" graze perfection. They show the mature Kipling as master of English plebeian settings and figures, but more important, as a sensibility matured and ripened, one that has worked its way out of the traps of enmity and touched compassion. "Friendly Brook," also a story of English plebeian life, though this time in the countryside, strongly recalls Hardy in its folk-like matching of naturalist detail and a touch of the eerie. And the tour de force "Dayspring Mishandled" figures crucially in the Kipling canon as evidence of a struggle against hardened judgments; in this instance, a struggle to shed earlier dispositions toward the savoring of revenge.

Revenge, or some emotion like it, forms the substance of "Mary Postgate," a story dated 1915 (the date signifies) and perhaps the single most brilliant piece of short fiction Kipling ever wrote. It is worth stopping for a moment with this story, since it brings to high focus the problems we repeatedly encounter in reading Kipling,

Wizened, undemanding, lifeless, Mary Postgate works as a "companion" to a wealthy woman in an English village. Whatever stopped-up emotions Mary Postgate has, she pours out in a blind adoration for the son of the house. The First World War breaks out; the boy joins the air force and is killed on a trial flight; there follows a raid by German planes over a nearby village, where Mary witnesses the death of a child from a bomb's explosion. Still without speech or visible emotion, she goes about the business of burning the clothes of the beloved son. "As she lit the match that would burn her heart to ashes, she heard a groan or a grunt behind the dense Portugal laurels." It comes from a downed German airman, badly wounded, begging for help. Pistol in hand, Mary refuses—with the wrenched, memorable German words "Ich haben der todt Kinder gesehn." The German boy dies.

But that is not all. More terrible even than Mary Postgate's refusal to help is the relish with which she attends his death. "She gave herself up to feel. Her long pleasure was broken by a sound that she had waited for in agony several times in her life. She leaned forward and listened, smiling. There could be no mistake. She closed her eyes and drank it in."

This savage story creates a lasting disturbance in the

mind. At the very least, it is an astonishing portrait of a gnarled consciousness reaching assertion through hatred. Mary Postgate's spasm of hatred as "she drank it in" comes to seem, in some deeply perverse way, a break-through into sentience, a moment of orgasmic discovery. Where the customary pattern of nineteenth-century fiction had proposed growth through understanding, Kipling offers here growth through an exertion of brutality.

Now, if we choose to take Kipling as properly distanced from his character, as the narrative voice simply observing Mary Postgate's dreadful climax, there are no serious difficulties and we can simply admire the brilliance of his representation. But can we really suppose him properly distanced?

I see no way of denying that Kipling lends a grim, despairing assent (not at all a savoring) to Mary's terrible refusal. I say "grim, despairing" because the perverse pleasure that Mary takes in being present at the German boy's death agony may be the price that has to be paid for making the decision not to help him. And that decision Kipling seems to have meant as a surrogate for a collective English response to German "barbarism" in the war. It is a terrible reply, of course, and by showing the moral and psychic deformation that accompanies it ("she ... drank it in"), Kipling refuses to make things easy for himself. He acknowledges the price; but it is a price, he implies, that is necessary for the defense of civilization.

Leave aside the question whether Kipling was right in his understanding of the First World War; that is not crucial to our problem here. Surely he knew the traditional moral argument against revenge, that it corrupts the agent without repairing his loss. Indeed, the dreadful ending is there to show this process of corruption. Yet, if I read the story correctly, Kipling seems to be suggesting that the moral argument against revenge may have to be suspended (not rejected) in order to summon the primitive, uncivilized energies which in extreme circumstances are needed for defending civilization. And for him, a lover of children all his life, the fact that a child can be killed from the air is a clear sign that the old, familiar world, the one in which revenge would be condemned, is gravely threatened and that new, intolerable responses are needed.

For a civilized reader, trained to place a high value on compassion, the story is very painful. Does not one's sense of humanity require a moral repudiation of its underlying idea even as one acknowledges the skill with which Kipling has written? Yes; such a repudiation comes directly, quickly. And yet ... We must search our inner hearts, asking whether that is all we feel about the story, asking whether Kipling has not had the courage to open up responses we find it prudent not to acknowledge. May not, in extreme circumstances, the inconceivable become conceivable? And may it not then become satisfying?

History adds a brutal complication. Suppose (only a few details would have to be changed) we were to transpose this story to the Second World War and see the fallen German flyer with, or even without, an SS armband. Would we then remain quite so eager to condemn Mary Postgate's shameful act?

Some readers may feel that I have abstracted the problem of the story too much from the story itself; but I would reply that precisely the success of Kipling's rendering forces the problem squarely upon us. Others may say that modern civilization has indeed sunk very low for this kind of problem to take on the cogency that it apparently has. To which there is no answer but a weary assent.

There is a common recognition that Kipling's poetry occupies an uncomfortable, even odd place in the course of recent English literature. It is difficult to connect Kipling's poetry with most of the poetry written by his contemporaries, and it is foolish to dismiss his poetry because of that difficulty.

It's reasonable to suppose that a good many of the people picking up this book will be sophisticated readers more or less at ease with Yeats and Eliot, Stevens and Auden, perhaps Cavafy and Montale. Such readers may be tempted to say about Kipling's poetry, "But it's not poetry," quite as an earlier generation said the same about the work of Yeats and Eliot. Yet both Yeats and Eliot, especially the latter, had a healthy appreciation of Kipling's poetry, and Eliot in a famous essay struggled manfully to grasp its distinctive character by calling it "verse" rather than "poetry," while adding that this "verse" at its best takes on the qualities of "poetry." Whether this elaborate maneuver really helped much is a question, since Eliot entangled himself in a confusion between "poetry" as description of kind and "poetry" as attribution of value.

Written at a time when the greatest English poets were turning inward, toward contemplative allusion and indirection, Kipling's poetry constitutes a public art. It is thereby sharply distinct from most of the poetry we cherish. Kipling's poetry is immediately accessible—or so it seems—to reasonably literate people, though in fact a closer scrutiny will often reveal the kind of textual intricacy relished by modern critics and readers: sudden bits of ambiguous heightened speech, phrasings that surprise through multiplicity of suggestion, subtle and even sly variations in refrains.

Kipling's verse is public in that it deals with communal and plebeian life in its large, rough outlines, taking for granted the continued vitality of the commonplace, refusing intuitively all variants of the "wasteland" vision. Famous or once-famous poems such as "Mandalay" and "Danny Deever" differ from most English poetry of the last century not only in their language and rhythms but, at least as important, in the modes of life they find absorbing. There is still, in Kipling, some remnant of the idea of a common culture, in which poet and soldier, poet and plebeian may find a shared feeling.

Kipling's poetry constitutes a public act in still another way: it draws much of its metrical arrangement and rhythmic strength from the popular culture of late-nineteenth-century England, the songs sung in music halls and the tunes of universally known hymns. There is some—but not nearly enough—scholarly literature on this matter, for instance, a few pages by Kipling's first biographer, Charles Carrington, which have a tone of authority. Carrington writes:

> Kipling went into barrooms and barrack-rooms and music-halls to find out the songs the people were really singing, and fitted new words to them. The tunes they knew best were hymn-tunes, and after that the range of popular songs, largely American in origin, that arose about the time of the Civil War and are still not forgotten—such songs as "John Brown's Body," "Marching Through Georgia," and "Tramp, tramp, tramp, the boys are marching," the songs that the boys had shouted in chorus at Westward Ho! Then there were the music-hall ditties, as strongly traditional as the evangelical hymns. At the end of the century, "The Man that Broke the Bank at Monte Carlo," and "Knocked 'em in the Old Kent Road," were the direct successors of "Vilikins and his Dinah" which dated back to the beginning of it. Since childhood Kipling had been fascinated by the London music-halls—too much fascinated, his father thought—and when he returned to London in 1889 he told a friend that he found them more satisfying than the theatre. During his lonely year in London his solace was Gatti's, the same music-hall which Sickert was to "discover" and depict in another medium a few years later. The *Barrack-Room Ballads* essentially are songs for the "Halls" in which the "patter" dominates the musical setting.

Carrington proceeds to link "Danny Deever" with popular soldiers' songs of the time. This is illuminating, but most such observations remain tantalizingly general, and more work remains to be done.

There is also a point in noticing Kipling's debt to (or kinship with) Sir Walter Scott and Robert Burns; but it may be useful here to suggest that Kipling was doing something with his ballads more original than has commonly been supposed. Bertolt Brecht, the sophisticated, even decadent left-wing German dramatist and poet, admired Kipling enormously and borrowed from him heavily. One of Brecht's biographers, Martin Esslin, provides a clue: "The same impulse that drove [Brecht] from the drab respectability of provincial society to the vagabonds among the poets, street entertainers, and fair-ground comics also made Brecht dream of the wide, wide world he found in Kipling's *Barrack-Room Ballads*. There too he met a vigorous plebeian language—spiced with delicately exotic names of places and things that breathed an air of boundless freedom and adventure."

What Brecht recognized in Kipling—and without worrying at all about their political differences (they did share a contempt for liberalism)—was that Kipling had not just drawn from or been merely influenced by the traditional ballad. Kipling *transformed* the ballad. Kipling made it into something closely linked with the plebeian life and demotic language of the twentieth century; something that smacked of smoky cities and rough army camps rather than farm and village; something that had the crude but invigorating beat of contemporary culture; something that escaped the depressiveness of naturalism by treating the plebes not so much as victims (though that, too, occasionally) but as figures of energy, humor, and irony; something, in short, of this time, this place. Irony is an important term here, the usually affectionate, sometimes abrasively distancing irony that Kipling brought to his songs.

Kipling, then, recreated the voice of the balladeer, giving it his own idiosyncratic accent in place of traditional anonymity. There is, of course, some continuity with the traditional ballad; but there is a break, too. Kipling was perhaps the first of a number of twentieth-century writers to do this: others include Brecht, who gave the Kipling-esque ballad a satiric-didactic turn and a nihilist under-current, and the Yiddish poet Itsik Manger, who wrote ballads desacralizing Biblical stories by setting them in a commonplace *shtetl.* All of these writers make of the ballad something new, a kind of personal, yet not introspective, poetry.

There are at least two other genres in which Kipling excelled as poet. One is the hymnlike declamation, open to the charge of sententiousness, but sometimes redeemed by a genuine sincerity of supplication. The famous "Reces-sional," which stirred all of England with its confession of imperial guilt and plea for some redemptive touch at a moment before the ebbing of power, is an impressive ex-ample. The refrain of "Lest we forget—lest we forget!" makes this poem not at all the jingo hymn that careless readers have seen in it, but a kind of public apologia, a half-atonement for the misuse of power and the arrogance of office:

> The tumult and the shouting dies;
>   The Captains and the Kings depart:
> Still stands Thine ancient sacrifice,
>   An humble and a contrite heart.
> Lord God of Hosts, be with us yet,
> Lest we forget—lest we forget!

And then there are Kipling's epigrams, a form which, except in the skilled contemporary hands of J. V. Cun-ningham, has not much flourished in the twentieth cen-tury. Kipling is not always successful with this form, perhaps because he lacks the complete focusing of vi-sion—a focusing purchased at a price—which this form demands. But here are two of his successful epigrams:

THE COWARD
I could not look on Death, which being known,
Men led me to him, blindfold and alone.

THE BEGINNER
On the first hour of my first day
In the front trench I fell.
(Children in boxes at a play
Stand up to watch it well.)

Apart from these forms, Kipling seems an oddly decen-
tralized sort of poet, one who tries his hand at almost
everything, shows his skill at almost everything, but then
flits on impatiently. There are many influences, briefly
accepted and then dropped; there are many ventures into
verse forms, often accomplished with virtuoso finish but
not persisted in. (Kipling admired engineers; sometimes
he seems to have regarded himself as an engineer of
verse.) "Harp Song of the Dane Women" opens with
lines that bear the clear, rich imprint of Hardy:

What is a woman that you forsake her,
And the hearth-fire and the home-acre,
To go with the old grey Widow-maker?

There is an equally clear imprint from Browning in the
form of Kipling's two dramatic monologues, "McAndrew's Hymn" and "The 'Mary Gloster.'" There are
surprises like "A Charm," in which Kipling writes as if he
had been reading Auden before Auden wrote:

Take of English earth as much
As either hand may rightly clutch.
In the taking of it breathe
Prayer for all who lie beneath.
. . . .
Lay that earth upon thy heart,
And thy sickness shall depart!

Finally, we have to say that while Kipling succeeds in doing a wide range of unexpected things in his poetry, the main interest of his career as poet lies with his popular work, the ballads preeminently and then the hymnlike verses.

I have been making high claims for Kipling in the hope that my reader, his reading done, will find them largely justified. But an honest appraisal must also speak of limits, and that means ending with a recognition that in the main Kipling cannot be placed among the very greatest writers of the modern era. He is not in the company of Chekhov and Melville, Joyce and Proust, Eliot and Lawrence.

This is not for lack of skill. Kipling's prose is a superbly vigorous and supple instrument; his imaginings or fables are usually cogent and frequently vivid. Yet some element is too often missing. One does not feel regularly in reading Kipling the presence of an enlarging, liberating sensibility. One does not encounter a world view embracing at once the glories and shames of humanity and reconciling us, insofar as we can be, to the limits of our existence. Nor does one meet a mind which, agree with its conclusions or not, changes deeply and forever our way of looking at the world. Yet, in the portion of his work that lives, there are both peaks of greatness and extended plateaus of high accomplishment. There are intimations of a harmonious life short of the corruptions of maturity, and when Kipling reaches these, his work can rightly be called sublime. And, as with every writer, he must be read and remembered for his best work.

William Hazlitt writes that upon first hearing Coleridge speak he felt as if he had been witness to "Truth and Genius embraced." It isn't an embrace that occurs very often, in literature or anywhere else; now and again it did in Kipling's work, enough so to make him precious in our eyes.

IRVING HOWE

CHRONOLOGY WITH
DATES OF
MAJOR PUBLICATIONS*

~~~~~~~~~~~~~~~~~~~~~~~~~~~~~~~~~~

1865   Born December 30, in Bombay, India. First child
       of John Lockwood and Alice MacDonald Kipling.
1868   Birth of sister Alice, known as Trix.
1872   Sent with sister to live in Southsea, England.
1877   To United Services College, Devon, a boarding
       school for children of Anglo-Indians.
1882   Returns to India. Journalism in Lahore.
1886   Publication of *Departmental Ditties* (poems).
1888   *Plain Tales from the Hills* (stories); *Soldiers
       Three* (stories).
1889   Returns to England, settles in London.
1890   *The Light That Failed* (novel).
1891   *Life's Handicap* (stories).
1892   *Barrack-Room Ballads* (poems).
1892   Marries Caroline Balestier, an American. Move to
       Brattleboro, Vermont.
1894   *The Jungle Book; The Second Jungle Book* pub-
       lished in 1895.
1896   *The Seven Seas* (poems).
1896   Returns to England.
1897   *Captains Courageous* (novel).
1899   Death of daughter, Josephine, at the age of seven.

_____

* Dates given in the text refer to each work's first appearance,
whether in periodical or book form; those in the Chronology refer to
complete volumes.

1901   *Kim* (novel).

1902   Moves to Burwash, Sussex.

1902   *Just So Stories.*

1904   *Traffics and Discoveries* (stories).

1906   *Puck of Pook's Hill* (stories).

1907   Receives Nobel Prize, the first English-language laureate.

1910   *Rewards and Fairies* (stories).

1915   Death of son, John, in World War I.

1917   *A Diversity of Creatures* (stories).

1919   *The Years Between* (poems).

1926   *Debits and Credits* (stories).

1932   *Limits and Renewals* (stories).

1936   Dies on January 18, in London. Buried in Westminster Abbey.

Stories

Stories of India

THE STRANGE RIDE OF MORROWBIE JUKES

Alive or dead—there is no other way.
Native Proverb

There is no invention about this tale. Jukes by accident stumbled upon a village that is well known to exist, though he is the only Englishman who has been there. A somewhat similar institution used to flourish on the outskirts of Calcutta, and there is a story that if you go into the heart of Bikanir, which is in the heart of the Great Indian Desert, you shall come across not a village but a town where the Dead who did not die but may not live have established their headquarters. And, since it is perfectly true that in the same Desert is a wonderful city where all the rich money-lenders retreat after they have made their fortunes (fortunes so vast that the owners cannot trust even the strong hand of the Government to protect them, but take refuge in the waterless sands), and drive sumptuous C-spring barouches, and buy beautiful girls and decorate their palaces with gold and ivory and Minton tiles and mother-o'-pearl, I do not see why Jukes's tale should not be true. He is a Civil Engineer, with a head for plans and distances and things of that kind, and he certainly would not take the trouble to invent imaginary traps. He could earn more by doing his legitimate work. He never varies the tale in the telling, and grows very hot and indignant when he thinks of the disrespectful treatment he received. He wrote this quite straightforwardly at first, but he has touched it up in places and introduced Moral Reflections: thus:—

In the beginning it all arose from a slight attack of fever. My work necessitated my being in camp for some months between Pakpattan and Mubarakpur—a desolate sandy stretch of country, as every one who has had the misfortune to go there may know. My coolies were neither more nor less exasperating than other gangs, and my work demanded sufficient attention to keep me from moping, had I been inclined to so unmanly a weakness.

On the 23rd December, 1884, I felt a little feverish. There was a full moon at the time, and, in consequence, every dog near my tent was baying it. The brutes assembled in twos and threes and drove me frantic. A few days previously I had shot one loud-mouthed singer and suspended his carcass *in terrorem* about fifty yards from my tent-door, but his friends fell upon, fought for, and ultimately devoured the body: and, as it seemed to me, sang their hymns of thanksgiving afterwards with renewed energy.

The light-headedness which accompanies fever acts differently on different men. My irritation gave way, after a short time, to a fixed determination to slaughter one huge black-and-white beast who had been foremost in song and first in flight throughout the evening. Thanks to a shaking hand and a giddy head, I had already missed him twice with both barrels of my shot-gun, when it struck me that my best plan would be to ride him down in the open and finish him off with a hog-spear. This, of course, was merely the semi-delirious notion of a fever-patient; but I remember that it struck me at the time as being eminently practical and feasible.

I therefore ordered my groom to saddle Pornic and

bring him round quietly to the rear of my tent. When the pony was ready, I stood at his head prepared to mount and dash out as soon as the dog should again lift up his voice. Pornic, by the way, had not been out of his pickets for a couple of days; the night air was crisp and chilly; and I was armed with a specially long and sharp pair of persuaders with which I had been rousing a sluggish cob that afternoon. You will easily believe, then, that when he was let go he went quickly. In one moment, for the brute bolted as straight as a die, the tent was left far behind, and we were flying over the smooth sandy soil at racing speed. In another we had passed the wretched dog, and I had almost forgotten why it was that I had taken horse and hog-spear.

The delirium of fever and the excitement of rapid motion through the air must have taken away the remnant of my senses. I have a faint recollection of standing upright in my stirrups, and of brandishing my hog-spear at the great white Moon that looked down so calmly on my mad gallop; and of shouting challenges to the camel-thorn bushes as they whizzed past. Once or twice, I believe, I swayed forward on Pornic's neck, and literally hung on by my spurs—as the marks next morning showed.

The wretched beast went forward like a thing possessed, over what seemed to be a limitless expanse of moonlit sand. Next, I remember, the ground rose suddenly in front of us, and as we topped the ascent I saw the waters of the Sutlej shining like a silver bar below. Then Pornic blundered heavily on his nose, and we rolled together down some unseen slope.

I must have lost consciousness, for when I recovered I was lying on my stomach in a heap of soft white sand, and the dawn was beginning to break dimly over the edge of the slope down which I had fallen. As the light grew stronger I saw I was at the bottom of a horseshoe-shaped crater of sand, opening on one side directly on to the shoals of the Sutlej. My fever had altogether left me, and, with the exception of a slight dizziness in the head, I felt no bad effects from the fall over night.

Pornic, who was standing a few yards away, was naturally a good deal exhausted, but had not hurt himself in the least. His saddle, a favourite polo one, was much knocked about, and had been twisted under his belly. It took me some time to put him to rights, and in the meantime I had ample opportunities of observing the spot into which I had so foolishly dropped.

At the risk of being considered tedious, I must describe it at length, inasmuch as an accurate mental picture of its peculiarities will be of material assistance in enabling the reader to understand what follows.

Imagine then, as I have said before, a horseshoe-shaped crater of sand with steeply-graded sand walls about thirty-five feet high. (The slope, I fancy, must have been about 65°.) This crater enclosed a level piece of ground about fifty yards long by thirty at its broadest part, with a rude well in the centre. Round the bottom of the crater, about three feet from the level of the ground proper, ran a series of eighty-three semicircular, ovoid, square, and multilateral holes, all about three feet at the mouth. Each hole on inspection showed that it was carefully shored internally with drift-wood and bamboos, and over the mouth a wooden drip-board projected, like the peak of a jockey's cap, for two feet. No sign of life was visible in these tunnels, but a most sickening stench pervaded the entire amphitheatre—a stench fouler than any which my wanderings in Indian villages have introduced me to.

Having remounted Pornic, who was as anxious as I to get back to camp, I rode round the base of the horseshoe to find some place whence an exit would be practicable. The inhabitants, whoever they might be, had not thought fit to put in an appearance, so I was left to my own devices. My first attempt to 'rush' Pornic up the steep sand-banks showed me that I had fallen into a trap exactly on the same model as that which the ant-lion sets for its prey. At each step the shifting sand poured down from above in tons, and rattled on the drip-boards of the holes like small shot. A couple of ineffectual charges sent us both rolling down to the bottom, half choked with the torrents of sand; and I was constrained to turn my attention to the river-bank.

Here everything seemed easy enough. The sand-hills ran down to the river edge, it is true, but there were plenty of shoals and shallows across which I could gallop Pornic, and find my way back to *terra firma* by turning sharply to the right or the left. As I led Pornic over the sands I was startled by the faint pop of a rifle across the river; and at the same moment a bullet dropped with a sharp '*whit*' close to Pornic's head.

There was no mistaking the nature of the missile—a regulation Martini-Henry 'picket.' About five hundred yards away a country-boat was anchored in midstream; and a jet of smoke drifting away from its bows in the still morning air showed me whence the delicate attention had come. Was ever a respectable gentleman in such an *impasse?* The treacherous sand slope allowed no escape from a spot which I had visited most involuntarily, and a promenade on the river frontage was the signal for a bombardment from some insane native in a boat. I'm afraid that I lost my temper very much indeed.

Another bullet reminded me that I had better save my breath to cool my porridge; and I retreated hastily up the sands and back to the horseshoe, where I saw that the noise of the rifle had drawn sixty-five human beings from the badger-holes which I had up till that point supposed to be untenanted. I found myself in the midst of a crowd of spectators—about forty men, twenty women, and one child who could not have been more than five years old. They were all scantily clothed in that salmon-coloured cloth which one associates with Hindu mendicants, and, at first sight, gave me the impression of a band of loathsome *fakirs*. The filth and repulsiveness of the assembly were beyond all description, and I shuddered to think what their life in the badger-holes must be.

Even in these days, when local self-government has destroyed the greater part of a native's respect for a Sahib, I have been accustomed to a certain amount of civility from my inferiors, and on approaching the crowd naturally expected that there would be some recognition of my presence. As a matter of fact, there was; but it was by no means what I had looked for.

The ragged crew actually laughed at me—such laughter I hope I may never hear again. They cackled, yelled, whistled, and howled as I walked into their midst; some of them literally throwing themselves down on the ground in convulsions of unholy mirth. In a moment I had let go Pornic's head, and, irritated beyond expression at the morning's adventure, commenced cuffing those nearest to me with all the force I could. The wretches dropped under my blows like nine-pins, and the laughter gave place to wails for mercy; while those yet untouched clasped me round the knees, imploring me in all sorts of uncouth tongues to spare them.

In the tumult, and just when I was feeling very much ashamed of myself for having thus easily given way to my temper, a thin, high voice murmured in English from behind my shoulder: 'Sahib! Sahib! Do you not know me? Sahib, it is Gunga Dass, the telegraph-master.'

I spun round quickly and faced the speaker.

Gunga Dass (I have, of course, no hesitation in mentioning the man's real name) I had known four years before as a Deccanee Brahmin lent by the Punjab Government to one of the Khalsia States. He was in charge of a branch telegraph-office there, and when I had last met him was a jovial, full-stomached portly Government servant with a marvellous capacity for making bad puns in English—a peculiarity which made me remember him

long after I had forgotten his services to me in his official
capacity. It is seldom that a Hindu makes English puns.

Now, however, the man was changed beyond all recognition. Caste-mark, stomach, slate-coloured continuations,
and unctuous speech were all gone. I looked at a withered
skeleton, turbanless and almost naked, with long matted
hair and deep-set codfish-eyes. But for a crescent-shaped
scar on the left cheek—the result of an accident for which
I was responsible—I should never have known him. But it
was indubitably Gunga Dass, and—for this I was thankful—an English-speaking native who might at least tell me
the meaning of all that I had gone through that day.

The crowd retreated to some distance as I turned towards the miserable figure and ordered him to show me
some method of escaping from the crater. He held a
freshly-plucked crow in his hand, and in reply to my
question climbed slowly on a platform of sand which ran
in front of the holes, and commenced lighting a fire there
in silence. Dried bents, sand-poppies, and driftwood burn
quickly; and I derived much consolation from the fact that
he lit them with an ordinary sulphur match. When they
were in a bright glow, and the crow was neatly spitted in
front thereof, Gunga Dass began without a word of pre-
amble:—

'There are only two kinds of men, Sar. The alive and
the dead. When you are dead you are dead, but when you
are alive you live.' (Here the crow demanded his attention
for an instant as it twirled before the fire in danger of
being burnt to a cinder.) 'If you die at home and do not
die when you come to the ghât to be burnt, you come
here.'

The nature of the reeking village was made plain now,
and all that I had known or read of the grotesque and
the horrible paled before the fact just communicated
by the ex-Brahmin. Sixteen years ago, when I first landed
in Bombay, I had been told by a wandering Armenian of

the existence, somewhere in India, of a place to which such Hindus as had the misfortune to recover from trance or catalepsy were conveyed and kept, and I recollect laughing heartily at what I was then pleased to consider a traveller's tale. Sitting at the bottom of the sand-trap, the memory of Watson's Hotel, with its swinging punkahs, white-robed servants, and the sallow-faced Armenian, rose up in my mind as vividly as a photograph, and I burst into a loud fit of laughter. The contrast was too absurd!

Gunga Dass, as he bent over the unclean bird, watched me curiously. Hindus seldom laugh, and his surroundings were not such as to move him that way. He removed the crow solemnly from the wooden spit and as solemnly devoured it. Then he continued his story, which I give in his own words:—

'In epidemics of the cholera you are carried to be burnt almost before you are dead. When you come to the riverside the cold air, perhaps, makes you alive, and then, if you are only little alive, mud is put on your nose and mouth and you die conclusively. If you are rather more alive, more mud is put; but if you are too lively they let you go and take you away. I was too lively, and made protestation with anger against the indignities that they endeavoured to press upon me. In those days I was Brahmin and proud man. Now I am dead man and eat'—here he eyed the well-gnawed breast-bone with the first sign of emotion that I had seen in him since we met—'crows, and—other things. They took me from my sheets when they saw that I was too lively and gave me medicines for one week, and I survived successfully. Then they sent me by rail from my place to Okara Station, with a man to take care of me; and at Okara Station we met two other men, and they conducted we three on camels, in the night, from Okara Station to this place, and they propelled me from the top to the bottom, and the other two succeeded, and I have been here ever since two and a half years. Once I was Brahmin and proud man, and now I eat crows.'

'There is no way of getting out?'

'None of what kind at all. When I first came I made experiments frequently, and all the others also, but we have always succumbed to the sand which is precipitated upon our heads.'

'But surely,' I broke in at this point, 'the river-front is open, and it is worth while dodging the bullets; while at night—'

I had already matured a rough plan of escape which a natural instinct of selfishness forbade me sharing with Gunga Dass. He, however, divined my unspoken thought almost as soon as it was formed; and, to my intense astonishment, gave vent to a long, low chuckle of derision—the laughter, be it understood, of a superior or at least of an equal.

'You will not'—he had dropped the Sir after his first sentence—'make any escape that way. But you can try. I have tried. Once only.'

The sensation of nameless terror which I had in vain attempted to strive against overmastered me completely. My long fast—it was now close upon ten o'clock, and I had eaten nothing since tiffin on the previous day—combined with the violent agitation of the ride had exhausted me, and I verily believe that, for a few minutes, I acted as one mad. I hurled myself against the sand-slope. I ran round the base of the crater, blaspheming and praying by turns. I crawled out among the sedges of the river-front, only to be driven back each time in an agony of nervous dread by the rifle-bullets which cut up the sand round me—for I dared not face the death of a mad dog among that hideous crowd—and so fell, spent and raving, at the curb of the well. No one had taken the slightest notice of an exhibition which makes me blush hotly even when I think of it now.

Two or three men trod on my panting body as they drew water, but they were evidently used to this sort of thing, and had no time to waste upon me. Gunga Dass, indeed, when he had banked the embers of his fire with sand, was at some pains to throw half a cupful of fetid water over my head, an attention for which I could have fallen on my knees and thanked him, but he was laughing all the while in the same mirthless, wheezy key that greeted me on my first attempt to force the shoals. And so, in a half-fainting state, I lay till noon. Then, being only a man after all, I felt hungry, and said as much to Gunga Dass, whom I had begun to regard as my natural protector. Following the impulse of the outer world when dealing with natives, I put my hand into my pocket and drew out four annas. The absurdity of the gift struck me at once, and I was about to replace the money.

Gunga Dass, however, cried: 'Give me the money, all you have, or I will get help, and we will kill you!'

A Briton's first impulse, I believe, is to guard the contents of his pockets; but a moment's thought showed me the folly of differing with the one man who had it in his power to make me comfortable, and with whose help it was possible that I might eventually escape from the crater. I gave him all the money in my possession, Rs. 9-8-5 —nine rupees, eight annas, and five pie—for I always keep small change as *bakshish* when I am in camp. Gunga Dass clutched the coins, and hid them at once in his ragged loin-cloth, looking round to assure himself that no one had observed us.

'*Now* I will give you something to eat,' said he.

What pleasure my money could have given him I am unable to say; but inasmuch as it did please him, I was not sorry that I had parted with it so readily, for I had no doubt that he would have had me killed if I had refused. One does not protest against the doings of a den of wild beasts; and my companions were lower than any beasts. While I ate what Gunga Dass had provided, a coarse *chapatti* and a cupful of the foul well-water, the people showed not the faintest sign of curiosity—that curiosity which is so rampant, as a rule, in an Indian village.

I could even fancy that they despised me. At all events, they treated me with the most chilling indifference, and Gunga Dass was nearly as bad. I plied him with questions about the terrible village, and received extremely unsatis-factory answers. So far as I could gather, it had been in existence from time immemorial—whence I concluded that it was at least a century old—and during that time no one had ever been known to escape from it. (I had to con-trol myself here with both hands, lest the blind terror should lay hold of me a second time and drive me raving round the crater.) Gunga Dass took a malicious pleasure in emphasising this point and in watching me wince. Nothing that I could do would induce him to tell me who the mysterious 'They' were.

'It is so ordered,' he would reply, 'and I do not yet know any one who has disobeyed the orders.'

'Only wait till my servant finds that I am missing,' I re-torted, 'and I promise you that this place shall be cleared off the face of the earth, and I'll give you a lesson in civil-ity, too, my friend.'

'Your servants would be torn in pieces before they came near this place; and, besides, you are dead, my dear friend. It is not your fault, of course, but none the less you are dead *and* buried.'

At irregular intervals supplies of food, I was told, were dropped down from the land side into the amphitheatre, and the inhabitants fought for them like wild beasts. When a man felt his death coming on he retreated to his lair and died there. The body was sometimes dragged out of the hole and thrown on to the sand, or allowed to rot where it lay.

The phrase 'thrown on to the sand' caught my atten-tion, and I asked Gunga Dass whether this sort of thing was not likely to breed a pestilence.

'That,' said he, with another of his wheezy chuckles, 'you may see for yourself subsequently. You will have much time to make observations.'

Whereat, to his great delight, I winced once more and hastily continued the conversation: 'And how do you live here from day to day? What do you do?' The question elicited exactly the same answer as before—coupled with the information that 'this place is like your European heaven; there is neither marrying nor giving in marriage.'

Gunga Dass had been educated at a Mission School, and, as he himself admitted, had he only changed his religion 'like a wise man,' might have avoided the living grave which was now his portion. But as long as I was with him I fancy he was happy.

Here was a Sahib, a representative of the dominant race, helpless as a child and completely at the mercy of his native neighbours. In a deliberate, lazy way he set himself to torture me as a schoolboy would devote a rapturous half-hour to watching the agonies of an impaled beetle, or as a ferret in a blind burrow might glue himself comfortably to the neck of a rabbit. The burden of his conversation was that there was no escape 'of no kind whatever,' and that I should stay here till I died and was 'thrown on to the sand.' If it were possible to forejudge the conversation of the Damned on the advent of a new soul in their abode, I should say that they would speak as Gunga Dass did to me throughout that long afternoon. I was powerless to protest or answer; all my energies being devoted to a struggle against the inexplicable terror that threatened to overwhelm me again and again. I can compare the feeling to nothing except the struggles of a man against the overpowering nausea of the Channel passage—only my agony was of the spirit and infinitely more terrible.

As the day wore on, the inhabitants began to appear in full strength to catch the rays of the afternoon sun, which were now sloping in at the mouth of the crater. They assembled by little knots, and talked among themselves without even throwing a glance in my direction. About four o'clock, so far as I could judge, Gunga Dass rose and dived into his lair for a moment, emerging with a live crow in his hands. The wretched bird was in a most draggled and deplorable condition, but seemed to be in no way afraid of its master. Advancing cautiously to the river-front, Gunga Dass stepped from tussock to tussock until he had reached a smooth patch of sand directly in the line of the boat's fire. The occupants of the boat took no notice. Here he stopped, and, with a couple of dexterous turns of the wrist, pegged the bird on its back with outstretched wings. As was only natural, the crow began to shriek at once and beat the air with its claws. In a few seconds the clamour had attracted the attention of a bevy of wild crows on a shoal a few hundred yards away, where they were discussing something that looked like a corpse. Half a dozen crows flew over at once to see what was going on, and also, as it proved, to attack the pinioned bird. Gunga Dass, who had lain down on a tussock, motioned to me to be quiet, though I fancy this was a needless precaution. In a moment, and before I could see how it happened, a wild crow, who had grappled with the shrieking and helpless bird, was entangled in the latter's claws, swiftly disengaged by Gunga Dass, and pegged down beside its companion in adversity. Curiosity, it seemed, overpowered the rest of the flock, and almost before Gunga Dass and I had time to withdraw to the tussock, two more captives were struggling in the upturned claws of the decoys. So the chase—if I can give it so dignified a name—continued until Gunga Dass had captured seven crows. Five of them he throttled at once, reserving two for further operations another day. I was a good deal impressed by this, to me, novel method of securing food, and complimented Gunga Dass on his skill.

'It is nothing to do,' said he. 'To-morrow you must do it for me. You are stronger than I am.'

This calm assumption of superiority upset me not a little, and I answered peremptorily: 'Indeed, you old ruffian? What do you think I have given you money for?'

'Very well,' was the unmoved reply. 'Perhaps not to-morrow, nor the day after, nor subsequently; but in the end, and for many years, you will catch crows and eat crows, and you will thank your European God that you have crows to catch and eat.'

I could have cheerfully strangled him for this; but judged it best under the circumstances to smother my resentment. An hour later I was eating one of the crows; and, as Gunga Dass had said, thanking my God that I had a crow to eat. Never as long as I live shall I forget that evening meal. The whole population were squatting on the hard sand platform opposite their dens, huddled over tiny fires of refuse and dried rushes. Death, having once laid his hand upon these men and forborne to strike, seemed to stand aloof from them now; for most of our company were old men, bent and worn and twisted with years, and women aged to all appearance as the Fates themselves. They sat together in knots and talked—God only knows what they found to discuss—in low equable tones, curiously in contrast to the strident babble with which natives are accustomed to make day hideous. Now and then an access of that sudden fury which had possessed me in the morning would lay hold on a man or woman; and with yells and imprecations the sufferer would attack the steep slope until, baffled and bleeding, he fell back on the platform incapable of moving a limb. The others would never even raise their eyes when this happened, as men too well aware of the futility of their fellows' attempts and wearied with their useless repetition. I saw four such outbursts in the course of that evening.

Gunga Dass took an eminently business-like view of my situation, and while we were dining—I can afford to laugh at the recollection now, but it was painful enough at the time—propounded the terms on which he would consent to 'do' for me. My nine rupees, eight annas, he argued, at the rate of three annas a day, would provide me with food for fifty-one days, or about seven weeks; that is to say, he would be willing to cater for me for that length of time. At

the end of it I was to look after myself. For a further consideration—*videlicet* my boots—he would be willing to
allow me to occupy the den next to his own, and would
supply me with as much dried grass for bedding as he
could spare.

'Very well, Gunga Dass,' I replied; 'to the first terms I
cheerfully agree, but, as there is nothing on earth to prevent my killing you as you sit here and taking everything
that you have'·(I thought of the two invaluable crows at
the time), 'I flatly refuse to give you my boots and shall
take whichever den I please.'

The stroke was a bold one, and I was glad when I saw
that it had succeeded. Gunga Dass changed his tone immediately, and disavowed all intention of asking for my
boots. At the time it did not strike me as at all strange that
I, a Civil Engineer, a man of thirteen years' standing in the
Service, and, I trust, an average Englishman, should thus
calmly threaten murder and violence against the man who
had, for a consideration it is true, taken me under his
wing. I had left the world, it seemed, for centuries. I was
as certain then, as I am now of my own existence, that in
the accursed settlement there was no law save that of the
strongest; that the living dead men had thrown behind
them every canon of the world which had cast them
out; and that I had to depend for my own life on my
strength and vigilance alone. The crew of the ill-fated *Mi-
gnonette* are the only men who would understand my
frame of mind. 'At present,' I argued to myself, 'I am
strong and a match for six of these wretches. It is impera-
tively necessary that I should, for my own sake, keep both
health and strength until the hour of my release comes—if
it ever does.'

Fortified with these resolutions, I ate and drank as
much as I could, and made Gunga Dass understand that I
intended to be his master, and that the least sign of insub-
ordination on his part would be visited with the only
punishment I had it in my power to inflict—sudden and

violent death. Shortly after this I went to bed. That is to say, Gunga Dass gave me a double armful of dried bents which I thrust down the mouth of the lair to the right of his, and followed myself, feet foremost; the hole running about nine feet into the sand with a slight downward inclination, and being neatly shored with timbers. From my den, which faced the river-front, I was able to watch the waters of the Sutlej flowing past under the light of a young moon and compose myself to sleep as best I might.

The horrors of that night I shall never forget. My den was nearly as narrow as a coffin, and the sides had been worn smooth and greasy by the contact of innumerable naked bodies, added to which it smelt abominably. Sleep was altogether out of the question to one in my excited frame of mind. As the night wore on, it seemed that the entire amphitheatre was filled with legions of unclean devils that, trooping up from the shoals below, mocked the unfortunates in their lairs.

Personally I am not of an imaginative temperament—very few Engineers are—but on that occasion I was as completely prostrated with nervous terror as any woman. After half an hour or so, however, I was able once more to calmly review my chances of escape. Any exit by the steep sand walls was, of course, impracticable. I had been thoroughly convinced of this some time before. It was possible, just possible, that I might, in the uncertain moonlight, safely run the gauntlet of the rifle-shots. The place was so full of terror for me that I was prepared to undergo any risk in leaving it. Imagine my delight, then, when after creeping stealthily to the river-front I found that the infernal boat was not there. My freedom lay before me in the next few steps!

By walking out to the first shallow pool that lay at the foot of the projecting left horn of the horseshoe, I could wade across, turn the flank of the crater, and make my way inland. Without a moment's hesitation I marched briskly past the tussocks where Gunga Dass had snared the crows, and out in the direction of the smooth white sand beyond. My first step from the tufts of dried grass showed me how utterly futile was any hope of escape; for, as I put my foot down, I felt an indescribable drawing, sucking motion of the sand below. Another moment, and my leg was swallowed up nearly to the knee. In the moonlight the whole surface of the sand seemed to be shaken with devilish delight at my disappointment. I struggled clear, sweating with terror and exertion, back to the tussocks behind me, and fell on my face.

My only means of escape from the semicircle was protected with a quicksand!

How long I lay I have not the faintest idea; but I was roused at the last by the malevolent chuckle of Gunga Dass at my ear. 'I would advise you, Protector of the Poor' (the ruffian was speaking English), 'to return to your house. It is unhealthy to lie down here. Moreover, when the boat returns, you will most certainly be rifled at.' He stood over me in the dim light of the dawn, chuckling and laughing to himself. Suppressing my first impulse to catch the man by the neck and throw him on to the quicksand, I rose sullenly and followed him to the platform below the burrows.

Suddenly, and futilely as I thought while I spoke, I asked: 'Gunga Dass, what is the good of the boat if I can't get out *anyhow?*' I recollect that even in my deepest trouble I had been speculating vaguely on the waste of ammunition in guarding an already well protected foreshore.

Gunga Dass laughed again and made answer: 'They have the boat only in daytime. It is for the reason that *there is a way.* I hope we shall have the pleasure of your company for much longer time. It is a pleasant spot when you have been here some years and eaten roast crow long enough.'

I staggered, numbed and helpless, towards the fetid burrow allotted to me, and fell asleep. An hour or so later I was awakened by a piercing scream—the shrill, high-pitched scream of a horse in pain. Those who have once heard that will never forget the sound. I found some little difficulty in scrambling out of the burrow. When I was in the open, I saw Pornic, my poor old Pornic, lying dead on the sandy soil. How they had killed him I cannot guess. Gunga Dass explained that horse was better than crow, and 'greatest good of greatest number is political maxim. We are now Republic, Mister Jukes, and you are entitled to a fair share of the beast. If you like, we will pass a vote of thanks. Shall I propose?'

Yes, we were a Republic indeed! A Republic of wild beasts penned at the bottom of a pit, to eat and fight and sleep till we died. I attempted no protest of any kind, but sat down and stared at the hideous sight in front of me. In less time almost than it takes me to write this, Pornic's body was divided, in some unclean way or other; the men and women had dragged the fragments on to the platform and were preparing their morning meal. Gunga Dass cooked mine. The almost irresistible impulse to fly at the sand walls until I was wearied laid hold of me afresh, and I had to struggle against it with all my might. Gunga Dass was offensively jocular till I told him that if he addressed another remark of any kind whatever to me I should strangle him where he sat. This silenced him till silence became insupportable, and I bade him say something.

'You will live here till you die like the other Feringhi,' he said coolly, watching me over the fragment of gristle that he was gnawing.

'What other Sahib, you swine? Speak at once, and don't stop to tell me a lie.'

'He is over there,' answered Gunga Dass, pointing to a burrow-mouth about four doors to the left of my own. 'You can see for yourself. He died in the burrow as you will die, and I will die, and as all these men and women and the one child will also die.'

'For pity's sake tell me all you know about him. Who was he? When did he come, and when did he die?'

This appeal was a weak step on my part. Gunga Dass only leered and replied: 'I will not—unless you give me something first.'

Then I recollected where I was, and struck the man between the eyes, partially stunning him. He stepped down from the platform at once, and, cringing and fawning and weeping and attempting to embrace my feet, led me round to the burrow which he had indicated.

'I know nothing whatever about the gentleman. Your God be my witness that I do not. He was as anxious to escape as you were, and he was shot from the boat, though we all did all things to prevent him from attempting. He was shot here.' Gunga Dass laid his hand on his lean stomach and bowed to the earth.

'Well, and what then? Go on!'

'And then—and then, Your Honour, we carried him into his house and gave him water, and put wet cloths on the wound, and he laid down in his house and gave up the ghost.'

'In how long? In how long?'

'About half an hour after he received his wound. I call Vishnu to witness,' yelled the wretched man, 'that I did everything for him. Everything which was possible, that I did!'

He threw himself down on the ground and clasped my ankles. But I had my doubts about Gunga Dass's benevolence, and kicked him off as he lay protesting.

'I believe you robbed him of everything he had. But I can find out in a minute or two. How long was the Sahib here?'

'Nearly a year and a half. I think he must have gone mad. But hear me swear, Protector of the Poor! Won't Your Honour hear me swear that I never touched an article that belonged to him? What is Your Worship going to do?'

I had taken Gunga Dass by the waist and had hauled him on to the platform opposite the deserted burrow. As I did so I thought of my wretched fellow-prisoner's unspeakable misery among all these horrors for eighteen months, and the final agony of dying like a rat in a hole, with a bullet-wound in the stomach. Gunga Dass fancied I was going to kill him, and howled pitifully. The rest of the population, in the plethora that follows a full flesh meal, watched us without stirring.

'Go inside, Gunga Dass,' said I, 'and fetch it out.'

I was feeling sick and faint with horror now. Gunga Dass nearly rolled off the platform, and howled aloud.

'But I am Brahmin, Sahib—a high-caste Brahmin. By your soul, by your father's soul, do not make me do this thing!'

'Brahmin or no Brahmin, by my soul and my father's soul, in you go!' I said, and, seizing him by the shoulders, I crammed his head into the mouth of the burrow, kicked the rest of him in, and, sitting down, covered my face with my hands.

At the end of a few minutes I heard a rustle and a creak; then Gunga Dass in a sobbing, choking whisper speaking to himself; then a soft thud—and I uncovered my eyes.

The dry sand had turned the corpse entrusted to its keeping into a yellow-brown mummy. I told Gunga Dass to stand off while I examined it. The body—clad in an olive-green hunting-suit much stained and worn, with leather pads on the shoulders—was that of a man between thirty and forty, above middle height, with light, sandy hair, long moustache, and a rough, unkempt beard. The left canine of the upper jaw was missing, and a portion of the lobe of the right ear was gone. On the second finger of the left hand was a ring—a shield-shaped blood-stone set in gold, with a monogram that might have been either 'B.K.' or 'B.L.' On the third finger of the right hand was a silver ring in the shape of a coiled cobra, much worn and tarnished. Gunga Dass deposited a handful of trifles he had picked out of the burrow at my feet, and, covering the face of the body with my handkerchief, I turned to examine these. I give the full list in the hope that it may lead to the identification of the unfortunate man:—

1. Bowl of a brierwood pipe, serrated at the edge; much worn and blackened; bound with string at the screw.

2. Two patent-lever keys; wards of both broken.

3. Tortoise-shell-handled penknife, silver or nickel, name-plate marked with monogram 'B.K.'

4. Envelope, postmark undecipherable, bearing a Victorian stamp, addressed to 'Miss Mon——' (rest illegible)—'ham'—'nt.'

5. Imitation crocodile-skin notebook with pencil. First forty-five pages blank; four and a half illegible; fifteen others filled with private memoranda relating chiefly to three persons—a Mrs. L. Singleton, abbreviated several times to 'Lot Single,' 'Mrs. S. May,' and 'Garmison,' referred to in places as 'Jerry' or 'Jack.'

6. Handle of small-sized hunting-knife. Blade snapped short. Buck's horn, diamond-cut, with swivel and ring on the butt; fragment of cotton cord attached.

It must not be supposed that I inventoried all these things on the spot as fully as I have here written them down. The notebook first attracted my attention, and I put it in my pocket with a view to studying it later on. The rest of the articles I conveyed to my burrow for safety's sake, and there, being a methodical man, I inventoried them. I then returned to the corpse and ordered Gunga Dass to help me to carry it out to the river-front. While we were engaged in this, the exploded shell of an old brown cartridge dropped out of one of the pockets and rolled at my feet. Gunga Dass had not seen it; and I fell to thinking that a man does not carry exploded cartridge-cases, especially 'browns,' which will not bear loading twice, about with him when shooting. In other words, that cartridge-case had been fired inside the crater. Consequently there must be a gun somewhere. I was on the

verge of asking Gunga Dass, but checked myself, knowing
that he would lie. We laid the body down on the edge of
the quicksand by the tussocks. It was my intention to
push it out and let it be swallowed up—the only possible
mode of burial that I could think of. I ordered Gunga Dass
to go away.

Then I gingerly put the corpse out on the quicksand. In
doing so—it was lying face downward—I tore the frail
and rotten khaki shooting-coat open, disclosing a hideous
cavity in the back. I have already told you that the dry
sand had, as it were, mummified the body. A moment's
glance showed that the gaping hole had been caused by a
gunshot wound; the gun must have been fired with the
muzzle almost touching the back. The shooting-coat,
being intact, had been drawn over the body after death,
which must have been instantaneous. The secret of the
poor wretch's death was plain to me in a flash. Some one
of the crater, presumably Gunga Dass, must have shot
him with his own gun—the gun that fitted the brown cartridges. He had never attempted to escape in the face of
the rifle-fire from the boat.

I pushed the corpse out hastily, and saw it sink from
sight literally in a few seconds. I shuddered as I watched.
In a dazed, half-conscious way I turned to peruse the note-
book. A stained and discoloured slip of paper had been in-
serted between the binding and the back, and dropped out
as I opened the pages. This is what it contained: *'Four out
from crow-clump; three left; nine out; two right; three
back; two left; fourteen out; two left; seven out; one left;
nine back; two right; six back; four right; seven back.'*
The paper had been burnt and charred at the edges. What
it meant I could not understand. I sat down on the dried
bents, turning it over and over between my fingers, until I
was aware of Gunga Dass standing immediately behind
me with glowing eyes and outstretched hands.

'Have you got it?' he panted. 'Will you not let me look
at it also? I swear that I will return it.'

'Got what? Return what?' I asked.

'That which you have in your hands. It will help us both.' He stretched out his long, bird-like talons, trembling with eagerness.

'I could never find it,' he continued. 'He had secreted it about his person. Therefore I shot him, but nevertheless I was unable to obtain it.'

Gunga Dass had quite forgotten his little fiction about the rifle-bullet. I heard him calmly. Morality is blunted by consorting with the Dead who are alive.

'What on earth are you raving about? What is it you want me to give you?'

'The piece of paper in the notebook. It will help us both. Oh, you fool! You fool! Can you not see what it will do for us? We shall escape!'

His voice rose almost to a scream, and he danced with excitement before me. I own I was moved at the chance of getting away.

'Do you mean to say that this slip of paper will help us? What does it mean?'

'Read it aloud! Read it aloud! I beg and I pray to you to read it aloud.'

I did so. Gunga Dass listened delightedly, and drew an irregular line in the sand with his fingers.

'See now! It was the length of his gun-barrels without the stock. I have those barrels. Four gun-barrels out from the place where I caught crows. Straight out; do you mind me? Then three left. Ah! Now well I remember how that man worked it out night after night. Then nine out, and so on. Out is always straight before you across the quicksand to the North. He told me so before I killed him.'

'But if you knew all this why didn't you get out before?'

'I did *not* know it. He told me that he was working it out a year and a half ago, and how he was working it out night after night when the boat had gone away, and he could get out near the quicksand safely. Then he said that we would get away together. But I was afraid that he would leave me behind one night when he had worked it all out, and so I shot him. Besides, it is not advisable that the men who once get in here should escape. Only I, and *I* am a Brahmin.'

The hope of escape had brought Gunga Dass's caste back to him. He stood up, walked about, and gesticulated violently. Eventually I managed to make him talk soberly, and he told me how this Englishman had spent six months night after night in exploring, inch by inch, the passage across the quicksand; how he had declared it to be simplicity itself up to within about twenty yards of the river-bank after turning the flank of the left horn of the horseshoe. This much he had evidently not completed when Gunga Dass shot him with his own gun.

In my frenzy of delight at the possibilities of escape I recollect shaking hands wildly with Gunga Dass, after we had decided that we were to make an attempt to get away that very night. It was weary work waiting throughout the afternoon.

About ten o'clock, as far as I could judge, when the Moon had just risen above the lip of the crater, Gunga Dass made a move for his burrow to bring out the gun-barrels whereby to measure our path. All the other wretched inhabitants had retired to their lairs long ago. The guardian boat had drifted down-stream some hours before, and we were utterly alone by the crow-clump. Gunga Dass, while carrying the gun-barrels, let slip the piece of paper which was to be our guide. I stooped down hastily to recover it, and, as I did so, I was aware that the creature was aiming a violent blow at the back of my head with the gun-barrels. It was too late to turn round. I must have received the blow somewhere on the nape of my neck, for I fell senseless at the edge of the quicksand.

When I recovered consciousness, the Moon was going down, and I was sensible of intolerable pain in the back of my head. Gunga Dass had disappeared, and my mouth was full of blood. I lay down again and prayed that I might die without more ado. Then the unreasoning fury which I have before mentioned laid hold upon me, and I staggered inland towards the walls of the crater. It seemed that some one was calling to me in a whisper—'Sahib! Sahib! Sahib!' exactly as my bearer used to call me in the mornings. I fancied that I was delirious until a handful of sand fell at my feet. Then I looked up and saw a head peering down into the amphitheatre—the head of Dunnoo, my dog-boy, who attended to my collies. As soon as he had attracted my attention, he held up his hand and showed a rope. I motioned, staggering to and fro the while, that he should throw it down. It was a couple of leather punkah-ropes knotted together, with a loop at one end. I slipped the loop over my head and under my arms; heard Dunnoo urge something forward; was conscious that I was being dragged, face downward, up the steep sand-slope, and the next instant found myself choked and half-fainting on the sand-hills overlooking the crater. Dunnoo, with his face ashy gray in the moonlight, implored me not to stay, but to get back to my tent at once.

It seems that he had tracked Pornic's footprints fourteen miles across the sands to the crater; had returned and told my servants, who flatly refused to meddle with any one, white or black, once fallen into the hideous Village of the Dead; whereupon Dunnoo had taken one of my ponies and a couple of punkah-ropes, returned to the crater, and hauled me out as I have described.

1885

THE MAN WHO WOULD
BE KING

~~~~~~~~~~~~~~~~~~~~~~~~~~~~~~~~~~

Brother to a Prince and fellow to a beggar if he be
found worthy.

The Law, as quoted, lays down a fair conduct of life, and
one not easy to follow. I have been fellow to a beggar again
and again under circumstances which prevented either of
us finding out whether the other was worthy. I have still
to be brother to a Prince, though I once came near to kinship with what might have been a veritable King and was
promised the reversion of a Kingdom—army, law-courts,
revenue and policy all complete. But, to-day, I greatly fear
that my King is dead, and if I want a crown I must go
hunt it for myself.

The beginning of everything was in a railway train
upon the road to Mhow from Ajmir. There had been a
Deficit in the Budget, which necessitated travelling, not
Second-class, which is only half as dear as First-class, but
by Intermediate, which is very awful indeed. There are no
cushions in the Intermediate class, and the population are
either Intermediate, which is Eurasian, or native, which
for a long night journey is nasty, or Loafer, which is
amusing though intoxicated. Intermediates do not buy
from refreshment-rooms. They carry their food in bundles and pots, and buy sweets from the native sweetmeat-
sellers, and drink the roadside water. That is why in
hot weather Intermediates are taken out of the carriages
dead, and in all weathers are most properly looked down
upon.

My particular Intermediate happened to be empty till I reached Nasirabad, when a big black-browed gentleman in shirt-sleeves entered, and, following the custom of Intermediates, passed the time of day. He was a wanderer and a vagabond like myself, but with an educated taste for whiskey. He told tales of things he had seen and done, of out-of-the-way corners of the Empire into which he had penetrated, and of adventures in which he risked his life for a few days' food.

'If India was filled with men like you and me, not knowing more than the crows where they'd get their next day's rations, it isn't seventy millions of revenue the land would be paying—it's seven hundred millions,' said he; and as I looked at his mouth and chin I was disposed to agree with him.

We talked politics—the politics of Loaferdom, that sees things from the underside where the lath and plaster are not smoothed off—and we talked postal arrangements because my friend wanted to send a telegram back from the next station to Ajmir, the turning-off place from the Bombay to the Mhow line as you travel westward. My friend had no money beyond eight annas which he wanted for dinner, and I had no money at all, owing to the hitch in the Budget before mentioned. Further, I was going into a wilderness where, though I should resume touch with the Treasury, there were no telegraph offices. I was, therefore, unable to help him in any way.

'We might threaten a Station-master, and make him send a wire on tick,' said my friend, 'but that'd mean enquiries for you and for me, and *I*'ve got my hands full these days. Did you say you were travelling back along this line within any days?'

'Within ten,' I said.

'Can't you make it eight?' said he. 'Mine is rather urgent business.'

'I can send your telegram within ten days if that will serve you,' I said.

'I couldn't trust the wire to fetch him now I think of it. It's this way. He leaves Delhi on the 23d for Bombay. That means he'll be running through Ajmir about the night of the 23d.'

'But I'm going into the Indian Desert,' I explained.

'Well *and* good,' said he. 'You'll be changing at Marwar Junction to get into Jodhpore territory—you must do that—and he'll be coming through Marwar Junction in the early morning of the 24th by the Bombay Mail. Can you be at Marwar Junction on that time? 'Twon't be inconveniencing you because I know that there's precious few pickings to be got out of these Central India States— even though you pretend to be correspondent of the "Backwoodsman." '

'Have you ever tried that trick?' I asked.

'Again and again, but the Residents find you out, and then you get escorted to the Border before you've time to get your knife into them. But about my friend here. I *must* give him a word o' mouth to tell him what's come to me, or else he won't know where to go. I would take it more than kind of you if you was to come out of Central India in time to catch him at Marwar Junction, and say to him: "He has gone South for the week." He'll know what that means. He's a big man with a red beard, and a great swell he is. You'll find him sleeping like a gentleman with all his luggage round him in a Second-class apartment. But don't you be afraid. Slip down the window and say: "He has gone South for the week," and he'll tumble. It's only cutting your time of stay in those parts by two days. I ask you as a stranger—going to the West,' he said with emphasis.

'Where have *you* come from?' said I.

'From the East,' said he, 'and I am hoping that you will give him the message on the Square—for the sake of my Mother as well as your own.'

Englishmen are not usually softened by appeals to the

memory of their mothers; but for certain reasons, which will be fully apparent, I saw fit to agree.

'It's more than a little matter,' said he, 'and that's why I asked you to do it—and now I know that I can depend on you doing it. A Second-class carriage at Marwar Junction, and a red-haired man asleep in it. You'll be sure to remember. I get out at the next station, and I must hold on there till he comes or sends me what I want.'

'I'll give the message if I catch him,' I said, 'and for the sake of your Mother as well as mine I'll give you a word of advice. Don't try to run the Central India States just now as the correspondent of the "Backwoodsman." There's a real one knocking about here, and it might lead to trouble.'

'Thank you,' said he simply, 'and when will the swine be gone? I can't starve because he's ruining my work. I wanted to get hold of the Degumber Rajah down here about his father's widow, and give him a jump.'

'What did he do to his father's widow, then?'

'Filled her up with red pepper and slippered her to death as she hung from a beam. I found that out myself, and I'm the only man that would dare going into the State to get hush-money for it. They'll try to poison me, same as they did in Chortumna when I went on the loot there. But you'll give the man at Marwar Junction my message?'

He got out at a little roadside station, and I reflected. I had heard, more than once, of men personating correspondents of newspapers and bleeding small Native States with threats of exposure, but I had never met any of the caste before. They lead a hard life, and generally die with great suddenness. The Native States have a wholesome horror of English newspapers, which may throw light on their peculiar methods of government, and do their best to choke correspondents with champagne, or drive them out of their mind with four-in-hand barouches. They do not understand that nobody cares a straw for the internal administration of Native States so long as oppression and crime are kept within decent limits, and the ruler is not drugged, drunk, or diseased from one end of the year to the other. They are the dark places of the earth, full of unimaginable cruelty, touching the Railway and the Telegraph on one side, and, on the other, the days of Harun-al-Raschid. When I left the train I did business with divers Kings, and in eight days passed through many changes of life. Sometimes I wore dress-clothes and consorted with Princes and Politicals, drinking from crystal and eating from silver. Sometimes I lay out upon the ground and devoured what I could get, from a plate made of leaves, and drank the running water, and slept under the same rug as my servant. It was all in the day's work.

Then I headed for the Great Indian Desert upon the proper date, as I had promised, and the night Mail set me down at Marwar Junction, where a funny little, happy-go-lucky, native-managed railway runs to Jodhpore. The Bombay Mail from Delhi makes a short halt at Marwar. She arrived as I got in, and I had just time to hurry to her platform and go down the carriages. There was only one Second-class on the train. I slipped the window and looked down upon a flaming red beard, half covered by a railway rug. That was my man, fast asleep, and I dug him gently in the ribs. He woke with a grunt, and I saw his face in the light of the lamps. It was a great and shining face.

'Tickets again?' said he.

'No,' said I. 'I am to tell you that he is gone South for the week. He has gone South for the week!'

The train had begun to move out. The red man rubbed his eyes. 'He has gone South for the week,' he repeated. 'Now that's just like his impidence. Did he say that I was to give you anything? 'Cause I won't.'

'He didn't,' I said, and dropped away, and watched the red lights die out in the dark. It was horribly cold because the wind was blowing off the sands. I climbed into my

own train—not an Intermediate carriage this time—and
went to sleep.

If the man with the beard had given me a rupee I should
have kept it as a memento of a rather curious affair. But
the consciousness of having done my duty was my only
reward.

Later on I reflected that two gentlemen like my friends
could not do any good if they foregathered and personated
correspondents of newspapers, and might, if they black-
mailed one of the little rat-trap states of Central India or
Southern Rajputana, get themselves into serious difficulties. I therefore took some trouble to describe them as ac-
curately as I could remember to people who would be
interested in deporting them: and succeeded, so I was later
informed, in having them headed back from the Degumber borders.

Then I became respectable, and returned to an Office
where there were no Kings and no incidents outside the
daily manufacture of a newspaper. A newspaper office
seems to attract every conceivable sort of person, to the
prejudice of discipline. Zenana-mission ladies arrive, and
beg that the Editor will instantly abandon all his duties to
describe a Christian prize-giving in a back slum of a perfectly inaccessible village; Colonels who have been over-
passed for command sit down and sketch the outline of a
series of ten, twelve, or twenty-four leading articles on Se-
niority *versus* Selection; missionaries wish to know why
they have not been permitted to escape from their regular
vehicles of abuse and swear at a brother-missionary under
special patronage of the editorial We; stranded theatrical
companies troop up to explain that they cannot pay for
their advertisements, but on their return from New Zealand or Tahiti will do so with interest; inventors of patent
punkah-pulling machines, carriage couplings and unbreakable swords and axle-trees call with specifications in
their pockets and hours at their disposal; tea-companies

enter and elaborate their prospectuses with the office pens; secretaries of ball-committees clamour to have the glories of their last dance more fully described; strange ladies rustle in and say: 'I want a hundred lady's cards printed *at once*, please,' which is manifestly part of an Editor's duty; and every dissolute ruffian that ever tramped the Grand Trunk Road makes it his business to ask for employment as a proof-reader. And, all the time, the telephone-bell is ringing madly, and Kings are being killed on the Continent, and Empires are saying—'You're another,' and Mr. Gladstone is calling down brimstone upon the British Dominions, and the little black copy-boys are whining, '*kaa-pi chay-ha-yeh*' (copy wanted) like tired bees, and most of the paper is as blank as Modred's shield.

But that is the amusing part of the year. There are six other months when none ever come to call, and the thermometer walks inch by inch up to the top of the glass, and the office is darkened to just above reading-light, and the press-machines are red-hot of touch, and nobody writes anything but accounts of amusements in the Hill-stations or obituary notices. Then the telephone becomes a tinkling terror, because it tells you of the sudden deaths of men and women that you knew intimately, and the prickly-heat covers you with a garment, and you sit down and write: 'A slight increase of sickness is reported from the Khuda Janta Khan District. The outbreak is purely sporadic in its nature, and, thanks to the energetic efforts of the District authorities, is now almost at an end. It is, however, with deep regret we record the death,' etc.

Then the sickness really breaks out, and the less recording and reporting the better for the peace of the subscribers. But the Empires and the Kings continue to divert themselves as selfishly as before, and the Foreman thinks that a daily paper really ought to come out once in twenty-four hours, and all the people at the Hill-stations in the middle of their amusements say: 'Good gracious!

Why can't the paper be sparkling? I'm sure there's plenty going on up here.'

That is the dark half of the moon, and, as the advertisements say, 'must be experienced to be appreciated.'

It was in that season, and a remarkably evil season, that the paper began running the last issue of the week on Saturday night, which is to say Sunday morning, after the custom of a London paper. This was a great convenience, for immediately after the paper was put to bed, the dawn would lower the thermometer from 96° to almost 84° for half an hour, and in that chill—you have no idea how cold is 84° on the grass until you begin to pray for it—a very tired man could get off to sleep ere the heat roused him.

One Saturday night it was my pleasant duty to put the paper to bed alone. A King or courtier or a courtesan or a Community was going to die or get a new Constitution, or do something that was important on the other side of the world, and the paper was to be held open till the latest possible minute in order to catch the telegram.

It was a pitchy-black night, as stifling as a June night can be, and the *loo,* the red-hot wind from the westward, was booming among the tinder-dry trees and pretending that the rain was on its heels. Now and again a spot of almost boiling water would fall on the dust with the flop of a frog, but all our weary world knew that was only pretence. It was a shade cooler in the press-room than the office, so I sat there, while the type ticked and clicked, and the night-jars hooted at the windows, and the all but naked compositors wiped the sweat from their foreheads, and called for water. The thing that was keeping us back, whatever it was, would not come off, though the *loo* dropped and the last type was set, and the whole round earth stood still in the choking heat, with its finger on its lip, to wait the event. I drowsed, and wondered whether the telegraph was a blessing, and whether this dying man, or struggling people, might be aware of the inconvenience

the delay was causing. There was no special reason beyond the heat and worry to make tension, but, as the
clock-hands crept up to three o'clock and the machines
spun their fly-wheels two and three times to see that all
was in order, before I said the word that would set them
off, I could have shrieked aloud.

Then the roar and rattle of the wheels shivered the
quiet into little bits. I rose to go away, but two men in
white clothes stood in front of me. The first one said: 'It's
him!' The second said: 'So it is!' And they both laughed
almost as loudly as the machinery roared, and mopped
their foreheads. 'We seed there was a light burning across
the road, and we were sleeping in that ditch there for
coolness, and I said to my friend here, "The office is open.
Let's come along and speak to him as turned us back from
the Degumber State," ' said the smaller of the two. He
was the man I had met in the Mhow train, and his fellow
was the red-bearded man of Marwar Junction. There was
no mistaking the eyebrows of the one or the beard of the
other.

I was not pleased, because I wished to go to sleep, not to
squabble with loafers. 'What do you want?' I asked.

'Half an hour's talk with you, cool and comfortable, in
the office,' said the red-bearded man. 'We'd *like* some
drink—the Contrack doesn't begin yet, Peachey, so you
needn't look—but what we really want is advice. We don't
want money. We ask you as a favour, because we found
out you did us a bad turn about Degumber State.'

I led from the press-room to the stifling office with the
maps on the walls, and the red-haired man rubbed his
hands. 'That's something like,' said he. 'This was the
proper shop to come to. Now, Sir, let me introduce to you
Brother Peachey Carnehan, that's him, and Brother Daniel Dravot, that is *me*, and the less said about our profes-
sions the better, for we have been most things in our time.
Soldier, sailor, compositor, photographer, proof-reader,
street-preacher, and correspondents of the "Backwoods-

man" when we thought the paper wanted one. Carnehan
is sober, and so am I. Look at us first, and see that's sure. It
will save you cutting into my talk. We'll take one of your
cigars apiece, and you shall see us light up.'

I watched the test. The men were absolutely sober, so I
gave them each a tepid whiskey and soda.

'Well *and* good,' said Carnehan of the eyebrows, wiping
the froth from his moustache. 'Let me talk now, Dan. We
have been all over India, mostly on foot. We have been
boiler-fitters, engine-drivers, petty contractors, and all
that, and we have decided that India isn't big enough for
such as us.'

They certainly were too big for the office. Dravot's
beard seemed to fill half the room and Carnehan's shoulders the other half, as they sat on the big table. Carnehan
continued: 'The country isn't half worked out because
they that governs it won't let you touch it. They spend all
their blessed time in governing it, and you can't lift a
spade, nor chip a rock, nor look for oil, nor anything like
that without all the Government saying—"Leave it alone,
and let us govern." Therefore, such *as* it is, we will let it
alone, and go away to some other place where a man isn't
crowded and can come to his own. We are not little men,
and there is nothing that we are afraid of except Drink,
and we have signed a Contrack on that. *Therefore*, we are
going away to be Kings.'

'Kings in our own right,' muttered Dravot.

'Yes, of course,' I said. 'You've been tramping in the
sun, and it's a very warm night, and hadn't you better
sleep over the notion? Come to-morrow.'

'Neither drunk nor sunstruck,' said Dravot. 'We have
slept over the notion half a year, and require to see Books
and Atlases, and we have decided that there is only one
place now in the world that two strong men can Sar-a-
whack. They call it Kafiristan. By my reckoning it's the
top right-hand corner of Afghanistan, not more than three
hundred miles from Peshawar. They have two-and-thirty

heathen idols there, and we'll be the thirty-third and
fourth. It's a mountaineous country, and the women of
those parts are very beautiful.'

'But that is provided against in the Contrack,' said Carnehan. 'Neither Woman nor Liqu-or, Daniel.'

'And that's all we know, except that no one has gone
there, and they fight, and in any place where they fight a
man who knows how to drill men can always be a King.
We shall go to those parts and say to any King we find—
"D'you want to vanquish your foes?" and we will show
him how to drill men; for that we know better than anything else. Then we will subvert that King and seize his
Throne and establish a Dy-nasty.'

'You'll be cut to pieces before you're fifty miles across
the Border,' I said. 'You have to travel through Afghanistan to get to that country. It's one mass of mountains and
peaks and glaciers, and no Englishman has been through
it. The people are utter brutes, and even if you reached
them you couldn't do anything.'

'That's more like,' said Carnehan. 'If you could think us
a little more mad we would be more pleased. We have
come to you to know about this country, to read a book
about it, and to be shown maps. We want you to tell us
that we are fools and to show us your books.' He turned to
the book-cases.

'Are you at all in earnest?' I said.

'A little,' said Dravot sweetly. 'As big a map as you
have got, even if it's all blank where Kafiristan is, and any
books you've got. We can read, though we aren't very
educated.'

I uncased the big thirty-two-miles-to-the-inch map of
India, and two smaller Frontier maps, hauled down volume INF–KAN of the 'Encyclopædia Britannica,' and
the men consulted them.

'See here!' said Dravot, his thumb on the map. 'Up to
Jagdallak, Peachey and me know the road. We was there

with Roberts' Army. We'll have to turn off to the right at Jagdallak through Laghmann territory. Then we get among the hills—fourteen thousand feet—fifteen thousand—it will be cold work there, but it don't look very far on the map.'

I handed him Wood on the 'Sources of the Oxus.' Carnehan was deep in the 'Encyclopædia.'

'They're a mixed lot,' said Dravot reflectively; 'and it won't help us to know the names of their tribes. The more tribes the more they'll fight, and the better for us. From Jagdallak to Ashang. H'mm!'

'But all the information about the country is as sketchy and inaccurate as can be,' I protested. 'No one knows anything about it really. Here's the file of the "United Services' Institute." Read what Bellew says.'

'Blow Bellew!' said Carnehan. 'Dan, they're a stinkin' lot of heathens, but this book here says they think they're related to us English.'

I smoked while the men pored over 'Raverty,' 'Wood,' the maps, and the 'Encyclopædia.'

'There is no use your waiting,' said Dravot politely. "It's about four o'clock now. We'll go before six o'clock if you want to sleep, and we won't steal any of the papers. Don't you sit up. We're two harmless lunatics, and if you come to-morrow evening down to the Serai we'll say good-bye to you.'

'You *are* two fools,' I answered. 'You'll be turned back at the Frontier or cut up the minute you set foot in Afghanistan. Do you want any money or a recommendation down-country? I can help you to the chance of work next week.'

'Next week we shall be hard at work ourselves, thank you,' said Dravot. 'It isn't so easy being a King as it looks. When we've got our Kingdom in going order we'll let you know, and you can come up and help us to govern it.'

'Would two lunatics make a Contrack like that?' said

Carnehan, with subdued pride, showing me a greasy half-sheet of notepaper on which was written the following. I copied it, then and there, as a curiosity—

This Contract between me and you persuing witnesseth in the name of God—Amen and so forth.

(*One*)   *That me and you will settle this matter to-gether; i. e., to be Kings of Kafiristan.*

(*Two*)   *That you and me will not, while this matter is being settled, look at any Liquor, nor any Woman black, white, or brown, so as to get mixed up with one or the other harmful.*

(*Three*)   *That we conduct ourselves with Dignity and Discretion, and if one of us gets into trouble the other will stay by him.*

Signed by you and me this day.
Peachey Taliaferro Carnehan.
Daniel Dravot.
Both Gentlemen at Large.

'There was no need for the last article,' said Carnehan, blushing modestly; 'but it looks regular. Now you know the sort of men that loafers are—we *are* loafers, Dan, until we get out of India—and *do* you think that we would sign a Contrack like that unless we was in earnest? We have kept away from the two things that make life worth having.'

'You won't enjoy your lives much longer if you are going to try this idiotic adventure. Don't set the office on fire,' I said, 'and go away before nine o'clock.'

I left them still poring over the maps and making notes on the back of the 'Contrack.' 'Be sure to come down to the Serai to-morrow,' were their parting words.

The Kumharsen Serai is the great four-square sink of humanity where the strings of camels and horses from the North load and unload. All the nationalities of Central

Asia may be found there, and most of the folk of India
proper. Balkh and Bokhara there meet Bengal and Bombay, and try to draw eye-teeth. You can buy ponics, turquoises, Persian pussy-cats, saddle-bags, fat-tailed sheep
and musk in the Kumharsen Serai, and get many strange
things for nothing. In the afternoon I went down to see
whether my friends intended to keep their word or were
lying there drunk.

A priest attired in fragments of ribbons and rags stalked
up to me, gravely twisting a child's paper whirligig. Behind him was his servant bending under the load of a crate
of mud toys. The two were loading up two camels, and
the inhabitants of the Serai watched them with shrieks of
laughter.

'The priest is mad,' said a horse-dealer to me. 'He is
going up to Kabul to sell toys to the Amir. He will either
be raised to honour or have his head cut off. He came in
here this morning and has been behaving madly ever
since.'

'The witless are under the protection of God,' stammered a flat-cheeked Usbeg in broken Hindi. 'They fore-
tell future events.'

'Would they could have foretold that my caravan would
have been cut up by the Shinwaris almost within shadow
of the Pass!' grunted the Eusufzai agent of a Rajputana
trading-house whose goods had been diverted into the
hands of other robbers just across the Border, and whose
misfortunes were the laughing-stock of the bazar. 'Ohé,
priest, whence come you and whither do you go?'

'From Roum have I come,' shouted the priest, waving
his whirligig; 'from Roum, blown by the breath of a hundred devils across the sea! O thieves, robbers, liars, the
blessing of Pir Khan on pigs, dogs, and perjurers! Who
will take the Protected of God to the North to sell charms
that are never still to the Amir? The camels shall not gall,
the sons shall not fall sick, and the wives shall remain
faithful while they are away, of the men who give me

place in their caravan. Who will assist me to slipper the King of the Roos with a golden slipper with a silver heel? The protection of Pir Khan be upon his labours!' He spread out the skirts of his gaberdine and pirouetted between the lines of tethered horses.

'There starts a caravan from Peshawar to Kabul in twenty days, *Huzrut*,' said the Eusufzai trader. 'My camels go therewith. Do thou also go and bring us good luck.'

'I will go even now!' shouted the priest. 'I will depart upon my winged camels, and be at Peshawar in a day! Ho! Hazar Mir Khan,' he yelled to his servant, 'drive out the camels, but let me first mount my own.'

He leaped on the back of his beast as it knelt, and, turning round to me, cried: 'Come thou also, Sahib, a little along the road, and I will sell thee a charm—an amulet that shall make thee King of Kafiristan.'

Then the light broke upon me, and I followed the two camels out of the Serai till we reached open road and the priest halted.

'What d'you think o' that?' said he in English. 'Carnehan can't talk their patter, so I've made him my servant. He makes a handsome servant. 'Tisn't for nothing that I've been knocking about the country for fourteen years. Didn't I do that talk neat? We'll hitch on to a caravan at Peshawar till we get to Jagdallak, and then we'll see if we can get donkeys for our camels, and strike into Kafiristan. Whirligigs for the Amir, O Lor! Put your hand under the camel-bags and tell me what you feel.'

I felt the butt of a Martini, and another and another.

'Twenty of 'em,' said Dravot placidly. 'Twenty of 'em and ammunition to correspond, under the whirligigs and the mud dolls.'

'Heaven help you if you are caught with those things!' I said. 'A Martini is worth her weight in silver among the Pathans.'

'Fifteen hundred rupees of capital—every rupee we

could beg, borrow, or steal—are invested on these two camels,' said Dravot. 'We won't get caught. We're going through the Khaiber with a regular caravan. Who'd touch a poor mad priest?'

'Have you got everything you want?' I asked, overcome with astonishment.

'Not yet, but we shall soon. Give us a memento of your kindness, *Brother*. You did me a service yesterday, and that time in Marwar. Half my Kingdom shall you have, as the saying is.' I slipped a small charm compass from my watch-chain and handed it up to the priest.

'Good-bye,' said Dravot, giving me his hand cautiously. 'It's the last time we'll shake hands with an Englishman these many days. Shake hands with him, Carnehan,' he cried, as the second camel passed me.

Carnehan leaned down and shook hands. Then the camels passed away along the dusty road, and I was left alone to wonder. My eye could detect no failure in the disguises. The scene in the Serai proved that they were complete to the native mind. There was just the chance, therefore, that Carnehan and Dravot would be able to wander through Afghanistan without detection. But, beyond, they would find death—certain and awful death.

Ten days later a native correspondent, giving me the news of the day from Peshawar, wound up his letter with: 'There has been much laughter here on account of a certain mad priest who is going in his estimation to sell petty gauds and insignificant trinkets which he ascribes as great charms to H. H. the Amir of Bokhara. He passed through Peshawar and associated himself to the Second Summer caravan that goes to Kabul. The merchants are pleased because through superstition they imagine that such mad fellows bring good fortune.'

The two, then, were beyond the Border. I would have prayed for them, but, that night, a real King died in Europe, and demanded an obituary notice.

* * *

The wheel of the world swings through the same phases again and again. Summer passed and winter thereafter, and came and passed again. The daily paper continued, and I with it, and upon the third summer there fell a hot night, a night-issue, and a strained waiting for something to be telegraphed from the other side of the world, exactly as had happened before. A few great men had died in the past two years, the machines worked with more clatter, and some of the trees in the Office garden were a few feet taller. But that was all the difference.

I passed over to the press-room, and went through just such a scene as I have already described. The nervous tension was stronger than it had been two years before, and I felt the heat more acutely. At three o'clock I cried, 'Print off,' and turned to go, when there crept to my chair what was left of a man. He was bent into a circle, his head was sunk between his shoulders, and he moved his feet one over the other like a bear. I could hardly see whether he walked or crawled—this rag-wrapped, whining cripple who addressed me by name, crying that he was come back. 'Can you give me a drink?' he whimpered. 'For the Lord's sake, give me a drink!'

I went back to the office, the man following with groans of pain, and I turned up the lamp.

'Don't you know me?' he gasped, dropping into a chair, and he turned his drawn face, surmounted by a shock of gray hair, to the light.

I looked at him intently. Once before had I seen eyebrows that met over the nose in an inch-broad black band, but for the life of me I could not tell where.

'I don't know you,' I said, handing him the whiskey. 'What can I do for you?'

He took a gulp of the spirit raw, and shivered in spite of the suffocating heat.

'I've come back,' he repeated; 'and I was the King of Kafiristan—me and Dravot—crowned Kings we was! In this office we settled it—you setting there and giving us the books. I am Peachey—Peachey-Taliaferro Carnehan, and you've been setting here ever since—O Lord!'

I was more than a little astonished, and expressed my feelings accordingly.

'It's true,' said Carnehan, with a dry cackle, nursing his feet, which were wrapped in rags. 'True as gospel. Kings we were, with crowns upon our heads—me and Dravot—poor Dan—oh, poor, poor Dan, that would never take advice, not though I begged of him!'

'Take the whiskey,' I said, 'and take your own time. Tell me all you can recollect of everything from beginning to end. You got across the border on your camels. Dravot dressed as a mad priest and you his servant. Do you remember that?'

'I ain't mad—yet, but I shall be that way soon. Of course I remember. Keep looking at me, or maybe my words will go all to pieces. Keep looking at me in my eyes, and don't say anything.'

I leaned forward and looked into his face as steadily as I could. He dropped one hand upon the table and I grasped it by the wrist. It was twisted like a bird's claw, and upon the back was a ragged, red, diamond-shaped scar.

'No, don't look there. Look at *me*,' said Carnehan. 'That comes afterwards, but for the Lord's sake don't distrack me! We left with that caravan, me and Dravot playing all sorts of antics to amuse the people we were with. Dravot used to make us laugh in the evenings when all the people was cooking their dinners—cooking their dinners, and . . . what did they do then? They lit little fires with sparks that went into Dravot's beard, and we all laughed—fit to die. Little red fires they was, going into Dravot's big red beard—so funny.' His eyes left mine, and he smiled foolishly.

'You went as far as Jagdallak with that caravan,' I said at a venture, 'after you had lit those fires. To Jagdallak, where you turned off to try to get into Kafiristan.'

'No, we didn't neither. What are you talking about? We

turned off before Jagdallak, because we heard the roads
was good. But they wasn't good enough for our two
camels—mine and Dravot's. When we left the caravan,
Dravot took off all his clothes and mine too, and said we
would be heathen, because the Kafirs didn't allow Mohammedans to talk to them. So we dressed betwixt and
between, and such a sight as Daniel Dravot I never saw
yet nor expect to see again. He burned half his beard, and
slung a sheep-skin over his shoulder, and shaved his head
into patterns. He shaved mine, too, and made me wear
outrageous things to look like a heathen. That was in a
most mountaineous country, and our camels couldn't go
along any more because of the mountains. They were tall
and black, and coming home I saw them fight like wild
goats—there are lots of goats in Kafiristan. And these
mountains, they never keep still, no more than the goats.
Always fighting they are, and don't let you sleep at night.'

'Take some more whiskey,' I said very slowly. 'What
did you and Daniel Dravot do when the camels could go
no further because of the rough roads that led into
Kafiristan?'

'What did which do? There was a party called Peachey
Taliaferro Carnehan that was with Dravot. Shall I tell you
about him? He died out there in the cold. Slap from the
bridge fell old Peachey, turning and twisting in the air like
a penny whirligig that you can sell to the Amir. No; they
was two for three ha'pence, those whirligigs, or I am much
mistaken and woeful sore . . . And then these camels were
no use, and Peachey said to Dravot—"For the Lord's sake
let's get out of this before our heads are chopped off," and
with that they killed the camels all among the mountains,
not having anything in particular to eat, but first they took
off the boxes with the guns and the ammunition, till two
men came along driving four mules. Dravot up and dances
in front of them, singing—"Sell me four mules." Says the
first man—"If you are rich enough to buy, you are rich
enough to rob;" but before ever he could put his hand to

his knife, Dravot breaks his neck over his knee, and the other party runs away. So Carnehan loaded the mules with the rifles that was taken off the camels, and together we starts forward into those bitter cold mountaineous parts, and never a road broader than the back of your hand.'

He paused for a moment, while I asked him if he could remember the nature of the country through which he had journeyed.

'I am telling you as straight as I can, but my head isn't as good as it might be. They drove nails through it to make me hear better how Dravot died. The country was mountaineous and the mules were most contrary, and the inhabitants was dispersed and solitary. They went up and up, and down and down, and that other party, Carnehan, was imploring of Dravot not to sing and whistle so loud, for fear of bringing down the tremenjus avalanches. But Dravot says that if a King couldn't sing it wasn't worth being King, and whacked the mules over the rump, and never took no heed for ten cold days. We came to a big level valley all among the mountains, and the mules were near dead, so we killed them, not having anything in special for them or us to eat. We sat upon the boxes, and played odd and even with the cartridges that was jolted out.

'Then ten men with bows and arrows ran down that valley, chasing twenty men with bows and arrows, and the row was tremenjus. They was fair men—fairer than you or me—with yellow hair and remarkable well built. Says Dravot, unpacking the guns—"This is the beginning of the business. We'll fight for the ten men," and with that he fires two rifles at the twenty men, and drops one of them at two hundred yards from the rock where he was sitting. The other men began to run, but Carnehan and Dravot sits on the boxes picking them off at all ranges, up and down the valley. Then we goes up to the ten men that had run across the snow too, and they fires a footy little arrow at us. Dravot he shoots above their heads, and they all falls down flat. Then he walks over them and kicks them, and then he lifts them up and shakes hands all round to make them friendly like. He calls them and gives them the boxes to carry, and waves his hand for all the world as though he was King already. They takes the boxes and him across the valley and up the hill into a pine wood on the top, where there was half a dozen big stone idols. Dravot he goes to the biggest—a fellow they call Imbra—and lays a rifle and a cartridge at his feet, rubbing his nose respectful with his own nose, patting him on the head, and saluting in front of it. He turns round to the men and nods his head, and says—"That's all right. I'm in the know too, and all these old jim-jams are my friends." Then he opens his mouth and points down it, and when the first man brings him food, he says—"No;" and when the second man brings him food he says—"No;" but when one of the old priests and the boss of the village brings him food, he says—"Yes;" very haughty, and eats it slow. That was how we came to our first village, without any trouble, just as though we had tumbled from the skies. But we tumbled from one of those damned rope-bridges, you see, and—you couldn't expect a man to laugh much after that?'

'Take some more whiskey and go on,' I said. 'That was the first village you came into. How did you get to be King?'

'I wasn't King,' said Carnehan. 'Dravot he was the King, and a handsome man he looked with the gold crown on his head, and all. Him and the other party stayed in that village, and every morning Dravot sat by the side of old Imbra, and the people came and worshipped. That was Dravot's order. Then a lot of men came into the valley, and Carnehan and Dravot picks them off with the rifles before they knew where they was, and runs down into the valley and up again the other side and finds another village, same as the first one, and the people all falls down flat on their faces and Dravot says—"Now what is the trouble between you two villages?" and the people points to a woman, as fair as you or me, that was carried off, and Dravot takes her back to the first village and counts up the dead—eight there was. For each dead man Dravot pours a little milk on the ground and waves his arms like a whirligig, and "That's all right," says he. Then he and Carnehan takes the big boss of each village by the arm and walks them down into the valley, and shows them how to scratch a line with a spear right down the valley, and gives each a sod of turf from both sides of the line. Then all the people comes down and shouts like the devil and all, and Dravot says—"Go and dig the land, and be fruitful and multiply," which they did, though they didn't understand. Then we asks the names of things in their lingo—bread and water and fire and idols and such, and Dravot leads the priest of each village up to the idol, and says he must sit there and judge the people, and if anything goes wrong he is to be shot.

'Next week they was all turning up the land in the valley as quiet as bees and much prettier, and the priests heard all the complaints and told Dravot in dumb show what it was about. "That's just the beginning," says Dravot. "They think we're Gods." He and Carnehan picks out twenty good men and shows them how to click off a rifle, and form fours, and advance in line, and they was very pleased to do so, and clever to see the hang of it. Then he takes out his pipe and his baccy-pouch and leaves one at one village, and one at the other, and off we two goes to see what was to be done in the next valley. That was all rock, and there was a little village there, and Carnehan says —"Send 'em to the old valley to plant," and takes 'em there and gives 'em some land that wasn't took before. They were a poor lot, and we blooded 'em with a kid before letting 'em into the new Kingdom. That was to impress the people, and then they settled down quiet, and Carnehan went back to Dravot, who had got into another valley, all snow and ice and most mountaineous. There was no people there, and the Army got afraid, so Dravot shoots one of them, and goes on till he finds some people in a village, and the Army explains that unless the people wants to be killed they had better not shoot their little matchlocks; for they had matchlocks. We makes friends with the priest, and I stays there alone with two of the Army, teaching the men how to drill; and a thundering big Chief comes across the snow with kettle-drums and horns twanging, because he heard there was a new God kicking about. Carnehan sights for the brown of the men half a mile across the snow and wings one of them. Then he sends a message to the Chief that, unless he wished to be killed, he must come and shake hands with me and leave his arms behind. The Chief comes alone first, and Carnehan shakes hands with him and whirls his arms about, same as Dravot used, and very much surprised that Chief was, and strokes my eyebrows. Then Carnehan goes alone to the Chief, and asks him in dumb show if he had an enemy he hated. "I have," says the Chief. So Carnehan weeds out the pick of his men, and sets the two of the Army to show them drill, and at the end of two weeks the men can manoeuvre about as well as Volunteers. So he marches with the Chief to a great big plain on the top of a mountain, and the Chief's men rushes into a village and takes it; we three Martinis firing into the brown of the enemy. So we took that village too, and I gives the Chief a rag from my coat and says, "Occupy till I come;" which was scriptural. By way of a reminder, when me and the Army was eighteen hundred yards away, I drops a bullet near him standing on the snow, and all the people falls flat on their faces. Then I sends a letter to Dravot wherever he be by land or sea.'

At the risk of throwing the creature out of train, I interrupted—'How could you write a letter up yonder?'

'The letter?—Oh!—The letter! Keep looking at me between the eyes, please. It was a string-talk letter, that we'd learned the way of it from a blind beggar in the Punjab.'

I remember that there had once come to the office a blind man with a knotted twig and a piece of string which he wound round the twig according to some cipher of his own. He could, after the lapse of days or hours, repeat the sentence which he had reeled up. He had reduced the alphabet to eleven primitive sounds; and he tried to teach me his method, but I could not understand.

'I sent that letter to Dravot,' said Carnehan; 'and told him to come back because this Kingdom was growing too big for me to handle, and then I struck for the first valley, to see how the priests were working. They called the village we took along with the Chief, Bashkai, and the first village we took, Er-Heb. The priests at Er-Heb was doing all right, but they had a lot of pending cases about land to show me, and some men from another village had been firing arrows at night. I went out and looked for that village, and fired four rounds at it from a thousand yards. That used all the cartridges I cared to spend, and I waited for Dravot, who had been away two or three months, and I kept my people quiet.

'One morning I heard the devil's own noise of drums and horns, and Dan Dravot marches down the hill with his Army and a tail of hundreds of men, and, which was the most amazing, a great gold crown on his head. "My Gord, Carnehan," says Daniel, "this is a tremenjus business, and we've got the whole country as far as it's worth having. I am the son of Alexander by Queen Semiramis, and you're my younger brother and a God too! It's the biggest thing we've ever seen. I've been marching and fighting for six weeks with the Army, and every footy little village for fifty miles has come in rejoiceful; and more than that, I've got the key of the whole show, as you'll see, and I've got a crown for you! I told em to make two of 'em at a place called Shu, where the gold lies in the rock like suet in mutton. Gold I've seen, and turquoise I've kicked out of the cliffs, and there's garnets in the sands of the river, and here's a chunk of amber that a man brought me. Call up all the priests and, here, take your crown."

'One of the men opens a black hair bag, and I slips the crown on. It was too small and too heavy, but I wore it for the glory. Hammered gold it was—five pound weight, like a hoop of a barrel.

' "Peachey," says Dravot, "we don't want to fight no more. The Craft's the trick, so help me!" and he brings forward that same Chief that I left at Bashkai—Billy Fish we called him afterwards, because he was so like Billy Fish that drove the big tank-engine at Mach on the Bolan in the old days. "Shake hands with him," says Dravot, and I shook hands and nearly dropped, for Billy Fish gave me the Grip. I said nothing, but tried him with the Fellow Craft Grip. He answers all right, and I tried the Master's Grip, but that was a slip. "A Fellow Craft he is!" I says to Dan. "Does he know the word?"—"He does," says Dan, "and all the priests know. It's a miracle! The Chiefs and the priests can work a Fellow Craft Lodge in a way that's very like ours, and they've cut the marks on the rocks, but they don't know the Third Degree, and they've come to find out. It's Gord's Truth. I've known these long years that the Afghans knew up to the Fellow Craft Degree, but this is a miracle. A God and a Grand-Master of the Craft am I, and a Lodge in the Third Degree I will open, and we'll raise the head priests and the Chiefs of the villages."

'It's against all the law,' I says, 'holding a Lodge without warrant from any one; and you know we never held office in any Lodge.'

' "It's a master-stroke o' policy," says Dravot. "It means running the country as easy as a four-wheeled bogie on a down grade. We can't stop to enquire now, or they'll turn against us. I've forty Chiefs at my heel, and passed and raised according to their merit they shall be. Billet these men on the villages, and see that we run up a Lodge of some kind. The temple of Imbra will do for the Lodge-room. The women must make aprons as you show them. I'll hold a levee of Chiefs to-night and Lodge to-morrow."

'I was fair run off my legs, but I wasn't such a fool as not to see what a pull this Craft business gave us. I showed the priests' families how to make aprons of the degrees, but for Dravot's apron the blue border and marks was made of turquoise lumps on white hide, not cloth. We took a great square stone in the temple for the Master's chair, and little stones for the officers' chairs, and painted the black pavement with white squares, and did what we could to make things regular.

'At the levee which was held that night on the hillside with big bonfires, Dravot gives out that him and me were Gods and sons of Alexander, and Past Grand-Masters in the Craft, and was come to make Kafiristan a country where every man should eat in peace and drink in quiet, and specially obey us. Then the Chiefs come round to shake hands, and they were so hairy and white and fair it was just shaking hands with old friends. We gave them names according as they was like men we had known in India—Billy Fish, Holly Dilworth, Pikky Kergan, that was Bazar-master when I was at Mhow, and so on, and so on.

'*The* most amazing miracles was at Lodge next night. One of the old priests was watching us continuous, and I felt uneasy, for I knew we'd have to fudge the Ritual, and I didn't know what the men knew. The old priest was a stranger come in from beyond the village of Bashkai. The minute Dravot puts on the Master's apron that the girls had made for him, the priest fetches a whoop and a howl, and tries to overturn the stone that Dravot was sitting on. "It's all up now," I says. "That comes of meddling with the Craft without warrant!" Dravot never winked an eye, not when ten priests took and tilted over the Grand-Master's chair—which was to say the stone of Imbra. The priest begins rubbing the bottom end of it to clear away the black dirt, and presently he shows all the other priests

the Master's Mark, same as was on Dravot's apron, cut
into the stone. Not even the priests of the temple of Imbra
knew it was there. The old chap falls flat on his face at
Dravot's feet and kisses 'em. "Luck again," says Dravot,
across the Lodge to me; "they say it's the missing Mark
that no one could understand the why of. We're more than
safe now." Then he bangs the butt of his gun for a gavel
and says: "By virtue of the authority vested in me by my
own right hand and the help of Peachey, I declare myself
Grand-Master of all Freemasonry in Kafiristan in this the
Mother Lodge o' the country, and King of Kafiristan
equally with Peachey!" At that he puts on his crown and I
puts on mine—I was doing Senior Warden—and we
opens the Lodge in most ample form. It was a amazing
miracle! The priests moved in Lodge through the first two
degrees almost without telling, as if the memory was
coming back to them. After that, Peachey and Dravot
raised such as was worthy—high priests and Chiefs of
far-off villages. Billy Fish was the first, and I can tell you
we scared the soul out of him. It was not in any way according to Ritual, but it served our turn. We didn't raise
more than ten of the biggest men, because we didn't want
to make the Degree common. And they was clamouring to
be raised.

' "In another six months," says Dravot, "we'll hold
another Communication, and see how you are working."
Then he asks them about their villages, and learns that
they was fighting one against the other, and were sick and
tired of it. And when they wasn't doing that they was
fighting with the Mohammedans. "You can fight those
when they come into our country," says Dravot. "Tell off
every tenth man of your tribes for a Frontier guard, and
send two hundred at a time to this valley to be drilled.
Nobody is going to be shot or speared any more so long as
he does well, and I know that you won't cheat me, because
you're white people—sons of Alexander—and not like
common, black Mohammedans. You are *my* people, and

by God," says he, running off into English at the end—
"I'll make a damned fine Nation of you, or I'll die in the
making!"

'I can't tell all we did for the next six months, because
Dravot did a lot I couldn't see the hang of, and he learned
their lingo in a way I never could. My work was to help
the people plough, and now and again go out with some
of the Army and see what the other villages were doing,
and make 'em throw rope-bridges across the ravines which
cut up the country horrid. Dravot was very kind to me,
but when he walked up and down in the pine wood pulling that bloody red beard of his with both fists I knew he
was thinking plans I could not advise about, and I just
waited for orders.

'But Dravot never showed me disrespect before the
people. They were afraid of me and the Army, but they
loved Dan. He was the best of friends with the priests and
the Chiefs; but any one could come across the hills with a
complaint, and Dravot would hear him out fair, and call
four priests together and say what was to be done. He
used to call in Billy Fish from Bashkai, and Pikky Kergan
from Shu, and an old Chief we called Kafuzelum—it was
like enough to his real name—and hold councils with 'em
when there was any fighting to be done in small villages.
That was his Council of War, and the four priests of
Bashkai, Shu, Khawak, and Madora was his Privy Council. Between the lot of 'em they sent me, with forty men
and twenty rifles, and sixty men carrying turquoises, into
the Ghorband country to buy those hand-made Martini
rifles, that come out of the Amir's workshops at Kabul,
from one of the Amir's Herati regiments that would have
sold the very teeth out of their mouths for turquoises.

'I stayed in Ghorband a month, and gave the Governor
there the pick of my baskets for hush-money, and bribed
the Colonel of the regiment some more, and, between the
two and the tribes-people, we got more than a hundred
hand-made Martinis, a hundred good Kohat Jezails that'll

throw to six hundred yards, and forty man-loads of very bad ammunition for the rifles. I came back with what I had, and distributed 'em among the men that the Chiefs sent in to me to drill. Dravot was too busy to attend to those things, but the old Army that we first made helped me, and we turned out five hundred men that could drill, and two hundred that knew how to hold arms pretty straight. Even those corkscrewed, hand-made guns was a miracle to them. Dravot talked big about powder-shops and factories, walking up and down in the pine wood when the winter was coming on.

' "I won't make a Nation," says he; "I'll make an Empire! These men aren't niggers; they're English! Look at their eyes—look at their mouths. Look at the way they stand up. They sit on chairs in their own houses. They're the Lost Tribes, or something like it, and they've grown to be English. I'll take a census in the spring if the priests don't get frightened. There must be a fair two million of 'em in these hills. The villages are full o' little children. Two million people—two hundred and fifty thousand fighting men—and all English! They only want the rifles and a little drilling. Two hundred and fifty thousand men ready to cut in on Russia's right flank when she tries for India! Peachey, man," he says, chewing his beard in great hunks, "we shall be Emperors—Emperors of the Earth! Rajah Brooke will be a suckling to us. I'll treat with the Viceroy on equal terms. I'll ask him to send me twelve picked English—twelve that I know of—to help us govern a bit. There's Mackray, Sergeant-pensioner at Segowli— many's the good dinner he's given me, and his wife a pair of trousers. There's Donkin, the Warder of Tounghoo Jail; there's hundreds that I could lay my hand on if I was in India. The Viceroy shall do it for me; I'll send a man through in the spring for those men, and I'll write for a dispensation from the Grand Lodge for what I've done as Grand-Master. That—and all the Sniders that'll be thrown out when the native troops in India take up the Martini. They'll be worn smooth, but they'll do for fighting in these hills. Twelve English, a hundred thousand Sniders run through the Amir's country in driblets—I'd be content with twenty thousand in one year—and we'd be an Empire. When everything was shipshape, I'd hand over the crown—this crown I'm wearing now—to Queen Victoria on my knees, and she'd say: 'Rise up, Sir Daniel Dravot.' Oh, it's big! It's big, I tell you! But there's so much to be done in every place—Bashkai, Khawak, Shu, and everywhere else."

' "What is it?" I says. "There are no more men coming in to be drilled this autumn. Look at those fat, black clouds. They're bringing the snow."

' "It isn't that," says Daniel, putting his hand very hard on my shoulder; "and I don't wish to say anything that's against you, for no other living man would have followed me and made me what I am as you have done. You're a first-class Commander-in-Chief, and the people know you; but—it's a big country, and somehow you can't help me, Peachey, in the way I want to be helped."

' "Go to your blasted priests, then!" I said, and I was sorry when I made that remark, but it did hurt me sore to find Daniel talking so superior when I'd drilled all the men, and done all he told me.

' "Don't let's quarrel, Peachey," says Daniel, without cursing. "You're a King too, and the half of this Kingdom is yours; but can't you see, Peachey, we want cleverer men than us now—three or four of 'em, that we can scatter about for our Deputies. It's a hugeous great State, and I can't always tell the right thing to do, and I haven't time for all I want to do, and here's the winter coming on, and all." He put half his beard into his mouth, all red like the gold of his crown.

' "I'm sorry, Daniel," says I. "I've done all I could. I've drilled the men and shown the people how to stack their oats better; and I've brought in those tinware rifles from Ghorband—but I know what you're driving at. I take it Kings always feel oppressed that way."

'"There's another thing too," says Dravot, walking up and down. "The winter's coming, and these people won't be giving much trouble, and if they do we can't move about. I want a wife."

'"For Gord's sake leave the women alone!" I says. "We've both got all the work we can, though I *am* a fool. Remember the Contrack, and keep clear o' women."

'"The Contrack only lasted till such time as we was Kings; and Kings we have been these months past," says Dravot, weighing his crown in his hand. "You go get a wife too, Peachey—a nice, strappin', plump girl that'll keep you warm in the winter. They're prettier than English girls, and we can take the pick of 'em. Boil 'em once or twice in hot water, and they'll come out like chicken and ham."

'"Don't tempt me!" I says. "I will not have any dealings with a woman not till we are a dam' side more settled than we are now. I've been doing the work o' two men, and you've been doing the work o' three. Let's lie off a bit, and see if we can get some better tobacco from Afghan country and run in some good liquor; but no women."

'"Who's talking o' *women?*" says Dravot. "I said *wife*—a Queen to breed a King's son for the King. A Queen out of the strongest tribe, that'll make them your blood-brothers, and that'll lie by your side and tell you all the people thinks about you and their own affairs. That's what I want."

'"Do you remember that Bengali woman I kept at Mogul Serai when I was a plate-layer?" says I. "A fat lot o' good she was to me. She taught me the lingo and one or two other things; but what happened? She ran away with the Station-Master's servant and half my month's pay. Then she turned up at Dadur Junction in tow of a half-

caste, and had the impidence to say I was her husband—
all among the drivers in the running-shed too!"

' "We've done with that," says Dravot; "these women
are whiter than you or me, and a Queen I will have for the
winter months."

' "For the last time o' asking, Dan, do *not*," I says. "It'll
only bring us harm. The Bible says that Kings ain't to
waste their strength on women, 'specially when they've
got a new raw Kingdom to work over."

' "For the last time of answering, I will," said Dravot,
and he went away through the pine-trees looking like a big
red devil, the sun being on his crown and beard and all.

'But getting a wife was not as easy as Dan thought. He
put it before the Council, and there was no answer till
Billy Fish said that he'd better ask the girls. Dravot
damned them all round. "What's wrong with me?" he
shouts, standing by the idol Imbra. "Am I a dog or am I
not enough of a man for your wenches? Haven't I put the
shadow of my hand over this country? Who stopped the
last Afghan raid?" It was me really, but Dravot was too
angry to remember. "Who bought your guns? Who re-
paired the bridges? Who's the Grand-Master of the sign
cut in the stone?" says he, and he thumped his hand on
the block that he used to sit on in Lodge, and at Council,
which opened like Lodge always. Billy Fish said nothing,
and no more did the others. "Keep your hair on, Dan,"
said I; "and ask the girls. That's how it's done at Home,
and these people are quite English."

' "The marriage of the King is a matter of State," says
Dan, in a white-hot rage, for he could feel, I hope, that he
was going against his better mind. He walked out of the
Council-room, and the others sat still, looking at the
ground.

' "Billy Fish," says I to the Chief of Bashkai, "what's
the difficulty here? A straight answer to a true friend."

' "You know," says Billy Fish. "How should a man tell

you who knows everything? How can daughters of men marry Gods or Devils? It's not proper."

'I remembered something like that in the Bible; but if, after seeing us as long as they had, they still believed we were Gods, it wasn't for me to undeceive them.

' "A God can do anything," says I. "If the King is fond of a girl he'll not let her die."

' "She'll have to," said Billy Fish. "There are all sorts of Gods and Devils in these mountains, and now and again a girl marries one of them and isn't seen any more. Besides, you two know the Mark cut in the stone. Only the Gods know that. We thought you were men till you showed the sign of the Master."

'I wished then that we had explained about the loss of the genuine secrets of a Master-Mason at the first go-off; but I said nothing. All that night there was a blowing of horns in a little dark temple half-way down the hill, and I heard a girl crying fit to die. One of the priests told us that she was being prepared to marry the King.

' "I'll have no nonsense of that kind," says Dan. "I don't want to interfere with your customs, but I'll take my own wife."

' "The girl's a little bit afraid," says the priest. "She thinks she's going to die, and they are a-heartening of her up down in the temple."

' "Hearten her very tender, then," says Dravot, "or I'll hearten you with the butt of a gun so you'll never want to be heartened again." He licked his lips, did Dan, and stayed up walking about more than half the night, thinking of the wife that he was going to get in the morning. I wasn't any means comfortable, for I knew that dealings with a woman in foreign parts, though you was a crowned King twenty times over, could not but be risky. I got up very early in the morning while Dravot was asleep, and I saw the priests talking together in whispers, and the Chiefs talking together too, and they looked at me out of the corners of their eyes.

' "What is up, Fish?" I says to the Bashkai man, who was wrapped up in his furs and looking splendid to behold.

' "I can't rightly say," says he; "but if you can make the King drop all this nonsense about marriage, you'll be doing him and me and yourself a great service."

' "That I do believe," says I. "But sure, you know, Billy, as well as me, having fought against and for us, that the King and me are nothing more than two of the finest men that God Almighty ever made. Nothing more, I do assure you."

' "That may be," says Billy Fish, "and yet I should be sorry if it was." He sinks his head upon his great fur cloak for a minute and thinks. "King," says he, "be you man or God or Devil, I'll stick by you to-day. I have twenty of my men with me, and they will follow me. We'll go to Bashkai until the storm blows over."

'A little snow had fallen in the night, and everything was white except the greasy fat clouds that blew down and down from the north. Dravot came out with his crown on his head, swinging his arms and stamping his feet, and looking more pleased than Punch.

' "For the last time, drop it, Dan," says I in a whisper; "Billy Fish here says that there will be a row."

' "A row among my people!" says Dravot. "Not much. Peachey, you're a fool not to get a wife too. Where's the girl?" says he with a voice as loud as the braying of a jack-ass. "Call up all the Chiefs and priests, and let the Emperor see if his wife suits him."

'There was no need to call any one. They were all there leaning on their guns and spears round the clearing in the centre of the pine wood. A lot of priests went down to the little temple to bring up the girl, and the horns blew fit to wake the dead. Billy Fish saunters round and gets as close to Daniel as he could, and behind him stood his twenty men with matchlocks. Not a man of them under six feet. I was next to Dravot, and behind me was twenty men of the regular Army. Up comes the girl, and a strapping wench she was, covered with silver and turquoises, but white as death, and looking back every minute at the priests.

' "She'll do," said Dan, looking her over. "What's to be afraid of, lass? Come and kiss me." He puts his arm round her. She shuts her eyes, gives a bit of a squeak, and down goes her face in the side of Dan's flaming red beard.

' "The slut's bitten me!" says he, clapping his hand to his neck, and, sure enough, his hand was red with blood. Billy Fish and two of his matchlock-men catches hold of Dan by the shoulders and drags him into the Bashkai lot, while the priests howls in their lingo,—"Neither God nor Devil, but a man!" I was all taken aback, for a priest cut at me in front, and the Army behind began firing into the Bashkai men.

' "God A'mighty!" says Dan. "What is the meaning o' this?"

' "Come back! Come away!" says Billy Fish. "Ruin and Mutiny is the matter. We'll break for Bashkai if we can."

'I tried to give some sort of orders to my men—the men o' the regular Army—but it was no use, so I fired into the brown of 'em with an English Martini and drilled three beggars in a line. The valley was full of shouting, howling creatures, and every soul was shrieking, "Not a God nor a Devil, but only a man!" The Bashkai troops stuck to Billy Fish all they were worth, but their matchlocks wasn't half as good as the Kabul breech-loaders, and four of them dropped. Dan was bellowing like a bull, for he was very wrathy; and Billy Fish had a hard job to prevent him running out at the crowd.

' "We can't stand," says Billy Fish. "Make a run for it down the valley! The whole place is against us." The matchlock-men ran, and we went down the valley in spite of Dravot. He was swearing horrible and crying out he was a King. The priests rolled great stones on us, and the regular Army fired hard, and there wasn't more than six men, not counting Dan, Billy Fish, and Me, that came down to the bottom of the valley alive.

'Then they stopped firing, and the horns in the temple blew again. "Come away—for Gord's sake come away!" says Billy Fish. "They'll send runners out to all the villages before ever we get to Bashkai. I can protect you there, but I can't do anything now."

'My own notion is that Dan began to go mad in his head from that hour. He stared up and down like a stuck pig. Then he was all for walking back alone and killing the priests with his bare hands; which he could have done. "An Emperor am I," says Daniel, "and next year I shall be a Knight of the Queen."

' "All right, Dan," says I; "but come along now while there's time."

' "It's your fault," says he, "for not looking after your Army better. There was mutiny in the midst, and you didn't know—you damned engine-driving, plate-laying, missionary's-pass-hunting hound." He sat upon a rock and called me every foul name he could lay tongue to. I was too heart-sick to care, though it was all his foolishness that brought the smash.

' "I'm sorry, Dan," says I, "but there's no accounting for natives. This business is our Fifty-Seven. Maybe we'll make something out of it yet, when we've got to Bashkai."

' "Let's get to Bashkai, then," says Dan, "and, by God, when I come back here again I'll sweep the valley so there isn't a bug in a blanket left!"

'We walked all that day, and all that night Dan was stumping up and down on the snow, chewing his beard and muttering to himself.

' "There's no hope o' getting clear," said Billy Fish. "The priests will have sent runners to the villages to say that you are only men. Why didn't you stick on as Gods till things was more settled? I'm a dead man," says Billy Fish, and he throws himself down on the snow and begins to pray to his Gods.

'Next morning we was in a cruel bad country—all up and down, no level ground at all, and no food either. The

six Bashkai men looked at Billy Fish hungry-way as if
they wanted to ask something, but they said never a word.
At noon we came to the top of a flat mountain all covered
with snow, and when we climbed up into it, behold, there
was an Army in position waiting in the middle!

'"The runners have been very quick," says Billy Fish,
with a little bit of a laugh. "They are waiting for us."

'Three or four men began to fire from the enemy's side,
and a chance shot took Daniel in the calf of the leg. That
brought him to his senses. He looks across the snow at the
Army, and sees the rifles that we had brought into the
country.

'"We're done for," says he. "They are Englishmen,
these people,—and it's my blasted nonsense that has
brought you to this. Get back, Billy Fish, and take your
men away; you've done what you could, and now cut for
it. Carnehan," says he, "shake hands with me and go along
with Billy. Maybe they won't kill you. I'll go and meet
'em alone. It's me that did it. Me, the King!"

'"Go!" says I. "Go to Hell, Dan. I'm with you here.
Billy Fish, you clear out, and we two will meet those folk."

'"I'm a Chief," says Billy Fish, quite quiet. "I stay with
you. My men can go."

'The Bashkai fellows didn't wait for a second word, but
ran off; and Dan and Me and Billy Fish walked across to
where the drums were drumming and the horns were
horning. It was cold—awful cold. I've got that cold in the
back of my head now. There's a lump of it there.'

The punkah-coolies had gone to sleep. Two kerosene
lamps were blazing in the office, and the perspiration
poured down my face and splashed on the blotter as I
leaned forward. Carnehan was shivering, and I feared that
his mind might go. I wiped my face, took a fresh grip of
the piteously mangled hands, and said: 'What happened
after that?'

The momentary shift of my eyes had broken the clear
current.

'What was you pleased to say?' whined Carnehan. 'They took them without any sound. Not a little whisper all along the snow, not though the King knocked down the first man that set hand on him—not though old Peachey fired his last cartridge into the brown of 'em. Not a single solitary sound did those swines make. They just closed up tight, and I tell you their furs stunk. There was a man called Billy Fish, a good friend of us all, and they cut his throat, Sir, then and there, like a pig; and the King kicks up the bloody snow and says: "We've had a dashed fine run for our money. What's coming next?" But Peachey, Peachey Taliaferro, I tell you, Sir, in confidence as be-twixt two friends, he lost his head, Sir. No, he didn't nei-ther. The King lost his head, so he did, all along o' one of those cunning rope-bridges. Kindly let me have the paper-cutter, Sir. It tilted this way. They marched him a mile across that snow to a rope-bridge over a ravine with a river at the bottom. You may have seen such. They prod-ded him behind like an ox. "Damn your eyes!" says the King. "D'you suppose I can't die like a gentleman?" He turns to Peachey—Peachey that was crying like a child. "I've brought you to this, Peachey," says he. "Brought you out of your happy life to be killed in Kafiristan, where you was late Commander-in-Chief of the Emperor's forces. Say you forgive me, Peachey."—"I do," says Peachey. "Fully and freely do I forgive you, Dan."— "Shake hands, Peachey," says he. "I'm going now." Out he goes, looking neither right nor left, and when he was plumb in the middle of those dizzy dancing ropes, "Cut, you beggars," he shouts; and they cut, and old Dan fell, turning round and round and round, twenty thousand miles, for he took half an hour to fall till he struck the water, and I could see his body caught on a rock with the gold crown close beside.

'But do you know what they did to Peachey between two pine-trees? They crucified him, Sir, as Peachey's hands will show. They used wooden pegs for his hands

and his feet; and he didn't die. He hung there and
screamed, and they took him down next day, and said it
was a miracle that he wasn't dead. They took him
down—poor old Peachey that hadn't done them any
harm—that hadn't done them any—'

He rocked to and fro and wept bitterly, wiping his eyes
with the back of his scarred hands and moaning like a
child for some ten minutes.

'They was cruel enough to feed him up in the temple,
because they said he was more of a God than old Daniel
that was a man. Then they turned him out on the snow,
and told him to go home, and Peachey came home in
about a year, begging along the roads quite safe; for Daniel Dravot he walked before and said: "Come along,
Peachey. It's a big thing we're doing." The mountains
they danced at night, and the mountains they tried to fall
on Peachey's head, but Dan he held up his hand, and
Peachey came along bent double. He never let go of Dan's
hand, and he never let go of Dan's head. They gave it to
him as a present in the temple, to remind him not to come
again, and though the crown was pure gold, and Peachey
was starving, never would Peachey sell the same. You
knew Dravot, Sir! You knew Right Worshipful Brother
Dravot! Look at him now!'

He fumbled in the mass of rags round his bent waist;
brought out a black horsehair bag embroidered with silver
thread; and shook therefrom on to my table—the dried,
withered head of Daniel Dravot! The morning sun that
had long been paling the lamps struck the red beard and
blind, sunken eyes; struck, too, a heavy circlet of gold
studded with raw turquoises, that Carnehan placed tenderly on the battered temples.

'You be'old now,' said Carnehan, 'the Emperor in his
'abit as he lived—the King of Kafiristan with his crown
upon his head. Poor old Daniel that was a monarch once!'

I shuddered, for, in spite of defacements manifold, I
recognised the head of the man of Marwar Junction. Car-

nehan rose to go. I attempted to stop him. He was not fit to walk abroad. 'Let me take away the whiskey, and give me a little money,' he gasped. 'I was a King once. I'll go to the Deputy Commissioner and ask to set in the Poorhouse till I get my health. No, thank you, I can't wait till you get a carriage for me. I've urgent private affairs—in the south—at Marwar.'

He shambled out of the office and departed in the direction of the Deputy Commissioner's house. That day at noon I had occasion to go down the blinding hot Mall, and I saw a crooked man crawling along the white dust of the roadside, his hat in his hand, quavering dolorously after the fashion of street-singers at Home. There was not a soul in sight, and he was out of all possible earshot of the houses. And he sang through his nose, turning his head from right to left:

> 'The Son of Man goes forth to war,
>   A golden crown to gain;
> His blood-red banner streams afar—
>   Who follows in his train?'

I waited to hear no more, but put the poor wretch into my carriage and drove him off to the nearest missionary for eventual transfer to the Asylum. He repeated the hymn twice while he was with me, whom he did not in the least recognise, and I left him singing it to the missionary.

Two days later I enquired after his welfare of the Superintendent of the Asylum.

'He was admitted suffering from sun-stroke. He died early yesterday morning,' said the Superintendent. 'Is it true that he was half an hour bareheaded in the sun at midday?'

'Yes,' said I, 'but do you happen to know if he had anything upon him by any chance when he died?'

'Not to my knowledge,' said the Superintendent.

And there the matter rests.

1888

WITHOUT BENEFIT OF CLERGY

~~~~~~

Before my Spring I garnered Autumn's gain,
Out of her time my field was white with grain,
   The year gave up her secrets to my woe,
Forced and deflowered each sick season lay,
In mystery of increase and decay;
I saw the sunset ere men saw the day,
   Who am too wise in that I should not know.

Bitter Waters

I

'But if it be a girl?'

'Lord of my life, it cannot be. I have prayed for so many nights, and sent gifts to Sheikh Badl's shrine so often, that I know God will give us a son—a man-child that shall grow into a man. Think of this and be glad. My mother shall be his mother till I can take him again, and the mullah of the Pattan mosque shall cast his nativity—God send he be born in an auspicious hour!—and then, and then thou wilt never weary of me, thy slave.'

'Since when hast thou been a slave, my queen?'

'Since the beginning—till this mercy came to me. How could I be sure of thy love when I knew that I had been bought with silver?'

'Nay, that was the dowry. I paid it to thy mother.'

'And she has buried it, and sits upon it all day long like a hen. What talk is yours of dower! I was bought as though I had been a Lucknow dancing-girl instead of a child.'

'Art thou sorry for the sale?'

'I have sorrowed; but to-day I am glad. Thou wilt never cease to love me now?—answer, my king.'

'Never—never. No.'

'Not even though the *mem-log*—the white women of thy own blood—love thee? And remember, I have watched them driving in the evening; they are very fair.'

'I have seen fire-balloons by the hundred. I have seen the moon, and—then I saw no more fire-balloons.'

Ameera clapped her hands and laughed. 'Very good talk,' she said. Then with an assumption of great stateliness, 'It is enough. Thou hast my permission to depart,—if thou wilt.'

The man did not move. He was sitting on a low red-lacquered couch in a room furnished only with a blue and white floor-cloth, some rugs, and a very complete collection of native cushions. At his feet sat a woman of sixteen, and she was all but all the world in his eyes. By every rule and law she should have been otherwise, for he was an Englishman, and she a Mussulman's daughter bought two years before from her mother, who, being left without money, would have sold Ameera shrieking to the Prince of Darkness if the price had been sufficient.

It was a contract entered into with a light heart; but even before the girl had reached her bloom she came to fill the greater portion of John Holden's life. For her, and the withered hag her mother, he had taken a little house overlooking the great red-walled city, and found,—when the marigolds had sprung up by the well in the courtyard and Ameera had established herself according to her own ideas of comfort, and her mother had ceased grumbling at the inadequacy of the cooking-places, the distance from the daily market, and at matters of house-keeping in general,—that the house was to him his home. Any one could enter his bachelor's bungalow by day or night, and the life that he led there was an unlovely one. In the house in the city his feet only could pass beyond the outer courtyard to the women's rooms; and when the big wooden gate was bolted behind him he was king in his own territory, with Ameera for queen. And there was going to be added to this kingdom a third person whose arrival Holden felt inclined to resent. It interfered with his perfect happiness. It disarranged the orderly peace of the house that was his own. But Ameera was wild with delight at the thought of it, and her mother not less so. The love of a man, and particularly a white man, was at the best an inconstant affair, but it might, both women argued, be held fast by a baby's hands. 'And then,' Ameera would always say, 'then he will never care for the white _mem-log_. I hate them all—I hate them all.'

'He will go back to his own people in time,' said the mother; 'but by the blessing of God that time is yet afar off.'

Holden sat silent on the couch thinking of the future, and his thoughts were not pleasant. The drawbacks of a double life are manifold. The Government, with singular care, had ordered him out of the station for a fortnight on special duty in the place of a man who was watching by the bedside of a sick wife. The verbal notification of the transfer had been edged by a cheerful remark that Holden ought to think himself lucky in being a bachelor and a free man. He came to break the news to Ameera.

'It is not good,' she said slowly, 'but it is not all bad. There is my mother here, and no harm will come to me— unless I die of pure joy. Go thou to thy work and think no troublesome thoughts. When the days are done I believe . . . nay, I am sure. And—and then I shall lay _him_ in thy arms, and thou wilt love me for ever. The train goes to-night, at midnight is it not? Go now, and do not let thy heart be heavy by cause of me. But thou wilt not delay in returning? Thou wilt not stay on the road to talk to the bold white _mem-log_. Come back to me swiftly, my life.'

As he left the courtyard to reach his horse that was

tethered to the gate-post, Holden spoke to the white-haired old watchman who guarded the house, and bade him under certain contingencies despatch the filled-up telegraph-form that Holden gave him. It was all that could be done, and with the sensations of a man who has attended his own funeral Holden went away by the night mail to his exile. Every hour of the day he dreaded the arrival of the telegram, and every hour of the night he pictured to himself the death of Ameera. In consequence his work for the State was not of first-rate quality, nor was his temper towards his colleagues of the most amiable. The fortnight ended without a sign from his home, and, torn to pieces by his anxieties, Holden returned to be swallowed up for two precious hours by a dinner at the club, wherein he heard, as a man hears in a swoon, voices telling him how execrably he had performed the other man's duties, and how he had endeared himself to all his associates. Then he fled on horseback through the night with his heart in his mouth. There was no answer at first to his blows on the gate, and he had just wheeled his horse round to kick it in when Pir Khan appeared with a lantern and held his stirrup.

'Has aught occurred?' said Holden.

'The news does not come from my mouth, Protector of the Poor, but—' He held out his shaking hand as befitted the bearer of good news who is entitled to a reward.

Holden hurried through the courtyard. A light burned in the upper room. His horse neighed in the gateway, and he heard a shrill little wail that sent all the blood into the apple of his throat. It was a new voice, but it did not prove that Ameera was alive.

'Who is there?' he called up the narrow brick staircase.

There was a cry of delight from Ameera, and then the voice of the mother, tremulous with old age and pride—'We be two women and—the—man—thy—son.'

On the threshold of the room Holden stepped on a

naked dagger, that was laid there to avert ill-luck, and it broke at the hilt under his impatient heel.

'God is great!' cooed Ameera in the half-light. 'Thou hast taken his misfortunes on thy head.'

'Ay, but how is it with thee, life of my life? Old woman, how is it with her?'

'She has forgotten her sufferings for joy that the child is born. There is no harm; but speak softly,' said the mother.

'It only needed thy presence to make me all well,' said Ameera. 'My king, thou hast been very long away. What gifts hast thou for me? Ah, ah! It is I that bring gifts this time. Look, my life, look. Was there ever such a babe? Nay, I am too weak even to clear my arm from him.'

'Rest then, and do not talk. I am here, *bachari* [little woman].'

'Well said, for there is a bond and a heel-rope [*pee-charee*] between us now that nothing can break. Look— canst thou see in this light? He is without spot or blemish. Never was such a man-child. *Ya illah!* he shall be a pundit—no, a trooper of the Queen. And, my life, dost thou love me as well as ever, though I am faint and sick and worn? Answer truly.'

'Yea. I love as I have loved, with all my soul. Lie still, pearl, and rest.'

'Then do not go. Sit by my side here—so. Mother, the lord of this house needs a cushion. Bring it.' There was an almost imperceptible movement on the part of the new life that lay in the hollow of Ameera's arm. 'Aho!' she said, her voice breaking with love. 'The babe is a champion from his birth. He is kicking me in the side with mighty kicks. Was there ever such a babe! And he is ours to us— thine and mine. Put thy hand on his head, but carefully, for he is very young, and men are unskilled in such matters.'

Very cautiously Holden touched with the tips of his fingers the downy head.

'He is of the faith,' said Ameera; 'for lying here in the night-watches I whispered the call to prayer and the profession of faith into his ears. And it is most marvellous that he was born upon a Friday, as I was born. Be careful of him, my life; but he can almost grip with his hands.'

Holden found one helpless little hand that closed feebly on his finger. And the clutch ran through his body till it settled about his heart. Till then his sole thought had been for Ameera. He began to realise that there was some one else in the world, but he could not feel that it was a veritable son with a soul. He sat down to think, and Ameera dozed lightly.

'Get hence, *sahib*,' said her mother under her breath. 'It is not good that she should find you here on waking. She must be still.'

'I go,' said Holden submissively. 'Here be rupees. See that my *baba* gets fat and finds all that he needs.'

The chink of the silver roused Ameera. 'I am his mother, and no hireling,' she said weakly. 'Shall I look to him more or less for the sake of money? Mother, give it back. I have born my lord a son.'

The deep sleep of weakness came upon her almost before the sentence was completed. Holden went down to the courtyard very softly with his heart at ease. Pir Khan, the old watchman, was chuckling with delight. 'This house is now complete,' he said, and without further comment thrust into Holden's hands the hilt of a sabre worn many years ago when he, Pir Khan, served the Queen in the police. The bleat of a tethered goat came from the well-kerb.

'There be two,' said Pir Khan, 'two goats of the best. I bought them, and they cost much money; and since there is no birth-party assembled their flesh will be all mine. Strike craftily, *sahib!* 'Tis an ill-balanced sabre at the best. Wait till they raise their heads from cropping the marigolds.'

'And why?' said Holden, bewildered.

'For the birth-sacrifice. What else? Otherwise the child being unguarded from fate may die. The Protector of the Poor knows the fitting words to be said.'

Holden had learned them once with little thought that he would ever speak them in earnest. The touch of the cold sabre-hilt in his palm turned suddenly to the clinging grip of the child up-stairs—the child that was his own son—and a dread of loss filled him.

'Strike!' said Pir Khan. 'Never life came into the world but life was paid for it. See, the goats have raised their heads. Now! With a drawing cut!'

Hardly knowing what he did Holden cut twice as he muttered the Mahomedan prayer that runs: 'Almighty! In place of this my son I offer life for life, blood for blood, head for head, bone for bone, hair for hair, skin for skin.' The waiting horse snorted and bounded in his pickets at the smell of the raw blood that spirted over Holden's riding-boots.

'Well smitten!' said Pir Khan, wiping the sabre. 'A swordsman was lost in thee. Go with a light heart, Heaven-born. I am thy servant, and the servant of thy son. May the Presence live a thousand years and . . . the flesh of the goats is all mine?' Pir Khan drew back richer by a month's pay. Holden swung himself into the saddle and rode off through the low-hanging wood-smoke of the evening. He was full of riotous exultation, alternating with a vast vague tenderness directed towards no particular object, that made him choke as he bent over the neck of his uneasy horse. 'I never felt like this in my life,' he thought. 'I'll go to the club and pull myself together.'

A game of pool was beginning, and the room was full of men. Holden entered, eager to get to the light and the company of his fellows, singing at the top of his voice—

'In Baltimore a-walking, a lady I did meet!'

'Did you?' said the club-secretary from his corner. 'Did she happen to tell you that your boots were wringing wet? Great goodness, man, it's blood!'

'Bosh!' said Holden, picking his cue from the rack. 'May I cut in? It's dew. I've been riding through high crops. My faith! my boots are in a mess though!

> 'And if it be a girl she shall wear a wedding-ring,
> And if it be a boy he shall fight for his king,
> With his dirk, and his cap, and his little jacket blue,
> He shall walk the quarter-deck—'

'Yellow on blue—green next player,' said the marker monotonously.

'He shall walk the quarter-deck,—Am I green, marker? *He shall walk the quarter-deck,*—eh! that's a bad shot,— *As his daddy used to do!'*

'I don't see that you have anything to crow about,' said a zealous junior civilian acidly. 'The Government is not exactly pleased with your work when you relieved Sanders.'

'Does that mean a wigging from headquarters?' said Holden with an abstracted smile. 'I think I can stand it.'

The talk beat up round the ever-fresh subject of each man's work, and steadied Holden till it was time to go to his dark empty bungalow, where his butler received him as one who knew all his affairs. Holden remained awake for the greater part of the night, and his dreams were pleasant ones.

II

'How old is he now?'

'*Ya illah!* What a man's question! He is all but six weeks old; and on this night I go up to the house-top with thee, my life, to count the stars. For that is auspicious. And he was born on a Friday under the sign of the Sun, and it has been told to me that he will outlive us both and get wealth. Can we wish for aught better, beloved?'

'There is nothing better. Let us go up to the roof, and thou shalt count the stars—but a few only, for the sky is heavy with cloud.'

'The winter rains are late, and maybe they come out of season. Come, before all the stars are hid. I have put on my richest jewels.'

'Thou hast forgotten the best of all.'

'*Ai!* Ours. He comes also. He has never yet seen the skies.'

'Ameera climbed the narrow staircase that led to the flat roof. The child, placid and unwinking, lay in the hollow of her right arm, gorgeous in silver-fringed muslin with a small skull-cap on his head. Ameera wore all that she valued most. The diamond nose-stud that takes the place of the Western patch in drawing attention to the curve of the nostril, the gold ornament in the centre of the forehead studded with tallow-drop emeralds and flawed rubies, the heavy circlet of beaten gold that was fastened round her neck by the softness of the pure metal, and the chinking curb-patterned silver anklets hanging low over the rosy ankle-bone. She was dressed in jade-green muslin as befitted a daughter of the Faith, and from shoulder to elbow and elbow to wrist ran bracelets of silver tied with floss silk, frail glass bangles slipped over the wrist in proof of the slenderness of the hand, and certain heavy gold bracelets that had no part in her country's ornaments but, since they were Holden's gift and fastened with a cunning European snap, delighted her immensely.

They sat down by the low white parapet of the roof, overlooking the city and its lights.

'They are happy down there,' said Ameera. 'But I do not think that they are as happy as we. Nor do I think the white *mem-log* are as happy. And thou?'

'I know they are not.'

'How dost thou know?'

'They give their children over to the nurses.'

'I have never seen that,' said Ameera with a sigh, 'nor do I wish to see. *Ahi!*'—she dropped her head on Holden's shoulder,—'I have counted forty stars, and I am tired. Look at the child, love of my life, he is counting too.'

The baby was staring with round eyes at the dark of the heavens. Ameera placed him in Holden's arms, and he lay there without a cry.

'What shall we call him among ourselves?' she said. 'Look! Art thou ever tired of looking? He carries thy very eyes. But the mouth—'

'Is thine, most dear. Who should know better than I?'

' "Tis such a feeble mouth. Oh, so small! And yet it holds my heart between its lips. Give him to me now. He has been too long away.'

'Nay, let him lie; he has not yet begun to cry.'

'When he cries thou wilt give him back—eh? What a man of mankind thou art! If he cried he were only the dearer to me. But, my life, what little name shall we give him?'

The small body lay close to Holden's heart. It was utterly helpless and very soft. He scarcely dared to breathe for fear of crushing it. The caged green parrot that is regarded as a sort of guardian-spirit in most native households moved on its perch and fluttered a drowsy wing.

'There is the answer,' said Holden. 'Mian Mittu has spoken. He shall be the parrot. When he is ready he will talk mightily and run about. Mian Mittu is the parrot in thy—in the Mussulman tongue, is it not?'

'Why put me so far off?' said Ameera fretfully. 'Let it be like unto some English name—but now wholly. For he is mine.'

'Then call him Tota, for that is likest English.'

'Ay, Tota, and that is still the parrot. Forgive me, my lord, for a minute ago, but in truth he is too little to wear all the weight of Mian Mittu for name. He shall be Tota—our Tota to us. Hearest thou, O small one? Littlest, thou art Tota.' She touched the child's cheek, and he waking wailed, and it was necessary to return him to his mother, who soothed him with the wonderful rhyme of *Aré koko, Jaré koko!* which says:

> Oh crow! Go crow! Baby's sleeping sound,
> And the wild plums grow in the jungle, only a penny a pound.
> Only a penny a pound, *baba*, only a penny a pound.

Reassured many times as to the price of those plums, Tota cuddled himself down to sleep. The two sleek, white well-bullocks in the courtyard were steadily chewing the cud of their evening meal; old Pir Khan squatted at the head of Holden's horse, his police sabre across his knees, pulling drowsily at a big water-pipe that croaked like a bull-frog in a pond. Ameera's mother sat spinning in the lower verandah, and the wooden gate was shut and barred. The music of a marriage-procession came to the roof above the gentle hum of the city, and a string of flying-foxes crossed the face of the low moon.

'I have prayed,' said Ameera after a long pause, 'I have prayed for two things. First, that I may die in thy stead if thy death is demanded, and in the second that I may die in the place of the child. I have prayed to the Prophet and to Beebee Miriam [the Virgin Mary]. Thinkest thou either will hear?'

'From thy lips who would not hear the lightest word?'

'I asked for straight talk, and thou hast given me sweet talk. Will my prayers be heard?'

'How can I say? God is very good.'

'Of that I am not sure. Listen now. When I die, or the child dies, what is thy fate? Living, thou wilt return to the bold white *mem-log*, for kind calls to kind.'

'Not always.'

'With a woman, no; with a man it is otherwise. Thou wilt in this life, later on, go back to thine own folk. That I could almost endure, for I should be dead. But in thy very death thou wilt be taken away to a strange place and a paradise that I do not know.'

'Will it be paradise?'

'Surely, for who would harm thee? But we two—I and the child—shall be elsewhere, and we cannot come to thee, nor canst thou come to us. In the old days, before the child was born, I did not think of these things; but now I think of them always. It is very hard talk.'

'It will fall as it will fall. To-morrow we do not know, but to-day and love we know well. Surely we are happy now.'

'So happy that it were well to make our happiness assured. And thy Beebee Miriam should listen to me; for she is also a woman. But then she would envy me! It is not seemly for men to worship a woman.'

Holden laughed aloud at Ameera's little spasm of jealousy.

'Is it not seemly? Why didst thou not turn me from worship of thee, then?'

'Thou a worshipper! And of me? My king, for all thy sweet words, well I know that I am thy servant and thy slave, and the dust under thy feet. And I would not have it otherwise. See!'

Before Holden could prevent her she stooped forward and touched his feet; recovering herself with a little laugh she hugged Tota closer to her bosom. Then, almost savagely—

'Is it true that the bold white *mem-log* live for three times the length of my life? Is it true that they make their marriages not before they are old women?'

'They marry as do others—when they are women.'

'That I know, but they wed when they are twenty-five. Is that true?'

'That is true.'

'*Ya illah!* At twenty-five! Who would of his own will take a wife even of eighteen? She is a woman—aging every hour. Twenty-five! I shall be an old woman at that age, and—— Those *mem-log* remain young for ever. How I hate them!'

'What have they to do with us?'

'I cannot tell. I know only that there may now be alive on this earth a woman ten years older than I who may come to thee and take thy love ten years after I am an old woman, gray-headed, and the nurse of Tota's son. That is unjust and evil. They should die too.'

'Now, for all thy years thou art a child, and shalt be picked up and carried down the staircase.'

'Tota! Have a care for Tota, my lord! Thou at least art as foolish as any babe!' Ameera tucked Tota out of harm's way in the hollow of her neck, and was carried downstairs laughing in Holden's arms, while Tota opened his eyes and smiled after the manner of the lesser angels.

He was a silent infant, and, almost before Holden could realise that he was in the world, developed into a small gold-coloured little god and unquestioned despot of the house overlooking the city. Those were months of absolute happiness to Holden and Ameera—happiness withdrawn from the world, shut in behind the wooden gate that Pir Khan guarded. By day Holden did his work with an immense pity for such as were not so fortunate as himself, and a sympathy for small children that amazed and amused many mothers at the little station-gatherings. At nightfall he returned to Ameera,—Ameera, full of the wondrous doings of Tota; how he had been seen to clap his hands together and move his fingers with intention and purpose—which was manifestly a miracle—how later, he had of his own initiative crawled out of his low bedstead on to the floor and swayed on both feet for the space of three breaths.

'And they were long breaths, for my heart stood still with delight,' said Ameera.

Then Tota took the beasts into his councils—the well-bullocks, the little gray squirrels, the mongoose that lived in a hole near the well, and especially Mian Mittu, the parrot, whose tail he grievously pulled, and Mian Mittu screamed till Ameera and Holden arrived.

'O villain! Child of strength! This to thy brother on the house-top! *Tobah, tobah!* Fie! Fie! But I know a charm to make him wise as Suleiman and Aflatoun [Solomon and Plato]. Now look,' said Ameera. She drew from an embroidered bag a handful of almonds. 'See! we count seven. In the name of God!'

She placed Mian Mittu, very angry and rumpled, on the top of his cage, and seating herself between the babe and the bird she cracked and peeled an almond less white than her teeth. 'This is a true charm, my life, and do not laugh. See! I give the parrot one half and Tota the other.' Mian Mittu with careful beak took his share from between Ameera's lips, and she kissed the other half into the mouth of the child, who ate it slowly with wondering eyes. 'This I will do each day of seven, and without doubt he who is ours will be a bold speaker and wise. Eh, Tota, what wilt thou be when thou art a man and I am gray-headed?' Tota tucked his fat legs into adorable creases. He could crawl, but he was not going to waste the spring of his youth in idle speech. He wanted Mian Mittu's tail to tweak.

When he was advanced to the dignity of a silver belt— which, with a magic square engraved on silver and hung round his neck, made up the greater part of his clothing— he staggered on a perilous journey down the garden to Pir Khan and proffered him all his jewels in exchange for one little ride on Holden's horse, having seen his mother's mother chaffering with pedlars in the verandah. Pir Khan wept and set the untried feet on his own gray head in sign of fealty, and brought the bold adventurer to his mother's arms, vowing that Tota would be a leader of men ere his beard was grown.

One hot evening, while he sat on the roof between his father and mother watching the never-ending warfare of the kites that the city boys flew, he demanded a kite of his

own with Pir Khan to fly it, because he had a fear of dealing with anything larger than himself, and when Holden
called him a 'spark,' he rose to his feet and answered
slowly in defence of his new-found individuality,
'*Hum'park nahin hai. Hum admi hai* [I am no spark, but
a man].'

The protest made Holden choke and devote himself
very seriously to a consideration of Tota's future. He need
hardly have taken the trouble. The delight of that life was
too perfect to endure. Therefore it was taken away as
many things are taken away in India—suddenly and
without warning. The little lord of the house, as Pir Khan
called him, grew sorrowful and complained of pains who
had never known the meaning of pain. Ameera, wild with
terror, watched him through the night, and in the dawning of the second day the life was shaken out of him by
fever—the seasonal autumn fever. It seemed altogether
impossible that he could die, and neither Ameera nor
Holden at first believed the evidence of the little body on
the bedstead. Then Ameera beat her head against the wall
and would have flung herself down the well in the garden
had Holden not restrained her by main force.

One mercy only was granted to Holden. He rode to his
office in broad daylight and found waiting him an unusually heavy mail that demanded concentrated attention
and hard work. He was not, however, alive to this kindness of the gods.

III

The first shock of a bullet is no more than a brisk pinch.
The wrecked body does not send in its protest to the soul
till ten or fifteen seconds later. Holden realised his pain
slowly, exactly as he had realised his happiness, and with
the same imperious necessity for hiding all trace of it. In
the beginning he only felt that there had been a loss, and
that Ameera needed comforting, where she sat with her

head on her knees shivering as Mian Mittu from the house-top called, *Tota! Tota! Tota!* Later all his world and the daily life of it rose up to hurt him. It was an outrage that any one of the children at the band-stand in the evening should be alive and clamorous, when his own child lay dead. It was more than mere pain when one of them touched him, and stories told by over-fond fathers of their children's latest performances cut him to the quick. He could not declare his pain. He had neither help, comfort, nor sympathy; and Ameera at the end of each weary day would lead him through the hell of self-questioning reproach which is reserved for those who have lost a child, and believe that with a little—just a little—more care it might have been saved.

'Perhaps,' Ameera would say, 'I did not take sufficient heed. Did I, or did I not? The sun on the roof that day when he played so long alone and I was—*ahi!* braiding my hair—it may be that the sun then bred the fever. If I had warned him from the sun he might have lived. But, oh my life, say that I am guiltless! Thou knowest that I loved him as I love thee. Say that there is no blame on me, or I shall die—I shall die!'

'There is no blame,—before God, none. It was written and how could we do aught to save? What has been, has been. Let it go, beloved.'

'He was all my heart to me. How can I let the thought go when my arm tells me every night that he is not here? *Ahi! Ahi!* O Tota, come back to me—come back again, and let us be all together as it was before!'

'Peace, peace! For thine own sake, and for mine also, if thou lovest me—rest.'

'By this I know thou dost not care; and how shouldst thou? The white men have hearts of stone and souls of iron. Oh, that I had married a man of mine own people— though he beat me—and had never eaten the bread of an alien!'

'Am I an alien—mother of my son?'

'What else—*Sahib?* ... Oh, forgive me—forgive! The
death has driven me mad. Thou are the life of my heart,
and the light of my eyes, and the breath of my life, and—
and I have put thee from me, though it was but for a moment. If thou goest away, to whom shall I look for help?
Do not be angry. Indeed, it was the pain that spoke and
not thy slave.'

'I know, I know. We be two who were three. The
greater need therefore that we should be one.'

They were sitting on the roof as of custom. The night
was a warm one in early spring, and sheet-lightning was
dancing on the horizon to a broken tune played by far-off
thunder. Ameera settled herself in Holden's arms.

'The dry earth is lowing like a cow for the rain, and I—I
am afraid. It was not like this when we counted the stars.
But thou lovest me as much as before, though a bond is
taken away? Answer!'

'I love more because a new bond has come out of the
sorrow that we have eaten together, and that thou
knowest.'

'Yes, I knew,' said Ameera in a very small whisper. 'But
it is good to hear thee say so, my life, who art so strong to
help. I will be a child no more, but a woman and an aid to
thee. Listen! Give me my *sitar* and I will sing bravely.'

She took the light silver-studded *sitar* and began a song
of the great hero Rajah Rasalu. The hand failed on the
strings, the tune halted, checked, and at a low note turned
off to the poor little nursery-rhyme about the wicked
crow—

> And the wild plums grow in the jungle, only a
> penny a pound.
> Only a penny a pound, *baba*—only ...

Then came the tears, and the piteous rebellion against
fate till she slept, moaning a little in her sleep, with the

right arm thrown clear of the body as though it protected something that was not there. It was after this night that life became a little easier for Holden. The ever-present pain of loss drove him into his work, and the work repaid him by filling up his mind for nine or ten hours a day. Ameera sat alone in the house and brooded, but grew happier when she understood that Holden was more at ease, according to the custom of women. They touched happiness again, but this time with caution.

'It was because we loved Tota that he died. The jealousy of God was upon us,' said Ameera. 'I have hung up a large black jar before our window to turn the evil eye from us, and we must make no protestations of delight, but go softly underneath the stars, lest God find us out. Is that not good talk, worthless one?'

She had shifted the accent on the word that means 'beloved,' in proof of the sincerity of her purpose. But the kiss that followed the new christening was a thing that any deity might have envied. They went about henceforward saying, 'It is naught, it is naught;' and hoping that all the Powers heard.

The Powers were busy on other things. They had allowed thirty million people four years of plenty wherein men fed well and the crops were certain, and the birthrate rose year by year; the districts reported a purely agricultural population varying from nine hundred to two thousand to the square mile of the overburdened earth; and the Member for Lower Tooting, wandering about India in pot-hat and frock-coat, talked largely of the benefits of British rule and suggested as the one thing needful the establishment of a duly qualified electoral system and a general bestowal of the franchise. His long-suffering hosts smiled and made him welcome, and when he paused to admire, with pretty picked words, the blossom of the blood-red *dhak*-tree that had flowered untimely for a sign of what was coming, they smiled more than ever.

It was the Deputy Commissioner of Kot-Kumharsen, staying at the club for a day, who lightly told a tale that made Holden's blood run cold as he overheard the end.

'He won't bother any one any more. Never saw a man so astonished in my life. By Jove, I thought he meant to ask a question in the House about it. Fellow-passenger in his ship—dined next him—bowled over by cholera and died in eighteen hours. You needn't laugh, you fellows. The Member for Lower Tooting is awfully angry about it; but he's more scared. I think he's going to take his enlightened self out of India.'

'I'd give a good deal if he were knocked over. It might keep a few vestrymen of his kidney to their own parish. But what's this about cholera? It's full early for anything of that kind,' said the warden of an unprofitable salt-lick.

'Don't know,' said the Deputy Commissioner reflectively. 'We've got locusts with us. There's sporadic cholera all along the north—at least we're calling it sporadic for decency's sake. The spring crops are short in five districts, and nobody seems to know where the rains are. It's nearly March now. I don't want to scare anybody, but it seems to me that Nature's going to audit her accounts with a big red pencil this summer.'

'Just when I wanted to take leave, too!' said a voice across the room.

'There won't be much leave this year, but there ought to be a great deal of promotion. I've come in to persuade the Government to put my pet canal on the list of famine-relief works. It's an ill-wind that blows no good. I shall get that canal finished at last.'

'Is it the old programme then,' said Holden; 'famine, fever, and cholera?'

'Oh no. Only local scarcity and an unusual prevalence of seasonal sickness. You'll find it all in the reports if you live till next year. You're a lucky chap. *You* haven't got a wife to send out of harm's way. The hill-stations ought to be full of women this year.'

'I think you're inclined to exaggerate the talk in the *bazars*,' said a young civilian in the Secretariat. 'Now I have observed——'

'I daresay you have,' said the Deputy Commissioner, 'but you've a great deal more to observe, my son. In the meantime, I wish to observe to you——' and he drew him aside to discuss the construction of the canal that was so dear to his heart. Holden went to his bungalow and began to understand that he was not alone in the world, and also that he was afraid for the sake of another,—which is the most soul-satisfying fear known to man.

Two months later, as the Deputy had foretold, Nature began to audit her accounts with a red pencil. On the heels of the spring-reapings came a cry for bread, and the Government, which had decreed that no man should die of want, sent wheat. Then came the cholera from all four quarters of the compass. It struck a pilgrim-gathering of half a million at a sacred shrine. Many died at the feet of their god; the others broke and ran over the face of the land carrying the pestilence with them. It smote a walled city and killed two hundred a day. The people crowded the trains, hanging on to the footboards and squatting on the roofs of the carriages, and the cholera followed them, for at each station they dragged out the dead and the dying. They died by the roadside, and the horses of the Englishmen shied at the corpses in the grass The rains did not come, and the earth turned to iron lest man should escape death by hiding in her. The English sent their wives away to the hills and went about their work, coming forward as they were bidden to fill the gaps in the fighting-line. Holden, sick with fear of losing his chiefest treasure on earth, had done his best to persuade Ameera to go away with her mother to the Himalayas.

'Why should I go?' said she one evening on the roof.

'There is sickness, and people are dying, and all the white *mem-log* have gone.'

All of them?'

'All—unless perhaps there remain some old scald-head who vexes her husband's heart by running risk of death.'

'Nay; who stays is my sister, and thou must not abuse her, for I will be a scald-head too. I am glad all the bold *mem-log* are gone.'

'Do I speak to a woman or a babe? Go to the hills and I will see to it that thou goest like a queen's daughter. Think, child. In a red-lacquered bullock-cart, veiled and curtained, with brass peacocks upon the pole and red cloth hangings. I will send two orderlies for guard, and——'

'Peace! Thou art the babe in speaking thus. What use are those toys to me? *He* would have patted the bullocks and played with the housings. For his sake, perhaps,—thou hast made me very English—I might have gone. Now, I will not. Let the *mem-log* run.'

'Their husbands are sending them, beloved.'

'Very good talk. Since when hast thou been my husband to tell me what to do? I have but borne thee a son. Thou art only all the desire of my soul to me. How shall I depart when I know that if evil befall thee by the breadth of so much as my littlest finger-nail—is that not small?—I should be aware of it though I were in paradise. And here, this summer thou mayest die—*ai, janee*, die! and in dying they might call to tend thee a white woman, and she would rob me in the last of thy love!'

'But love is not born in a moment or on a death-bed!'

'What dost thou know of love, stoneheart? She would take thy thanks at least and, by God and the Prophet and Beebee Miriam the mother of thy Prophet, that I will never endure. My lord and my love, let there be no more foolish talk of going away. Where thou art, I am. It is enough.' She put an arm round his neck and a hand on his mouth.

There are not many happinesses so complete as those that are snatched under the shadow of the sword. They sat together and laughed, calling each other openly by every pet name that could move the wrath of the gods. The city below them was locked up in its own torments. Sulphur fires blazed in the streets; the conches in the Hindu temples screamed and bellowed, for the gods were inattentive in those days. There was a service in the great Mahomedan shrine, and the call to prayer from the minarets was almost unceasing. They heard the wailing in the houses of the dead, and once the shriek of a mother who had lost a child and was calling for its return. In the gray dawn they saw the dead borne out through the city gates, each litter with its own little knot of mourners. Wherefore they kissed each other and shivered.

It was a red and heavy audit, for the land was very sick and needed a little breathing-space ere the torrent of cheap life should flood it anew. The children of immature fathers and undeveloped mothers made no resistance. They were cowed and sat still, waiting till the sword should be sheathed in November if it were so willed. There were gaps among the English, but the gaps were filled. The work of superintending famine-relief, cholera-sheds, medicine-distribution, and what little sanitation was possible, went forward because it was so ordered.

Holden had been told to keep himself in readiness to move to replace the next man who should fall. There were twelve hours in each day when he could not see Ameera, and she might die in three. He was considering what his pain would be if he could not see her for three months, or if she died out of his sight. He was absolutely certain that her death would be demanded—so certain that when he looked up from the telegram and saw Pir Khan breathless in the doorway, he laughed aloud. 'And?' said he,—

'When there is a cry in the night and the spirit flutters into the throat, who has a charm that will restore? Come swiftly, Heaven-born! It is the black cholera.'

Holden galloped to his home. The sky was heavy with clouds, for the long-deferred rains were near and the heat

was stifling. Ameera's mother met him in the courtyard,
whimpering, 'She is dying. She is nursing herself into
death. She is all but dead. What shall I do, *sahib?*'

Ameera was lying in the room in which Tota had been
born. She made no sign when Holden entered, because
the human soul is a very lonely thing and, when it is getting ready to go away, hides itself in a misty borderland
where the living may not follow. The black cholera does
its work quietly and without explanation. Ameera was
being thrust out of life as though the Angel of Death had
himself put his hand upon her. The quick breathing
seemed to show that she was either afraid or in pain, but
neither eyes nor mouth gave any answer to Holden's
kisses. There was nothing to be said or done. Holden
could only wait and suffer. The first drops of the rain
began to fall on the roof, and he could hear shouts of joy in
the parched city.

The soul came back a little and the lips moved. Holden
bent down to listen. 'Keep nothing of mine,' said Ameera.
'Take no hair from my head. *She* would make thee burn it
later on. That flame I should feel. Lower! Stoop lower! Remember only that I was thine and bore thee a son.
Though thou wed a white woman to-morrow, the pleasure of receiving in thy arms thy first son is taken from
thee for ever. Remember me when thy son is born—the
one that shall carry thy name before all men. His misfortunes be on my head. I bear witness—I bear witness'—the
lips were forming the words on his ear—'that there is no
God but—thee, beloved!'

Then she died. Holden sat still, and all thought was
taken from him,—till he heard Ameera's mother lift the
curtain.

'Is she dead, *sahib?*'

'She is dead.'

'Then I will mourn, and afterwards take an inventory of
the furniture in this house. For that will be mine. The

sahib does not mean to resume it? It is so little, so very little, *sahib*, and I am an old woman. I would like to lie softly.'

'For the mercy of God be silent a while. Go out and mourn where I cannot hear.'

'*Sahib*, she will be buried in four hours.'

'I know the custom. I shall go ere she is taken away. That matter is in thy hands. Look to it, that the bed on which—on which she lies——'

'Aha! That beautiful red-lacquered bed. I have long desired——'

'That the bed is left here untouched for my disposal. All else in the house is thine. Hire a cart, take everything, go hence, and before sunrise let there be nothing in this house but that which I have ordered thee to respect.'

'I am an old woman. I would stay at least for the days of mourning, and the rains have just broken. Whither shall I go?'

'What is that to me? My order is that there is a going. The house-gear is worth a thousand rupees and my orderly shall bring thee a hundred rupees to-night.'

'That is very little. Think of the cart-hire.'

'It shall be nothing unless thou goest, and with speed. O woman, get hence and leave me with my dead!'

The mother shuffled down the staircase, and in her anxiety to take stock of the house-fittings forgot to mourn. Holden stayed by Ameera's side and the rain roared on the roof. He could not think connectedly by reason of the noise, though he made many attempts to do so. Then four sheeted ghosts glided dripping into the room and stared at him through their veils. They were the washers of the dead. Holden left the room and went out to his horse. He had come in a dead, stifling calm through ankle-deep dust. He found the courtyard a rain-lashed pond alive with frogs; a torrent of yellow water ran under the gate, and a roaring wind drove the bolts of the rain like buckshot against the mud-walls. Pir Khan was shivering in his little hut by the gate, and the horse was stamping uneasily in the water.

'I have been told the *sahib's* order,' said Pir Khan. 'It is well. This house is now desolate. I go also, for my monkey-face would be a reminder of that which has been. Concerning the bed, I will bring that to thy house yonder in the morning; but remember, *sahib*, it will be to thee a knife turning in a green wound. I go upon a pilgrimage, and I will take no money. I have grown fat in the protection of the Presence whose sorrow is my sorrow. For the last time I hold his stirrup.'

He touched Holden's foot with both hands and the horse sprang out into the road, where the creaking bamboos were whipping the sky and all the frogs were chuckling. Holden could not see for the rain in his face. He put his hands before his eyes and muttered—

'Oh you brute! You utter brute!'

The news of his trouble was already in his bungalow. He read the knowledge in his butler's eyes when Ahmed Khan brought in food, and for the first and last time in his life laid a hand upon his master's shoulder, saying, 'Eat, *sahib*, eat. Meat is good against sorrow. I also have known. Moreover the shadows come and go, *sahib*; the shadows come and go. These be curried eggs.'

Holden could neither eat nor sleep. The heavens sent down eight inches of rain in that night and washed the earth clean. The waters tore down walls, broke roads, and scoured open the shallow graves on the Mahomedan burying-ground. All next day it rained, and Holden sat still in his house considering his sorrow. On the morning of the third day he received a telegram which said only, 'Ricketts, Myndonie. Dying. Holden relieve. Immediate.' Then he thought that before he departed he would look at the house wherein he had been master and lord. There was a break in the weather, and the rank earth steamed with vapour.

He found that the rains had torn down the mud pillars of the gateway, and the heavy wooden gate that had guarded his life hung lazily from one hinge. There was grass three inches high in the courtyard; Pir Khan's lodge was empty, and the sodden thatch sagged between the beams. A gray squirrel was in possession of the verandah, as if the house had been untenanted for thirty years instead of three days. Ameera's mother had removed everything except some mildewed matting. The *tick-tick* of the little scorpions as they hurried across the floor was the only sound in the house. Ameera's room and the other one where Tota had lived were heavy with mildew; and the narrow staircase leading to the roof was streaked and stained with rain-borne mud. Holden saw all these things, and came out again to meet in the road Durga Dass, his landlord,—portly, affable, clothed in white muslin, and driving a Cee-spring buggy. He was overlooking his property to see how the roofs stood the stress of the first rains.

'I have heard,' said he, 'you will not take this place any more, *sahib?*'

'What are you going to do with it?'

'Perhaps I shall let it again.'

'Then I will keep it on while I am away.'

Durga Dass was silent for some time. 'You shall not take it on, *sahib*,' he said. 'When I was a young man I also——, but to-day I am a member of the Municipality. Ho! Ho! No. When the birds have gone what need to keep the nest? I will have it pulled down—the timber will sell for something always. It shall be pulled down, and the Municipality shall make a road across, as they desire, from the burning-ghaut to the city wall, so that no man may say where this house stood.'

1890

LISPETH

Look, you have cast out Love! What Gods are these
　　You bid me please?
The Three in One, the One in Three? Not so!
　　To my own gods I go.
It may be they shall give me greater ease
Than your cold Christ and tangled Trinities.
The Convert

She was the daughter of Sonoo, a Hill-man of the Himalayas, and Jadéh his wife. One year their maize failed, and
two bears spent the night in their only opium poppy-field
just above the Sutlej Valley on the Kotgarh side; so, next
season, they turned Christian, and brought their baby to
the Mission to be baptized. The Kotgarh Chaplain christened her Elizabeth, and 'Lispeth' is the Hill or *pahari*
pronunciation.

Later, cholera came into the Kotgarh Valley and carried
off Sonoo and Jadéh, and Lispeth became half servant, half
companion, to the wife of the then Chaplain of Kotgarh.
This was after the reign of the Moravian missionaries in
that place, but before Kotgarh had quite forgotten her title
of 'Mistress of the Northern Hills.'

Whether Christianity improved Lispeth, or whether the
gods of her own people would have done as much for her
under any circumstances, I do not know; but she grew
very lovely. When a Hill-girl grows lovely, she is worth
travelling fifty miles over bad ground to look upon. Lispeth had a Greek face—one of those faces people paint so
often, and see so seldom. She was of a pale, ivory colour,
and, for her race, extremely tall. Also, she possessed eyes

that were wonderful; and, had she not been dressed in the abominable print-cloths affected by Missions, you would, meeting her on the hillside unexpectedly, have thought her the original Diana of the Romans going out to slay.

Lispeth took to Christianity readily, and did not abandon it when she reached womanhood, as do some Hill-girls. Her own people hated her because she had, they said, become a white woman and washed herself daily; and the Chaplain's wife did not know what to do with her. One cannot ask a stately goddess, five feet ten in her shoes, to clean plates and dishes. She played with the Chaplain's children and took classes in the Sunday School, and read all the books in the house, and grew more and more beautiful, like the Princesses in fairy tales. The Chaplain's wife said that the girl ought to take service in Simla as a nurse or something 'genteel.' But Lispeth did not want to take service. She was very happy where she was.

When travellers—there were not many in those years—came in to Kotgarh, Lispeth used to lock herself into her own room for fear they might take her away to Simla, or out into the unknown world.

One day, a few months after she was seventeen years old, Lispeth went out for a walk. She did not walk in the manner of English ladies—a mile and a half out, with a carriage-ride back again. She covered between twenty and thirty miles in her little constitutionals, all about and about, between Kotgarh and Narkanda. This time she came back at full dusk, stepping down the break-neck descent into Kotgarh with something heavy in her arms. The Chaplain's wife was dozing in the drawing-room when Lispeth came in breathing heavily and very exhausted with her burden. Lispeth put it down on the sofa, and said simply, 'This is my husband. I found him on the Bagi Road. He has hurt himself. We will nurse him, and when he is well your husband shall marry him to me.'

This was the first mention Lispeth had ever made of her matrimonial views, and the Chaplain's wife shrieked with horror. However, the man on the sofa needed attention first. He was a young Englishman, and his head had been cut to the bone by something jagged. Lispeth said she had found him down the hillside, and had brought him in. He was breathing queerly and was unconscious.

He was put to bed and tended by the Chaplain, who knew something of medicine; and Lispeth waited outside the door in case she could be useful. She explained to the Chaplain that this was the man she meant to marry; and the Chaplain and his wife lectured her severely on the impropriety of her conduct. Lispeth listened quietly, and repeated her first proposition. It takes a great deal of Christianity to wipe out uncivilised Eastern instincts, such as falling in love at first sight. Lispeth, having found the man she worshipped, did not see why she should keep silent as to her choice. She had no intention of being sent away, either. She was going to nurse that Englishman until he was well enough to marry her. This was her programme.

After a fortnight of slight fever and inflammation, the Englishman recovered coherence and thanked the Chaplain and his wife, and Lispeth—especially Lispeth—for their kindness. He was a traveller in the East, he said—they never talked about 'globe-trotters' in those days, when the P. & O. fleet was young and small—and had come from Dehra Dun to hunt for plants and butterflies among the Simla hills. No one at Simla, therefore, knew anything about him. He fancied that he must have fallen over the cliff while reaching out for a fern on a rotten tree-trunk, and that his coolies must have stolen his baggage and fled. He thought he would go back to Simla when he was a little stronger. He desired no more mountaineering.

He made small haste to go away, and recovered his strength slowly. Lispeth objected to being advised either by the Chaplain or his wife; therefore the latter spoke to the Englishman, and told him how matters stood in Lispeth's heart. He laughed a good deal, and said it was very pretty and romantic, but, as he was engaged to a girl at Home, he fancied that nothing would happen. Certainly he would behave with discretion. He did that. Still he found it very pleasant to talk to Lispeth, and walk with Lispeth, and say nice things to her, and call her pet names while he was getting strong enough to go away. It meant nothing at all to him, and everything in the world to Lispeth. She was very happy while the fortnight lasted, because she had found a man to love.

Being a savage by birth, she took no trouble to hide her feelings, and the Englishman was amused. When he went away, Lispeth walked with him up the Hill as far as Narkanda, very troubled and very miserable. The Chaplain's wife, being a good Christian and disliking anything in the shape of fuss or scandal—Lispeth was beyond her management entirely—had told the Englishman to tell Lispeth that he was coming back to marry her. 'She is but a child, you know, and, I fear, at heart a heathen,' said the Chaplain's wife. So all the twelve miles up the Hill the Englishman, with his arm around Lispeth's waist, was assuring the girl that he would come back and marry her; and Lispeth made him promise over and over again. She wept on the Narkanda Ridge till he had passed out of sight along the Muttiani path.

Then she dried her tears and went in to Kotgarh again, and said to the Chaplain's wife, 'He will come back and marry me. He has gone to his own people to tell them so.' And the Chaplain's wife soothed Lispeth and said, 'He will come back.' At the end of two months Lispeth grew impatient, and was told that the Englishman had gone over the seas to England. She knew where England was, because she had read little geography primers; but, of course, she had no conception of the nature of the sea, being a Hill-girl. There was an old puzzle-map of the

World in the house. Lispeth had played with it when she was a child. She unearthed it again, and put it together of evenings, and cried to herself, and tried to imagine where her Englishman was. As she had no ideas of distance or steamboats her notions were somewhat wild. It would not have made the least difference had she been perfectly correct; for the Englishman had no intention of coming back to marry a Hill-girl. He forgot all about her by the time he was butterfly-hunting in Assam. He wrote a book on the East afterwards. Lispeth's name did not appear there.

At the end of three months Lispeth made daily pilgrimage to Narkanda to see if her Englishman was coming along the road. It gave her comfort, and the Chaplain's wife finding her happier thought that she was getting over her 'barbarous and most indelicate folly.' A little later the walks ceased to help Lispeth, and her temper grew very bad. The Chaplain's wife thought this a profitable time to let her know the real state of affairs—that the Englishman had only promised his love to keep her quiet—that he had never meant anything, and that it was wrong and improper of Lispeth to think of marrige with an Englishman, who was of a superior clay, besides being promised in marriage to a girl of his own people. Lispeth said that all this was clearly impossible because he had said he loved her, and the Chaplain's wife had, with her own lips, asserted that the Englishman was coming back.

'How can what he and you said be untrue?' asked Lispeth.

'We said it as an excuse to keep you quiet, child,' said the Chaplain's wife.

'Then you have lied to me,' said Lispeth, 'you and he?'

The Chaplain's wife bowed her head, and said nothing. Lispeth was silent too for a little time; then she went out down the valley, and returned in the dress of a Hill-girl—infamously dirty, but without the nose-stud and ear-rings. She had her hair braided into the long pigtail, helped out with black thread, that Hill-women wear.

'I am going back to my own people,' said she. 'You have killed Lispeth. There is only left old Jadéh's daughter—the daughter of a *pahari* and the servant of *Tarka Devi.* You are all liars, you English.'

By the time that the Chaplain's wife had recovered from the shock of the announcement that Lispeth had 'verted to her mother's gods the girl had gone; and she never came back.

She took to her own unclean people savagely, as if to make up the arrears of the life she had stepped out of; and, in a little time, she married a wood-cutter who beat her after the manner of *paharis,* and her beauty faded soon.

'There is no law whereby you can account for the vagaries of the heathen,' said the Chaplain's wife, 'and I believe that Lispeth was always at heart an infidel.' Seeing she had been taken into the Church of England at the mature age of five weeks, this statement does not do credit to the Chaplain's wife.

Lispeth was a very old woman when she died. She had always a perfect command of English, and when she was sufficiently drunk could sometimes be induced to tell the story of her first love-affair.

It was hard then to realise that the bleared, wrinkled creature, exactly like a wisp of charred rag, could ever have been 'Lispeth of the Kotgarh Mission.'

1886

THE HEAD
OF THE DISTRICT

~~~~~~~~~~~~~~~~~~~~~~~~~~~~~~~~

There's a convict more in the Central Jail,
  Behind the old mud wall;
There's a lifter less on the Border trail,
  And the Queen's Peace over all,
                              Dear boys,
    The Queen's Peace over all.

For we must bear our leader's blame,
  On us the shame will fall,
If we lift our hand from a fettered land
  And the Queen's Peace over all,
                              Dear boys,
    The Queen's Peace over all!
                    The Running of Shindand

I

The Indus had risen in flood without warning. Last night
it was a fordable shallow; to-night five miles of raving
muddy water parted bank and caving bank, and the river
was still rising under the moon. A litter borne by six
bearded men, all unused to the work, stopped in the white
sand that bordered the whiter plain.

'It's God's will,' they said. 'We dare not cross to-night,
even in a boat. Let us light a fire and cook food. We be
tired men.'

They looked at the litter inquiringly. Within, the Deputy Commissioner of the Kot-Kumharsen district lay
dying of fever. They had brought him across country, six

fighting-men of a frontier clan that he had won over to the paths of a moderate righteousness, when he had broken down at the foot of their inhospitable hills. And Tallantire, his assistant, rode with them, heavy-hearted as heavy-eyed with sorrow and lack of sleep. He had served under the sick man for three years, and had learned to love him as men associated in toil of the hardest learn to love— or hate. Dropping from his horse he parted the curtains of the litter and peered inside.

'Orde—Orde, old man, can you hear? We have to wait till the river goes down, worse luck.'

'I hear,' returned a dry whisper. 'Wait till the river goes down. I thought we should reach camp before the dawn. Polly knows. She'll meet me.'

One of the litter-men stared across the river and caught a faint twinkle of light on the far side. He whispered to Tallantire, 'There are his camp-fires, and his wife. They will cross in the morning, for they have better boats. Can he live so long?'

Tallantire shook his head. Yardley-Orde was very near to death. What need to vex his soul with hopes of a meeting that could not be? The river gulped at the banks, brought down a cliff of sand, and snarled the more hungrily. The litter-men sought for fuel in the waste—dried camel-thorn and refuse of the camps that had waited at the ford. Their sword-belts clinked as they moved softly in the haze of the moonlight, and Tallantire's horse coughed to explain that he would like a blanket.

'I'm cold too,' said the voice from the litter. 'I fancy this is the end. Poor Polly!'

Tallantire rearranged the blankets; Khoda Dad Khan, seeing this, stripped off his own heavy-wadded sheepskin coat and added it to the pile. 'I shall be warm by the fire presently,' said he. Tallantire took the wasted body of his chief into his arms and held it against his breast. Perhaps if they kept him very warm Orde might live to see his wife once more. If only blind Providence would send a three-foot fall in the river!

'That's better,' said Orde faintly. 'Sorry to be a nuisance, but is—is there anything to drink?'

They gave him milk and whisky, and Tallantire felt a little warmth against his own breast. Orde began to mutter.

'It isn't that I mind dying,' he said. 'It's leaving Polly and the district. Thank God! we have no children. Dick, you know, I'm dipped—awfully dipped—debts in my first five years' service. It isn't much of a pension, but enough for her. She has her mother at home. Getting there is the difficulty. And—and—you see, not being a soldier's wife——'

'We'll arrange the passage home, of course,' said Tallantire quietly.

'It's not nice to think of sending round the hat; but, good Lord! how many men I lie here and remember that had to do it! Morten's dead—he was of my year. Shaughnessy is dead, and he had children; I remember he used to read us their school-letters; what a bore we thought him! Evans is dead—Kot-Kumharsen killed him! Ricketts of Myndonie is dead—and I'm going too. "Man that is born of a woman is small potatoes and few in the hill." That reminds me, Dick; the four Khusru Kheyl villages in our border want a one-third remittance this spring. That's fair; their crops are bad. See that they get it, and speak to Ferris about the canal. I should like to have lived till that was finished; it means so much for the North-Indus villages—but Ferris is an idle beggar—wake him up. You'll have charge of the district till my successor comes. I wish they would appoint you permanently; you know the folk. I suppose it will be Bullows, though. 'Good man, but too weak for frontier work; and he doesn't understand the priests. The blind priest at Jagai will bear watching. You'll find it in my papers,—in the uniform-case, I think.

Call the Khusru Kheyl men up; I'll hold my last public audience. Khoda Dad Khan!'

The leader of the men sprang to the side of the litter, his companions following.

'Men, I'm dying,' said Orde quickly, in the vernacular; 'and soon there will be no more Orde Sahib to twist your tails and prevent you from raiding cattle.'

'God forbid this thing!' broke out the deep bass chorus. 'The Sahib is not going to die.'

'Yes, he is; and then he will know whether Mahomed speaks truth, or Moses. But you must be good men, when I am not here. Such of you as live in our borders must pay your taxes quietly as before. I have spoken of the villages to be gently treated this year. Such of you as live in the hills must refrain from cattle-lifting, and burn no more thatch, and turn a deaf ear to the voice of the priests, who, not knowing the strength of the Government, would lead you into foolish wars, wherein you will surely die and your crops be eaten by strangers. And you must not sack any caravans, and must leave your arms at the police-post when you come in; as has been your custom, and my order. And Tallantire Sahib will be with you, but I do not know who takes my place. I speak now true talk, for I am as it were already dead, my children,—for though ye be strong men, ye are children.'

'And thou art our father and our mother,' broke in Khoda Dad Khan with an oath. 'What shall we do, now there is no one to speak for us, or to teach us to go wisely!'

'There remains Tallantire Sahib. Go to him; he knows your talk and your heart. Keep the young men quiet, listen to the old men, and obey. Khoda Dad Khan, take my ring. The watch and chain go to thy brother. Keep those things for my sake, and I will speak to whatever God I may encounter and tell him that the Khusru Kheyl are good men. Ye have my leave to go.'

Khoda Dad Khan, the ring upon his finger, choked audibly as he caught the well-known formula that closed an interview. His brother turned to look across the river. The dawn was breaking, and a speck of white showed on the dull silver of the stream. 'She comes,' said the man under his breath. 'Can he live for another two hours?' And he pulled the newly-acquired watch out of his belt and looked uncomprehendingly at the dial, as he had seen Englishmen do.

For two hours the bellying sail tacked and blundered up and down the river, Tallantire still clasping Orde in his arms, and Khoda Dad Khan chafing his feet. He spoke now and again of the district and his wife, but, as the end neared, more frequently of the latter. They hoped he did not know that she was even then risking her life in a crazy native boat to regain him. But the awful foreknowledge of the dying deceived them. Wrenching himself forward, Orde looked through the curtains and saw how near was the sail. 'That's Polly,' he said simply, though his mouth was wried with agony. 'Polly and—the grimmest practical joke ever played on a man. Dick—you'll—have—to—explain.'

And an hour later Tallantire met on the bank a woman in a gingham riding-habit and a sun-hat who cried out to him for her husband—her boy and her darling—while Khoda Dad Khan threw himself face-down on the sand and covered his eyes.

II

The very simplicity of the notion was its charm. What more easy to win a reputation for far-seeing statesmanship, originality, and, above all, deference to the desires of the people, than by appointing a child of the country to the rule of that country? Two hundred millions of the most loving and grateful folk under Her Majesty's dominion would laud the fact, and their praise would endure for ever. Yet he was indifferent to praise or blame, as befitted the Very Greatest of All the Viceroys. His administration was based upon principle, and the principle must be enforced in season and out of season. His pen and tongue had created the New India, teeming with possibilities—loud-voiced, insistent, a nation among nations—all his very own. Wherefore the Very Greatest of All the Viceroys took another step in advance, and with it counsel of those who should have advised him on the appointment of a successor to Yardley-Orde. There was a gentleman and a member of the Bengal Civil Service who had won his place and a university degree to boot in fair and open competition with the sons of the English. He was cultured, of the world, and, if report spoke truly, had wisely and, above all, sympathetically ruled a crowded district in South-Eastern Bengal. He had been to England and charmed many drawing-rooms there. His name, if the Viceroy recollected aright, was Mr. Grish Chunder Dé, M.A. In short, did anybody see any objection to the appointment, always on principle, of a man of the people to rule the people? The district in South-Eastern Bengal might with advantage, he apprehended, pass over to a younger civilian of Mr. G. C. Dé's nationality (who had written a remarkably clever pamphlet on the political value of sympathy in administration); and Mr. G. C. Dé could be transferred northward to Kot-Kumharsen. The Viceroy was averse, on principle, to interfering with appointments under control of the Provincial Governments. He wished it to be understood that he merely recommended and advised in this instance. As regarded the mere question of race, Mr. Grish Chunder Dé was more English than the English, and yet possessed of that peculiar sympathy and insight which the best among the best Service in the world could only win to at the end of their service.

The stern, black-bearded kings who sit about the Council-board of India divided on the step, with the inevitable result of driving the Very Greatest of All the Vice-

roys into the borders of hysteria, and a bewildered obsti-
nacy pathetic as that of a child.

'The principle is sound enough,' said the weary-eyed
Head of the Red Provinces in which Kot-Kumharsen lay,
for he too held theories. 'The only difficulty is——'

'Put the screw on the District officials; brigade Dé with
a very strong Deputy Commissioner on each side of him;
give him the best assistant in the Province; rub the fear of
God into the people beforehand; and if anything goes
wrong, say that his colleagues didn't back him up. All
these lovely little experiments recoil on the District-
Officer in the end,' said the Knight of the Drawn Sword
with a truthful brutality that made the Head of the Red
Provinces shudder. And on a tacit understanding of this
kind the transfer was accomplished, as quietly as might be
for many reasons.

It is sad to think that what goes for public opinion in
India did not generally see the wisdom of the Viceroy's
appointment. There were not lacking indeed hireling
organs, notoriously in the pay of a tyrannous bureaucracy,
who more than hinted that His Excellency was a fool, a
dreamer of dreams, a doctrinaire, and, worst of all, a trifler
with the lives of men. 'The Viceroy's Excellence Gazette,'
published in Calcutta, was at pains to thank 'Our beloved
Viceroy for once more and again thus gloriously vindicat-
ing the potentialities of the Bengali nations for extended
executive and administrative duties in foreign parts beyond our ken. We do not at all doubt that our excellent
fellow-townsman, Mr. Grish Chunder Dé, Esq., M.A.,
will uphold the prestige of the Bengali, notwithstanding
what underhand intrigue and *peshbundi* may be set on
foot to insidiously nip his fame and blast his prospects
among the proud civilians, some of which will now have
to serve under a despised native and take orders too. How
will you like that, Misters? We entreat our beloved Viceroy still to substantiate himself superiorly to race-
prejudice and colour-blindness, and to allow the flower

of this now *our* Civil Service all the full pays and allowances granted to his more fortunate brethren.'

III

'When does this man take over charge? I'm alone just now, and I gather that I'm to stand fast under him.'

'Would you have cared for a transfer?' said Bullows keenly. Then, laying his hand on Tallantire's shoulder: 'We're all in the same boat; don't desert us. And yet, why the devil should you stay, if you can get another charge?'

'It was Orde's,' said Tallantire simply.

'Well, it's Dé's now. He's a Bengali of the Bengalis, crammed with code and case law; a beautiful man so far as routine and deskwork go, and pleasant to talk to. They naturally have always kept him in his own home district, where all his sisters and his cousins and his aunts lived, somewhere south of Dacca. He did no more than turn the place into a pleasant little family preserve, allowed his subordinates to do what they liked, and let everybody have a chance at the shekels. Consequently he's immensely popular down there.'

'I've nothing to do with that. How on earth am I to explain to the district that they are going to be governed by a Bengali? Do you—does the Government, I mean—suppose that the Khusru Kheyl will sit quiet when they once know? What will the Mahomedan heads of villages say? How will the police—Muzbi Sikhs and Pathans—how will *they* work under him? We couldn't say anything if the Government appointed a sweeper; but my people will say a good deal, you know that. It's a piece of cruel folly!'

'My dear boy, I know all that, and more. I've represented it, and have been told that I am exhibiting "culpable and puerile prejudice." By Jove, if the Khusru Kheyl don't exhibit something worse than that I don't know the Border! The chances are that you have the district alight on your hands, and I shall have to leave my work and help you pull through. I needn't ask you to stand by the Bengali man in every possible way. You'll do that for your own sake.'

'For Orde's. I can't say that I care twopence personally.'

'Don't be an ass. It's grievous enough, God knows, and the Government will know later on; but that's no reason for your sulking. *You* must try to run the district; *you* must stand between him and as much insult as possible; *you* must show him the ropes; *you* must pacify the Khusru Kheyl, and just warn Curbar of the Police to look out for trouble by the way. I'm always at the end of a telegraph-wire, and willing to peril my reputation to hold the district together. You'll lose yours, of course. If you keep things straight, and he isn't actually beaten with a stick when he's on tour, he'll get all the credit. If anything goes wrong, you'll be told that you didn't support him loyally.'

'I know what I've got to do,' said Tallantire wearily, 'and I am going to do it. But it's hard.'

'The work is with us, the event is with Allah,—as Orde used to say when he was more than usually in hot water.' And Bullows rode away.

That two gentlemen in Her Majesty's Bengal Civil Service should thus discuss a third, also in that service, and a cultured and affable man withal, seems strange and saddening. Yet listen to the artless babble of the Blind Mullah of Jagai, the priest of the Khusru Kheyl, sitting upon a rock overlooking the Border. Five years before, a chance-hurled shell from a screw-gun battery had dashed earth in the face of the Mullah, then urging a rush of Ghazis against half a dozen British bayonets. So he became blind, and hated the English none the less for the little accident. Yardley-Orde knew his failing, and had many times laughed at him therefor.

'Dogs you are,' said the Blind Mullah to the listening tribesmen round the fire. 'Whipped dogs! Because you listened to Orde Sahib and called him father and behaved as his children, the British Government have proven how they regard you. Orde Sahib ye know is dead.'

'Ai! ai! ai!' said half a dozen voices.

'He was a man. Comes now in his stead, whom think ye? A Bengali of Bengal—an eater of fish from the South.'

'A lie!' said Khoda Dad Khan. 'And but for the small matter of thy priesthood, I'd drive my gun butt-first down thy throat!'

'Oho, art thou there, lickspittle of the English? Go in to-morrow across the Border to pay service to Orde Sahib's successor, and thou shalt slip thy shoes at the tent-door of a Bengali, as thou shalt hand thy offering to a Bengali's black fist. This I know; and in my youth, when a young man spoke evil to a Mullah holding the doors of Heaven and Hell, the gun-butt was not rammed down the Mullah's gullet. No!'

The Blind Mullah hated Khoda Dad Khan with Afghan hatred; both being rivals for the headship of the tribe; but the latter was feared for bodily as the other for spiritual gifts. Khoda Dad Khan looked at Orde's ring and grunted, 'I go in to-morrow because I am not an old fool, preaching war against the English. If the Government, smitten with madness, have done this, then . . .'

'Then,' croaked the Mullah, 'thou wilt take out the young men and strike at the four villages within the Border?'

'Or wring thy neck, black raven of Jehannum, for a bearer of ill-tidings.'

Khoda Dad Khan oiled his long locks with great care, put on his best Bokhara belt, a new turban-cap and fine green shoes, and accompanied by a few friends came down from the hills to pay a visit to the new Deputy Commissioner of Kot-Kumharsen. Also he bore tribute—four or five priceless gold mohurs of Akbar's time in a white handkerchief. These the Deputy Commissioner would touch and remit. The little ceremony used to be a sign that, so far as Khoda Dad Khan's personal influence went, the Khusru Kheyl would be good boys,—till the next time; especially if Khoda Dad Khan happened to like the new Deputy Commissioner. In Yardley-Orde's consulship his visit concluded with a sumptuous dinner and perhaps forbidden liquors; certainly with some wonderful tales and great good-fellowship. Then Khoda Dad Khan would swagger back to his hold, vowing that Orde Sahib was one prince and Tallantire Sahib another, and that whosoever went a-raiding into British territory would be flayed alive. On this occasion he found the Deputy Commissioner's tents looking much as usual. Regarding himself as privileged he strode through the open door to confront a suave, portly Bengali in English costume writing at a table. Unversed in the elevating influence of education, and not in the least caring for university degrees, Khoda Dad Khan promptly set the man down for a Babu—the native clerk of the Deputy Commissioner—a hated and despised animal.

'Ugh!' said he cheerfully. 'Where's your master, Babu-jee?'

'I am the Deputy Commissioner,' said the gentleman in English.

Now he overvalued the effects of university degrees, and stared Khoda Dad Khan in the face. But if from your earliest infancy you have been accustomed to look on battle, murder, and sudden death, if spilt blood affects your nerves as much as red paint, and, above all, if you have faithfully believed that the Bengali was the servant of all Hindustan, and that all Hindustan was vastly inferior to your own large, lustful self, you can endure, even though uneducated, a very large amount of looking over. You can even stare down a graduate of an Oxford College if the latter has been born in a hothouse, of stock bred in a hothouse, and fearing physical pain as some men fear sin; especially if your opponent's mother has frightened him to sleep in his youth with horrible stories of devils inhabiting Afghanistan, and dismal legends of the black North.

The eyes behind the gold spectacles sought the floor. Khoda Dad Khan chuckled, and swung out to find Tallantire hard by. 'Here,' said he roughly, thrusting the coins before him, 'touch and remit. That answers for *my* good behaviour. But, O Sahib, has the Government gone mad to send a black Bengali dog to us? And am I to pay service to such an one? And are you to work under him? What does it mean?'

'It is an order,' said Tallantire. He had expected something of this kind. 'He is a very clever S-sahib.'

'He a Sahib! He's a *kala admi*—a black man—unfit to run at the tail of a potter's donkey. All the peoples of the earth have harried Bengal. It is written. Thou knowest when we of the North wanted women or plunder whither went we? To Bengal—where else? What child's talk is this of Sahibdom—after Orde Sahib too! Of a truth the Blind Mullah was right.'

'What of him?' asked Tallantire uneasily. He mistrusted that old man with his dead eyes and his deadly tongue.

'Nay, now, because of the oath that I sware to Orde Sahib when we watched him die by the river yonder, I will tell. In the first place, is it true that the English have set the heel of the Bengali on their own neck, and that there is no more English rule in the land?'

'I am here,' said Tallantire, 'and I serve the Maharanee of England.'

'The Mullah said otherwise, and further that because we loved Orde Sahib the Government sent us a pig to show that we were dogs, who till now have been held by the strong hand. Also that they were taking away the white soldiers, that more Hindustanis might come, and that all was changing.'

This is the worst of ill-considered handling of a very large country. What looks so feasible in Calcutta, so right in Bombay, so unassailable in Madras, is misunderstood by the North and entirely changes its complexion on the

banks of the Indus. Khoda Dad Khan explained as clearly
as he could that, though he himself intended to be good,
he really could not answer for the more reckless members
of his tribe under the leadership of the Blind Mullah.
They might or they might not give trouble, but they certainly had no intention whatever of obeying the new Deputy Commissioner. Was Tallantire perfectly sure that in
the event of any systematic border-raiding the force in the
district could put it down promptly?

'Tell the Mullah if he talks any more fool's talk,' said
Tallantire curtly, 'that he takes his men on to certain
death, and his tribe to blockade, trespass-fine, and blood-
money. But why do I talk to one who no longer carries
weight in the counsels of the tribe?'

Khoda Dad Khan pocketed that insult. He had learned
something that he much wanted to know, and returned to
his hills to be sarcastically complimented by the Mullah,
whose tongue raging round the camp-fires was deadlier
flame than ever dung-cake fed.

IV

Be pleased to consider here for a moment the unknown
district of Kot-Kumharsen. It lay cut lengthways by the
Indus under the line of the Khusru hills—ramparts of
useless earth and tumbled stone. It was seventy miles long
by fifty broad, maintained a population of something less
than two hundred thousand, and paid taxes to the extent
of forty thousand pounds a year on an area that was by
rather more than half sheer, hopeless waste. The cultiva-
tors were not gentle people, the miners for salt were less
gentle still, and the cattle-breeders least gentle of all. A
police-post in the top right-hand corner and a tiny mud
fort in the top left-hand corner prevented as much salt-
smuggling and cattle-lifting as the influence of the civilians could not put down; and in the bottom right-hand
corner lay Jumala, the district headquarters—a pitiful

knot of lime-washed barns facetiously rented as houses, reeking with frontier fever, leaking in the rain, and ovens in the summer.

It was to this place that Grish Chunder Dé was travelling, there formally to take over charge of the district. But the news of his coming had gone before. Bengalis were as scarce as poodles among the simple Borderers, who cut each other's heads open with their long spades and worshipped impartially at Hindu and Mahomedan shrines. They crowded to see him, pointing at him, and diversely comparing him to a gravid milch-buffalo, or a broken-down horse, as their limited range of metaphor prompted. They laughed at his police-guard, and wished to know how long the burly Sikhs were going to lead Bengali apes. They inquired whether he had brought his women with him, and advised him explicitly not to tamper with theirs. It remained for a wrinkled hag by the road-side to slap her lean breasts as he passed, crying, 'I have suckled six that could have eaten six thousand of *him*. The Government shot them, and made this That a king!' Whereat a blue-turbaned huge-boned plough-mender shouted, 'Have hope, mother o' mine! He may yet go the way of thy wastrels.' And the children, the little brown puff-balls, regarded curiously. It was generally a good thing for infancy to stray into Orde Sahib's tent, where copper coins were to be won for the mere wishing, and tales of the most authentic, such as even their mothers knew but the first half of. No! This fat black man could never tell them how Pir Prith hauled the eye-teeth out of ten devils; how the big stones came to lie all in a row on top of the Khusru hills, and what happened if you shouted through the village-gate to the gray wolf at even 'Badl Khas is dead.' Meantime Grish Chunder Dé talked hastily and much to Tallantire, after the manner of those who are 'more English than the English,'—of Oxford and 'home,' with much curious book-knowledge of bump-suppers, cricket-matches, hunting-runs, and other unholy sports of the alien. 'We

must get these fellows in hand,' he said once or twice uneasily; 'get them well in hand, and drive them on a tight
rein. No use, you know, being slack with your district.'

And a moment later Tallantire heard Debendra Nath
Dé, who brotherliwise had followed his kinsman's fortune
and hoped for the shadow of his protection as a pleader,
whisper in Bengali, 'Better are dried fish at Dacca than
drawn swords at Delhi. Brother of mine, these men are
devils, as our mother said And you will always have to
ride upon a horse!'

That night there was a public audience in a broken-
down little town thirty miles from Jumala, when the new
Deputy Commissioner, in reply to the greetings of the
subordinate native officials, delivered a speech. It was a
carefully thought-out speech, which would have been
very valuable had not his third sentence begun with three
innocent words, '*Hamara hookum hai*—It is my order.'
Then there was a laugh, clear and bell-like, from the back
of the big tent, where a few border landholders sat, and
the laugh grew and scorn mingled with it, and the lean,
keen face of Debendra Nath Dé paled, and Grish Chunder
turning to Tallantire spake: '*You*—you put up this arrangement.' Upon that instant the noise of hoofs rang
without, and there entered Curbar, the District Superintendent of Police, sweating and dusty. The State had
tossed him into a corner of the province for seventeen
weary years, there to check smuggling of salt, and to hope
for promotion that never came. He had forgotten how to
keep his white uniform clean, had screwed rusty spurs
into patent-leather shoes, and clothed his head indif-
ferently with a helmet or a turban. Soured, old, worn with
heat and cold, he waited till he should be entitled to sufficient pension to keep him from starving.

'Tallantire,' said he, disregarding Grish Chunder Dé,
'come outside. I want to speak to you.' They withdrew.
'It's this,' continued Curbar. 'The Khusru Kheyl have

rushed and cut up half a dozen of the coolies on Ferris's new canal-embankment; killed a couple of men and carried off a woman. I wouldn't trouble you about that—Ferris is after them and Hugonin, my assistant, with ten mounted police. But that's only the beginning, I fancy. Their fires are out on the Hassan Ardeb heights, and unless we're pretty quick there'll be a flare-up all along our Border. They are sure to raid the four Khusru villages on our side of the line; there's been bad blood between them for years; and you know the Blind Mullah has been preaching a holy war since Orde went out. What's your notion?'

'Damn!' said Tallantire thoughtfully. 'They've begun quick. Well, it seems to me I'd better ride off to Fort Ziar and get what men I can there to picket among the lowland villages, if it's not too late. Tommy Dodd commands at Fort Ziar, I think. Ferris and Hugonin ought to teach the canal-thieves a lesson, and—— No, we can't have the Head of the Police ostentatiously guarding the Treasury. You go back to the canal. I'll wire Bullows to come into Jumala with a strong police-guard, and sit on the Treasury. They won't touch the place, but it looks well.'

'I—I—I insist upon knowing what this means,' said the voice of the Deputy Commissioner, who had followed the speakers.

'Oh!' said Curbar, who being in the Police could not understand that fifteen years of education must, on principle, change the Bengali into a Briton. 'There has been a fight on the Border, and heaps of men are killed. There's going to be another fight, and heaps more will be killed.'

'What for?'

'Because the teeming millions of this district don't exactly approve of you, and think that under your benign rule they are going to have a good time. It strikes me that you had better make arrangements. I act, as you know, by your orders. What do you advise?'

'I—I take you all to witness that I have not yet assumed charge of the district,' stammered the Deputy Commissioner, not in the tones of the 'more English.'

'Ah, I thought so. Well, as I was saying, Tallantire, your plan is sound. Carry it out. Do you want an escort?'

'No; only a decent horse. But how about wiring to headquarters?'

'I fancy, from the colour of his cheeks, that your superior officer will send some wonderful telegrams before the night's over. Let him do that, and we shall have half the troops of the province coming up to see what's the trouble. Well, run along, and take care of yourself—the Khusru Kheyl jab upwards from below, remember. Ho! Mir Khan, give Tallantire Sahib the best of the horses, and tell five men to ride to Jumala with the Deputy Commissioner Sahib Bahadur. There is a hurry toward.'

There was; and it was not in the least bettered by Debendra Nath Dé clinging to a policeman's bridle and demanding the shortest, the very shortest way to Jumala. Now originality is fatal to the Bengali. Debendra Nath should have stayed with his brother, who rode steadfastly for Jumala on the railway-line, thanking gods entirely unknown to the most catholic of universities that he had not taken charge of the district, and could still—happy resource of a fertile race!—fall sick.

And I grieve to say that when he reached his goal two policemen, not devoid of rude wit, who had been conferring together as they bumped in their saddles, arranged an entertainment for his behoof. It consisted of first one and then the other entering his room with prodigious details of war, the massing of bloodthirsty and devilish tribes, and the burning of towns. It was almost as good, said these scamps, as riding with Curbar after evasive Afghans. Each invention kept the hearer at work for half an hour on telegrams which the sack of Delhi would hardly have justified. To every power that could move a bayonet or transfer a terrified man, Grish Chunder Dé appealed tele-graphically. He was alone, his assistants had fled, and in truth he had not taken over charge of the district. Had the telegrams been despatched many things would have oc-curred; but since the only signaller in Jumala had gone to bed, and the station-master, after one look at the tremen-dous pile of paper, discovered that railway regulations forbade the forwarding of imperial messages, policemen Ram Singh and Nihal Singh were fain to turn the stuff into a pillow and slept on it very comfortably.

Tallantire drove his spurs into a rampant skewbald stallion with china-blue eyes, and settled himself for the forty-mile ride to Fort Ziar. Knowing his district blind-fold, he wasted no time hunting for short cuts, but headed across the richer grazing-ground to the ford where Orde had died and been buried. The dusty ground deadened the noise of his horse's hoofs, the moon threw his shadow, a restless goblin, before him, and the heavy dew drenched him to the skin. Hillock, scrub that brushed against the horse's belly, unmetalled road where the whip-like foliage of the tamarisks lashed his forehead, illimitable levels of lowland furred with bent and speckled with drowsing cat-tle, waste, and hillock anew, dragged themselves past, and the skewbald was labouring in the deep sand of the Indus-ford. Tallantire was conscious of no distinct thought till the nose of the dawdling ferry-boat grounded on the farther side, and his horse shied snorting at the white headstone of Orde's grave. Then he uncovered, and shouted that the dead might hear, 'They're out, old man! Wish me luck.' In the chill of the dawn he was hammering with a stirrup-iron at the gate of Fort Ziar, where fifty sabres of that tattered regiment, the Belooch Beshaklis were supposed to guard Her Majesty's interests along a few hundred miles of Border. This particular fort was commanded by a subaltern, who, born of the ancient fam-ily of the Derouletts, naturally answered to the name of

Tommy Dodd. Him Tallantire found robed in a sheep-skin coat, shaking with fever like an aspen, and trying to read the native apothecary's list of invalids.

'So you've come, too,' said he. 'Well, we're all sick here, and I don't think I can horse thirty men; but we're bub—bub—bub blessed willing. Stop, does this impress you as a trap or a lie?' He tossed a scrap of paper to Tallantire, on which was written painfully in crabbed Gurmukhi, 'We cannot hold young horses. They will feed after the moon goes down in the four border villages issuing from the Jagai pass on the next night.' Then in English round hand—'Your sincere friend.'

'Good man!' said Tallantire. 'That's Khoda Dad Khan's work, I know. It's the only piece of English he could ever keep in his head, and he is immensely proud of it. He is playing against the Blind Mullah for his own hand—the treacherous young ruffian!'

'Don't know the politics of the Khusru Kheyl, but if you're satisfied, I am. That was pitched in over the gate-head last night, and I thought we might pull ourselves together and see what was on. Oh, but we're sick with fever here and no mistake! Is this going to be a big business, think you?' said Tommy Dodd.

Tallantire gave him briefly the outlines of the case, and Tommy Dodd whistled and shook with fever alternately. That day he devoted to strategy, the art of war, and the enlivenment of the invalids, till at dusk there stood ready forty-two troopers, lean, worn, and dishevelled, whom Tommy Dodd surveyed with pride, and addressed thus: 'O men! If you die you will go to Hell. Therefore endeavour to keep alive. But if you go to Hell that place cannot be hotter than this place, and we are not told that we shall there suffer from fever. Consequently be not afraid of dying. File out there!' They grinned, and went.

V

It will be long ere the Khusru Kheyl forget their night attack on the lowland villages. The Mullah had promised an easy victory and unlimited plunder; but behold, armed troopers of the Queen had risen out of the very earth, cutting, slashing, and riding down under the stars, so that no man knew where to turn, and all feared that they had brought an army about their ears, and ran back to the hills. In the panic of that flight more men were seen to drop from wounds inflicted by an Afghan knife jabbed upwards, and yet more from long-range carbine-fire. Then there rose a cry of treachery, and when they reached their own guarded heights, they had left, with some forty dead and sixty wounded, all their confidence in the Blind Mullah on the plains below. They clamoured, swore, and argued round the fires; the women wailing for the lost, and the Mullah shrieking curses on the returned.

Then Khoda Dad Khan, eloquent and unbreathed, for he had taken no part in the fight, rose to improve the occasion. He pointed out that the tribe owed every item of its present misfortune to the Blind Mullah, who had lied in every possible particular and talked them into a trap. It was undoubtedly an insult that a Bengali, the son of a Bengali, should presume to administer the Border, but that fact did not, as the Mullah pretended, herald a general time of license and lifting; and the inexplicable madness of the English had not in the least impaired their power of guarding their marches. On the contrary, the baffled and out-generalled tribe would now, just when their food-stock was lowest, be blockaded from any trade with Hindustan until they had sent hostages for good behaviour, paid compensation for disturbance, and blood-money at the rate of thirty-six English pounds per head for every villager that they might have slain. 'And ye know that those lowland dogs will make oath that we have slain scores. Will the Mullah pay the fines or must we sell our guns?' A low growl ran round the fires. 'Now, seeing that all this is the Mullah's work, and that we have gained nothing but promises of Paradise thereby, it is in my heart that we of the Khusru Kheyl lack a shrine whereat to pray. We are weakened, and henceforth how shall we dare to cross into the Madar Kheyl border, as has been our custom, to kneel to Pir Sajji's tomb? The Madar men will fall upon us, and rightly. But our Mullah is a holy man. He has helped two score of us into Paradise this night. Let him therefore accompany his flock, and we will build over his body a dome of the blue tiles of Mooltan, and burn lamps at his feet every Friday night. He shall be a saint: we shall have a shrine; and there our women shall pray for fresh seed to fill the gaps in our fighting-tale. How think you?'

A grim chuckle followed the suggestion, and the soft *wheep, wheep* of unscabbarded knives followed the chuckle. It was an excellent notion, and met a long felt want of the tribe. The Mullah sprang to his feet, glaring with withered eyeballs at the drawn death he could not see, and calling down the curses of God and Mahomed on the tribe. Then began a game of blind man's buff round and between the fires, whereof Khuruk Shah, the tribal poet, has sung in verse that will not die.

They tickled him gently under the armpit with the knife-point. He leaped aside screaming, only to feel a cold blade drawn lightly over the back of his neck, or a rifle-muzzle rubbing his beard. He called on his adherents to aid him, but most of these lay dead on the plains, for Khoda Dad Khan had been at some pains to arrange their decease. Men described to him the glories of the shrine they would build, and the little children clapping their hands cried, 'Run, Mullah, run! There's a man behind you!' In the end, when the sport wearied, Khoda Dad Khan's brother sent a knife home between his ribs. 'Wherefore,' said Khoda Dad Khan with charming simplicity, 'I am now Chief of the Khusru Kheyl!' No man gainsaid him; and they all went to sleep very stiff and sore.

On the plain below Tommy Dodd was lecturing on the beauties of a cavalry charge by night, and Tallantire, bowed on his saddle, was gasping hysterically because there was a sword dangling from his wrist flecked with the blood of the Khusru Kheyl, the tribe that Orde had kept in leash so well. When a Rajpoot trooper pointed out that the skewbald's right ear had been taken off at the root by some blind slash of its unskilled rider, Tallantire broke down altogether, and laughed and sobbed till Tommy Dodd made him lie down and rest.

'We must wait about till the morning,' said he. 'I wired to the Colonel just before we left, to send a wing of the Beshaklis after us. He'll be furious with me for monopolising the fun, though. Those beggars in the hills won't give us any more trouble.'

'Then tell the Beshaklis to go on and see what has happened to Curbar on the canal. We must patrol the whole line of the Border. You're quite sure, Tommy, that—that stuff was—was only the skewbald's ear?'

'Oh, quite,' said Tommy. 'You just missed cutting off his head. *I* saw you when we went into the mess. Sleep, old man.'

Noon brought two squadrons of Beshaklis and a knot of furious brother officers demanding the court-martial of Tommy Dodd for 'spoiling the picnic,' and a gallop across country to the canal-works where Ferris, Curbar, and Hugonin were haranguing the terror-stricken coolies on the enormity of abandoning good work and high pay, merely because half a dozen of their fellows had been cut down. The sight of a troop of the Beshaklis restored wavering confidence, and the police-hunted section of the Khusru Kheyl had the joy of watching the canal-bank humming with life as usual, while such of their men as had taken refuge in the water-courses and ravines were being driven out by the troopers. By sundown began the remorseless patrol of the Border by police and trooper, most like the cow-boys' eternal ride round restless cattle.

'Now,' said Khoda Dad Khan to his fellows, pointing out a line of twinkling fires below, 'ye may see how far the old order changes. After their horse will come the little devil-guns that they can drag up to the tops of the hills, and, for aught I know, to the clouds when we crown the hills. If the tribe-council thinks good, I will go to Tallantire Sahib—who loves me—and see if I can stave off at least the blockade. Do I speak for the tribe?'

'Ay, speak for the tribe in God's name. How those accursed fires wink! Do the English send their troops on the wire—or is this the work of the Bengali?'

As Khoda Dad Khan went down the hill he was delayed by an interview with a hard-pressed tribesman, which caused him to return hastily for something he had forgotten. Then, handing himself over to the two troopers who had been chasing his friend, he claimed escort to Tallantire Sahib, then with Bullows at Jumala. The Border was safe, and the time for reasons in writing had begun.

'Thank Heaven!' said Bullows, 'that the trouble came at once. Of course we can never put down the reason in black and white, but all India will understand. And it is better to have a sharp short outbreak than five years of impotent administration inside the Border. It costs less. Grish Chunder Dé has reported himself sick, and has been transferred to his own province without any sort of reprimand. He was strong on not having taken over the district.'

'Of course,' said Tallantire bitterly. 'Well, what am I supposed to have done that was wrong?'

'Oh, you will be told that you exceeded all your powers, and should have reported, and written, and advised for three weeks until the Khusru Kheyl could really come down in force. But I don't think the authorities will dare to make a fuss about it. They've had their lesson. Have you seen Curbar's version of the affair? He can't write a report, but he can speak the truth.'

'What's the use of the truth? He'd much better tear up the report. I'm sick and heartbroken over it all. It was so utterly unnecessary—except in that it rid us of that Babu.'

Entered unabashed Khoda Dad Khan, a stuffed forage-net in his hand, and the troopers behind him.

'May you never be tired!' said he cheerily. 'Well, Sahibs, that was a good fight, and Naim Shah's mother is in debt to you, Tallantire Sahib. A clean cut, they tell me, through jaw, wadded coat, and deep into the collar-bone. Well done! But I speak for the tribe. There has been a fault—a great fault. Thou knowest that I and mine, Tallantire Sahib, kept the oath we sware to Orde Sahib on the banks of the Indus.'

'As an Afghan keeps his knife—sharp on one side, blunt on the other,' said Tallantire.

'The better swing in the blow, then. But I speak God's truth. Only the Blind Mullah carried the young men on the tip of his tongue, and said that there was no more Border-law because a Bengali had been sent, and we need not fear the English at all. So they came down to avenge that insult and get plunder. Ye know what befell, and how far I helped. Now five score of us are dead or wounded, and we are all shamed and sorry, and desire no further war. Moreover, that ye may better listen to us, we have taken off the head of the Blind Mullah, whose evil counsels have led us to folly. I bring it for proof,'—and he heaved on the floor the head. 'He will give no more trouble, for *I* am chief now, and so I sit in a higher place at all audiences. Yet there is an offset to this head. That was another fault. One of the men found that black Bengali beast, through whom this trouble arose, wandering on horseback and weeping. Reflecting that he had caused loss of much good life, Alla Dad Khan, whom, if you choose, I will to-morrow shoot, whipped off this head, and I bring it to you to cover your shame, that ye may bury it. See, no man kept the spectacles, though they were of gold.'

Slowly rolled to Tallantire's feet the crop-haired head of a spectacled Bengali gentleman, open-eyed, open-mouthed—the head of Terror incarnate. Bullows bent down. 'Yet another blood-fine and a heavy one, Khoda Dad Khan, for this is the head of Debendra Nath, the man's brother. The Babu is safe long since. All but the fools of the Khusru Kheyl know that.'

'Well, I care not for carrion. Quick meat for me. The thing was under our hills asking the road to Jumala and Alla Dad Khan showed him the road to Jehannum, being, as thou sayest, but a fool. Remains now what the Government will do to us. As to the blockade——'

'Who art thou, seller of dog's flesh,' thundered Tallantire, 'to speak of terms and treaties? Get hence to the hills—go, and wait there starving, till it shall please the Government to call thy people out for punishment—children and fools that ye be! Count your dead, and be still. Rest assured that the Government will send you a *man!*'

'Ay,' returned Khoda Dad Khan, 'for we also be men.' As he looked Tallantire between the eyes, he added, 'And by God, Sahib, may thou be that man!'

1890

THE MIRACLE OF
PURUN BHAGAT

There was once a man in India who was Prime Minister of
one of the semi-independent native States in the north-
western part of the country. He was a Brahmin, so high-
caste that caste ceased to have any particular meaning for
him; and his father had been an important official in the
gay-colored tag-rag and bobtail of an old-fashioned Hindu
Court. But as Purun Dass grew up he felt that the old
order of things was changing, and that if any one wished
to get on in the world he must stand well with the English,
and imitate all that the English believed to be good. At the
same time a native official must keep his own master's
favor. This was a difficult game, but the quiet, close-
mouthed young Brahmin, helped by a good English education at a Bombay University, played it coolly, and rose,
step by step, to be Prime Minister of the kingdom. That is
to say, he held more real power than his master, the Maharajah.

When the old king—who was suspicious of the English,
their railways and telegraphs—died, Purun Dass stood
high with his young successor, who had been tutored by
an Englishman; and between them, though he always took
care that his master should have the credit, they established schools for little girls, made roads, and started State
dispensaries and shows of agricultural implements, and
published a yearly blue-book on the 'Moral and Material
Progress of the State,' and the Foreign Office and the Government of India were delighted. Very few native States

take up English progress altogether, for they will not believe, as Purun Dass showed he did, that what was good for the Englishman must be twice as good for the Asiatic. The Prime Minister became the honored friend of Viceroys and Governors, and Lieutenant-Governors, and medical missionaries, and common missionaries, and hard-riding English officers who came to shoot in the State preserves, as well as of whole hosts of tourists who traveled up and down India in the cold weather, showing how things ought to be managed. In his spare time he would endow scholarships for the study of medicine and manufactures on strictly English lines, and write letters to the 'Pioneer,' the greatest Indian daily paper, explaining his master's aims and objects.

At last he went to England on a visit, and had to pay enormous sums to the priests when he came back; for even so high-caste a Brahmin as Purun Dass lost caste by crossing the black sea. In London he met and talked with every one worth knowing—men whose names go all over the world—and saw a great deal more than he said. He was given honorary degrees by learned universities, and he made speeches and talked of Hindu social reform to English ladies in evening dress, till all London cried, 'This is the most fascinating man we have ever met at dinner since cloths were first laid.'

When he returned to India there was a blaze of glory, for the Viceroy himself made a special visit to confer upon the Maharajah the Grand Cross of the Star of India—all diamonds and ribbons and enamel; and at the same ceremony, while the cannon boomed, Purun Dass was made a Knight Commander of the Order of the Indian Empire; so that his name stood Sir Purun Dass, K. C. I. E.

That evening, at dinner in the big Viceregal tent, he stood up with the badge and the collar of the Order on his breast, and replying to the toast of his master's health, made a speech few Englishmen could have bettered.

Next month, when the city had returned to its sun-baked quiet, he did a thing no Englishman would have dreamed of doing; for, so far as the world's affairs went, he died. The jeweled order of his knighthood went back to the Indian Government, and a new Prime Minister was appointed to the charge of affairs, and a great game of General Post began in all the subordinate appointments. The priests knew what had happened and the people guessed; but India is the one place in the world where a man can do as he pleases and nobody asks why; and the fact that Dewan Sir Purun Dass, K. C. I. E., had resigned position, palace, and power, and taken up the begging-bowl and ocher-colored dress of a Sunnyasi or holy man, was considered nothing extraordinary. He had been, as the Old Law recommends, twenty years a youth, twenty years a fighter,—though he had never carried a weapon in his life,—and twenty years head of a household. He had used his wealth and his power for what he knew both to be worth; he had taken honor when it came his way; he had seen men and cities far and near, and men and cities had stood up and honored him. Now he would let these things go, as a man drops the cloak he no longer needs.

Behind him, as he walked through the city gates, an antelope skin and brass-handled crutch under his arm, and a begging-bowl of polished brown *coco-de-mer* in his hand, barefoot, alone, with eyes cast on the ground—behind him they were firing salutes from the bastions in honor of his happy successor. Purun Dass nodded. All that life was ended; and he bore it no more ill-will or good-will than a man bears to a colorless dream of the night. He was a Sunnyasi—a houseless wandering mendicant, depending on his neighbors for his daily bread; and so long as there is a morsel to divide in India neither priest nor beggar starves. He had never in his life tasted meat, and very seldom eaten even fish. A five-pound note would have covered his personal expenses for food through any one of the many years in which he had been absolute master of millions of money. Even when he was being lionized in London he had held before him his dream of peace and quiet—the long, white, dusty Indian road, printed all over with bare feet, the incessant, slow-moving traffic, and the sharp-smelling wood smoke curling up under the fig-trees in the twilight, where the wayfarers sit at their evening meal.

When the time came to make that dream true the Prime Minister took the proper steps, and in three days you might more easily have found a bubble in the trough of the long Atlantic seas than Purun Dass among the roving, gathering, separating millions of India.

At night his antelope skin was spread where the darkness overtook him—sometimes in a Sunnyasi monastery by the roadside; sometimes by a mud pillar shrine of Kala Pir, where the Jogis, who are another misty division of holy men, would receive him as they do those who know what castes and divisions are worth; sometimes on the outskirts of a little Hindu village, where the children would steal up with the food their parents had prepared; and sometimes on the pitch of the bare grazing-grounds, where the flame of his stick fire waked the drowsy camels. It was all one to Purun Dass—or Purun Bhagat, as he called himself now. Earth, people, and food were all one. But unconsciously his feet drew him away northward and eastward; from the south to Rohtak; from Rohtak to Kurnool; from Kurnool to ruined Samanah, and then upstream along the dried bed of the Gugger river that fills only when the rain falls in the hills, till one day he saw the far line of the great Himalayas.

Then Purun Bhagat smiled, for he remembered that his mother was of Rajput Brahmin birth, from Kulu way—a Hill-woman, always homesick for the snows—and that the least touch of Hill blood draws a man at the end back to where he belongs.

'Yonder,' said Purun Bhagat, breasting the lower slopes of the Sewaliks, where the cacti stand up like seven-branched candlesticks—'yonder I shall sit down and get knowledge'; and the cool wind of the Himalayas whistled about his ears as he trod the road that led to Simla.

The last time he had come that way it had been in state, with a clattering cavalry escort, to visit the gentlest and most affable of Viceroys; and the two had talked for an hour together about mutual friends in London, and what the Indian common folk really thought of things. This time Purun Bhagat paid no calls, but leaned on the rail of the Mall, watching that glorious view of the Plains spread out forty miles below, till a native Mohammedan police-man told him he was obstructing traffic; and Purun Bhagat salaamed reverently to the Law, because he knew the value of it, and was seeking for a Law of his own. Then he moved on, and slept that night in an empty hut at Chota Simla, which looks like the very last end of the earth, but it was only the beginning of his journey.

He followed the Himalaya-Thibet road, the little ten-foot track that is blasted out of solid rock, or strutted out on timbers over gulfs a thousand feet deep; that dips into warm, wet, shut-in valleys, and climbs out across bare, grassy hill-shoulders where the sun strikes like a burning-glass; or turns through dripping, dark forests where the tree-ferns dress the trunks from head to heel, and the pheasant calls to his mate. And he met Thibetan herds-men with their dogs and flocks of sheep, each sheep with a little bag of borax on his back, and wandering wood-cut-ters, and cloaked and blanketed Lamas from Thibet, com-ing into India on pilgrimage, and envoys of little solitary Hill-states, posting furiously on ring-streaked and piebald ponies, or the cavalcade of a Rajah paying a visit; or else for a long, clear day he would see nothing more than a black bear grunting and rooting below in the valley. When he first started, the roar of the world he had left still rang in his ears, as the roar of a tunnel rings long after the train has passed through; but when he had put the Mutteeanee Pass behind him that was all done, and Purun Bhagat was alone with himself, walking, wondering, and thinking, his eyes on the ground, and his thoughts with the clouds.

One evening he crossed the highest pass he had met till then—it had been a two days' climb—and came out on a line of snow-peaks that banded all the horizon—mountains from fifteen to twenty thousand feet high, looking almost near enough to hit with a stone, though they were fifty or sixty miles away. The pass was crowned with dense, dark forest—deodar, walnut, wild cherry, wild olive, and wild pear, but mostly deodar, which is the Himalayan cedar; and under the shadow of the deodars stood a deserted shrine to Kali—who is Durga, who is Sitala, who is sometimes worshiped against the smallpox.

Purun Dass swept the stone floor clean, smiled at the grinning statue, made himself a little mud fireplace at the back of the shrine, spread his antelope skin on a bed of fresh pine-needles, tucked his *bairagi*—his brass-handled crutch—under his armpit, and sat down to rest.

Immediately below him the hillside fell away, clean and cleared for fifteen hundred feet, where a little village of stone-walled houses, with roofs of beaten earth, clung to the steep tilt. All round it the tiny terraced fields lay out like aprons of patchwork on the knees of the mountain, and cows no bigger than beetles grazed between the smooth stone circles of the threshing-floors. Looking across the valley, the eye was deceived by the size of things, and could not at first realize that what seemed to be low scrub, on the opposite mountain-flank, was in truth a forest of hundred-foot pines. Purun Bhagat saw an eagle swoop across the gigantic hollow, but the great bird dwindled to a dot ere it was half-way over. A few bands of scattered clouds strung up and down the valley, catching on a shoulder of the hills, or rising up and dying out when they were level with the head of the pass. And 'Here shall I find peace,' said Purun Bhagat.

Now, a Hill-man makes nothing of a few hundred feet up or down, and as soon as the villagers saw the smoke in the deserted shrine, the village priest climbed up the terraced hillside to welcome the stranger.

When he met Purun Bhagat's eyes—the eyes of a man used to control thousands—he bowed to the earth, took the begging-bowl without a word, and returned to the village, saying, 'We have at last a holy man. Never have I seen such a man. He is of the Plains—but pale-colored—a Brahmin of the Brahmins.' Then all the housewives of the village said, 'Think you he will stay with us?' and each did her best to cook the most savory meal for the Bhagat. Hill-food is very simple, but with buckwheat and Indian corn, and rice and red pepper, and little fish out of the stream in the valley, and honey from the flue-like hives built in the stone walls, and dried apricots, and turmeric, and wild ginger, and bannocks of flour, a devout woman can make good things, and it was a full bowl that the priest carried to the Bhagat. Was he going to stay? asked the priest. Would he need a *chela*—a disciple—to beg for him? Had he a blanket against the cold weather? Was the food good?

Purun Bhagat ate, and thanked the giver. It was in his mind to stay. That was sufficient, said the priest. Let the begging-bowl be placed outside the shrine, in the hollow made by those two twisted roots, and daily should the Bhagat be fed; for the village felt honored that such a man—he looked timidly into the Bhagat's face—should tarry among them.

That day saw the end of Purun Bhagat's wanderings. He had come to the place appointed for him—the silence and the space. After this, time stopped, and he, sitting at the mouth of the shrine, could not tell whether he were alive or dead; a man with control of his limbs, or a part of the hills, and the clouds, and the shifting rain and sunlight. He would repeat a Name softly to himself a hundred hundred times, till, at each repetition, he seemed to move more and more out of his body, sweeping up to the doors of some tremendous discovery; but, just as the door was opening, his body would drag him back, and, with grief, he felt he was locked up again in the flesh and bones of Purun Bhagat.

Every morning the filled begging-bowl was laid silently in the crutch of the roots outside the shrine. Sometimes the priest brought it; sometimes a Ladakhi trader, lodging in the village, and anxious to get merit, trudged up the path; but, more often, it was the woman who had cooked the meal overnight; and she would murmur, hardly above her breath: 'Speak for me before the gods, Bhagat. Speak for such a one, the wife of so-and-so!' Now and then some bold child would be allowed the honor, and Purun Bhagat would hear him drop the bowl and run as fast as his little legs could carry him, but the Bhagat never came down to the village. It was laid out like a map at his feet. He could see the evening gatherings, held on the circle of the threshing-floors because that was the only level ground; could see the wonderful unnamed green of the young rice, the indigo blues of the Indian corn, the dock-like patches of buckwheat, and, in its season, the red bloom of the amaranth, whose tiny seeds, being neither grain nor pulse, make a food that can be lawfully eaten by Hindus in time of fasts.

When the year turned, the roofs of the huts were all little squares of purest gold, for it was on the roofs that they laid out their cobs of the corn to dry. Hiving and harvest, rice-sowing and husking, passed before his eyes, all embroidered down there on the many-sided plots of fields, and he thought of them all, and wondered what they all led to at the long last.

Even in populated India a man cannot a day sit still before the wild things run over him as though he were a rock; and in that wilderness very soon the wild things, who knew Kali's Shrine well, came back to look at the intruder. The *langurs*, the big gray-whiskered monkeys of the Himalayas, were, naturally, the first, for they are alive with curiosity; and when they had upset the begging-bowl, and rolled it round the floor, and tried their teeth on the brass-handled crutch, and made faces at the antelope skin, they decided that the human being who sat so still was harmless. At evening, they would leap down from the pines, and beg with their hands for things to eat, and then swing off in graceful curves. They liked the warmth of the fire, too, and huddled round it till Purun Bhagat had to push them aside to throw on more fuel; and in the morning, as often as not, he would find a furry ape sharing his blanket. All day long, one or other of the tribe would sit by his side, staring out at the snows, crooning and looking unspeakably wise and sorrowful.

After the monkeys came the *barasingh*, that big deer which is like our red deer, but stronger. He wished to rub off the velvet of his horns against the cold stones of Kali's statue, and stamped his feet when he saw the man at the shrine. But Purun Bhagat never moved, and, little by little, the royal stag edged up and nuzzled his shoulder. Purun Bhagat slid one cool hand along the hot antlers, and the touch soothed the fretted beast, who bowed his head, and Purun Bhagat very softly rubbed and raveled off the velvet. Afterward, the *barasingh* brought his doe and fawn—gentle things that mumbled on the holy man's blanket—or would come alone at night, his eyes green in the fire-flicker, to take his share of fresh walnuts. At last, the musk-deer, the shyest and almost the smallest of the deerlets, came, too, her big rabbity ears erect; even brindled, silent *mushick-nabha* must needs find out what the light in the shrine meant, and drop her moose-like nose into Purun Bhagat's lap, coming and going with the shadows of the fire. Purun Bhagat called them all 'my brothers,' and his low call of '*Bhai! Bhai!*' would draw them from the forest at noon if they were within earshot. The Himalayan black bear, moody and suspicious—Sona, who has the V-shaped white mark under his chin—passed that way more than once; and since the Bhagat showed no fear, Sona showed no anger, but watched him, and came closer, and begged a share of the caresses, and a dole of bread or wild berries. Often, in the still dawns, when the Bhagat would climb to the very crest of the pass to watch the red day walking along the peaks of the snows, he would find Sona shuffling and grunting at his heels, thrusting a curious fore-paw under fallen trunks, and bringing it away with a *whoof* of impatience; or his early steps would wake Sona where he lay curled up, and the great brute, rising erect, would think to fight, till he heard the Bhagat's voice and knew his best friend.

Nearly all hermits and holy men who live apart from the big cities have the reputation of being able to work miracles with the wild things, but all the miracle lies in keeping still, in never making a hasty movement, and, for a long time, at least, in never looking directly at a visitor. The villagers saw the outline of the *barasingh* stalking like a shadow through the dark forest behind the shrine; saw the *minaul,* the Himalayan pheasant, blazing in her best colors before Kali's statue; and the *langurs* on their haunches, inside, playing with the walnut shells. Some of the children, too, had heard Sona singing to himself, bear-fashion, behind the fallen rocks, and the Bhagat's reputation as miracle-worker stood firm.

Yet nothing was further from his mind than miracles. He believed that all things were one big Miracle, and when a man knows that much he knows something to go upon. He knew for a certainty that there was nothing great and nothing little in this world; and day and night he strove to think out his way into the heart of things, back to the place whence his soul had come.

So thinking, his untrimmed hair fell down about his shoulders, the stone slab at the side of the antelope skin was dented into a little hole by the foot of his brass-handled crutch, and the place between the tree-trunks, where the begging-bowl rested day after day, sunk and wore into a hollow almost as smooth as the brown shell itself; and each beast knew his exact place at the fire. The fields changed their colors with the seasons; the threshing-floors filled and emptied, and filled again and again; and again and again, when winter came, the *langurs* frisked among the branches feathered with light snow, till the mother-monkeys brought their sad-eyed little babies up from the warmer valleys with the spring. There were few changes in the village. The priest was older, and many of the little children who used to come with the begging-dish sent their own children now; and when you asked of the villagers how long their holy man had lived in Kali's Shrine at the head of the pass, they answered, 'Always.'

Then came such summer rains as had not been known in the Hills for many seasons. Through three good months the valley was wrapped in cloud and soaking mist—steady, unrelenting downfall, breaking off into thunder-shower after thunder-shower. Kali's Shrine stood above the clouds, for the most part, and there was a whole month in which the Bhagat never saw his village. It was packed away under a white floor of cloud that swayed and shifted and rolled on itself and bulged upward, but never broke from its piers—the streaming flanks of the valley.

All that time he heard nothing but the sound of a million little waters, overhead from the trees, and underfoot along the ground, soaking through the pine-needles, dripping from the tongues of draggled fern, and spouting in newly torn muddy channels down the slopes. Then the sun came out, and drew forth the good incense of the deodars and the rhododendrons, and that far-off, clean smell which the Hill people call 'the smell of the snows.' The hot sunshine lasted for a week, and then the rains gathered together for their last downpour, and the water fell in sheets that flayed off the skin of the ground and leaped back in mud. Purun Bhagat heaped his fire high that night, for he was sure his brothers would need warmth; but never a beast came to the shrine, though he called and called till he dropped asleep, wondering what had happened in the woods.

It was in the black heart of the night, the rain drumming like a thousand drums, that he was roused by a plucking at his blanket, and, stretching out, felt the little hand of a *langur*. 'It is better here than in the trees,' he said sleepily, loosening a fold of blanket; 'take it and be warm.' The monkey caught his hand and pulled hard. 'Is it food, then?' said Purun Bhagat. 'Wait awhile, and I will prepare some.' As he kneeled to throw fuel on the fire the *langur* ran to the door of the shrine, crooned, and ran back again, plucking at the man's knee.

'What is it? What is thy trouble, Brother?' said Purun Bhagat, for the *langur's* eyes were full of things that he could not tell. 'Unless one of thy caste be in a trap—and none set traps here—I will not go into that weather. Look, Brother, even the *barasingh* comes for shelter!'

The deer's antlers clashed as he strode into the shrine, clashed against the grinning statue of Kali. He lowered them in Purun Bhagat's direction and stamped uneasily, hissing through his half-shut nostils.

'Hai! Hai! Hai!' said the Bhagat, snapping his fingers. 'Is *this* payment for a night's lodging?' But the deer pushed him toward the door, and as he did so Purun Bhagat heard the sound of something opening with a sigh, and saw two slabs of the floor draw away from each other, while the sticky earth below smacked its lips.

'Now I see,' said Purun Bhagat. 'No blame to my brothers that they did not sit by the fire to-night. The mountain is falling. And yet—why should I go?' His eye fell on the empty begging-bowl, and his face changed. 'They have given me good food daily since—since I came, and, if I am not swift, to-morrow there will not be one mouth in the valley. Indeed, I must go and warn them below. Back there, Brother! Let me get to the fire.'

The *barasingh* backed unwillingly as Purun Bhagat drove a pine torch deep into the flame, twirling it till it was well lit. 'Ah! ye came to warn me,' he said, rising.

'Better than that we shall do; better than that. Out, now, and lend me thy neck, Brother, for I have but two feet.'

He clutched the bristling withers of the *barasingh* with his right hand, held the torch away with his left, and stepped out of the shrine into the desperate night. There was no breath of wind, but the rain nearly drowned the flare as the great deer hurried down the slope, sliding on his haunches. As soon as they were clear of the forest more of the Bhagat's brothers joined them. He heard, though he could not see, the *langurs* pressing about him, and behind them the *uhh! uhh!* of Sona. The rain matted his long white hair into ropes; the water splashed beneath his bare feet, and his yellow robe clung to his frail old body, but he stepped down steadily, leaning against the *barasingh*. He was no longer a holy man, but Sir Purun Dass, K. C. I. E., Prime Minister of no small State, a man accustomed to command, going out to save life. Down the steep, plashy path they poured all together, the Bhagat and his brothers, down and down till the deer's feet clicked and stumbled on the wall of a threshing-floor, and he snorted because he smelt Man. Now they were at the head of the one crooked village street, and the Bhagat beat with his crutch on the barred windows of the blacksmith's house as his torch blazed up in the shelter of the eaves. 'Up and out!' cried Purun Bhagat; and he did not know his own voice, for it was years since he had spoken aloud to a man. 'The hill falls! The hill is falling! Up and out, oh, you within!'

'It is our Bhagat,' said the blacksmith's wife. 'He stands among his beasts. Gather the little ones and give the call.'

It ran from house to house, while the beasts, cramped in the narrow way, surged and huddled round the Bhagat, and Sona puffed impatiently.

The people hurried into the street—they were no more than seventy souls all told—and in the glare of the torches they saw their Bhagat holding back the terrified *bara-*

singh, while the monkeys plucked piteously at his skirts, and Sona sat on his haunches and roared.

'Across the valley and up the next hill!' shouted Purun Bhagat. 'Leave none behind! We follow!'

Then the people ran as only Hill folk can run, for they knew that in a landslip you must climb for the highest ground across the valley. They fled, splashing through the little river at the bottom, and panted up the terraced fields on the far side, while the Bhagat and his brethren followed. Up and up the opposite mountain they climbed, calling to each other by name—the roll-call of the village—and at their heels toiled the big *barasingh,* weighted by the failing strength of Purun Bhagat. At last the deer stopped in the shadow of a deep pine-wood, five hundred feet up the hillside. His instinct, that had warned him of the coming slide, told him he would be safe here.

Purun Bhagat dropped fainting by his side, for the chill of the rain and that fierce climb were killing him; but first he called to the scattered torches ahead, 'Stay and count your numbers'; then, whispering to the deer as he saw the lights gather in a cluster: 'Stay with me, Brother. Stay—till—I—go!'

There was a sigh in the air that grew to a mutter, and a mutter that grew to a roar, and a roar that passed all sense of hearing, and the hillside on which the villagers stood was hit in the darkness, and rocked to the blow. Then a note as steady, deep, and true as the deep C of the organ drowned everything for perhaps five minutes, while the very roots of the pines quivered to it. It died away, and the sound of the rain falling on miles of hard ground and grass changed to the muffled drum of water on soft earth. That told its own tale.

Never a villager—not even the priest—was bold enough to speak to the Bhagat who had saved their lives. They crouched under the pines and waited till the day. When it came they looked across the valley and saw that what had been forest, and terraced field, and track-threaded grazing-ground was one raw, red, fan-shaped smear, with a few trees flung head-down on the scarp. That red ran high up the hill of their refuge, damming back the little river, which had begun to spread into a brick-colored lake. Of the village, of the road to the shrine, of the shrine itself, and the forest behind, there was not trace. For one mile in width and two thousand feet in sheer depth the mountain-side had come away bodily, planed clean from head to heel.

And the villagers, one by one, crept through the wood to pray before their Bhagat. They saw the *barasingh* standing over him, who fled when they came near, and they heard the *langurs* wailing in the branches, and Sona moaning up the hill; but their Bhagat was dead, sitting cross-legged, his back against a tree, his crutch under his armpit, and his face turned to the northeast.

The priest said: 'Behold a miracle after a miracle, for in this very attitude must all Sunnyasis be buried! Therefore where he now is we will build the temple to our holy man.'

They built the temple before a year was ended—a little stone-and-earth shrine—and they called the hill the Bhagat's Hill, and they worship there with lights and flowers and offerings to this day. But they do not know that the saint of their worship is the late Sir Purun Dass, K. C. I. E., D. C. L., Ph. D., etc., once Prime Minister of the progressive and enlightened State of Mohiniwala, and honorary or corresponding member of more learned and scientific societies than will ever do any good in this world or the next.

1894

THE STORY OF
MUHAMMAD DIN

~~~~~~

Who is the happy man? He that sees in his own
house at home, little children crowned with dust, leaping and falling and crying.
                        Munichandra,
                        translated by Professor Peterson

The polo-ball was an old one, scarred, chipped, and
dinted. It stood on the mantelpiece among the pipe-stems
which Imam Din, *khitmatgar*, was cleaning for me.

'Does the Heaven-born want this ball?' said Imam Din
deferentially.

The Heaven-born set no particular store by it; but of
what use was a polo-ball to a *khitmatgar?*

'By Your Honour's favour, I have a little son. He has
seen this ball, and desires it to play with. I do not want it
for myself.'

No one would for an instant accuse portly old Imam
Din of wanting to play with polo-balls. He carried out the
battered thing into the verandah; and there followed a
hurricane of joyful squeaks, a patter of small feet, and the
thud-thud-thud of the ball rolling along the ground. Evidently the little son had been waiting outside the door to
secure his treasure. But how had he managed to see that
polo-ball?

Next day, coming back from office half an hour earlier
than usual, I was aware of a small figure in the dining-
room—a tiny, plump figure in a ridiculously inadequate
shirt which came, perhaps, half-way down the tubby

stomach. It wandered round the room, thumb in mouth, crooning to itself as it took stock of the pictures. Undoubtedly this was the 'little son.'

He had no business in my room, of course; but was so deeply absorbed in his discoveries that he never noticed me in the doorway. I stepped into the room and startled him nearly into a fit. He sat down on the ground with a gasp. His eyes opened, and his mouth followed suit. I knew what was coming, and fled, followed by a long, dry howl which reached the servants' quarters far more quickly than any command of mine had ever done. In ten seconds Imam Din was in the dining-room. Then despairing sobs arose, and I returned to find Imam Din admonishing the small sinner who was using most of his shirt as a handkerchief.

'This boy,' said Imam Din judicially, 'is a *budmash*—a big *budmash*. He will, without doubt, go to the *jail-khana* for his behaviour.' Renewed yells from the penitent, and an elaborate apology to myself from Imam Din.

'Tell the baby,' said I, 'that the *Sahib* is not angry, and take him away.' Imam Din conveyed my forgiveness to the offender, who had now gathered all his shirt round his neck, stringwise, and the yell subsided into a sob. The two set off for the door. 'His name,' said Imam Din, as though the name were part of the crime, 'is Muhammad Din, and he is a *budmash*.' Freed from present danger, Muhammad Din turned round in his father's arms, and said gravely, 'It is true that my name is Muhammad Din, *Tahib*, but I am not a *budmash*. I am a *man!*'

From that day dated my acquaintance with Muhammad Din. Never again did he come into my dining-room, but on the neutral ground of the garden we greeted each other with much state, though our conversation was confined to '*Talaam, Tahib*' from his side, and '*Salaam, Muhammad Din*' from mine. Daily on my return from office, the little white shirt and the fat little body used to rise from the shade of the creeper-covered trellis where they had been hid; and daily I checked my horse here, that my salutation might not be slurred over or given unseemly.

Muhammad Din never had any companions. He used to trot about the compound, in and out of the castor-oil bushes, on mysterious errands of his own. One day I stumbled upon some of his handiwork far down the grounds. He had half buried the polo-ball in dust, and stuck six shrivelled old marigold flowers in a circle round it. Outside that circle again was a rude square, traced out in bits of red brick alternating with fragments of broken china; the whole bounded by a little bank of dust. The water-man from the well-curb put in a plea for the small architect, saying that it was only the play of a baby and did not much disfigure my garden.

Heaven knows that I had no intention of touching the child's work then or later; but, that evening, a stroll through the garden brought me unawares full on it; so that I trampled, before I knew, marigold-heads, dust-bank, and fragments of broken soap-dish into confusion past all hope of mending. Next morning, I came upon Muhammad Din crying softly to himself over the ruin I had wrought. Some one had cruelly told him that the *Sahib* was very angry with him for spoiling the garden, and had scattered his rubbish, using bad language the while. Muhammad Din laboured for an hour at effacing every trace of the dust-bank and pottery fragments, and it was with a tearful and apologetic face that he said, '*Talaam Tahib*,' when I came home from office. A hasty inquiry resulted in Imam Din informing Muhammad Din that, by my singular favour, he was permitted to disport himself as he pleased. Whereat the child took heart and fell to tracing the ground-plan of an edifice which was to eclipse the marigold-polo-ball creation.

For some months the chubby little eccentricity revolved in his humble orbit among the castor-oil bushes and in the dust; always fashioning magnificent palaces from stale flowers thrown away by the bearer, smooth water-worn pebbles, bits of broken glass, and feathers pulled, I fancy, from my fowls—always alone, and always crooning to himself.

A gaily-spotted sea-shell was dropped one day close to the last of his little buildings; and I looked that Muhammad Din should build something more than ordinarily splendid on the strength of it. Nor was I disappointed. He meditated for the better part of an hour, and his crooning rose to a jubilant song. Then he began tracing in the dust. It would certainly be a wondrous palace, this one, for it was two yards long and a yard broad in ground-plan. But the palace was never completed.

Next day there was no Muhammad Din at the head of the carriage-drive, and no '*Talaam, Tahib*' to welcome my return. I had grown accustomed to the greeting, and its omission troubled me. Next day Imam Din told me that the child was suffering slightly from fever and needed quinine. He got the medicine, and an English Doctor.

'They have no stamina, these brats,' said the Doctor, as he left Imam Din's quarters.

A week later, though I would have given much to have avoided it, I met on the road to the Mussulman burying-ground Imam Din, accompanied by one other friend, carrying in his arms, wrapped in a white cloth, all that was left of little Muhammad Din.

1888

JEWS IN SHUSHAN

My newly purchased house furniture was, at the least, in-
secure; the legs parted from the chairs, and the tops from
the tables, on the slightest provocation. But such as it was,
it was to be paid for, and Ephraim, agent and collector
for the local auctioneer, waited in the verandah with the
receipt. He was announced by the Mahomedan servant as
'Ephraim, Yahudi'—Ephraim the Jew. He who believes in
the Brotherhood of Man should hear my Elahi Pukhsh
grinding the second word through his white teeth with all
the scorn he dare show before his master. Ephraim was,
personally, meek in manner—so meek indeed that one
could not understand how he had fallen into the profession of bill-collecting. He resembled an over-fed sheep,
and his voice suited his figure. There was a fixed, unvary-
ing mask of childish wonder upon his face. If you paid
him, he was as one marvelling at your wealth; if you sent
him away, he seemed puzzled at your hard-heartedness.
Never was Jew more unlike his dread breed.

Ephraim wore list slippers and coats of duster-cloth, so
preposterously patterned that the most brazen of British
subalterns would have shied from them in fear. Very slow
and deliberate was his speech, and carefully guarded to
give offence to no one. After many weeks, Ephraim was
induced to speak to me of his friends.

'There be eight of us in Shushan, and we are waiting till
there are ten. Then we shall apply for a synagogue, and
get leave from Calcutta. To-day we have no synagogue;
and I, only I, am Priest and Butcher to our people. I am of
the tribe of Judah—I think, but I am not sure. My father

was of the tribe of Judah, and we wish much to get our synagogue. I shall be a priest of that synagogue.'

Shushan is a big city in the North of India, counting its dwellers by the ten thousand; and these eight of the Chosen People were shut up in its midst, waiting till time or chance sent them their full congregation.

Miriam the wife of Ephraim, two little children, an orphan boy of their people, Ephraim's uncle Jackrael Israel, a white-haired old man, his wife Hester, a Jew from Cutch, one Hyem Benjamin, and Ephraim, Priest and Butcher, made up the list of the Jews in Shushan. They lived in one house, on the outskirts of the great city, amid heaps of saltpetre, rotten bricks, herds of kine, and a fixed pillar of dust caused by the incessant passing of the beasts to the river to drink. In the evening the children of the City came to the waste place to fly their kites, and Ephraim's sons held aloof, watching the sport from the roof, but never descending to take part in them. At the back of the house stood a small brick enclosure, in which Ephraim prepared the daily meat for his people after the custom of the Jews. Once the rude door of the square was suddenly smashed open by a struggle from inside, and showed the meek bill-collector at his work, nostrils dilated, lips drawn back over his teeth, and his hands upon a half-maddened sheep. He was attired in strange raiment, having no relation whatever to duster coats or list slippers, and a knife was in his mouth. As he struggled with the animal between the walls, the breath came from him in thick sobs, and the nature of the man seemed changed. When the ordained slaughter was ended, he saw that the door was open and shut it hastily, his hand leaving a red mark on the timber, while his children from the neighbouring house-top looked down awe-stricken and open-eyed. A glimpse of Ephraim busied in one of his religious capacities was no thing to be desired twice.

Summer came upon Shushan, turning the trodden waste-ground to iron, and bringing sickness to the city.

'It will not touch us,' said Ephraim confidently. 'Before the winter we shall have our synagogue. My brother and his wife and children are coming up from Calcutta, and *then* I shall be the priest of the synagogue.'

Jackrael Israel, the old man, would crawl out in the stifling evenings to sit on the rubbish-heap and watch the corpses being borne down to the river.

'It will not come near us,' said Jackrael Israel feebly, 'for we are the People of God, and my nephew will be priest of our synagogue. Let them die.' He crept back to his house again and barred the door to shut himself off from the world of the Gentile.

But Miriam, the wife of Ephraim, looked out of the window at the dead as the biers passed and said that she was afraid. Ephraim comforted her with hopes of the synagogue to be, and collected bills as was his custom.

In one night, the two children died and were buried early in the morning by Ephraim. The deaths never appeared in the City returns. 'The sorrow is my sorrow,' said Ephraim; and this to him seemed a sufficient reason for setting at naught the sanitary regulations of a large, flourishing, and remarkably well-governed Empire.

The orphan boy, dependent on the charity of Ephraim and his wife, could have felt no gratitude, and must have been a ruffian. He begged for whatever money his protectors would give him, and with that fled down-country for his life. A week after the death of her children Miriam left her bed at night and wandered over the country to find them. She heard them crying behind every bush, or drowning in every pool of water in the fields, and she begged the cartmen on the Grand Trunk Road not to steal her little ones from her. In the morning the sun rose and beat upon her bare head, and she turned into the cool wet crops to lie down and never came back; though Hyem Benjamin and Ephraim sought her for two nights.

The look of patient wonder on Ephraim's face deepened, but he presently found an explanation. 'There are so few of us here, and these people are so many,' said he, 'that, it may be, our God has forgotten us.'

In the house on the outskirts of the city old Jackrael Israel and Hester grumbled that there was no one to wait on them, and that Miriam had been untrue to her race. Ephraim went out and collected bills, and in the evenings smoked with Hyem Benjamin till, one dawning, Hyem Benjamin died, having first paid all his debts to Ephraim. Jackrael Israel and Hester sat alone in the empty house all day, and, when Ephraim returned, wept the easy tears of age till they cried themselves asleep.

A week later Ephraim, staggering under a huge bundle of clothes and cooking-pots, led the old man and woman to the railway station, where the bustle and confusion made them whimper.

'We are going back to Calcutta,' said Ephraim, to whose sleeve Hester was clinging. 'There are more of us there, and here my house is empty.'

He helped Hester into the carriage and, turning back, said to me, 'I should have been priest of the synagogue if there had been ten of us. Surely we must have been forgotten by our God.'

The remnant of the broken colony passed out of the station on their journey south; while a subaltern, turning over the books on the bookstall, was whistling to himself 'The Ten Little Nigger Boys.'

But the tune sounded as solemn as the Dead March.

It was the dirge of the Jews in Shushan.

1887

Soldiers' Tales

~~~~~~~~~~~~~~~~~~~~~~~~~~~~~~~~~~

THE COURTING OF DINAH SHADD

What did the colonel's lady think?
  Nobody never knew.
Somebody asked the sergeant's wife
  An' she told 'em true.
When you git to a man in the case
  They're like a row o' pins,
For the colonel's lady an' Judy O'Grady
  Are sisters under their skins.
                    Barrack-Room Ballad

All day I had followed at the heels of a pursuing army engaged on one of the finest battles that ever camp of exercise beheld. Thirty thousand troops had by the wisdom of the Government of India had been turned loose over a few thousand square miles of country to practise in peace what they would never attempt in war. Consequently cavalry charged unshaken infantry at the trot. Infantry captured artillery by frontal attacks delivered in line of quarter columns, and mounted infantry skirmished up to the wheels of an armoured train which carried nothing more deadly than a twenty-five pounder Armstrong, two Nordenfeldts, and a few score volunteers all cased in three-eighths-inch boiler-plate. Yet it was a very lifelike camp. Operations did not cease at sundown; nobody knew the country and nobody spared man or horse. There was unending cavalry scouting and almost unending forced work over broken ground. The Army of the South had finally pierced the centre of the Army of the North, and was pouring through the gap hot-foot to capture a city of strategic importance. Its front extended fanwise, the sticks being represented by regiments strung out along the line of route backwards to the divisional transport columns and all the lumber that trails behind an army on the move. On its right the broken left of the Army of the North was flying in mass, chased by the Southern horse and hammered by the Southern guns till these had been pushed far beyond the limits of their last support. Then the flying sat down to rest, while the elated commandant of the pursuing force telegraphed that he held all in check and observation.

Unluckily he did not observe that three miles to his right flank a flying column of Northern horse with a detachment of Ghoorkhas and British troops had been pushed round, as fast as the failing light allowed, to cut across the entire rear of the Southern Army, to break, as it were, all the ribs of the fan where they converged by striking at the transport, reserve ammunition, and artillery supplies. Their instructions were to go in, avoiding the few scouts who might not have been drawn off by the pursuit, and create sufficient excitement to impress the Southern Army with the wisdom of guarding their own flank and rear before they captured cities. It was a pretty manœuvre, neatly carried out.

Speaking for the second division of the Southern Army, our first intimation of the attack was at twilight, when the artillery were labouring in deep sand, most of the escort were trying to help them out, and the main body of the infantry had gone on. A Noah's Ark of elephants, camels, and the mixed menagerie of an Indian transport-train bubbled and squealed behind the guns, when there appeared from nowhere in particular British infantry to the extent of three companies, who sprang to the heads of the gun-horses and brought all to a standstill amid oaths and cheers.

'How's that, umpire?' said the major commanding the attack, and with one voice the drivers and limber gunners answered 'Hout!' while the colonel of artillery sputtered.

'All your scouts are charging our main body,' said the major. 'Your flanks are unprotected for two miles. I think we've broken the back of this division. And listen,—there go the Ghoorkhas!'

A weak fire broke from the rear-guard more than a mile away, and was answered by cheerful howlings. The Ghoorkhas, who should have swung clear of the second division, had stepped on its tail in the dark, but drawing off hastened to reach the next line of attack, which lay almost parallel to us five or six miles away.

Our column swayed and surged irresolutely,—three batteries, the divisional ammunition reserve, the baggage, and a section of the hospital and bearer corps. The commandant ruefully promised to report himself 'cut up' to the nearest umpire, and commending his cavalry and all other cavalry to the special care of Eblis, toiled on to resume touch with the rest of the division.

'We'll bivouac here to-night,' said the major, 'I have a notion that the Ghoorkhas will get caught. They may want us to re-form on. Stand easy till the transport gets away.'

A hand caught my beast's bridle and led him out of the choking dust; a larger hand deftly canted me out of the saddle; and two of the hugest hands in the world received me sliding. Pleasant is the lot of the special correspondent who falls into such hands as those of Privates Mulvaney, Ortheris, and Learoyd.

'An' that's all right,' said the Irishman calmly. 'We

thought we'd find you somewheres here by. Is there anything av yours in the transport? Orth'ris 'll fetch ut out.'

Ortheris did 'fetch ut out,' from under the trunk of an elephant, in the shape of a servant and an animal both laden with medical comforts. The little man's eyes sparkled.

'If the brutil an' licentious soldiery av these parts gets sight av the thruck,' said Mulvaney, making practised investigation, 'they'll loot ev'rything. They're bein' fed on iron-filin's an' dog-biscuit these days, but glory's no compensation for a belly-ache. Praise be, we're here to protect you, sorr. Beer, sausage, bread (soft an' that's a cur'osity), soup in a tin, whisky by the smell av ut, an' fowls! Mother av Moses, but ye take the field like a confectioner! 'Tis scand'lus.'

' 'Ere's a orficer,' said Ortheris significantly. 'When the sergent's done lushin' the privit may clean the pot.'

I bundled several things into Mulvaney's haversack before the major's hand fell on my shoulder and he said tenderly, 'Requisitioned for the Queen's service. Wolseley was quite wrong about special correspondents: they are the solder's best friends. Come and take pot-luck with us to-night.'

And so it happened amid laughter and shoutings that my well-considered commissariat melted away to reappear later at the mess-table, which was a waterproof sheet spread on the ground. The flying column had taken three days' rations with it, and there be few things nastier than government rations—especially when government is experimenting with German toys. Erbsenwurst, tinned beef of surpassing tinniness, compressed vegetables, and meat-biscuits may be nourishing, but what Thomas Atkins needs is bulk in his inside. The major, assisted by his brother officers, purchased goats for the camp and so made the experiment of no effect. Long before the fatigue-party sent to collect brushwood had returned, the men were settled down by their valises, kettles and pots had appeared from the surrounding country and were dangling over fires as the kid and the compressed vegetable bubbled together; there rose a cheerful clinking of mess-tins; outrageous demands for 'a little more stuffin' with that there liver-wing;' and gust on gust of chaff as pointed as a bayonet and as delicate as a gun-butt.

'The boys are in a good temper,' said the major. 'They'll be singing presently. Well, a night like this is enough to keep them happy.'

Over our heads burned the wonderful Indian stars, which are not all pricked in on one plane, but, preserving an orderly perspective, draw the eye through the velvet darkness of the void up to the barred doors of heaven itself. The earth was a gray shadow more unreal than the sky. We could hear her breathing lightly in the pauses between the howling of the jackals, the movement of the wind in the tamarisks, and the fitful mutter of musketry-fire leagues away to the left. A native woman from some unseen hut began to sing, the mail-train thundered past on its way to Delhi, and a roosting crow cawed drowsily. Then there was a belt-loosening silence about the fires, and the even breathing of the crowded earth took up the story.

The men, full fed, turned to tobacco and song,—their officers with them. The subaltern is happy who can win the approval of the musical critics in his regiment, and is honoured among the more intricate step-dancers. By him, as by him who plays cricket cleverly, Thomas Atkins will stand in time of need, when he will let a better officer go on alone. The ruined tombs of forgotten Mussulman saints heard the ballad of *Agra Town, The Buffalo Battery, Marching to Kabul, The long, long Indian Day, The Place where the Punkah-coolie died,* and that crashing chorus which announces,

Youth's daring spirit, manhood's fire,
　　Firm hand and eagle eye,
Must he acquire who would aspire,
　　To see the gray boar die.

To-day, of all those jovial thieves who appropriated my commissariat and lay and laughed round that waterproof sheet, not one remains. They went to camps that were not of exercise and battles without umpires. Burmah, the Soudan, and the frontier,—fever and fight,—took them in their time.

I drifted across to the men's fires in search of Mulvaney, whom I found strategically greasing his feet by the blaze. There is nothing particularly lovely in the sight of a private thus engaged after a long day's march, but when you reflect on the exact proportion of the 'might, majesty, dominion, and power' of the British Empire which stands on those feet you take an interest in the proceedings.

'There's a blister, bad luck to ut, on the heel,' said Mulvaney. 'I can't touch ut. Prick ut out, little man.'

Ortheris took out his house-wife, eased the trouble with a needle, stabbed Mulvaney in the calf with the same weapon, and was swiftly kicked into the fire.

'I've bruk the best av my toes over you, ye grinnin' child av disruption,' said Mulvaney, sitting cross-legged and nursing his feet; then seeing me, 'Oh, ut's you, sorr! Be welkim, an' take that maraudin' scutt's place. Jock, hold him down on the cindhers for a bit.'

But Ortheris escaped and went elsewhere, as I took possession of the hollow he had scraped for himself and lined with his greatcoat. Learoyd on the other side of the fire grinned affably and in a minute fell fast asleep.

'There's the height av politeness for you,' said Mulvaney, lighting his pipe with a flaming branch. 'But Jock's eaten half a box av your sardines at wan gulp, an' I think the tin too. What's the best wid you, sorr, an' how did you happen to be on the losin' side this day whin we captured you?'

'The Army of the South is winning all along the line,' I said.

'Then that line's the hangman's rope, savin' your presence. You'll learn to-morrow how we rethreated to dhraw thim on before we made thim trouble, an' that's what a woman does. By the same tokin, we'll be attacked before the dawnin' an' ut would be betther not to slip your boots. How do I know that? By the light av pure reason. Here are three companies av us ever so far inside av the enemy's flank an' a crowd av roarin', tarin', squealin' cavalry gone on just to turn out the whole hornet's nest av them. Av course the enemy will pursue, by brigades like as not, an' thin we'll have to run for ut. Mark my words. I am av the opinion av Polonius whin he said, "Don't fight wid ivry scutt for the pure joy av fightin', but if you do, knock the nose av him first an' frequint." We ought to ha' gone on an' helped the Ghoorkhas.'

'But what do you know about Polonius?' I demanded. This was a new side of Mulvaney's character.

'All that Shakespeare iver wrote an' a dale more that the gallery shouted,' said the man of war, carefully lacing his boots. 'Did I not tell you av Silver's theatre in Dublin, whin I was younger than I am now an' a patron av the drama? Ould Silver wud never pay actor-man or woman their just dues, an' by consequince his comp'nies was collapsible at the last minut. Thin the bhoys wud clamour to take a part, an' oft as not ould Silver made them pay for the fun. Faith, I've seen Hamlut played wid a new black eye an' the queen as full as a cornucopia. I remimber wanst Hogin that 'listed in the Black Tyrone an' was shot in South Africa, he sejuced ould Silver into givin' him Hamlut's part instid av me that had a fine fancy for rhetoric in those days. Av course I wint into the gallery an' began to fill the pit wid other people's hats, an' I passed the time av day to Hogin walkin' through Denmark like a hamstrung mule wid a pall on his back. "Hamlut," sez I, "there's a hole in your heel. Pull up your shtockin's, Hamlut," sez I. "Hamlut, Hamlut, for the love av decincy dhrop that skull an' pull up your shtockin's." The whole house begun to tell him that. He stopped his soliloquishms mid-between. "My shtockin's may be comin' down or they may not," sez he, screwin' his eye into the gallery, for well he knew who I was. "But afther this performince is over me an' the Ghost 'll trample the tripes out av you, Terence, wid your ass's bray!" An' that's how I come to know about Hamlut. Eyah! Those days, those days! Did you iver have onendin' devilmint an' nothing' to pay for it in your life, sorr?'

'Never, without having to pay,' I said.

'That's thrue! 'Tis mane whin you considher on ut; but ut's the same wid horse or fut. A headache if you dhrink, an' a belly-ache if you eat too much, an' a heart-ache to kape all down. Faith, the beast only gets the colic, an' he's the lucky man.'

He dropped his head and stared into the fire, fingering his moustache the while. From the far side of the bivouac the voice of Corbet-Nolan, senior subaltern of B company, uplifted itself in an ancient and much appreciated song of sentiment, the men moaning melodiously behind him.

> The north wind blew coldly, she drooped from that
> hour,
> My own little Kathleen, my sweet little Kathleen,
> Kathleen, my Kathleen, Kathleen O'Moore!

With forty-five O's in the last word: even at that distance you might have cut the soft South Irish accent with a shovel.

'For all we take we must pay, but the price is cruel high,' murmured Mulvaney when the chorus had ceased.

'What's the trouble?' I said gently, for I knew that he was a man of an inextinguishable sorrow.

'Hear now,' said he. 'Ye know what I am now. *I* know what I mint to be at the beginnin' av my service. I've tould you time an' again, an' what I have not Dinah Shadd has. An' what am I? Oh, Mary Mother av Hiven, an ould dhrunken, untrustable baste av a privit that has seen the reg'ment change out from colonel to drummer-boy, not wanst or twice, but scores av times! Ay, scores! An' me not so near gettin' promotion as in the first! An' me livin' on an' kapin' clear av clink, not by my own good conduck, but the kindness av some orf'cer-bhoy young enough to be son to me! Do I not know ut? Can I not tell whin I'm passed over at p'rade, tho' I'm rockin' full av liquor an' ready to fall all in wan piece, such as even a suckin' child might see, bekaze, "Oh, 'tis only ould Mulvaney!" An' whin I'm let off in ord'ly-room through some thrick of the tongue an' a ready answer an' the ould man's mercy, is ut smilin' I feel whin I fall away an' go back to Dinah Shadd, thryin' to carry ut all off as a joke? Not I! 'Tis hell to me, dumb hell through ut all; an' next time whin the fit comes I will be as bad again. Good cause the reg'ment has to know me for the best soldier in ut. Better cause have I to know mesilf for the worst man. I'm only fit to tache the new drafts what I'll niver learn mesilf; an' I am sure, as tho' I heard ut, that the minut wan av these pink-eyed recruities gets away from my "Mind ye now," an' "Listen to this, Jim, bhoy,"—sure I am that the sergint houlds me up to him for a warnin'.' So I tache, as they say at musketry-instruction, by direct and ricochet fire. Lord be good to me, for I have stud some throuble!'

'Lie down and go to sleep,' said I, not being able to comfort or advise. 'You're the best man in the regiment, and, next to Ortheris, the biggest fool. Lie down and wait till we're attacked. What force will they turn out? Guns, think you?'

'Try that wid your lorrds an' ladies, twistin' an' turnin'

the talk, tho' you mint ut well. Ye cud say nothin' to help me, an' yet ye niver knew what cause I had to be what I am.'

'Begin at the beginning and go on to the end,' I said royally. 'But rake up the fire a bit first.'

I passed Ortheris's bayonet for a poker.

'That shows how little we know what we do,' said Mulvaney, putting it aside. 'Fire takes all the heart out av the steel, an' the next time, may be, that our little man is fighting for his life his bradawl 'll break, an' so you'll ha' killed him, manin' no more than to kape yourself warm. 'Tis a recruity's thrick that. Pass the clanin'-rod, sorr.'

I snuggled down abased; and after an interval the voice of Mulvaney began.

'Did I iver tell you how Dinah Shadd came to be wife av mine?'

I dissembled a burning anxiety that I had felt for some months—ever since Dinah Shadd, the strong, the patient, and the infinitely tender, had of her own good love and free will washed a shirt for me, moving in a barren land where washing was not.

'I can't remember,' I said casually. 'Was it before or after you make love to Annie Bragin, and got no satisfaction?'

The story of Annie Bragin is written in another place. It is one of the many less respectable episodes in Mulvaney's chequered career.

'Before—before—long before, was that business av Annie Bragin an' the corp'ril's ghost. Niver woman was the worse for me whin I had married Dinah. There's a time for all things, an' I know how to kape all things in place—barrin' the dhrink, that kapes me in my place wid no hope av comin' to be aught else.'

'Begin at the beginning,' I insisted. 'Mrs. Mulvaney told me that you married her when you were quartered in Krab Bokhar barracks.'

'An' the same is a cess-pit,' said Mulvaney piously. 'She

spoke thrue, did Dinah. 'Twas this way. Talkin' av that, have ye iver fallen in love, sorr?'

I preserved the silence of the damned. Mulvaney continued—

'Thin I will assume that ye have not. *I* did. In the days av my youth, as I have more than wanst tould you, I was a man that filled the eye an' delighted the sowl av women. Niver man was hated as I have bin. Niver man was loved as I—no, not within half a day's march av ut! For the first five years av my service, whin I was what I wud give my sowl to be now, I tuk whatever was within my reach an' digested ut—an' that's more than most men can say. Dhrink I tuk, an' ut did me no harm. By the Hollow av Hiven, I cud play wid four women at wanst, an' kape them from findin' out anythin' about the other three, an' smile like a full-blown marigold through ut all. Dick Coulhan, av the battery we'll have down on us to-night, could drive his team no better than I mine, an' I hild the worser cattle! An' so I lived, an' so I was happy till afther that business wid Annie Bragin—she that turned me off as cool as a meat-safe, an' taught me where I stud in the mind av an honest woman. 'Twas no sweet dose to swallow.

'Afther that I sickened awhile an' tuk thought to my reg'mental work; conceiting mesilf I wud study an' be a sargint, an' a major-giniral twinty minutes afther that. But on top av my ambitiousness there was an empty place in my sowl, an' me own opinion av mesilf cud not fill ut. Sez I to mesilf, "Terence, you're a great man an' the best set-up in the reg'mint. Go on an' get promotion." Sez mesilf to me, "What for?" Sez I to mesilf, "For the glory av ut!" Sez mesilf to me, "Will that fill these two strong arrums av yours, Terence?" "Go to the devil," sez I to mesilf. "Go to the married lines," sez mesilf to me. " 'Tis the same thing," sez I to mesilf. "Av you're the same man, ut is," said mesilf to me; an' wid that I considhered on ut a long while. Did you iver feel that way, sorr?'

I snored gently, knowing that if Mulvaney were

uninterrupted he would go on. The clamour from the bivouac fires beat up to the stars, as the rival singers of the companies were pitted against each other.

'So I felt that way an' a bad time ut was. Wanst, bein' a fool, I wint into the married lines more for the sake av spakin' to our ould colour-sergint Shadd than for any thruck wid women-folk. I was a corp'ril then—rejuced aftherwards, but a corp'ril then. I've got a photograft av mesilf to prove ut. "You'll take a cup av tay wid us?" sez Shadd. "I will that," I sez, "tho' tay is not my divarsion."

' " " 'Twud be better for you if ut were," sez ould Mother Shadd, an' she had ought to know, for Shadd, in the ind av his service, dhrank bung-full each night.

'Wid that I tuk off my gloves—there was pipeclay in thim, so that they stud alone—an' pulled up my chair, lookin' round at the china ornaments an' bits av things in the Shadds' quarters. They were things that belonged to a man, an' no camp-kit, here to-day an' dishipated next. "You're comfortable in this place, sergint," sez I. " 'Tis the wife that did ut, boy," sez he, pointin' the stem av his pipe to ould Mother Shadd, an' she smacked the top av his bald head apon the compliment. "That manes you want money," sez she.

'An' thin—an' thin whin the kettle was to be filled, Dinah came in—my Dinah—her sleeves rowled up to the elbow an' her hair in a winkin' glory over her forehead, the big blue eyes beneath twinklin' like stars on a frosty night, an' the tread av her two feet lighter than waste-paper from the colonel's basket in ord'ly-room whin ut's emptied. Bein' but a shlip av a girl she went pink at seein' me, an' I twisted me moustache an' looked at a picture forninst the wall. Niver show a woman that ye care the snap av a finger for her, an' begad she'll come bleatin' to your boot-heels!'

'I suppose that's why you followed Annie Bragin till everybody in the married quarters laughed at you,' said I, remembering that unhallowed wooing and casting off the disguise of drowsiness.

'I'm layin' down the gin'ral theory av the attack,' said Mulvaney, driving his boot into the dying fire. 'If you read the *Soldier's Pocket Book*, which niver any soldier reads, you'll see that there are exceptions. Whin Dinah was out av the door (an' 'twas as tho' the sunlight had shut too)—"Mother av Hiven, sergint," sez I, "but is that your daughter?"—"I've believed that way these eighteen years," sez ould Shadd, his eyes twinklin'; "but Mrs. Shadd has her own opinion, like iv'ry woman."—" 'Tis wid yours this time, for a mericle," sez Mother Shadd. "Thin why in the name av fortune did I niver see her before?" sez I. "Bekaze you've been thrapesin' round wid the married women these three years past. She was a bit av a child till last year, an' she shot up wid the spring," sez ould Mother Shadd. "I'll thrapese no more," sez I. "D'you mane that?" sez ould Mother Shadd, lookin' at me side-ways like a hen looks at a hawk whin the chickens are runnin' free. "Try me, an' tell," sez I. Wid that I pulled on my gloves, dhrank off the tay, an' went out av the house as stiff as at gin'ral p'rade, for well I knew that Dinah Shadd's eyes were in the small av my back out av the scullery window. Faith! that was the only time I mourned I was not a cav'l'ry man for the pride av the spurs to jingle.

'I wint out to think, an' I did a powerful lot av thinkin', but ut all came round to that shlip av a girl in the dotted blue dhress, wid the blue eyes an' the sparkil in them. Thin I kept off canteen, an' I kept to the married quarthers, or near by, on the chanst av meetin' Dinah. Did I meet her? Oh, my time past, did I not; wid a lump in my throat as big as my valise an' my heart goin' like a farrier's forge on a Satuday morning? 'Twas "Good day to ye, Miss Dinah," an' "Good day t'you, corp'ril," for a week or two, and divil a bit further could I get bekaze av the respect I had to that girl that I cud ha' broken betune finger an' thumb.'

Here I giggled as I recalled the gigantic figure of Dinah Shadd when she handed me my shirt.

'Ye may laugh,' grunted Mulvaney. 'But I'm speakin' the trut', an' 'tis you that are in fault. Dinah was a girl that wud ha' taken the imperiousness out av the Duchess av Clonmel in those days. Flower hand, foot av shod air, an' the eyes av the livin' mornin' she had that is my wife to-day—ould Dinah, and niver aught else than Dinah Shadd to me.

' 'Twas after three weeks standin' off an' on, an' niver makin' headway excipt through the eyes, that a little drummer-boy grinned in me face whin I had admonished him wid the buckle av my belt for riotin' all over the place. "An' I'm not the only wan that doesn't kape to barricks," sez he. I tuk him by the scruff av his neck,—my heart was hung on a hair-thrigger those days, you will onderstand—an' "Out wid ut," sez I, "or I'll lave no bone av you unbreakable."—"Speak to Dempsey," sez he howlin'. "Dempsey which?" sez I, "ye unwashed limb av Satan."—"Av the Bob-tailed Dhragoons," sez he. "He's seen her home from her aunt's house in the civil lines four times this fortnight."—"Child!" sez I, dhroppin' him, "your tongue's stronger than your body. Go to your quarters. I'm sorry I dhressed you down."

'At that I went four ways to wanst huntin' Dempsey. I was mad to think that wid all my airs among women I shud ha' been chated by a basin-faced fool av a cav'lry-man not fit to trust on a trunk. Presently I found him in our lines—the Bobtails was quartered next us—an' a tallowy, topheavy son av a she-mule he was wid his big brass spurs an' his plastrons on his epigastrons an' all. But he niver flinched a hair.

' "A word with you, Dempsey," sez I. "You've walked wid Dinah Shadd four times this fortnight gone."

' "What's that to you?" sez he. "I'll walk forty times

more, an' forty on top av that, ye shovel-futted clod-breakin' infantry lance-copr'ril."

'Before I cud gyard he had his gloved fist home on my cheek an' down I went full-sprawl. "Will that content you?" sez he, blowin' on his knuckles for all the world like a Scots Greys orf'cer. "Content!" sez I. "For your own sake, man, take off your spurs, peel your jackut, an' on-glove. 'Tis the beginnin' av the overture; stand up!"

'He stud all he know, but he niver peeled his jacket, an' his shoulders had no fair play. I was fightin' for Dinah Shadd an' that cut on my cheek. What hope had he for-ninst me? "Stand up," sez I, time an' again whin he was beginnin' to quarter the ground an' gyard high an' go large. "This isn't ridin'-school," I sez. "O man, stand up an' let me get in at ye." But whin I saw he wud be runnin' about, I grup his shtock in my left an' his waist-belt in my right an' swung him clear to my right front, head undher, he hammerin' my nose till the wind was knocked out av him on the bare ground. "Stand up," sez I, "or I'll kick your head into your chest!" and I wud ha' done ut too, so ragin' mad I was.

' "My collar-bone's bruk," sez he. "Help me back to lines. I'll walk wid her no more." So I helped him back.'

'And was his collar-bone broken?' I asked, for I fancied that only Learoyd could neatly accomplish that terrible throw.

'He pitched on his left shoulder-point. Ut was. Next day the news was in both barricks, an' whin I met Dinah Shadd wid a cheek on me like all the reg'mintal tailor's samples there was no "Good mornin', corp'ril," or aught else. "An' what have I done, Miss Shadd," sez I, very bould, plantin' mesilf forninst her, "that ye should not pass the time of day?"

' "Ye've half-killed rough-rider Dempsey," sez she, her dear blue eyes fillin' up.

' "May be," sez I. "Was he a friend av yours that saw ye home four times in the fortnight?"

' "Yes," sez she, but her mouth was down at the corners. "An'—an' what's that to you?" she sez.

' "Ask Dempsey," sez I, purtendin' to go away.

' "Did you fight for me then, ye silly man?" she sez, tho' she knew ut all along.

' "Who else?" sez I, an' I tuk wan pace to the front.

' "I wasn't worth ut," sez she, fingerin' in her apron.

' "That's for me to say," sez I. "Shall I say ut?"

' "Yes," sez she in a saint's whisper, an' at that I explained mesilf; and she tould me what ivry man that is a man, an' many that is a woman, hears wanst in his life.

' "But what made ye cry at startin', Dinah, darlin'?" sez I.

' "Your—your bloody cheek," sez she, duckin' her little head down on my sash (I was on duty for the day) an' whimperin' like a sorrowful angil.

'Now a man cud take that two ways. I tuk ut as pleased me best an' my first kiss wid ut. Mother av Innocence! but I kissed her on the tip av the nose an' undher the eye; an' a girl that let's a kiss come tumbleways like that has never been kissed before. Take note av that, sorr. Thin we wint hand in hand to ould Mother Shadd like two little childher, an' she said 'twas no bad thing, an' ould Shadd nodded behind his pipe, an' Dinah ran away to her own room. That day I throd on rollin' clouds. All earth was too small to hould me. Begad, I cud ha' hiked the sun out av the sky for a live coal to my pipe, so magnificent I was. But I tuk recruities at squad-drill instid, an' began wid general battalion advance whin I shud ha' been balance-steppin' them. Eyah! that day! that day!'

A very long pause. 'Well?' said I.

' 'Twas all wrong,' said Mulvaney, with an enormous sigh. 'An' I know that ev'ry bit av ut was my own foolishness. That night I tuk maybe the half av three pints—not enough to turn the hair of a man in his natural senses. But I was more than half drunk wid pure joy, an' that canteen beer was so much whisky to me. I can't tell how it came about, but *bekaze* I had no thought for anywan except Dinah, *bekaze* I hadn't slipped her little white arms from my neck five minuts, *bekaze* the breath of her kiss was not gone from my mouth, I must go through the married lines on my way to quarters an' I must stay talkin' to a red-headed Mullingar heifer av a girl, Judy Sheehy, that was daughter to Mother Sheehy, the wife of Nick Sheehy, the canteen-sergint—the Black Curse av Shielygh be on the whole brood that are above groun' this day!

' "An' what are ye houldin' your head that high for, corp'ril?" sez Judy. "Come in an' thry a cup av tay," she sez, standin' in the doorway. Bein' an ontrustable fool, an' thinkin' av anything but tay, I wint.

' "Mother's at canteen," sez Judy, smoothin' the hair av hers that was like red snakes, an' lookin' at me cornerways out av her green cats' eyes. 'Ye will not mind, corp'ril?"

' "I can endure," sez I; ould Mother Sheehy bein' no divarsion av mine, nor her daughter too. Judy fetched the tea things an' put thim on the table, leanin' over me very close to get thim square. I dhrew back, thinkin' av Dinah.

' "Is ut afraid you are av a girl alone?" sez Judy.

' "No," sez I. "Why should I be?"

' "That rests wid the girl," sez Judy, dhrawin' her chair next to mine.

' "Thin there let ut rest," sez I; an' thinkin' I'd been a trifle onpolite, I sez, "The tay's not quite sweet enough for my taste. Put your little finger in the cup, Judy. 'Twill make ut necthar."

' "What's necthar?" sez she.

' "Somethin' very sweet," sez I; an' for the sinful life av me I cud not help lookin' at her out av the corner av my eye, as I was used to look at a woman.

' "Go on wid ye, corp'ril," sez she. "You're a flirrt."

' "On me sowl I'm not," sez I.

' "Then you're a cruel handsome man, an' that's worse," sez she, heaving big sighs an' lookin' crossways.

' "You know your own mind," sez I.

' " 'Twud be better for me if I did not," she sez.

' "There's a dale to be said on both sides av that," sez I, unthinkin'.

' "Say your own part av ut, then, Terence, darlin'," sez she; "for begad I'm thinkin I've said too much or too little for an honest girl," an' wid that she put her arms round my neck an' kissed me.

' "There's no more to be said afther that," sez I, kissin' her back again—Oh the mane scutt that I was, my head ringin' wid Dinah Shadd! How does ut come about, sorr, that when a man has put the comether on wan woman, he's sure bound to put it on another? 'Tis the same thing at musketry. Wan day ivry shot goes wide or into the bank, an' the next, lay high lay low, sight or snap, ye can't get off the bull's-eye for ten shots runnin'.'

'That only happens to a man who has had a good deal of experience. He does it without thinking,' I replied.

'Thankin' you for the complimint, sorr, ut may be so. But I'm doubtful whether you mint ut for a complimint. Hear now; I sat there wid Judy on my knee tellin' me all manner av nonsinse an' only sayin' "yes" an' "no," when I'd much better ha' kept tongue betune teeth. An' that was not an hour afther I had left Dinah! What I was thinkin' av I cannot say. Presintly, quiet as a cat, ould Mother Sheehy came in velvet-dhrunk. She had her daughter's red hair, but 'twas bald in patches, an' I cud see in her wicked ould face, clear as lightnin', what Judy wud be twenty years to come. I was for jumpin' up, but Judy niver moved.

' "Terence has promust, mother," sez she, an' the could sweat bruk out all over me. Ould Mother Sheehy sat down of a heap an' began playin' wid the cups. "Thin you're a well-matched pair," she sez very thick. "For he's the biggest rogue that iver spoiled the queen's shoe-leather," an'——

' "I'm off, Judy," sez I. "Ye should not talk nonsinse to your mother. Get her to bed, girl."

' "Nonsinse!" sez the ould woman, prickin' up her ears like a cat an' grippin' the table-edge. " 'Twill be the most nonsinsical nonsinse for you, ye grinnin' badger, if non-sinse 'tis. Git clear, you. I'm goin' to bed."

'I ran out into the dhark, my head in a stew an' my heart sick, but I had sinse enough to see that I'd brought ut all on mysilf. "It's this to pass the time av day to a pan-jandhrum av hell-cats," sez I. "What I've said, an' what I've not said do not matther. Judy an' her dam will hould me for a promust man, an' Dinah will give me the go, an' I desarve ut. I will go an' get dhrunk," sez I, "an' forget about ut, for 'tis plain I'm not a marrin' man."

'On my way to canteen I ran against Lascelles, colour-sergeant that was av E Comp'ny, a hard, hard man, wid a torment av a wife. "You've the head av a drowned man on your shoulders," sez he; "an' you're goin' where you'll get a worse wan. Come back," sez he. "Let me go," sez I. "I've thrown my luck over the wall wid my own hand!"— "Then that's not the way to get ut back again," sez he. "Have out wid your throuble, ye fool-bhoy." An' I tould him how the matther was.

'He sucked in his lower lip. "You've been thrapped," sez he. "Ju Sheehy wud be the betther for a man's name to hers as soon as can. An ye thought ye'd put the comether on her,—that's the natural vanity of the baste. Terence, you're a big born fool, but you're not bad enough to marry into that comp'ny. If you said anythin, an' for all your protestations I'm sure ye did—or did not, which is worse,—eat ut all—lie like the father of all lies, but come out av ut free of Judy. Do I not know what ut is to marry a woman that was the very spit an' image av Judy whin she was young? I'm gettin' old an' I've larnt patience, but you, Terence, you'd raise hand on Judy an' kill her in a year. Never mind if Dinah gives you the go, you've desarved ut; never mind if the whole reg'mint laughs you all day. Get shut av Judy an' her mother. They can't dhrag you to church, but if they do, they'll dhrag you to hell. Go back to your quarters and lie down," sez he. Thin over his shoulder, "You *must* ha' done with thim."

'Next day I wint to see Dinah, but there was no tucker in me as I walked. I knew the throuble wud come soon enough widout any handlin' av mine, an' I dreaded ut sore.

'I heard Judy callin' me, but I hild straight on to the Shadds' quarthers, an' Dinah wud ha' kissed me but I put her back.

' "Whin all's said, darlin'," sez I, "you can give ut me if ye will, tho' I misdoubt 'twill be so easy to come by then."

'I had scarce begun to put the explanation into shape before Judy an' her mother came to the door. I think there was a verandah, but I'm forgettin'.

' "Will ye not step in?" sez Dinah, pretty and polite, though the Shadds had no dealin's with the Sheehys. Old Mother Shadd looked up quick, an' she was the fust to see the throuble; for Dinah was her daughter.

' "I'm pressed for time to-day," sez Judy as bould as brass; "an' I've only come for Terence,—my promust man. 'Tis strange to find him here the day afther the day."

'Dinah looked at me as though I had hit her, an' I answered straight.

' "There was some nonsinse last night at the Sheehys' quarthers, an' Judy's carryin' on the joke, darlin'," sez I.

' "At the Sheehys' quarthers?" sez Dinah very slow, an' Judy cut in wid: "He was there from nine till ten, Dinah Shadd, an' the betther half av that time I was sittin' on his knee, Dinah Shadd. Ye may look and ye may look an' ye may look me up an' down, but ye won't look away that Terence is my promust man. Terence, darlin', 'tis time for us to be comin' home."

'Dinah Shadd niver said word to Judy. "Ye left me at half-past eight," she sez to me, "an' I niver thought that ye'd leave me for Judy,—promises or no promises. Go back wid her, you that have to be fetched by a girl! I'm done with you," sez she, and she ran into her own room, her mother followin'. So I was alone wid those two women and at liberty to spake my sentiments.

' "Judy Sheehy," sez I, "if you made a fool av me betune the lights you shall not do ut in the day. I niver promised you words or lines."

' "You lie," sez ould Mother Sheehy, "an' may ut choke you where you stand!" She was far gone in dhrink.

' "An' tho' ut choked me where I stud I'd not change," sez I. "Go home, Judy. I take shame for a decent girl like you dhraggin' your mother out bare-headed on this errand. Hear now, and have ut for an answer. I gave my word to Dinah Shadd yesterday, an', more blame to me, I was wid you last night talkin' nonsinse but nothin' more. You've chosen to thry to hould me on ut. I will not be held thereby for anythin' in the world. Is that enough?"

'Judy wint pink all over. "An' I wish you joy av the perjury," sez she, duckin' a curtsey. "You've lost a woman that would ha' wore her hand to the bone for your pleasure; an' 'deed, Terence, ye were not thrapped. . . ." Lascelles must ha' spoken plain to her. "I am such as Dinah is—'deed I am! Ye've lost a fool av a girl that'll niver look at you again, an' ye've lost what he niver had,—your common honesty. If you manage your men as you manage your love-makin', small wondher they call you the worst corp'ril in the comp'ny. Come away, mother," sez she.

'But divil a fut would the ould woman budge! "D'you hould by that?" sez she, peerin' up under her thick gray eyebrows.

' "Ay, an' wud," sez I, "tho' Dinah give me the go twinty times. I'll have no thruck with you or yours," sez I. "Take your child away, ye shameless woman."

' "An' am I shameless?" sez she, bringin' her hands up above her head. "Thin what are you, ye lyin', schamin', weak-kneed, dhirty-souled son av a sutler? Am *I* shameless? Who put the open shame on me an' my child that we shud go beggin' through the lines in the broad daylight for the broken word of a man? Double portion of my shame be on you, Terence Mulvaney, that think yourself so strong! By Mary and the saints, by blood and water an' by ivry sorrow that came into the world since the beginnin', the black blight fall on you and yours, so that you may niver be free from pain for another when ut's not your own! May your heart bleed in your breast drop by drop wid all your friends laughin' at the bleedin'! Strong you think yourself? May your strength be a curse to you to dhrive you into the divil's hands against your own will! Clear-eyed you are? May your eyes see clear evry step av the dark path you take till the hot cindhers av hell put thim out! May the ragin' dry thirst in my own ould bones go to you that you shall niver pass bottle full nor glass empty. God preserve the light av your onderstandin' to you, my jewel av a bhoy, that ye may niver forget what you mint to be an' do, whin you're wallowin' in the muck! May ye see the betther and follow the worse as long as there's breath in your body; an' may ye die quick in a strange land, watchin' your death before ut takes you, an' onable to stir hand or foot!"

'I heard a scufflin' in the room behind, and thin Dinah Shadd's hand dhropped into mine like a rose-leaf into a muddy road.

' "The half av that I'll take," sez she, "an' more too if I can. Go home, ye silly talkin' woman,—go home an' confess."

' "Come away! Come away!" sez Judy, pullin' her mother by the shawl. " 'Twas none av Terence's fault. For the love av Mary stop the talkin'."

' "An' you!" said ould Mother Sheehy, spinnin' round forninst Dinah. "Will ye take the half av that man's load? Stand off from him, Dinah Shadd, before he takes you down too—you that look to be a quarther-master-sergeant's wife in five years. You look too high, child. You shall *wash* for the quarther-master-sergeant, whin he plases to give you the job out av charity; but a privit's wife you shall be to the end, an' evry sorrow of a privit's wife you shall know and niver a joy but wan, that shall go from you like the running tide from a rock. The pain av bearin' you shall know but niver the pleasure av giving the breast; an' you shall put away a man-child into the common ground wid niver a priest to say a prayer over him, an' on that man-child ye shall think ivry day av your life. Think long, Dinah Shadd, for you'll niver have another tho' you pray till your knees are bleedin'. The mothers av childer shall mock you behind your back when you're wringing over the washtub. You shall know what ut is to help a dhrunken husband home an' see him go to the gyard-room. Will that plase you, Dinah Shadd, that won't be seen talkin' to my daughter? You shall talk to worse than Judy before all's over. The sergints' wives shall look down on you contemptuous, daughter av a sergint, an' you shall cover ut all up wid a smiling face when your heart's burstin'. Stand off av him, Dinah Shadd, for I've put the Black Curse of Shielygh upon him an' his own mouth shall make ut good."

'She pitched forward on her head an' began foamin' at the mouth. Dinah Shadd ran out wid water, an' Judy dhragged the ould woman into the verandah till she sat up.

' "I'm old an' forlore," she sez, thremblin' an' cryin', "and 'tis like I say a dale more than I mane."

' "When you're able to walk,—go," says ould Mother Shadd. "This house has no place for the likes av you that have cursed my daughter."

' "Eyah!" said the ould woman. "Hard words break no bones, an' Dinah Shadd 'll kape the love av her husband till my bones are green corn. Judy darlin', I misremember what I came here for. Can you lend us the bottom av a taycup av tay, Mrs. Shadd?"

'But Judy dhragged her off cryin' as tho' her heart wud break. An' Dinah Shadd an' I, in ten minutes we had forgot ut all.'

'Then why do you remember it now?' said I.

'Is ut like I'd forget? Ivry word that wicked ould woman spoke fell thrue in my life afterwards, an' I cud ha' stud ut all—stud ut all—excipt when my little Shadd was born. That was on the line av march three months afther the regiment was taken with cholera. We were betune Umballa an' Kalka thin, an' I was on picket. Whin I came off duty the women showed me the child, an' ut turned on uts side an' died as I looked. We buried him by the road, an' Father Victor was a day's march behind wid the heavy baggage, so the comp'ny captain read a prayer. An' since then I've been a childless man, an' all else that ould Mother Sheehy put upon me an' Dinah Shadd. What do you think, sorr?'

I thought a good deal, but it seemed better then to reach out for Mulvaney's hand. The demonstration nearly cost me the use of three fingers. Whatever he knows of his weaknesses, Mulvaney is entirely ignorant of his strength.

'But what do you think?' he repeated, as I was straightening out the crushed fingers.

My reply was drowned in yells and outcries from the next fire, where ten men were shouting for 'Orth'ris,' 'Privit Orth'ris,' 'Mistah Or—ther—ris!' 'Deah boy,' 'Cap'n Orth'ris,' 'Field-Marshal Orth'ris,' 'Stanley, you pen'north o' pop, come 'ere to your own comp'ny!' And the cockney, who had been delighting another audience with recondite and Rabelaisian yarns, was shot down among his admirers by the major force.

'You've crumpled my dress-shirt 'orrid,' said he, 'an' I shan't sing no more to this 'ere bloomin' drawin'-room.'

Learoyd, roused by the confusion, uncoiled himself, crept behind Ortheris, and slung him aloft on his shoulders.

'Sing, ye bloomin' hummin' bird!' said he, and Ortheris, beating time on Learoyd's skull, delivered himself, in the raucous voice of the Ratcliffe Highway, of this song:—

My girl she give me the go onst,
  When I was a London lad,
An' I went on the drink for a fortnight,
  An' then I went to the bad.
The Queen she give me a shillin'
  To fight for 'er over the seas;
But Guv'ment built me a fever-trap,
  An' Injia give me disease.

Chorus.

Ho! don't you 'eed what a girl says,
  An' don't you go for the beer;
But I was an ass when I was at grass,
  An' that is why I'm here.

I fired a shot at a Afghan,
  The beggar 'e fired again,
An' I lay on my bed with a 'ole in my 'ed,
  An' missed the next campaign!

I up with my gun at a Burman
  Who carried a bloomin' *dah*,
But the cartridge stuck and the bay'nit bruk,
  An' all I got was the scar.

Chorus.

Ho! don't you aim at a Afghan
  When you stand on the sky-line clear;
An' don't you go for a Burman
  If none o' your friends is near.

I served my time for a corp'ral,
  An' wetted my stripes with pop,
For I went on the bend with a intimate friend,
  An' finished the night in the 'shop.'
I served my time for a sergeant;
  The colonel 'e sez 'No!
The most you'll see is a full C.B.'[1]
  An' ... very next night 'twas so.

_____

[1] Confined to barracks.

Chorus.

Ho! don't you go for a corp'ral
    Unless your 'ed is clear;
But I was an ass when I was at grass,
    An' that is why I'm 'ere.

I've tasted the luck o' the army
    In barrack an' camp an' clink,
An' I lost my tip through the bloomin' trip
    Along o' the women an' drink.
I'm down at the heel o' my service
    An' when I am laid on the shelf,
My very wust friend from beginning to end
    By the blood of a mouse was myself!

Chorus.

Ho! don't you 'eed what a girl says,
    An' don't you go for the beer;
But I was an ass when I was at grass,
    An' that is why I'm 'ere.

'Ay, listen to our little man now, singin' an' shoutin' as tho' trouble had niver touched him. D' you remember when he went mad with the home-sickness?' said Mulvaney, recalling a never-to-be-forgotten season when Ortheris waded through the deep waters of affliction and behaved abominably. 'But he's talkin' bitter truth, though. Eyah!

    'My very worst frind from beginnin' to ind
      By the blood av a mouse was mesilf!'

When I woke I saw Mulvaney, the night-dew gemming his moustache, leaning on his rifle at picket, lonely as Prometheus on his rock, with I know not what vultures tearing his liver.

                                   1890

ON GREENHOW HILL

To Love's low voice she lent a careless ear;
Her hand within his rosy fingers lay,
A chilling weight. She would not turn or hear;
But with averted face went on her way.
But when pale Death, all featureless and grim,
Lifted his bony hand, and beckoning
Held out his cypress-wreath, she followed him,
And Love was left forlorn and wondering,
That she who for his bidding would not stay,
At Death's first whisper rose and went away.
                                        Rivals

'*Ohé, Ahmed Din! Shafiz Ullah ahoo!* Bahadur Khan, where are you? Come out of the tents, as I have done, and fight against the English. Don't kill your own kin! Come out to me!'

The deserter from a native corps was crawling round the outskirts of the camp, firing at intervals, and shouting invitations to his old comrades. Misled by the rain and the darkness, he came to the English wing of the camp, and with his yelping and rifle-practice disturbed the men. They had been making roads all day, and were tired.

Ortheris was sleeping at Learoyd's feet. 'Wot's all that?' he said thickly. Learoyd snored, and a Snider bullet ripped its way through the tent wall. The men swore. 'It's that bloomin' deserter from the Aurangabadis,' said Ortheris. 'Git up, some one, an' tell 'im 'e's come to the wrong shop.'

'Go to sleep, little man,' said Mulvaney, who was steaming nearest the door. 'I can't arise an' expaytiate with him. 'Tis rainin' entrenchin' tools outside.'

' 'Tain't because you bloomin' can't. It's 'cause you bloomin' won't, ye long, limp, lousy, lazy beggar, you. 'Ark to 'im 'owlin'!'

'Wot's the good of argifying? Put a bullet into the swine! 'E's keepin' us awake!' said another voice.

A subaltern shouted angrily, and a dripping sentry whined from the darkness—

' 'Tain't no good, sir. I can't see 'im. 'E's 'idin' some-where down 'ill.'

Ortheris tumbled out of his blanket. 'Shall I try to get 'im, sir?' said he.

'No,' was the answer. 'Lie down. I won't have the whole camp shooting all round the clock. Tell him to go and pot his friends.'

Ortheris considered for a moment. Then, putting his head under the tent wall, he called, as a 'bus conductor calls in a block, ' 'Igher up, there! 'Igher up!'

The men laughed, and the laughter was carried down wind to the deserter, who, hearing that he had made a mistake, went off to worry his own regiment half a mile away. He was received with shots; the Aurangabadis were very angry with him for disgracing their colours.

'An' that's all right,' said Ortheris, withdrawing his head as he heard the hiccough of the Sniders in the dis-tance. 'S'elp me Gawd, tho', that man's not fit to live— messin' with my beauty-sleep this way.'

'Go out and shoot him in the morning, then,' said the subaltern incautiously. 'Silence in the tents now. Get your rest, men.'

Ortheris lay down with a happy little sigh, and in two minutes there was no sound except the rain on the canvas and the all-embracing and elemental snoring of Learoyd.

The camp lay on a bare ridge of the Himalayas, and for a week had been waiting for a flying column to make connection. The nightly rounds of the deserter and his friends had become a nuisance.

In the morning the men dried themselves in hot sunshine and cleaned their grimy accoutrements. The native regiment was to take its turn of road-making that day while the Old Regiment loafed.

'I'm goin' to lay for a shot at that man,' said Ortheris, when he had finished washing out his rifle. ' 'E comes up the watercourse every evenin' about five o'clock. If we go and lie out on the north 'ill a bit this afternoon we'll get 'im.'

'You're a bloodthirsty little mosquito,' said Mulvaney, blowing blue clouds into the air. 'But I suppose I will have to come wid you. Fwhere's Jock?'

'Gone out with the Mixed Pickles, 'cause 'e thinks 'isself a bloomin' marksman,' said Ortheris with scorn.

The 'Mixed Pickles' were a detachment of picked shots, generally employed in clearing spurs of hills when the enemy were too impertinent. This taught the young officers how to handle men, and did not do the enemy much harm. Mulvaney and Ortheris strolled out of camp, and passed the Aurangabadis going to their road-making.

'You've got to sweat to-day,' said Ortheris genially. 'We're going to get your man. You didn't knock 'im out last night by any chance, any of you?'

'No. The pig went away mocking us. I had one shot at him,' said a private. 'He's my cousin, and *I* ought to have cleared our dishonour. But good luck to you.'

They went cautiously to the north hill, Ortheris leading, because, as he explained, 'this is a long-range show, an' I've got to do it.' His was an almost passionate devotion to his rifle, which, by barrack-room report, he was supposed to kiss every night before turning in. Charges and scuffles he held in contempt, and, when they were inevitable, slipped between Mulvaney and Learoyd, bidding them to fight for his skin as well as their own. They never failed him. He trotted along, questing like a hound on a broken trail, through the wood of the north hill. At last he was satisfied, and threw himself down on the soft pine-needled slope that commanded a clear view of the water-course and a brown, bare hillside beyond it. The trees made a scented darkness in which an army corps could have hidden from the sun-glare without.

' 'Ere's the tail o' the wood,' said Ortheris. ' 'E's got to come up the watercourse, 'cause it gives 'im cover. We'll lay 'ere. 'Tain't not arf so bloomin' dusty neither.'

He buried his nose in a clump of scentless white violets. No one had come to tell the flowers that the season of their strength was long past, and they had bloomed merrily in the twilight of the pines.

'This is something like,' he said luxuriously. 'Wot a 'evinly clear drop for a bullet acrost! How much d'you make it, Mulvaney?'

'Seven hunder. Maybe a trifle less, bekaze the air's so thin.'

Wop! wop! wop! went a volley of musketry on the rear face of the north hill.

'Curse them Mixed Pickles firin' at nothin'! They'll scare arf the country.'

'Thry a sightin' shot in the middle of the row,' said Mulvaney, the man of many wiles. 'There's a red rock yonder he'll be sure to pass. Quick!'

Ortheris ran his sight up to six hundred yards and fired. The bullet threw up a feather of dust by a clump of gentians at the base of the rock.

'Good enough!' said Ortheris, snapping the scale down. 'You snick your sights to mine or a little lower. You're always firin' high. But remember, first shot to me. O Lordy! but it's a lovely afternoon.'

The noise of the firing grew louder, and there was a tramping of men in the wood. The two lay very quiet, for they knew that the British soldier is desperately prone to fire at anything that moves or calls. Then Learoyd appeared, his tunic ripped across the breast by a bullet, looking ashamed of himself. He flung down on the pine-needles, breathing in snorts.

'One o' them damned gardeners o' th' Pickles,' said he, fingering the rent. 'Firin' to th' right flank, when he knowed I was there. If I knew who he was I'd 'a' rippen the hide offan him. Look at ma tunic!'

'That's the spishil trustability av a marksman. Train him to hit a fly wid a stiddy rest at seven hunder, an' he loose on anythin' he sees or hears up to th' mile. You're well out av that fancy-firin' gang, Jock. Stay here.'

'Bin firin' at the bloomin' wind in the bloomin' tree-tops,' said Ortheris with a chuckle 'I'll show you some firin' later on.'

They wallowed in the pine-needles, and the sun warmed them where they lay. The Mixed Pickles ceased firing, and returned to camp, and left the wood to a few scared apes. The watercourse lifted up its voice in the silence, and talked foolishly to the rocks. Now and again the dull thump of a blasting charge three miles away told that the Aurangabadis were in difficulties with their road-making. The men smiled as they listened and lay still, soaking in the warm leisure. Presently Learoyd, between the whiffs of his pipe—

'Seems queer—about 'im yonder—desertin' at all.'

' 'E'll be a bloomin' side queerer when I've done with 'im,' said Ortheris. They were talking in whispers, for the stillness of the wood and the desire of slaughter lay heavy upon them.

'I make no doubt he had his reasons for desertin'; but, my faith! I make less doubt ivry man has good reason for killin' him,' said Mulvaney.

'Happen there was a lass tewed up wi' it. Men do more than more for th' sake of a lass.'

'They make most av us 'list. They've no manner av right to make us desert.'

'Ah; they make us 'list, or their fathers do,' said Learoyd softly, his helmet over his eyes.

Ortheris's brows contracted savagely. He was watching the valley. 'If it's a girl I'll shoot the beggar twice over, an' second time for bein' a fool. You're blasted sentimental all of a sudden. Thinkin' o' your last near shave?'

'Nay, lad; ah was but thinkin' o' what had happened.'

'An' fwhat has happened, ye lumberin' child av calamity, that you're lowing like a cow-calf at the back av the pasture, an' suggestin' invidious excuses for the man Stanley's goin' to kill. Ye'll have to wait another hour yet, little man. Spit it out, Jock, an' bellow melojus to the moon. It takes an earthquake or a bullet graze to fetch aught out av you. Discourse, Don Juan! The a-moors av Lotharius Learoyd! Stanley, kape a rowlin' rig'mental eye on the valley.'

'It's along o' yon hill there,' said Learoyd, watching the bare sub-Himalayan spur that reminded him of his Yorkshire moors. He was speaking more to himself than his fellows. 'Ay,' said he, 'Rumbolds Moor stands up ower Skipton town, an' Greenhow Hill stands up ower Pately Brig. I reckon you've never heeard tell o' Greenhow Hill, but yon bit o' bare stuff if there was nobbut a white road windin' is like ut; strangely like. Moors an' moors an' moors, wi' never a tree for shelter, an' gray houses wi' flagstone rooves, and pewits cryin', an' a windhover goin' to and fro just like these kites. And cold! A wind that cuts you like a knife. You could tell Greenhow Hill folk by the red-apple colour o' their cheeks an' nose tips, and their blue eyes, driven into pin-points by the wind. Miners mostly, burrowin' for lead i' th' hillsides, followin' the trail of th' ore vein same as a field-rat. It was the roughest minin' I ever seen. Yo'd come on a bit o' creakin' wood windlass like a well-head, an' you was let down i' th' bight of a rope, fendin' yoursen off the side wi' one hand, carryin' a candle stuck in a lump o' clay with t'other, an' clickin' hold of a rope with t'other hand.'

'An' that's three of them,' said Mulvaney. 'Must be a good climate in those parts.'

Learoyd took no heed.

'An' then yo' came to a level, where you crept on your hands and knees through a mile o' windin' drift, an' you come out into a cave-place as big as Leeds Townhall, with a engine pumpin' water from workin's 'at went deeper still. It's a queer country, let alone minin', for the hill is full of those natural caves, an' the rivers an' the becks drops into what they call pot-holes, an' come out again miles away.'

'Wot was you doin' there?' said Ortheris.

'I was a young chap then, an' mostly went wi' 'osses, leadin' coal and lead ore; but at th' time I'm tellin' on I was drivin' the waggon-team i' th' big sumph. I didn't belong to that country-side by rights. I went there because of a little difference at home, an' at fust I took up wi' a rough lot. One night we'd been drinkin', an' I must ha' hed more than I could stand, or happen th' ale was none so good. Though i' them days, By for God, I never seed bad ale.' He flung his arms over his head, and gripped a vast handful a white violets. 'Nah,' said he, 'I never seed the ale I could not drink, the bacca I could not smoke, nor the lass I could not kiss. Well, we mun have a race home, the lot on us. I lost all th' others, an' when I was climbin' ower one of them walls built o' loose stones, I comes down into the ditch, stones and all, an' broke my arm. Not as I knawed much about it, for I fell on th' back of my head, an' was knocked stupid like. An' when I come to mysen it were mornin', an' I were lyin' on the settle i' Jesse Roantree's houseplace, an' 'Liza Roantree was settin' sewin'. I ached all ovver, and my mouth were like a lime-kiln. She gave me a drink out of a china mug wi' gold letters—"A Present from Leeds"—as I looked at many and many a time at after. "Yo're to lie still while Dr. Warbottom comes, because your arm's broken, and father has sent a lad to fetch him. He found yo' when he was goin' to work, an' carried you here on his back," sez she. "Oa!" sez I; an' I shet my eyes, for I felt ashamed o' mysen. "Father's gone to his work these three hours, an' he said he'd tell 'em to get somebody to drive the tram." The clock ticked, an' a bee comed in the house, an' they rung i' my head like mill-wheels. An' she give me another drink an' settled the pillow. "Eh, but yo're young to be getten drunk an' such like, but yo' won't do it again, will yo'?"—"Noa," sez I, "I wouldn't if she'd not but stop they mill-wheels clatterin'." '

'Faith, it's a good thing to be nursed by a woman when you're sick!' said Mulvaney. 'Dir' cheap at the price av twenty broken heads.'

Ortheris turned to frown across the valley. He had not been nursed by many women in his life.

'An' then Dr. Warbottom comes ridin' up, an' Jesse Roantree along with 'im. He was a high-larned doctor, but he talked wi' poor folk same as theirsens. "What's ta bin agaate on naa?" he sings out. "Brekkin' tha thick head?" An' he felt me all ovver. "That's none broken. Tha' nobbut knocked a bit sillier than ordinary, an' that's daaft eneaf." An' soa he went on, callin' me all the names he could think on, but settin' my arm, wi' Jesse's help, as careful as could be. "Yo' mun let the big oaf bide here a bit, Jesse," he says, when he hed strapped me up an' given me a dose o' physic; "an' you an' Liza will tend him, though he's scarcelins worth the trouble. An' tha'll lose tha work," sez he, "an' tha'll be upon th' Sick Club for a couple o' months an' more. Doesn't tha think tha's a fool?" '

'But whin was a young man, high or low, the other av a fool, I'd like to know?' said Mulvaney. 'Sure, folly's the only safe way to wisdom, for I've thried it.'

'Wisdom!' grinned Ortheris, scanning his comrades with uplifted chin. 'You're bloomin' Solomons, you two, ain't you?'

Learoyd went calmly on, with a steady eye like an ox chewing the cud.

'And that was how I come to know 'Liza Roantree.

There's some tunes as she used to sing—aw, she were always singin'—that fetches Greenhow Hill before my eyes as fair as yon brow across there. And she would learn me to sing bass, an' I was to go to th' chapel wi' 'em where Jesse and she led the singin', th' old man playin' the fiddle. He was a strange chap, old Jesse, fair mad wi' music, an' he made me promise to learn the big fiddle when my arm was better. It belonged to him, and it stood up in a big case alongside o' th' eight-day clock, but Willie Satterthwaite, as played it in the chapel, had getten deaf as a door-post, and it vexed Jesse, as he had to rap him ower his head wi' th' fiddle-stick to make him give ower sawin' at th' right time.

'But there was a black drop in it all, an' it was a man in a black coat that brought it. When th' Primitive Methodist preacher came to Greenhow, he would always stop wi' Jesse Roantree, an' he laid hold of me from th' beginning. It seemed I wor a soul to be saved, and he meaned to do it. At th' same time I jealoused 'at he were keen o' savin' 'Liza Roantree's soul as well, and I could ha' killed him many a time. An' this went on till one day I broke out, an' borrowed th' brass for a drink from 'Liza. After fower days I come back, wi' my tail between my legs, just to see 'Liza again. But Jesse were at home an' th' preacher—th' Reverend Amos Barraclough. 'Liza said naught, but a bit o' red come into her face as were white of a regular thing. Says Jesse, tryin' his best to be civil, "Nay, lad, it's like this. You've getten to choose which way it's goin' to be. I'll ha' nobody across ma doorstep as goes a-drinkin', an' borrows my lass's money to spend i' their drink. Ho'd tha tongue, 'Liza," sez he, when she wanted to put in a word 'at I were welcome to th' brass, and she were none afraid that I wouldn't pay it back. Then the Reverend cuts in, seein' as Jesse were losin' his temper, an' they fair beat me among them. But it were 'Liza, as looked an' said naught, as did more than either o' their tongues, an' soa I concluded to get converted.'

'Fwhat?' shouted Mulvaney. Then, checking himself, he said softly, 'Let it be! Let it be! Sure the Blessed Virgin is the mother of all religion an' most women; an' there's a dale av piety in a girl if the men would only let ut stay there. I'd ha' been converted myself under the circumstances.'

'Nay, but,' pursued Learoyd with a blush, 'I meaned it.'

Ortheris laughed as loudly as he dared, having regard to his business at the time.

'Ay, Ortheris, you may laugh, but you didn't know yon preacher Barraclough—a little white-faced chap, wi' a voice as 'ud wile a bird off an a bush, and a way o' layin' hold of folks as made them think they'd never had a live man for a friend before. You never saw him, an'—an' you never seed 'Liza Roantree—never seed 'Liza Roantree.... Happen it was as much 'Liza as th' preacher and her father, but anyways they all meaned it, an' I was fair shamed o' mysen, an' so I become what they call a changed charácter. And when I think on, it's hard to believe as yon chap going to prayer-meetin's, chapel, and class-meetin's were me. But I never had naught to say for mysen, though there was a deal o' shoutin', and old Sammy Strother, as were almost clemmed to death and doubled up with the rheumatics, would sing out, "Joyful! Joyful!" and 'at it were better to go up to heaven in a coal-basket than down to hell i' a coach an' six. And he would put his poor old claw on my shoulder, sayin', "Doesn't tha feel it, tha great lump? Doesn't tha feel it?" An' sometimes I thought I did, and then again I thought I didn't, an' how was that?'

'The iverlastin' nature av mankind,' said Mulvaney. 'An', furthermore, I misdoubt you were built for the Primitive Methodians. They're a new corps anyways. I hold by the Ould Church, for she's the mother of them all—ay, an' the father, too. I like her bekaze she's most remarkable regimental in her fittings. I may die in Honolulu, Nova Zambra, or Cape Cayenne, but wherever I die, me bein' fwhat I am, an' a priest handy, I go under the same orders an' the same words an' the same unction as tho' the Pope himself come down from the roof av St. Peter's to see me off. There's neither high nor low, nor broad nor deep, nor betwixt nor between wid her, an' that's what I like. But mark you, she's no manner av Church for a wake man, bekaze she takes the body and the soul av him, onless he has his proper work to do. I remember when my father died that was three months comin' to his grave; begad he'd ha' sold the shebeen above our heads for ten minutes' quittance of purgathory. An' he did all he could. That's why I say ut takes a strong man to deal with the Ould Church, an' for that reason you'll find so many women go there. An' that same's a conundrum.'

'Wot's the use o' worritin' 'bout these things?' said Ortheris. 'You're bound to find all out quicker nor you want to, any'ow.' He jerked the cartridge out of the breech-block into the palm of his hand. ' 'Ere's my chaplain,' he said, and made the venomous black-headed bullet bow like a marionette. ' 'E's goin' to teach a man all about which is which, an' wot's true, after all, before sundown. But wot 'appened after that, Jock?'

'There was one thing they boggled at, and almost shut th' gate i' my face for, and that were my dog Blast, th' only one saved out o' a litter o' pups as was blowed up when a keg o' minin' powder loosed off in th' storekeeper's hut. They liked his name no better than his business, which were fightin' every dog he comed across; a rare good dog, wi' spots o' black and pink on his face, one ear gone, and lame o' one side wi' being driven in a basket through an iron roof, a matter of half a mile.

'They said I mun give him up 'cause he were worldly and low; and would I let mysen be shut out of heaven for the sake on a dog? "Nay," says I, "if th' door isn't wide enough for th' pair on us, we'll stop outside, for we'll none be parted." And th' preacher spoke up for Blast, as had a likin' for him from th' first—I reckon that was why I come to like th' preacher—and wouldn't hear o' changin' his name to Bless, as some o' them wanted. So th' pair on us became reg'lar chapel-members. But it's hard for a young chap o' my build to cut traces from the world, th' flesh, an' the devil all uv a heap. Yet I stuck to it for a long time, while th' lads as used to stand about th' town-end an' lean ower th' bridge, spittin' into th' beck o' a Sunday, would call after me, "Sitha, Learoyd, when's ta bean to preach, 'cause we're comin' to hear tha."—"Ho'd tha jaw. He hasn't getten th' white choaker on ta morn," another lad would say, and I had to double my fists hard i' th' bottom of my Sunday coat, and say to mysen, "If 'twere Monday and I warn't a member o' the Primitive Methodists, I'd leather all th' lot of yond'." That was th' hardest of all—to know that I could fight and I mustn't fight.'

Sympathetic grunts from Mulvaney.

'So what wi' singin', practisin', and class-meetin's, and th' big fiddle, as he made me take between my knees, I spend a deal o' time i' Jesse Roantree's house-place. But often as I was there, th' preacher fared to me to go oftener, and both th' old man an' th' young woman were pleased to have him. He lived i' Pately Brig, as were a goodish step off, but he come. He come all the same. I liked him as well or better as any man I'd ever seen i' one way, and yet I hated him wi' all my heart i' t'other, and we watched each other like cat and mouse, but civil as you please, for I was on my best behaviour, and he was that fair and open that I was bound to be fair with him. Rare good company he was, if I hadn't wanted to wring his cliver little neck half of the time. Often and often when he was goin' from Jesse's I'd set him a bit on the road.'

'See 'im 'come, you mean?' said Ortheris.

'Ay. It's a way we have i' Yorkshire o' seein' friends off. You was a friend as I didn't want to come back, and he didn't want me to come back neither, and so we'd walk together towards Pately, and then he'd set me back again, and there we'd be wal two o'clock i' the mornin' settin' each other to an' fro like a blasted pair o' pendulums twixt hill and valley, long after th' light had gone out i' 'Liza's window, as both on us had been looking at, pretending to watch the moon.'

'Ah!' broke in Mulvaney, 'ye'd no chanst against the maraudin' psalm-singer. They'll take the airs an' the graces instid av the man nine times out av ten, an' they only find the blunder later—the wimmen.'

'That's just where yo're wrong,' said Learoyd, reddening under the freckled tan of his cheeks. 'I was th' first wi' 'Liza, an' yo'd think that were enough. But th' parson were a steady-gaited sort o' chap, and Jesse were strong o' his side, and all th' women i' the congregation dinned it to 'Liza 'at she were fair fond to take up wi' a wastrel ne'er-do-weel like me, as was scarcelins respectable an' a fighting dog at his heels. It was all very well for her to be doing me good and saving my soul, but she must mind as she didn't do herself harm. They talk o' rich folk bein' stuck up an' genteel, but for cast-iron pride o' respectability there's naught like poor chapel folk. It's as cold as th' wind o' Greenhow Hill—ay, and colder, for 'twill never change. And now I come to think on it, one at strangest things I know is 'at they couldn't abide th' thought o' soldiering. There's a vast o' fightin' i' th' Bible, and there's a deal of Methodists i' th' army; but to hear chapel folk talk yo'd think that soldierin' were next door, an' t'other side, to hangin'. I' their meetin's all their talk is o' fightin'. When Sammy Strother were stuck for summat to say in his prayers, he'd sing out, "Th' sword o' th' Lord and o' Gideon." They were allus at it about puttin' on th' whole armour o' righteousness, an' fightin' the good fight o' faith. And then, atop o' 't all, they held a prayer-meetin' ower a young chap as wanted to 'list, and nearly deafened him, till he picked up his hat and fair ran away. And they'd tell tales in th' Sunday-school o' bad lads as had been thumped and brayed for bird-nesting o' Sundays and playin' truant o' week-days, and how they took to wrestlin', dog-fightin', rabbit-runnin', and drinkin', till at last, as if 'twere a hepitaph on a gravestone, they damned him across th' moors wi', "an' then he went and 'listed for a soldier," an' they'd all fetch a deep breath, and throw up their eyes like a hen drinkin'.'

'Fwhy is ut?' said Mulvaney, bringing down his hand on his thigh with a crack. 'In the name av God, fwhy is ut? I've seen ut, tu. They cheat an' they swindle an' they lie an' they slander, an' fifty things fifty times worse; but the last an' the worst by their reckonin' is to serve the Widdy honest. It's like the talk av childer—seein' things all round.'

'Plucky lot of fightin' good fights whatsername they'd do if we didn't see they had a quiet place to fight in. And such fightin' as theirs is! Cats on the tiles. T'other callin' to which to come on. I'd give a month's pay to get some o' them broad-backed beggars in London sweatin' through a day's road-makin' an' a night's rain. They'd carry on a deal afterwards—same as we're supposed to carry on. I've bin turned out of a measly arf-license pub down Lambeth way, full o' greasy kebmen, 'fore now,' said Ortheris with an oath.

'Maybe you were dhrunk,' said Mulvaney soothingly.

'Worse nor that. The Forders were drunk. *I* was wearin' the Queen's uniform.'

'I'd no particular thought to be a soldier i' them days,' said Learoyd, still keeping his eye on the bare hill opposite, 'but this sort o' talk put it i' my head. They was so good, th' chapel folk, that they tumbled ower t'other side. But I stuck to it for 'Liza's sake, specially as she was learning me to sing the bass part in a horotorio as Jesse were gettin' up. She sung like a throstle hersen, and we had practisin's night after night for a matter of three months.'

'I know what a horotorio is,' said Ortheris pertly. 'It's a sort of chaplain's sing-song—words all out of the Bible, and hullabaloojah choruses.'

'Most Greenhow Hill folks played some instrument or t'other, an' they all sung so you might have heard them miles away, and they were so pleased wi' the noise they made they didn't fair to want anybody to listen. The preacher sung high seconds when he wasn't playin' the flute, an' they set me, as hadn't got far with big fiddle, again Willie Satterthwaite, to jog his elbow when he had to get a' gate playin'. Old Jesse was happy if ever a man was, for he were th' conductor an' th' first fiddle an' th' leadin' singer, beatin' time wi' his fiddle-stick, till at times he'd rap with it on the table, and cry out, "Now, you mun all stop; it's my turn." And he'd face round to his front, fair sweating wi' pride, to sing th' tenor solos. But he were grandest i' th' choruses, waggin' his head, flinging his arms round like a windmill, and singin' hisself black in the face. A rare singer were Jesse.

'Yo' see, I was not o' much account wi' 'em all exceptin' to 'Liza Roantree, and I had a deal o' time settin' quiet at meetings and horotorio practises to hearken their talk, and if it were strange to me at beginnin', it got stranger still at after, when I was shut on it, and could study what it meaned.

'Just after th' horotorios come off, 'Liza, as had allus been weakly like, was took very bad. I walked Dr. War-bottom's horse up and down a deal of times while he were inside, where they wouldn't let me go, though I fair ached to see her.

' "She'll be better i' noo, lad—better i' noo," he used to say. "Tha mun ha' patience." Then they said if I was quiet I might go in, and th' Reverernd Amos Barraclough used to read to her lyin' propped up among th' pillows. Then she began to mend a bit, and they let me carry her on to th' settle, and when it got warm again she went about same as afore. Th' preacher and me and Blast was a deal together i' them days, and i' one way we was rare good comrades. But I could ha' stretched him time and again with a good will. I mind one day he said he would like to go down into th' bowels o' th' earth, and see how th' Lord had builded th' framework o' th' everlastin' hills. He were one of them chaps as had a gift o' sayin' things. They rolled off the tip of his clever tongue, same as Mulvaney here, as would ha' made a rare good preacher if he had nobbut given his mind to it. I lent him a suit o' miner's kit as almost buried th' little man, and his white face down i' th' coat-collar and hat-flap looked like the face of a boggart, and he cowered down i' th' bottom o' the waggon. I was drivin' a tram as led up a bit of an incline up to th' cave where the engine was pumpin', and where th' ore was brought up and put into th' waggons as went down o' themselves, me puttin' th' brake on and th' horses a-trottin' after. Long as it was daylight we were good friends, but when we got fair into th' dark, and could nobbut see th' day shinin' at the hole like a lamp at a street-end, I feeled downright wicked. Ma religion dropped all away from me when I looked back at him as were always comin' between me and 'Liza. The talk was 'at they were to be wed when she got better, an' I couldn't get her to say yes or nay to it. He began to sing a hymn in his thin voice, and I came out wi' a chorus that was all cussin' an' swearin' at my horses, an' I began to know how I hated him. He were such a little chap, too. I could drop him wi' one hand down Garstang's Copper-hole—a place where th' beck slithered ower th' edge on a rock, and fell wi' a bit of whisper into a pit as no rope i' Greenhow could plumb.'

Again Learoyd rooted up the innocent violets. 'Ay, he should see th' bowels o' th' earth an' never naught else. I could take him a mile or two along th' drift, and leave him wi' his candle doused to cry hallelujah, wi' none to hear him and say amen. I was to lead him down th' ladder-way to th' drift where Jesse Roantree was workin', and why shouldn't he slip on th' ladder, wi' my feet on his fingers till they loosed grip, and I put him down wi' my heel? If I went fust down th' ladder I could click hold on him and chuck him over my head, so as he should go squshin' down the shaft, breakin' his bones at ev'ry timberin' as Bill Appleton did when he was fresh, and hadn't a bone left when he wrought to th' bottom. Niver a blasted leg to walk from Pately. Niver an arm to put round 'Liza Roantree's waist. Niver no more—niver no more.'

The thick lips curled back over the yellow teeth, and that flushed face was not pretty to look upon. Mulvaney nodded sympathy, and Ortheris, moved by his comrade's passion, brought up the rifle to his shoulder, and searched the hillside for his quarry, muttering ribaldry about a sparrow, a spout, and a thunder-storm. The voice of the watercourse supplied the necessary small talk till Learoyd picked up his story.

'But it's none so easy to kill a man like yon. When I'd given up my horses to th' lad as took my place and I was showin' th' preacher th' workin's, shoutin' into his ear across th' clang o' th' pumpin' engines, I saw he were afraid o' naught; and when the lamplight showed his black eyes, I could feel as he was masterin' me again. I were no better nor Blast chained up short and growlin' i' the depths of him while a strange dog went safe past.

' "Th'art a coward and a fool," I said to mysen; an' I restled i' my mind again' him till, when we come to Garstang's Copper-hole, I laid hold o' the preacher and lifted him up over my head and held him into the darkest on it. "Now, lad," I says, "it's to be one or t'other on us—thee or me—for 'Liza Roantree. Why, isn't thee afraid for thysen?" I says, for he were still i' my arms as a sack. "Nay; I'm but afraid for thee, my poor lad, as knows naught," says he. I set him down on th' edge, an' th' beck run stiller, an' there was no more buzzin' in my head like when th' bee come through th' window o' Jesse's house. "What dost tha mean?" says I.

' "I've often thought as thou ought to know," says he, "but 'twas hard to tell thee. 'Liza Roantree's for neither on us, nor for nobody o' this earth. Dr. Warbottom says—

and he knows her, and her mother before her—that she is in a decline, and she cannot live six months longer. He's known it for many a day. Steady, John! Steady!" says he. And that weak little man pulled me further back and set me again' him, and talked it all over quiet and still, me turnin' a bunch o' candles in my hand, and counting them ower and ower again as I listened. A deal on it were th' regular preachin' talk, but there were a vast lot as made me begin to think as he were more of a man than I'd ever given him credit for, till I were cut as deep for him as I were for mysen.

'Six candles we had, and we crawled and climbed all that day while they lasted, and I said to mysen, " 'Liza Roantree hasn't six months to live." And when we came into th' daylight again we were like dead men to look at, an' Blast come behind us without so much as waggin' his tail. When I saw 'Liza again she looked at me a minute and says, "Who's telled tha? For I see tha knows." And she tried to smile as she kissed me, and I fair broke down.

'Yo' see, I was a young chap i' them days, and had seen naught o' life, let alone death, as is allus a-waitin'. She told me as Dr. Warbottom said as Greenhow air was too keen, and they were goin' to Bradford, to Jesse's brother David, as worked i' a mill, and I mun hold up like a man and a Christian, and she'd pray for me. Well, and they went away, and the preacher that same back end o' th' year were appointed to another circuit, as they call it, and I were left alone on Greenhow Hill.

'I tried, and I tried hard, to stick to th' chapel, but 'tweren't th' same thing at after. I hadn't 'Liza's voice to follow i' th' singin', nor her eyes a-shinin' acrost their heads. And i' th' class-meetings they said as I mun have some experiences to tell, and I hadn't a word to say for mysen.

'Blast and me moped a good deal, and happen we didn't behave ourselves over well, for they dropped us and wondered however they'd come to take us up. I can't tell how we got through th' time, while i' th' winter I gave up my job and went to Bradford. Old Jesse were at th' door o' th' house, in a long street o' little houses. He'd been sendin' th' children 'way as were clatterin' their clogs in th' causeway, for she were asleep.

' "Is it thee?" he says; "but you're not to see her. I'll none have her wakened for a nowt like thee. She's goin' fast, and she mun go in peace. Thou'lt never be good for naught i' th' world, and as long as thou lives thou'll never play the big fiddle. Get away, lad, get away!" So he shut the door softly i' my face.

'Nobody never made Jesse my master, but it seemed to me he was about right, and I went away into the town and knocked up against a recruiting sergeant. The old tales o' th' chapel folk came buzzin' into my head. I was to get away, and this were th' regular road for the likes o' me. I 'listed there and then, took th' Widow's shillin', and had a bunch o' ribbons pinned i' my hat.

'But next day I found my way to David Roantree's door, and Jesse came to open it. Says he, "Thou's come back again wi' th' devil's colours flyin'—thy true colours, as I always telled thee."

'But I begged and prayed of him to let me see her nobbut to say good-bye, till a woman calls down th' stairway, "She says John Learoyd's to come up." Th' old man shifts aside in a flash, and lays his hand on my arm, quite gentle like. "But thou'lt be quiet, John," says he, "for she's rare weak. Thou was allus a good lad."

'Her eyes were all alive wi' light, and her hair was thick on the pillow round her, but her cheeks were thin—thin to frighten a man that's strong. "Nay, father, yo mayn't say th' devil's colours. Them ribbons is pretty." An' she held out her hands for th' hat, an' she put all straight as a woman will wi' ribbons. "Nay, but what they're pretty," she says. "Eh, but I'd ha' liked to see thee i' thy red coat, John, for thou was allus my own lad—my very own lad, and none else."

'She lifted up her arms, and they come round my neck i' a gentle grip, and they slacked away, and she seemed fainting. "Now yo' mun get away, lad," says Jesse, and I picked up my hat and I came downstairs.

'Th' recruiting sergeant were waiting' for me at th' corner public-house. "Yo've seen your sweetheart?" says he. "Yes, I've seen her," says I. "Well, we'll have a quart now, and you'll do your best to forget her," says he, bein' one o' them smart, bustlin' chaps. "Ay, sergeant," says I. "Forget her." And I've been forgettin' her ever since.'

He threw away the wilted clump of white violets as he spoke. Ortheris suddenly rose to his knees, his rifle at his shoulder, and peered across the valley in the clear afternoon light. His chin cuddled the stock, and there was a twitching of the muscles of the right cheek as he sighted; Private Stanley Ortheris was engaged on his business. A speck of white crawled up the watercourse.

'See that beggar? . . . Got 'im.'

Seven hundred yards away, and a full two hundred down the hillside, the deserter of the Aurangabadis pitched forward, rolled down a red rock, and lay very still, with his face in a clump of blue gentians, while a big raven flapped out of the pine wood to make investigation.

'That's a clean shot, little man,' said Mulvaney.

Learoyd thoughtfully watched the smoke clear away. 'Happen there was a lass tewed up wi' him, too,' said he.

Ortheris did not reply. He was staring across the valley, with the smile of the artist who looks on the completed work.

                                                    1890

BLACK JACK

~~~~~~

To the wake av Tim O'Hara
    Came company,
All St. Patrick's Alley
    Was there to see.
                Robert Buchanan

As the Three Musketeers share their silver, tobacco, and liquor together, as they protect each other in barracks or camp, and as they rejoice together over the joy of one, so do they divide their sorrows. When Ortheris's irrepressible tongue has brought him into cells for a season, or Learoyd has run amok through his kit and accoutrements, or Mulvaney has indulged in strong waters, and under their influence reproved his Commanding Officer, you can see the trouble in the faces of the untouched two. And the rest of the regiment know that comment or jest is unsafe. Generally the three avoid Orderly Room and the Corner Shop that follows, leaving both to the young bloods who have not sown their wild oats; but there are occasions—

For instance, Ortheris was sitting on the drawbridge of the main gate of Fort Amara, with his hands in his pockets and his pipe, bowl down, in his mouth. Learoyd was lying at full length on the turf of the glacis, kicking his heels in the air, and I came round the corner and asked for Mulvaney.

Ortheris spat into the ditch and shook his head. 'No good seein' 'im now,' said Ortheris; ' 'e's a bloomin' camel. Listen.'

I heard on the flags of the veranda opposite to the cells, which are close to the Guard-Room, a measured step that

I could have identified in the tramp of an army. There were twenty paces *crescendo*, a pause, and then twenty *diminuendo*.

'That's 'im,' said Ortheris; 'my Gawd, that's 'im! All for a bloomin' button you could see your face in an' a bit o' lip that a bloomin' Harkangel would 'a' guv back.'

Mulvaney was doing pack-drill—was compelled, that is to say, to walk up and down for certain hours in full marching order, with rifle, bayonet, ammunition, knapsack, and overcoat. And his offence was being dirty on parade! I nearly fell into the Fort Ditch with astonishment and wrath, for Mulvaney is the smartest man that ever mounted guard, and would as soon think of turning out uncleanly as of dispensing with his trousers.

'Who was the Sergeant that checked him?' I asked.

'Mullins, o' course,' said Ortheris. 'There ain't no other man would whip 'im on the peg so. But Mullins ain't a man. 'E's a dirty little pigscraper, that's wot 'e is.'

'What did Mulvaney say? He's not the make of man to take that quietly.'

'Said! Bin better for 'im if 'e'd shut 'is mouth. Lord, 'ow we laughed! "Sargint," 'e sez, "ye say I'm dirty. Well," sez 'e, "when your wife lets you blow your own nose for yourself, perhaps you'll know wot dirt is. You're himperfectly eddicated, Sargint," sez 'e, an' then we fell in. But after p'rade, 'e was up an' Mullins was swearin' 'imself black in the face at Ord'ly Room that Mulvaney 'ad called 'im a swine an' Lord knows wot all. You know Mullins. 'E'll 'ave 'is 'ead broke in one o' these days. 'E's too big a bloomin' liar for ord'nary consumption. "Three hours' can an' kit," sez the Colonel; "not for bein' dirty on p'rade, but for 'avin' said somethin' to Mullins, tho' I do not believe," sez 'e, "you said wot 'e said you said." An' Mulvaney fell away sayin' nothin'. You know 'e never speaks to the Colonel for fear o' gettin' 'imself fresh copped.'

Mullins, a very young and very much married Sergeant,

whose manners were partly the result of innate depravity
and partly of imperfectly digested Board School, came
over the bridge, and most rudely asked Ortheris what he
was doing.

'Me?' said Ortheris. 'Ow! I'm waiting for my C'mission.
'Seed it comin' along yit?'

Mullins turned purple and passed on. There was the
sound of a gentle chuckle from the glacis where Learoyd
lay.

' 'E expects to get 'is C'mission some day,' explained
Orth'ris; 'Gawd 'elp the Mess that 'ave to put their 'ands
into the same kiddy as 'im! Wot time d'you make it, Sir?
Fower! Mulvancy'll be out in 'arf an hour. You don't want
to buy a dorg, Sir, do you? A pup you can trust—'arf
Rampore by the Colonel's grey'ound.'

'Ortheris,' I answered sternly, for I knew what was in
his mind, 'do you mean to say that——'

'I didn't mean to arx money o' you, any'ow,' said Ortheris; 'I'd 'a' sold you the dorg good an' cheap, but—but—I
know Mulvaney'll want somethin' after we've walked 'im
orf, an' I ain't got nothin', nor 'e 'asn't neither. I'd sooner
sell you the dorg, Sir. 'S trewth I would!'

A shadow fell on the drawbridge, and Ortheris began to
rise into the air, lifted by a huge hand upon his collar.

'Onything but t' braass,' said Learoyd quietly, as he
held the Londoner over the ditch. 'Onything but t' braass,'
Orth'ris, ma son! Ah've got one rupee eight annas of ma
own.' He showed two coins, and replaced Ortheris on the
drawbridge rail.

'Very good,' I said; 'where are you going to?'

'Goin' to walk 'im orf wen 'e comes out—two miles or
three or fower,' said Ortheris.

The footsteps within ceased. I heard the dull thud of a
knapsack falling on a bedstead, followed by the rattle of
arms. Ten minutes later, Mulvaney, faultlessly dressed,
his lips tight and his face as black as a thunderstorm,

stalked into the sunshine on the drawbridge. Learoyd and
Ortheris sprang from my side and closed in upon him,
both leaning towards as horses lean upon the pole. In an
instant they had disappeared down the sunken road to the
cantonments, and I was left alone. Mulvaney had not seen
fit to recognise me; so I knew that his trouble must be
heavy upon him.

I climbed one of the bastions and watched the figures of
the Three Musketeers grow smaller and smaller across the
plain. They were walking as fast as they could put foot to
the ground, and their heads were bowed. They fetched a
great compass round the parade-ground, skirted the Cavalry lines, and vanished in the belt of trees that fringes the
low land by the river.

I followed slowly, and sighted them—dusty, sweating,
but still keeping up their long, swinging tramp—on the
river bank. They crashed through the Forest Reserve,
headed towards the Bridge of Boats, and presently established themselves on the bow of one of the pontoons. I
rode cautiously till I saw three puffs of white smoke rise
and die out in the clear evening air, and knew that peace
had come again. At the bridge-head they waved me
forward with gestures of welcome.

'Tie up your 'orse,' shouted Ortheris, 'an' come on, Sir.
We're all goin' 'ome in this 'ere bloomin' boat.'

From the bridge-head to the Forest Officer's bungalow
is but a step. The mess-man was there, and would see that
a man held my horse. Did the Sahib require aught else—a
peg, or beer? Ritchie Sahib had left half a dozen bottles of
the latter, but since the Sahib was a friend of Ritchie
Sahib, and he, the mess-man, was a poor man——

I gave my order quietly, and returned to the bridge.
Mulvaney had taken off his boots, and was dabbling his
toes in the water; Learoyd was lying on his back on the
pontoon; and Ortheris was pretending to row with a big
bamboo.

'I'm an ould fool,' said Mulvaney, reflectively, 'dhraggin' you two out here bekaze I was undher the Black Dog—sulkin' like a child. Me that was soldierin' when Mullins, an' be damned to him, was shqualin' on a counterpin for five shillin' a week—an' that not paid! Bhoys, I've took you five miles out av natural pevarsity. Phew!'

'Wot's the odds so long as you're 'appy?' said Ortheris, applying himself afresh to the bamboo. 'As well 'ere as anywhere else.'

Learoyd held up a rupee and an eight-anna bit, and shook his head sorrowfully. 'Five mile from t' Canteen, all along o' Mulvaney's blaasted pride.'

'I know ut,' said Mulvaney penitently. 'Why will ye come wid me? An' yet I wud be mortial sorry if ye did not—any time—though I am ould enough to know betther. But I will do penance. I will take a dhrink av wather.'

Ortheris squeaked shrilly. The butler of the Forest bungalow was standing near the railings with a basket, uncertain how to clamber down to the pontoon. 'Might 'a' know'd you'd 'a' got liquor out o' bloomin' desert, Sir,' said Ortheris, gracefully, to me. Then to the mess-man: 'Easy with them there bottles. They're worth their weight in gold. Jock, ye long-armed beggar, get out o' that an' hike 'em down.'

Learoyd had the basket on the pontoon in an instant, and the Three Musketeers gathered round it with dry lips. They drank my health in due and ancient form, and thereafter tobacco tasted sweeter than ever. They absorbed all the beer, and disposed themselves in picturesque attitudes to admire the setting sun—no man speaking for a while.

Mulvaney's head dropped upon his chest, and we thought that he was asleep.

'What on earth did you come so far for?' I whispered to Ortheris.

'To walk 'im orf, o' course. When 'e's been checked we

allus walks 'im orf. 'E ain't fit to be spoke to those times —nor 'e ain't fit to leave alone neither. So we takes 'im till 'e is.'

Mulvaney raised his head, and stared straight into the sunset. 'I had my rifle,' said he dreamily, 'an' I had my bay'nit, an' Mullins came round the corner, an' he looked in my face an' grinned dishpiteful. "*You* can't blow your own nose," sez he. Now, I cannot tell fwhat Mullins's ex-payrience may ha' been, but, Mother av God, he was nearer to his death that minut' than I have iver been to mine—and that's less than the thicknuss av a hair!'

'Yes,' said Ortheris calmly, 'you'd look fine with all your buttons took orf, an' the Band in front o' you walkin' roun' slow time. We're both front-rank men, me an' Jock, when the rig'ment's in 'ollow square. Bloomin' fine you'd look. "The Lord giveth an' the Lord taketh awai,—Heasy with that there drop!—Blessed be the naime o' the Lord," he gulped in a quaint and suggestive fashion.

'Mullins! Wot's Mullins?' said Learoyd slowly 'Ah'd take a coomp'ny o' Mullinses—ma hand behind me. Sitha, Mulvaney, don't be a fool.'

'*You* were not checked for fwhat you did not do, an' made a mock av afther. 'Twas for less than that the Tyrone wud ha' sent O'Hara to hell, instid av lettin' him go by his own choosin', whin Rafferty shot him,' retorted Mulvaney.

'And who stopped the Tyrone from doing it?' I asked.

'That ould fool who's sorry he didn't stick the pig Mullins.' His head dropped again. When he raised it he shivered and put his hands on the shoulders of his two companions.

'Ye've walked the Divil out av me, bhoys,' said he.

Ortheris shot out the red-hot dottel of his pipe on the back of the hairy fist. 'They say 'Ell's 'otter than that,' said he, as Mulvaney swore aloud. 'You be warned so. Look yonder!'—he pointed across the river to a ruined tem-ple—'Me an' you an' '*im*'—he indicated me by a jerk of his head—'was there one day when Hi made a bloomin' show o' myself. You an' 'im stopped me doin' such—an' Hi was on'y wishful for to desert. You are makin' a bigger bloomin' show o' yourself now.'

'Don't mind him, Mulvaney,' I said; 'Dinah Shadd won't let you hang yourself yet awhile, and you don't intend to try it either. Let's hear about the Tyrone and O'Hara. Rafferty shot him for fooling with his wife. What happened before that?'

'There's no fool like an ould fool. You know you can do anythin' wid me whin I'm talkin'. Did I say I wud like to cut Mullins's liver out? I deny the imputashin, for fear that Orth'ris here wud report me—Ah! You wud tip me into the river, wud you? Sit quiet, little man. Anyways, Mullins is not worth the trouble av an extry p'rade, an' I will trate him wid outrajis contimpt. The Tyrone an' O'Hara! O'Hara an' the Tyrone, begad! Ould days are hard to bring back into the mouth, but they're always inside the head.'

Followed a long pause.

'O'Hara was a Divil. Though I saved him, for the honour av the rig'mint, from his death that time, I say it now. He was a Divil—a long, bould, black-haired Divil.'

'Which way?' asked Ortheris.

'Women.'

'Then I know another.'

'Not more than in reason, if you mane me, ye warped walkin'-shtick. I have been young, an' for why should I not have tuk what I cud? Did I iver, whin I was Corp'ril, use the rise av my rank—wan step an' that taken away, more's the sorrow an' the fault av me!—to prosecute a nefarious inthrigue, as O'Hara did? Did I, whin I was Corp'ril, lay my spite upon a man an' make his life a dog's life from day to day? Did I lie, as O'Hara lied, till the young wans in the Tyrone turned white wid the fear av the Judgment av God killin' thim all in a lump, as ut killed the woman at Devizes? I did not! I have sinned my sins an' I have made my confesshin, an' Father Victor knows the worst av me. O'Hara was tuk, before he cud spake, on Rafferty's doorstep, an' no man knows the worst av him. But this much I know!

'The Tyrone was recruited any fashion in the ould days. A draf' from Connemara—a draf' from Portsmouth—a draf' from Kerry, an' that was a blazin' bad draf'—here, there and iverywhere—but the large av thim was Oirish—Black Oirish. Now there are Oirish an' Oirish. The good are good as the best, but the bad are wurrst than the wurrst. 'Tis this way. They clog together in pieces as fast as thieves, an' no wan knows fwhat they will do till wan turns informer an' the gang is bruk. But ut begins again, a day later, meetin' in holes an' corners an' swearin' bloody oaths an' shtickin' a man in the back an' runnin' away, an' thin waitin' for the blood-money on the reward papers—to see if ut's worth enough. Those are the Black Oirish, an' 'tis they that bring dishgrace upon the name av Oireland, an' thim I wud kill—as I nearly killed wan wanst.

'But to reshume. My room—'twas before I was married—was wid twelve av the scum av the earth—the pickin's av the gutter—mane men that wud neither laugh nor talk nor yet get dhrunk as a man shud. They thried some av their dog's thricks on me, but I dhrew a line round my cot, an' the man that thransgressed ut wint into hospital for three days good.

'O'Hara had put his spite on the room—he was my Colour Sargint—an' nothin' cud we do to plaze him. I was younger than I am now, an' I tuk what I got in the way av dressing down and punishmint-dhrill wid my tongue in my cheek. But it was diff'rint wid the others, an' why I cannot say, excipt that some men are borrun mane an' go to dhirty murdher where a fist is more than enough. Afther a whoile, they changed their chune to me an' was desp'rit frien'ly—all twelve av thim cursin' O'Hara in chorus.

' "Eyah," sez I, "O'Hara's a divil an' I'm not for denyin' ut, but is he the only man in the wurruld? Let him go. He'll get tired av findin' our kit foul an' our 'coutrements onproperly kep'."

' "We will *not* let him go," sez they.

' "Thin take him," sez I, "an' a dashed poor yield you will get for your throuble."

' "Is he not misconductin' himself wid Slimmy's wife?" sez another.

' "She's common to the rig'mint," sez I. "Fwhat has made ye this partic'lar on a suddint?"

' "Has he not put his spite on the roomful av us? Can we do anythin' that he will not check us for?" sez another.

' "That's thrue," sez I.

' "Will ye not help us to do aught," sez another—"a big bould man like you?"

' "I will break his head upon his shoulthers av he puts hand on me," sez I. "I will give him the lie av he says that I'm dhirty, an' I wud not mind duckin' him in the Artillery troughs if ut was not that I'm thryin' for my shtripes."

' "Is that all ye will do?" sez another. "Have ye no more spunk than that, ye blood-dhrawn calf?"

' "Blood-dhrawn I may be," sez I, gettin' back to my cot an' makin' my line round ut; "but ye know that the man who comes acrost this mark will be more blood-dhrawn than me. No man gives me the name in my mouth," I sez. "Ondersthand, I will have no part wid you in anythin' ye do, nor will I raise my fist to my shuperior. Is any wan comin' on?" sez I.

'They made no move, tho' I gave them full time, but stud growlin' an' snarlin' together at wan ind av the room. I tuk up my cap and wint out to Canteen, thinkin' no little av mesilf, and there I grew most ondacintly dhrunk in my legs. My head was all reasonable.

' "Houligan," I sez to a man in E Comp'ny that was by way av bein' a frind av mine; "I'm overtuk from the belt down. Do you give me the touch av your shoulther to presarve my formation an' march me acrost the ground into the high grass. I'll sleep ut off there," sez I; an' Houligan—he's dead now, but good he was while he lasted— walked wid me, givin' me the touch whin I wint wide, ontil we came to the high grass, an', my faith, the sky an' the earth was fair rowlin' undher me. I made for where the grass was thickust, an' there I slep' off my liquor wid an easy conscience. I did not desire to come on books too frequent; my characther havin' been shpotless for the good half av a year.

'Whin I roused, the dhrink was dyin' out in me, an' I felt as though a she-cat had littered in my mouth. I had not learned to hould my liquor wid comfort in thim days. 'Tis little betther I am now. "I will get Houligan to pour a bucket over my head," thinks I, an' I wud ha' risen, but I hears some wan say: "Mulvaney can take the blame av ut for the backslidin' hound he is."

' "Oho!" sez I, an' my head rang like a guard-room gong: "fwhat is the blame that this young man must take to oblige Tim Vulmea?" For 'twas Tim Vulmea that shpoke.

'I turned on my belly an' crawled through the grass, a bit at a time, to where the spache came from. There was the twelve av my room sittin' down in a little patch, the dhry grass wavin' above their heads an' the sin av black murdher in their hearts. I put the stuff aside to get a clear view.

' "Fwhat's that?" sez wan man, jumpin' up.

' "A dog," says Vulmea. "You're a nice hand to this job! As I said, Mulvaney will take the blame—av ut comes to a pinch."

' " 'Tis harrd to swear a man's life away," sez a young wan.

' "Thank ye for that," thinks I. "Now, fwhat the divil are you paragins conthrivin' against me?"

' " 'Tis as easy as dhrinkin' your quart," sez Vulmea. "At seven or thereon, O'Hara will come acrost to the Married Quarters, goin' to call on Slimmy's wife, the swine! Wan av us'll pass the wurrd to the room an' we shtart the divil an' all av a shine—laughin' an' crackin' on an' t'rowin' our boots about. Thin O'Hara will come to give us the ordher to be quiet, the more by token bekaze the room-lamp will be knocked over in the larkin'. He will take the straight road to the ind door where there's the lamp in the veranda, an' that'll bring him clear against the light as he shtands. He will not be able to look into the dhark. Wan av us will loose off, an' a close shot ut will be, an' shame to the man that misses. 'Twill be Mulvaney's rifle, she that is at the head av the rack—there's no mistakin' that long-shtocked, cross-eyed bitch even in the dhark."

'The thief misnamed my ould firin'-piece out av jealousy—I was pershuaded av that—an' ut made me more angry than all.

'But Vulmea goes on: "O'Hara will dhrop, an' by the time the light's lit again, there'll be some six av us on the chest av Mulvancy, cryin' murdher an' rape. Mulvaney's cot is near the ind door, an' the shmokin' rifle will be lyin' undher him whin we've knocked him over. We know, an' all the rig'mint knows, that Mulvaney has given O'Hara more lip than any man av us. Will there be any doubt at the Coort-Martial? Wud twelve honust sodger-bhoys swear away the life av a dear, quiet, swate-timpered man such as is Mulvaney—wid his line av pipe-clay roun' his cot, threatenin' us wid murdher av we overshtepped ut, as we can truthful testify?"

' "Mary, Mother av Mercy!" thinks I to mesilf; "it is this to have an unruly mimber an' fistes fit to use! Oh the sneakin' hounds!"

'The big dhrops ran down my face, for I was wake wid the liquor an' had not the full av my wits about me. I laid shtill an' heard thim workin' themselves up to swear my life by tellin' tales av ivry time I had put my mark on wan or another; an' my faith, they was few that was not so dishtinguished. 'Twas all in the way av fair fight, though, for niver did I raise my hand excipt whin they had provoked me to ut.

' " 'Tis all well," sez wan av thim, "but who's to do this shootin'?"

'Fwhat matther?" sez Vulmea. " 'Tis Mulvaney will do that—at the Coort-Martial."

' "He will so," sez the man, "but whose hand is put to the trigger—*in the room?*"

' "Who'll do ut?" sez Vulmea, lookin' round, but divil a man answeared. They began to dishpute till Kiss, that was always playin' Shpoil Five, sez: "Thry the kyards!" Wid that he opined his tunic an' tuk out the greasy palammers, an' they all fell in wid the notion.

' "Deal on!" sez Vulmea, wid a big rattlin' oath, "an' the Black Curse av Shielygh come to the man that will not do his duty as the kyards say. Amin!"

' "Black Jack is the masther," sez Kiss, dealin'. Black Jack, Sorr, I shud expaytiate to you, is the Ace av Shpades which from time immimorial has been intimately connect wid battle, murdher an' suddin death.

'*Wanst* Kiss dealt an' there was no sign, but the men was whoite wid the workin's av their sowls. *Twice* Kiss dealt, an' there was a gray shine on their cheeks like the mess av an egg. *Three* times Kiss dealt an' they was blue. "Have ye not lost him?" sez Vulmea, wipin' the sweat on him; "Let's ha' done quick!" "Quick ut it," sez Kiss t'rowin' him the kyard; an' ut fell face up on his knee— Black Jack!

'Thin they all cackled wid laughin'. "Duty thrippence," sez wan av thim, "an' damned cheap at that price!" But I cud see they all dhrew a little away from Vulmea an' lef' him sittin' playin' wid the kyard. Vulmea sez no word for a whoile but licked his lips—cat-ways. Thin he threw up his head an' made the men swear by ivry oath known to stand by him not alone in the room but at the Coort-Martial that was to set on *me!* He tould off five av the biggest to stretch me on my cot whin the shot was fired, an' another man he tould off to put out the light, an' yet another to load my rifle. He wud not do that himself; an' that was quare, for 'twas but a little thing considerin'.

'Thin they swore over again that they wud not bethray wan another, an' crep' out av the grass in diff'rint ways, two by two. A mercy ut was that they did not come on me. I was sick wid fear in the pit av my stummick—sick, sick, sick! Afther they was all gone, I wint back to Canteen an' called for a quart to put a thought in me. Vulmea was there, dhrinkin' heavy, an' politeful to me beyond reason. "Fwhat will I do—fwhat will I do?" thinks I to mesilf whin Vulmea wint away.

'Presently the Arm'rer Sargint comes in stiffin' an' crackin' on, not pleased wid any wan, bekaze the Martini Henri bein' new to the rig'mint in those days we used to play the mischief wid her arrangemints. 'Twas a long time before I cud get out av the way av thryin' to pull back the back-sight an' turnin' her over afther firin'—as if she was a Snider.

' "Fwhat tailor-men do they give me to work wid?" sez the Arm'rer Sargint. "Here's Hogan, his nose flat as a table, laid by for a week, an' ivry Comp'ny sendin' their arrums in knocked to small shivreens."

' "Fwhat's wrong wid Hogan, Sargint?" sez I.

' "Wrong!" sez the Arm'rer Sargint; "I showed him, as though I had been his mother, the way av shtrippin' a 'Tini, an' he shtrup her clane an' easy. I tould him to put her to again an' fire a blank into the blow-pit to show how the dirt hung on the groovin'. He did that, but he did not put in the pin av the fallin'-block, an' av coorse whin he fired he was strook by the block jumpin' clear. Well for him 'twas but a blank—a full charge wud ha' cut his oi out."

'I looked a thrifle wiser than a boiled sheep's head. "Hows that, Sargint?" sez I.

' "This way, ye blundherin' man, an' don't you be doin' ut," sez he. Wid that he shows me a Waster action—the breech av her all cut away to show the inside—an' so plazed he was to grumble that he dimonstrated fwhat Hogan had done twice over. "An' that comes av not knowin' the wepping you're purvided wid," sez he.

' "Thank ye, Sargint," sez I; "I will come to you again for further information."

' "Ye will not," sez he. "Kape your clanin'-rod away from the breech-pin or you will get into throuble."

'I wint outside an' I could ha' danced wid delight for the grandeur av ut. "They will load my rifle, good luck to thim, whoile I'm away," thinks I, and back I wint to the Canteen to give them their clear chanst.

'The Canteen was fillin' wid men at the ind av the day. I made feign to be far gone in dhrink, an', wan by wan, all my roomful came in wid Vulmea. I wint away, walkin' thick an' heavy, but not so thick an' heavy that any wan cud ha' tuk me. Sure and thrue, there was a kyartridge gone from my pouch an' lyin' snug in my rifle. I was hot wid rage against thim all, an' I worried the bullet out wid my teeth as fast as I cud, the room bein' empty. Then I tuk my boot an' the clanin'-rod and knocked out the pin av the fallin'-block. Oh, 'twas music when that pin rowled on the flure! I put ut into my pouch an' stuck a dab av dirt on the holes in the plate, puttin' the fallin'-block back. "That'll do your business, Vulmea," sez I, lyin' easy on the cot. "Come an' sit on my chest the whole room av you, an' I will take you to my bosom for the biggest divils that iver cheated halter." I wud have no mercy on Vulmea. His oi or his life—little I cared!

'At dusk they came back, the twelve av thim, an' they

had all been dhrinkin'. I was shammin' sleep on the cot. Wan man wint outside in the veranda. Whin he whishtled they began to rage roun' the room an' carry on tremenjus. But I niver want to hear men laugh as they did—sky-larkin' too! 'Twas like mad jackals.

' "Shtop that blasted noise!" sez O'Hara in the dark, an' pop goes the room lamp. I cud hear O'Hara runnin' up an' the rattlin' av my rifle in the rack an' the men breathin' heavy as they stud roun' my cot. I cud see O'Hara in the light av the veranda lamp, an' thin I heard the crack av my rifle. She cried loud, poor darlint, bein' mishandled. Next minut' five men were houldin' me down. "Go easy," I sez; "fwhat's ut all about?"

'Thin Vulmea, on the flure, raised a howl you cud hear from wan ind av cantonmints to the other. "I'm dead, I'm butchered, I'm blind!" sez he. "Saints have mercy on my sinful sowl! Sind for Father Constant! Oh sind for Father Constant an' let me go clean!" By that I knew he was not so dead as I cud ha' wished.

'O'Hara picks up the lamp in the veranda wid a hand as stiddy as a rest. "Fwhat damned dog's thrick is this av yours?" sez he, and turns the light on Tim Vulmea that was shwimmin' in blood from top to toe. The fallin'-block had sprung free behin' a full charge av powther—good care I tuk to bite down the brass afther takin' out the bullet that there might be somethin' to give ut full worth—an' had cut Tim from the lip to the corner av the right eye, lavin' the eyelid in tatthers, an' so up an' along by the forehead to the hair. 'Twas more av a rakin' plough, if you will ondherstand, than a clean cut; an' niver did I see a man bleed as Vulmea did. The dhrink an' the stew that he was in pumped the blood strong. The minut' the men sittin' on my chest heard O'Hara spakin' they scatthered each wan to his cot, an' cried out very politeful: "Fwhat is ut, Sargint?"

' "Fwhat is ut!" sez O'Hara, shakin' Tim. "Well an' good do you know fwhat ut is, ye skulkin' ditch-lurkin' dogs! Get a *doolie*, an' take this whimperin' scutt away. There will be more heard av ut than any av you will care for."

'Vulmea sat up rockin' his head in his hand an' moanin' for Father Constant.

' "Be done!" sez O'Hara, dhraggin' him up by the hair. "You're none so dead that you cannot go fifteen years for thryin' to shoot me."

' "I did not," sez Vulmea; "I was shootin' mesilf."

' "That's quare," sez O'Hara, "for the front av my jackut is black wid your powther." He tuk up the rifle that was still warm an' began to laugh. "I'll make your life Hell to you," sez he, "for attempted murdher an' kapin' your rifle onproperly. You'll be hanged first an' thin put undher stoppages for four fifteen. The rifle's done for," sez he.

' "Why, 'tis my rifle!" sez I, comin' up to look; "Vulmea, ye divil, fwhat were you doin' wid her—answer me that?"

' "Lave me alone," sez Vulmea; "I'm dyin'!"

' "I'll wait till you're betther," sez I, "an' thin we two will talk ut out umbrageous."

'O'Hara pitched Tim into the *doolie*, none too tinder, but all the bhoys kep' by their cots, which was not the sign av innocint men. I was huntin' ivrywhere for my fallin'-block, but not findin' ut at all. I niver found ut.

' "*Now* fwhat will I do?" sez O'Hara, swinging the veranda light in his hand an' lookin' down the room. I had hate and contimpt av O'Hara an' I have now, dead tho' he is, but, for all that, will I say he was a brave man. He is baskin' in Purgathory this tide, but I wish he cud hear that, whin he stud lookin' down the room an' the bhoys shivered before the oi av him, I knew him for a brave man an' I liked him *so*.

' "Fwhat will I do?" sez O'Hara agin, an' we heard the voice av a woman low an' sof' in the veranda. 'Twas Slimmy's wife, come over at the shot, sittin' on wan av the benches an' scarce able to walk.

' "O Denny!—Denny, dear," sez she, "have they kilt you?"

'O'Hara looked down the room again an' showed his teeth to the gum. Then he spat on the flure.

' "You're not worth ut," sez he. "Light that lamp, ye dogs," an' wid that he turned away, an' I saw him walkin' off wid Slimmy's wife; she thryin' to wipe off the powther-black on the front av his jackut wid her handker-chief. "A brave man you are," thinks I—"a brave man an' a bad woman."

'No wan said a word for a time. They was all ashamed, past spache.

' "Fwhat d'you think he will do?" sez wan av thim at last. "He knows we're all in ut."

' "Are we so?" sez I from my cot. "The man that sez that to me will be hurt. I do not know," sez I, "fwhat on-derhand divilmint you have conthrived, but by what I've seen I know that you cannot commit murdher wid another man's rifle—such shakin' cowards you are. I'm goin' to slape," I sez, "an' you can blow my head off whoile I lay." I did not slape, though, for a long time. Can ye wonder?

'Next morn the news was through all the rig'mint, an' there was nothin' that the men did not tell. O'Hara re-ports, fair an' easy, that Vulmea was come to grief through tamperin' wid his rifle in barracks, all for to show the mechanism. An' by my sowl, he had the impart'nince to say that he was on the shpot at the time an' cud certify that ut was an accidint! You might ha' knocked my room-ful down wid a straw whin they heard that. 'Twas lucky for thim that the bhoys were always thryin' to find out how the new rifle was made, an' a lot av thim had come up for easin' the pull by shtickin' bits av grass an' such in the part av the lock that showed near the thrigger. The first issues of the 'Tinis was not covered in, an' I mesilf have eased the pull av mine time an' agin. A light pull is ten points on the range to me.

' "I will not have this foolishness!" sez the Colonel. "I

will twist the tail off Vulmea!" sez he; but whin he saw him, all tied up an' groanin' in hospital, he changed his will. "Make him an early convalescint," sez he to the Doctor, an' Vulmea was made so for a warnin'. His big bloody bandages an' face puckered up to wan side did more to kape the bhoys from messin' wid the insides ave their rifles than any punishmint.

'O'Hara gave no reason for fwhat he'd said, an' all my roomful were too glad to inquire, tho' he put his spite upon thim more wearin' than before. Wan day, howiver, he tuk me apart very polite, for he cud be that at the choosin.'

' "You're a good sodger, tho' you're a damned insolint man," sez he.

' "Fair words, Sargint," sez I, "or I may be insolint again."

' " 'Tis not like you," sez he, "to lave your rifle in the rack widout the breech-pin, for widout the breech-pin she was whin Vulmea fired. I should ha' found the break av ut in the eyes av the holes, else," he sez.

' "Sargint," sez I, "fwhat wud your life ha' been worth av the breech-pin had been in place, for, on my sowl, my life wud be worth just as much to me av I tould you whether ut was or was not. Be thankful the bullet was not there," I sez.

' "That's thrue," sez he, pulling his moustache; "but I do not believe that you, for all your lip, was in that business."

' "Sargint," sez I, "I cud hammer the life out av a man in ten minuts wid my fistes if that man dishpleased me; for I am a good sodger, an' I will be threated as such, an' whoile my fistes are my own they're strong enough for all work I have to do. They do not fly back towards me!" sez I, lookin' him betune the eyes.

' "You're a good man," sez he, lookin' me betune the eyes—an' oh he was a gran'-built man to see!—"you're a good man," he sez, "an' I cud wish, for the pure frolic av ut, that I was not a Sargint, or that you were not a Privit; an' you will think me no coward whin I say this thing."

' "I do not," sez I. "I saw you whin Vulmea mishandled the rifle. But, Sargint," I sez, "take the wurrd from me now, spakin' as man to man wid the shtripes off, tho' 'tis little right I have to talk, me being fwhat I am by natur'. This time ye tuk no harm, an' next time ye may not, but, in the ind, so sure as Slimmy's wife came into the veranda, so sure will ye take harm—an' bad harm. Have thought, Sargint," sez I. "Is ut worth ut?"

' "Ye're a bould man," sez he, breathin' harrd. "A very bould man. But I am a bould man tu. Do you go your way, Privit Mulvaney, an' I will go mine."

'We had no further spache thin or afther, but, wan by another, he drafted the twelve av my room out into other rooms an' got thim spread among the Comp'nies, for they was not a good breed to live together, an' the Comp'ny orf'cers saw ut. They wud ha' shot me in the night av they had known fwhat I knew; but that they did not.

'An', in the ind, as I said, O'Hara met his death from Rafferty for foolin' wid his wife. He wint his own way too well—Eyah, too well! Shtraight to that affair, widout turnin' to the right or to the lef', he wint, an' may the Lord have mercy on his sowl. Amin!'

' 'Ear! 'Ear!' said Ortheris, pointing the moral with a wave of his pipe. 'An' this is 'im 'oo would be a bloomin' Vulmea all for the sake of Mullins an' a bloomin' button! Mullins never went after a woman in his life. Mrs. Mullins, she saw 'im one day——'

'Ortheris,' I said, hastily, for the romances of Private Ortheris are all too daring for publication, 'look at the sun. It's a quarter past six!'

'O Lord! Three quarters of an hour for five an' a 'arf miles! We'll 'ave to run like Jimmy O.'

The Three Musketeers clambered on to the bridge, and departed hastily in the direction of the cantonment road. When I overtook them I offered them two stirrups and a tail, which they accepted enthusiastically. Ortheris held the tail, and in this manner we trotted steadily through the shadows by an unfrequented road.

At the turn into the cantonments we heard carriage wheels. It was the Colonel's barouche, and in it sat the Colonel's wife and daughter. I caught a suppressed chuckle, and my beast sprang forward with a lighter step.

The Three Musketeers had vanished into the night.

1888

From
The Jungle Books

~~~~~~

TOOMAI OF
THE ELEPHANTS

I will remember what I was. I am sick of rope and
chain.
I will remember my old strength and all my forest
affairs.
I will not sell my back to man for a bundle of sugar-
cane.
I will go out to my own kind, and the wood-folk in
their lairs.

I will go out until the day, until the morning break—
Out to the winds' untainted kiss, the waters' clean
caress—
I will forget my ankle-ring and snap my picket-stake.
I will revisit my lost loves, and playmates masterless!

Kala Nag, which means Black Snake, had served the
Indian Government in every way that an elephant could
serve it for forty-seven years, and as he was fully twenty
years old when he was caught, that makes him nearly
seventy—a ripe age for an elephant. He remembered
pushing, with a big leather pad on his forehead, at a gun
stuck in deep mud, and that was before the Afghan War of

1842, and he had not then come to his full strength. His mother Radha Pyari—Radha the Darling—who had been caught in the same drive with Kala Nag, told him, before his little milk tusks had dropped out, that elephants who were afraid always got hurt. And Kala Nag knew that that advice was good, for the first time that he saw a shell burst he backed, screaming, into a stand of piled rifles, and the bayonets pricked him in all his softest places. So, before he was twenty-five, he gave up being afraid, and so he was the best-loved and the best-looked-after elephant in the service of the Government of India. He had carried tents, twelve hundred pounds' weight of tents, on the march in Upper India. He had been hoisted into a ship at the end of a steam-crane and taken for days across the water, and made to carry a mortar on his back in a strange and rocky country very far from India, and had seen the Emperor Theodore lying dead in Magdala, and had come back again in the steamer entitled, so the soldiers said, to the Abyssinian War medal. He had seen his fellow-elephants die of cold and epilepsy and starvation and sunstroke up at a place called Ali Masjid, ten years later, and afterwards he had been sent down thousands of miles south to haul and pile big baulks of teak in the timber-yards at Moulmein. There he had half killed an insubordinate young elephant who was shirking his fair share of work.

After that he was taken off timber-hauling, and employed, with a few score other elephants who were trained to the business, in helping to catch wild elephants among the Garo Hills. Elephants are very strictly preserved by the Indian Government. There is one whole department which does nothing else but hunt them, and catch them, and break them in, and send them up and down the country as they are needed for work. Kala Nag stood ten fair feet at the shoulders, and his tusks had been cut off short at five feet, and bound round the ends, to prevent them splitting, with bands of copper, but he could do more with those stumps than any untrained elephant could do with the real sharpened ones. When, after weeks and weeks of cautious driving of scattered elephants across the hills, the forty or fifty wild monsters were driven into the last stockade, and the big drop-gate, made of tree-trunks lashed together, jarred down behind them, Kala Nag, at the word of command, would go into that flaring, trumpeting pandemonium (generally at night, when the flicker of the torches made it difficult to judge distances), and, picking out the biggest and wildest tusker of the mob, would hammer him and hustle him into quiet while the men on the backs of the other elephants roped and tied the smaller ones. There was nothing in the way of fighting that Kala Nag, the old wise Black Snake, did not know, for he had stood up more than once in his time to the charge of the wounded tiger, and, curling up his soft trunk to be out of harm's way, had knocked the springing brute sideways in mid-air with a quick sickle-cut of his head, that he had invented all by himself; had knocked him over, and kneeled upon him with his huge knees till the life went out with a gasp and a howl, and there was only a fluffy striped thing on the ground for Kala Nag to pull by the tail.

'Yes,' said Big Toomai, his driver, the son of Black Toomai who had taken him to Abyssinia, and grandson of Toomai of the Elephants who had seen him caught, 'there is nothing that the Black Snake fears except me. He has seen three generations of us feed him and groom him, and he will live to see four.'

'He is afraid of *me* also,' said Little Toomai, standing up to his full height of four feet, with only one rag upon him. He was ten years old, the eldest son of Big Toomai, and, according to custom, he would take his father's place on Kala Nag's neck when he grew up, and would handle the heavy iron *ankus*, the elephant-goad, that had been worn smooth by his father, and his grandfather, and his great-grandfather. He knew what he was talking of, for he had been born under Kala Nag's shadow, had played with the end of his trunk before he could walk, had taken him down to water as soon as he could walk, and Kala Nag would no more have dreamed of disobeying his shrill little orders than he would have dreamed of killing him on that day when Big Toomai carried the little brown baby under Kala Nag's tusks, and told him to salute his master that was to be. 'Yes,' said Little Toomai, 'he is afraid of *me*.' And he took long strides up to Kala Nag, called him a fat old pig, and made him lift up his feet one after the other.

'*Wah!*' said Little Toomai, 'thou art a big elephant.' And he wagged his fluffy head, quoting his father. 'The Government may pay for elephants, but they belong to us mahouts. When thou art old, Kala Nag, there will come some rich rajah, and he will buy thee from the Government, on account of thy size and thy manners, and then thou wilt have nothing to do but to carry gold earrings in thy ears, and a gold howdah on thy back, and a red cloth covered with gold on thy sides, and walk at the head of the processions of the king. Then I shall sit on thy neck, O Kala Nag, with a silver *ankus*, and men will run before us with golden sticks, crying: 'Room for the King's elephant!' That will be good, Kala Nag, but not so good as this hunting in the jungles.'

'*Umph!*' said Big Toomai. 'Thou art a boy, and as wild as a buffalo-calf. This running up and down among the hills is not the best Government service. I am getting old, and I do not love wild elephants. Give me brick elephant-lines, one stall to each elephant, and big stumps to tie them to safely, and flat, broad roads to exercise upon, instead of this come-and-go camping. *Aha*, the Cawnpore barracks were good. There was a bazaar close by, and only three hours' work a day.'

Little Toomai remembered the Cawnpore elephant-lines and said nothing. He very much preferred the camp life, and hated those broad, flat roads, with the daily grubbing for grass in the forage-reserve, and the long hours when there was nothing to do except to watch Kala Nag fidgeting in his pickets. What Little Toomai liked was to scramble up bridle-paths that only an elephant could take; the dip into the valley below; the glimpses of the wild elephants browsing miles away; the rush of the frightened pig and peacock under Kala Nag's feet; the blinding warm rains, when all the hills and valleys smoked; the beautiful misty mornings when nobody knew where he would camp that night; the steady, cautious drive of the wild elephants, and the mad rush and blaze and hullaballoo of the last night's drive, when the elephants poured into the stockade like boulders in a landslide, found that they could not get out, and flung themselves at the heavy posts only to be driven back by yells and flaring torches and volleys of blank cartridge. Even a little boy could not be of use there, and Toomai was as useful as three boys. He would get his torch and wave it, and yell with the best. But the really good time came when the driving out began, and the keddah, that is, the stockade, looked like a picture of the end of the world, and men had to make signs to one another, because they could not hear themselves speak. Then Little Toomai would climb up to the top of one of the quivering stockade-posts, his sun-bleached brown hair flying loose all over his shoulders, and he looking like a goblin in the torch-light. And as soon as there was a lull you could hear his high-pitched yells of encouragement to Kala Nag, above the trumpeting and crashing, and snapping of ropes, and groans of the tethered elephants. '*Maíl, maíl, Kala Nag!* [Go on, go on, Black Snake!] *Dant do!* [Give him the tusk!] *Somalo! Somalo!* [Careful, careful!] *Maro! Mar!* [Hit him, hit him!] Mind the post! *Arré! Arré! Hai! Yai! Kya-a-ah!*' he would shout, and the big fight between Kala Nag and the wild elephant would sway to and fro across the keddah, and the old elephant-catchers would wipe the sweat out of their eyes, and find time to nod to Little Toomai wriggling with joy on the top of the posts.

He did more than wriggle. One night he slid down from

the post and slipped in between the elephants, and threw up the loose end of a rope, which had dropped, to a driver who was trying to get a purchase on the leg of a kicking young calf (calves always give more trouble than full-grown animals). Kala Nag saw him, caught him in his trunk, and handed him up to Big Toomai, who slapped him then and there, and put him back on the post. Next morning he gave him a scolding, and said: 'Are not good brick elephant-lines and a little tent-carrying enough, that thou must needs go elephant-catching on thy own account, little worthless? Now those foolish hunters, whose pay is less than my pay, have spoken to Petersen Sahib of the matter.' Little Toomai was frightened. He did not know much of white men, but Petersen Sahib was the greatest white man in the world to him. He was the head of all the keddah operations—the man who caught all the elephants for the Government of India, and who knew more about the ways of elephants than any living man.

'What—what will happen?' said Little Toomai.

'Happen! The worst that can happen. Petersen Sahib is a madman; else why should he go hunting these wild devils? He may even require thee to be an elephant-catcher, to sleep anywhere in these fever-filled jungles, and at last to be trampled to death in the keddah. It is well that this nonsense ends safely. Next week the catching is over, and we of the plains are sent back to our stations. Then we will march on smooth roads, and forget all this hunting. But, Son, I am angry that thou shouldst meddle in the business that belongs to these dirty Assamese jungle-folk. Kala Nag will obey none but me, so I must go with him into the keddah, but he is only a fighting elephant, and he does not help to rope them. So I sit at my ease, as befits a mahout—not a mere hunter—a mahout, I say, and a man who gets a pension at the end of his service. Is the family of Toomai of the Elephants to be trodden underfoot in the dirt of a keddah? Bad one!

Wicked one! Worthless son! Go and wash Kala Nag and attend to his ears, and see that there are no thorns in his feet, or else Petersen Sahib will surely catch thee and make thee a wild hunter—a follower of elephant's foot-tracks, a jungle-bear. *Bah!* Shame! Go!'

Little Toomai went off without saying a word, but he told Kala Nag all his grievances while he was examining his feet. 'No matter,' said Little Toomai, turning up the fringe of Kala Nag's huge right ear. 'They have said my name to Petersen Sahib, and perhaps—and perhaps—and perhaps—who knows? *Hai!* That is a big thorn that I have pulled out!'

The next few days were spent in getting the elephants together, in walking the newly caught wild elephants up and down between a couple of tame ones, to prevent them giving too much trouble on the downward march to the plains, and in taking stock of the blankets and ropes and things that had been worn out or lost in the forest. Petersen Sahib came in on his clever she-elephant Pudmini. He had been paying off other camps among the hills, for the season was coming to an end, and there was a native clerk sitting at a table under a tree, to pay the drivers their wages. As each man was paid he went back to his elephant, and joined the line that stood ready to start. The catchers, and hunters, and beaters, the men of the regular keddah, who stayed in the jungle year in and year out, sat on the backs of the elephants that belonged to Petersen Sahib's permanent force, or leaned against the trees with their guns across their arms, and made fun of the drivers who were going away, and laughed when the newly caught elephants broke the line and ran about. Big Toomai went up to the clerk with Little Toomai behind him, and Machua Appa, the head-tracker, said in an undertone to a friend of his: 'There goes one piece of good elephant-stuff at least. 'Tis a pity to send that young jungle-cock to moult in the plains.'

Now Petersen Sahib had ears all over him, as a man

must have who listens to the most silent of all living things—the wild elephant. He turned where he was lying all along on Pudmini's back, and said: 'What is that? I did not know of a man among the plains-drivers who had wit enough to rope even a dead elephant.'

'This is not a man, but a boy. He went into the keddah at the last drive, and threw Barmao there the rope, when we were trying to get that young calf with the blotch on his shoulder away from his mother.' Machua Appa pointed at Little Toomai, and Petersen Sahib looked, and Little Toomai bowed to the earth.

'He throw a rope? He is smaller than a picket-pin. Little one, what is thy name?' said Petersen Sahib. Little Toomai was too frightened to speak, but Kala Nag was behind him, and Toomai made a sign with his hand, and the elephant caught him up in his trunk and held him level with Pudmini's forehead, in front of the great Petersen Sahib. Then Little Toomai covered his face with his hands, for he was only a child, and except where elephants were concerned, he was just as bashful as a child could be.

'Oho!' said Petersen Sahib, smiling underneath his moustache, 'and why didst thou teach thy elephant *that* trick? Was it to help thee steal green corn from the roofs of the houses when the ears are put out to dry?'

'Not green corn, Protector of the Poor—melons,' said Little Toomai, and all the men sitting about broke into a roar of laughter. Most of them had taught their elephants that trick when they were boys. Little Toomai was hanging eight feet up in the air, and he wished very much that he were eight feet under ground.

'He is Toomai, my son, Sahib,' said Big Toomai, scowling. 'He is a very bad boy, and he will end in a gaol, Sahib.'

'Of that I have my doubts,' said Petersen Sahib. 'A boy who can face a full keddah at his age does not end in gaols. See, little one, here are four annas to spend on sweetmeats because thou hast a little head under that great thatch of hair. In time thou mayest become a hunter too.' Big Toomai scowled more than ever. 'Remember, though, that keddahs are not good for children to play in,' Petersen Sahib went on.

'Must I never go there, Sahib?' asked Little Toomai, with a big gasp.

'Yes.' Petersen Sahib smiled again. 'When thou hast seen the elephants dance. That is the proper time. Come to me when thou hast seen the elephants dance, and then I will let thee go into all the keddahs.'

There was another roar of laughter, for that is an old joke among elephant-catchers, and it means just never. There are great cleared flat places hidden away in the forests that are called elephants' ball-rooms, but even these are only found by accident, and no man has ever seen the elephants dance. When a driver boasts of his skill and bravery the other drivers say: 'And when didst *thou* see the elephants dance?'

Kala Nag put Little Toomai down, and he bowed to the earth again and went away with his father, and gave the silver four-anna piece to his mother, who was nursing his baby-brother, and they all were put up on Kala Nag's back, and the line of grunting, squealing elephants rolled down the hill-path to the plains. It was a very lively march on account of the new elephants, who gave trouble at every ford, and needed coaxing or beating every other minute.

Big Toomai prodded Kala Nag spitefully, for he was very angry, but Little Toomai was too happy to speak. Petersen Sahib had noticed him, and given him money, so he felt as a private soldier would feel if he had been called out of the ranks and praised by his commander-in-chief.

'What did Petersen Sahib mean by the elephant-dance?' he said, at last, softly to his mother.

Big Toomai heard him and grunted. 'That thou

shouldst never be one of these hill-buffaloes of trackers. *That* was what he meant. Oh you in front, what is blocking the way?'

An Assamese driver, two or three elephants ahead, turned round angrily, crying: 'Bring up Kala Nag, and knock this youngster of mine into good behaviour. Why should Petersen Sahib have chosen *me* to go down with you donkeys of the rice-fields? Lay your beast alongside, Toomai, and let him prod with his tusks. By all the Gods of the Hills, these new elephants are possessed, or else they can smell their companions in the jungle.'

Kala Nag hit the new elephant in the ribs and knocked the wind out of him, as Big Toomai said: 'We have swept the hills of wild elephants at the last catch. It is only your carelessness in driving. Must I keep order along the whole line?'

'Hear him!' said the other driver. '*We* have swept the hills! Ho! Ho! You are very wise, you plains-people. Any one but a mud-head who never saw the jungle would know that *they* know that the drives are ended for the season. Therefore all the wild elephants to-night will— but why should I waste wisdom on a river-turtle?'

'What will they do?' Little Toomai called out.

'*Ohé*, little one. Art thou there? Well, I will tell thee, for thou hast a cool head. They will dance, and it behoves thy father and son, who has swept *all* the hills of *all* the elephants, to double-chain his pickets to-night.'

'What talk is this?' said Big Toomai. 'For forty years, father and son, we have tended elephants, and we have never heard such moonshine about dances.'

'Yes, but a plains-man who lives in a hut knows only the four walls of his hut. Well, leave thy elephants unshackled to-night and see what comes. As for their dancing, I have seen the place where—*Bapree bap!* How many windings has the Dihang River? Here is another ford, and we must swim the calves. Stop still, you behind there.'

And in this way, talking and wrangling and splashing through the rivers, they made their first march to a sort of receiving-camp for the new elephants. But they lost their tempers long before they got there.

Then the elephants were chained by their hind legs to their big stumps of pickets, and extra ropes were fitted to the new elephants, and the fodder was piled before them, and the hill-drivers went back to Petersen Sahib through the afternoon light, telling the plains-drivers to be extra careful that night, and laughing when the plains-drivers asked the reason.

Little Toomai attended to Kala Nag's supper, and as evening fell, wandered through the camp, unspeakably happy, in search of a tom-tom. When an Indian child's heart is full, he does not run about and make a noise in an irregular fashion. He sits down to a sort of revel all by himself. And Little Toomai had been spoken to by Petersen Sahib! If he had not found what he wanted I believe he would have been ill. But the sweetmeat-seller in the camp lent him a little tom-tom—a drum beaten with the flat of the hand—and he sat down, cross-legged, before Kala Nag as the stars began to come out, the tom-tom in his lap, and he thumped and he thumped and he thumped, and the more he thought of the great honour that had been done to him, the more he thumped, all alone among the elephant-fodder. There was no tune and no words, but the thumping made him happy. The new elephants strained at their ropes, and squealed and trumpeted from time to time, and he could hear his mother in the ´camp hut putting his small brother to sleep with an old, old song about the great God Shiv, who once told all the animals what they should eat. It is a very soothing lullaby, and the first verse says:

Shiv, who poured the harvest and made the winds to blow,
Sitting at the doorways of a day of long ago,
Gave to each his portion, food and toil and fate,

From the king upon the *guddee* to the beggar at the gate.
  All things made he—Shiva the Preserver.
  Mahadeo! Mahadeo! He made all—
  Thorn for the camel, fodder for the kine,
  And mother's heart for sleepy head, O little son of mine!

Little Toomai came in from a joyous *tunk-a-tunk* at the end of each verse, till he felt sleepy and stretched himself on the fodder at Kala Nag's side. At last the elephants began to lie down one after another as is their custom, till only Kala Nag at the right of the line was left standing up, and he rocked slowly from side to side, his ears put forward to listen to the night wind as it blew very slowly across the hills. The air was full of all the night noises that, taken together, make one big silence—the click of one bamboo-stem against the other, the rustle of something alive in the undergrowth, the scratch and squawk of a half-waked bird (birds are awake in the night much more often than we imagine), and the fall of water ever so far away. Little Toomai slept for some time, and when he waked it was brilliant moonlight, and Kala Nag was still standing up with his ears cocked. Little Toomai turned, rustling in the fodder, and watched the curve of his big back against half the stars in heaven, and while he watched he heard, so far away that it sounded no more than a pinhole of noise pricked through the stillness, the 'hoot-toot' of a wild elephant. All the elephants in the lines jumped up as if they had been shot, and their grunts at last waked the sleeping mahouts, and they came out and drove in the picket-pegs with big mallets, and tightened this rope and knotted that till all was quiet. One new elephant had nearly grubbed up his picket, and Big Toomai took off Kala Nag's leg-chain and shackled that elephant fore foot to hind foot, but slipped a loop of grass-string round Kala Nag's leg, and told him to remember that he was tied fast. He knew that he and his father and his grandfather had done the very same thing hundreds of times before.

Kala Nag did not answer to the order by gurgling, as he usually did. He stood still, looking out across the moonlight, his head a little raised and his ears spread like fans, up to the great folds of the Garo Hills.

'Tend to him if he grows restless in the night,' said Big Toomai to Little Toomai, and he went into the hut and slept. Little Toomai was just going to sleep, too, when he heard the coir-string snap with a little *ting*, and Kala Nag rolled out of his pickets as slowly and as silently as a cloud rolls out of the mouth of a valley. Little Toomai pattered after him, barefooted, down the road in the moonlight, calling under his breath: 'Kala Nag! Kala Nag! Take me with you, O Kala Nag!' The elephant turned, without a sound, took three strides back to the boy in the moonlight, put down his trunk, swung him up to his neck, and almost before Little Toomai had settled his knees, slipped into the forest.

There was one blast of furious trumpeting from the lines, and then the silence shut down on everything, and Kala Nag began to move. Sometimes a tuft of high grass washed along his sides as a wave washes along the sides of a ship, and sometimes a cluster of wild-pepper vines would scrape along his back, or a bamboo would creak where his shoulder touched it, but between those times he moved absolutely without any sound, drifting through the thick Garo Forest as though it has been smoke. He was going up hill, but though Little Toomai watched the stars in the rifts of the trees, he could not tell in what direction. Then Kala Nag reached the crest of the ascent and stopped for a minute, and Little Toomai could see the tops of the trees lying all speckled and furry under the moonlight for miles and miles, and the blue-white mist over the river in the hollow. Toomai leaned forward and looked, and he felt that the forest was awake below him—awake and alive and crowded. A big brown fruit-eating bat brushed past his ear; a porcupine's quills rattled in the thicket, and in the darkness between the tree-stems he heard a hog-bear digging hard in the moist warm earth, and snuffing as it digged. Then the branches closed over his head again, and Kala Nag began to go down into the valley—not quietly this time, but as a runaway gun goes down a steep bank—in one rush. The huge limbs moved as steadily as pistons, eight feet to each stride, and the wrinkled skin of the elbow-points rustled. The undergrowth on either side of him ripped with a noise like torn canvas, and the saplings that he heaved away right and left with his shoulders sprang back again, and banged him on the flank, and great trails of creepers, all matted together, hung from his tusks as he threw his head from side to side and ploughed out his pathway. Then Little Toomai laid himself down close the great neck lest a swinging bough should sweep him to the ground, and he wished that he were back in the lines again. The grass began to get squashy, and Kala Nag's feet sucked and squelched as he put them down, and the night mist at the bottom of the valley chilled Little Toomai. There was a splash and a trample, and the rush of running water, and Kala Nag strode through the bed of a river, feeling his way at each step. Above the noise of the water, as it swirled round the elephant's legs, Little Toomai could hear more splashing and some trumpeting both up-stream and down—great grunts and angry snortings, and all the mist about him seemed to be full of rolling wavy shadows. '*Ai!*' he said, half aloud, his teeth chattering. 'The Elephant-Folk are out to-night. It *is* a dance, then!'

Kala Nag swashed out of the water, blew his trunk clear, and began another climb, but this time he was not alone, and he had not to make his path. That was made already, six feet wide, in front of him, where the bent jungle-grass was trying to recover itself and stand up. Many elephants must have gone that way only a few minutes before. Little Toomai looked back, and behind him a great wild tusker, with his little pig's eyes glowing like hot coals, was just lifting himself out of the misty river. Then the trees closed up again, and they went on and up, with trumpetings and crashings, and the sound of breaking branches on every side of them. At last Kala Nag stood still between two tree-trunks at the very top of the hill. They were part of a circle of trees that grew round an irregular space of some three or four acres, and in all that space, as Little Toomai could see, the ground had been trampled down as hard as a brick floor. Some trees grew in the centre of the clearing, but their bark was rubbed away, and the white wood beneath showed all shiny and polished in the patches of moonlight. There were creepers hanging from the upper branches, and the bells of the flowers of the creepers, great waxy white things like convolvuluses, hung down fast asleep, but within the limits of the clearing there was not a single blade of green—nothing but the trampled earth. The moonlight showed it all iron-grey, except where some elephants stood upon it, and their shadows were inky black. Little Toomai looked, holding his breath, with his eyes starting out of his head, and as he looked, more and more and more elephants swung out into the open from between the tree-trunks. Little Toomai could only count up to ten, and he counted again and again on his fingers till he lost count of the tens, and his head began to swim. Outside the clearing he could hear them crashing in the undergrowth as they worked their way up the hillside, but as soon as they were within the circle of the tree-trunks they moved like ghosts.

There were white-tusked wild males, with fallen leaves and nuts and twigs lying in the wrinkles of their necks and the folds of their ears; fat slow-footed she-elephants, with restless, little pinky-black calves only three or four feet high running under their stomachs; young elephants with their tusks just beginning to show, and very proud of them; lanky, scraggy old-maid elephants, with their hollow anxious faces, and trunks like rough bark; savage old bull elephants, scarred from shoulder to flank with great weals and cuts of bygone fights, and the caked dirt of their solitary mud-baths dropping from their shoulders; and there was one with a broken tusk and the marks of the full-stroke, the terrible drawing scrape, of a tiger's claws on his side. They were standing head to head, or walking to and fro across the ground in couples, or rocking and swaying all by themselves—scores and scores of elephants. Toomai knew that so long as he lay still on Kala Nag's neck nothing would happen to him, for even in the rush and scramble of a keddah-drive a wild elephant does not reach up with his trunk and drag a man off the neck of a tame elephant. And these elephants were not thinking of men that night. Once they started and put their ears forward when they heard the chinking of a leg-iron in the forest, but it was Pudmini, Petersen Sahib's pet elephant, her chain snapped short off, grunting, snuffling up the hillside. She must have broken her pickets, and come straight from Petersen Sahib's camp. And Little Toomai saw another elephant, one that he did not know, with deep rope-galls on his back and breast. He, too, must have run away from some camp in the hills about.

At last there was no sound of any more elephants moving in the forest, and Kala Nag rolled out from his station between the trees and went into the middle of the crowd, clucking and gurgling, and all the elephants began to talk in their own tongue, and to move about. Still lying down, Little Toomai looked down upon scores and scores of broad backs, and wagging ears, and tossing trunks, and little rolling eyes. He heard the click of tusks as they crossed other tusks by accident, and the dry rustle of trunks twined together, and the chafing of enormous sides and shoulders in the crowd, and the incessant flick and *hissh* of the great tails. Then a cloud came over the moon, and he sat in black darkness. But the quiet, steady hustling and pushing and gurgling went on just the same. He knew that there were elephants all round Kala Nag, and that there was no chance of backing him out of the assembly; so he set his teeth and shivered. In a keddah at least there was torch-light and shouting, but here he was all alone in the dark, and once a trunk came up and touched him on the knee. Then an elephant trumpeted, and they all took it up for five or ten terrible seconds. The dew from the trees above spattered down like rain on the unseen backs, and a dull booming noise began, not very loud at first, and Little Toomai could not tell what it was. But it grew and grew, and Kala Nag lifted up one fore foot and then the other, and brought them down on the ground—one-two, one-two, as steadily as trip-hammers. The elephants were stamping altogether now, and it sounded like a war-drum beaten at the mouth of a cave. The dew fell from the trees till there was no more left to fall, and the booming went on, and the ground rocked and shivered, and Little Toomai put his hands up to his ears to shut out the sound. But it was all one gigantic jar that ran through him—this stamp of hundreds of heavy feet on the raw earth. Once or twice he could feel Kala Nag and all the others surge forward a few strides, and the thumping would change to the crushing sound of juicy green things being bruised, but in a minute or two the boom of feet on hard earth began again. A tree was creaking and groaning somewhere near him. He put out his arm and felt the bark, but Kala Nag moved forward still tramping, and he could not tell where he was in the clearing. There was no sound from the elephants, except once, when two or three little calves squeaked together. Then he heard a thump and a shuffle, and the booming went on. It must have lasted fully two hours, and Little Toomai ached in every nerve, but he knew by the smell of the night air that the dawn was coming.

The morning broke in one sheet of pale yellow behind the green hills, and the booming stopped with the first ray, as though the light had been an order. Before Little Toomai had got the ringing out of his head, before even he had shifted his position, there was not an elephant in sight except Kala Nag, Pudmini, and the elephant with the rope-galls, and there was neither sign nor rustle nor whisper down the hillsides to show where the others had gone. Little Toomai stared again and again. The clearing, as he remembered it, had grown in the night. More trees stood in the middle of it, but the undergrowth and the jungle-grass at the sides had been rolled back. Little Toomai stared once more. Now he understood the trampling. The elephants had stamped out more room— had stamped the thick grasses and juicy cane to trash, the trash into slivers, the slivers into tiny fibres, and the fibres into hard earth.

'*Wah!*' said Little Toomai, and his eyes were very heavy. 'Kala Nag, my lord, let us keep by Pudmini and go to Petersen Sahib's camp, or I shall drop from thy neck.'

The third elephant watched the two go away, snorted, wheeled round, and took his own path. He may have belonged to some little native king's establishment, fifty or sixty or a hundred miles away.

Two hours later, as Petersen Sahib was eating early breakfast, his elephants, who had been double-chained that night, began to trumpet, and Pudmini, mired to the shoulders, with Kala Nag, very footsore, shambled into the camp. Little Toomai's face was grey and pinched, and his hair was full of leaves and drenched with dew, but he tried to salute to Petersen Sahib, and cried faintly: 'The dance—the elephant-dance! I have seen it, and—I die!' As Kala Nag sat down, he slid off his neck in a dead faint.

But, since native children have no nerves worth speaking of, in two hours he was lying very contented-ly in Petersen Sahib's hammock with Petersen Sahib's shooting-coat under his head, and a glass of warm milk, a little brandy, with a dash of quinine inside of him, and while the old hairy, scarred hunters of the jungles sat three deep before him, looking at him as though he were a spirit, he told his tale in short words, as a child will, and wound up with:

'Now, if I lie in one word, send men to see, and they will find that the Elephant-Folk have trampled down more room in their dance-room, and they will find ten and ten, and many times ten, tracks leading to that dance-room. They made more room with their feet. I have seen it. Kala Nag took me, and I saw. Also Kala Nag is very leg-weary!'

Little Toomai lay back and slept all through the long afternoon and into the twilight, and while he slept Petersen Sahib and Machua Appa followed the track of the two elephants for fifteen miles across the hills. Petersen Sahib had spent eighteen years in catching elephants, and he had only once before found such a dance-place. Machua Appa had no need to look twice at the clearing to see what had been done there, or to scratch with his toe in the packed, rammed earth.

'The child speaks truth,' said he. 'All this was done last night, and I have counted seventy tracks crossing the river. See, Sahib, where Pudmini's leg-iron cut the bark of that tree! Yes, she was there too.' They looked at one another and up and down, and they wondered, for the ways of elephants are beyond the wit of any man, black or white, to fathom.

'Forty years and five,' said Machua Appa, 'have I followed my lord the elephant, but never have I heard that any child of man had seen what this child has seen. By all the Gods of the Hills, it is—what can we say?' And he shook his head.

When they got back to camp it was time for the evening meal. Petersen Sahib ate alone in his tent, but he gave orders that the camp should have two sheep and some fowls, as well as a double ration of flour and rice and salt, for he knew that there would be a feast. Big Toomai had come up hot-foot from the camp in the plains to search for his son and his elephant, and now that he had found them he looked at them as though he were afraid of them both. And there was a feast by the blazing camp-fires in front of the lines of picketed elephants, and Little Toomai was the hero of it all. And the big brown elephant-catchers, the trackers and drivers and ropers, and the men who know all the secrets of breaking the wildest elephants, passed him from one to the other, and they marked his forehead with blood from the breast of a newly killed jungle-cock, to show that he was a forester, initiated and free of all the jungles.

And at last, when the flames died down, and the red light of the logs made the elephants look as though they had been dipped in blood too, Machua Appa, the head of all the drivers of all the keddahs—Machua Appa, Petersen Sahib's other self, who had never seen a made road in forty years: Machua Appa, who was so great that he had no other name than Machua Appa—leaped to his feet, with Little Toomai held high in the air above his head, and shouted: 'Listen, my brothers. Listen, too, you my lords in the lines there, for I, Machua Appa, am speaking! This little one shall no more be called Little Toomai, but Toomai of the Elephants, as his great grandfather was called before him. What never man has seen he has seen through the long night, and the favour of the Elephant-Folk and of the Gods of the Jungles is with him. He shall become a great tracker; he shall become greater than I, even I, Machua Appa! He shall follow the new trail, and the stale trail, and the mixed trail, with a clear eye! He shall take no harm in the keddah when he runs under their bellies to rope the wild tuskers. And if he slips before the feet of the charging bull-elephant, the bull-elephant shall know who he is and shall not crush him. *Aihai!* My lords in the chains'—he whirled up the line of pickets—'here is the little one that has seen your dances in your hidden places—the sight that never man saw! Give him honour, my lords! *Salaam karo*, my children. Make your salute to Toomai of the Elephants!

Gunga Pershad, *ahaa!* Hira Guj, Birchi Guj, Kuttar Guj, *ahaa!* Pudmini—thou hast seen him at the dance, and thou too, Kala Nag, my pearl among elephants! *Ahaa!* Together! To Toomai of the Elephants. *Barrao!*'

And at that last wild yell the whole line flung up their trunks till the tips touched their foreheads, and broke out into the full salute—the crashing trumpet-peal that only the Viceroy of India hears, the salaamut of the keddah.

But it was all for the sake of Little Toomai, who had seen what never man had seen before—the dance of the elephants at night and alone in the heart of the Garo Hills!

1893

THE KING'S ANKUS

~~~~~~~~~~~~~~~~~~~~~~~~~~~~~~~~~~~~~~~

Kaa, the big Rock Python, had changed his skin for perhaps the two hundredth time since his birth; and Mowgli, who never forgot that he owed his life to Kaa for a night's work at Cold Lairs, which you may perhaps remember, went to congratulate him. Skin-changing always makes a snake moody and depressed till the new skin begins to shine and look beautiful. Kaa never made fun of Mowgli any more, but accepted him, as the other Jungle People did, for the Master of the Jungle, and brought him all the news that a python of his size would naturally hear. What Kaa did not know about the Middle Jungle, as they call it,—the life that runs close to the earth or under it, the boulder, burrow, and the tree-bole life,—might have been written upon the smallest of his scales.

That afternoon Mowgli was sitting in the circle of Kaa's great coils, fingering the flaked and broken old skin that lay all looped and twisted among the rocks just as Kaa had left it. Kaa had very courteously packed himself under Mowgli's broad, bare shoulders, so that the boy was really resting in a living arm-chair.

'Even to the scales of the eyes it is perfect,' said Mowgli, under his breath, playing with the old skin. 'Strange to see the covering of one's own head at one's own feet!'

'Aye, but I lack feet,' said Kaa; 'and since this is the custom of all my people, I do not find it strange. Does thy skin never feel old and harsh?'

'Then go I and wash, Flathead; but, it is true, in the great heats I have wished I could slough my skin without pain, and run skinless.'

'I wash, and *also* I take off my skin. How looks the new coat?'

Mowgli ran his hand down the diagonal checkerings of the immense back. 'The Turtle is harder-backed, but not so gay,' he said judgmatically. 'The Frog, my name-bearer, is more gay, but not so hard. It is very beautiful to see—like the mottling in the mouth of a lily.'

'It needs water. A new skin never comes to full color before the first bath. Let us go bathe.'

'I will carry thee,' said Mowgli; and he stooped down, laughing, to lift the middle section of Kaa's great body, just where the barrel was thickest. A man might just as well have tried to heave up a two-foot water-main; and Kaa lay still, puffing with quiet amusement. Then the regular evening game began—the boy in the flush of his great strength, and the Python in his sumptuous new skin, standing up one against the other for a wrestling-match— a trial of eye and strength. Of course, Kaa could have crushed a dozen Mowglis if he had let himself go; but he played carefully, and never loosed one tenth of his power. Ever since Mowgli was strong enough to endure a little rough handling, Kaa had taught him this game, and it supplied his limbs as nothing else could. Sometimes Mowgli would stand lapped almost to his throat in Kaa's shifting coils, striving to get one arm free and catch him by the throat. Then Kaa would give way limply, and Mowgli, with both quick-moving feet, would try to cramp the purchase of that huge tail as it flung backward feeling for a rock or a stump. They would rock to and fro, head to head, each waiting for his chance, till the beautiful, statue-like group melted in a whirl of black-and-yellow coils and struggling legs and arms, to rise up again and again. 'Now! now! now!' said Kaa, making feints with his head that even Mowgli's quick hand could not turn aside. 'Look! I touch thee here, Little Brother! Here, and here! Are thy hands numb? Here again!'

The game always ended in one way—with a straight,

driving blow of the head that knocked the boy over and over. Mowgli could never learn the guard for that lightning lunge, and, as Kaa said, there was not the least use in trying.

'Good hunting!' Kaa grunted at last; and Mowgli, as usual, was shot away half a dozen yards, gasping and laughing. He rose with his fingers full of grass, and followed Kaa to the wise snake's pet bathing-place—a deep, pitchy-black pool surrounded with rocks, and made interesting by sunken tree-stumps. The boy slipped in, Jungle-fashion, without a sound, and dived across; rose, too, without a sound, and turned on his back, his arms behind his head, watching the moon rising above the rocks, and breaking up her reflection in the water with his toes. Kaa's diamond-shaped head cut the pool like a razor, and came out to rest on Mowgli's shoulder. They lay still, soaking luxuriously in the cool water.

'It is *very* good,' said Mowgli at last, sleepily. 'Now, in the Man-Pack, at this hour, as I remember, they laid them down upon hard pieces of wood in the inside of a mud-trap, and, having carefully shut out all the clean winds, drew foul cloth over their heavy heads, and made evil songs through their noses. It is better in the Jungle.'

A hurrying cobra slipped down over a rock and drank, gave them 'Good hunting!' and went away.

'Sssh!' said Kaa, as though he had suddenly remembered something. 'So the Jungle gives thee all that thou hast ever desired, Little Brother?'

'Not all,' said Mowgli, laughing; 'else there would be a new and strong Shere Khan to kill once a moon. Now, I could kill with my own hands, asking no help of buffaloes. And also I have wished the sun to shine in the middle of the Rains, and the Rains to cover the sun in the deep of summer; and also I have never gone empty but I wished that I had killed a goat; and also I have never killed a goat but I wished it had been buck; nor buck but I wished it had been nilghai. But thus do we feel, all of us.'

'Thou hast no other desire?' the big snake demanded.

'What more can I wish? I have the Jungle, and the favor of the Jungle! Is there more anywhere between sunrise and sunset?'

'Now, the Cobra said—' Kaa began.

'What cobra? He that went away just now said nothing. He was hunting.'

'It was another.'

'Hast thou many dealings with the Poison People? I give them their own path. They carry death in the fore-tooth, and that is not good—for they are so small. But what hood is this thou hast spoken with?'

Kaa rolled slowly in the water like a steamer in a beam sea. 'Three or four moons since,' said he, 'I hunted in Cold Lairs, which place thou hast not forgotten. And the thing I hunted fled shrieking past the tanks and to that house whose side I once broke for thy sake, and ran into the ground.'

'But the people of Cold Lairs do not live in burrows.' Mowgli knew that Kaa was talking of the Monkey People.

'This thing was not living, but seeking to live,' Kaa replied, with a quiver of his tongue. 'He ran into a burrow that led very far. I followed, and having killed, I slept. When I waked I went forward.'

'Under the earth?'

'Even so, coming at last upon a White Hood [a white cobra], who spoke of things beyond my knowledge, and showed me many things I had never before seen.'

'New game? Was it good hunting?' Mowgli turned quickly on his side.

'It was no game, and would have broken all my teeth; but the White Hood said that a man—he spoke as one that knew the breed—that a man would give the breath under his ribs for only the sight of those things.'

'We will look,' said Mowgli. 'I now remember that I was once a man.'

'Slowly—slowly. It was haste killed the Yellow Snake

that ate the sun. We two spoke together under the earth, and I spoke of thee, naming thee as a man. Said the White Hood (and he is indeed as old as the Jungle): "It is long since I have seen a man. Let him come, and he shall see all these things, for the least of which very many men would die."

'That *must* be new game. And yet the Poison People do not tell us when game is afoot. They are an unfriendly folk.'

'It is *not* game. It is—it is—I cannot say what it is.'

'We will go there. I have never seen a White Hood, and I wish to see the other things. Did he kill them?'

'They are all dead things. He says he is the keeper of them all.'

'Ah! As a wolf stands above meat he has taken to his own lair. Let us go.'

Mowgli swam to bank, rolled on the grass to dry himself, and the two set off for Cold Lairs, the deserted city of which you may have heard. Mowgli was not the least afraid of the Monkey People in those days, but the Monkey People had the liveliest horror of Mowgli. Their tribes, however, were raiding in the Jungle, and so Cold Lairs stood empty and silent in the moonlight. Kaa led up to the ruins of the queen's pavilion that stood on the terrace, slipped over the rubbish, and dived down the half-choked staircase that went underground from the center of the pavilion. Mowgli gave the snake-call—'We be of one blood, ye and I,'—and followed on his hands and knees. They crawled a long distance down a sloping passage that turned and twisted several times, and at last came to where the root of some great tree, growing thirty feet overhead, had forced out a solid stone in the wall. They crept through the gap, and found themselves in a large vault, whose domed roof had been also broken away by tree-roots so that a few streaks of light dropped down into the darkness.

'A safe lair,' said Mowgli, rising to his firm feet, 'but over far to visit daily. And now what do we see?'

'Am I nothing?' said a voice in the middle of the vault; and Mowgli saw something white move till, little by little, there stood up the hugest cobra he had ever set eyes on— a creature nearly eight feet long, and bleached by being in darkness to an old ivory-white. Even the spectacle-marks of his spread hood had faded to faint yellow. His eyes were as red as rubies, and altogether he was most wonderful.

'Good hunting!' said Mowgli, who carried his manners with his knife, and that never left him.

'What of my city?' said the White Cobra, without an-swering the greeting. 'What of the great, the walled city— the city of a hundred elephants and twenty thousand horses, and cattle past counting—the city of the King of Twenty Kings? I grow deaf here, and it is long since I heard their war-gongs.'

'The Jungle is above our heads,' said Mowgli. 'I know only Hathi and his sons among elephants. Bagheera has slain all the horses in one village, and—what is a King?'

'I told thee,' said Kaa softly to the Cobra—'I told thee, four moons ago, that thy city was not.'

'The city—the great city of the forest whose gates are guarded by the King's towers—can never pass. They builded it before my father's father came from the egg, and it shall endure when my son's sons are as white as I! Salomdhi, son of Chandrabija, son of Viyeja, son of Yega-suri, made it in the days of Bappa Rawal. Whose cattle are *ye?*'

'It is a lost trail,' said Mowgli, turning to Kaa. 'I know not his talk.'

'Nor I. He is very old. Father of Cobras, there is only the Jungle here, as it has been since the beginning.'

'Then who is *he,*' said the White Cobra, 'sitting down before me, unafraid, knowing not the name of the King, talking our talk through a man's lips? Who is he with the knife and the snake's tongue?'

'Mowgli they call me,' was the answer. 'I am of the Jungle. The Wolves are my people, and Kaa here is my brother. Father of Cobras, who art thou?'

'I am the Warden of the King's Treasure. Kurrun Raja builded the stone above me, in the days when my skin was dark, that I might teach death to those who came to steal. Then they let down the treasure through the stone, and I heard the song of the Brahmins my masters.'

'Umm!' said Mowgli to himself. 'I have dealt with one Brahmin already, in the Man-Pack, and—I know what I know. Evil comes here in a little.'

'Five times since I came here has the stone been lifted, but always to let down more, and never to take away. There are no riches like these riches—the treasures of a hundred kings. But it is long and long since the stone was last moved, and I think that my city has forgotten.'

'There is no city. Look up. Yonder are roots of the great trees tearing the stones apart. Trees and men do not grow together,' Kaa insisted.

'Twice and thrice have men found their way here,' the White Cobra answered savagely; 'but they never spoke till I came upon them groping in the dark, and then they cried only a little time. But *ye* come with lies, Man and Snake both, and would have me believe the city is not, and that my wardship ends. Little do men change in the years. But *I* change never! Till the stone is lifted, and the Brahmins come down singing the songs that I know, and feed me with warm milk, and take me to the light again, I—I—*I*, and no other, am the Warden of the King's Treasure! The city is dead, ye say, and here are the roots of the trees? Stoop down, then, and take what ye will. Earth has no treasure like to these. Man with the snake's tongue, if thou canst go alive by the way that thou hast entered at, the lesser Kings will be thy servants!'

'Again the trail is lost,' said Mowgli, coolly. 'Can any

jackal have burrowed so deep and bitten this great White Hood? He is surely mad. Father of Cobras, I see nothing here to take away.'

'By the Gods of the Sun and Moon, it is the madness of death upon the boy!' hissed the Cobra. 'Before thine eyes close I will allow thee this favor. Look thou, and see what man has never seen before!'

'They do not well in the Jungle who speak to Mowgli of favors,' said the boy, between his teeth; 'but the dark changes all, as I know. I will look, if that please thee.'

He stared with puckered-up eyes round the vault, and then lifted up from the floor a handful of something that glittered.

'Oho!' said he, 'this is like the stuff they play with in the Man-Pack: only this is yellow and the other was brown.'

He let the gold pieces fall, and moved forward. The floor of the vault was buried some five or six feet deep in coined gold and silver that had burst from the sacks it had been originally stored in, and, in the long years, the metal had packed and settled as sand packs at low tide. On it and in it, and rising through it, as wrecks lift through the sand, were jeweled elephant-howdahs of embossed silver, studded with plates of hammered gold, and adorned with carbuncles and turquoises. There were palanquins and litters for carrying queens, framed and braced with silver and enamel, with jade-handled poles and amber curtain-rings; there were golden candlesticks hung with pierced emeralds that quivered on the branches; there were studded images, five feet high, of forgotten gods, silver with jeweled eyes; there were coats of mail, gold inlaid on steel, and fringed with rotted and blackened seed-pearls; there were helmets, crested and beaded with pigeon's-blood rubies; there were shields of lacquer, of tortoise-shell and rhinoceros-hide, strapped and bossed with red gold and set with emeralds at the edge; there were sheaves of diamond-hilted swords, daggers, and hunting-knives; there were golden sacrificial bowls and ladles, and portable altars of a shape that never see the light of day; there were jade cups and bracelets; there were incense-burners, combs, and pots for perfume, henna, and eye-powder, all in embossed gold; there were nose-rings, armlets, head-bands, finger-rings, and girdles past any counting; there were belts, seven fingers broad, of square-cut diamonds and rubies, and wooden boxes, trebly clamped with iron, from which the wood had fallen away in powder, showing the pile of uncut star-sapphires, opals, cat's-eyes, sap-phires, rubies, diamonds, emeralds, and garnets within.

The White Cobra was right. No mere money would begin to pay the value of this treasure, the sifted pickings of centuries of war, plunder, trade, and taxation. The coins alone were priceless, leaving out of count all the precious stones; and the dead weight of the gold and silver alone might be two or three hundred tons. Every native ruler in India to-day, however poor, has a hoard to which he is always adding; and though, once in a long while, some enlightened prince may send off forty or fifty bullock-cart loads of silver to be exchanged for Govern-ment securities, the bulk of them keep their treasure and the knowledge of it very closely to themselves.

But Mowgli naturally did not understand what these things meant. The knives interested him a little, but they did not balance so well as his own, and so he dropped them. At last he found something really fascinating laid on the front of a howdah half buried in the coins. It was a three-foot ankus, or elephant-goad—something like a small boat-hook. The top was one round shining ruby, and twelve inches of the handle below it were studded with rough turquoises close together, giving a most satis-factory grip. Below them was a rim of jade with a flower-pattern running round it—only the leaves were emeralds, and the blossoms were rubies sunk in the cool, green stone. The rest of the handle was a shaft of pure ivory, while the point—the spike and hook—was gold-inlaid steel with pictures of elephant-catching; and the pictures attracted Mowgli, who saw that they had something to do with his friend Hathi the Silent.

The White Cobra had been following him closely.

'Is this not worth dying to behold?' he said. 'Have I not done thee a great favor?'

'I do not understand,' said Mowgli. 'The things are hard and cold, and by no means good to eat. But this'—he lifted the ankus—'I desire to take away, that I may see it in the sun. Thou sayest they are all thine? Wilt thou give it to me, and I will bring thee frogs to eat?'

The White Cobra fairly shook with evil delight. 'Assuredly I will give it,' he said. 'All that is here I will give thee—till thou goest away.'

'But I go now. This place is dark and cold, and I wish to take the thorn-pointed thing to the Jungle.'

'Look by thy foot! What is that there?'

Mowgli picked up something white and smooth. 'It is the bone of a man's head,' he said quietly. 'And here are two more.'

'They came to take the treasure away many years ago. I spoke to them in the dark, and they lay still.'

'But what do I need of this that is called treasure? If thou wilt give me the ankus to take away, it is good hunting. If not, it is good hunting none the less. I do not fight with the Poison People, and I was also taught the Master-word of thy tribe.'

'There is but one Master-word here. It is mine!'

Kaa flung himself forward with blazing eyes. 'Who bade me bring the Man?' he hissed.

'I surely,' the old Cobra lisped. 'It is long since I have seen Man, and this Man speaks our tongue.'

'But there was no talk of killing. How can I go to the Jungle and say that I have led him to his death?' said Kaa.

'I talk not of killing till the time. And as to thy going or not going, there is the hole in the wall. Peace, now, thou fat monkey-killer! I have but to touch thy neck, and the Jungle will know thee no longer. Never Man came here that went away with the breath under his ribs. I am the Warden of the Treasure of the King's City!'

'But, thou white worm of the dark, I tell thee there is neither king nor city! The Jungle is all about us!' cried Kaa.

'There is still the Treasure. But this can be done. Wait a while, Kaa of the Rocks, and see the boy run. There is room for great sport here. Life is good. Run to and fro a while, and make sport, boy!'

Mowgli put his hand on Kaa's head quietly.

'The white thing has dealt with men of the Man-Pack until now. He does not know me,' he whispered. 'He has asked for this hunting. Let him have it.' Mowgli had been standing with the ankus held point down. He flung it from him quickly, and it dropped crossways just behind the great snake's hood, pinning him to the floor. In a flash, Kaa's weight was upon the writhing body, paralyzing it from hood to tail. The red eyes burned, and the six spare inches of the head struck furiously right and left.

'Kill!' said Kaa, as Mowgli's hand went to his knife.

'No,' he said, as he drew the blade; 'I will never kill again save for food. But look you, Kaa!' He caught the snake behind the hood, forced the mouth open with the blade of the knife, and showed the terrible poison-fangs of the upper jaw lying black and withered in the gum. The White Cobra had outlived his poison, as a snake will.

'*Thuu*' ('It is dried up'),[1] said Mowgli; and motioning Kaa away, he picked up the ankus, setting the White Cobra free.

'The King's Treasure needs a new Warden,' he said gravely. 'Thuu, thou hast not done well. Run to and fro and make sport, Thuu!'

'I am ashamed. Kill me!' hissed the White Cobra.

'There has been too much talk of killing. We will go

---

[1] Literally, a rotted out tree-stump.

now. I take the thorn-pointed thing, Thuu, because I have fought and worsted thee.'

'See, then, that the thing does not kill thee at last. It is Death! Remember, it is Death! There is enough in that thing to kill the men of all my city. Not long wilt thou hold it, Jungle Man, nor he who takes it from thee. They will kill, and kill, and kill for its sake! My strength is dried up, but the ankus will do my work. It is Death! It is Death! It is Death!'

Mowgli crawled out through the hole into the passage again, and the last that he saw was the White Cobra striking furiously with his harmless fangs at the stolid golden faces of the gods that lay on the floor, and hissing, 'It is Death!'

They were glad to get to the light of day once more; and when they were back in their own Jungle and Mowgli made the ankus glitter in the morning light, he was almost as pleased as though he had found a bunch of new flowers to stick in his hair.

'This is brighter than Bagheera's eyes,' he said delightedly, as he twirled the ruby. 'I will show it to him; but what did the Thuu mean when he talked of death?'

'I cannot say. I am sorrowful to my tail's tail that he felt not thy knife. There is always evil at Cold Lairs—above ground or below. But now I am hungry. Dost thou hunt with me this dawn?' said Kaa.

'No; Bagheera must see this thing. Good hunting!' Mowgli danced off, flourishing the great ankus, and stopping from time to time to admire it, till he came to that part of the Jungle Bagheera chiefly used, and found him drinking after a heavy kill. Mowgli told him all his adventures from beginning to end, and Bagheera sniffed at the ankus between whiles. When Mowgli came to the White Cobra's last words, the Panther purred approvingly.

'Then the White Hood spoke the thing which is?' Mowgli asked quickly.

'I was born in the King's cages at Oodeypore, and it is in my stomach that I know some little of Man. Very many men would kill thrice in a night for the sake of that one big red stone alone.'

'But the stone makes it heavy to the hand. My little bright knife is better; and—see! the red stone is not good to eat. Then *why* would they kill?'

'Mowgli, go thou and sleep. Thou hast lived among men, and—'

'I remember. Men kill because they are not hunting;—for idleness and pleasure. Wake again, Bagheera. For what use was this thorn-pointed thing made?'

Bagheera half opened his eyes—he was very sleepy—with a malicious twinkle.

'It was made by men to thrust into the head of the sons of Hathi, so that the blood should pour out. I have seen the like in the street of Oodeypore, before our cages. That thing has tasted the blood of many such as Hathi.'

'But why do they thrust into the heads of elephants?'

'To teach them Man's Law. Having neither claws nor teeth, men make these things—and worse.'

'Always more blood when I come near, even to the things the Man-Pack have made,' said Mowgli, disgustedly. He was getting a little tired of the weight of the ankus. 'If I had known this, I would not have taken it. First it was Messua's blood on the thongs, and now it is Hathi's. I will use it no more. Look!'

The ankus flew sparkling, and buried itself point down thirty yards away, between the trees. 'So my hands are clean of Death,' said Mowgli, rubbing his palms on the fresh, moist earth. 'The Thuu said Death would follow me. He is old and white and mad.'

'White or black, or death or life, *I* am going to sleep, Little Brother. I cannot hunt all night and howl all day, as do some folk.'

Bagheera went off to a hunting-lair that he knew, about

two miles off. Mowgli made an easy way for himself up a convenient tree, knotted three or four creepers together, and in less time than it takes to tell was swinging in a hammock fifty feet above ground. Though he had no positive objection to strong daylight, Mowgli followed the custom of his friends, and used it as little as he could. When he waked among the very loud-voiced peoples that live in the trees, it was twilight once more, and he had been dreaming of the beautiful pebbles he had thrown away.

'At least I will look at the thing again,' he said, and slid down a creeper to the earth; but Bagheera was before him. Mowgli could hear him snuffing in the half light.

'Where is the thorn-pointed thing?' cried Mowgli.

'A man has taken it. Here is the trail.'

'Now we shall see whether the Thuu spoke truth. If the pointed thing is Death, that man will die. Let us follow.'

'Kill first,' said Bagheera. 'An empty stomach makes a careless eye. Men go very slowly, and the Jungle is wet enough to hold the lightest mark.'

They killed as soon as they could, but it was nearly three hours before they finished their meat and drink and buckled down to the trail. The Jungle People know that nothing makes up for being hurried over your meals.

'Think you the pointed thing will turn in the man's hand and kill him?' Mowgli asked. 'The Thuu said it was Death.'

'We shall see when we find,' said Bagheera, trotting with his head low. 'It is single-foot' (he meant that there was only one man), 'and the weight of the thing has pressed his heel far into the ground.'

'Hai! This is as clear as summer lightning,' Mowgli answered; and they fell into the quick, choppy trail-trot in and out through the checkers of the moonlight, following the marks of those two bare feet.

'Now he runs swiftly,' said Mowgli. 'The toes are

spread apart.' They went on over some wet ground. 'Now why does he turn aside here?'

'Wait!' said Bagheera, and flung himself forward with one superb bound as far as ever he could. The first thing to do when a trail ceases to explain itself is to cast forward without leaving your own confusing foot-marks on the ground. Bagheera turned as he landed, and faced Mowgli, crying, 'Here comes another trail to meet him. It is a smaller foot, this second trail, and the toes turn inward.'

Then Mowgli ran up and looked. 'It is the foot of a Gond hunter,' he said. 'Look! Here he dragged his bow on the grass. That is why the first trail turned aside so quickly. Big Foot hid from Little Foot.'

'That is true,' said Bagheera. 'Now, lest by crossing each other's tracks we foul the signs, let each take one trail. I am Big Foot, Little Brother, and thou art Little Foot, the Gond.'

Bagheera leaped back to the original trail, leaving Mowgli stooping above the curious narrow track of the wild little man of the woods.

'Now,' said Bagheera, moving step by step along the chain of footprints, 'I, Big Foot, turn aside here. Now I hide me behind a rock and stand still, not daring to shift my feet. Cry thy trail, Little Brother.'

'Now, I, Little Foot, come to the rock,' said Mowgli, running up his trail. 'Now, I sit down under the rock, leaning upon my right hand, and resting my bow between my toes. I wait long, for the mark of my feet is deep here.'

'I also,' said Bagheera, hidden behind the rock. 'I wait, resting the end of the thorn-pointed thing upon a stone. It slips, for here is a scratch upon the stone. Cry thy trail, Little Brother.'

'One, two twigs and a big branch are broken here,' said Mowgli, in an undertone. 'Now, how shall I cry *that*? Ah! It is plain now. I, Little Foot, go away making noises and tramplings so that Big Foot may hear me.' He moved away from the rock pace by pace among the trees, his voice rising in the distance as he approached a little cascade. 'I—go—far—away—to—where—the—noise—of—falling—water—covers—my—noise; and—here—I—wait. Cry thy trail, Bagheera, Big Foot!'

The panther had been casting in every direction to see how Big Foot's trail led away from behind the rock. Then he gave tongue:

'I come from behind the rock upon my knees, dragging the thorn-pointed thing. Seeing no one, I run. I, Big Foot, run swiftly. The trail is clear. Let each follow his own. I run!'

Bagheera swept on along the clearly marked trail, and Mowgli followed the steps of the Gond. For some time there was silence in the Jungle.

'Where art thou, Little Foot?' cried Bagheera. Mowgli's voice answered him not fifty yards to the right.

'Um!' said the panther, with a deep cough. 'The two run side by side, drawing nearer!'

They raced on another half mile, always keeping about the same distance, till Mowgli, whose head was not so close to the ground as Bagheera's, cried: 'They have met. Good hunting—look! Here stood Little Foot, with his knee on a rock—and yonder is Big Foot indeed!'

Not ten yards in front of them, stretched across a pile of broken rocks, lay the body of a villager of the district, a long, small-feathered Gond arrow through his back and breast.

'Was the Thuu so old and so mad, Little Brother?' said Bagheera gently. 'Here is one death, at least.'

'Follow on. But where is the drinker of elephant's blood—the red-eyed thorn?'

'Little Foot has it—perhaps. It is single-foot again now.'

The single trail of a light man who had been running quickly and bearing a burden on his left shoulder, held on round a long, low spur of dried grass, where each footfall seemed, to the sharp eyes of the trackers, marked in hot iron.

Neither spoke till the trail ran up to the ashes of a camp-fire hidden in a ravine.

'Again!' said Bagheera, checking as though he had been turned into stone.

The body of a little wizened Gond lay with its feet in the ashes, and Bagheera looked inquiringly at Mowgli.

'That was done with a bamboo,' said the boy, after one glance. 'I have used such a thing among the buffaloes when I served in the Man-Pack. The Father of Cobras—I am sorrowful that I made a jest of him—knew the breed well, as I might have known. Said I not that men kill for idleness?'

'Indeed, they killed for the sake of the red and blue stones,' Bagheera answered. 'Remember, I was in the King's cages at Oodeypore.'

'One, two, three, four tracks,' said Mowgli, stooping over the ashes. 'Four tracks of men with shod feet. They do not go so quickly as Gonds. Now, what evil had the little woodman done to them? See, they talked together, all five, standing up, before they killed him. Bagheera, let us go back. My stomach is heavy in me, and yet it heaves up and down like an oriole's nest at the end of a branch.'

'It is not good hunting to leave game afoot. Follow!' said the panther. 'Those eight shod feet have not gone far.'

No more was said for fully an hour, as they worked up the broad trail of the four men with shod feet.

It was clear, hot daylight now, and Bagheera said, 'I smell smoke.'

'Men are always more ready to eat than to run,' Mowgli answered, trotting in and out between the low scrub bushes of the new Jungle they were exploring. Bagheera, a little to his left, made an indescribable noise in his throat.

'Here is one that has done with feeding,' said he. A tumbled bundle of gay-colored clothes lay under a bush, and round it was some spilt flour.

'That was done by the bamboo again,' said Mowgli. 'See! that white dust is what men eat. They have taken the kill from this one,—he carried their food,—and given him for a kill to Chil, the Kite.'

'It is the third,' said Bagheera.

'I will go with new, big frogs to the Father of Cobras, and feed him fat,' said Mowgli to himself. 'The drinker of elephant's blood is Death himself—but still I do not understand!'

'Follow!' said Bagheera.

They had not gone half a mile further when they heard Ko, the Crow, singing the death-song in the top of a tamarisk under whose shade three men were lying. A half-dead fire smoked in the center of the circle, under an iron plate which held a blackened and burned cake of unleavened bread. Close to the fire, and blazing in the sunshine, lay the ruby-and-turquoise ankus.

'The thing works quickly; all ends here,' said Bagheera. 'How did *these* die, Mowgli? There is no mark on any.'

A Jungle-dweller gets to learn by experience as much as many doctors know of poisonous plants and berries. Mowgli sniffed the smoke that came up from the fire, broke off a morsel of the blackened bread, tasted it, and spat it out again.

'Apple of Death,' he coughed. 'The first must have made it ready in the food for *these*, who killed him, having first killed the Gond.'

'Good hunting, indeed! The kills follow close,' said Bagheera.

'Apple of Death' is what the Jungle call thorn-apple or dhatura, the readiest poison in all India.

'What now?' said the panther. 'Must thou and I kill each other for yonder red-eyed slayer?'

'Can it speak?' said Mowgli, in a whisper. 'Did I do it a wrong when I threw it away? Between us two it can do no wrong, for we do not desire what men desire. If it be left here, it will assuredly continue to kill men one after another as fast as nuts fall in a high wind. I have no love to men, but even I would not have them die six in a night.'

'What matter? They are only men. They killed one another and were well pleased,' said Bagheera. 'That first little woodman hunted well.'

'They are cubs none the less; and a cub will drown himself to bite the moon's light on the water. The fault was mine,' said Mowgli, who spoke as though he knew all about everything. 'I will never again bring into the Jungle strange things—not though they be as beautiful as flowers. This'—he handled the ankus gingerly—'goes back to the Father of Cobras. But first we must sleep, and we cannot sleep near these sleepers. Also we must bury *him*, lest he run away and kill another six. Dig me a hole under that tree.'

'But, Little Brother,' said Bagheera, moving off to the spot, 'I tell thee it is no fault of the blood-drinker. The trouble is with men.'

'All one,' said Mowgli. 'Dig the hole deep. When we wake I will take him up and carry him back.'

Two nights later, as the White Cobra sat mourning in the darkness of the vault, ashamed, and robbed, and alone, the turquoise ankus whirled through the hole in the wall, and clashed on the floor of golden coins.

'Father of Cobras,' said Mowgli (he was careful to keep the other side of the wall), 'get thee a young and ripe one of thine own people to help thee guard the King's Treasure so that no man may come away alive any more.'

'Ah-ha! It returns, then. I said the thing was Death. How comes it that thou art still alive?' the old Cobra mumbled, twining lovingly round the ankus-haft.

'By the Bull that bought me, I do not know! That thing has killed six times in a night. Let him go out no more.'

1895

From
Just So Stories

~~~~~~~~~~~~~~~~~~~~~~

HOW THE RHINOCEROS
GOT HIS SKIN

Once upon a time, on an uninhabited island on the shores
of the Red Sea, there lived a Parsee from whose hat the
rays of the sun were reflected in more-than-oriental splendour. And the Parsee lived by the Red Sea with nothing
but his hat and his knife and a cooking-stove of the kind
that you must particularly never touch. And one day he
took flour and water and currants and plums and sugar
and things, and made himself one cake which was two feet
across and three feet thick. It was indeed a Superior Co-
mestible (*that's* magic) and he put it on the stove because
he was allowed to cook on that stove, and he baked it and
he baked it till it was all done brown and smelt most sentimental. But just as he was going to eat it there came
down to the beach from the Altogether Uninhabited Interior one Rhinoceros with a horn on his nose, two piggy
eyes, and few manners. In those days the Rhinoceros's
skin fitted him quite tight. There were no wrinkles in it
anywhere. He looked exactly like a Noah's Ark Rhinoceros, but of course much bigger. All the same, he had no
manners then, and he has no manners now, and he never
will have any manners. He said, 'How!' and the Parsee left
that cake and climbed to the top of a palm tree with noth-

ing on but his hat, from which the rays of the sun were always reflected in more-than-oriental splendour. And the Rhinoceros upset the oil-stove with his nose, and the cake rolled on the sand, and he spiked that cake on the horn of his nose, and he ate it, and he went away, waving his tail to the desolate and Exclusively Uninhabited Interior which abuts on the islands of Mazanderan, Socotra, and the Promontories of the Larger Equinox. Then the Parsee came down from his palm-tree and put the stove on its legs and recited the following *Sloka,* which, as you have not heard, I will now proceed to relate:—

> Them that takes cakes
> Which the Parsee-man bakes
> Makes dreadful mistakes.

And there was a great deal more in that than you would think.

Because, five weeks later, there was a heat wave in the Red Sea, and everybody took off all the clothes they had. The Parsee took off his hat; but the Rhinoceros took off his skin and carried it over his shoulder as he came down to the beach to bathe. In those days it buttoned underneath with three buttons and looked like a waterproof. He said nothing whatever about the Parsee's cake, because he had eaten it all; and he never had any manners, then, since, or henceforward. He waddled straight into the water and blew bubbles through his nose, leaving his skin on the beach.

Presently the Parsee came by and found the skin, and he smiled one smile that ran all round his face two times. Then he danced three times round the skin and rubbed his hands. Then he went to his camp and filled his hat with cake-crumbs, for the Parsee never ate anything but cake, and never swept out his camp. He took that skin, and he rubbed that skin just as full of old, dry, stale, tickly cake-crumbs and some burned currants as ever it could *possibly* hold. Then he climbed to the top of his palm-tree and waited for the Rhinoceros to come out of the water and put it on.

And the Rhinoceros did. He buttoned it up with the three buttons, and it tickled like cake-crumbs in bed. Then he wanted to scratch, but that made it worse; and then he lay down on the sands and rolled and rolled and rolled, and every time he rolled the cake crumbs tickled him worse and worse and worse. Then he ran to the palm-tree and rubbed and rubbed and rubbed himself against it. He rubbed so much and so hard that he rubbed his skin into a great fold over his shoulders, and another fold underneath, where the buttons used to be (but he rubbed the buttons off), and he rubbed some more folds over his legs. And it spoiled his temper, but it didn't make the least difference to the cake-crumbs. They were inside his skin and they tickled. So he went home, very angry indeed and horribly scratchy; and from that day to this every rhinoceros has great folds in his skin and a very bad temper, all on account of the cake-crumbs inside.

But the Parsee came down from his palm-tree, wearing his hat, from which the rays of the sun were reflected in more-than-oriental splendour, packed up his cooking-stove, and went away in the direction of Orotavo, Amygdala, the Upland Meadows of Anantarivo, and the Marshes of Sonaput.

This Uninhabited Island
   Is off Cape Gardafui.
By the Beaches of Socotra
   And the Pink Arabian Sea:
But it's hot—too hot from Suez
   For the likes of you and me
      Ever to go
      In a P. and O.
And call on the Cake-Parsee!

1897

THE CAT THAT
WALKED BY HIMSELF

Hear and attend and listen; for this befell and behappened and became and was, O my Best Beloved, when the Tame animals were wild. The Dog was wild, and the Horse was wild, and the Cow was wild, and the Sheep was wild, and the Pig was wild—as wild as wild could be—and they walked in the Wet Wild Woods by their wild lones. But the wildest of all the wild animals was the Cat. He walked by himself, and all places were alike to him.

Of course the Man was wild too. He was dreadfully wild. He didn't even begin to be tame till he met the Woman, and she told him that she did not like living in his wild ways. She picked out a nice dry Cave, instead of a heap of wet leaves, to lie down in; and she lit a nice fire of wood at the back of the Cave; and she hung a dried wild-horse skin, tail-down, across the opening of the Cave; and she said, 'Wipe your feet, dear, when you come in, and now we'll keep house.'

That night, Best Beloved, they ate wild sheep roasted on the hot stones, and flavoured with wild garlic and wild pepper; and wild duck stuffed with wild rice and wild fenugreek and wild coriander; and marrow-bones of wild oxen; and wild cherries, and wild grenadillas. Then the Man went to sleep in front of the fire ever so happy; but the Woman sat up, combing her hair. She took the bone of the shoulder of mutton—the big fat blade-bone— and she looked at the wonderful marks on it, and she threw more wood on the fire, and she made a Magic. She made the First Singing Magic in the world.

Out in the Wet Wild Woods all the wild animals gathered together where they could see the light of the fire a long way off, and they wondered what it meant.

Then Wild Horse stamped with his wild foot and said, 'O my Friends and O my Enemies, why have the Man and the Woman made that great light in that great Cave, and what harm will it do us?'

Wild Dog lifted up his wild nose and smelled the smell of roast mutton, and said, 'I will go up and see and look, and say; for I think it is good. Cat, come with me.'

'Nenni!' said the Cat. 'I am the Cat who walks by himself, and all places are alike to me. I will not come.'

'Then we can never be friends again,' said Wild Dog, and he trotted off to the Cave. But when he had gone a little way the Cat said to himself, 'All places are alike to me. Why should I not go too and see and look and come away at my own liking.' So he slipped after Wild Dog softly, very softly, and hid himself where he could hear everything.

When Wild Dog reached the mouth of the Cave he lifted up the dried horse-skin with his nose and sniffed the beautiful smell of the roast mutton, and the Woman, looking at the blade-bone, heard him, and laughed, and said, 'Here comes the first. Wild Thing out of the Wild Woods, what do you want?'

Wild Dog said, 'O my Enemy and Wife of my Enemy, what is this that smells so good in the Wild Woods?'

Then the Woman picked up a roasted mutton-bone and threw it to Wild Dog, and said, 'Wild Thing out of the Wild Woods, taste and try.' Wild Dog gnawed the bone, and it was more delicious than anything he had ever tasted, and he said, 'O my Enemy and Wife of my Enemy, give me another.'

The Woman said, 'Wild Thing out of the Wild Woods, help my Man to hunt through the day and guard this Cave at night, and I will give you as many roast bones as you need.'

'Ah!' said the Cat, listening. 'This is a very wise Woman, but she is not so wise as I am.'

Wild Dog crawled into the Cave and laid his head on the Woman's lap, and said, 'O my Friend and Wife of my Friend, I will help your Man to hunt through the day, and at night I will guard your Cave.'

'Ah!' said the Cat, listening. 'That is a very foolish Dog.' And he went back through the Wet Wild Woods waving his wild tail, and walking by his wild lone. But he never told anybody.

When the Man waked up he said, 'What is Wild Dog doing here?' And the Woman said, 'His name is not Wild Dog any more, but the First Friend, because he will be our friend for always and always and always. Take him with you when you go hunting.'

Next night the Woman cut great green armfuls of fresh grass from the water-meadows, and dried it before the fire, so that it smelt like new-mown hay, and she sat at the mouth of the Cave and plaited a halter out of horse-hide, and she looked at the shoulder of mutton-bone—at the big broad blade-bone—and she made a Magic. She made the Second Singing Magic in the world.

Out in the Wild Woods all the wild animals wondered what had happened to Wild Dog, and at last Wild Horse stamped with his foot and said, 'I will go and see and say why Wild Dog has not returned. Cat, come with me.'

'Nenni!' said the Cat. 'I am the Cat who walks by himself, and all places are alike to me. I will not come.' But all the same he followed Wild Horse softly, very softly, and hid himself where he could hear everything.

When the Woman heard Wild Horse tripping and stumbling on his long mane, she laughed and said, 'Here comes the second. Wild Thing out of the Wild Woods, what do you want?'

Wild Horse said, 'O my Enemy and Wife of my Enemy, where is Wild Dog?'

The Woman laughed, and picked up the blade-bone and looked at it, and said, 'Wild Thing out of the Wild Woods, you did not come here for Wild Dog, but for the sake of this good grass.'

And Wild Horse, tripping and stumbling on his long mane, said, 'That is true; give it me to eat.'

The Woman said, 'Wild Thing out of the Wild Woods, bend your wild head and wear what I give you, and you shall eat the wonderful grass three times a day.'

'Ah,' said the Cat, listening, 'this is a clever Woman, but she is not so clever as I am.'

Wild Horse bent his wild head, and the Woman slipped the plaited hide halter over it, and Wild Horse breathed on the Woman's feet and said, 'O my Mistress, and Wife of my Master, I will be your servant for the sake of the wonderful grass.'

'Ah,' said the Cat, listening, 'that is a very foolish Horse.' And he went back through the Wet Wild Woods, waving his wild tail and walking by his wild lone. But he never told anybody.

When the Man and the Dog came back from hunting, the Man said, 'What is Wild Horse doing here?' And the Woman said, 'His name is not Wild Horse any more, but the First Servant, because he will carry us from place to place for always and always and always. Ride on his back when you go hunting.'

Next day, holding her wild head high that her wild horns should not catch in the wild trees, Wild Cow came up to the Cave, and the Cat followed, and hid himself just the same as before; and everything happened just the same as before; and the Cat said the same things as before, and when Wild Cow had promised to give her milk to the Woman every day in exchange for the wonderful grass, the Cat went back through the Wet Wild Woods waving his wild tail and walking by his wild lone, just the same as before. But he never told anybody. And when the Man and the Horse and the Dog came home from hunting and asked the same questions same as before, the Woman said, 'Her name is not Wild Cow any more, but the Giver of Good Food. She will give us the warm white milk for always and always and always, and I will take care of her while you and the First Friend and the First Servant go hunting.'

Next day the Cat waited to see if any other Wild thing would go up to the Cave, but no one moved in the Wet Wild Woods, so the Cat walked there by himself; and he saw the Woman milking the Cow, and he saw the light of the fire in the Cave, and he smelt the smell of the warm white milk.

Cat said, 'O my Enemy and Wife of my Enemy, where did Wild Cow go?'

The Woman laughed and said, 'Wild Thing out of the Wild Woods, go back to the Woods again, for I have braided up my hair, and I have put away the magic blade-bone, and we have no more need of either friends or servants in our Cave.'

Cat said, 'I am not a friend, and I am not a servant. I am the Cat who walks by himself, and I wish to come into your cave.'

Woman said, 'Then why did you not come with First Friend on the first night?'

Cat grew very angry and said, 'Has Wild Dog told tales of me?'

Then the Woman laughed and said, 'You are the Cat who walks by himself, and all places are alike to you. You are neither a friend nor a servant. You have said it yourself. Go away and walk by yourself in all places alike.'

Then Cat pretended to be sorry and said, 'Must I never come into the Cave? Must I never sit by the warm fire? Must I never drink the warm white milk? You are very wise and very beautiful. You should not be cruel even to a Cat.'

Woman said, 'I knew I was wise, but I did not know I was beautiful. So I will make a bargain with you. If ever I say one word in your praise you may come into the Cave.'

'And if you say two words in my praise?' said the Cat.

'I never shall,' said the Woman, 'but if I say two words in your praise, you may sit by the fire in the Cave.'

'And if you say three words?' said the Cat.

'I never shall,' said the Woman, 'but if I say three words in your praise, you may drink the warm white milk three times a day for always and always and always.'

Then the Cat arched his back and said, 'Now let the Curtain at the mouth of the Cave, and the Fire at the back of the Cave, and the Milk-pots that stand beside the Fire, remember what my Enemy and the Wife of my Enemy has said.' And he went away through the Wet Wild Woods waving his wild tail and walking by his wild lone.

That night when the Man and the Horse and the Dog came home from hunting, the Woman did not tell them of the bargain that she had made with the Cat, because she was afraid that they might not like it.

Cat went far and far away and hid himself in the Wet Wild Woods by his wild lone for a long time till the woman forgot all about him. Only the Bat—the little upside-down Bat—that hung inside the Cave, knew where Cat hid; and every evening Bat would fly to Cat with news of what was happening.

One evening Bat said, 'There is a Baby in the Cave. He is new and pink and fat and small, and the Woman is very fond of him.'

'Ah,' said the Cat, listening, 'but what is the Baby fond of?'

'He is fond of things that are soft and tickle,' said the Bat. 'He is fond of warm things to hold in his arms when he goes to sleep. He is fond of being played with. He is fond of all those things.'

'Ah,' said the Cat, listening, 'then my time has come.'

Next night Cat walked through the Wet Wild Woods and hid very near the Cave till morning-time, and Man and Dog and Horse went hunting. The Woman was busy cooking that morning, and the Baby cried and interrupted. So she carried him outside the Cave and gave him a handful of pebbles to play with. But still the Baby cried.

Then the Cat put out his paddy paw and patted the Baby on the cheek, and it cooed; and the Cat rubbed against its fat knees and tickled it under its fat chin with his tail. And the Baby laughed and the Woman heard him and smiled.

Then the Bat—the little upside-down Bat—that hung in the mouth of the Cave said, 'O my Hostess and Wife of my Host and Mother of my Host's Son, a Wild Thing from the Wild Woods is most beautifully playing with your Baby.'

'A blessing on that Wild Thing whoever he may be,' said the Woman, straightening her back, 'for I was a busy woman this morning and he has done me a service.'

The very minute and second, Best Beloved, the dried horse-skin Curtain that was stretched tail-down at the mouth of the Cave fell down—*woosh!*—because it remembered the bargain she had made with the Cat, and when the Woman went to pick it up—lo and behold!—the Cat was sitting quite comfy inside the Cave.

'O my Enemy and Wife of my Enemy and Mother of my Enemy,' said the Cat, 'it is I: for you have spoken a word in my praise, and now I can sit within the Cave for always and always and always. But still I am the Cat who walks by himself, and all places are alike to me.

The Woman was very angry, and shut her lips tight and took up her spinning-wheel and began to spin.

But the Baby cried because the Cat had gone away, and

the Woman could not hush it, for it struggled and kicked and grew black in the face.

'O my Enemy and Wife of my Enemy and Mother of my Enemy,' said the Cat, 'take a strand of the wire that you are spinning and tie it to your spinning-whorl and drag it along the floor, and I will show you a magic that shall make your Baby laugh as loudly as he is now crying.'

'I will do so,' said the Woman, 'because I am at my wits' end; but I will not thank you for it.'

She tied the thread to the little clay spindle-whorl and drew it across the floor, and the Cat ran after it and patted it with his paws and rolled head over heels, and tossed it backward over his shoulder and chased it between his hind-legs and pretended to lose it, and pounced down upon it again, till the Baby laughed as loudly as it had been crying, and scrambled after the Cat and frolicked all over the Cave till it grew tired and settled down to sleep with the Cat in its arms.

'Now,' said the Cat, 'I will sing the Baby a song that shall keep him asleep for an hour.' And he began to purr, loud and low, low and loud, till the Baby fell fast asleep. The Woman smiled as she looked down upon the two of them and said, 'That was wonderfully done. No question but you are very clever, O Cat.'

That very minute and second, Best Beloved, the smoke of the fire at the back of the Cave came down in clouds from the roof—*puff!*—because it remembered the bargain she had made with the Cat, and when it had cleared away—lo and behold!—the Cat was sitting quite comfy close to the fire.

'O my Enemy and Wife of my Enemy and Mother of my Enemy,' said the Cat, 'it is I, for you have spoken a second word in my praise, and now I can sit by the warm fire at the back of the Cave for always and always and always. But still I am the Cat who walks by himself, and all places are alike to me.'

Then the Woman was very very angry, and let down her hair and put more wood on the fire and brought out the broad blade-bone of the shoulder of mutton and began to make a Magic that should prevent her from saying a third word in praise of the Cat. It was not a Singing Magic, Best Beloved, it was a Still Magic; and by and by the Cave grew so still that a little wee-wee mouse crept out of a corner and ran across the floor.

'O my Enemy and Wife of my Enemy and Mother of my Enemy,' said the Cat, 'is that little mouse part of your magic?'

'Ouh! Chee! No indeed!' said the Woman, and she dropped the blade-bone and jumped upon the footstool in front of the fire and braided up her hair very quick for fear that the mouse should run up it.

'Ah,' said the Cat, watching, 'then the mouse will do me no harm if I eat it?'

'No,' said the Woman, braiding up her hair, 'eat it quickly and I will ever be grateful to you.'

Cat made one jump and caught the little mouse, and the Woman said, 'A hundred thanks. Even the First Friend is not quick enough to catch little mice as you have done. You must be very wise.'

That very moment and second, O Best Beloved, the Milk-pot that stood by the fire cracked in two pieces—*ffft*—because it remembered the bargain she had made with the Cat, and when the Woman jumped down from the footstool—lo and behold!—the Cat was lapping up the warm white milk that lay in one of the broken pieces.

'O my Enemy and Wife of my Enemy and Mother of my Enemy,' said the Cat, 'it is I; for you have spoken three words in my praise, and now I can drink the warm white milk three times a day for always and always and always. But *still* I am the Cat who walks by himself, and all places are alike to me.'

Then the Woman laughed and set the Cat a bowl of the warm white milk and said, 'O Cat, you are as clever as a man, but remember that your bargain was not made with the Man or the Dog, and I do not know what they will do when they come home.'

'What is that to me?' said the Cat. 'If I have my place in the Cave by the fire and my warm white milk three times a day I do not care what the Man or the Dog can do.'

That evening when the Man and the Dog came into the Cave, the Woman told them all the story of the bargain while the Cat sat by the fire and smiled. Then the Man said, 'Yes, but he has not made a bargain with *me* or with all proper Men after me.' Then he took off his two leather boots and he took up his little stone axe (that makes three) and he fetched a piece of wood and a hatchet (that is five altogether), and he set them out in a row and he said, 'Now we will make *our* bargain. If you do not catch mice when you are in the Cave for always and always and always, I will throw these five things at you whenever I see you, and so shall all proper Men do after me.'

'Ah,' said the Woman, listening, 'this is a very clever Cat, but he is not so clever as my Man.'

The Cat counted the five things (and they looked very knobby) and he said, 'I will catch mice when I am in the Cave for always and always and always; but *still* I am the Cat who walks by himself, and all places are alike to me.'

'Not when I am near,' said the Man. "If you had not said that last I would have put all these things away for always and always and always; but I am now going to throw my two boots and my little stone axe (that makes three) at you whenever I meet you. And so shall all proper Men do after me!'

Then the Dog said, 'Wait a minute. He has not made a bargain with *me* or with all proper Dogs after me.' And he showed his teeth and said, 'If you are not kind to the Baby while I am in the Cave for always and always and always, I will hunt you till I catch you, and when I catch you I will bite you. And so shall all proper Dogs do after me.'

'Ah,' said the Woman, listening, 'this is a very clever Cat, but he is not so clever as the Dog.'

Cat counted the Dog's teeth (and they looked very pointed) and he said, 'I will be kind to the Baby while I am in the Cave, as long as he does not pull my tail too hard, for always and always and always. But *still* I am the Cat that walks by himself, and all places are alike to me.'

'Not when I am near,' said the Dog. 'If you had not said that last I would have shut my mouth for always and always and always; but *now* I am going to hunt you up a tree whenever I meet you. And so shall all proper Dogs do after me.'

Then the Man threw his two boots and his little stone axe (that makes three) at the Cat, and the Cat ran out of the Cave and the Dog chased him up a tree; and from that day to this, Best Beloved, three proper Men out of five will always throw things at a Cat whenever they meet him, and all proper Dogs will chase him up a tree. But the Cat keeps his side of the bargain too. He will kill mice and he will be kind to Babies when he is in the house, just as long as they do not pull his tail too hard. But when he has done that, and between times, and when the moon gets up and night comes, he is the Cat that walks by himself, and all places are alike to him. Then he goes out to the Wet Wild Woods or up the Wet Wild Trees or on the Wet Wild Roofs, waving his wild tail and walking by his wild lone.

1902

Entertainments

~~~~~~~~~~~~~~~~~~~~~~~~~~~~~~~~

THE VILLAGE THAT
VOTED THE
EARTH WAS FLAT

Our drive till then had been quite a success. The other
men in the car were my friend Woodhouse, young Ollyett, a distant connection of his, and Pallant, the M.P.
Woodhouse's business was the treatment and cure of sick
journals. He knew by instinct the precise moment in a
newspaper's life when the impetus of past good management is exhausted and it fetches up on the dead-centre between slow and expensive collapse and the new start
which can be given by gold injections—and genius. He
was wisely ignorant of journalism; but when he stooped
on a carcase there was sure to be meat. He had that week
added a half-dead, halfpenny evening paper to his collection, which consisted of a prosperous London daily, one
provincial ditto, and a limp-bodied weekly of commercial
leanings. He had also, that very hour, planted me with a
large block of the evening paper's common shares, and
was explaining the whole art of editorship to Ollyett, a
young man three years from Oxford, with coir-matting-
coloured hair and a face harshly modelled by harsh experiences, who, I understood, was assisting in the new venture. Pallant, the long, wrinkled M.P., whose voice is more

like a crane's than a peacock's, took no shares, but gave us all advice.

'You'll find it rather a knacker's yard,' Woodhouse was saying. 'Yes, I know they call me The Knacker; but it will pay inside a year. All my papers do. I've only one motto: Back your luck and back your staff. It'll come out all right.'

Then the car stopped, and a policeman asked our names and addresses for exceeding the speed-limit. We pointed out that the road ran absolutely straight for half a mile ahead without even a side-lane. 'That's just what we depend on,' said the policeman unpleasantly.

'The usual swindle,' said Woodhouse under his breath. 'What's the name of this place?'

'Huckley,' said the policeman. 'H-u-c-k-l-e-y,' and wrote something in his note-book at which young Ollyett protested. A large red man on a grey horse who had been watching us from the other side of the hedge shouted an order we could not catch. The policeman laid his hand on the rim of the right driving-door (Woodhouse carries his spare tyres aft), and it closed on the button of the electric horn. The grey horse at once bolted, and we could hear the rider swearing all across the landscape.

'Damn it, man, you've got your silly fist on it! Take it off!' Woodhouse shouted.

'Ho!' said the constable, looking carefully at his fingers as though we had trapped them. 'That won't do you any good either,' and he wrote once more in his note-book before he allowed us to go.

This was Woodhouse's first brush with motor law, and since I expected no ill consequences to myself, I pointed out that it was very serious. I took the same view myself when in due time I found that I, too, was summonsed on charges ranging from the use of obscene language to endangering traffic.

Judgment was done in a little pale-yellow market-town with a small, Jubilee clock-tower and a large corn-exchange. Woodhouse drove us there in his car. Pallant, who had not been included in the summons, came with us as moral support. While we waited outside, the fat man on the grey horse rode up and entered into loud talk with his brother magistrates. He said to one of them—for I took the trouble to note it down—'It falls away from my lodge-gates, dead straight, three-quarters of a mile. I'd defy any one to resist it. We rooked seventy pounds out of 'em last month. No car can resist the temptation. You ought to have one your side the county, Mike. They simply can't resist it.'

'Whew!' said Woodhouse. 'We're in for trouble. Don't you say a word—or Ollyett either! I'll pay the fines and we'll get it over as soon as possible. Where's Pallant?'

'At the back of the court somewhere,' said Ollyett. 'I saw him slip in just now.'

The fat man then took his seat on the Bench, of which he was chairman, and I gathered from a bystander that his name was Sir Thomas Ingell, Bart., M.P., of Ingell Park, Huckley. He began with an allocution pitched in a tone that would have justified revolt throughout empires. Evidence, when the crowded little court did not drown it with applause, was given in the pauses of the address. They were all very proud of their Sir Thomas, and looked from him to us, wondering why we did not applaud too.

Taking its time from the chairman, the Bench rollicked with us for seventeen minutes. Sir Thomas explained that he was sick and tired of processions of cads of our type, who would be better employed breaking stones on the road than in frightening horses worth more than themselves or their ancestors. This was after it had been proved that Woodhouse's man had turned on the horn purposely to annoy Sir Thomas, who 'happened to be riding by'! There were other remarks too—primitive enough,—but it was the unspeakable brutality of the tone, even more than the quality of the justice, or the laughter of the audience, that stung our souls out of all reason. When we were dismissed—to the tune of twenty-three pounds, twelve shillings and sixpence—we waited for Pallant to join us, while we listened to the next case—one of driving without a licence. Ollyett, with an eye to his evening paper, had already taken very full notes of our own, but we did not wish to seem prejudiced.

'It's all right,' said the reporter of the local paper soothingly. 'We never report Sir Thomas *in extenso*. Only the fines and charges.'

'Oh, thank you,' Ollyett replied, and I heard him ask who every one in court might be. The local reporter was very communicative.

The new victim, a large, flaxen-haired man in somewhat striking clothes, to which Sir Thomas, now thoroughly warmed, drew public attention, said that he had left his licence at home. Sir Thomas asked him if he expected the police to go to his home address at Jerusalem to find it for him; and the court roared. Nor did Sir Thomas approve of the man's name, but insisted on calling him 'Mr. Masquerader,' and every time he did so, all his people shouted. Evidently this was their established *auto-da-fé*.

'He didn't summons me—because I'm in the House, I suppose. I think I shall have to ask a Question,' said Pallant, reappearing at the close of the case.

'I think *I* shall have to give it a little publicity too,' said Woodhouse. 'We can't have this kind of thing going on, you know.' His face was set and quite white. Pallant's, on the other hand, was black, and I know that my very stomach had turned with rage. Ollyett was dumb.

'Well, let's have lunch,' Woodhouse said at last. 'Then we can get away before the show breaks up.'

We drew Ollyett from the arms of the local reporter, crossed the Market Square to the Red Lion and found Sir Thomas's 'Mr. Masquerader' just sitting down to beer, beef and pickles.

'Ah!' said he, in a large voice. 'Companions in misfortune. Won't you gentlemen join me?'

'Delighted,' said Woodhouse. 'What did you get?'

'I haven't decided. It might make a good turn, but—the public aren't educated up to it yet. It's beyond 'em. If it wasn't, that red dub on the Bench would be worth fifty a week.'

'Where?' said Woodhouse. The man looked at him with unaffected surprise.

'At any one of My places,' he replied. 'But perhaps you live here?'

'Good heavens!' cried young Ollyett suddenly. 'You *are* Masquerier, then? I thought you were!'

'Bat Masquerier.' He let the words fall with the weight of an international ultimatum. 'Yes, that's all I am. But you have the advantage of me, gentlemen.'

For the moment, while we were introducing ourselves, I was puzzled. Then I recalled prismatic music-hall posters—of enormous acreage—that had been the unnoticed background of my visits to London for years past. Posters of men and women, singers, jongleurs, impersonators and audacities of every draped and undraped brand, all moved on and off in London and the Provinces by Bat Masquerier—with the long wedge-tailed flourish following the final 'r.'

'*I* knew you at once,' said Pallant, the trained M.P., and I promptly backed the lie. Woodhouse mumbled excuses. Bat Masquerier was not moved for or against us any more than the frontage of one of his own palaces.

'I always tell My people there's a limit to the size of the lettering,' he said. 'Overdo that and the ret'na doesn't take it in. Advertisin' is the most delicate of all the sciences.'

'There's one man in the world who is going to get a little of it if I live for the next twenty-four hours,' said Woodhouse, and explained how this would come about.

Masquerier stared at him lengthily with gun-metal-blue eyes.

'You mean it?' he drawled; the voice was as magnetic as the look.

'*I* do,' said Ollyett. 'That business of the horn alone ought to have him off the Bench in three months.' Masquerier looked at him even longer than he had looked at Woodhouse.

'He told *me*,' he said suddenly, 'that my home address was Jerusalem. You heard that?'

'But it was the tone—the tone,' Ollyett cried.

'You noticed that, too, did you?' said Masquerier. 'That's the artistic temperament. You can do a lot with it. And I'm Bat Masquerier,' he went on. He dropped his chin in his fists and scowled straight in front of him. . . . 'I made the Silhouettes—I made the Trefoil and the Jocunda. I made 'Dal Benzaguen.' Here Ollyett sat straight up, for in common with the youth of that year he worshipped Miss Vidal Benzaguen of the Trefoil immensely and unreservedly. ' "*Is* that a dressing-gown or an ulster you're supposed to be wearing?" You heard *that?* . . . "And I suppose you hadn't time to brush your hair either?" You heard *that?* . . . Now, you hear *me!*' His voice filled the coffee-room, then dropped to a whisper as dreadful as a surgeon's before an operation. He spoke for several minutes. Pallant muttered 'Hear! hear!' I saw Ollyett's eye flash—it was to Ollyett that Masquerier addressed himself chiefly,—and Woodhouse leaned forward with joined hands.

'Are you *with* me?' he went on, gathering us all up in one sweep of the arm. 'When I begin a thing I see it through, gentlemen. What Bat can't break, breaks him! But I haven't struck that thing yet. This is no one-turn turn-it-down show. This is business to the dead finish. Are you with me, gentlemen? Good! Now, we'll pool our assets. One London morning, and one provincial daily, didn't you say? One weekly commercial ditto and one M.P.'

'Not much use, I'm afraid,' Pallant smirked.

'But privileged. *But* privileged,' he returned. 'And we have also my little team—London, Blackburn, Liverpool,

Leeds—I'll tell you about Manchester later—and Me! Bat Masquerier.' He breathed the name reverently into his tankard. 'Gentlemen, when our combination has finished with Sir Thomas Ingell, Bart., M.P., and everything else that is his, Sodom and Gomorrah will be a winsome bit of Merrie England beside 'em. I must go back to town now, but I trust you gentlemen will give me the pleasure of your company at dinner to-night at the Chop Suey—the Red Amber Room—and we'll block out the scenario.' He laid his hand on young Ollyett's shoulder and added: 'It's your brains I want.' Then he left, in a good deal of astrachan collar and nickel-plated limousine, and the place felt less crowded.

We ordered our car a few minutes later. As Woodhouse, Ollyett and I were getting in, Sir Thomas Ingell, Bart., M.P., came out of the Hall of Justice across the square and mounted his horse. I have sometimes thought that if he had gone in silence he might even then have been saved, but as he settled himself in the saddle he caught sight of us and must needs shout: 'Not off yet? You'd better get away and you'd better be careful.' At that moment Pallant, who had been buying picture-postcards, came out of the inn, took Sir Thomas's eye and very leisurely entered the car. It seemed to me that for one instant there was a shade of uneasiness on the baronet's grey-whiskered face.

'I hope,' said Woodhouse after several miles, 'I hope he's a widower.'

'Yes,' said Pallant. 'For his poor, dear wife's sake I hope that, very much indeed. I suppose he didn't see me in Court. Oh, here's the parish history of Huckley written by the Rector and here's your share of the picture-postcards. Are we all dining with this Mr. Masquerier to-night?'

'Yes!' said we all.

If Woodhouse knew nothing of journalism, young Ollyett, who had graduated in a hard school, knew a good deal. Our halfpenny evening paper, which we will call *The Bun* to distinguish her from her prosperous morning sister, *The Cake*, was not only diseased but corrupt. We found this out when a man brought us the prospectus of a new oil-field and demanded sub-leaders on its prosperity. Ollyett talked pure Brasenose to him for three minutes. Otherwise he spoke and wrote trade-English —a toothsome amalgam of Americanisms and epigrams. But though the slang changes the game never alters, and Ollyett and I and, in the end, some others enjoyed it immensely. It was weeks ere we could see the wood for the trees, but so soon as the staff realised that they had proprietors who backed them right or wrong, and specially when they were wrong (which is the sole secret of journalism), and that their fate did not hang on any passing owner's passing mood, they did miracles.

But we did not neglect Huckley. As Ollyett said, our first care was to create an 'arresting atmosphere' round it. He used to visit the village of week-ends, on a motor-bicycle with a side-car; for which reason I left the actual place alone and dealt with it in the abstract. Yet it was I who drew first blood. Two inhabitants of Huckley wrote to contradict a small, quite solid paragraph in *The Bun* that a hoopoe had been seen at Huckley and had, 'of course, been shot by the local sportsmen.' There was some heat in their letters, both of which we published. Our version of how the hoopoe got his crest from King Solomon was, I grieve to say, so inaccurate that the Rector himself—no sportsman as he pointed out, but a lover of accuracy—wrote to us to correct it. We gave his letter good space and thanked him.

'This priest is going to be useful,' said Ollyett. 'He has the impartial mind. I shall vitalise him.'

Forthwith he created M. L. Sigden, a recluse of refined tastes who in *The Bun* demanded to know whether this Huckley-of-the-Hoopoe was the Hugly of his boyhood and whether, by any chance, the fell change of name had been wrought by collusion between a local magnate and the railway, in the mistaken interests of spurious refinement. 'For I knew it and loved it with the maidens of my day—*eheu ab angulo!*—as Hugly,' wrote M. L. Sigden from Oxford.

Though other papers scoffed, *The Bun* was gravely sympathetic. Several people wrote to deny that Huckley had been changed at birth. Only the Rector—no philosopher as he pointed out, but a lover of accuracy—had his doubts, which he laid publicly before Mr. M. L. Sigden, who suggested, through *The Bun*, that the little place might have begun life in Anglo-Saxon days as 'Hogslea' or among the Normans as 'Argilé,' on account of its much clay. The Rector had his own ideas too (he said it was mostly gravel), and M. L. Sigden had a fund of reminiscences. Oddly enough—which is seldom the case with free reading-matter—our subscribers rather relished the correspondence, and contemporaries quoted freely.

'The secret of power,' said Ollyett, 'is not the big stick. It's the liftable stick.' (This means the 'arresting' quotation of six or seven lines.) 'Did you see the *Spec.* had a middle on 'Rural Tenacities' last week? That was all Huckley. I'm doing a 'Mobiquity' on Huckley next week.'

Our 'Mobiquities' were Friday evening accounts of easy motor-bike-*cum*-side-car trips round London, illustrated (we could never get that machine to work properly) by smudgy maps. Ollyett wrote the stuff with a fervour and a delicacy which I always ascribed to the side-car. His account of Epping Forest, for instance, was simply young love with its soul at its lips. But his Huckley "Mobiquity" would have sickened a soap-boiler. It chemically combined loathsome familiarity, leering suggestion, slimy piety and rancid 'social service' in one fuming compost that fairly lifted me off my feet.

'Yes,' said he, after compliments. 'It's the most vital, arresting and dynamic bit of tump I've done up to date. *Non nobis gloria!* I met Sir Thomas Ingell in his own park. He talked to me again. He inspired most of it.'

'Which? The "glutinous native drawl," or "the neglected adenoids of the village children"?' I demanded.

'Oh, no! That's only to bring in the panel doctor. It's the last flight we—I'm proudest of.'

This dealt with 'the crepuscular penumbra spreading her dim limbs over the boskage'; with 'jolly rabbits'; with a herd of 'gravid polled Angus'; and with the 'arresting, gipsy-like face of their swart, scholarly owner—as well known at the Royal Agricultural Shows as that of our late King-Emperor.'

' "Swart" is good and so's "gravid," ' said I, 'but the panel doctor will be annoyed about the adenoids.'

'Not half as much as Sir Thomas will about his face,' said Ollyett. 'And if you only knew what I've left out!'

He was right. The panel doctor spent his week-end (this is the advantage of Friday articles) in overwhelming us with a professional counterblast of no interest whatever to our subscribers. We told him so, and he, then and there, battered his way with it into the *Lancet,* where they are keen on glands, and forgot us altogether. But Sir Thomas Ingell was of sterner stuff. He must have spent a happy week-end too. The letter which we received from him on Monday proved him to be a kinless loon of upright life, for no woman, however remotely interested in a man, would have let it pass the home wastepaper-basket. He objected to our references to his own herd, to his own labours in his own village, which he said was a Model Village, and to our infernal insolence; but he objected most to our invoice of his features. We wrote him courteously to ask whether the letter was meant for publication. He, remembering, I presume, the Duke of Wellington, wrote back, 'Publish and be damned.'

'Oh! This is too easy,' Ollyett said as he began heading the letter.

'Stop a minute,' I said. 'The game is getting a little beyond us. To-night's the Bat dinner.' (I may have forgotten to tell you that our dinner with Bat Masquerier in the Red Amber Room of the Chop Suey had come to be a weekly affair.) 'Hold it over till they've all seen it.'

'Perhaps you're right,' he said. 'You might waste it.'

At dinner, then, Sir Thomas's letter was handed round. Bat seemed to be thinking of other matters, but Pallant was very interested.

'I've got an idea,' he said presently. 'Could you put something into *The Bun* to-morrow about foot-and-mouth disease in that fellow's herd?'

'Oh, plague if you like,' Ollyett replied. 'They're only five measly Shorthorns. I saw one lying down in the park. She'll serve as a substratum of fact.'

'Then, do that; and hold the letter over meanwhile. I think *I* come in here,' said Pallant.

'Why?' said I.

'Because there's something coming up in the House about foot-and-mouth, and because he wrote me a letter after that little affair when he fined you. 'Took ten days to think it over. Here you are,' said Pallant. 'House of Commons paper, you see.'

We read:

DEAR PALLANT—Although in the past our paths have not lain much together, I am sure you will agree with me that on the floor of the House all members are on a footing of equality. I make bold, therefore, to approach you in a matter which I think capable of a very different interpretation from that which perhaps was put upon it by your friends. Will you let them know that that was the case and that I was in no way swayed by animus in the exercise of my magisterial duties, which as you, as a brother magistrate, can imagine are frequently very distasteful to—Yours very sincerely,

T. INGELL.

P.S.—I have seen to it that the motor vigilance to which your friends took exception has been considerably relaxed in my district.

'What did you answer?' said Ollyett, when all our opinions had been expressed.

'I told him I couldn't do anything in the matter. And I couldn't—then. But you'll remember to put in that foot-and-mouth paragraph. I want something to work upon.'

'It seems to me *The Bun* has done all the work up to date,' I suggested. 'When does *The Cake* come in?'

'*The Cake,*' said Woodhouse, and I remembered afterwards that he spoke like a Cabinet Minister on the eve of a Budget, 'reserves to itself the fullest right to deal with situations as they arise.'

'Ye-eh!' Bat Masquerier shook himself out of his thoughts. ' "Situations as they arise." I ain't idle either. But there's no use fishing till the swim's baited. You'—he turned to Ollyett—'manufacture very good ground-bait. . . . I always tell My people—What the deuce is that?'

There was a burst of song from another private dining-room across the landing. 'It ees some ladies from the Tre-foil,' the waiter began.

'Oh, I know that. What are they singing, though?'

He rose and went out, to be greeted by shouts of applause from that merry company. Then there was silence, such as one hears in the form-room after a master's entry. Then a voice that we loved began again: 'Here we go gathering nuts in May—nuts in May—nuts in May!'

'It's only 'Dal—and some nuts,' he explained when he returned. 'She says she's coming in to dessert.' He sat down, humming the old tune to himself, and till Miss Vidal Benzaguen entered, he held us speechless with tales of the artistic temperament.

We obeyed Pallant to the extent of slipping into *The*

Bun a wary paragraph about cows lying down and dripping at the mouth, which might be read either as an unkind libel or, in the hands of a capable lawyer, as a piece of
faithful nature-study.

'And besides,' said Ollyett, 'we allude to "gravid polled
Angus." I am advised that no action can lie in respect of
virgin Shorthorns. Pallant wants us to come to the House
to-night. He's got us places for the Strangers' Gallery. I'm
beginning to like Pallant.'

'Masquerier seems to like you,' I said.

'Yes, but I'm afraid of him,' Ollyett answered with perfect sincerity. 'I am. He's the Absolutely Amoral Soul.
I've never met one yet.'

We went to the House together. It happened to be an
Irish afternoon, and as soon as I had got the cries and the
faces a little sorted out, I gathered there were grievances in
the air, but how many of them was beyond me.

'It's all right,' said Ollyett of the trained ear. 'They've
shut their ports against—oh yes—export of Irish cattle!
Foot-and-mouth disease at Ballyhellion. *I* see Pallant's
idea!'

The House was certainly all mouth for the moment,
but, as I could feel, quite in earnest. A Minister with a
piece of typewritten paper seemed to be fending off volleys of insults. He reminded me somehow of a nervous
huntsman breaking up a fox in the face of rabid hounds.

'It's question-time. They're asking questions,' said
Ollyett. 'Look! Pallant's up.'

There was no mistaking it. His voice, which his enemies
said was his one parliamentary asset, silenced the hubbub
as toothache silences mere singing in the ears. He said:

'Arising out of that, may I ask if any special consideration has recently been shown in regard to any suspected
outbreak of this disease on *this* side of the Channel?'

He raised his hand; it held a noon edition of *The Bun.*
We had thought it best to drop the paragraph out of the

later ones. He would have continued, but something in a grey frock-coat roared and bounded on a bench opposite, and waved another *Bun*. It was Sir Thomas Ingell.

'As the owner of the herd so dastardly implicated—' His voice was drowned in shouts of 'Order!'—the Irish leading.

'What's wrong?' I asked Ollyett. 'He's got his hat on his head, hasn't he?'

'Yes, but his wrath should have been put as a question.'

'Arising out of that, Mr. Speaker, Sirrr!' Sir Thomas bellowed through a lull, 'are you aware that—that all this is a conspiracy—part of a dastardly conspiracy to make Huckley ridiculous—to make *us* ridiculous? Part of a deep-laid plot to make *me* ridiculous, Mr. Speaker, Sir!'

The man's face showed almost black against his white whiskers, and he struck out swimmingly with his arms. His vehemence puzzled and held the House for an instant, and the Speaker took advantage of it to lift his pack from Ireland to a new scent. He addressed Sir Thomas Ingell in tones of measured rebuke, meant also, I imagine, for the whole House, which lowered its hackles at the word. Then Pallant, shocked and pained: 'I can only express my profound surprise that in response to my simple question the honourable member should have thought fit to indulge in a personal attack. If I have in any way offended—'

Again the Speaker intervened, for it appeared that he regulated these matters.

He, too, expressed surprise, and Sir Thomas sat back in a hush of reprobation that seemed to have the chill of the centuries behind it. The Empire's work was resumed.

'Beautiful!' said I, and I felt hot and cold up my back.

'And now we'll publish his letter,' said Ollyett.

We did—on the heels of his carefully reported outburst. We made no comment. With that rare instinct for grasping the heart of a situation which is the mark of the Anglo-Saxon, all our contemporaries and, I should say, two-thirds of our correspondents demanded how such a person could be made more ridiculous than he had already proved himself to be. But beyond spelling his name 'Injle,' we alone refused to hit a man when he was down.

'There's no need,' said Ollyett. 'The whole press is on the huckle from end to end.'

Even Woodhouse was a little astonished at the ease with which it had come about, and said as much.

'Rot!' said Ollyett. 'We haven't really begun. Huckley isn't news yet.'

'What do you mean?' said Woodhouse, who had grown to have great respect for his young but by no means distant connection.

'Mean? By the grace of God, Master Ridley, I mean to have it so that when Huckley turns over in its sleep, Reuters and the Press Association jump out of bed to cable.' Then he went off at score about certain restorations in Huckley Church which, he said—and he seemed to spend his every weekend there—had been perpetrated by the Rector's predecessor, who had abolished a 'leper-window' or a 'squinch-hole' (whatever these may be) to institute a lavatory in the vestry. It did not strike me as stuff for which Reuters or the Press Association would lose much sleep, and I left him declaiming to Woodhouse about a fourteenth-century font which, he said, he had unearthed in the sexton's tool-shed.

My methods were more on the lines of peaceful penetration. An odd copy, in *The Bun's* rag-and-bone library, of Hone's *Every-Day Book* had revealed to me the existence of a village dance founded, like all village dances, on Druidical mysteries connected with the Solar Solstice (which is always unchallengeable) and Midsummer Morning, which is dewy and refreshing to the London eye. For this I take no credit—Hone being a mine any one can work—but that I rechristened that dance, after I had revised it, 'The Gubby' is my title to immortal fame. It was still to be witnessed, I wrote, 'in all its poignant purity at Huckley, that last home of significant mediæval survivals'; and I fell so in love with my creation that I kept it back for days, enamelling and burnishing.

'You'd better put it in,' said Ollyett at last. 'It's time we asserted ourselves again. The other fellows are beginning to poach. You saw that thing in the *Pinnacle* about Sir Thomas's Model Village? He must have got one of their chaps down to do it.'

' 'Nothing like the wounds of a friend,' I said. 'That account of the non-alcoholic pub alone was—'

'I liked the bit best about the white-tiled laundry and the Fallen Virgins who wash Sir Thomas's dress shirts. Our side couldn't come within a mile of that, you know. We haven't the proper flair for sexual slobber.'

'That's what I'm always saying,' I retorted. 'Leave 'em alone. The other fellows are doing our work for us now. Besides I want to touch up my "Gubby Dance" a little more.'

'No. You'll spoil it. Let's shove it in to-day. For one thing it's Literature. I don't go in for compliments as you know, but, etc., etc.'

I had a healthy suspicion of young Ollyett in every aspect, but though I knew that I should have to pay for it, I fell to his flattery, and my priceless article on the 'Gubby Dance' appeared. Next Saturday he asked me to bring out *The Bun* in his absence, which I naturally assumed would be connected with the little maroon side-car. I was wrong.

On the following Monday I glanced at *The Cake* at breakfast-time to make sure, as usual, of her inferiority to my beloved but unremunerative *Bun*. I opened on a heading: 'The Village that Voted the Earth was Flat.' I read . . . I read that the Geoplanarian Society—a society devoted to the proposition that the earth is flat—had held its Annual Banquet and Exercises at Huckley on Saturday, when after convincing addresses, amid scenes of the greatest enthusiasm, Huckley village had decided by an unanimous vote of 438 that the earth was flat. I do not remember that I breathed again till I had finished the two columns of description that followed. Only one man could have written them. They were flawless—crisp, nervous, austere yet human, poignant, vital, arresting—most distinctly arresting—dynamic enough to shift a city—and quotable by whole sticks at a time. And there was a leader, a grave and poised leader, which tore me in two with mirth, until I remembered that I had been left out—infamously and unjustifiably dropped. I went to Ollyett's rooms. He was breakfasting and, to do him justice, looked conscience-stricken.

'It wasn't my fault,' he began. 'It was Bat Masquerier. I swear *I* would have asked you to come if—'

'Never mind that,' I said. 'It's the best bit of work you've ever done or will do. Did any of it happen?'

'Happen? Heavens! D'you think even *I* could have invented it?'

'Is it exclusive to *The Cake?*' I cried.

'It cost Bat Masquerier two thousand,' Ollyett replied. 'D'you think he'd let any one else in on that? But I give you my sacred word I knew nothing about it till he asked me to come down and cover it. He had Huckley posted in three colours, 'The Geoplanarians' Annual Banquet and Exercises.' Yes, he invented 'Geoplanarians.' He wanted Huckley to think it meant aeroplanes. Yes, I know that there is a real Society that thinks the world's flat—they ought to be grateful for the lift—but Bat made his own. He did! He created the whole show, I tell you. He swept out half his Halls for the job. Think of that—on a Saturday! They—we went down in motor char-à-bancs—three of 'em—one pink, one primrose, and one forget-me-not blue—twenty people in each one and 'The Earth *is* Flat' on each side and across the back. I went with Teddy Rickets and Lafone from the Trefoil, and both the Silhouette Sisters, and—wait a minute!—the Crossleigh Trio. You know the Every-Day Dramas Trio at the Jocunda—Ada Crossleigh, 'Bunt' Crossleigh, and little Victorine? Them. And there was Hoke Ramsden, the lightning-change chap in *Morgiana and Drexel*—and there was Billy Turpeen. Yes, you know him! The North London Star. 'I'm the Referee that got himself disliked at Blackheath.' *That* chap! And there was Mackaye—that one-eyed Scotch fellow that all Glasgow is crazy about. Talk of subordinating yourself for Art's sake! Mackaye was the earnest inquirer who got converted at the end of the meeting. And there was quite a lot of girls I didn't know, and—oh, yes—there was 'Dal! 'Dal Benzaguen herself! We sat together, going and coming. She's all the darling there ever was. She sent you her love, and she told me to tell you that she won't forget about Nellie Farren. She says you've given her an ideal to work for. She? Oh, she was the Lady Secretary to the Geoplanarians, of course. I forget who were in the other brakes—provincial stars mostly—but they played up gorgeously. The art of the music-hall's changed since your day. They didn't overdo it a bit. You see, people who believe the earth is flat don't dress quite like other people. You may have noticed that I hinted at that in my account. It's a rather flat-fronted Ionic style—neo-Victorian, except for the bustles, 'Dal told me,—but 'Dal looked heavenly in it! So did little Victorine. And there was a girl in the blue brake—she's a provincial—but she's coming to town this winter and she'll knock 'em—Winnie Deans. Remember that! She told Huckley how she had suffered for the Cause as a governess in a rich family where they believed that the world is round, and how she threw up her job sooner than teach immoral geography. That was at the overflow meeting outside the Baptist chapel. She knocked 'em to sawdust! We must look out for Winnie. . . . But Lafone! Lafone was beyond everything. Impact, personality—conviction—the whole bag o' tricks! He sweated conviction. Gad, he convinced *me* while he was speaking! (Him? He was President of the Geoplanarians, of course. Haven't you read my account?) It *is* an infernally plausible theory. After all, no one has actually proved the earth is round, have they?'

'Never mind the earth. What about Huckley?'

'Oh, Huckley got tight. That's the worst of these model villages if you let 'em smell fire-water. There's one alcoholic pub in the place that Sir Thomas can't get rid of. Bat made it his base. He sent down the banquet in two motor lorries—dinner for five hundred and drinks for ten thousand. Huckley voted all right. Don't you make any mistake about that. No vote, no dinner. A unanimous vote—exactly as I've said. At least, the Rector and the Doctor were the only dissentients. We didn't count them. Oh yes, Sir Thomas was there. He came and grinned at us through his park gates. He'll grin worse to-day. There's an aniline dye that you rub through a stencil-plate that eats about a foot into any stone and wears good to the last. Bat had both the lodge-gates stencilled "The Earth *is* flat!" and all the barns and walls they could get at. . . . Oh Lord, but Huckley was drunk! We had to fill 'em up to make 'em forgive us for not being aeroplanes. Unthankful yokels! D'you realise that Emperors couldn't have commanded the talent Bat decanted on 'em? Why, 'Dal alone was. . . . And by eight o'clock not even a bit of paper left! The whole show packed up and gone, and Huckley hooraying for the earth being flat.'

'Very good,' I began. 'I am, as you know, a one-third proprietor of *The Bun*.'

'I didn't forget that,' Ollyett interrupted. 'That was uppermost in my mind all the time. I've got a special account for *The Bun* to-day—it's an idyll—and just to show how I thought of you, I told 'Dal, coming home, about your Gubby Dance, and she told Winnie. Winnie came back in our char-à-banc. After a bit we had to get out and dance it in a field. It's quite a dance the way we did it—and Lafone invented a sort of gorilla lock-step procession at the end. Bat had sent down a film-chap on the chance of getting something. He was the son of a clergyman—a most dynamic personality. He said there isn't anything for the cinema in meetings *qua* meetings—they lack action. Films are a branch of art by themselves. But he went wild over the Gubby. He said it was like Peter's vision at Joppa. He took about a million feet of it. Then I photoed it exclusive for *The Bun*. I've sent 'em in already, only remember we must eliminate Winnie's left leg in the first figure. It's too arresting. . . . And there you are! But I tell you I'm afraid of Bat. That man's the Personal Devil. He did it all. He didn't even come down himself. He said he'd distract his people.'

'Why didn't he ask me to come?' I persisted.

'Because he said you'd distract me. He said he wanted my brains on ice. He got 'em. I believe it's the best thing I've ever done.' He reached for *The Cake* and re-read it luxuriously. 'Yes, out and away the best—supremely quotable,' he concluded, and—after another survey—'By God, what a genius I was yesterday!'

I would have been angry, but I had not the time. That morning, Press agencies grovelled to me in *The Bun* office for leave to use certain photos, which, they understood, I controlled, of a certain village dance. When I had sent the fifth man away on the edge of tears, my self-respect came back a little. Then there was *The Bun's* poster to get out. Art being elimination, I fined it down to two words (one too many, as it proved—'The Gubby!' in red, at which our manager protested; but by five o'clock he told me that I was *the* Napoleon of Fleet Street. Ollyett's account in *The Bun* of the Geoplanarians' Exercises and Love Feast lacked the supreme shock of his version in *The Cake* but it bruised more; while the photos of 'The Gubby' (which, with Winnie's left leg, was why I had set the doubtful press to work so early) were beyond praise and, next day, beyond price. But even then I did not understand.

A week later, I think it was, Bat Masquerier telephoned to me to come to the Trefoil.

'It's your turn now,' he said. 'I'm not asking Ollyett. Come to the stage-box.'

I went, and, as Bat's guest, was received as Royalty is not. We sat well back and looked out on the packed thousands. It was *Morgiana and Drexel*, that fluid and electric review which Bat—though he gave Lafone the credit—really created.

'Ye-es,' said Bat dreamily, after Morgiana had given 'the nasty jar' to the Forty Thieves in their forty oil 'combinations.' 'As you say, I've got 'em and I can hold 'em. What a man does doesn't matter much; and how he does it don't matter either. It's the *when*—the psychological moment. 'Press can't make up for it; money can't; brains can't. A lot's luck, but all the rest is genius. I'm not speaking about My people now. I'm talking of Myself.'

Then 'Dal—she was the only one who dared—knocked at the door and stood behind us all alive and panting as Morgiana. Lafone was carrying the police-court scene, and the house was ripped up crossways with laughter.

'Ah! Tell a fellow now,' she asked me for the twentieth time, 'did you love Nellie Farren when you were young?'

'Did we love her?' I answered. ' "If the earth and the sky and the sea"—There were three million of us, 'Dal, and we worshipped her.'

'How did she get it across?' 'Dal went on.

'She was Nellie. The houses used to coo over her when she came on.'

'I've had a good deal, but I've never been cooed over yet,' said 'Dal wistfully.

'It isn't the how, it's the when,' Bat repeated. 'Ah!'

He leaned forward as the house began to rock and peal full-throatedly. 'Dal fled. A sinuous and silent procession was filing into the police-court to a scarcely audible accompaniment. It was dressed—but the world and all its picture-palaces know how it was dressed. It danced and it danced, and it danced the dance which bit all humanity in the leg for half a year, and it wound up with the lock-step finale that mowed the house down in swathes, sobbing and aching. Somebody in the gallery moaned. 'Oh Gord, the Gubby!' and we heard the word run like a shudder, for they had not a full breath left among them. Then 'Dal came on, an electric star in her dark hair, the diamonds flashing in her three-inch heels—a vision that made no sign for thirty counted seconds while the police-court scene dissolved behind her into Morgiana's Manicure Palace, and they recovered themselves. The star on her forehead went out, and a soft light bathed her as she took—slowly, slowly to the croon of adoring strings—the eighteen paces forward. We saw her first as a queen alone; next as a queen for the first time conscious of her subjects, and at the end, when her hands fluttered, as a woman delighted, awed not a little, but transfigured and illuminated with sheer, compelling affection and goodwill. I caught the broken mutter of welcome—the coo which is more than tornadoes of applause. It died and rose and died again lovingly.

'She's got it across,' Bat whispered. 'I've never seen her like this. I told her to light up the star, but I was wrong, and she knew it. She's an artist.'

' 'Dal, you darling!' some one spoke, not loudly but it carried through the house.

'Thank *you!*' 'Dal answered, and in that broken tone one heard the last fetter riveted. 'Good evening, boys! I've just come from—now—where the dooce was it I have come from?' She turned to the impassive files of the Gubby dancers, and went on: 'Ah, so good of you to remind me, you dear, bun-faced things. I've just come from the village—The Village that Voted the Earth was Flat.'

She swept into that song with the full orchestra. It devastated the habitable earth for the next six months. Imagine, then, what its rage and pulse must have been at the incandescent hour of its birth! She only gave the chorus once. At the end of the second verse, 'Are you *with* me, boys?' she cried, and the house tore it clean away from her—'*Earth* was flat—*Earth* was flat. Flat as my hat—

Flatter than that'—drowning all but the bassoons and double-basses that marked the word.

'Wonderful,' I said to Bat. 'And it's only "Nuts in May" with variations.'

'Yes—but *I* did the variations,' he replied.

At the last verse she gestured to Carlini the conductor, who threw her up his baton. She caught it with a boy's ease. 'Are you *with* me?' she cried once more, and—the maddened house behind her—abolished all the instruments except the guttural belch of the double-basses on '*Earth*'—'The Village that voted the *Earth* was flat— *Earth* was flat!' It was delirium. Then she picked up the Gubby dancers and led them in a clattering improvised lock-step thrice round the stage till her last kick sent her diamond-hilted shoe catherine-wheeling to the electrolier. I saw the forest of hands raised to catch it, heard the roaring and stamping pass through hurricanes to full typhoon; heard the song, pinned down by the faithful double-basses as the bull-dog pins down the bellowing bull, overbear even those; till at last the curtain fell and Bat took me round to her dressing-room where she lay spent after her seventh call. Still the song, through all those white-washed walls, shook the reinforced concrete of the Trefoil as steam pile-drivers shake the flanks of a dock.

'I'm all out—first time in my life. Ah! Tell a fellow now, did I get it across?' she whispered huskily.

'You know you did,' I replied as she dipped her nose deep in a beaker of barley-water. 'They cooed over you.'

Bat nodded. 'And poor Nellie's dead—in Africa, ain't it?'

'I hope I'll die before they stop cooing,' said 'Dal.

' "*Earth* was flat—*Earth* was flat!" ' Now it was more like mine-pumps in flood.

'They'll have the house down if you don't take another,' some one called.

'Bless 'em!' said 'Dal, and went out for her eighth, when

in the face of that cataract she said yawning, 'I don't know how *you* feel, children, but *I'm* dead. You be quiet.'

'Hold a minute,' said Bat to me. 'I've got to hear how it went in the provinces. Winnie Deans had it in Manchester, and Ramsden at Glasgow—and there are all the films too. I had rather a heavy week-end.'

The telephones presently reassured him.

'It'll do,' said he. 'And *he* said my home address was Jerusalem.' He left me humming the refrain of 'The Holy City.' Like Ollyett I found myself afraid of that man.

When I got out into the street and met the disgorging picture-palaces capering on the pavements and humming it (for he had put the gramophones on with the films), and when I saw far to the south the red electrics flash 'Gubby' across the Thames, I feared more than ever.

A few days passed which were like nothing except, perhaps, a suspense of fever in which the sick man perceives the searchlights of the world's assembled navies in act to converge on one minute fragment of wreckage—one only in all the black and agony-strewn sea. Then those beams focussed themselves. Earth as we knew it—the full circuit of our orb—laid the weight of its impersonal and searing curiosity on this Huckley which had voted that it was flat. It asked for news about Huckley—where and what it might be, and how it talked—it knew how it danced—and how it thought in its wonderful soul. And then, in all the zealous, merciless press, Huckley was laid out for it to look at, as a drop of pond water is exposed on the sheet of a magic-lantern show. But Huckley's sheet was only coterminous with the use of type among mankind. For the precise moment that was necessary, Fate ruled it that there should be nothing of first importance in the world's idle eye. One atrocious murder, a political crisis, an incautious or heady continental statesman, the mere catarrh of a king, would have wiped out the significance of our message, as a passing cloud annuls the urgent helio. But it was halcyon weather in every respect. Ollyett and I did not need to lift our little fingers any more than the Alpine climber whose last sentence has unkeyed the arch of the avalanche. The thing roared and pulverised and swept beyond eyesight all by itself—all by itself. And once well away, the fall of kingdoms could not have diverted it.

Ours is, after all, a kindly earth. While The Song ran and raped it with the cataleptic kick of 'Ta-ra-ra-boom-de-ay,' multiplied by the West African significance of 'Everybody's doing it,' plus twice the infernal elementality of a certain tune in *Dona et Gamma;* when for all practical purposes, literary, dramatic, artistic, social, municipal, political, commercial, and administrative, the Earth *was* flat, the Rector of Huckley wrote to us—again as a lover of accuracy—to point out that the Huckley vote on 'the alleged flatness of this scene of our labours here below' was *not* unanimous; he and the doctor having voted against it. And the great Baron Reuter himself (I am sure it could have been none other) flashed that letter in full to the front, back, and both wings of this scene of our labours. For Huckley was News. *The Bun* also contributed a photograph which cost me some trouble to fake.

'We are a vital nation,' said Ollyett while we were discussing affairs at a Bat dinner. 'Only an Englishman could have written that letter at this present juncture.'

'It reminded me of a tourist in the Cave of the Winds under Niagara. Just one figure in a mackintosh. But perhaps you saw our photo?' I said proudly.

'Yes,' Bat replied. 'I've been to Niagara, too. And how's Huckley taking it?'

'They don't quite understand, of course,' said Ollyett. 'But it's bringing pots of money into the place. Ever since the motor-bus excursions were started—'

'I didn't know they had been,' said Pallant.

'Oh yes. Motor char-à-bancs—uniformed guides and key-bugles included. They're getting a bit fed up with the tune there nowadays,' Ollyett added.

'They play it under his windows, don't they?' Bat asked. 'He can't stop the right of way across his park.'

'He cannot,' Ollyett answered. 'By the way, Wood-house, I've bought that font for you from the sexton. I paid fifteen pounds for it.'

'What am I supposed to do with it?' asked Woodhouse.

'You give it to the Victoria and Albert Museum. It is fourteenth-century work all right. You can trust me.'

'Is it worth it—now?' said Pallant. 'Not that I'm weak-ening, but merely as a matter of tactics?'

'But this is true,' said Ollyett. 'Besides, it is my hobby, I always wanted to be an architect. I'll attend to it myself. It's too serious for *The Bun* and miles too good for *The Cake*.'

He broke ground in a ponderous architectural weekly, which had never heard of Huckley. There was no passion in his statement, but mere fact backed by a wide range of authorities. He established beyond doubt that the old font at Huckley had been thrown out, on Sir Thomas's insti-gation, twenty years ago, to make room for a new one of Bath stone adorned with Limoges enamels; and that it had lain ever since in a corner of the sexton's shed. He proved, with learned men to support him, that there was only one other font in all England to compare with it. So Wood-house bought it and presented it to a grateful South Ken-sington which said it would see the earth still flatter before it returned the treasure to purblind Huckley. Bishops by the benchful and most of the Royal Academy, not to mention 'Margaritas ante Porcos,' wrote fervently to the papers. *Punch* based a political cartoon on it; the *Times* a third leader, 'The Lust of Newness;' and the *Spectator* a scholarly and delightful middle, 'Village Hausmania.' The vast amused outside world said in all its tongues and types: 'Of course! This is just what Huckley would do!' And neither Sir Thomas nor the Rector nor the sexton nor any one else wrote to deny it.

'You see,' said Ollyett, 'this is much more of a blow to Huckley than it looks—because every word of it's true. Your Gubby dance was inspiration, I admit, but it hadn't its roots in—'

'Two hemispheres and four continents so far,' I pointed out.

'Its roots in the hearts of Huckley was what I was going to say. Why don't you ever come down and look at the place? You've never seen it since we were stopped there.'

'I've only my week-ends free,' I said, 'and you seem to spend yours there pretty regularly—with the side-car. I was afraid—'

'Oh, *that's* all right,' he said cheerily. 'We're quite an old engaged couple now. As a matter of fact, it happened after "the gravid polled Angus" business. Come along this Saturday. Woodhouse says he'll run us down after lunch. He wants to see Huckley too.'

Pallant could not accompany us, but Bat took his place.

'It's odd,' said Bat, 'that none of us except Ollyett has ever set eyes on Huckley since that time. That's what I always tell My people. Local colour is all right after you've got your idea. Before that, it's a mere nuisance.' He regaled us on the way down with panoramic views of the success—geographical and financial—of 'The Gubby' and The Song.

'By the way,' said he, 'I've assigned 'Dal all the gramophone rights of "The Earth." She's a born artist. 'Hadn't sense enough to hit me for tripledubs the morning after. She'd have taken it out in coos.'

'Bless her! And what'll she make out of the gramophone rights?' I asked.

'Lord knows!' he replied. 'I've made fifty-four thousand my little end of the business, and it's only just beginning. Hear *that!*'

A shell-pink motor-brake roared up behind us to the music on a key-bugle of 'The Village that Voted the Earth was Flat.' In a few minutes we overtook another, in natural wood, whose occupants were singing it through their noses.

'I don't know that agency. It must be Cook's,' said Ollyett. 'They *do* suffer.' We were never out of ear-shot of the tune the rest of the way to Huckley.

Though I knew it would be so, I was disappointed with the actual aspect of the spot we had—it is not too much to say—created in the face of the nations. The alcoholic pub; the village green; the Baptist chapel; the church; the sexton's shed; the Rectory whence the so-wonderful letters had come; Sir Thomas's park gate-pillars still violently declaring 'The Earth *is* flat,' were as mean, as average, as ordinary as the photograph of a room where a murder has been committed. Ollyett, who, of course, knew the place specially well, made the most of it to us. Bat, who had employed it as a back-cloth to one of his own dramas, dismissed it as a thing used and emptied, but Woodhouse expressed my feelings when he said: 'Is that all—after all we've done?'

'*I* know,' said Ollyett soothingly. ' "Like that strange song I heard Apollo sing: When Ilion like a mist rose into towers." I've felt the same sometimes, though it has been Paradise for me. But they *do* suffer.'

The fourth brake in thirty minutes had just turned into Sir Thomas's park to tell the Hall that 'The *Earth* was flat'; a knot of obviously American tourists were kodaking his lodge gates; while the tea-shop opposite the lych-gate was full of people buying postcards of the old font as it had lain twenty years in the sexton's shed. We went to the alcoholic pub and congratulated the proprietor.

'It's bringin' money to the place,' said he. 'But in a sense you can buy money too dear. It isn't doin' us any good. People are laughin' at us. That's what they're doin'. . . . Now, with regard to that Vote of ours you may have heard talk about . . .'

'For Gorze sake, chuck that votin' business,' cried an elderly man at the door. 'Money-gettin' or no money-gettin', we're fed up with it.'

'Well, I do think,' said the publican, shifting his ground, 'I do think Sir Thomas might ha' managed better in some things.'

'He tole me,'—the elderly man shouldered his way to the bar—'he tole me twenty years ago to take an' lay that font in my tool-shed. He *tole* me so himself. An' now, after twenty years, me own wife makin' me out little better than the common 'angman!'

'That's the sexton,' the publican explained. 'His good lady sells the postcards—if you 'aven't got some. But we feel Sir Thomas might ha' done better.'

'What's he got to do with it?' said Woodhouse.

'There's nothin' we can trace 'ome to 'im in so many words, but we think he might 'ave saved us the font business. Now, in regard to that votin' business—'

'Chuck it! Oh, chuck it!' the sexton roared, 'or you'll 'ave me cuttin' my throat at cock-crow. 'Erc's another parcel of fun-makers!'

A motor-brake had pulled up at the door and a multitude of men and women immediately descended. We went out to look. They bore rolled banners, a reading-desk in three pieces and, I specially noticed, a collapsible harmonium, such as is used on ships at sea.

'Salvation Army?' I said, though I saw no uniforms.

Two of them unfurled a banner between poles which bore the legend: 'The Earth *is* flat.' Woodhouse and I turned to Bat. He shook his head. 'No, no! Not me. . . . If I had only seen their costumes in advance!'

'Good Lord!' said Ollyett. 'It's the genuine Society!'

The company advanced on the green with the precision of people well broke to these movements. Scene-shifters could not have been quicker with the three-piece rostrum, nor stewards with the harmonium. Almost before its

cross-legs had been kicked into their catches, certainly before the tourists by the lodge-gates had begun to move
over, a woman sat down to it and struck up a hymn:

> Hear ther truth our tongues are telling,
>   Spread ther light from shore to shore,
> God hath given man a dwelling
>   Flat and flat forevermore.
>
> When ther Primal Dark retreated,
>   When ther deeps were undesigned,
> He with rule and level meted
>   Habitation for mankind!

I saw sick envy on Bat's face. 'Curse Nature,' he muttered. 'She gets ahead of you every time. To think *I* forgot
hymns and a harmonium!'

Then came the chorus:

> Hear ther truth our tongues are telling,
>   Spread ther light from shore to shore—
> Oh, be faithful! Oh, be truthful—
>   Earth is flat forevermore.

They sang several verses with the fervour of Christians
awaiting their lions. Then there were growlings in the air.
The sexton, embraced by the landlord, two-stepped out of
the pub-door. Each was trying to outroar the other.
'Apologising in advarnce for what he says,' the landlord
shouted. 'You'd better go away' (here the sexton began to
speak words). 'This isn't the time nor yet the place for—
for any more o' this chat.'

The crowd thickened. I saw the village police-sergeant
come out of his cottage buckling his belt.

'But surely,' said the woman at the harmonium, 'there
must be some mistake. We are not suffragettes.'

'Damn it! They'd be a change,' cried the sexton. 'You

get out of this! Don't talk! *I* can't stand it for one! Get right out, or we'll font you!'

The crowd which was being recruited from every house in sight echoed the invitation. The sergeant pushed forward. A man beside the reading-desk said: 'But surely we are among dear friends and sympathisers. Listen to me for a moment.'

It was the moment that a passing char-à-banc chose to strike into The Song. The effect was instantaneous. Bat, Ollyett, and I, who by divers roads have learned the psychology of crowds, retreated towards the tavern door. Woodhouse, the newspaper proprietor, anxious, I presume, to keep touch with the public, dived into the thick of it. Every one else told the Society to go away at once. When the lady at the harmonium (I began to understand why it is sometimes necessary to kill women) pointed at the stencilled park pillars and called them 'the cromlechs of our common faith,' there was a snarl and a rush. The police-sergeant checked it, but advised the Society to keep on going. The Society withdrew into the brake fighting, as it were, a rearguard action of oratory up each step. The collapsed harmonium was hauled in last, and with the perfect unreason of crowds, they cheered it loudly, till the chauffeur slipped in his clutch and sped away. Then the crowd broke up, congratulating all concerned except the sexton, who was held to have disgraced his office by having sworn at ladies. We strolled across the green towards Woodhouse, who was talking to the police-sergeant near the park-gates. We were not twenty yards from him when we saw Sir Thomas Ingell emerge from the lodge and rush furiously at Woodhouse with an uplifted stick, at the same time shrieking: 'I'll teach you to laugh, you—' but Ollyett has the record of the language. By the time we reached them, Sir Thomas was on the ground; Woodhouse, very white, held the walking-stick and was saying to the sergeant:

'I give this person in charge for assault.'

'But, good Lord!' said the sergeant, whiter than Wood-house. 'It's Sir Thomas.'

'Whoever it is, it isn't fit to be at large,' said Wood-house. The crowd suspecting something wrong began to reassemble, and all the English horror of a row in public moved us, headed by the sergeant, inside the lodge. We shut both park-gates and lodge-door.

'You saw the assault, sergeant,' Woodhouse went on. 'You can testify I used no more force than was necessary to protect myself. You can testify that I have not even damaged this person's property. (Here! take your stick, you!) You heard the filthy language he used.'

'I—I can't say I did,' the sergeant stammered.

'Oh, but *we* did!' said Ollyett, and repeated it, to the apron-veiled horror of the lodge-keeper's wife.

Sir Thomas on a hard kitchen chair began to talk. He said he had 'stood enough of being photographed like a wild beast,' and expressed loud regret that he had not killed 'that man,' who was 'conspiring with the sergeant to laugh at him.'

' 'Ad you ever seen 'im before, Sir Thomas?' the sergeant asked.

'No! But it's time an example was made here. I've never seen the sweep in my life.'

I think it was Bat Masquerier's magnetic eye that re-called the past to him, for his face changed and his jaw dropped. 'But I have!' he groaned. 'I remember now.'

Here a writhing man entered by the back door. He was, he said, the village solicitor. I do not assert that he licked Woodhouse's boots, but we should have respected him more if he had and been done with it. His notion was that the matter could be accommodated, arranged and com-promised for gold, and yet more gold. The sergeant thought so too. Woodhouse undeceived them both. To the sergeant he said, 'Will you or will you not enter the charge?' To the village solicitor he gave the name of his lawyers, at which the man wrung his hands and cried, 'Oh, Sir T., Sir T.!' in a miserable falsetto, for it was a Bat Masquerier of a firm. They conferred together in tragic whispers.

'I don't dive after Dickens,' said Ollyett to Bat and me by the window, 'but every time *I* get into a row I notice the police-court always fills up with his characters.'

'I've noticed that too,' said Bat. 'But the odd thing is you mustn't give the public straight Dickens—not in My business. I wonder why that is.'

Then Sir Thomas got his second wind and cursed the day that he, or it may have been we, were born. I feared that though he was a Radical he might apologise and, since he was an M.P., might lie his way out of the difficulty. But he was utterly and truthfully beside himself. He asked foolish questions—such as what we were doing in the village at all, and how much blackmail Woodhouse expected to make out of him. But neither Woodhouse nor the sergeant nor the writhing solicitor listened. The upshot of their talk, in the chimney-corner, was that Sir Thomas stood engaged to appear next Monday before his brother magistrates on charges of assault, disorderly conduct, and language calculated, etc. Ollyett was specially careful about the language.

Then we left. The village looked very pretty in the late night—pretty and tuneful as a nest of nightingales.

'You'll turn up on Monday, I hope,' said Woodhouse, when we reached town. That was his only allusion to the affair.

So we turned up—through a world still singing that the Earth was flat—at the little clay-coloured market-town with the large Corn Exchange and the small Jubilee memorial. We had some difficulty in getting seats in the court. Woodhouse's imported London lawyer was a man of commanding personality, with a voice trained to convey blasting imputations by tone. When the case was called, he rose and stated his client's intention not to proceed with the charge. His client, he went on to say, had not entertained, and, of course, in the circumstances could not have entertained, any suggestion of accepting on behalf of public charities any monies that might have been offered to him on the part of Sir Thomas's estate. At the same time, no one acknowledged more sincerely than his client the spirit in which those offers had been made by those entitled to make them. But, as a matter of fact—here he became the man of the world colloguing with his equals—certain—er—details had come to his client's knowledge *since* the lamentable outburst, which ... He shrugged his shoulders. Nothing was served by going into them, but he ventured to say that, had those painful circumstances only been known earlier, his client would—again 'of course'—never have dreamed— A gesture concluded the sentence, and the ensnared Bench looked at Sir Thomas with new and withdrawing eyes. Frankly, as they could see, it would be nothing less than cruelty to proceed further with this—er—unfortunate affair. He asked leave, therefore, to withdraw the charge *in toto*, and at the same time to express his client's deepest sympathy with all who had been in any way distressed, as his client had been, by the fact and the publicity of proceedings which he could, of course, again assure them that his client would never have dreamed of instituting if, as he hoped he had made plain, certain facts had been before his client at the time when ... But he had said enough. For his fee it seemed to me that he had.

Heaven inspired Sir Thomas's lawyer—all of a sweat lest his client's language should come out—to rise up and thank him. Then, Sir Thomas—not yet aware what leprosy had been laid upon him, but grateful to escape on any terms—followed suit. He was heard in interested silence, and people drew back a pace as Gehazi passed forth.

'You hit hard,' said Bat to Woodhouse afterwards. 'His own people think he's mad.'

'You don't say so? I'll show you some of his letters to-night at dinner,' he replied.

He brought them to the Red Amber Room of the Chop Suey. We forgot to be amazed, as till then we had been amazed, over the Song or 'The Gubby,' or the full tide of Fate that seemed to run only for our sakes. It did not even interest Ollyett that the verb 'to huckle' had passed into the English leader-writers' language. We were studying the interior of a soul, flash-lighted to its grimiest corners by the dread of 'losing its position.'

'And then it thanked you, didn't it, for dropping the case?' said Pallant.

'Yes, and it sent me a telegram to confirm.' Woodhouse turned to Bat. 'Now d'you think I hit too hard?' he asked.

'No—o!' said Bat. 'After all—I'm talking of every one's business now—one can't ever do anything in Art that comes up to Nature in any game in life. Just think how this thing has—'

'Just let me run through that little case of yours again,' said Pallant, and picked up *The Bun* which had it set out in full.

'Any chance of 'Dal looking in on us to-night?' Ollyett began.

'She's occupied with her Art too,' Bat answered bitterly. 'What's the use of Art? Tell me, some one!' A barrel-organ outside promptly pointed out that the *Earth* was flat. 'The gramophone's killing street organs, but I let loose a hundred-and-seventy-four of those hurdygurdys twelve hours after The Song,' said Bat. 'Not counting the Provinces.' His face brightened a little.

'Look here!' said Pallant over the paper. 'I don't suppose you or those asinine J.P.'s knew it—but your lawyer ought to have known that you've all put your foot in it most confoundedly over this assault case.'

'What's the matter?' said Woodhouse.

'It's ludicrous. It's insane. There isn't two penn'orth of

legality in the whole thing. Of course, you could have withdrawn the charge, but the way you went about it is childish—besides being illegal. What on earth was the Chief Constable thinking of?'

'Oh, he was a friend of Sir Thomas's. They all were for that matter,' I replied.

'He ought to be hanged. So ought the Chairman of the Bench. I'm talking as a lawyer now.'

'Why, what have we been guilty of? Misprision of treason or compounding a felony—or what?' said Ollyett.

'I'll tell you later.' Pallant went back to the paper with knitted brows, smiling unpleasantly from time to time. At last he laughed.

'Thank you!' he said to Woodhouse. 'It ought to be pretty useful—for us.'

'What d'you mean?' said Ollyett.

'For our side. They are all Rads who are mixed up in this—from the Chief Constable down. There must be a Question. There must be a Question.'

'Yes, but I wanted the charge withdrawn in my own way,' Woodhouse insisted.

'That's nothing to do with the case. It's the legality of your silly methods. You wouldn't understand if I talked till morning.' He began to pace the room, his hands behind him. 'I wonder if I can get it through our Whip's thick head that it's a chance. . . . That comes of stuffing the Bench with radical tinkers,' he muttered.

'Oh, sit down!' said Woodhouse.

'Where's your lawyer to be found now?' he jerked out.

'At the Trefoil,' said Bat promptly. 'I gave him the stage-box for to-night. He's an artist too.'

'Then I'm going to see him,' said Pallant. 'Properly handled this ought to be a godsend for our side.' He withdrew without apology.

'Certainly, this thing keeps on opening up, and up,' I remarked inanely.

'It's beyond me!' said Bat. 'I don't think if I'd known I'd have ever . . . Yes, I would, though. He said my home address was—'

'It was his tone—his tone!' Ollyett almost shouted. Woodhouse said nothing, but his face whitened as he brooded.

'Well, any way,' Bat went on, 'I'm glad I always believed in God and Providence and all those things. Else I should lose my nerve. We've put it over the whole world—the full extent of the geographical globe. We couldn't stop it if we wanted to now. It's got to burn itself out. I'm not in charge any more. What d'you expect'll happen next? Angels?'

I expected nothing. Nothing that I expected approached what I got. Politics are not my concern, but, for the moment, since it seemed that they were going to 'huckle' with the rest, I took an interest in them. They impressed me as a dog's life without a dog's decencies, and I was confirmed in this when an unshaven and unwashen Pallant called on me at ten o'clock one morning, begging for a bath and a couch.

'Bail too?' I asked. He was in evening dress and his eyes were sunk feet in his head.

'No,' he said hoarsely. 'All night sitting. Fifteen divisions. 'Nother to-night. Your place was nearer than mine, so—' He began to undress in the hall.

When he awoke at one o'clock he gave me lurid accounts of what he said was history, but which was obviously collective hysteria. There had been a political crisis. He and his fellow M.P.'s had 'done things'—I never quite got at the things—for eighteen hours on end, and the pitiless Whips were even then at the telephones to herd 'em up to another dog-fight. So he snorted and grew hot all over again while he might have been resting.

'I'm going to pitch in my question about that miscarriage of justice at Huckley this afternoon, if you care to listen to it,' he said. 'It'll be absolutely thrown away—in our present state. I told 'em so; but it's my only chance for weeks. P'raps Woodhouse would like to come.'

'I'm sure he would. Anything to do with Huckley interests us,' I said.

'It'll miss fire, I'm afraid. Both sides are absolutely cooked. The present situation has been working up for some time. You see the row was bound to come, etc., etc.,' and he flew off the handle once more.

I telephoned to Woodhouse, and we went to the House together. It was a dull, sticky afternoon with thunder in the air. For some reason or other, each side was determined to prove its virtue and endurance to the utmost. I heard men snarling about it all round me. 'If they won't spare us, we'll show 'em no mercy.' 'Break the brutes up from the start. They can't stand late hours.' 'Come on! No shirking! I know *you*'ve had a Turkish bath,' were some of the sentences I caught on our way. The House was packed already, and one could feel the negative electricity of a jaded crowd wrenching at one's own nerves, and depressing the afternoon soul.

'This is bad!' Woodhouse whispered. 'There'll be a row before they've finished. Look at the Front Benches!' And he pointed out little personal signs by which I was to know that each man was on edge. He might have spared himself. The House was ready to snap before a bone had been thrown. A sullen minister rose to reply to a staccato question. His supporters cheered defiantly. 'None o' that! None o' that!' came from the Back Benches. I saw the Speaker's face stiffen like the face of a helmsman as he humours a hard-mouthed yacht after a sudden following sea. The trouble was barely met in time. There came a fresh, apparently causeless gust a few minutes later—savage, threatening, but futile. It died out—one could hear the sigh—in sudden wrathful realisation of the dreary hours ahead, and the ship of state drifted on.

Then Pallant—and the raw House winced at the torture

of his voice—rose. It was a twenty-line question, studded with legal technicalities. The gist of it was that he wished to know whether the appropriate Minister was aware that there had been a grave miscarriage of justice on such and such a date, at such and such a place, before such and such justices of the peace, in regard to a case which arose—

I heard one desperate, weary 'damn!' float up from the pit of that torment. Pallant sawed on—'out of certain events which occurred at the village of Huckley.'

The House came to attention with a parting of the lips like a hiccough, and it flashed through my mind . . . Pallant repeated, 'Huckley. The village—'

'That voted the *Earth* was flat.' A single voice from a Back Bench sang it once like a lone frog in a far pool.

'*Earth* was flat,' croaked another voice opposite.

'*Earth* was flat.' There were several. Then several more.

It was, you understand, the collective, over-strained nerve of the House, snapping, strand by strand to various notes, as the hawser parts from its moorings.

'The Village that voted the *Earth* was flat.' The tune was beginning to shape itself. More voices were raised and feet began to beat time. Even so it did not occur to me that the thing would—

'The Village that voted the *Earth* was flat!' It was easier now to see who were not singing. There were still a few. Of a sudden (and this proves the fundamental instability of the cross-bench mind) a cross-bencher leaped on his seat and there played an imaginary double-bass with tremendous maestro-like wagglings of the elbow.

The last strand parted. The ship of state drifted out helpless on the rocking tide of melody.

'The Village that voted the *Earth* was flat!
The Village that voted the *Earth* was flat!'

The Irish first conceived the idea of using their order-papers as funnels wherewith to reach the correct '*vroom—vroom*' on '*Earth.*' Labour, always conservative and respectable at a crisis, stood out longer than any other section, but when it came in it was howling syndicalism. Then, without distinction of Party, fear of constituents, desire for office, or hope of emolument, the House sang at the tops and at the bottoms of their voices, swaying their stale bodies and epileptically beating with their swelled feet. They sang 'The Village that voted the *Earth* was flat': first, because they wanted to, and secondly—which is the terror of that song—because they could not stop. For no consideration could they stop.

Pallant was still standing up. Some one pointed at him and they laughed. Others began to point, lunging, as it were, in time with the tune. At this moment two persons came in practically abreast from behind the Speaker's chair, and halted appalled. One happened to be the Prime Minister and the other a messenger. The House, with tears running down their cheeks, transferred their attention to the paralysed couple. They pointed six hundred forefingers at them. They rocked, they waved, and they rolled while they pointed, but still they sang. When they weakened for an instant, Ireland would yell: 'Are ye *with* me, bhoys?' and they all renewed their strength like Antaeus. No man could say afterwards what happened in the Press or the Strangers' Gallery. It was the House, the hysterical and abandoned House of Commons that held all eyes, as it deafened all ears. I saw both Front Benches bend forward, some with their foreheads on their despatch-boxes, the rest with their faces in their hands; and their moving shoulders jolted the House out of its last rag of decency. Only the Speaker remained unmoved. The entire press of Great Britain bore witness next day that he had not even bowed his head. The Angel of the Constitution, for vain was the help of man, foretold him the exact moment at which the House would have broken into 'The Gubby.' He is reported to have said: 'I heard the Irish beginning to shuffle it. So I adjourned.' Pallant's version is that he added: 'And I was never so grateful to a private member in all my life as I was to Mr. Pallant.'

He made no explanation. He did not refer to orders or disorders. He simply adjourned the House till six that evening. And the House adjourned—some of it nearly on all fours.

I was not correct when I said that the Speaker was the only man who did not laugh. Woodhouse was beside me all the time. His face was set and quite white—as white, they told me, as Sir Thomas Ingell's when he went, by request, to a private interview with his Chief Whip.

1917

BRUGGLESMITH

~~~~~~

This day the ship went down, and all hands was drowned but me.

Clark Russell

The first officer of the *Breslau* asked me to dinner on board, before the ship went round to Southampton to pick up her passengers. The *Breslau* was lying below London Bridge, her fore-hatches opened for cargo, and her deck littered with nuts and bolts, and screws and chains. The Black M'Phee had been putting some finishing touches to his adored engines, and M'Phee is the most tidy of chief engineers. If the leg of a cockroach gets into one of his slide-valves the whole ship knows it, and half the ship has to clean up the mess.

After dinner, which the first officer, M'Phee, and I ate in one little corner of the empty saloon, M'Phee returned to the engine-room to attend to some brass-fitters. The first officer and I smoked on the bridge and watched the lights of the crowded shipping till it was time for me to go home. It seemed, in the pauses of our conversation, that I could catch an echo of fearful bellowings from the engine-room, and the voice of M'Phee singing of home and the domestic affections.

'M'Phee has a friend aboard to-night—a man who was a boiler-maker at Greenock when M'Phee was a 'prentice,' said the first officer. 'I didn't ask him to dine with us be-cause——'

'I see—I mean I hear,' I answered. We talked on for a

few minutes longer, and M'Phee came up from the engine-room with his friend on his arm.

'Let me present ye to this gentleman,' said M'Phee. 'He's a great admirer o' your wor-rks. He has just hear-rd o' them.'

M'Phee could never pay a compliment prettily. The friend sat down suddenly on a bollard, saying that M'Phee had under-stated the truth. Personally, he on the bollard considered that Shakespeare was trembling in the balance solely on my account, and if the first officer wished to dispute this he was prepared to fight the first officer then or later, 'as per invoice.' 'Man, if ye only knew,' said he, wagging his head, 'the times I've lain in my lonely bunk reading *Vanity Fair* an' sobbin'—ay, weepin' bitterly, at the pure fascination of it.'

He shed a few tears for guarantee of good faith, and the first officer laughed. M'Phee resettled the man's hat, that had tilted over one eyebrow, and said:

'That'll wear off in a little. It's just the smell o' the engine-room,' said M'Phee.

'I think I'll wear off myself,' I whispered to the first officer. 'Is the dinghy ready?'

The dinghy was at the gangway, which was down, and the first officer went forward to find a man to row me to the bank. He returned with a very sleepy Lascar, who knew the river.

'Are you going?' said the man on the bollard. 'Well, I'll just see ye home. M'Phee, help me down the gangway. It has as many ends as a cat-o'-nine tails, and—losh!—how innumerable are the dinghys!'

'You'd better let him come with you,' said the first officer. 'Muhammad Jan, put the drunk sahib ashore first. Take the sober sahib to the next stairs.'

I had my foot in the bow of the dinghy, the tide was making up-stream, when the man cannoned against me, pushed the Lascar back on the gangway, cast loose the painter, and the dinghy began to saw, stern-first, along the side of the *Breslau*.

'We'll have no exter-r-raneous races here,' said the man. 'I've known the Thames for thirty years——'

There was no time for argument. We were drifting under the *Breslau's* stern, and I knew that her propeller was half out of water, in the midst of an inky tangle of buoys, low-lying hawsers, and moored ships, with the tide roaring about them.

'What shall I do?' I shouted to the first officer.

'Find the Police Boat as soon as you can, and for God's sake get way on the dinghy. Steer with the oar. The rudder's unshipped and—'

I could hear no more. The dinghy slid away, bumped on a mooring-buoy, swung round and jigged off irresponsibly as I hunted for the oar. The man sat in the bow, his chin on his hands, smiling.

'Row, you ruffian,' I said. 'Get her out into the middle of the river—'

'It's a preevilege to gaze on the face o' genius. Let me go on thinking. There was "Little Bar-rnaby Dorrit" and "The Mystery o' the Bleak Druid." I sailed in a ship called the *Druid* once—badly found she was. It all comes back to me so sweet. It all comes back to me. Man, ye steer like a genius!'

We just bumped another mooring-buoy and drifted on to the bows of a Norwegian timber-ship—I could see the great square holes on either side of the cutwater. Then we dived into a string of barges and scraped through them by the paint on our planks. It was a consolation to think that the dinghy was being reduced in value at every bump, but the question before me was when she would begin to leak. The man looked ahead into the pitchy darkness and whistled.

'Yon's a Castle liner; her ties are black. She's swinging across stream. Keep her port light on our starboard bow, and go large,' he said.

'How can I keep anything anywhere? You're sitting on the oars. Row, man, if you don't want to drown.'

He took the sculls, saying sweetly: 'No harm comes to a drunken man. That's why I wished to come with *you*. Man, ye're not fit to be alone in a boat.'

He flirted the dinghy round the big ship, and for the next ten minutes I enjoyed—positively enjoyed—an exhibition of first-class steering. We threaded in and out of the mercantile marine of Great Britain as a ferret threads a rabbit-hole, and we, he that is to say, sang joyously to each ship till men looked over bulwarks and cursed us. When we came to some moderately clear water he gave the sculls to me, and said:

'If ye could row as ye write, I'd respect you for all your vices. Yon's London Bridge. Take her through.'

We shot under the dark ringing arch, and came out the other side, going up swiftly with the tide chanting songs of victory. Except that I wished to get home before morning, I was growing reconciled to the jaunt. There were one or two stars visible, and by keeping into the centre of the stream, I could not come to any very serious danger.

The man began to sing loudly:—

> 'The smartest clipper that you could find,
>   Yo ho! Oho!
> Was the *Marg'ret Evans* of the Black X Line
>   A hundred years ago!

Incorporate that in your next book. Which is marvellous.' Here he stood up in the bows and declaimed:—

> 'Ye Towers o' Julia, London's lasting wrong,
>   By mony a foul an' midnight murder fed—
> Sweet Thames run softly till I end my song—
>   And yon's the grave as little as my bed.

I'm a poet mysel an' I can feel for others.'

'Sit down,' said I. 'You'll have the boat over.'

'Ay, I'm settin'—settin' like a hen.' He plumped down heavily, and added, shaking his forefinger at me:—

> 'Lear-rn, prudent, cautious self-control
> Is wisdom's root.

How did a man o' your parts come to be so drunk? Oh, it's a sinfu' thing, an' ye may thank God on all fours that I'm wi' you. What's yon boat?'

We had drifted far up the river, and a boat manned by four men, who rowed with a soothingly regular stroke, was overhauling us.

'It's the River Police,' I said, at the top of my voice.

'Oh ay! If your sin do not find you out on dry land, it will find you out in the deep waters. Is it like they'll give us drink?'

'Exceedingly likely. I'll hail them.' I hailed.

'What are you doing?' was the answer from the boat.

'It's the *Breslau's* dinghy broken loose,' I began.

'It's a vara drunken man broke loose,' roared my companion, 'and I'm taking him home by water, for he cannot stand on dry land.' Here he shouted my name twenty times running, and I could feel the blushes racing over my body three deep.

'You'll be locked up in ten minutes, my friend,' I said, 'and I don't think you'll be bailed either.'

'H'sh, man, h'sh. They think I'm your uncle.' He caught up a scull and began splashing the boat as it ranged alongside.

'You're a nice pair,' said the sergeant at last.

'I am anything you please so long as you take this fiend away. Tow us in to the nearest station, and I'll make it worth your while,' I said.

'Corruption—corruption,' roared the man, throwing himself flat in the bottom of the boat. 'Like unto the worms that perish, so is man. And all for the sake of a filthy half-crown to be arrested by the River Police at my time o' life!'

'For pity's sake, row,' I shouted. 'The man's drunk.'

They rowed us to a flat—a fire or a police-station; it was too dark to see which. I could feel that they regarded me in no better light than my companion, and I could not explain, for I was holding the far end of the painter, ten long feet from all respectability.

We got out of the boat, my companion falling flat on his wicked face, and the sergeant asked us rude questions about the dinghy. My companion washed his hands of all responsibility. He was an old man; he had been lured into a stolen boat by a young man—probably a thief—he had saved the boat from wreck (this was absolutely true), and now he expected salvage in the shape of hot whisky and water. The sergeant turned to me. Fortunately I was in evening dress, and had a card to show. More fortunately still, the sergeant happened to know the *Breslau* and M'Phee. He promised to send the dinghy down next tide, and was not beyond accepting my thanks, in silver.

As this was satisfactorily arranged, I heard my companion say angrily to a constable, 'If you will not give it to a dry man, ye maun to a drookit.' Then he walked deliberately off the edge of the flat into the water. Somebody stuck a boat-hook into his clothes and hauled him out.

'Now,' said he triumphantly, 'under the rules o' the R-royal Humane Society, ye must give me hot whisky and water. Do not put temptation before the laddie. He's my nephew an' a good boy i' the main. Tho' why he should masquerade as Mister Thackeray on the high seas is beyond my comprehension. Oh the vanity o' youth! M'Phee told me ye were as vain as a peacock. I mind that now.'

'You had better give him something to drink and wrap him up for the night. I don't know who he is,' I said desperately, and when the man had settled down to a drink supplied on my representations, I escaped and found that I was near a bridge.

I went towards Fleet Street, intending to take a hansom and go home. After the first feeling of indignation died out, the absurdity of the experience struck me fully and I began to laugh aloud in the empty streets, to the scandal of a policeman. The more I reflected the more heartily I laughed, till my mirth was quenched by a hand on my shoulder, and turning I saw him who should have been in bed at the river police-station. He was damp all over; his wet silk hat rode far at the back of his head, and round his shoulders hung a striped yellow blanket, evidently the property of the State.

'The crackling o' thorns under a pot,' said he, solemnly. 'Laddie, have ye not thought o' the sin of idle laughter? My heart misgave me that ever ye'd get home, an' I've just come to convoy you a piece. They're sore uneducate down there by the river. They would na listen to me when I talked o' your wor-rks, so I e'en left them. Cast the blanket about you, laddie. It's fine and cold.'

I groaned inwardly. Providence evidently intended that I should frolic through eternity with M'Phee's infamous acquaintance.

'Go away,' I said; 'go home, or I'll give you in charge.'

He leaned against a lamp-post and laid his finger to his nose—his dishonourable, carnelian neb.

'I mind now that M'Phee told me ye were vainer than a peacock, an' your castin' me adrift in a boat shows ye were drunker than an owl. A good name is as a savoury bake-meat. I ha' nane.' He smacked his lips joyously.

'Well, I know that,' I said.

'Ay, but *ye* have. I mind now that M'Phee spoke o' your reputation that you're so proud of. Laddie, if ye gie me in charge—I'm old enough to be your father—I'll bla-ast your reputation as far as my voice can carry; for I'll call you by name till the cows come hame. It's no jestin' mat-ter to be a friend to me. If you discard my friendship, ye must come to Vine Street wi' me for stealin' the *Breslau's* dinghy.'

Then he sang at the top of his voice:—

'In the mor-nin'
I' the mor-rnin' by the black van—
We'll toodle up to Vine Street i' the mornin'!

Yon's my own composeetion, but *I'm* not vain. We'll go home together, laddie, we'll go home together.' And he sang 'Auld Lang Syne' to show that he meant it.

A policeman suggested that we had better move on, and we moved on to the Law Courts near St. Clement Danes. My companion was quieter now, and his speech which up till that time had been distinct—it was a marvel to see how in his condition he could talk dialect—began to slur and slide and slummock. He bade me observe the architecture of the Law Courts and linked himself lovingly to my arm. Then he saw a policeman, and before I could shake him off, whirled me up to the man singing:—

'Every member of the Force,
Has a watch and chain of course—'

and threw his dripping blanket over the helmet of the Law. In any other country in the world we should have run an exceedingly good chance of being shot, or dirked, or clubbed—and clubbing is worse than being shot. But I reflected in that wet-cloth tangle that this was England, where the police are made to be banged and battered and bruised, that they may the better endure a police-court reprimand next morning. We three fell in a tangle, he calling on me by name—that was the tingling horror of it—to sit on the policeman's head and cut the traces. I wriggled clear first and shouted to the policeman to kill the blanket-man.

Naturally the policeman answered: 'You're as bad as

'im,' and chased me, as the smaller man, round St. Clement Danes into Holywell Street, where I ran into the arms of another policeman. That flight could not have lasted more than a minute and a half, but it seemed to me as long and as wearisome as the foot-bound flight of a nightmare. I had leisure to think of a thousand things as I ran, but most I thought of the great and god-like man who held a sitting in the north gallery of St. Clement Danes a hundred years ago. I know that he at least would have felt for me. So occupied was I with these considerations, that when the other policeman hugged me to his bosom and said: 'What are you tryin' to do?' I answered with exquisite politeness: 'Sir, let us take a walk down Fleet Street.' 'Bow Street'll do *your* business, I think,' was the answer, and for a moment I thought so too, till it seemed I might wriggle out of it. Then there was a hideous scene, and it was complicated by my companion hurrying up with the blanket and telling me—always by name—that he would rescue me or perish in the attempt.

'Knock him down,' I pleaded. 'Club his head open first and I'll explain afterwards.'

The first policeman, the one who had been outraged, drew his truncheon and cut my companion's head. The high silk hat crackled and the owner dropped like a log.

'Now you've done it,' I said. 'You've probably killed him.'

Holywell Street never goes to bed. A small crowd gathered on the spot, and some one of German extraction cried: 'You haf killed the man.'

Another cried: 'Take his bloomin' number. I saw him strook cruel 'ard. Yah!'

Now the street was empty when the trouble began, and, saving the two policemen and myself, no one had seen the blow. I said, therefore, in a loud and cheerful voice:—

'The man's a friend of mine. He's fallen down in a fit. Bobby, will you bring the ambulance?' Under my breath

I added: 'It's five shillings apiece, and the man didn't hit you.'

'No, but 'im and you tried to scrob me,' said the policeman.

This was not a thing to argue about.

'Is Dempsey on duty at Charing Cross?' I said.

'Wot d'you know of Dempsey, you bloomin' garrotter?' said the policeman.

'If Dempsey's there, he knows me. Get the ambulance quick, and I'll take him to Charing Cross.'

'You're coming to Bow Street, *you* are,' said the policeman crisply.

'The man's dying'—he lay groaning on the pavement— 'get the ambulance,' said I.

There is an ambulance at the back of St. Clement Danes, whereof I know more than most people. The policeman seemed to possess the keys of the box in which it lived. We trundled it out—it was a three-wheeled affair with a hood—and we bundled the body of the man upon it.

A body in an ambulance looks very extremely dead. The policeman softened at the sight of the stiff boot-heels.

'Now, then,' said they, and I fancied that they still meant Bow Street.

'Let me see Dempsey for three minutes if he's on duty,' I answered.

'Very good. He is.'

Then I knew that all would be well, but before we started I put my head under the ambulance-hood to see if the man were alive. A guarded whisper caught my ear.

'Laddie, you maun pay me for a new hat. They've broken it. Dinna desert me now, laddie. I'm o'er old to go to Bow Street in my gray hairs for a fault of yours. Laddie, dinna desert me.'

'You'll be lucky if you get off under seven years,' I said to the policeman.

Moved by a very lively fear of having exceeded their
duty, the two policeman left their beats, and the mournful
procession wound down the empty Strand. Once west of
the Adelphi, I knew I should be in my own country; and
the policemen had reason to know that too, for as I was
pacing proudly a little ahead of the catafalque, another policeman said 'Good night, sir,' to me as he passed.

'Now, you see,' I said, with condescension. 'I wouldn't
be in your shoes for something. On my word, I've a great
mind to march you two down to Scotland Yard.'

'If the gentleman's a friend o' yours, per'aps—' said the
policeman who had given the blow, and was reflecting on
the consequences.

'Perhaps you'd like me to go away and say nothing
about it,' I said. Then there hove into view the figure of
Constable Dempsey, glittering in his oilskins, and an angel
of light to me. I had known him for months; he was an es-
teemed friend of mine, and we used to talk together in the
early mornings. The fool seeks to ingratiate himself with
Princes and Ministers; and courts and cabinets leave him
to perish miserably. The wise man makes allies among the
police and the hansoms, so that his friends spring up from
the round-house and the cab-rank, and even his offences
become triumphal processions.

'Dempsey,' said I, 'have the Police been on strike again?
They've put some things on duty at St. Clement Danes
that want to take me to Bow Street for garrotting.'

'Lor, sir!' said Dempsey indignantly.

'Tell them I'm not a garrotter, nor a thief. It's simply
disgraceful that a gentleman can't walk down the Strand
without being man-handled by these roughs. One of them
has done his best to kill my friend here; and I'm taking the
body home. Speak for me, Dempsey.'

There was no time for the much misrepresented policemen to say a word. Dempsey spoke to them in language
calculated to alarm. They tried to explain, but Dempsey
launched into a glowing catalogue of my virtues, as noted

by him in the early hours. 'And,' he concluded vehemently, ' 'e writes for the papers, too. How'd *you* like to be written for in the papers—in verse, too, which is 'is 'abit. You leave 'im alone. 'Im an' me have been friends for months.'

'What about the dead man?' said the policeman who had not given the blow.

'I'll tell you,' I said relenting, and to the three policemen under the lights of Charing Cross assembled, I recounted faithfully and at length the adventures of the night, beginning with the *Breslau* and ending at St. Clement Danes. I described the sinful old ruffian in the ambulance in terms that made him wriggle where he lay, and never since the Metropolitan Police was founded did three policemen laugh as those three laughed. The Strand echoed to it, and the unclean birds of the night stood and wondered.

'Oh lor'!' said Dempsey wiping his eyes, 'I'd ha' given anything to see that old man runnin' about with a wet blanket an' all! Excuse me, sir, but you ought to get took up every night for to make us 'appy.' He dissolved into fresh guffaws.

There was a clinking of silver and the two policemen of St. Clement Danes hurried back to their beats, laughing as they ran.

'Take 'im to Charing Cross,' said Dempsey between shouts. 'They'll send the ambulance back in the morning.'

'Laddie, ye've misca'ed me shameful names, but I'm o'er old to go to a hospital. Dinna desert me, laddie, tak me home to my wife,' said the voice in the ambulance.

'He's none so bad. 'Is wife'll comb 'is hair for 'im proper,' said Dempsey, who was a married man.

'Where d'you live?' I demanded

'Brugglesmith,' was the answer.

'What's that?' I said to Dempsey, more skilled than I in the portmanteau words of early dawn.

'Brook Green, 'Ammersmith,' Dempsey translated promptly.

'Of course,' I said. 'That's just the sort of place he would choose to live in. I only wonder it was not Kew.'

'Are you going to wheel him 'ome, sir?' said Dempsey.

'I'd wheel him home if he lived in——Paradise. He's not going to get out of this ambulance while I'm here. He'd drag me into a murder for tuppence.'

'Then strap 'im up an' make sure,' said Dempsey, and he deftly buckled two straps, that hung by the side of the ambulance, over the man's body. Brugglesmith—I know not his other name—was sleeping deeply. He even smiled in his sleep.

'That's all right,' said Dempsey, and I moved off, wheeling my devil's perambulator before me. Trafalgar Square was empty except for the few that slept in the open. One of these wretches ranged alongside and begged for money, asserting that he had once been a gentleman.

'So have I,' I said. 'That was long ago. I'll give you a shilling if you'll help me to push this thing.'

'Is it a murder?' said the vagabond, shrinking back. 'I've not got to *that* yet.'

'No. It's going to be one,' I answered. 'I have.'

The man slunk back into the darkness and I pressed on, through Cockspur Street, and up to Piccadilly Circus, wondering what I should do with my treasure. All London was asleep, and I had only this drunken carcase to bear me company. It was silent—silent as chaste Piccadilly. A young man of my acquaintance came out of a pink-brick club as I passed. A faded carnation drooped from his button-hole; he had been playing cards, and was walking home before the dawn, when he overtook me.

'What are you doing?' he said.

I was far beyond any feeling of shame. 'It's for a bet,' said I. 'Come and help.'

'Laddie, who's yon?' said the voice beneath the hood.

'Good Lord!' said the young man, leaping across the pavement. Perhaps card-losses had told on his nerves. Mine were steel that night.

'The Lord, the Lord?' the passionless, incurious voice went on. 'Dinna be profane, laddie. He'll come in His ain good time.'

The young man looked at me with horror.

'It's all part of the bet,' I answered. 'Do come and push.'

'W—where are you going to?' said he.

'Brugglesmith,' said the voice within. 'Laddie, d'ye ken my wife?'

'No,' said I.

'Well, she's just a tremenjus wumman. Laddie, I want a drink. Knock at one o' these braw houses, laddie, an'—an'—ye may kiss the girl for your pains.'

'Lie still, or I'll gag you,' I said, savagely.

The young man with the carnation crossed to the other side of Piccadilly, and hailed the only hansom visible for miles. What he thought I cannot tell. Later I was told.

I pressed on—wheeling, eternally—to Brook Green, Hammersmith. There I would abandon Brugglesmith to the gods of that desolate land. We had been through so much together that I could not leave him bound in the street. Besides, he would call after me, and oh! it is a shameful thing to hear one's name ringing down the emptiness of London in the dawn.

So I went on, past Apsley House, even to the coffee-stall, but there was no coffee for Brugglesmith. And into Knightsbridge—respectable Knightsbridge—I wheeled my burden, the body of Brugglesmith.

'Laddie, what are ye going to do to me?' he said when opposite the barracks.

'Kill you,' I said briefly, 'or hand you over to your wife. Be quiet.'

He would not obey. He talked incessantly—sliding in one sentence from clear cut dialect to wild and drunken jumble. At the Albert Hall he said that I was the 'Hattle Gardle buggle,' which I apprehend is the Hatton Garden burglar. At Kensington High Street he loved me as a son, but when my weary legs came to the Addison Road

Bridge he implored me with tears to unloose the straps and to fight against the sin of vanity. No man molested us. It was as though a bar had been set between myself and all humanity till I had cleared my account with Bruggle-smith. The glimmering of light grew in the sky; the cloudy brown of the wood pavement turned to heather-purple; I made no doubt that I should be allowed vengeance on Brugglesmith ere the evening.

At Hammersmith the heavens were steel-gray, and the day came weeping. All the tides of the sadness of an unprofitable dawning poured into the soul of Brugglesmith. He wept bitterly, because the puddles looked cold and houseless. I entered a half-waked public-house—in evening dress and an ulster, I marched to the bar—and got him whisky on condition that he should cease kicking at the canvas of the ambulance. Then he wept more bitterly, for that he had ever been associated with me, and so seduced into stealing the *Breslau's* dinghy.

The day was white and wan when I reached my long journey's end, and, putting back the hood, bade Bruggle-smith declare where he lived. His eyes wandered disconsolately round the red and gray houses till they fell on a villa in whose garden stood a staggering board with the legend 'To Let.' It needed only this to break him down utterly, and with that breakage fled his fine fluency in his guttural northern tongue; for liquor levels all.

'Olely lil while,' he sobbed. 'Olely lil while. Home— falmy—besht of falmies—wife, too—*you* dole know my wife! Left them all a lil while ago. Now everything's sold—all sold. Wife—falmy—all sold. Lemmegellup!'

I unbuckled the straps cautiously. Brugglesmith rolled off his resting-place and staggered to the house.

'Wattle I do?' he said.

Then I understood the baser depths in the mind of Mephistopheles.

'Ring,' I said; 'perhaps they are in the attic or the cellar.'

'You do' know my wife. She shleeps on soful in the dorlin' room waitin' meculhome. *You* do' know my wife.'

He took off his boots, covered them with his tall hat, and craftily as a Red Indian picked his way up the garden path and smote the bell marked 'Visitors' a severe blow with his clenched fist.

'Bell sole too. Sole electick bell! Wassor bell this? I can't riggle bell,' he moaned despairingly.

'You pull it—pull it hard,' I repeated, keeping a wary eye down the road. Vengeance was coming and I desired no witnesses.

'Yes, I'll pull it hard.' He slapped his forehead with inspiration. 'I'll pull it out.'

Leaning back he grasped the knob with both hands and pulled. A wild ringing in the kitchen was his answer. Spitting on his hands he pulled with renewed strength, and shouted for his wife. Then he bent his ear to the knob, shook his head, drew out an enormous yellow and red handkerchief, tied it round the knob, turned his back to the door, and pulled over his shoulder.

Either the handkerchief or the wire, it seemed to me, was bound to give way. But I had forgotten the bell. Something cracked in the kitchen, and Brugglesmith moved slowly down the doorsteps, pulling valiantly. Three feet of wire followed him.

'Pull, oh pull!' I cried. 'It's coming now!'

'Qui' ri',' he said. '*I'll* riggle bell.'

He bowed forward, the wire creaking and straining behind him, the bell-knob clasped to his bosom, and from the noises within I fancied the bell was taking away with it half the wood-work of the kitchen and all the basement banisters as it came up.

'Get a purchase on her,' I shouted, and he spun round, lapping that good copper wire about him. I opened the garden gate politely, and he passed out, spinning his own cocoon. Still the bell came up, hand over hand, and still the wire held fast. He was in the middle of the road now, whirling like an impaled cockchafer, and shouting madly for his wife and family. There he met with the ambulance, the bell within the house gave one last peal, and bounded from the far end of the hall to the inner side of the hall door, when it stayed fast. So did not my friend Brugglesmith. He fell upon his face embracing the ambulance as he did so, and the two turned over together in the toils of the never-sufficiently-to-be-advertised copper wire.

'Laddie,' he gasped, his speech returning, 'have I a legal remedy?'

'I will go and look for one,' I said, and, departing, found two policemen, whom I told that daylight had surprised a burglar in Brook Green while he was stealing lead from an empty house. Perhaps they had better take care of that bootless thief. He seemed to be in difficulties.

I led the way to the spot, and behold! in the splendour of the dawning, the ambulance, wheels uppermost, was walking down the muddy road on two stockinged feet— was shuffling to and fro in a quarter of a circle whose radius was copper wire, and whose centre was the bell-plate of the empty house.

Next to the amazing ingenuity with which Brugglesmith had contrived to lash himself under the ambulance, the thing that appeared to impress the constables most was the fact of the St. Clement Danes ambulance being at Brook Green, Hammersmith.

They even asked me, of all people in the world, whether I knew anything about it.

They extricated him; not without pain and dirt. He explained that he was repelling boarding-attacks by a 'Hattle Gardle buggle' who had sold his house, wife, and family. As to the bell-wire, he offered no explanation, and was borne off shoulder-high between the two policemen. Though his feet were not within six inches of the ground, they paddled swiftly, and I saw that in his magnificent mind he was running—furiously running.

Sometimes I have wondered whether he wished to find me.

1891

BROTHER
SQUARE-TOES

~~~~~~

It was almost the end of their visit to the seaside. They had turned themselves out of doors while their trunks were being packed, and strolled over the Downs toward the dull evening sea. The tide was dead low under the chalk cliffs, and the little wrinkled waves grieved along the sands up the coast to Newhaven and down the coast to long, grey Brighton, whose smoke trailed out across the Channel.

They walked to The Gap where the cliff is only a few feet high. A windlass for hoisting shingle from the beach below stands at the edge of it. The Coastguard cottages are a little farther on, and an old ship's figure-head of a Turk in a turban stared at them over the wall.

'This time to-morrow we shall be at home, thank goodness,' said Una. 'I hate the sea!'

'I believe it's all right in the middle,' said Dan. 'The edges are the sorrowful parts.'

Cordery, the coastguard, came out of the cottage, levelled his telescope at some fishing-boats, shut it with a click and walked away. He grew smaller and smaller along the edge of the cliff, where neat piles of white chalk every few yards show the path even on the darkest night.

'Where's Cordery going?' said Una.

'Half-way to Newhaven,' said Dan. 'Then he'll meet the Newhaven coastguard and turn back. He says if coastguards were done away with, smuggling would start up at once.'

A voice on the beach under the cliff began to sing:

> 'The moon she shined on Telscombe Tye—
>   On Telscombe Tye at night it was—
> She saw the smugglers riding by,
>   A very pretty sight it was!'

Feet scrabbled on the flinty path. A dark, thin-faced man in very neat brown clothes and broad-toed shoes came up, followed by Puck.

> 'Three Dunkirk boats was standin' in!'

the man went on.

'Hssh!' said Puck. 'You'll shock these nice young people.'

'Oh! Shall I? Mille pardons!' He shrugged his shoulders almost up to his ears—spread his hands abroad, and jabbered in French. 'No comprenny?' he said. 'I'll give it you in Low German.' And he went off in another language, changing his voice and manner so completely that they hardly knew him for the same person. But his dark, beady-brown eyes still twinkled merrily in his lean face, and the children felt that they did not suit the straight, plain, snuffy-brown coat, brown knee-breeches and broad-brimmed hat. His hair was tied in a short pig-tail which danced wickedly when he turned his head.

'Ha' done!' said Puck, laughing. 'Be one thing or t'other. Pharaoh. French or English or German—no great odds which.'

'Oh, but it is, though,' said Una quickly. 'We haven't begun German yet, and—and we're going back to our French next week.'

'Aren't you English?' said Dan. 'We heard you singing just now.'

'Aha! That was the Sussex side o' me. Dad he married a French girl out o' Boulogne, and French she stayed till her dyin' day. She was an Aurette, of course. We Lees mostly marry Aurettes. Haven't you ever come across the saying:

> "Aurettes and Lees,
>   Like as two peas.
>   What they can't smuggle,
>   They'll run over seas?" '

'Then, are you a smuggler?' Una cried; and, 'Have you smuggled much?' said Dan.

Mr. Lee nodded solemnly.

'Mind you,' said he, 'I don't uphold smuggling for the generality o' mankind—mostly they can't make a do of it—but I was brought up to the trade, d'ye see, in a lawful line o' descent on'—he waved across the Channel—'on both sides the water. 'Twas all in the families, same as fiddling. The Aurettes used mostly to run the stuff across from Boulogne, and we Lees landed it here and ran it up to London town, by the safest road.'

'Then where did you live?' said Una.

'You mustn't ever live too close to your business in *our* trade. We kept our little fishing smack at Shoreham, but otherwise we Lees was all honest cottager folk—at Warminghurst under Washington—Bramber way—on the old Penn estate.'

'Ah!' said Puck, squatted by the windlass. 'I remember a piece about the Lees at Warminghurst, I do:

> "There was never a Lee to Warminghurst,
>   That wasn't a gipsy last and first."

I reckon that's truth, Pharaoh.'

Pharaoh laughed. 'Admettin' that's true,' he said, 'my gipsy blood must be wore pretty thin, for I've made and kept a worldly fortune.'

'By smuggling?' Dan asked.

'No, in the tobacco trade.'

'You don't mean to say you gave up smuggling just to go and be a tobacconist!' Dan looked so disappointed they all had to laugh.

'I'm sorry; but there's all sorts of tobacconists,' Pharaoh replied. 'How far out, now, would you call that smack with the patch on her foresail?' He pointed to the fishing-boats.

'A scant mile,' said Puck after a quick look.

'Just about. It's seven fathom under her—clean sand. That was where Uncle Aurette used to sink his brandy kegs from Boulogne, and we fished 'em up and rowed 'em into The Gap here for the ponies to run inland. One thickish night in January of '93, Dad and Uncle Lot and me came over from Shoreham in the smack, and we found Uncle Aurette and the L'Estranges, my cousins, waiting for us in their lugger with New Year's presents from mother's folk in Boulogne. I remember Aunt Cecile she'd sent me a fine new red knitted cap which I put on then and there, for the French was having their Revolution in those days, and red caps was all the fashion. Uncle Aurette tells us that they had cut off their King Louis' head, and, more-over, the Brest forts had fired on an English man-o'-war. The news wasn't a week old.

' "That means war again, when we was only just getting used to the peace," says Dad. "Why can't King George's men and King Louis' men do on their uniforms and fight it out over our heads?"

' "Me too, I wish that," says Uncle Aurette. "But they'll be pressing better men than themselves to fight for 'em. The press-gangs are out already on our side: you look out for yours."

' "I'll have to bide ashore and grow cabbages for a while, after I've run this cargo; but I *do* wish"—Dad says, going over the lugger's side with our New Year presents under his arm and young L'Estrange holding the lantern—

"I just do wish that those folk which make war so easy had to run one cargo a month all this winter. It 'ud show 'em what honest work means."

' "Well, I've warned ye," says Uncle Aurette. "I'll be slipping off now before your Revenue cutter comes. Give my love to sister and take care o' the kegs. It's thicking to southward."

'I remember him waving to us and young Stephen L'Estrange blowing out the lantern. By the time we'd fished up the kegs, the fog came down so thick Dad judged it risky for me to row 'em ashore, even though we could hear the ponies stamping on the beach. So he and Uncle Lot took the dinghy and left me in the smack playing on my fiddle to guide 'em back.

'Presently I heard guns. Two of 'em sounded mighty like Uncle Aurette's three-pounders. He didn't go naked about the seas after dark. Then come more, which I reckoned was Captain Giddens in the Revenue cutter. He was open-handed with his compliments, but he *would* lay his guns himself. I stopped fiddling to listen, and I heard a whole skyful o' French up in the fog—and a high bow come down on top o' the smack. I hadn't time to call or think. I remember the smack heeling over, and me standing on the gunwale pushing against the ship's side as if I hoped to bear her off. Then the square of an open port, with a lantern in it, slid by in front of my nose. I kicked back on our gunwale as it went under and slipped through that port into the French ship—me and my fiddle.'

'Gracious!' said Una. 'What an adventure!'

'Didn't anybody see you come in?' said Dan.

'There wasn't any one there. I'd made use of an orlop deck port—that's the next deck below the gun-deck, which by rights it shouldn't have been open at all. The crew was standing by their guns up above. I rolled on to a pile of dunnage in the dark and I went to sleep. When I woke, men was talking all round me, telling each other their names and sorrows just like Dad told me pressed

men used to talk in the last war. Pretty soon I made out
they'd all been hove aboard together by the press-gangs,
and left to sort 'emselves. The ship she was the *Embuscade*, a thirty-six gun Republican frigate, Captain Jean
Baptiste Bompard, two days out of Le Havre, going to the
United States with a Republican French Ambassador of
the name of Genêt. They had been up all night clearing
for action on account of hearing guns in the fog. Uncle
Aurette and Captain Giddens must have been passing the
time o' day with each other off Newhaven, and the frigate
had drifted past 'em. She never knew she'd run down our
smack. Seeing so many aboard was total strangers to each
other, I thought one more mightn't be noticed; so I put
Aunt Cecile's red cap on the back of my head, and my
hands in my pockets like the rest, and, as we French say, I
circulated till I found the galley.

'What! Here's one of 'em that isn't sick!' says a cook.
'Take his breakfast to Citizen Bompard.'

'I carried the tray to the cabin but I didn't call this
Bompard "Citizen." Oh no! "Mon Capitaine" was my little word, same as Uncle Aurette used to answer in King
Louis' Navy. Bompard, he liked it; he took me on for
cabin servant, and after that no one asked questions; and
thus I got good victuals and light work all the way across
to America. He talked a heap of politics, and so did his officers; and when this Ambassador Genêt got rid of his land
stomach and laid down the law after dinner, a rook's parliament was nothing compared to their cabin. I learned to
know most of the men which had worked the French Revolution, through waiting at table and hearing talk about
'em. One of our forecas'le six-pounders was called Danton
and t'other Marat. I used to play the fiddle between 'em,
sitting on the capstan. Day in and day out, Bompard and
Monsieur Genêt talked o' what France had done, and how
the United States was going to join her to finish off the
English in this war. Monsieur Genêt said he'd just about
make the United States fight for France. He was a rude

common man. But I liked listening. I always helped drink any healths that was proposed—specially Citizen Danton's, who'd cut off King Louis' head. An all-Englishman might have been shocked—but that's where my French blood saved me.

'It didn't save me from getting a dose of ship's fever though, the week before we put Monsieur Genêt ashore at Charleston; and what was left of me after bleeding and pills took the dumb horrors from living 'tween decks. The surgeon, Karaguen his name was, kept me down there to help him with his plasters—I was too weak to wait on Bompard. I don't remember much of any account for the next few weeks, till I smelled lilacs, and I looked out of the port, and we was moored to a wharf-edge and there was a town o' fine gardens and red-brick houses and all the green leaves in God's world waiting for me outside.

' "What's this?" I said to the sick-bay man—old Pierre Tiphaigne he was. "Philadelphia," says Pierre. "You've missed it all. We're sailing next week."

'I just turned round and cried for longing to be amongst the laylocks.

' "If that's your trouble," says old Pierre, "you go straight ashore. None'll hinder you. They're all gone mad on these coasts—French and American together. 'Tisn't *my* notion o' war." Pierre was an old King Louis man.

'My legs was pretty tottly, but I made shift to go on deck, which it was like a fair. The frigate was crowded with fine gentlemen and ladies pouring in and out. They sung and they waved French flags, while Captain Bompard and his officers—yes, and some of the men—speechified to all and sundry about war with England. They shouted, "Down with England!"—"Down with Washington!"—"Hurrah for France and the Republic!" I couldn't make sense of it. I wanted to get out from that crunch of swords and petticoats and sit in a field. One of the gentlemen said to me, "Is that a genuine cap o' Liberty you're wearing?" 'Twas Aunt Cecile's red one, and pretty near

wore out. "Oh, yes!" I says, "straight from France." "I'll
give you a shilling for it," he says, and with that money in
my hand and my fiddle under my arm I squeezed past the
entry-port and went ashore. It was like a dream—meadows, trees, flowers, birds, houses and people *all* different! I
sat me down in a meadow and fiddled a bit, and then I
went in and out the streets, looking and smelling and
touching, like a little dog at a fair. Fine fold was setting on
the white stone doorsteps of their houses, and a girl threw
me a handful of laylock sprays, and when I said "Merci"
without thinking, she said she loved the French. They was
all the fashion in the city. I saw more tricolour flags in
Philadelphia than ever I'd seen in Boulogne, and every one
was shouting for war with England. A crowd o' folk was
cheering after our French ambassador—that same Monsieur Genêt which we'd left at Charleston. He was
a-horseback, behaving as if the place belonged to him—
and commanding all and sundry to fight the British. But
I'd heard that often. I got into a long straight street as
wide as the Broyle, where gentlemen was racing horses.
I'm fond o' horses. Nobody hindered 'em, and a man told
me it was called Race Street o' purpose for that. Then I
followed some black niggers, which I'd never seen close
before; but I left them to run after a great, proud, copper-
faced man with feathers in his hair and a red blanket trail-
ing behind him. A man told me he was a real Red Indian
called Red Jacket, and I followed him into an alley-way off
Race Street by Second Street, where there was a fiddle
playing. I'm fond o' fiddling. The Indian stopped at a
baker's shop—Conrad Gerhard's it was—and bought
some sugary cakes. Hearing what the price was I was
going to have some too, but the Indian asked me in
English if I was hungry. "Oh yes!" I says. I must have
looked a sore scrattel. He opens a door on to a staircase
and leads the way up. We walked into a dirty little room
full of flutes and fiddles and a fat man fiddling by
the window, in a smell of cheese and medicines fit to

knock you down. I *was* knocked down too, for the fat man jumped up and hit me a smack in the face. I fell against an old spinet covered with pill-boxes, and the pills rolled about the floor. The Indian never moved an eyelid.

' "Pick up the pills! Pick up the pills!" the fat man screeches.

'I started picking 'em up—hundreds of 'em—meaning to run out under the Indian's arm, but I came on giddy all over and I sat down. The fat man went back to his fiddling.

' "Toby!" says the Indian after quite a while. "I brought the boy to be fed, not hit."

' "What?" says Toby. "I thought it was Gert Schwankfelder." He put down his fiddle and took a good look at me. "Himmel!" he says. "I have hit the wrong boy. It is not the new boy. Why are you not the new boy? Why are you not Gert Schwankfelder?"

' "I don't know," I said. "The gentleman in the pink blanket brought me."

'Says the Indian, "He is hungry, Toby. Christians always feed the hungry. So I bring him."

' "You should have said that first," said Toby. He pushed plates at me and the Indian put bread and pork on them, and a glass of Madeira wine. I told him I was off the French ship, which I had joined on account of my mother being French. That was true enough when you think of it, and besides I saw that the French was all the fashion in Philadelphia. Toby and the Indian whispered and I went on picking up the pills.

' "You like pills—eh?" says Toby.

' "No," I says. "I've seen our ship's doctor roll too many of 'em."

' "Ho!" he says and he shoves two bottles at me. "What's those?"

' "Calomel," I says. "And t'other's senna."

' "Right," he says. "One week have I tried to teach Gert

Schwankfelder the difference between them, yet he cannot tell. You like to fiddle?" he says. He'd just seen my kit on the floor.

' "Oh yes!" says I.

' "Oho!" he says. "What note is this?" drawing his bow acrost.

'He meant it for A, so I told him it was.

' "My brother," he says to the Indian, "I think this is the hand of Providence! I warned that Gert if he went to play upon the wharves any more he would hear from me. Now look at this boy and say what you think."

'The Indian looked me over whole minutes—there was a musical clock on the wall, and dolls came out and hopped while the hour struck. He looked me over all the while they did it.

' "Good," he says at last. "This boy is good."

' "Good, then," says Toby. "Now I shall play my fiddle and you shall sing your hymn, brother. Boy, go down to the bakery and tell them you are young Gert Schwankfelder that was. The horses are in Davy Jones's locker. If you ask any questions you shall hear from me."

'I left 'em singing hymns and I went down to old Conrad Gerhard. He wasn't at all surprised when I told him I was young Gert Schwankfelder that was. He knew Toby. His wife she walked me into the back yard without a word, and she washed me and she cut my hair to the edge of a basin, and she put me to bed, and oh! how I slept—how I slept in that little room behind the oven looking on the flower garden! I didn't know Toby went to the *Embuscade* that night and bought me off Dr. Karaguen for twelve dollars and a dozen bottles of Seneca Oil. Karaguen wanted a new lace to his coat, and he reckoned I hadn't long to live; so he put me down as "discharged sick." '

'I like Toby,' said Una.

'Who was he?' said Puck.

'Apothecary Tobias Hirte,' Pharaoh replied. 'One Hun-

dred and Eighteen, Second Street—the famous Seneca Oil
man, that lived half of every year among the Indians. But
let me tell my tale my own way, same as his brown mare
used to go to Lebanon.'

'Then why did he keep her in Davy Jones's locker?'
Dan asked.

'That was his joke. He kept her under David Jones's hat
shop in the "Buck" tavern yard, and his Indian friends
kept their ponies there when they visited him. I looked
after the horses, when I wasn't rolling pills on top of the
old spinet while he played his fiddle and Red Jacket sang
hymns. I liked it. I had good victuals, light work, a suit o'
clean clothes, a plenty music, and quiet smiling German
folk all around that let me sit in their gardens. My first
Sunday, Toby took me to his church in Moravian Alley;
and that was in a garden too. The women wore long-eared
caps and handkerchiefs. They came in at one door and the
men at another, and there was a brass chandeller you
could see your face in, and a nigger-boy to blow the
organ-bellows. I carried Toby's fiddle and he played
pretty much as he chose all against the organ and the
singing. He was the only one they let do it, for they was a
simple-minded folk. They used to wash each other's feet
up in the attic to keep 'emselves humble: which Lord
knows they didn't need.'

'How very queer,' said Una.

Pharaoh's eyes twinkled. 'I've met many and seen
much,' he said. 'But I haven't yet found any better or
quieter or forbearinger people than the Brethern and Sis-
tern of the Moravian Church in Philadelphia. Nor will I
ever forget my first Sunday—the service was in English
that week—with the smell of the flowers coming in from
Pastor Meder's garden where the big peach tree is, and me
looking at all the clean strangeness and thinking of 'tween
decks on the *Embuscade* only six days ago. Being a boy, it
seemed to me it had lasted for ever, and was going on for
ever. But I didn't know Toby then. As soon as the dancing

clock struck midnight that Sunday—I was lying under the
spinet—I heard Toby's fiddle. He'd just done his supper
which he always took late and heavy. "Gert," says he, "get
the horses. Liberty and Independence for ever! The flowers appear upon the earth and the time of the singing of
birds is come. We are going to my country seat in Lebanon."

'I rubbed my eyes, and fetched 'em out of the "Buck"
stable. Red Jacket was there saddling his, and when I'd
packed the saddle-bags we three rode up Race Street to
the Ferry by starlight. So we went travelling. It's a kindly,
soft country there, back of Philadelphia among the German towns, Lancaster way. Little houses and bursting big
barns, fat cattle, fat women, and all as peaceful as Heaven
might be if they farmed there. Toby sold medicines out of
his saddle-bags, and gave the French war-news to folk
along the roads. Him and his long-hilted umberell was as
well known as the stage coaches. He took orders for that
famous Seneca Oil which he had the secret of from Red
Jacket's Indians, and he slept in friends' farmhouses, but
he *would* shut all the windows: so Red Jacket and me slept
outside. There's nothing to hurt except snakes—and they
slip away quick enough if you thrash in the bushes.'

'I'd have liked that!' said Dan.

'I'd no fault to find with those days. In the cool o' the
morning the cat-bird sings. He's something to listen to.
And there's a smell of wild grape-vine growing in damp
hollows which you drop into, after long rides in the heat,
which is beyond compare for sweetness. So's the puffs out
of the pine woods of afternoons. Come sundown, the
frogs strike up, and later on the fireflies dance in the
corn. Oh me, the fireflies in the corn! We were a week or
ten days on the road, tacking from one place to another—
such as Lancaster, Bethlehem-Ephrata—'thou Bethlehem-
Ephrata'—no odds—I loved the going about: and so we
jogged into dozy little Lebanon by the Blue Mountains
where Toby had a cottage and a garden of all fruits. He

come north every year for this wonderful Seneca Oil the Seneca Indians made for him. They'd never sell to any one else, and he doctored 'em with von Swieten pills which they valued more than their own oil. He could do what he chose with them, and, of course, he tried to make them Moravians. The Senecas are a seemly, quiet people, and they'd had trouble enough from white men—Americans and English—during the wars, to keep 'em in that walk. They lived on a Reservation by themselves, away off on their lake. Toby took me up there, and they treated me as if I was their own blood brother. Red Jacket said the mark of my bare feet in the dust was just like an Indian's and my style of walking was similar. I know I took to their ways all over.'

'Maybe the gipsy drop in your blood helped you?' said Puck.

'Sometimes I think it did,' Pharaoh went on. 'Anyhow, Red Jacket and Cornplanter, the other Seneca chief, they let me be adopted into the tribe. It's only a compliment, of course, but Toby was angry when I showed up with my face painted. They gave me a side-name which means "Two Tongues" because, d'ye see, I talked French and English.

'They had their own opinions (*I*'ve heard 'em) about the French and the English, *and* the Americans. They'd suffered from all of 'em during the wars, and they only wished to be left alone. But they thought a heap of the President of the United States. Cornplanter had had dealings with him in some French wars out West when General Washington was only a lad. His being President afterward made no odds to 'em. They always called him Big Hand, for he was a large-fisted man, and he was all of their notion of a white chief. Cornplanter 'ud sweep his blanket round him, and after I'd filled his pipe he'd begin—"In the old days, long ago, when braves were many and blankets were few, Big Hand said——" If Red Jacket agreed to the say-so he'd trickle a little smoke out of the

corners of his mouth. If he didn't he'd blow through his
nostrils. Then Cornplanter 'ud stop and Red Jacket 'ud
take on. Red Jacket was the better talker of the two. I've
laid and listened to 'em for hours. Oh! they knew General
Washington well. Cornplanter used to meet him at
Epply's—the great dancing place in the city before District Marshal William Nichols bought it. They told me he
was always glad to see 'em, and he'd hear 'em out to the
end if they had anything on their minds. They had a good
deal in those days. I came at it by degrees, after I was
adopted into the tribe. The talk up in Lebanon and everywhere else that summer was about the French war with
England and whether the United States 'ud join in with
France or make a peace-treaty with England. Toby
wanted peace so as he could go about the Reservation
buying his oils. But most of the white men wished for
war, and they was angry because the President wouldn't
give the sign for it. The newspaper said men was burning
Guy Fawkes images of General Washington and yelling
after him in the streets of Philadelphia. You'd have been
astonished what those two fine old chiefs knew of the ins
and outs of such matters. The little I've learned of politics
I picked up from Cornplanter and Red Jacket on the Reservation. Toby used to read the *Aurora* newspaper. He
was what they call a "Democrat," though our Church is
against the Brethren concerning themselves with politics.'

'I hate politics, too,' said Una, and Pharaoh laughed.

'I might ha' guessed it,' he said. 'But here's something
that isn't politics. One hot evening late in August, Toby
was reading the newspaper on the stoop and Red Jacket
was smoking under a peach tree and I was fiddling. Of a
sudden Toby drops his *Aurora*.'

' "I am an oldish man, too fond of my own comforts,"
he says. "I will go to the church which is in Philadelphia.
My brother, lend me a spare pony. I must be there to-
morrow night."

' "Good!" says Red Jacket looking at the sun. "My

brother shall be there. I will ride with him and bring back the ponies."

'I went to pack the saddle-bags. Toby had cured me of asking questions. He stopped my fiddling if I did. Besides, Indians don't ask questions much, and I wanted to be like 'em.

'When the horses were ready I jumped up.

' "Get off," says Toby. "Stay and mind the cottage till I come back. The Lord has laid this on me, not on you. I wish He hadn't."

'He powders off down the Lancaster road, and I sat on the door-step wondering after him. When I picked up the paper to wrap his fiddle-strings in I spelled out a piece about the yellow fever being in Philadelphia so dreadful every one was running away. I was scared, for I was fond of Toby. We never said much to each other, but we fiddled together; and music's as good as talking to them that understand.'

'Did Toby die of yellow fever?' Una asked.

'Not him! There's justice left in the world still! He went down to the City and bled 'em well again in heaps. He sent back word by Red Jacket that, if there was war or he died, I was to bring the oils along to the city, but till then I was to go on working in the garden and Red Jacket was to see me do it. Down at heart, all Indians reckon digging a squaw's business, and neither him nor Cornplanter, when he relieved watch, was a hard task-master. We hired a nigger-boy to do our work, and a lazy grinning runagate he was. When I found Toby didn't die the minute he reached town, why, boylike, I took him off my mind and went with my Indians again. Oh, those days up north at Canasedago, running races and gambling with the Senecas, or bee-hunting in the woods, or fishing in the lake!' Pharaoh sighed and looked across the water. 'But it's best,' he went on suddenly, 'after the first frostes. You roll out o' your blanket and find every leaf left green over night turned red and yellow, not by trees at a time, but hundreds and hundreds of miles of 'em, like sunsets splattered upside down. On one of such days—the maples was flaming scarlet and gold, and the sumach bushes were redder—Cornplanter and Red Jacket came out in full war-dress, making the very leaves look silly. Feathered war-bonnets, yellow doe-skin leggings, fringed and tasselled, red horse-blankets, and their bridles feathered and shelled and beaded no bounds. I thought it was war against the British till I saw their faces weren't painted, and they only carried wrist-whips. Then I hummed "Yankee Doodle" at 'em. They told me they was going to visit Big Hand and find out for sure whether he meant to join the French in fighting the English or make a peace treaty with England. I reckon those two would ha' gone out on the war-path at a nod from Big Hand, but they knew well, if there was war 'twixt England and the United States, their tribe 'ud catch it from both parties same as in all the other wars. They asked me to come along and hold the ponies. That puzzled me, because they always put their ponies up at the "Buck" or Epply's when they went to see General Washington in the city, and horse-holding is a nigger's job. Besides, I wasn't exactly dressed for it.'

'D'you mean you were dressed like an Indian?' Dan demanded.

Pharaoh looked a little abashed. 'This didn't happen at Lebanon,' he said, 'but a bit farther north, on the Reservation; and at that particular moment of time, so far as blanket, hair-band, moccasins and sunburn went, there wasn't much odds 'twix me and a young Seneca buck. You may laugh,' he smoothed down his long-skirted brown coat. 'But I told you I took to their ways all over. I said nothing, though I was bursting to let out the war-whoop like the young men had taught me.'

'No, and you don't let out one here, either,' said Puck before Dan could ask. 'Go on, Brother Square-toes.'

'We went on.' Pharaoh's narrow dark eyes gleamed and danced. 'We went on—forty, fifty miles a day, for days on

end—we three braves. And how a great tall Indian
a-horseback can carry his war-bonnet at a canter through
thick timber without brushing a feather beats *me!* My silly
head was banged often enough by low branches, but *they*
slipped through like running elks. We had evening hymn-
singing every night after they'd blown their pipe-smoke to
the quarters of Heaven. Where did we go? I'll tell you, but
don't blame me if you're no wiser. We took the old war-
trail from the end of the Lake along the East Susquehanna
through the Nantego country, right down to Fort Shamo-
kin on the Senachse river. We crossed the Juniata by Fort
Granville, got into Shippensberg over the hills by the
Ochwick trail, and then to Williams Ferry (it's a bad
one). From Williams Ferry, across the Shanedore, over
the Blue Mountains, through Ashby's Gap, and so south-
east by south from there, till we found the President at the
back of his own plantations. I'd hate to be trailed by Indians in earnest. They caught him like a partridge on a
stump. After we'd left our ponies, we scouted forward
through a woody piece and, creeping slower and slower, at
last if my moccasins even slipped Red Jacket 'ud turn and
frown. I heard voices—Monsieur Genêt's for choice—long
before I saw anything, and we pulled up at the edge of a
clearing where some niggers in grey and red liveries were
holding horses, and half-a-dozen gentlemen—but one was
Genêt—were talking among felled timber. I fancy they'd
come to see Genêt a piece on his road, for his portmantle
was with him. I hid in between two logs as near to the
company as I be to that old windlass there. I didn't need
anybody to show me Big Hand. He stood up, very still,
his legs a little apart, listening to Genêt, that French Ambassador, which never had more manners than a Bosham
tinker. Genêt was as good as ordering him to declare war
on England at once. I had heard that clack before on the
Embuscade. He said he'd stir up the whole United States
to have war with England, whether Big Hand liked it or
not.

'Big Hand heard him out to the last end. I looked behind me and my two chiefs had vanished like smoke. Says Big Hand, "That is very forcibly put, Monsieur Genêt——" "Citizen—citizen!" the fellow spits in. "*I*, at least, am a Republican!" "Citizen Genêt," he says, "you may be sure it will receive my fullest consideration." This seemed to take Citizen Genêt back a piece. He rode off grumbling, and never gave his nigger a penny. No gentleman!

'The others all assembled round Big Hand then, and, in their way, they said pretty much what Genêt had said. They put it to him, here was France and England at war, in a manner of speaking, right across the United States' stomach, and paying no regards to any one. The French was searching American ships on pretence they was helping England, but really for to steal the goods. The English was doing the same, only t'other way round; and, besides searching, they was pressing American citizens into their navy to help them fight France, on pretence that those Americans was lawful British subjects. His gentlemen put this very clear to Big Hand. It didn't look to *them*, they said, as though the United States trying to keep out of the fight was any advantage to *her*, because she only catched it from both French and English. They said that nine out of ten good Americans was crazy to fight the English then and there. They wouldn't say whether that was right or wrong, they only wanted Big Hand to turn it over in his mind. He did—for a while. I saw Red Jacket and Cornplanter watching him from the far side of the clearing, and how they had slipped round there was another mystery. Then Big Hand drew himself up, and he let his gentlemen have it.'

'Hit 'em?' Dan asked.

'No, nor yet was it what you might call swearing. He—he blasted 'em with his natural speech. He asked them, half a dozen times over, whether the United States had enough armed ships for any shape or sort of war with any one. He asked 'em, if they thought she *had* those ships, to *give* him those ships, and they looked on the ground, as if they expected to find 'em *there*. He put it to 'em whether, setting ships aside, their country—I reckon he gave 'em good reasons—whether the United States was ready or able to face a new big war; she having but so few years back wound up one against England, and being all holds full of her own troubles. As I said, the strong way he laid it all before 'em blasted 'em, and when he'd done it was like a still in the woods after a storm. A little man—but they all looked little—pipes up like a young rook in a blowed-down nest, "Nevertheless, General, it seems you will be compelled to fight England." Quick Big Hand wheels on him, "And is there anything in my past which makes you think I am averse to fighting Great Britain?"

'Everybody laughed except him. "Oh, General, you mistake us entirely!" they says. "I trust so," he says. "But I know my duty. We *must* have peace with England."

' "At any price?" says the man with the rook's voice.

' "At any price," says he word by word. "Our ships will be searched—our citizens will be pressed, but——"

' "Then what about the Declaration of Independence?" says one.

' "Deal with facts, not fancies," says Big Hand. "The United States are in no position to fight England."

' "But think of public opinion," another one starts up. "The feeling in Philadelphia alone is at fever heat."

'He held up one of his big hands. "Gentlemen," he says—slow he spoke, but his voice carried far—"I have to think of our country. Let me assure you that the treaty with Great Britain will be made though every city in the Union burn me in effigy."

' "At any price?" the actor-like chap keeps on croaking.

' "The treaty must be made on Great Britain's own terms. What else can I do?"

'He turns his back on 'em and they looked at each other and slinked off to the horses, leaving him alone: and then I saw he was an old man. Then Red Jacket and Cornplanter rode down the clearing from the far end as though they had just chanced along. Back went Big Hand's shoulders, up went his head and he stepped forward one single pace with a great deep Hough! so pleased he was. That was a statelified meeting to behold—three big men, and two of 'em looking like jewelled images among the spattle of gay-coloured leaves. I saw my chiefs' war-bonnets sinking together, down and down. Then they made the sign which no Indian makes outside of the Medicine Lodges—a sweep of the right hand just clear of the dust and an inbend of the left knee at the same time, and those proud eagle feathers almost touched his boot-top.'

'What did it mean?' said Dan.

'Mean!' Pharaoh cried. 'Why it's what you—what we—it's the Sachems' way of sprinkling the sacred corn-meal in front of—Oh! it's a piece of Indian compliment really, and it signifies that you are a very big chief.

'Big Hand looked down on 'em. First he says quite softly, "My brothers know it is not easy to be a chief." Then his voice grew. "My children," says he, "what is in your minds?"

'Says Cornplanter, "We came to ask whether there will be war with King George's men, but we have heard what our Father has said to his chiefs. We will carry away that talk in our hearts to tell our people."'

1910

'A PRIEST
IN SPITE OF HIMSELF'

The day after they came home from the seaside they set
out on a tour of inspection to make sure everything was as
they had left it. Soon they discovered that old Hobden had
blocked their best hedge-gaps with stakes and thorn-
bundles, and had trimmed up the hedges where the black-
berries were setting.

'It can't be time for the gipsies to come along,' said Una.
'Why, it was summer only the other day!'

'There's smoke in Low Shaw!' said Dan, sniffing. 'Let's
make sure!'

They crossed the fields toward the thin line of blue
smoke that leaned above the hollow of Low Shaw which
lies beside the King's Hill road. It used to be an old quarry
till somebody planted it, and you can look straight down
into it from the edge of Banky Meadow.

'I thought so,' Dan whispered, as they came up to the
fence at the edge of the larches. A gipsy-van—not the
showman's sort, but the old black kind, with little windows high up and a baby-gate across the door—was getting ready to leave. A man was harnessing the horses; an
old woman crouched over the ashes of a fire made out of
broken fence-rails; and a girl sat on the van-steps singing
to a baby on her lap. A wise-looking, thin dog snuffed at a
patch of fur on the ground till the old woman put it carefully in the middle of the fire. The girl reached back inside

the van and tossed her a paper parcel. This was laid on the fire too, and they smelt singed feathers.

'Chicken feathers!' said Dan. 'I wonder if they are old Hobden's.'

Una sneezed. The dog growled and crawled to the girl's feet, the old woman fanned the fire with her hat, while the man led the horses up to the shafts. They all moved as quickly and quietly as snakes over moss.

'Ah!' said the girl. 'I'll teach you!' She beat the dog, who seemed to expect it.

'Don't do that,' Una called down. 'It wasn't his fault.'

'How do you know what I'm beating him for?' she answered.

'For not seeing us,' said Dan. 'He was standing right in the smoke, and the wind was wrong for his nose, anyhow.'

The girl stopped beating the dog, and the old woman fanned faster than ever.

'You've fanned some of your feathers out of the fire,' said Una. 'There's a tail-feather by that chestnut-tot.'

'What of it?' said the old woman, as she grabbed it.

'Oh, nothing!' said Dan. 'Only I've heard say that tail-feathers are as bad as the whole bird, sometimes.'

That was a saying of Hobden's about pheasants. Old Hobden always burned all feather and fur before he sat down to eat.

'Come on, mother,' the man whispered. The old woman climbed into the van and the horses drew it out of the deep-rutted shaw on to the hard road.

The girl waved her hands and shouted something they could not catch.

'That was gipsy for "Thank you kindly, Brother and Sister," ' said Pharaoh Lee.

He was standing behind them, his fiddle under his arm.

'Gracious, you startled me!' said Una.

'*You* startled old Priscilla Savile,' Puck called from

below them. 'Come and sit by their fire. She ought to have put it out before they left.'

They dropped down the ferny side of the shaw. Una raked the ashes together, Dan found a dead wormy oak branch that burns without flame, and they watched the smoke while Pharaoh played a curious wavery air.

'That's what the girl was humming to the baby,' said Una.

'I know it,' he nodded, and went on—

> 'Ai Lumai, Lumai, Lumai! Luludia!
> Ai Luludia!'

He passed from one odd tune to another, and quite forgot the children. At last Puck asked him to go on with his adventures in Philadelphia and among the Seneca Indians.

'I'm telling it,' he said, staring straight in front of him as he played. 'Can't you hear?'

'Maybe, but *they* can't. Tell it aloud,' said Puck.

Pharaoh shook himself, laid his fiddle beside him, and began:

'I'd left Red Jacket and Cornplanter riding home with me after Big Hand had said that there wouldn't be any war. That's all there was to it. We believed Big Hand and we went home again—we three braves. When we reached Lebanon we found Toby at the cottage with his waistcoat a foot too big for him—so hard he had worked amongst the yellow-fever people. He beat me for running off with the Indians, but 'twas worth it—I was glad to see him—and when we went back to Philadelphia for the winter, and I was told how he'd sacrificed himself over sick people in the yellow fever, I thought the world and all of him. No I didn't neither. I'd thought that all along. That yellow fever must have been something dreadful. Even in December people had no more than begun to trinkle back to town. Whole houses stood empty and the niggers was

robbing them out. But I can't call to mind that any of the
Moravian Brethren had died. It seemed like they had just
kept on with their own concerns, and the good Lord He'd
just looked after 'em. That was the winter—yes, winter of
Ninety-three—the Brethren bought a stove for the
Church. Toby spoke in favour of it because the cold
spoiled his fiddle hand, but many thought stove-heat
not in the Bible, and there was yet a third party which always brought hickory-coal foot-warmers to service and
wouldn't speak either way. They ended by casting the Lot
for it, which is like pitch and toss. After my summer with
the Senecas, church-stoves didn't highly interest me, so I
took to haunting around among the French *émigrés* which
Philadelphia was full of. My French and my fiddling
helped me there, d'ye see. They come over in shiploads
from France, where, by what I made out, every one was
killing every one else by any means, and they spread 'emselves about the city—mostly in Drinker's Alley and El-
frith's Alley—and they did odd jobs till times should
mend. But whatever they stooped to, they were gentry
and kept a cheerful countenance, and after an evening's
fiddling at one of their poor little proud parties, the Brethren seemed old-fashioned. Pastor Meder and Brother
Adam Goose didn't like my fiddling for hire, but Toby
said it was lawful in me to earn my living by exercising
my talents. He never let me be put upon.

'In February of Ninety-four—no, March it must have
been, because a new ambassador called Fauchet had come
from France, with no more manners than Genêt the old
one—in March, Red Jacket came in from the Reservation
bringing news of all kind friends there. I showed him
round the city, and we saw General Washington riding
through a crowd of folk that shouted for war with
England. They gave him quite rough music, but he looked
'twixt his horse's ears and made out not to notice. His
stirrup brished Red Jacket's elbow, and Red Jacket whis-

pered up, "My brother knows it is not easy to be a chief?"
Big Hand shot just one look at him and nodded. Then there
was a scuffle behind us over some one who wasn't hooting
at Washington loud enough to please the people. We went
away to be out of the fight. Indians won't risk being hit.'

'What do they do if they are?' Dan asked.

'Kill, of course. That's why they have such proper
manners. Well, then, coming home by Drinker's Alley to
get a new shirt which a French Vicomte's lady was washing to take the stiff out of (I'm always choice in my body-
linen), a lame Frenchman pushes a paper of buttons at us.
He hadn't long landed in the United States, and please
would we buy. He sure-ly was a pitiful scrattel—his coat
half torn off, his face cut, but his hands steady; so I knew
it wasn't drink. He said his name was Peringuey, and he'd
been knocked about in the crowd round the Stadt—Independence Hall. One thing leading to another we took him
up to Toby's rooms, same as Red Jacket had taken me the
year before. The compliments he paid to Toby's Madeira
wine fairly conquered the old man, for he opened a second
bottle and he told this Monsieur Peringuey all about our
great stove dispute in the Church. I remember Pastor
Meder and Brother Adam Goose dropped in, and although they and Toby were direct opposite sides regarding stoves, yet this Monsieur Peringuey he made 'em feel
as if he thought each one was in the right of it. He said he
had been a clergyman before he had to leave France. He
admired at Toby's fiddling and he asked if Red Jacket, sitting by the spinet, was a simple Huron. Senecas aren't
Hurons, they're Iroquois, of course, and Toby told him
so. Well, then, in due time he arose and left in a style
which made us feel he'd been favouring us, instead of us
feeding him. I've never seen that so strong before—in a
man. We all talked him over but couldn't make head or tail
of him; and Red Jacket come out to walk with me to the
French quarter when I was due to fiddle at a party. Passing Drinker's Alley again, we saw a naked window with a

light in it, and there sat our button-selling Monsieur Peringuey throwing dice all alone, right hand against left.

'Says Red Jacket, keeping back in the dark, "Look at his face!"

'I was looking. I protest to you I wasn't frightened like I was when Big Hand talked to his gentlemen. I—I only looked, and I only wondered that even those dead dumb dice 'ud dare to fall different from what that face wished. It—it *was* a face!

' "He is bad," says Red Jacket. "But he is a great chief. The French have sent away a great chief. I thought so when he told us his lies. Now I know."

'I had to go on to the party, so I asked him to call round for me afterward and we'd have hymn-singing at Toby's as usual.

' "No," he says. "Tell Toby I am not Christian to-night. All Indian." He had those fits sometimes. I wanted to know more about Monsieur Peringuey, and the *émigré* party was the very place to find out. It's neither here nor there of course, but those French *émigré* parties they almost make you cry. The men that you bought fruit of in Market Street, the hair-dressers and fencing-masters and French teachers, they turn back again by candlelight to what they used to be at home, and you catch their real names. There wasn't much room in the wash-house, so I sat on top of the copper and played 'em the tunes they called for—"*Si le Roi m'avait donné*," and such nursery stuff. They cried sometimes. It hurt me to take their money afterward, indeed it did. And there I found out about Monsieur Peringuey. He was a proper rogue too! None of 'em had a good word for him except the Marquise that kept the French boarding-house on Fourth Street. I made out that his real name was the Count Talleyrand de Périgord—a priest right enough, but sorely come down in the world. He'd been King Louis's Ambassador to England a year or two back, before the French had cut off King Louis's head; and, by what I heard, that head wasn't hardly more than hanging loose before he'd run back to Paris and prevailed on Danton, the very man which did the murder, to send him back to England again as Ambassador of the French Republic! That was too much for the English, so they kicked him out by Act of Parliament, and he'd fled to the Americas without money or friends or prospects. I'm telling you the talk in the wash-house. Some of 'em was laughing over it. Says the French Marquise, "My friends, you laugh too soon. That man will be on the winning side before any of us."

' "I did not know you were so fond of priests, Marquise," says the Vicomte. His lady did my washing, as I've told you.

' "I have my reasons," says the Marquise. "He sent my uncle and my two brothers to Heaven by the little door,"—that was one of the *émigré* names for the guillotine. "He will be on the winning side if it costs him the blood of every friend he has in the world."

' "Then what does he want here?" says one of 'em. "We have all lost our game."

' "My faith!" says the Marquise. "He will find out, if any one can, whether this canaille of a Washington means to help us to fight England. Genêt (that was my ambassador in the *Embuscade*) has failed and gone off disgraced; Fauchet (he was the new man) hasn't done any better, but our abbé will find out, and he will make his profit out of the news. Such a man does not fail."

' "He begins unluckily," says the Vicomte. "He was set upon to-day in the street for not hooting your Washington." They all laughed again, and one remarks, "How does the poor devil keep himself?"

'He must have slipped in through the wash-house door, for he flits past me and joins 'em, cold as ice.

' "One does what one can," he says. "I sell buttons. And you, Marquise?"

' "I?"—she waves her poor white hands all burned—

"I am a cook—a very bad one—at your service, abbé. We were just talking about you."

'They didn't treat him like they talked of him. They backed off and stood still.

' "I have missed something then," he says. "But I spent this last hour playing—only for buttons, Marquise— against a noble savage, the veritable Huron himself."

' "You had your usual luck, I hope?" she says.

' "Certainly," he says. "I cannot afford to lose even buttons in these days."

' "Then I suppose the child of nature does not know that your dice are usually loaded, Father Tout-a-tous," she continues. I don't know whether she meant to accuse him of cheating. He only bows.

' "Not yet, Mademoiselle Cunegonde," he says, and goes on to make himself agreeable to the rest of the company. And that was how I found out our Monsieur Peringuey was Count Charles Maurice Talleyrand de Périgord.'

Pharaoh stopped, but the children said nothing.

'You've heard of him?' said Pharaoh.

Una shook her head.

'Was Red Jacket the Indian he played dice with?' Dan asked.

'He was. Red Jacket told me the next time we met. I asked if the lame man had cheated. Red Jacket said no—he had played quite fair and was a master player. I allow Red Jacket knew. I've seen him, on the Reservation, play himself out of everything he had and in again. Then I told Red Jacket all I'd heard at the party concerning Talleyrand.

' "I was right," he says. "I saw the man's war-face when he thought he was alone. That is why I played him. I played him face to face. He is a great chief. Do they say why he comes here?"

' "They say he comes to find out if Big Hand makes war against the English," I said.

'Red Jacket grunted. "Yes," he says. "He asked me that

too. If he had been a small chief I should have lied. But he is a great chief. He knew I was a chief, so I told him the truth. I told him what Big Hand said to Cornplanter and me in the clearing—'There will be no war.' I could not see what he thought. I could not see behind his face. But he is a great chief. He will believe."

' "Will he believe that Big Hand can keep his people back from war?" I said, thinking of the crowds that hooted Big Hand whenever he rode out.

' "He is as bad as Big Hand is good, but he is not as strong as Big Hand," says Red Jacket. "When he talks with Big Hand he will feel this in his heart. The French have sent away a great chief. Presently he will go back and make them afraid."

'Now wasn't that comical? The French woman that knew him and owed all her losses to him; the Indian that picked him up, cut and muddy on the street, and played dice with him; they neither of 'em doubted that Talleyrand was something by himself—appearances notwithstanding.'

'And was he something by himself?' asked Una.

Pharaoh began to laugh, but stopped. 'The way *I* look at it,' he said, 'Talleyrand was one of just three men in this world who are quite by themselves. Big Hand I put first, because I've seen him.'

'Ay,' said Puck. 'I'm sorry we lost him out of Old England. Who d'you put second?'

'Talleyrand: maybe because I've seen him too,' said Pharaoh.

'Who's third?' said Puck.

'Boney—even though I've seen him.'

'Whew!' said Puck. 'Every man has his own weights and measures, but that's queer reckoning.'

'Boney?' said Una. 'You don't mean you've ever met Napoleon Bonaparte?'

'There! I knew you wouldn't have patience with the

rest of my tale after hearing that! But wait a minute. Talleyrand he come round to Hundred and Eighteen Second Street in a day or two to thank Toby for his kindness. I didn't mention the dice-playing, but I could see that Red Jacket's doings had made Talleyrand highly curious about Indians—though he *would* call him the Huron. Toby, as you may believe, was all holds full of knowledge concerning their manners and habits. He only needed a listener. The Brethren don't study Indians much till they join the church, but Toby knew 'em wild. So evening after evening Talleyrand crossed his sound leg over his game one and Toby poured forth. Having been adopted into the Senecas I, naturally, kept still; but Toby 'ud call on me to back up some of his remarks, and by that means, and a habit he had of drawing you on in talk, Talleyrand saw I knew something of his noble savages too. Then he tried a trick. Coming back from an *émigré* party he turns into his little shop and puts it to me, laughing like, that I'd gone with the two chiefs on their visit to Big Hand. *I* hadn't told. Red Jacket hadn't told, and Toby, of course, didn't know. 'Twas just Talleyrand's guess. "Now," he says, "my English and Red Jacket's French was so bad that I am not sure I got the rights of what the President really said to the unsophisticated Huron. Do me the favour of telling it again." I told him every word Red Jacket had told him and not one word more. I had my suspicions, having just come from an *émigré* party where the Marquise was hating and praising him as usual.

' "Much obliged," he said. "But I couldn't gather from Red Jacket exactly what the President said to Monsieur Genêt, or to his American gentlemen after Monsieur Genêt had ridden away."

'I saw Talleyrand was guessing again, for Red Jacket hadn't told him a word about the white man's pow-wow.'

'Why hadn't he?' Puck asked.

'Because Red Jacket was a chief. He told Talleyrand

what the President had said to him and Cornplanter, but
he didn't repeat the talk, between the white men, that Big
Hand ordered him to leave behind.'

'Oh!' Puck. 'I see. What did *you* do?'

'First I was going to make some sort of tale round it, but
Talleyrand was a chief too. So I said, "As soon as I get
Red Jacket's permission to tell that part of the tale, I'll be
delighted to refresh your memory, abbé." What else could
I have done?

' "Is that all?" he says, laughing. "Let me refresh your
memory. In a month from now I can give you a hundred
dollars for your account of the conversation."

' "Make it five hundred, abbé," I says.

' "Five, then," says he.

' "That will suit me admirably," I says. "Red Jacket
will be in town again by then, and the moment he gives
me leave I'll claim the money."

'He had a hard fight to be civil, but he come out smiling.

' "Monsieur," he says. "I beg your pardon as sincerely
as I envy the noble Huron your loyalty. Do me the honour to sit down while I explain."

'There wasn't another chair, so I sat on the button-box.

'He was a clever man. He had got hold of the gossip that
the President meant to make a peace treaty with England
at any cost. He had found out—from Genêt, I reckon—
who was with the President on the day the two chiefs met
him. He'd heard that Genêt had had a huff with the President and had ridden off leaving his business at loose ends.
What he wanted—what he begged and blustered to
know—was just the very words which the President had
said to his gentlemen *after* Genêt had left, concerning the
peace treaty with England. He put it to me that in helping
him to those very words I'd be helping three great countries as well as mankind. The room was as bare as the
palm of your hand, but I couldn't laugh.

' "I'm sorry," I says, when he wiped his forehead, "As soon as Red Jacket gives permission——"

' "You don't believe me, then?" he cuts in.

' "Not one little, little word, abbé," I says. "Except that you mean to be on the winning side. Remember, I've been fiddling to all your old friends for months."

'Well, then, his temper fled him and he called me names.

' "Wait a minute, ci-devant," I says at last. "I *am* half English and half French, but I am not the half of a man. I will tell thee something the Indian told me. Has thee seen the President?"

' "Oh yes!" he sneers, "I had letters from the Lord Lansdowne to that estimable old man."

' "Then," I says, "thee will understand. The Red Skin said that when thee has met the President thee will feel in thy heart he is a stronger man than thee."

' "Go!" he whispers. "Before I kill thee, go."

'He looked like it. So I left him.'

'Why did he want to know so badly?' said Dan.

'The way I look at it is that if he *had* known for certain that Washington meant to make the peace-treaty with England at any price, he'd ha' left old Fauchet fumbling about in Philadelphia while he went straight back to France and told old Danton—"It's no good your wasting time and hopes on the United States because she won't fight on our side—that I've proof of!" Then Danton might have been grateful and given Talleyrand a job, because a whole mass of things hang on knowing for sure who's your friend and who's your enemy. Just think of us poor shopkeepers, for instance.'

'Did Red Jacket let you tell, when he came back?' Una asked.

'Of course not. He said, "When Cornplanter and I ask you what Big Hand said to the whites you can tell the Lame Chief. All that talk was left behind in the timber, as

Big Hand ordered. Tell the Lame Chief there will be no war. He can go back to France with that word."

'Talleyrand and me hadn't met for a long time except at *émigré* parties. When I give him the message he just shook his head. He was sorting buttons in the shop.

' "I cannot return to France with nothing better than the word of an unsophisticated savage," he says.

' "Hasn't the President said anything to you?" I asked him.

' "He has said everything that one in his position ought to say, but—but if only I knew what he said to his Cabinet after Genêt rode off I believe I could change Europe—the world, maybe."

' "I'm sorry," I says. "Maybe you'll do that without my help."

'He looked at me hard. "Either you have unusual observation for one so young, or you choose to be insolent," he says.

' "It was intended for a compliment," I says. "But no odds. We're off in a few days for our summer trip, and I've come to make my goodbyes."

' "I go on my travels too," he says. "If ever we meet again you may be sure I will do my best to repay what I owe you."

' "Without malice, abbé, I hope," I says.

' "None whatever," says he. "Give my respects to your adorable Dr. Pangloss (that was one of his side-names for Toby) and the Huron." I never *could* teach him the difference betwixt Hurons and Senecas.

'Then Sister Haga came in for a paper of what we call "pilly buttons" and that was the last I saw of Talleyrand in those parts.'

'But after that you met Napoleon, didn't you?' said Una.

'Wait just a little, dearie. After that, Toby and I went to Lebanon and the Reservation, and, being older and knowing better how to manage him, I enjoyed myself well that summer with fiddling and fun. When we came back, the Brethren got after Toby because I wasn't learning any lawful trade, and he had hard work to save me from being apprenticed to Helmbold and Geyer the printers. 'Twould have ruined our music together, indeed it would; and when we escaped that, old Mattes Roush, the leatherbreeches maker round the corner, took a notion I was cut out for skin-dressing. But we were rescued. Along toward Christmas, there comes a big sealed letter from the Bank saying that a Monsieur Talleyrand had put five hundred dollars—a hundred pounds—to my credit there to use as I pleased. There was a little note from him inside—he didn't give any address—to thank me for past kindnesses and my believing in his future which he said was pretty cloudy at the time of writing. I wished Toby to share the money. *I* hadn't done more than bring Talleyrand up to Hundred and Eighteen. The kindnesses were Toby's. But Toby said, "No! Liberty and Independence for ever. I have all my wants, my son." So I gave him a set of new fiddle-strings and the Brethren didn't advise us any more. Only Pastor Meder he preached about the deceitfulness of riches, and Brother Adam Goose said if there was war the English 'ud surely shoot down the Bank. *I* knew there wasn't going to be any war, but I drew the money out, and on Red Jacket's advice I put it into horse-flesh, which I sold to Bob Bicknell for the Baltimore stage-coaches. That way, I doubled my money inside the twelvemonth.'

'You gipsy! You proper gipsy!' Puck shouted.

'Why not? 'Twas fair buying and selling. Well, one thing leading to another, in a few years I had made the beginning of a worldly fortune and was in the tobacco trade.'

'Ah!' said Puck, suddenly. 'Might I inquire if you'd ever sent any news to your people in England—or in France?'

'O' course I had. I wrote regular every three months after I'd made money in the horse-trade. We Lees don't like coming home empty-handed. If it's only a turnip or

an egg, it's something. Oh yes, I wrote good and plenty to
Uncle Aurette and—Dad don't read very quickly—Uncle
used to slip over Newhaven way and tell Dad what was
going on in the tobacco trade.'

'I see—

> "Aurettes and Lees—
> Like as two peas."

Go on, Brother Square-toes,' said Puck. Pharaoh laughed
and went on.

'Talleyrand he'd gone up in the world same as me. He'd
sailed to France again, and was a great man in the Government there awhile, but they had to turn him out on account of some story about bribes from American shippers.
All our poor *émigrés* said he was surely finished this time,
but Red Jacket and me we didn't think it likely, not unless
he was quite dead. Big Hand had made his peace-treaty
with Great Britain, just *as* he said he would, and there was
a roaring trade 'twixt England and the United States for
such as 'ud take the risk of being searched by British and
French men-of-wars. Those two was fighting and, just *as*
his gentlemen told Big Hand 'ud happen—the United
States was catching it from both. If an English man-o'-war
met an American ship he'd press half the best men out of
her, and swear they was British subjects. Most of 'em was!
If a Frenchman met her he'd, likely, have the cargo out of
her, swearing it was meant to aid and comfort the English:
and if a Spaniard or a Dutchman met her—they was
hanging on to England's coat-tails too—Lord only knows
what *they* wouldn't do! It came over me that what I
wanted in my tobacco trade was a fast-sailing ship and a
man who could be French, English or American at a
pinch. Luckily I could lay my hands on both articles. So
along toward the end of September in the year '99 I sailed
from Philadelphia with a hundred and eleven hogshead o'
good Virginia tobacco, in the brig *Berthe Aurette*, named

after mother's maiden name, hoping 'twould bring me luck, which she didn't—and yet she did.'

'Where was you bound for?' Puck asked.

'Er—any port I found handiest. I didn't tell Toby or the Brethren. They don't understand the ins and outs of the tobacco trade.'

Puck coughed a small cough as he shifted a piece of wood with his bare foot.

'It's easy for you to sit and judge,' Pharaoh cried. 'But think o' what *we* had to put up with! We spread our wings and run across the broad Atlantic like a hen through a horse-fair. Even so, we was stopped by an English frigate, three days out. He sent a boat alongside and pressed seven able seamen. I remarked it was hard on honest traders, but the officer said they was fighting all creation and hadn't time to argue. The next English frigate we escaped with no more than a shot in our quarter. Then we was chased two days and a night by a French privateer, firing between squalls, and the dirty little English ten-ton brig, which made him sheer off, had the impudence to press another five of our men. That's how we reached to the chops of the Channel. Twelve good men pressed out of thirty-five; an eighteen-pound shot-hole close beside our rudder; our mainsail looking like spectacles where the Frenchman had hit us—and the Channel crawling with short-handed British cruisers. Put *that* in your pipe and smoke it next time you grumble at the price of tobacco!

'Well, then, to top it off, while we was trying to get at our leaks, a French lugger come swooping at us out o' the dusk. We warned him to keep away, but he fell aboard us, and up climbed his jabbering red-caps. We couldn't endure any more—indeed we couldn't. We went at 'em with all we could lay hands on. It didn't last long. They was fifty odd to our twenty-three. Pretty soon I heard the cutlasses thrown down and some one bellowed for the *sacré* captain.

' "Here I am!" I says. "I don't suppose it makes any

odds to you thieves, but this is the United States brig *Berthe Aurette*."

' "My aunt!" the man says, laughing. "Why is she named that?"

' "Who's speaking?" I said. 'Twas too dark to see, but I thought I knew the voice.

' "Enseigne de Vaisseau Estephe L'Estrange," he sings out, and then I was sure.

' "Oh!" I says. "It's all in the family, I suppose, but you *have* done a fine day's work, Stephen."

'He whips out the binnacle-light and holds it to my face. He was young L'Estrange, my full cousin, that I hadn't seen since the night the smack sank off Telscombe Tye—six years ago.

' "Whew!" he says. "That's why she was named for Aunt Berthe, is it? What's your share in her, Pharaoh?"

' "Only half owner, but the cargo's mine."

' "That's bad," he says. "I'll do what I can, but you shouldn't have fought us."

' "Steve," I says, "you aren't ever going to report our little fall-out as a fight? Why, a Revenue cutter 'ud laugh at it!"

' "So'd I, if I wasn't in the Republican Navy," he says. "But two of our men are dead, d'ye see, and I'm afraid I'll have to take you to the Prize Court at Le Havre."

' "Will they condemn my 'baccy?" I asks.

' "To the last ounce. But I was thinking more of the ship. She'd make a sweet little craft for the Navy if the Prize Court 'ud let me have her," he says.

'Then I knew there was no hope. I don't blame him—a man must consider his own interests—but nigh every dollar I had was in ship or cargo, and Steve kept on saying, "You shouldn't have fought us."

'Well, then, the lugger took us to Le Havre, and that being the one time we *did* want a British ship to rescue us, why o' course we never saw one. My cousin spoke his best for us at the Prize Court. He owned he'd no right to rush alongside in the face o' the United States flag, but we couldn't get over those two men killed, d'ye see, and the Court condemned both ship and cargo. They was kind enough not to make us prisoners—only beggars—and young L'Estrange was given the *Berthe Aurette* to re-arm into the French Navy.

'"I'll take you round to Boulogne," he says. "Mother and the rest'll be glad to see you, and you can slip over to Newhaven with Uncle Aurette. Or you can ship with me, like most o' your men, and have a turn at King George's loose trade. There's plenty pickings," he says.

'Crazy as I was, I couldn't help laughing.

'"I've had my allowance of pickings and stealings," I says. "Where are they taking my tobacco?" 'Twas being loaded on to a barge.

'"Up the Seine to be sold in Paris," he says. "Neither you nor I will ever touch a penny of that money."

'"Get me leave to go with it," I says. "I'll see if there's justice to be gotten out of our American Ambassador."

'"There's not much justice in this world," he says, "without a Navy." But he got me leave to go with the barge and he gave me some money. That tobacco was all I had, and I followed it like a hound follows a snatched bone. Going up the river I fiddled a little to keep my spirits up, as well as to make friends with the guard. They was only doing their duty. Outside o' that they were the reasonablest o' God's creatures. They never even laughed at me. So we come to Paris, by river, along in November, which the French had christened Brumaire. They'd given new names to all the months, and after such an outrageous silly piece o' business as *that*, they wasn't likely to trouble 'emselves with my rights and wrongs. They didn't. The barge was laid up below Notre Dame Church in charge of a caretaker, and he let me sleep aboard after I'd run about all day from office to office, seeking justice and fair dealing, and getting speeches concerning liberty. None heeded me. Looking back on it I can't rightly blame 'em. I'd no money, my clothes was filthy mucked; I hadn't changed my linen in weeks, and I'd no proof of my claims except the ship's papers which, they said, I might have stolen. The thieves! The doorkeeper to the American Ambassador—for I never saw even the Secretary—he swore I spoke French a sight too well for an American citizen. Worse than that—I had spent my money, d'ye see, and I—I took to fiddling in the streets for my keep; and—and, a ship's captain with a fiddle under his arm—well, I *don't* blame 'em that they didn't believe me.

'I come back to the barge one day—late in this month Brumaire it was—fair beazled out. Old Maingon, the caretaker, he'd lit a fire in a bucket and was grilling a herring.

' "Courage, mon ami," he says. "Dinner is served."

' "I can't eat," I says. "I can't do any more. It's stronger than I am."

' "Bah!" he says. "Nothing's stronger than a man. Me, for example! Less than two years ago I was blown up in the *Orient* in Aboukir Bay, but I descended again and hit the water like a fairy. Look at me now," he says. He wasn't much to look at for he'd only one leg and one eye, but the cheerfullest soul that ever trod shoe-leather. "That's worse than a hundred and eleven hogshead of 'baccy," he goes on. "You're young, too! What wouldn't I give to be young in France at this hour! There's nothing you couldn't do," he says. "The ball's at your feet— kick it!" he says. He kicks the old firebucket with his peg-leg. "General Buonaparte, for example!" he goes on. "That man's a babe compared to me, and see what he's done already. He's conquered Egypt and Austria and Italy—oh! half Europe!" he says, "and now he sails back to Paris, and he sails out to St. Cloud down the river here—*don't* stare at the river, you young fool!— and all in front of these pig-jobbing lawyers and citizens he makes himself Consul, which is as good as a King. He'll *be* King, too, in the next three turns of the capstan—

King of France, England and the world! Think o' that!" he shouts, "and eat your herring."

'I says something about Boney. If he hadn't been fighting England I shouldn't have lost my 'baccy—should I?

' "Young fellow," says Maingon, "you don't understand."

'We heard cheering. A carriage passed over the bridge with two in it.

' "That's the man himself," says Maingon. "He'll give 'em something to cheer for soon." He stands at the salute.

' "Who's t'other in black beside him?" I asks, fairly shaking all over.

' "Ah! he's the clever one. You'll hear of him before long. He's that scoundrel-bishop, Talleyrand."

' "It is!" I said, and up the steps I went with my fiddle, and run after the carriage calling, "Abbé, abbé!"

'A soldier knocked the wind out of me with the back of his sword, but I had sense to keep on following till the carriage stopped—and there just was a crowd round the house-door! I must have been half-crazy else I wouldn't have struck up *Si le Roi m'avait donné, Paris la grande ville!* I thought it might remind him.

' "That is a good omen!" he says to Boney sitting all hunched up; and he looks straight at me.

' "Abbé—oh, abbé!" I says. "Don't you remember Toby and Hundred and Eighteen Second Street?"

'He said not a word. He just crooked his long white finger to the guard at the door while the carriage steps were let down, and I skipped into the house, and they slammed the door in the crowd's face.

' "You go there," says a soldier, and shoves me into an empty room, where I catched my first breath since I'd left the barge. Presently I heard plates rattling next door— there were only folding doors between—and a cork drawn. "I tell you," some one shouts with his mouth full, "it was all that sulky ass Sieyès' fault. Only my speech to the Five Hundred saved the situation."

' "Did it save your coat?" says Talleyrand. "I hear they

tore it when they threw you out. Don't gasconnade to me. You may be in the road of victory, but you aren't there yet."

'Then I guessed t'other man was Boney. He stamped about and swore at Talleyrand.

' "You forget yourself, Consul," says Talleyrand, "or rather you remember yourself—Corsican."

' "Pig!" says Boney, and worse.

' "Emperor!" says Talleyrand, but, the way he spoke, it sounded worst of all. Some one must have backed against the folding doors, for they flew open and showed me in the middle of the room. Boney whipped out his pistol before I could stand up. "General," says Talleyrand to him, "this gentleman has a habit of catching us canaille *en déshabille*. Put that thing down."

'Boney laid it on the table, so I guessed which was master. Talleyrand takes my hand—"Charmed to see you again, Candide," he says. "How is the adorable Dr. Pangloss and the noble Huron?"

' "They were doing very well when I left," I said. "But I'm not."

' "Do *you* sell buttons now?" he says, and fills me a glass of wine off the table.

' "Madeira," says he. "Not so good as some I have drunk."

' "You mountebank!" Boney roars. "Turn that out." (He didn't even say "man," but Talleyrand being gentle born, just went on.)

' "Pheasant is not so good as pork," he says. "You will find some at that table if you will do me the honour to sit down. Pass him a clean plate, General." And, as true as I'm here, Boney slid a plate along just like a sulky child. He was a lanky-haired, yellow-skinned, little man, as nervous as a cat—and as dangerous. I could feel that.

' "And now," said Talleyrand, crossing his game leg over his sound one, "will you tell me your story?"

'I was in a fluster, but I told him nearly everything from

the time he left me the five hundred dollars in Philadelphia up to my losing ship and cargo at Le Havre. Boney began by listening, but after a bit he dropped into his own thoughts and looked at the crowd sideways through the front-room curtains. Talleyrand called to him when I'd done.

' "Eh? What we need now," says Boney, "is peace for the next three or four years."

' "Quite so," says Talleyrand. "Meantime I want the Consul's order to the Prize Court at Le Havre to restore my friend here his ship."

' "Nonsense!" says Boney. "Give away an oak-built brig of two hundred and seven tons for sentiment? Certainly not! She must be armed into my Navy with ten— no, fourteen twelve-pounders and two long fours. Is she strong enough to bear a long twelve forward?"

'Now I could ha' sworn he'd paid no heed to my talk, but that wonderful head-piece of his seemingly skimmed off every word of it that was useful to him.

' "Ah, General!" says Talleyrand. "You are a magician—a magician without morals. But the brig is undoubtedly American, and we don't want to offend them more than we have."

' "Need anybody talk about the affair?" he says. He didn't look at me, but I knew what was in his mind—just cold murder because I worried him: and he'd order it as easy as ordering his carriage!

' "You can't stop 'em," I said. "There's twenty-two other men besides me." I felt a little more 'ud set me screaming like a wired hare.

' "Undoubtedly American," Talleyrand goes on. "You would gain something if you returned the ship—with a message of fraternal good-will—published in the *Moniteur*" (that's a French paper like the Philadelphia *Aurora*).

' "A good idea!" Boney answers. "One could say much in a message."

' "It might be useful," says Talleyrand. "Shall I have the message prepared?" He wrote something in a little pocket ledger.

' "Yes—for me to embellish this evening. The *Moniteur* will publish it to-night."

' "Certainly. Sign, please," says Talleyrand, tearing the leaf out.

' "But that's the order to return the brig," says Boney. "Is that necessary? Why should I lose a good ship? Haven't I lost enough ships already?"

'Talleyrand didn't answer any of those questions. Then Boney sidled up to the table and jabs his pen into the ink. Then he shies at the paper again: "My signature alone is useless," he says. "You must have the other two Consuls as well. Sieyès and Roger Ducos must sign. We must preserve the Laws."

' "By the time my friend presents it," says Talleyrand, still looking out of the window, "only one signature will be necessary."

'Boney smiles. "It's a swindle," says he, but he signed and pushed the paper across.

' "Give that to the President of the Prize Court at Le Havre," says Talleyrand, "and he will give you back your ship. I will settle for the cargo myself. You have told me how much it cost. What profit did you expect to make on it?"

'Well, then, as man to man, I was bound to warn him that I'd set out to run it into England without troubling the Revenue, and so I couldn't rightly set bounds to my profits.'

'I guessed that all along,' said Puck:

'There was never a Lee to Warminghurst—
That wasn't a smuggler last and first.'

The children laughed.

'It's comical enough now,' said Pharaoh, 'but I didn't

laugh then. Says Talleyrand after a minute, "I am a bad accountant and I have several calculations on hand at present. Shall we say twice the cost of the cargo?"

'Say? I couldn't say a word. I sat choking and nodding like a China image while he wrote an order to his secretary to pay me, I won't say how much, because you wouldn't believe it.

' "Oh! Bless you, abbé! God bless you!" I got it out at last.

' "Yes," he says, "I am a priest in spite of myself, but they call me bishop now. Take this for my episcopal blessing," and he hands me the paper.

' "He stole all that money from me," says Boney over my shoulder. "A Bank of France is another of the things we must make. Are you mad?" he shouts at Talleyrand.

' "Quite," says Talleyrand, getting up. "But be calm; the disease will never attack you. It is called gratitude. This gentleman found me in the street and fed me when I was hungry."

' "I see; and he has made a fine scene of it and you have paid him, I suppose. Meantime, France waits."

' "Oh! poor France!" says Talleyrand. "Goodbye, Candide," he says to me. "By the way," he says, "have you yet got Red Jacket's permission to tell me what the President said to his Cabinet after Monsieur Genêt rode away?"

'I couldn't speak, I could only shake my head, and Boney—so impatient he was to go on with his doings—he ran at me and fair pushed me out of the room. And that was all there was to it.'

Pharaoh stood up and slid his fiddle into one of his big skirt-pockets as though it were a dead hare.

'Oh! but we want to know lots and lots more,' said Dan. 'How you got home—and what old Maingon said on the barge—and wasn't your cousin surprised when he had to give back the *Berthe Aurette*, and——'

'Tell us more about Toby!' cried Una.

'Yes, and Red Jacket,' said Dan.

'Won't you tell us any more?' they both pleaded.

Puck kicked the oak branch on the fire, till it sent up a column of smoke that made them sneeze. When they had finished, the Shaw was empty except for old Hobden stamping through the larches.

'They gipsies have took two,' he said. 'My black pullet and my liddle gingy-speckled cockrel.'

'I thought so,' said Dan, picking up one tail-feather the old woman had overlooked.

'Which way did they go? Which way did the runagates go?' said Hobden.

'Hobby!' said Una. 'Would you like it if we told Keeper Ridley all your goings and comings?'

                                                        1910

Historical Stories

~~~~~~~~~~~~~~~~~~~~

THE CHURCH THAT WAS
AT ANTIOCH

But when Peter was come to Antioch, I withstood him
to the face, because he was to be blamed.
                    St. Paul's Epistle to the Galatians, ii. 11

His mother, a devout and well-born Roman widow, decided that he was doing himself no good in an Eastern Le-
gion so near to free-thinking Constantinople, and got him
seconded for civil duty in Antioch, where his uncle,
Lucius Sergius, was head of the urban Police. Valens
obeyed as a son and as a young man keen to see life, and,
presently, cast up at his uncle's door.

'That sister-in-law of mine,' said the elder, 'never remembers me till she wants something. What have you
been doing?'

'Nothing, Uncle.'

'Meaning everything?'

'That's what Mother thinks. But I haven't.'

'We shall see. Your quarters are across the inner courtyard. Your—er—baggage is there already. . . . Oh, I shan't
interfere with your private arrangements! I'm not the
uncle with the rough tongue. Get your bath. We'll talk at
supper.'

But before that hour 'Father Serga,' as the Prefect of

Police was called, learned from the Treasury that his nephew had marched overland from Constantinople in charge of a treasure-convoy which, after a brush with brigands in the pass outside Tarsus, he had duly delivered.

'Why didn't you tell me about it?' his uncle asked at the meal.

'I had to report to the Treasury first,' was the answer.

Serga looked at him. 'Gods! You *are* like your father,' said he. 'Cilicia is scandalously policed.'

'So I noticed. They ambushed us not five miles from Tarsus town. Are we given to that sort of thing here?'

'You make yourself at home early. No. *We* are not, but Syria is a Non-regulation Province—under the Emperor—not the Senate. We've the entire unaccountable East to one side; the scum of the Mediterranean on the other; and all hellicat Judaea southward. Anything can happen in Syria. D'you like the prospect?'

'I shall—under you.'

'It's in the blood. The same with men as horses. Now what have you done that distresses your mother so?'

'She's a little behind the times, sir. She follows the old school, of course—the home-worships, and the strict Latin Trinity. I don't think she recognises any Gods outside Jupiter, Juno, and Minerva.'

'I don't either—officially.'

'Nor I, as an officer, sir. But one wants more than that, and—and—what I learned in Byzant squared with what I saw with the Fifteenth.'

'You needn't go on. All Eastern Legions are alike. You mean you follow Mithras—eh?'

The young man bowed his head slightly.

'No harm, boy. It's a soldier's religion, even if it comes from outside.'

'So I thought. But Mother heard of it. She didn't approve and—I suppose that's why I'm here.'

'Off the trident and into the net! Just like a woman! All

Syria is stuffed with Mithraism. *My* objection to fancy religions is that they mostly meet after dark, and that means
more work for the Police. We've a College here of stiff-
necked Hebrews who call themselves Christians.'

'I've heard of them,' said Valens. 'There isn't a ceremony or symbol they haven't stolen from the Mithras ritual.'

' 'No news to *me!* Religions are part of my office-work;
and they'll be part of yours. Our Synagogue Jews are
fighting like Scythians over this new faith.'

'Does that matter much?'

'So long as they fight each other, we've only to keep the
ring. Divide and rule—especially with Hebrews. Even
these Christians are divided now. You see—one part of
their worship is to eat together.'

'Another theft! The Supper is the essential Symbol
with us,' Valens interrupted.

'With *us*, it's the essential symbol of trouble for your
uncle, my dear. Anyone can become a Christian. A Jew
may; but he still lives by his Law of Moses (I've had to
master that cursed code, too), and it regulates all his doings. Then he sits down at a Christian love-feast beside a
Greek or Westerner, who doesn't kill mutton or pig—No!
No! Jews don't touch pork—as the Jewish Law lays down.
Then the tables are broken up—but not by laughter—No!
No! Riot!'

'That's childish,' said Valens.

' 'Wish it were. But my lictors are called in to keep
order, and I have to take the depositions of Synagogue
Jews, denouncing Christians as traitors to Caesar. If I
chose to act on half the stuff their Rabbis swear to, I'd
have respectable little Jew shop-keepers up every week for
conspiracy. *Never* decide on the evidence, when you're
dealing with Hebrews! Oh, you'll get your bellyful of it!
You're for Market-duty to-morrow in the Little Circus
ward, all among 'em. And now, sleep you well! I've been
on this frontier as far back as anyone remembers—that's

why they call me the Father of Syria—and oh—it's good
to see a sample of the old stock again!'

Next morning, and for many weeks after, Valens found
himself on Market-inspection duty with a fat Aedile, who
flew into rages because the stalls were not flushed down at
the proper hour. A couple of his uncle's men were told off
to him, and, of course, introduced him to the thieves' and
prostitutes' quarters, to the leading gladiators, and so
forth.

One day, behind the Little Circus, near Singon Street,
he ran into a mob, where a race-course gang were trying to
collect, or evade, some bets on recent chariot-races. The
Aedile said it was none of his affair and turned back. The
lictors closed up behind Valens, but left the situation in
his charge. Then a small hard man with eyebrows was
punted on to his chest, amid howls from all around that he
was the ringleader of a conspiracy. 'Yes,' said Valens, 'that
was an old trick in Byzant; but I think we'll take *you*, my
friend.' Turning the small man loose, he gathered in the
loudest of his accusers to appear before his uncle.

'You were quite right,' said Serga next day. 'That gentleman was put up to the job—by someone else. I ordered
him one Roman dozen. Did you get the name of the man
they were trying to push off on you?'

'Yes. Gaius Julius Paulus. Why?'

'I guessed as much. He's an old acquaintance of mine, a
Cilician from Tarsus. Well-born—a citizen by descent,
and well-educated, but his people have disowned him. So
he works for his living.'

'He spoke like a well-born. He's in splendid training,
too. 'Felt him. All muscle.'

'Small wonder. He can outmarch a camel. He is really
the Prefect of this new sect. He travels all over our Eastern
Provinces starting their Colleges and keeping them up to
the mark. That's why the Synagogue Jews are hunting
him. If they could run him in on the political charge, it
would finish him.'

'Is he seditious, then?'

'Not in the least. Even if he were, I wouldn't feed him to the Jews just because they wanted it. One of our Governors tried that game down-coast—for the sake of peace—some years ago. He didn't get it. Do you like your Market-work, my boy?'

'It's interesting. D'you know, uncle, I think the Synagogue Jews are better at their slaughter-house arrangements than we.'

'They are. That's what makes 'em so tough. A dozen stripes are nothing to Apella, though he'll howl the yard down while he's getting 'em. You've the Christians' College in your quarter. How do they strike you?'

' 'Quiet enough. They're worrying a bit over what they ought to eat at their love-feasts.'

'I know it. Oh, I meant to tell you—we mustn't try 'em too high just now, Valens. My office reports that Paulus, your small friend, is going down-country for a few days to meet another priest of the College, and bring him back to help smooth over their difficulties about their victuals. That means their congregation will be at loose ends till they return. Mass without mind always comes a cropper. So, *now* is when the Synagogue Jews will try to compromise them. I don't want the poor devils stampeded into what can be made to look like political crime. 'Understand?'

Valens nodded. Between his uncle's discursive evening talks, studded with kitchen-Greek and out-of-date Roman society-verses; his morning tours with the puffing Aedile; and the confidences of his lictors at all hours; he fancied he understood Antioch.

So he kept an eye on the rooms in the colonnade behind the Little Circus, where the new faith gathered. One of the many Jew butchers told him that Paulus had left affairs in the hands of some man called Barnabas, but that he would come back with one, Petrus—evidently a well-known character—who would settle all the food-differences between Greek and Hebrew Christians. The butcher had no spite against Greek Christians as such, if they would only kill their meat like decent Jews.

Serga laughed at this talk, but lent Valens an extra man or two, and said that this lion would be his to tackle, before long.

The boy found himself rushed into the arena one hot dusk, when word had come that this was to be a night of trouble. He posted his lictors in an alley within signal, and entered the common-room of the College, where the love-feasts were held. Everyone seemed as friendly as a Christian—to use the slang of the quarter—and Barnabas, a smiling, stately man by the door, specially so.

'I am glad to meet you,' he said. 'You helped our Paulus in that scuffle the other day. We can't afford to lose *him*. I wish he were back!'

He looked nervously down the hall, as it filled with people, of middle and low degree, setting out their evening meal on the bare tables, and greeting each other with a special gesture.

'I assure you,' he went on, his eyes still astray, *'we've* no intention of offending any of the brethren. Our differences can be settled if only——'

As though on a signal, clamour rose from half a dozen tables at once, with cries of 'Pollution! Defilement! Heathen! The Law! The Law! Let Caesar know!' As Valens backed against the wall, the crowd pelted each other with broken meats and crockery, till at last stones appeared from nowhere.

'It's a put-up affair,' said Valens to Barnabas.

'Yes. They come in with stones in their breasts. Be careful! They're throwing your way,' Barnabas replied. The crowd was well-embroiled now. A section of it bore down to where they stood, yelling for the Justice of Rome. His two lictors slid in behind Valens, and a man leaped at him with a knife.

Valens struck up the hand, and the lictors had the man

helpless as the weapon fell on the floor. The clash of it
stilled the tumult a little. Valens caught the lull, speaking
slowly: 'Oh, citizens,' he called, *'must* you begin your
love-feasts with battle? Our tripe-sellers' burial-club has
better manners.'

A little laughter relieved the tension.

'The Synagogue has arranged this,' Barnabas muttered.
'The responsibility will be laid on me.'

'Who is the Head of your College?' Valens called to the
crowd.

The cries rose against each other.

'Paulus! Saul! *He* knows the world—— No! No! Petrus!
Our Rock! *He* won't betray us. Petrus, the Living Rock.'

'When do they come back?' Valens asked. Several dates
were given, sworn to, and denied.

'Wait to fight till they return. I'm not a priest; but if you
don't tidy up these rooms, our Aedile (Valens gave him
his gross nick-name in the quarter) will fine the sandals
off your feet. And you mustn't trample good food either.
When you've finished, I'll lock up after you. Be quick. *I*
know our Prefect if you don't.'

They toiled, like children rebuked. As they passed out
with baskets of rubbish, Valens smiled. The matter would
not be pressed further.

'Here is our key,' said Barnabas at the end. 'The Synagogue will swear I hired this man to kill you.'

'Will they? Let's look at him.'

The lictors pushed their prisoner forward.

'Ill-fortune!' said the man. 'I owed you for my brother's
death in Tarsus Pass.'

'Your brother tried to kill me,' Valens retorted.

The fellow nodded.

'Then we'll call it even-throws,' Valens signed to the
lictors, who loosed hold. 'Unless you *really* want to see
my uncle?'

The man vanished like a trout in the dusk. Valens returned the key to Barnabas, and said:

'If I were you, I shouldn't let your people in again till your leaders come back. You don't know Antioch as I do.'

He went home, the grinning lictors behind him, and they told his uncle, who grinned also, but said that he had done the right thing—even to patronising Barnabas.

'Of course, *I* don't know Antioch as you do; but, seriously, my dear, I think you've saved their Church for the Christians this time. I've had three depositions already that your Cilician friend was a Christian hired by Barnabas. 'Just as well for Barnabas that you let the brute go.'

'You told me you didn't want them stampeded into trouble. Besides, it was fair-throws. I may have killed his brother after all. We had to kill two of 'em.'

'Good! You keep a level head in a tight corner. You'll need it. There's no lying about in secluded parks for *us!* I've got to see Paulus and Petrus when they come back, and find out what they've decided about their infernal feasts. Why can't they all get decently drunk and be done with it?'

'They talk of them both down-town as though they were Gods. By the way, uncle, all the riot was worked up by Synagogue Jews sent from Jerusalem—not by our lot at all.'

'You *don't* say so? Now, perhaps, you understand why I put you on market-duty with old Sow-Belly! You'll make a Police-officer yet.'

Valens met the scared, mixed congregation round the fountains and stalls as he went about his quarter. They were rather relieved at being locked out of their rooms for the time; as well as by the news that Paulus and Petrus would report to the Prefect of Police before addressing them on the great food-question.

Valens was not present at the first part of that interview, which was official. The second, in the cool, awning-covered courtyard, with drinks and *hors-d'œuvre*, all set out beneath the vast lemon and lavender sunset, was much less formal.

'You have met, I think,' said Serga to the little lean Paulus as Valens entered.

'Indeed, yes. Under God, we are twice your debtors,' was the quick reply.

'Oh, that was part of my duty. I hope you found our roads good on your journey,' said Valens.

'Why, yes. I think they were.' Paulus spoke as if he had not noticed them.

'We should have done better to come by boat,' said his companion, Petrus, a large fleshy man, with eyes that seemed to see nothing, and a half-palsied right hand that lay idle in his lap.

'Valens came overland from Byzant,' said his uncle. 'He rather fancies his legs.'

'He ought to at his age. What was your best day's march on the Via Sebaste?' Paulus asked interestedly, and, before he knew, Valens was reeling off his mileage on mountain-roads every step of which Paulus seemed to have trod.

'That's good,' was the comment. 'And I expect you march in heavier order than I.'

'What would you call your best day's work?' Valens asked in turn.

'I have covered . . .' Paulus checked himself. 'And yet not I but the God,' he muttered. 'It's hard to cure oneself of boasting.'

A spasm wrenched Petrus' face.

'Hard indeed,' said he. Then he addressed himself to Paulus as though none other were present. 'It is true I have eaten with Gentiles and as the Gentiles ate. Yet, at the time, I doubted if it were wise.'

'That is behind us now,' said Paulus gently. 'The decision has been taken for the Church—that little Church which you saved, my son.' He turned on Valens with a smile that half-captured the boy's heart. 'Now—as a Roman and a Police-officer—what think you of us Christians?'

'That I have to keep order in my own ward.'

'Good! Caesar must be served. But—as a servant of Mithras, shall we say—how think you about our food-disputes?'

Valens hesitated. His uncle encouraged him with a nod. 'As a servant of Mithras I eat with any initiate, so long as the food is clean,' said Valens.

'But,' said Petrus, *'that* is the crux.'

'Mithras also tells us,' Valens went on, 'to share a bone covered with dirt, if better cannot be found.'

'You observe no difference, then, between peoples at your feasts?' Paulus demanded.

'How dare we? We are all His children. Men make laws. Not Gods,' Valens quoted from the old Ritual.

'Say that again, child!'

'Gods do not make laws. They change men's hearts. The rest is the Spirit.'

'You heard it, Petrus? You heard that? It is the utter Doctrine itself!' Paulus insisted to his dumb companion.

Valens, a little ashamed of having spoken of his faith, went on:

'They tell me the Jew butchers here want the monopoly of killing for your people. Trade feeling's at the bottom of most of it.'

'A little more than that perhaps,' said Paulus. 'Listen a minute.' He threw himself into a curious tale about the God of the Christians, Who, he said, had taken the shape of a Man, and Whom the Jerusalem Jews, years ago, had got the authorities to deal with as a conspirator. He said that he himself, at that time a right Jew, quite agreed with the sentence, and had denounced all who followed the new God. But one day the Light and the Voice of the God broke over him, and he experienced a rending change of heart—precisely as in the Mithras creed. Then he met, and had been initiated by, some men who had walked and talked and, more particularly, had eaten, with the new God before He was killed, and who had seen Him after, like Mithras, He had risen from His grave. Paulus and those others—Petrus was one of them—had next tried to preach Him to the Jews, but that was no success; and, one thing leading to another, Paulus had gone back to his home at Tarsus, where his people disowned him for a renegade. There he had broken down with overwork and despair. Till then, he said, it had never occurred to any of them to show the new religion to any except right Jews; for their God had been born in the shape of a Jew. Paulus himself only came to realise the possibilities of outside work, little by little. He said he had all the foreign preaching in his charge now, and was going to change the whole world by it.

Then he made Petrus finish the tale, who explained, speaking very slowly, that he had, some years ago, received orders from the God to preach to a Roman officer of Irregulars down-country; after which that officer and most of his people wanted to become Christians. So Petrus had initiated them the same night, although none of them were Hebrews. 'And,' Petrus ended, 'I saw there is nothing under heaven that we dare call unclean.'

Paulus turned on him like a flash and cried:

'You admit it! Out of your own mouth it is evident.' Petrus shook like a leaf and his right hand almost lifted.

'Do *you* too twit me with my accent?' he began, but his face worked and he choked.

'Nay! God forbid! And God once more forgive *me!*' Paulus seemed as distressed as he, while Valens stared at the extraordinary outbreak.

'Talking of clean and unclean,' his uncle said tactfully, 'there's that ugly song come up again in the City. They were singing it on the city-front yesterday, Valens. Did you notice?'

He looked at his nephew, who took the hint.

'If it was "Pickled Fish," sir, they were. Will it make trouble?'

'As surely as these fish'—a jar of them stood on the

table—'make one thirsty. How does it go? Oh yes.' Serga hummed:

> Oie-eaah!
> 'From the Shark and the Sardine—the clean and the unclean—
> To the Pickled Fish of Galilee, said Petrus, shall be mine.

He twanged it off to the proper gutter-drawl.

> (Ha-ow?)
> In the nets or on the line,
> Till the Gods Themselves decline.
> (Whe-en?)
> When the Pickled Fish of Galilee ascend the Esquiline!

That'll be something of a flood—worse than live fish in trees! Hey?'

'It will happen one day,' said Paulus.

He turned from Petrus, whom he had been soothing tenderly, and resumed in his natural, hardish voice:

'Yes. We owe a good deal to that Centurion being converted when he was. It taught us that the whole world could receive the God; and it showed *me* my next work. I came over from Tarsus to teach here for a while. And I shan't forget how good the Prefect of Police was to us then.'

'For one thing, Cornelius was an early colleague,' Serga smiled largely above his strong cup. ' "Prime companion"—how does it go?—"we drank the long, long Eastern day out together," and so on. For another, I know a good workman when I see him. That camel-kit you made for my desert-tours, Paul, is as sound as ever. And for a third—which to a man of my habits is most important—that Greek doctor you recommended me is the only one who understands my tumid liver.'

He passed a cup of all but unmixed wine, which Paulus

handed to Petrus, whose lips were flaky white at the corners

'But your trouble,' the Prefect went on, 'will come from your own people. Jerusalem never forgives. They'll get you run in on the charge of *laesa majestatis* soon or late.'

'Who knows better than I?' said Petrus. 'And the decision we *all* have taken about our love-feasts may unite Hebrew and Greek against us. As I told you, Prefect, we are asking Christian Greeks not to make the feasts difficult for Christian Hebrews by eating meat that has not been lawfully killed. (Our way is much more wholesome, anyhow.) Still, we may get round that. But there's *one* vital point. Some of our Greek Christians bring food to the love-feasts that they've bought from your priests, after your sacrifices have been offered. That we can't allow.'

Paulus turned to Valens imperiously.

'You mean they buy Altar-scraps,' the boy said. 'But only the very poor do it; and it's chiefly block-trimmings. The sale's a perquisite of the Altar-butchers. They wouldn't like its being stopped.'

'Permit separate tables for Hebrew and Greek, as I once said,' Petrus spoke suddenly.

'That would end in separate churches. There shall be but *one* Church,' Paulus spoke over his shoulder, and the words fell like rods. 'You think there may be trouble, Valens?'

'My uncle——' Valens began.

'No, no!' the Prefect laughed. 'Singon Street Markets are your Syria. Let's hear what our Legate thinks of his Province.'

Valens flushed and tried to pull his wits together.

'Primarily,' he said, 'it's pig, I suppose. Hebrews hate pork.'

'Quite right, too. Catch *me* eating pig east the Adriatic! *I* don't want to die of worms. Give me a young Sabine tush-ripe boar! I have spoken!'

Serga mixed himself another raw cup and took some pickled Lake fish to bring out the flavour.

'But, still,' Petrus leaned forward like a deaf man, 'if we admitted Hebrew and Greek Christians to separate tables we should escape——'

'Nothing, except salvation,' said Paulus. 'We have broken with the whole Law of Moses. We live in and through and by our God only. Else we are nothing. What is the sense of harking back to the Law at meal-times? Whom do we deceive? Jerusalem? Rome? The God? You yourself have eaten with Gentiles! You yourself have said——'

'One says more than one means when one is carried away,' Petrus answered, and his face worked again.

'This time you will say precisely what is meant,' Paulus spoke between his teeth. 'We will keep the Churches *one*—in and through the Lord. You dare not deny this?'

'I dare nothing—the God knows! But I have denied Him. . . . I denied Him. . . . And He said—He said I was the Rock on which His Church should stand.'

'*I* will see that it stands, and yet not I——' Paulus' voice dropped again. 'To-morrow you will speak to the one Church of the one Table the world over.'

'That's *your* business,' said the Prefect. 'But I warn you again, it's your own people who will make you trouble.'

Paulus rose to say farewell, but in the act he staggered, put his hand to his forehead and, as Valens steered him to a divan, collapsed in the grip of that deadly Syrian malaria which strikes like a snake. Valens, having suffered, called to his rooms for his heavy travelling-fur. His girl, whom he had bought in Constantinople a few months before, fetched it. Petrus tucked it awkwardly round the shivering little figure; the Prefect ordered lime-juice and hot water, and Paulus thanked them and apologised, while his teeth rattled on the cup.

'Better to-day than to-morrow,' said the Prefect. 'Drink—sweat—and sleep here the night. Shall I send for my doctor?'

But Paulus said that the fit would pass naturally, and as soon as he could stand he insisted on going away with Petrus, late though it was, to prepare their announcement to the Church.

'Who was that big, clumsy man?' his girl asked Valens as she took up the fur. 'He made more noise than the small one, who was really suffering.'

'He's a priest of the new College by the Little Circus, dear. He believes, uncle told me, that he once denied his God, Who, he says, died for him.'

She halted in the moonlight, the glossy jackal skins over her arm.

'Does he? *My* God bought me from the dealers like a horse. Too much, too, he paid. Didn't he? 'Fess, thou?'

'No, thee!' emphatically.

'But I wouldn't deny *my* God—living or dead! ... Oh—but *not* dead! My God's going to live—for me. Live—live Thou, my heart's blood, for ever!'

It would have been better had Paulus and Petrus not left the Prefect's house so late; for the rumour in the city, as the Prefect knew, and as the long conference seemed to confirm, was that Caesar's own Secretary of State in Rome was, through Paulus, arranging for a general defilement of the Hebrew with the Greek Christians, and that after this had been effected, by promiscuous eating of unlawful foods, all Jews would be lumped together as Christians—members, that is, of a mere free-thinking sect instead of the very particular and troublesome 'Nation of Jews within the Empire.' Eventually, the story went, they would lose their rights as Roman citizens, and could then be sold on any slave-stand.

'Of course,' Serga explained to Valens next day, 'that has been put about by the Jerusalem Synagogue. Our Antioch Jews aren't clever enough. Do you see their game? Petrus is a defiler of the Hebrew nation. If he is cut down to-night by some properly primed young zealot so much the better.'

'He won't be,' said Valens. 'I'm looking after him.'

' 'Hope so. But, if he isn't knifed,' Serga went on, 'they'll try to work up city riots on the grounds that, when all the Jews have lost their civil rights, he'll set up as a sort of King of the Christians.'

'At Antioch? In the present year of Rome? That's crazy, Uncle.'

'*Every* crowd is crazy. What else do we draw pay for? But, listen. Post a Mounted Police patrol at the back of the Little Circus. Use 'em to keep the people moving when the congregation comes out. Post two of your men in the Porch of their College itself. Tell Paulus and Petrus to wait there with them, till the streets are clear. Then fetch 'em both over here. Don't hit till you have to. Hit hard *before* the stones fly. Don't get my little horses knocked about more than you can help, and—look out for "Pickled Fish"!'

Knowing his own quarter, it seemed to Valens as he went on duty that evening, that his uncle's precautions had been excessive. The Christian Church, of course, was full, and a large crowd waited outside for word of the decision about the feasts. Most of them seemed to be Christians of sorts, but there was an element of gesticulating Antiochene loafers, and like all crowds they amused themselves with popular songs while they waited. Things went smoothly, till a group of Christians raised a rather explosive hymn, which ran:

> 'Enthroned above Caesar and Judge of the Earth!
>   We wait on Thy coming—oh tarry not long!
>   As the Kings of the Sunrise
>   Drew sword at Thy Birth,
>   So we arm in this midnight of insult and wrong!'

'Yes—and if one of their fish-stalls is bumped over by a camel—it's *my* fault!' said Valens. 'Now they've started it!' Sure enough, voices on the outskirts broke into 'Pickled

Fish,' but before Valens could speak, they were suppressed by someone crying:

'Quiet there, or you'll get your pickle before your fish.'

It was close on twilight when a cry rose from within the packed Church, and its congregation breasted out into the crowd. They all talked about the new orders for their love-feasts, most of them agreeing that they were sensible and easy. They agreed, too, that Petrus (Paulus did not seem to have taken much part in the debate) had spoken like one inspired, and they were all extremely proud of being Christians. Some of them began to link arms across the alley, and strike into the 'Enthroned above Caesar' chorus.

'And this, I *think*,' Valens called to the young Commandant of the Mounted Patrol, 'is where we'll begin to steer 'em home. Oh! And "Let night also have her well-earned hymn," as Uncle 'ud say.'

There filed out from behind the Little Circus four blaring trumpets, a standard, and a dozen Mounted Police. Their wise little grey Arabs sidled, passaged, shouldered, and nosed softly into the mob, as though they wanted petting, while the trumpets deafened the narrow street. An open square, near by, eased the pressure before long. Here the Patrol broke into fours, and gridironed it, saluting the images of the Gods at each corner and in the centre. People stopped, as usual, to watch how cleverly the incense was cast down over the withers into the spouting cressets; children reached up to pat horses which they said they knew; family groups re-found each other in the smoky dusk; hawkers offered cooked suppers; and soon the crowd melted into the main traffic avenues. Valens went over to the Church porch, where Petrus and Paulus waited between his lictors.

'That was well done,' Paulus began.

'How's the fever?' Valens asked.

'I was spared for to-day. I think, too, that by The Blessing we have carried our point.'

'Good hearing! My uncle bids me say you are welcome at his house.'

'That is always a command,' said Paulus, with a quick down-country gesture. 'Now that this day's burden is lifted, it will be a delight.'

Petrus joined up like a weary ox. Valens greeted him, but he did not answer.

'Leave him alone,' Paulus whispered. 'The virtue has gone out of me—him—for the while.' His own face looked pale and drawn.

The street was empty, and Valens took a short cut through an alley, where light ladies leaned out of windows and laughed. The three strolled easily together, the lictors behind them, and far off they heard the trumpets of the Night Horse saluting some statue of a Caesar, which marked the end of their round. Paulus was telling Valens how the whole Roman Empire would be changed by what the Christians had agreed to about their love-feasts, when an impudent little Jew boy stole up behind them, playing 'Pickled Fish' on some sort of desert bag-pipe.

'Can't you stop that young pest, one of you?' Valens asked laughing. 'You shan't be mocked on this great night of yours, Paulus.'

The lictors turned back a few paces, and shook a torch at the brat, but he retreated and drew them on. Then they heard Paulus shout, and when they hurried back, found Valens prostrate and coughing—his blood on the fringe of the kneeling Paul's robe. Petrus stooped, waving a helpless hand above them.

'Someone ran out from behind that well-head. He stabbed him as he ran, and ran on. Listen!' said Paulus.

But there was not even the echo of a footfall for clue, and the Jew boy had vanished like a bat. Said Valens from the ground:

'Home! Quick! I have it!'

They tore a shutter out of a shop-front, lifted and carried him, while Paulus walked beside. They set him down in the lighted inner courtyard of the Prefect's house, and a lictor hurried for the Prefect's physician.

Paulus watched the boy's face, and, as Valens shivered a little, called to the girl to fetch last night's fur rug. She brought it, laid the head on her breast, and cast herself beside Valens.

'It isn't bad. It doesn't bleed much. So it *can't* be bad—can it?' she repeated. Valens' smile reassured her, till the Prefect came and recognised the deadly upward thrust under the ribs. He turned on the Hebrews.

'To-morrow you will look for where your Church stood,' said he.

Valens lifted the hand that the girl was not kissing.

'No—no!' he gasped. 'The Cilician did it! For his brother! He said it.'

'The Cilician you let go to save these Christians because I——?' Valens signed to his uncle that it was so, while the girl begged him to steal strength from her till the doctor should come.

'Forgive me,' said Serga to Paulus. 'None the less I wish your God in Hades once for all. . . . But what am I to write his mother? Can't either of you two talking creatures tell me what I'm to tell his mother?'

'What has *she* to do with him?' the slave-girl cried. 'He is mine—mine! I testify before all Gods that he bought me! I am his. He is mine.'

'We can deal with the Cilician and his friends later,' said one of the lictors. 'But what now?'

For some reason, the man, though used to butcher-work, looked at Petrus.

'Give him drink and wait,' said Petrus. 'I have—seen such a wound.' Valens drank and a shade of colour came to him. He motioned the Prefect to stoop.

'What is it? Dearest of lives, what troubles?'

'The Cilician and his friends. . . . Don't be hard on them. . . . They get worked up. . . . They don't know what they are doing. . . . Promise!'

'This is not I, child. It is the Law.'

' 'No odds. You're Father's brother. . . . Men make laws—not Gods. . . . Promise! . . . It's finished with me.'

Valens' head eased back on its yearning pillow.

Petrus stood like one in a trance. The tremor left his face as he repeated:

' "Forgive them, for they know not what they do." Heard you *that*, Paulus? He, a heathen and an idolator, said it!'

'I heard. What hinders now that we should baptize him?' Paulus answered promptly.

Petrus stared at him as though he had come up out of the sea.

'Yes,' he said at last. 'It is the little maker of tents. . . . And what does he *now*—command?'

Paulus repeated the suggestion.

Painfully, that other raised the palsied hand that he had once held up in a hall to deny a charge.

'Quiet!' said he. 'Think you that one who has spoken Those Words needs such as *we* are to certify him to any God?'

Paulus cowered before the unknown colleague, vast and commanding, revealed after all these years.

'As you please—as you please,' he stammered, overlooking the blasphemy. 'Moreover there is the concubine.'

The girl did not heed, for the brow beneath her lips was chilling, even as she called on her God who had bought her at a price that he should not die but live.

1929

THE EYE OF ALLAH

The Cantor of St. Illod's being far too enthusiastic a musician to concern himself with its Library, the Sub-Cantor, who idolised every detail of the work, was tidying up, after two hours' writing and dictation in the Scriptorium. The copying-monks handed him in their sheets—it was a plain Four Gospels ordered by an Abbot at Evesham—and filed out to vespers. John Otho, better known as John of Burgos, took no heed. He was burnishing a tiny boss of gold in his miniature of the Annunciation for his Gospel of St. Luke, which it was hoped that Cardinal Falcodi, the Papal Legate, might later be pleased to accept.

'Break off, John,' said the Sub-Cantor in an undertone.

'Eh? Gone, have they? I never heard. Hold a minute, Clement.'

The Sub-Cantor waited patiently. He had known John more than a dozen years, coming and going at St. Illod's, to which monastery John, when abroad, always said he belonged. The claim was gladly allowed for, more even than other Fitz Otho's, he seemed to carry all the Arts under his hand, and most of their practical receipts under his hood.

The Sub-Cantor looked over his shoulder at the pinned-down sheet where the first words of the Magnificat were built up in gold washed with redlac for a background to the Virgin's hardly yet fired halo. She was shown, hands joined in wonder, at a lattice of infinitely intricate arabesque, round the edges of which sprays of orange-bloom seemed to load the blue hot air that carried back over the minute parched landscape in the middle distance.

'You've made her all Jewess,' said the Sub-Cantor, studying the olive-flushed cheek and the eyes charged with foreknowledge.

'What else was Our Lady?' John slipped out the pins. 'Listen, Clement. If I do not come back, this goes into my Great Luke, whoever finishes it.' He slid the drawing between its guard-papers.

'Then you're for Burgos again—as I heard?'

'In two days. The new Cathedral yonder—but they're slower than the Wrath of God, those masons—is good for the soul.'

'*Thy* soul?' The Sub-Cantor seemed doubtful.

'Even mine, by your permission. And down south—on the edge of the Conquered Countries—Granada way— there's some Moorish diaper-work that's wholesome. It allays vain thought and draws it toward the picture—as you felt, just now, in my Annunciation.'

'She—it was very beautiful. No wonder you go. But you'll not forget your absolution, John?'

'Surely.' This was a precaution John no more omitted on the eve of his travels than he did the recutting of the tonsure which he had provided himself with in his youth, somewhere near Ghent. The mark gave him privilege of clergy at a pinch, and a certain consideration on the road always.

'You'll not forget, either, what we need in the Scriptorium. There's no more true ultramarine in this world now. They mix it with that German blue. And as for vermilion——'

'I'll do my best always.'

'And Brother Thomas (this was the Infirmarian in charge of the monastery hospital) he needs——'

'He'll do his own asking. I'll go over his side now, and get me re-tonsured.'

John went down the stairs to the lane that divides the hospital and cook-house from the back-cloisters. While he was being barbered, Brother Thomas (St. Illod's meek but deadly persistent Infirmarian) gave him a list of drugs that he was to bring back from Spain by hook, crook, or lawful purchase. Here they were surprised by the lame, dark Abbot Stephen, in his fur-lined night-boots. Not that Stephen de Sautré was any spy; but as a young man he had shared an unlucky Crusade, which had ended, after a battle at Mansura, in two years' captivity among the Saracens at Cairo where men learn to walk softly. A fair huntsman and hawker, a reasonable disciplinarian but a man of science above all, and a Doctor of Medicine under one Ranulphus, Canon of St. Paul's, his heart was more in the monastery's hospital work than its religious. He checked their list interestedly, adding items of his own. After the Infirmarian had withdrawn he gave John generous absolution, to cover lapses by the way; for he did not hold with chance-bought Indulgences.

'And what seek you *this* journey?' he demanded, sitting on the bench beside the mortar and scales in the little warm cell for stored drugs.

'Devils, mostly,' said John, grinning.

'In Spain? Are not Abana and Pharphar——?'

John, to whom men were but matter for drawings, and well-born to boot (since he was a de Sanford on his mother's side), looked the Abbot full in the face and— 'Did *you* find it so?' said he.

'No. They were in Cairo too. But what's your special need of 'em?'

'For my Great Luke. He's the master-hand of all Four when it comes to devils.'

'No wonder. He was a physician. You're not.'

'Heaven forbid! But I'm weary of our Church-pattern

devils. They're only apes and goats and poultry conjoined. 'Good enough for plain red-and-black Hells and Judgment Days—but not for me.'

'What makes you so choice in them?'

'Because it stands to reason and Art that there are all musters of devils in Hell's dealings. Those Seven, for example, that were haled out of the Magdalene. They'd be she-devils—no kin at all to the beaked and horned and bearded devils-general.'

The Abbot laughed.

'And see again! The devil that came out of the dumb man. What use is snout or bill to *him?* He'd be faceless as a leper. Above all—God send I live to do it!—the devils that entered the Gadarene swine. They'd be—they'd be—I know not yet what they'd be, but they'd be surpassing devils. I'd have 'em diverse as the Saints themselves. But now, they're all one pattern, for wall, window, or picture-work.'

'Go on, John. You're deeper in this mystery than I.'

'Heaven forbid! But I say there's respect due to devils, damned tho' they be.'

'Dangerous doctrine.'

'My meaning is that if the shape of anything be worth man's thought to picture to man, it's worth his best thought.'

'That's safer. But I'm glad I've given you Absolution.'

'There's less risk for a craftsman who deals with the outside shapes of things—for Mother Church's glory.'

'Maybe so, but John'—the Abbot's hand almost touched John's sleeve—'tell me, now is—is she Moorish or—or Hebrew?'

'She's mine,' John returned.

'Is that enough?'

'I found it so.'

'Well—ah well! It's out of my jurisdiction but—how do they look at it down yonder?'

'Oh, they drive nothing to a head in Spain—neither

Church nor King, bless them! There's too many Moors and Jews to kill them all, and if they chased 'em away there'd be no trade nor farming. Trust me, in the Conquered Countries, from Seville to Granada, we live lovingly enough together—Spaniard, Moor, and Jew. Ye see, *we* ask no questions.'

'Yes—yes,' Stephen sighed. 'And always there's the hope, she may be converted.'

'Oh yes, there's always hope.'

The Abbot went on into the hospital. It was an easy age before Rome tightened the screw as to clerical connections. If the lady were not too forward, or the son too much his father's beneficiary in ecclesiastical preferments and levies, a good deal was overlooked. But, as the Abbot had reason to recall, unions between Christian and Infidel led to sorrow. None the less, when John with mule, mails, and man, clattered off down the lane for Southampton and the sea, Stephen envied him.

He was back, twenty months later, in good hard case, and loaded down with fairings. A lump of richest lazuli, a bar of orange-hearted vermilion, and a small packet of dried beetles which make most glorious scarlet, for the Sub-Cantor. Besides that, a few cubes of milky marble, with yet a pink flush in them, which could be slaked and ground down to incomparable background-stuff. There were quite half the drugs that the Abbot and Thomas had demanded, and there was a long deep-red cornelian necklace for the Abbot's Lady—Anne of Norton. She received it graciously, and asked where John had come by it.

'Near Granada,' he said.

'You left all well there?' Anne asked. (Maybe the Abbot had told her something of John's confession.)

'I left all in the hands of God.'

'Ah me! How long since?'

'Four months less eleven days.'

'Were you—with her?'

'In my arms. Childbed.'

'And?'

'The boy too. There is nothing now.'

Anne of Norton caught her breath.

'I think you'll be glad of that,' she said after a while.

'Give me time, and maybe I'll compass it. But not now.'

'You have your handwork and your art and—John—remember there's no jealousy in the grave.'

'Ye-es! I have my Art, and Heaven knows I'm jealous of none.'

'Thank God for that at least,' said Anne of Norton, the always ailing woman who followed the Abbot with her sunk eyes. 'And be sure I shall treasure this,' she touched the beads, 'as long as I shall live.'

'I brought—trusted—it to you for that,' he replied, and took leave. When she told the Abbot how she had come by it, he said nothing, but as he and Thomas were storing the drugs that John handed over in the cell which backs on to the hospital kitchen-chimney, he observed, of a cake of dried poppy-juice: 'This has power to cut off all pain from a man's body.'

'I have seen it,' said John.

'But for pain of the soul there is, outside God's Grace, but one drug; and that is a man's craft, learning, or other helpful motion of his own mind.'

'That is coming to me, too,' was the answer.

John spent the next fair May day out in the woods with the monastery swineherd and all the porkers; and returned, loaded with flowers and sprays of spring, to his own carefully kept place in the north bay of the Scriptorium. There with his travelling sketch-books under his left elbow, he sunk himself past all recollections in his Great Luke.

Brother Martin, Senior Copyist (who spoke about once a fortnight) ventured to ask, later, how the work was going.

'All here!' John tapped his forehead with his pencil. 'It

has been only waiting these months to—ah God!—be born. Are ye free of your plain-copying, Martin?'

Brother Martin nodded. It was his pride that John of Burgos turned to him, in spite of his seventy years, for really good page-work.

'Then see!' John laid out a new vellum—thin but flawless. 'There's no better than this sheet from here to Paris. Yes! Smell it if you choose. Wherefore—give me the compasses and I'll set it out for you—if ye make one letter lighter or darker than its next, I'll stick ye like a pig.'

'Never, John!' the old man beamed happily.

'But I will! Now, follow! Here and here, as I prick, and in script of just this height to the hair's-breadth, ye'll scribe the thirty-first and thirty-second verses of Eighth Luke.'

'Yes, the Gadarene Swine! "*And they besought him that he would not command them to go out into the abyss. And there was a herd of many swine*" '——Brother Martin naturally knew all the Gospels by heart.

'Just so! Down to "*and he suffered them.*" Take your time to it. My Magdalene has to come off my heart first.'

Brother Martin achieved the work so perfectly that John stole some soft sweetmeats from the Abbot's kitchen for his reward. The old man ate them; then repented; then confessed and insisted on penance. At which the Abbot, knowing there was but one way to reach the real sinner, set him a book called *De Virtutibus Herbarum* to fair-copy. St. Illod's had borrowed it from the gloomy Cistercians, who do not hold with pretty things, and the crabbed text kept Martin busy just when John wanted him for some rather specially spaced letterings.

'See now,' said the Sub-Cantor reprovingly. 'You should not do such things, John. Here's Brother Martin on penance for your sake——'

'No—for my Great Luke. But I've paid the Abbot's cook. I've drawn him till his own scullions cannot keep straight-faced. *He*'ll not tell again.'

'Unkindly done! And you're out of favour with the
Abbot too. He's made no sign to you since you came
back—never asked you to high table.'

'I've been busy. Having eyes in his head, Stephen knew
it. Clement, there's no Librarian from Durham to Torre
fit to clean up after you.'

The Sub-Cantor stood on guard; he knew where John's
compliments generally ended.

'But outside the Scriptorium——'

'Where I never go.' The Sub-Cantor had been excused
even digging in the garden, lest it should mar his wonderful book-binding hands.

'In all things outside the Scriptorium you are the mas-
ter-fool of Christendie. Take it from me, Clement. I've
met many.'

'I take everything from you,' Clement smiled benignly.
'You use me worse than a singing-boy.'

They could hear one of that suffering breed in the
cloister below, squalling as the Cantor pulled his hair.

'God love you! So I do! But have you ever thought
how I lie and steal daily on my travels—yes, and for
aught you know, murder—to fetch you colours and
earths?'

'True,' said just and conscience-stricken Clement. 'I
have often thought that were I in the world—which God
forbid!—I might be a strong thief in some matters.'

Even Brother Martin, bent above his loathed *De Virtutibus*, laughed.

But about mid-summer, Thomas the Infirmarian conveyed to John the Abbot's invitation to supper in his
house that night, with the request that he would bring
with him anything that he had done for his Great Luke.

'What's toward?' said John, who had been wholly shut
up in his work.

'Only one of his "wisdom" dinners. You've sat at a few
since you were a man.'

'True: and mostly good. How would Stephen have us——?'

'Gown and hood over all. There will be a doctor from Salerno—one Roger, an Italian. Wise and famous with the knife on the body. He's been in the Infirmary some ten days, helping me—even me!'

' 'Never heard the name. But our Stephen's *physicus* before *sacerdos,* always.'

'And his Lady has a sickness of some time. Roger came hither in chief because of her.'

'Did he? Now I think of it, I have not seen the Lady Anne for a while.'

'Ye've seen nothing for a long while. She has been housed near a month—they have to carry her abroad now.'

'So bad as that, then?'

'Roger of Salerno will not yet say what he thinks. But——'

'God pity Stephen! . . . Who else at table, beside thee?'

'An Oxford friar. Roger is his name also. A learned and famous philosopher. And he holds his liquor too, valiantly.'

'Three doctors—counting Stephen. I've always found that means two atheists.'

Thomas looked uneasily down his nose. 'That's a wicked proverb,' he stammered. 'You should not use it.'

'Hoh! Never come you the monk over me, Thomas! You've been Infirmarian at St. Illod's eleven years—and a lay-brother still. Why have you never taken orders, all this while?'

'I—I am not worthy.'

'Ten times worthier than that new fat swine—Henry Who's-his-name—that takes the Infirmary Masses. He bullocks in with the Viaticum, under your nose, when a sick man's only faint from being bled. So the man dies—of pure fear. Ye know it! I've watched your face at such times. Take Orders, Didymus. You'll have a little more

medicine and a little less Mass with your sick then; and
they'll live longer.'

'I am unworthy—unworthy,' Thomas repeated pitifully.

'Not you—but—to your own master you stand or fall.
And now that my work releases me for a while, I'll drink
with any philosopher out of any school. And Thomas,' he
coaxed, 'a hot bath for me in the Infirmary before vespers.'

When the Abbot's perfectly cooked and served meal
had ended, and the deep-fringed naperies were removed,
and the Prior had sent in the keys with word that all was
fast in the Monastery, and the keys had been duly returned with the word: 'Make it so till Prime,' the Abbot
and his guests went out to cool themselves in an upper
cloister that took them, by way of the leads, to the South
Choir side of the Triforium. The summer sun was still
strong, for it was barely six o'clock, but the Abbey
Church, of course, lay in her wonted darkness. Lights
were being lit for choir-practice thirty feet below.

'Our Cantor gives them no rest,' the Abbot whispered.
'Stand by this pillar and we'll hear what he's driving them
at now.'

'Remember all!' the Cantor's hard voice came up. 'This
is the soul of Bernard himself, attacking our evil world.
Take it quicker than yesterday, and throw all your words
clean-bitten from you. In the loft there! Begin!'

The organ broke out for an instant, alone and raging.
Then the voices crashed together into that first fierce line
of the *'De Contemptu Mundi.'*[1]

'Hora novissima—tempora pessima'—a dead pause till,
the assenting *sunt* broke, like a sob, out of the darkness,
and one boy's voice, clearer than silver trumpets, returned
the long-drawn *vigilemus.*

'Ecce minaciter, imminet Arbiter' (Organ and voices

---

[1] Hymn No. 226, A. and M., 'The world is very evil.'

were leashed together in terror and warning, breaking away liquidly to the *'ille supremus'*). Then the tone-colours shifted for the prelude to—*'Imminet, imminet, ut mala terminet——'*

'Stop! Again!' cried the Cantor; and gave his reasons a little more roundly than was natural at choir-practice.

'Ah! Pity o' man's vanity! He's guessed we are here. Come away!' said the Abbot. Anne of Norton, in her carried chair, had been listening too, further along the dark Triforium, with Roger of Salerno. John heard her sob. On the way back, he asked Thomas how her health stood. Before Thomas could reply the sharp-featured Italian doctor pushed between them. 'Following on our talk together, I judged it best to tell her,' said he to Thomas.

'What?' John asked simply enough.

'What she knew already.' Roger of Salerno launched into a Greek quotation to the effect that every woman knows all about everything.

'I have no Greek,' said John stiffly. Roger of Salerno had been giving them a good deal of it, at dinner.

'Then I'll come to you in Latin. Ovid hath it neatly. *"Utque malum late solet immedicabile cancer——"* but doubtless you know the rest, worthy Sir.'

'Alas! My school-Latin's but what I've gathered by the way from fools professing to heal sick women. *"Hocus-pocus——"* but doubtless you know the rest, worthy Sir.'

Roger of Salerno was quite quiet till they regained the dining-room, where the fire had been comforted and the dates, raisins, ginger, figs, and cinnamon-scented sweetmeats set out, with the choicer wines, on the after-table. The Abbot seated himself, drew off his ring, dropped it, that all might hear the tinkle, into an empty silver cup, stretched his feet towards the hearth, and looked at the great gilt and carved rose in the barrel-roof. The silence that keeps from Compline to Matins had closed on their world. The bull-necked Friar watched a ray of sunlight split itself into colours on the rim of a crystal salt-cellar;

Roger of Salerno had re-opened some discussion with Brother Thomas on a type of spotted fever that was baffling them both in England and abroad; John took note of the keen profile, and—it might serve as a note for the Great Luke—his hand moved to his bosom. The Abbot saw, and nodded permission. John whipped out silverpoint and sketch-book.

'Nay—modesty is good enough—but deliver your own opinion,' the Italian was urging the Infirmarian. Out of courtesy to the foreigner nearly all the talk was in table-Latin; more formal and more copious than monk's patter. Thomas began with his meek stammer.

'I confess myself at a loss for the cause of the fever unless—as Varro saith in his *De Re Rustica*—certain small animals which the eye cannot follow enter the body by the nose and mouth, and set up grave diseases. On the other hand, this is not in Scripture.'

Roger of Salerno hunched head and shoulders like an angry cat. 'Always *that!*' he said, and John snatched down the twist of the thin lips.

'Never at rest, John,' the Abbot smiled at the artist. 'You should break off every two hours for prayers, as we do. St. Benedict was no fool. Two hours is all that a man can carry the edge of his eye or hand.'

'For copyists—yes. Brother Martin is not sure after one hour. But when a man's work takes him, he must go on till it lets him go.'

'Yes, that is the Demon of Socrates,' the Friar from Oxford rumbled above his cup.

'The doctrine leans toward presumption,' said the Abbot. 'Remember, "Shall mortal man be more just than his Maker?"'

'There is no danger of justice'; the Friar spoke bitterly. 'But at least Man might be suffered to go forward in his Art or his thought. Yet if Mother Church sees or hears him move anyward, what says she? "No!" Always "No!"'

'But if the little animals of Varro be invisible'—this was

Roger of Salerno to Thomas—'how are we any nearer to a cure?'

'By experiment'—the Friar wheeled round on them suddenly. 'By reason and experiment. The one is useless without the other. But Mother Church——'

'Ay!' Roger de Salerno dashed at the fresh bait like a pike. 'Listen, Sirs. Her bishops—our Princes—strew our roads in Italy with carcasses that they make for their pleasure or wrath. Beautiful corpses! Yet if I—if we doctors—so much as raise the skin of one of them to look at God's fabric beneath, what says Mother Church? "Sacrilege! Stick to your pigs and dogs, or you burn!"'

'And not Mother Church only!' the Friar chimed in. '*Every* way we are barred—barred by the words of some man, dead a thousand years, which are held final. Who is any son of Adam that his one say-so should close a door towards truth? I would not except even Peter Peregrinus, my own great teacher.'

'Nor I Paul of Aegina,' Roger of Salerno cried. 'Listen, Sirs! Here is a case to the very point. Apuleius affirmeth, if a man eat fasting of the juice of the cut-leaved butter-cup—*sceleratus* we call it, which means "rascally"'—this with a condescending nod towards John—'his soul will leave his body laughing. Now this is the lie more danger-ous than truth, since truth of a sort is in it.'

'He's away!' whispered the Abbot despairingly.

'For the juice of that herb, I know by experiment, burns, blisters, and wries the mouth. I know also the *ric-tus*, or pseudo-laughter on the face of such as have perished by the strong poisons of herbs allied to this ra-nunculus. Certainly that spasm resembles laughter. It seems then, in my judgment, that Apuleius, having seen the body of one thus poisoned, went off at score and wrote that the man died laughing.'

'Neither staying to observe, nor to confirm observation by experiment,' added the Friar, frowning.

Stephen the Abbot cocked an eyebrow toward John.

'How think *you?*' said he.

'I'm no doctor,' John returned, 'but I'd say Apuleius in all these years might have been betrayed by his copyists. They take shortcuts to save 'emselves trouble. Put case that Apuleius wrote the soul *seems to* leave the body laughing, after this poison. There's not three copyists in five (*my* judgment) would not leave out the "seems to." For who'd question Apuleius? If it seemed so to him, so it must be. Otherwise any child knows cut-leaved buttercup.'

'Have you knowledge of herbs?' Roger of Salerno asked curtly.

'Only, that when I was a boy in convent, I've made tetters round my mouth and on my neck with buttercup-juice, to save going to prayer o' cold nights.'

'Ah!' said Roger. 'I profess no knowledge of tricks.' He turned aside, stiffly.

'No matter! Now for your own tricks, John,' the tactful Abbot broke in. 'You shall show the doctors your Magdalene and your Gadarene Swine and the devils.'

'Devils? Devils? *I* have produced devils by means of drugs; and have abolished them by the same means. Whether devils be external to mankind or immanent, I have not yet pronounced.' Roger of Salerno was still angry.

'Ye dare not,' snapped the Friar from Oxford. 'Mother Church makes Her own devils.'

'Not wholly! Our John has come back from Spain with brand-new ones.' Abbot Stephen took the vellum handed to him, and laid it tenderly on the table. They gathered to look. The Magdalene was drawn in palest, almost transparent, grisaille, against a raging, swaying background of woman-faced devils, each broke to and by her special sin, and each, one could see, frenziedly straining against the Power that compelled her.

'I've never seen the like of this grey shadow-work,' said the Abbot. 'How came you by it?'

'*Non nobis!* It came to me,' said John, not knowing he was a generation or so ahead of his time in the use of that medium.

'Why is she so pale?' the Friar demanded.

'Evil has all come out of her—she'd take any colour now.'

'Ay, like light through glass. *I* see.'

Roger of Salerno was looking in silence—his nose nearer and nearer the page. 'It is so,' he pronounced finally. 'Thus it is in epilepsy—mouth, eyes, and forehead—even to the droop of her wrist there. Every sign of it! She will need restoratives, that woman, and, afterwards, sleep natural. No poppy-juice, or she will vomit on her waking. And thereafter—but I am not in my Schools.' He drew himself up. 'Sir,' said he, 'you should be of Our calling. For, by the Snakes of Aesculapius, you *see!*'

The two struck hands as equals.

'And how think you of the Seven Devils?' the Abbot went on.

These melted into convoluted flower- or flame-like bodies, ranging in colour from phosphorescent green to the black purple of outworn iniquity, whose hearts could be traced beating through their substance. But, for sign of hope and the sane workings of life, to be regained, the deep border was of conventionalised spring flowers and birds, all crowned by a kingfisher in haste, atilt through a clump of yellow iris.

Roger of Salerno identified the herbs and spoke largely of their virtues.

'And now, the Gadarene Swine,' said Stephen. John laid the picture on the table.

Here were devils dishoused, in dread of being abolished to the Void, huddling and hurtling together to force lodgment by every opening into the brute bodies offered. Some of the swine fought the invasion, foaming and jerking; some were surrendering to it, sleepily, as to a luxurious back-scratching; others, wholly possessed, whirled off in bucking droves for the lake beneath. In one corner the freed man stretched out his limbs all restored to his control, and Our Lord, seated, looked at him as questioning what he would make of his deliverance.

'Devils indeed!' was the Friar's comment. 'But wholly a new sort.'

Some devils were mere lumps, with lobes and protuberances—a hint of a fiend's face peering through jelly-like walls. And there was a family of impatient, globular devillings who had burst open the belly of their smirking parent, and were revolving desperately towards their prey. Others patterned themselves into rods, chains and ladders, single or conjoined, round the throat and jaws of a shrieking sow, from whose ear emerged the lashing, glassy tail of a devil that had made good his refuge. And there were granulated and conglomerate devils, mixed up with the foam and slaver where the attack was fiercest. Thence the eye carried on to the insanely active backs of the downward-racing swine, the swineherd's aghast face, and his dog's terror.

Said Roger of Salerno, 'I pronounce that these were begotten of drugs. They stand outside the rational mind.'

'Not these,' said Thomas the Infirmarian, who as a servant of the Monastery should have asked his Abbot's leave to speak. 'Not *these*—look!—in the bordure.'

The border to the picture was a diaper of irregular but balanced compartments or cellules, where sat, swam, or weltered, devils in blank, so to say—things as yet uninspired by Evil—indifferent, but lawlessly outside imagination. Their shapes resembled, again, ladders, chains, scourges, diamonds, aborted buds, or gravid phosphorescent globes—some well-nigh star-like.

Roger of Salerno compared them to the obsessions of a Churchman's mind.

'Malignant?' the Friar from Oxford questioned.

' "Count everything unknown for horrible," ' Roger quoted with scorn.

'Not I. But they are marvellous—marvellous. I think——'

The Friar drew back. Thomas edged in to see better, and half opened his mouth.

'Speak,' said Stephen, who had been watching him. 'We are all in a sort doctors here.'

'I would say then'—Thomas rushed at it as one putting out his life's belief at the stake—'that these lower shapes in the bordure may not be so much hellish and malignant as models and patterns upon which John has tricked out and embellished his proper devils among the swine above there!'

'And that would signify?' said Roger of Salerno sharply.

'In my poor judgment, that he may have seen such shapes—without help of drugs.'

'Now who—*who*'—said John of Burgos, after a round and unregarded oath—'has made thee so wise of a sudden, my Doubter?'

'I wise? God forbid! Only John, remember—one winter six years ago—the snow-flakes melting on your sleeve at the cookhouse-door. You showed me them through a little crystal, that made small things larger.'

'Yes. The Moors call such a glass the Eye of Allah,' John confirmed.

'You showed me them melting—six-sided. You called them, then, your patterns.'

'True. Snow-flakes melt six-sided. I have used them for diaper-work often.'

'Melting snow-flakes as seen through a glass? By art optical?' the Friar asked.

'Art optical? *I* have never heard!' Roger of Salerno cried.

'John,' said the Abbot of St. Illod's commandingly, 'was it—is it so?'

'In some sort,' John replied, 'Thomas has the right of it. Those shapes in the bordure were my workshop-patterns for the devils above. In *my* craft, Salerno, we dare not drug. It kills hand and eye. My shapes are to be seen honestly, in nature.'

The Abbot drew a bowl of rose-water towards him. 'When I was prisoner with—with the Saracens after Mansura,' he began, turning up the fold of his long sleeve, 'there were certain magicians—physicians—who could show—' he dipped his third finger delicately in the water—'all the firmament of Hell, as it were, in—' he shook off one drop from his polished nail on to the polished table—'even such a supernaculum as this.'

'But it must be foul water—not clean,' said John.

'Show us then—all—all,' said Stephen. 'I would make sure—once more.' The Abbot's voice was official.

John drew from his bosom a stamped leather box, some six or eight inches long, wherein, bedded on faded velvet, lay what looked like silver-bound compasses of old boxwood, with a screw at the head which opened or closed the legs to minute fractions. The legs terminated, not in points, but spoon-shapedly, one spatula pierced with a metal-lined hole less than a quarter of an inch across, the other with a half-inch hole. Into this latter John, after carefully wiping with a silk rag, slipped a metal cylinder that carried glass or crystal, it seemed, at each end.

"Ah! Art optic!' said the Friar. 'But what is that beneath it?'

It was a small swivelling sheet of polished silver no bigger than a florin, which caught the light and concentrated it on the lesser hole. John adjusted it without the Friar's proffered help.

'And now to find a drop of water,' said he, picking up a small brush.

'Come to my upper cloister The sun is on the leads still,' said the Abbot, rising.

They followed him there. Half way along, a drip from a gutter had made a greenish puddle in a worn stone. Very

carefully, John dropped a drop of it into the smaller hole
of the compass-leg, and, steadying the apparatus on a cop-
ing, worked the screw in the compass-joint, screwed the
cylinder, and swung the swivel of the mirror till he was
satisfied.

'Good!' He peered through the thing. 'My Shapes are
all here. Now look, Father! If they do not meet your eye at
first, turn this nicked edge here, left or right-handed.'

'I have not forgotten,' said the Abbot, taking his place.
'Yes! They are here—as they were in my time—my time
past. There is no end to them, I was told. . . . There *is* no
end!'

'The light will go. Oh, let me look! Suffer me to see,
also!' the Friar pleaded, almost shouldering Stephen from
the eye-piece. The Abbot gave way. His eyes were on
time past. But the Friar, instead of looking, turned the apparatus in his capable hands. .

'Nay, nay,' John interrupted, for the man was already
fiddling at the screws. 'Let the Doctor see.'

Roger of Salerno looked, minute after minute. John saw
his blue-veined cheek-bones turn white. He stepped back
at last, as though stricken.

'It is a new world—a new world and—Oh, God Unjust!—I am old!'

'And now Thomas,' Stephen ordered.

John manipulated the tube for the Infirmarian, whose
hands shook, and he too looked long. 'It is Life,' he said
presently in a breaking voice. 'No Hell! Life created and
rejoicing—the work of the Creator. They live, even as I
have dreamed. Then it was no sin for me to dream. No
sin—O God—no sin!'

He flung himself on his knees and began hysterically
the *Benedicite omnia Opera*.

'And now I will see how it is actuated,' said the Friar
from Oxford, thrusting forward again.

'Bring it within. The place is all eyes and ears,' said
Stephen.

They walked quietly back along the leads, three English counties laid out in evening sunshine around them; church upon church, monastery upon monastery, cell after cell, and the bulk of a vast cathedral moored on the edge of the banked shoals of sunset.

When they were at the after-table once more they sat down, all except the Friar who went to the window and huddled bat-like over the thing. 'I see! I see!' he was repeating to himself.

'He'll not hurt it,' said John. But the Abbot, staring in front of him, like Roger of Salerno, did not hear. The Infirmarian's head was on the table between his shaking arms.

John reached for a cup of wine.

'It was shown to me,' the Abbot was speaking to himself, 'in Cairo, that man stands ever between two Infinities—of greatness and littleness. Therefore, there is no end—either to life—or——'

'And *I* stand on the edge of the grave,' snarled Roger of Salerno. 'Who pities *me?*'

'Hush!' said Thomas the Infirmarian. 'The little creatures shall be sanctified—sanctified to the service of His sick.'

'What need?' John of Burgos wiped his lips. 'It shows no more than the shapes of things. It gives good pictures. I had it at Granada. It was brought from the East, they told me.'

Roger of Salerno laughed with an old man's malice. 'What of Mother Church? Most Holy Mother Church? If it comes to Her ears that we have spied into Her Hell without Her leave, where do we stand?'

'At the stake,' said the Abbot of St. Illod's, and, raising his voice a trifle. 'You hear that? Roger Bacon, heard you that?'

The Friar turned from the window, clutching the compasses tighter.

'No, no!' he appealed. 'Not with Falcodi—not with our

English-hearted Foulkes made Pope. He's wise—he's learned. He reads what I have put forth. Foulkes would never suffer it.'

' "Holy Pope is one thing, Holy Church another," Roger quoted.

'But I—*I* can bear witness it is no Art Magic,' the Friar went on. 'Nothing is it, except Art optical—wisdom after trial and experiment, mark you. I can prove it, and—my name weighs with men who dare think.'

'Find them!' croaked Roger of Salerno. 'Five or six in all the world. That makes less than fifty pounds by weight of ashes at the stake. I have watched such men—reduced.'

'I will not give this up!' The Friar's voice cracked in passion and despair. 'It would be to sin against the Light.'

'No, no! Let us—let us sanctify the little animals of Varro,' said Thomas.

Stephen leaned forward, fished his ring out of the cup, and slipped it on his finger. 'My sons,' said he, 'we have seen what we have seen.'

'That it is no magic but simple Art,' the Friar persisted.

' 'Avails nothing. In the eyes of Mother Church we have seen more than is permitted to man.'

'But it was Life—created and rejoicing,' said Thomas.

'To look into Hell as we shall be judged—as we shall be proved—to have looked, is for priests only.'

'Or green-sick virgins on the road to sainthood who, for cause any mid-wife could give you——'

The Abbot's half-lifted hand checked Roger of Salerno's outpouring.

'Nor may even priests see more in Hell than Church knows to be there. John, there is respect due to Church as well as to Devils.'

'My trade's the outside of things,' said John quietly. 'I have my patterns.'

'But you may need to look again for more,' the Friar said.

'In my craft, a thing done is done with. We go on to new shapes after that.'

'And if we trespass beyond bounds, even in thought, we lie open to the judgment of the Church,' the Abbot continued.

'But thou knowest—*knowest!*' Roger of Salerno had returned to the attack. 'Here's all the world in darkness concerning the causes of things—from the fever across the lane to thy Lady's—thine own Lady's—eating malady. Think!'

'I have thought upon it, Salerno! I have thought indeed.'

Thomas the Infirmarian lifted his head again; and this time he did not stammer at all. 'As in the water, so in the blood must they rage and war with each other! I have dreamed these ten years—I thought it was a sin—but my dreams and Varro's are true! Think on it again! Here's the Light under our very hand!'

'Quench it! You'd no more stand to roasting than—any other. I'll give you the case as Church—as I myself—would frame it. Our John here returns from the Moors, and shows us a hell of devils contending in the compass of one drop of water. Magic past clearance! You can hear the faggots crackle.'

'But thou knowest! Thou hast seen it all before! For man's poor sake! For old friendship's sake—Stephen!' The Friar was trying to stuff the compasses into his bosom as he appealed.

'What Stephen de Sautré knows, you his friends know also. I would have you, now, obey the Abbot of St. Illod's. Give to me!' He held out his ringed hand.

'May I—may John here—not even make a drawing of one—one screw?' said the broken Friar, in spite of himself.

'Nowise!' Stephen took it over. 'Your dagger, John. Sheathed will serve.'

He unscrewed the metal cylinder, laid it on the table, and with the dagger's hilt smashed some crystal to sparkling dust which he swept into a scooped hand and cast behind the hearth.

'It would seem,' said he, 'the choice lies between two sins. To deny the world a Light which is under our hand, or to enlighten the world before her time. What you have seen, I saw long since among the physicians at Cairo. And I know what doctrine they drew from it. Hast *thou* dreamed, Thomas? I also—with fuller knowledge. But this birth, my sons, is untimely. It will be but the mother of more death, more torture, more division, and greater darkness in this dark age. Therefore I, who know both my world and the Church, take this Choice on my consience. Go! It is finished.'

He thrust the wooden part of the compasses deep among the beech logs till all was burned.

1926

Utopian/Antiutopian

AS EASY AS A.B.C.

The A.B.C., that semi-elected, semi-nominated body of a few score persons, controls the Planet. Transportation is Civilization, our motto runs. Theoretically we do what we please, so long as we do not interfere with the traffic and all it implies. Practically, the A.B.C. confirms or annuls all international arrangements, and, to judge from its last report, finds our tolerant, humorous, lazy little Planet only too ready to shift the whole burden of public administration on its shoulders.

'With the Night Mail'

Isn't it almost time that our Planet took some interest in the proceedings of the Aerial Board of Control? One knows that easy communications nowadays, and lack of privacy in the past, have killed all curiosity among mankind, but as the Board's Official Reporter I am bound to tell my tale.

At 9:30 a.m. August 26, A.D. 2065, the Board, sitting in London, was informed by De Forest that the District of Northern Illinois had riotously cut itself out of all systems and would remain disconnected till the Board should take over and administer it direct.

Every Northern Illinois freight and passenger tower was, he reported, out of action; all District main, local, and guiding lights had been extinguished; all General Communications were dumb, and through traffic had been diverted. No reason had been given, but he gathered unofficially from the Mayor of Chicago that the District complained of 'crowd-making and invasion of privacy'.

As a matter of fact, it is of no importance whether Northern Illinois stay in or out of planetary circuit; as a matter of policy, any complaint of invasion of privacy needs immediate investigation, lest worse follow.

By 9:45 a.m. De Forest, Dragomiroff (Russia), Takahira (Japan), and Pirolo (Italy) were empowered to visit Illinois and 'to take such steps as might be necessary for the resumption of traffic and *all that that implies*'. By 10 a.m. the Hall was empty, and the four Members and I were aboard what Pirolo insisted on calling 'my leetle godchild'—that is to say, the new *Victor Pirolo*. Our Planet prefers to know Victor Pirolo as a gentle, grey-haired enthusiast who spends his time near Foggia, inventing or creating new breeds of Spanish-Italian olive-trees; but there is another side to his nature—the manufacture of quaint inventions, of which the *Victor Pirolo* is, perhaps, not the least surprising. She and a few score sister-craft of the same type embody his latest ideas. But she is not comfortable. An A.B.C. boat does not take the air with the level-keeled lift of a liner, but shoots up rocket-fashion like the 'aeroplane' of our ancestors, and makes her height at top-speed from the first. That is why I found myself sitting suddenly on the large lap of Eustace Arnott, who commands the A.B.C. Fleet. One knows vaguely that there is such a thing as a Fleet somewhere on the Planet, and that, theoretically, it exists for the purposes of what used to be known as 'war'. Only a week before, while visiting a glacier sanatorium behind Gothaven, I had seen some squadrons making false auroras far to the north while they manoeuvred round the Pole; but, naturally, it had never occurred to me that the things could be used in earnest.

Said Arnott to De Forest as I staggered to a seat on the chart-room divan: 'We're tremendously grateful to 'em in

Illinois. We've never had a chance of exercising all the Fleet together. I've turned in a General Call, and I expect we'll have at least two hundred keels aloft this evening.'

'Well aloft?' De Forest asked.

'Of course, sir. Out of sight till they're called for.'

Arnott laughed as he lolled over the transparent chart-table where the map of the summer-blue Atlantic slid along, degree by degree, in exact answer to our progress. Our dial already showed 320 m.p.h. and we were two thousand feet above the uppermost traffic lines.

'Now, where is this Illinois District of yours?' said Dragomiroff. 'One travels so much, one sees so little. Oh, I remember! It is in North America.'

De Forest, whose business it is to know the out districts, told us that it lay at the foot of Lake Michigan, on a road to nowhere in particular, was about half an hour's run from end to end, and, except in one corner, as flat as the sea. Like most flat countries nowadays, it was heavily guarded against invasion of privacy by forced timber—fifty-foot spruce and tamarack, grown in five years. The population was close on two millions, largely migratory between Florida and California, with a backbone of small farms (they call a thousand acres a farm in Illinois) whose owners come into Chicago for amusements and society during the winter. They were, he said, noticeably kind, quiet folk, but a little exacting, as all flat countries must be, in their notions of privacy. There had, for instance, been no print news-sheet in Illinois for twenty-seven years. Chicago argued that engines for printed news sooner or later developed into engines for invasion of privacy, which in turn might bring the old terror of Crowds and blackmail back to the Planet. So news-sheets were not.

'And that's Illinois,' De Forest concluded. 'You see, in the Old Days, she was in the forefront of what they used to call "progress", and Chicago—'

'Chicago?' said Takahira. 'That's the little place where

there is Salati's Statue of the Nigger in Flames? A fine bit of old work.'

'When did you see it?' asked De Forest quickly. 'They only unveil it once a year.'

'I know. At Thanksgiving. It was then,' said Takahira, with a shudder. 'And they sang MacDonough's Song, too.'

'Whew!' De Forest whistled. 'I did not know that! I wish you'd told me before. MacDonough's Song may have had its uses when it was composed, but it was an infernal legacy for any man to leave behind.'

'It's protective instinct, my dear fellows,' said Pirolo, rolling a cigarette. 'The Planet, she has had her dose of popular government. She suffers from inherited agoraphobia. She has no—ah—use for crowds.'

Dragomiroff leaned forward to give him a light. 'Certainly,' said the white-bearded Russian, 'the Planet has taken all precautions against crowds for the past hundred years. What is our total population today? Six hundred million, we hope; five hundred, we think; but—but if next year's census shows more than four hundred and fifty, I myself will eat all the extra little babies. We have cut the birth-rate out—right out! For a long time we have said to Almighty God, "Thank You, Sir, but we do not much like Your game of life, so we will not play." '

'Anyhow,' said Arnott defiantly, 'men live a century apiece on the average now.'

'Oh, that is quite well! I am rich—you are rich—we are all rich and happy because we are so few and we live so long. Only *I* think Almighty God He will remember what the Planet was like in the time of Crowds and the Plague. Perhaps He will send us nerves. Eh, Pirolo?'

The Italian blinked into space. 'Perhaps,' he said, 'He has sent them already. Anyhow, you cannot argue with the Planet. She does not forget the Old Days, and—what can you do?'

'For sure we can't remake the world.' De Forest glanced

at the map flowing smoothly across the table from west to east. 'We ought to be over our ground by nine tonight. There won't be much sleep afterwards.'

On which hint we dispersed, and I slept till Takahira waked me for dinner. Our ancestors thought nine hours' sleep ample for their little lives. We, living thirty years longer, feel ourselves defrauded with less than eleven out of the twenty-four.

By ten o'clock we were over Lake Michigan. The west shore was lightless, except for a dull ground-glare at Chicago, and a single traffic-directing light—its leading beam pointing north—at Waukegan on our starboard bow. None of the Lake villages gave any sign of life; and inland, westward, so far as we could see, blackness lay unbroken on the level earth. We swooped down and skimmed low across the dark, throwing calls county by county. Now and again we picked up the faint glimmer of a house-light, or heard the rap and rend of a cultivator being played across the fields, but Northern Illinois as a whole was one inky, apparently uninhabited, waste of high, forced woods. Only our illuminated map, with its little pointer switching from county to county, as we wheeled and twisted, gave us any idea of our position. Our calls, urgent, pleading, coaxing or commanding, through the General Communicator brought no answer. Illinois strictly maintained her own privacy in the timber which she grew for that purpose.

'Oh, this is absurd!' said De Forest. 'We're like an owl trying to work a wheat-field. Is this Bureau Creek? Let's land, Arnott, and get hold of some one.'

We brushed over a belt of forced woodland—fifteen-year-old maple sixty feet high—grounded on a private meadow-dock, none too big, where we moored to our own grapnels, and hurried out through the warm dark night towards a light in a verandah. As we neared the garden gate I could have sworn we had stepped knee-deep in quicksand, for we could scarcely drag our feet against the

prickling currents that clogged them. After five paces we
stopped, wiping our foreheads, as hopelessly stuck on dry
smooth turf as so many cows in a bog.

'Pest!' cried Pirolo angrily. 'We are ground-circuited.
And it is my own system of ground-circuits too! I know
the pull.'

'Good evening,' said a girl's voice from the verandah.
'Oh, I'm sorry! We've locked up. Wait a minute.'

We heard the click of a switch, and almost fell forward
as the currents round our knees were withdrawn.

The girl laughed, and laid aside her knitting. An
old-fashioned Controller stood at her elbow, which she
reversed from time to time, and we could hear the snort
and clank of the obedient cultivator half a mile away, behind the guardian woods.

'Come in and sit down,' she said. 'I'm only playing a
plough. Dad's gone to Chicago to—Ah! Then it was *your*
call I heard just now!'

She had caught sight of Arnott's Board uniform, leaped
to the switch, and turned it full on.

We were checked, gasping, waist-deep in current this
time, three yards from the verandah.

'We only want to know what's the matter with Illinois,'
said De Forest placidly.

'Then hadn't you better go to Chicago and find out?'
she answered. 'There's nothing wrong here. We own ourselves.'

'How can we go anywhere if you won't loose us?' De
Forest went on, while Arnott scowled. Admirals of Fleets
are still quite human when their dignity is touched.

'Stop a minute—you don't know how funny you look!'
She put her hands on her hips and laughed mercilessly.

'Don't worry about that,' said Arnott, and whistled. A
voice answered from the *Victor Pirolo* in the meadow.

'Only a single-fuse ground-circuit!' Arnott called. 'Sort
it out gently, please.'

We heard the ping of a breaking lamp; a fuse blew out

somewhere in the verandah roof, frightening a nest full of birds. The ground-circuit was open. We stooped and rubbed our tingling ankles.

'How rude—how very rude of you!' the Maiden cried.

'Sorry, but we haven't time to look funny,' said Arnott. 'We've got to go to Chicago; and if I were you, young lady, I'd go into the cellars for the next two hours, and take mother with me.'

Off he strode, with us at his heels, muttering indignantly, till the humour of the thing struck and doubled him up with laughter at the foot of the gangway ladder.

'The Board hasn't shown what you might call a fat spark on this occasion,' said De Forest, wiping his eyes. 'I hope I didn't look as big a fool as you did, Arnott! Hullo! What on earth is that? Dad coming home from Chicago?'

There was a rattle and a rush, and a five-plough cultivator, blades in air like so many teeth, trundled itself at us round the edge of the timber, fuming and sparking furiously.

'Jump!' said Arnott, as we bundled ourselves through the none-too-wide door. 'Never mind about shutting it. Up!'

The *Victor Pirolo* lifted like a bubble, and the vicious machine shot just underneath us, clawing high as it passed.

'There's a nice little spit-kitten for you!' said Arnott, dusting his knees. 'We ask her a civil question. First she circuits us and then she plays a cultivator at us!'

'And then we fly,' said Dragomiroff. 'If I were forty years more young, I would go back and kiss her. Ho! Ho!'

'I,' said Pirolo, 'would smack her! My pet ship has been chased by a dirty plough; a—how do you say?—agricultural implement.'

'Oh, that is Illinois all over,' said De Forest. 'They don't content themselves with talking about privacy. They arrange to have it. And now, where's your alleged fleet, Arnott? We must assert ourselves against this wench.'

Arnott pointed to the black heavens.

'Waiting on—up there,' said he. 'Shall I give them the whole installation, sir?'

'Oh, I don't think the young lady is quite worth that,' said De Forest. 'Get over Chicago, and perhaps we'll see something.'

In a few minutes we were hanging at two thousand feet over an oblong block of incandescence in the centre of the little town.

'That looks like the old City Hall. Yes, there's Salati's Statue in front of it,' said Takahira. 'But what on earth are they doing to the place? I thought they used it for a market nowadays! Drop a little, please.'

We could hear the sputter and crackle of road-surfacing machines—the cheap Western type which fuse stone and rubbish into lava-like ribbed glass for their rough country roads. Three or four surfacers worked on each side of a square of ruins. The brick and stone wreckage crumbled, slid forward, and presently spread out into white-hot pools of sticky slag, which the levelling-rods smoothed more or less flat. Already a third of the big block had been so treated, and was cooling to dull red before our astonished eyes.

'It is the Old Market,' said De Forest. 'Well, there's nothing to prevent Illinois from making a road through a market. It doesn't interfere with traffic, that I can see.'

'Hsh!' said Arnott, gripping me by the shoulder. 'Listen! They're singing. Why on the earth are they singing?'

We dropped again till we could see the black fringe of people at the edge of that glowing square.

At first they only roared against the roar of the surfacers and levellers. Then the words came up clearly—the words of the Forbidden Song that all men knew, and none let pass their lips—poor Pat MacDonough's Song, made in the days of the Crowds and the Plague—every silly word of it loaded to sparking-point with the Planet's inherited memories of horror, panic, fear and cruelty. And Chicago—innocent, contented little Chicago—was singing it aloud to the infernal tune that carried riot, pestilence and lunacy round our Planet a few generations ago!

'Once there was The People—Terror gave it birth;
Once there was The People, and it made a hell of earth!'

(Then the stamp and pause):

'Earth arose and crushed it. Listen, oh, ye slain!
Once there was The People—it shall never be again!'

The levellers thrust in savagely against the ruins as the song renewed itself again, again and again, louder than the crash of the melting walls.

De Forest frowned.

'I don't like that,' he said. 'They've broken back to the Old Days! They'll be killing somebody soon. I think we'd better divert 'em, Arnott.'

'Ay, ay, sir,' Arnott's hand went to his cap, and we heard the hull of the *Victor Pirolo* ring to the command: 'Lamps! Both watches stand by! Lamps! Lamps! Lamps!'

'Keep still!' Takahira whispered to me. 'Blinkers, please, quartermaster.'

'It's all right—all right!' said Pirolo from behind, and to my horror slipped over my head some sort of rubber helmet that locked with a snap. I could feel thick colloid bosses before my eyes, but I stood in absolute darkness.

'To save the sight,' he explained, and pushed me on to the chart-room divan. 'You will see in a minute.'

As he spoke I became aware of a thin thread of almost intolerable light, let down from heaven at an immense distance—one vertical hairsbreadth of frozen lightning.

'Those are our flanking ships,' said Arnott at my elbow. 'That one is over Galena. Look south—that other one's over Keithburg. Vincennes is behind us, and north yonder is Winthrop Woods. The Fleet's in position, sir'—this to De Forest. 'As soon as you give the word.'

'Ah, no! No!' cried Dragomiroff at my side. I could feel the old man tremble. 'I do not know all that you can do, but be kind! I ask you to be a little kind to them below! This is horrible—horrible!'

> 'When a Woman kills a Chicken,
>   Dynasties and Empires sicken,'

Takahira quoted. 'It is too late to be gentle now.'

'Then take off my helmet! Take off my helmet!' Dragomiroff began hysterically.

Pirolo must have put his arm round him.

'Hush,' he said, 'I am here. It is all right, Ivan, my dear fellow.'

'I'll just send our little girl in Bureau County a warning,' said Arnott. 'She don't deserve it, but we'll allow her a minute or two to take mamma to the cellar.'

In the utter hush that followed the growling spark after Arnott had linked up his Service Communicator with the invisible Fleet, we heard MacDonough's Song from the city beneath us grow fainter as we rose to position. Then I clapped my hand before my mask lenses, for it was as though the floor of Heaven had been riddled and all the inconceivable blaze of suns in the making was poured through the manholes.

'You needn't count,' said Arnott. I had had no thought of such a thing. 'There are two hundred and fifty keels up there, five miles apart. Full power, please, for another twelve seconds.'

The firmament, as far as eye could reach, stood on pillars of white fire. One fell on the glowing square at Chicago, and turned it black.

'Oh! Oh! Oh! Can men be allowed to do such things?' Dragomiroff cried, and fell across our knees.

'Glass of water, please,' said Takahira to a helmeted shape that leaped forward. 'He is a little faint.'

The lights switched off, and the darkness stunned like an avalanche. We could hear Dragomiroff's teeth on the glass edge.

Pirolo was comforting him.

'All right, all ra-ight,' he repeated. 'Come and lie down. Come below and take off your mask. I give you my word, old friend, it is all right. They are my siege-lights. Little Victor Pirolo's leetle lights. You know *me!* I do not hurt people.'

'Pardon!' Dragomiroff moaned. 'I have never seen Death. I have never seen the Board take action. Shall we go down and burn them alive, or is that already done?'

'Oh, hush,' said Pirolo, and I think he rocked him in his arms.

'Do we repeat, sir?' Arnott asked De Forest.

'Give 'em a minute's break,' De Forest replied. 'They may need it.'

We waited a minute, and then MacDonough's Song, broken but defiant, rose from undefeated Chicago.

'They seem fond of that tune,' said De Forest. 'I should let 'em have it, Arnott.'

'Very good, sir,' said Arnott, and felt his way to the Communicator keys.

No lights broke forth, but the hollow of the skies made herself the mouth for one note that touched the raw fibre of the brain. Men hear such sounds in delirium, advancing like tides from horizons beyond the ruled foreshores of space.

'That's our pitch-pipe,' said Arnott. 'We may be a bit ragged. I've never conducted two hundred and fifty performers before.' He pulled out the couplers, and struck a full chord on the Service Communicators.

The beams of light leaped down again, and danced, solemnly and awfully, a stilt-dance, sweeping thirty or forty miles left and right at each stiff-legged kick, while the darkness delivered itself—there is no scale to measure against that utterance—of the tune to which they kept time. Certain notes—one learnt to expect them with terror—cut through one's marrow, but, after three minutes, thought and emotion passed in indescribable agony.

We saw, we heard, but I think we were in some sort swooning. The two hundred and fifty beams shifted, reformed, straddled and split, narrowed, widened, rippled in ribbons, broke into a thousand white-hot parallel lines, melted and revolved in interwoven rings like old-fashioned engine-turning, flung up to the zenith, made as if to descend and renew the torment, halted at the last instant, twizzled insanely round the horizon, and vanished, to bring back for the hundredth time darkness more shattering than their instantly renewed light over all Illinois. Then the tune and lights ceased together, and we heard one single devastating wail that shook all the horizon as a rubbed wet finger shakes the rim of a bowl.

'Ah, that is my new siren,' said Pirolo. 'You can break an iceberg in half, if you find the proper pitch. They will whistle by squadrons now. It is the wind through pierced shutters in the bows.'

I had collapsed beside Dragomiroff, broken and snivelling feebly, because I had been delivered before my time to all the terrors of Judgement Day, and the Archangels of the Resurrection were hailing me naked across the Universe to the sound of the music of the spheres.

Then I saw De Forest smacking Arnott's helmet with his open hand. The wailing died down in a long shriek as a black shadow swooped past us, and returned to her place above the lower clouds.

'I hate to interrupt a specialist when he's enjoying himself,' said De Forest. 'But, as a matter of fact, all Illinois has been asking us to stop for these last fifteen seconds.'

'What a pity.' Arnott slipped off his mask. 'I wanted you to hear us really hum. Our lower C can lift streetpaving.'

'It is Hell—Hell!' cried Dragomiroff, and sobbed aloud.

Arnott looked away as he answered:

'It's a few thousand volts ahead of the old shoot-'em-and-sink-'em game, but I should scarcely call it *that*. What shall I tell the Fleet, sir?'

'Tell 'em we're very pleased and impressed. I don't think they need wait on any longer. There isn't a spark left down there.' De Forest pointed. 'They'll be deaf and blind.'

'Oh, I think not, sir. The demonstration lasted less than ten minutes.'

'Marvellous!' Takahira sighed. 'I should have said it was half a night. Now, shall we go down and pick up the pieces?'

'But first a small drink,' said Pirolo. 'The Board must not arrive weeping at its own works.'

'I am an old fool—an old fool!' Dragomiroff began piteously. 'I did not know what would happen. It is all new to me. We reason with them in Little Russia.'

Chicago North landing-tower was unlighted, and Arnott worked his ship into the clips by her own lights. As soon as these broke out we heard groanings of horror and appeal from many people below.

'All right,' shouted Arnott into the darkness. 'We aren't beginning again!' We descended by the stairs, to find ourselves knee-deep in a grovelling crowd, some crying that they were blind, others beseeching us not to make any more noises, but the greater part writhing face downwards, their hands or their caps before their eyes.

It was Pirolo who came to our rescue. He climbed the side of a surfacing-machine, and there, gesticulating as though they could see, made oration to those afflicted people of Illinois.

'You stchewpids!' he began. 'There is nothing to fuss for. Of course, your eyes will smart and be red tomorrow. You will look as if you and your wives had drunk too

much, but in a little while you will see again as well as before. I tell you this, and I—*I* am Pirolo. Victor Pirolo!'

The crowd with one accord shuddered, for many legends attach to Victor Pirolo of Foggia, deep in the secrets
of God.

'Pirolo?' An unsteady voice lifted itself. 'Then tell us
was there anything except light in those lights of yours
just now?'

The question was repeated from every corner of the
darkness.

Pirolo laughed.

'No!' he thundered. (Why have small men such large
voices?) 'I give you my word and the Board's word that
there was nothing except light—just light! You stchewpids! Your birthrate is too low already as it is. Some day I
must invent something to send it up, but send it down—
never!'

'Is that true?—We thought—somebody said—'

One could feel the tension relax all round.

'You *too* big fools,' Pirolo cried. 'You could have sent us
a call and we would have told you.'

'Send you a call!' a deep voice shouted. 'I wish you had
been at our end of the wire.'

'I'm glad I wasn't,' said De Forest. 'It was bad enough
from behind the lamps. Never mind! It's over now. Is
there any one here I can talk business with? I'm De Forest—for the Board.'

'You might begin with me, for one—I'm Mayor,' the
bass voice replied.

A big man rose unsteadily from the street, and staggered towards us where we sat on the broad turf-edging,
in front of the garden fences.

'I ought to be the first on my feet. Am I?' said he.

'Yes,' said De Forest and steadied him as he dropped
down beside us.

'Hello, Andy. Is that you?' a voice called.

'Excuse me,' said the Mayor; 'that sounds like my Chief of Police, Bluthner!'

'Bluthner it is; and here's Mulligan and Keefe—on their feet.'

'Bring 'em up please, Blut. We're supposed to be the Four in charge of this hamlet. What we say, goes. And, De Forest, what do you say?'

'Nothing—yet,' De Forest answered, as we made room for the panting, reeling men. '*You*'ve cut out of system. Well?'

'Tell the steward to send down drinks, please,' Arnott whispered to an orderly at his side.

'Good!' said the Mayor, smacking his dry lips. 'Now I suppose we can take it, De Forest, that henceforward the Board will administer us direct?'

'Not if the Board can avoid it,' De Forest laughed. 'The A.B.C. is responsible for the planetary traffic only.'

'*And all that that implies.*' The big Four who ran Chicago chanted their Magna Charta like children at school.

'Well, get on,' said De Forest wearily. 'What is your silly trouble anyway?'

'Too much dam' Democracy,' said the Mayor, laying his hand on De Forest's knee.

'So? I thought Illinois had had her dose of that.'

'She has. That's why. Blut, what did you do with our prisoners last night?'

'Locked 'em in the water-tower to prevent the women killing 'em,' the Chief of Police replied. 'I'm too blind to move just yet, but—'

'Arnott, send some of your people, please, and fetch 'em along,' said De Forest.

'They're triple-circuited,' the Mayor called. 'You'll have to blow out three fuses.' He turned to De Forest, his large outline just visible in the paling darkness. 'I hate to throw any more work on the Board. I'm an administrator myself but we've had a little fuss with our Serviles. What?

In a big city there's bound to be a few men and women who can't live without listening to themselves, and who prefer drinking out of pipes they don't own both ends of. They inhabit flats and hotels all the year round. They say it saves 'em trouble. Anyway, it gives 'em more time to make trouble for their neighbours. We call 'em Serviles locally. And they are apt to be tuberculous.'

'Just so!' said the man called Mulligan. 'Transportation is Civilization. Democracy is Disease. I've proved it by the blood test, every time.'

'Mulligan's our Health Officer, and a one-idea man,' said the Mayor, laughing. 'But it's true that most Serviles haven't much control. They *will* talk; and when people take to talking as a business, anything may arrive—mayn't it, De Forest?'

'Anything—except the facts of the case,' said De Forest, laughing.

'I'll give you those in a minute,' said the Mayor. 'Our Serviles got to talking—first in their houses and then on the streets, telling men and women how to manage their own affairs. (You can't teach a Servile not to finger his neighbour's soul.) That's invasion of privacy, of course, but in Chicago we'll suffer anything sooner than make crowds. Nobody took much notice, and so I let 'em alone. My fault! I was warned there would be trouble, but there hasn't been a crowd or murder in Illinois for nineteen years.'

'Twenty-two,' said his Chief of Police.

'Likely. Anyway, we'd forgot such things. So, from talking in the houses and on the streets, our Serviles go to calling a meeting at the Old Market yonder.' He nodded across the square where the wrecked buildings heaved up grey in the dawn-glimmer behind the square-cased statue of The Negro in Flames. 'There's nothing to prevent any one calling meetings except that it's against human nature to stand in a crowd, besides being bad for the health. I ought to have known by the way our men and women attended that first meeting that trouble was brewing. There were as many as a thousand in the market-place, touching each other. Touching! Then the Serviles turned in all tongue-switches and talked, and we—'

'What did they talk about?' said Takahira.

'First, how badly things were managed in the city. That pleased us Four—we were on the platform—because we hoped to catch one or two good men for City work. You know how rare executive capacity is. Even if we didn't it's—its refreshing to find any one interested enough in our job to damn our eyes. You don't know what it means to work, year in, year out, without a spark of difference with a living soul.'

'Oh, don't we!' said De Forest. 'There are times on the Board when we'd give our positions if any one would kick us out and take hold of things themselves.'

'But they won't,' said the Mayor ruefully. 'I assure you, sir, we Four have done things in Chicago, in the hope of rousing people, that would have discredited Nero. But what do they say? "Very good, Andy. Have it your own way. Anything's better than a crowd. I'll go back to my land." You *can't* do anything with folk who can go where they please, and don't want anything on God's earth except their own way. There isn't a kick or a kicker left on the Planet.'

'Then I suppose that little shed yonder fell down by itself?' said De Forest. We could see the bare and still smoking ruins, and hear the slagpools crackle as they hardened and set.

'Oh, that's only amusement. 'Tell you later. As I was saying, our Serviles held the meeting, and pretty soon we had to ground-circuit the platform to save 'em from being killed. And that didn't make our people any more pacific.'

'How d'you mean?' I ventured to ask.

'If you've ever been ground-circuited,' said the Mayor, 'you'll know it don't improve any man's temper to be held up straining against nothing. No, sir! Eight or nine hun-

dred folk kept pawing and buzzing like flies in treacle for
two hours, while a pack of perfectly safe Serviles invades
their mental and spiritual privacy, may be amusing to
watch, but they are not pleasant to handle afterwards.'

Pirolo chuckled.

'Our fold own themselves. They were of opinion things
were going too far and too fiery. I warned the Serviles; but
they're born house-dwellers. Unless a fact hits 'em on the
head, they cannot see it. Would you believe me, they went
on to talk of what they called "popular government"?
They did! They wanted us to go back to the old Voodoo-
business of voting with papers and wooden boxes, and
word-drunk people and printed formulas, and news-
sheets! They said they practised it among themselves
about what they'd have to eat in their flats and hotels. Yes,
sir! They stood up behind Bluthner's doubled ground-circuits, and they said that, in this present year of grace, *to*
self-owning men and women, *on* that very spot! Then
they finished'—he lowered his voice cautiously—'by talking about "The People". And then Bluthner he had to sit
up all night in charge of the circuits because he couldn't
trust his men to keep 'em shut.'

'It was trying 'em too high,' the Chief of Police broke in.
'But we couldn't hold the crowd ground-circuited for
ever. I gathered in all the Serviles on charge of crowd-
making, and put 'em in the water-tower, and then I let
things cut loose. I had to! The District lit like a sparked
gas-tank!'

'The news was out over seven degrees of country,' the
Mayor continued: 'and when once it's a question of invasion of privacy, good-bye to right and reason in Illinois!
They began turning out traffic-lights and locking up
landing-towers on Thursday night. Friday, they stopped
all traffic and asked for the Board to take over. Then
they wanted to clean Chicago off the side of the Lake
and rebuild elsewhere—just for a souvenir of "The

People" that the Serviles talked about. I suggested that they should slag the Old Market where the meeting was held, while I turned in a call to you all on the Board. That kept 'em quiet till you came along. And—and now *you* can take hold of the situation.'

'Any chance of their quieting down?' De Forest asked.

'You can try,' said the Mayor.

De Forest raised his voice in the face of the reviving crowd that had edged in towards us. Day was come.

'Don't you think this business can be arranged?' he began. But there was a roar of angry voices:

'We've finished with Crowds! We aren't going back to the Old Days! Take us over! Take the Serviles away! Administer direct or we'll kill 'em! Down with The People!'

An attempt was made to begin MacDonough's Song. It got no further than the first line, for the *Victor Pirolo* sent down a warning drone on one stopped horn. A wrecked sidewall of the Old Market tottered and fell inwards on the slagpools. None spoke or moved till the last of the dust had settled down again, turning the steel case of Salati's Statue ashy grey.

'You see you'll just *have* to take us over,' the Mayor whispered.

De Forest shrugged his shoulders.

'You talk as if executive capacity could be snatched out of the air like so much horse-power. Can't you manage yourselves on any terms?' he said.

'We can, if you say so. It will only cost those few lives to begin with.'

The Mayor pointed across the square, where Arnott's men guided a stumbling group of ten or twelve men and women to the lake front and halted them under the Statue.

'Now I think,' said Takahira under his breath, 'there will be trouble.'

The mass in front of us growled like beasts.

At that moment the sun rose clear, and revealed the

blinking assembly to itself. As soon as it realized that it was a crowd we saw the shiver of horror and mutual repulsion shoot across it precisely as the steely flaws shot across the lake outside. Nothing was said, and, being half blind, of course it moved slowly. Yet in less than fifteen minutes most of that vast multitude—three thousand at the lowest count—melted away like frost on south eaves. The remnant stretched themselves on the grass, where a crowd feels and looks less like a crowd.

'These mean business,' the Mayor whispered to Takahira. 'There are a goodish few women there who've borne children. I don't like it.'

The morning draught off the lake stirred the trees round us with promise of a hot day; the sun reflected itself dazzlingly on the canister-shaped covering of Salati's Statue; cocks crew in the gardens, and we could hear gate-latches clicking in the distance as people stumblingly resought their homes.

'I'm afraid there won't be any morning deliveries,' said De Forest. 'We rather upset things in the country last night.'

'That makes no odds,' the Mayor returned. 'We're all provisioned for six months. *We* take no chances.'

Nor, when you come to think of it, does any one else. It must be three-quarters of a generation since any house or city faced a food shortage. Yet is there house or city on the Planet today that has not half a year's provisions laid in? We are like the shipwrecked seamen in the old books, who, having once nearly starved to death, ever afterwards hide away bits of food and biscuit. Truly we trust no Crowds, nor system based on Crowds!

De Forest waited till the last footstep had died away. Meantime the prisoners at the base of the Statue shuffled, posed and fidgeted, with the shamelessness of quite little children. None of them were more than six feet high, and many of them were as grey-haired as the ravaged, harassed heads of old pictures. They huddled together in actual touch, while the crowd, spaced at large intervals, looked at them with congested eyes.

Suddenly a man among them began to talk. The Mayor had not in the least exaggerated. It appeared that our Planet lay sunk in slavery beneath the heel of the Aerial Board of Control. The orator urged us to arise in our might, burst our prison doors and break our fetters (all his metaphors, by the way, were of the most medieval). Next he demanded that every matter of daily life, including most of the physical functions, should be submitted for decision at any time of the week, month, or year to, I gathered, anybody who happened to be passing by or residing within a certain radius, and that everybody should forthwith abandon his concerns to settle the matter, first by crowd-making, next by talking to the crowds made, and lastly by describing crosses on pieces of paper, which rubbish should later be counted with certain mystic ceremonies and oaths. Out of this amazing play, he assured us, would automatically arise a higher, nobler, and kinder world, based—he demonstrated this with the awful lucidity of the insane—based on the sanctity of the Crowd and the villainy of the single person. In conclusion, he called loudly upon God to testify to his personal merits and integrity. When the flow ceased, I turned bewildered to Takahira, who was nodding solemnly.

'Quite correct,' said he. 'It is all in the old books. He has left nothing out, not even the war-talk.'

'But I don't see how this stuff can upset a child, much less a district,' I replied.

'Ah, you are too young,' said Dragomiroff. 'For another thing, you are not a mamma. Please look at the mammas.'

Ten or fifteen women who remained had separated themselves from the silent men, and were drawing in towards the prisoners. It reminded one of the stealthy encircling, before the rush in at the quarry, of wolves round musk-oxen in the North. The prisoners saw, and drew together more closely. The Mayor covered his face with his hands for an instant. De Forest, bareheaded, stepped forward between the prisoners and the slowly, stiffly moving line.

'That's all very interesting,' he said to the dry-lipped orator. 'But the point seems that you've been making crowds and invading privacy.'

A woman stepped forward, and would have spoken, but there was a quick assenting murmur from the men, who realized that De Forest was trying to pull the situation down to ground-line.

'Yes! Yes!' they cried. 'We cut out because they made crowds and invaded privacy! Stick to that! Keep on that switch! Lift the Serviles out of this! The Board's in charge! Hsh!'

'Yes, the Board's in charge,' said De Forest. 'I'll take formal evidence of crowd-making if you like, but the Members of the Board can testify to it. Will that do?'

The women had closed in another pace, with hands that clenched and unclenched at their sides.

'Good! Good enough!' the men cried. 'We're content. Only take them away quickly.'

'Come along up!' said De Forest to the captives. 'Breakfast is quite ready.'

It appeared, however, that they did not wish to go. They intended to remain in Chicago and make crowds. They pointed out that De Forest's proposal was gross invasion of privacy.

'My dear fellow,' said Pirolo to the most voluble of the leaders, 'you hurry, or your crowd that can't be wrong will kill you!'

'But that would be murder,' answered the believer in crowds; and there was a roar of laughter from all sides that seemed to show the crisis had broken.

A woman stepped forward from the line of women, laughing, I protest, as merrily as any of the company. One hand, of course, shaded her eyes, the other was at her throat.

'Oh, they needn't be afraid of being killed!' she called.

'Not in the least,' said De Forest. 'But don't you think that, now the Board's in charge, you might go home while we get these people away?'

'I shall be home long before that. It—it has been rather a trying day.'

She stood up to her full height, dwarfing even De Forest's six-foot-eight, and smiled, with eyes closed against the fierce light.

'Yes, rather,' said De Forest. 'I'm afraid you feel the glare a little. We'll have the ship down.'

He motioned to the *Pirolo* to drop between us and the sun, and at the same time to loop-circuit the prisoners, who were a trifle unsteady. We saw them stiffen to the current where they stood. The woman's voice went on, sweet and deep and unshaken:

'I don't suppose you men realize how much this—this sort of thing means to a woman. I've borne three. We women don't want our children given to Crowds. It must be an inherited instinct. Crowds make trouble. They bring back the Old Days. Hate, fear, blackmail, publicity, "The People"—*That! That! That!*' She pointed to the Statue, and the crowd growled once more.

'Yes, if they are allowed to go on,' said De Forest. 'But this little affair—'

'It means so much to us women that this—this little affair should never happen again. Of course, never's a big word, but one feels so strongly that it is important to stop crowds at the very beginning. Those creatures'—she pointed with her left hand at the prisoners swaying like seaweed in a tideway as the circuit pulled them—'these people have friends and wives and children in the city and elsewhere. One doesn't want anything done to *them*, you know. It's terrible to force a human being out of fifty or sixty years of good life. I'm only forty myself. *I* know. But, at the same time, one feels that an example should be made, because no price is too heavy to pay if—if these people and *all that they imply* can be put an end to. Do you quite understand, or would you be kind enough to tell your men to take the casing off the Statue? It's worth looking at.'

'I understand perfectly. But I don't think anybody here wants to see the Statue on an empty stomach. Excuse me one moment.' De Forest called up to the ship, 'A flying loop ready on the port side, if you please.' Then to the woman he said with some crispness, 'You might leave us a little discretion in the matter.'

'Oh of course. Thank you for being so patient. I know my arguments are silly, but—' She half turned away and went on in a changed voice, 'Perhaps this will help you to decide.'

She threw out her right arm with a knife in it. Before the blade could be returned to her throat or her bosom it was twitched from her grip, sparked as it flew out of the shadow of the ship above, and fell flashing in the sunshine at the foot of the Statue fifty yards away. The outflung arm was arrested, rigid as a bar for an instant, till the releasing circuit permitted her to bring it slowly to her side. The other women shrank back silent among the men.

Pirolo rubbed his hands, and Takahira nodded.

'That was clever of you, De Forest,' said he.

'What a glorious pose!' Dragomiroff murmured, for the frightened woman was on the edge of tears.

'Why did you stop me? I would have done it!' she cried.

'I have no doubt you would,' said De Forest. 'But we can't waste a life like yours on these people. I hope the arrest didn't sprain your wrist; it's so hard to regulate a flying loop. But I think you are quite right about those persons' women and children. We'll take them all away with us if you promise not to do anything stupid to yourself.'

'I promise—I promise.' She controlled herself with an effort. 'But it is so important to us women. We know what it means; and I thought if you saw I was in earnest—'

'I saw you were, and you've gained your point. I shall take all your Serviles away with me at once. The Mayor will make lists of their friends and families in the city and the district, and he'll ship them after us this afternoon.'

'Sure,' said the Mayor, rising to his feet. 'Keefe, if you can see, hadn't you better finish levelling off the Old Market? It don't look slightly the way it is now, and we shan't use it for crowds any more.'

'I think you had better wipe out that Statue as well, Mr Mayor,' said De Forest. 'I don't question its merits as a work of art, but I believe it's a shade morbid.'

'Certainly, sir. Oh, Keefe! Slag the Nigger before you go on to fuse the Market. I'll get to the Communicators and tell the District that the Board is in charge. Are you making any special appointments, sir?'

'None. We haven't men to waste on these backwoods. Carry on as before, but under the Board. Arnott, run your Serviles aboard, please. Ground ship and pass them through the bilge-doors. We'll wait till we've finished with this work of art.'

The prisoners trailed past him, talking fluently, but unable to gesticulate in the drag of the current. Then the surfacers rolled up, two on each side of the Statue. With one accord the spectators looked elsewhere, but there was no need. Keefe turned on full power, and the thing simply melted within its case. All I saw was a surge of white-hot metal pouring over the plinth, a glimpse of Salati's inscription, 'To the Eternal Memory of the Justice of the People', ere the stone base itself cracked and powdered into finest lime. The crowd cheered.

'Thank you,' said De Forest; 'but we want our breakfasts, and I expect you do too. Good-bye, Mr Mayor! Delighted to see you at any time, but I hope I shan't have to, officially, for the next thirty years. Good-bye, madam. Yes. We're all given to nerves nowadays. I suffer from them myself. Good-bye, gentlemen all! You're under the tyrannous heel of the Board from this moment, but if ever you feel like breaking your fetters you've only to let us know. This is no treat to us. Good luck!'

We embarked amid shouts, and did not check our lift till they had dwindled into whispers. Then De Forest flung himself on the chartroom divan and mopped his forehead.

'I don't mind men,' he panted, 'but women are the devil!'

'Still the devil,' said Pirolo cheerfully. 'That one would have suicided.'

'I know it. That was why I signalled for the flying loop to be clapped on her. I owe you an apology for that, Arnott. I hadn't time to catch your eye, and you were busy with our caitiffs. By the way, who actually answered my signal? It was a smart piece of work.'

'Ilroy,' said Arnott; 'but he overloaded the wave. It may be pretty gallery-work to knock a knife out of a lady's hand, but didn't you noticed how she rubbed 'em? He scorched her fingers. Slovenly, I call it.'

'Far be it from me to interfere with Fleet discipline, but don't be too hard on the boy. If that woman had killed herself they would have killed every Servile and everything related to a Servile throughout the district by nightfall.'

'That was what she was playing for,' Takahira said. 'And with our Fleet gone we could have done nothing to hold them.'

'I may be ass enough to walk into a ground-circuit,' said Arnott, 'but I don't dismiss my Fleet till I'm reasonably sure that trouble is over. They're in position still, and I intend to keep 'em there till the Serviles are shipped out of the district. That last little crowd meant murder, my friends.'

'Nerves! All nerves!' said Pirolo. 'You cannot argue with agoraphobia.'

'And it is not as if they had seen much dead—or *is* it?' said Takahira.

'In all my ninety years I have never seen death.' Drago-miroff spoke as one who would excuse himself. 'Perhaps that was why—last night—'

Then it came out as we sat over breakfast, that, with the exception of Arnott and Pirolo, none of us had ever seen a corpse, or knew in what manner the spirit passes.

'We're a nice lot to flap about governing the Planet,' De Forest laughed. 'I confess, now it's all over, that my main fear was I mightn't be able to pull it off without losing a life.'

'I thought of that too,' said Arnott; 'but there's no death reported, and I've inquired everywhere. What are we sup-posed to do with our passengers? I've fed 'em.'

'We're between two switches,' De Forest drawled. 'If we drop them in any place that isn't under the Board, the natives will make their presence an excuse for cutting out, same as Illinois did, and forcing the Board to take over. If we drop them in any place under the Board's control they'll be killed as soon as our backs are turned.'

'If you say so,' said Pirolo thoughtfully, 'I can guarantee that they will become extinct in process of time, quite happily. What is their birth-rate now?'

'Go down and ask 'em,' said De Forest.

'I think they might become nervous and tear me to bits,' the philosopher of Foggia replied.

'Not really? Well?'

'Open the bilge-doors,' said Takahira with a downward jerk of the thumb.

'Scarcely—after all the trouble we've taken to save 'em,' said De Forest.

'Try London,' Arnott suggested. 'You could turn Satan himself loose there, and they'd only ask him to dinner.'

'Good man! You've given me an idea. Vincent! Oh, Vincent!' He threw the General Communicator open so that we could all hear, and in a few minutes the chartroom filled with the rich, fruity voice of Leopold Vincent, who has purveyed all London her choicest amusements for the last thirty years. We answered with expectant grins, as though we were actually in the stalls of, say, the Combination on a first night.

'We've picked up something in your line,' De Forest began.

'That's good, dear man. If it's old enough. There's nothing to beat the old things for business purposes. Have you see *London, Chatham, and Dover* at Earl's Court? No? I thought I missed you there. Im-mense! I've had the real steam locomotive engines built from the old designs and the iron rails cast specially by hand. Cloth cushions in the carriages, too! Im-mense! And paper railway tickets. And Polly Milton.'

'Polly Milton back again!' said Arnott rapturously. 'Book me two stalls for tomorrow night. What's she singing now, bless her?'

'The old songs. Nothing comes up to the old touch. Listen to this, dear men.' Vincent carolled with flourishes:

'Oh, cruel lamps of London,
    If tears your light could drown,
    Your victim's eyes would weep them,
    Oh, lights of London Town!'

'Then they weep.'

'You see?' Pirolo waved his hands at us. 'The old world always weeped when it saw crowds together. It did not know why, but it weeped. We know why, but we do not weep, except when we pay to be made to by fat, wicked old Vincent.'

'Old, yourself!' Vincent laughed. 'I'm a public benefactor, I keep the world soft and united.'

'And I'm De Forest of the Board,' said De Forest acidly, 'trying to get a little business done. As I was saying, I've picked up a few people in Chicago.'

'I cut out. Chicago is—'

'Do listen! They're perfectly unique.'

'Do they build houses of baked mudblocks while you wait—eh? That's an old contact.'

'They're an untouched primitive community, with all the old ideas.'

'Sewing-machines and maypole-dances? Cooking on coal-gas stoves, lighting pipes with matches, and driving horses? Gerolstein tried that last year. An absolute blow-out!'

De Forest plugged him wrathfully, and poured out the story of our doings for the last twenty-four hours on the top-note.

'And they do it *all* in public,' he concluded. 'You can't stop 'em. The more public, the better they are pleased. They'll talk for hours—like you! Now you can come in again!'

'Do you really mean they know how to vote?' said Vincent. 'Can they act it?'

'Act? It's their life to 'em! And you never saw such faces! Scarred like volcanoes. Envy, hatred, and malice in plain sight. Wonderfully flexible voices. They weep, too.'

'Aloud? In public?'

'I guarantee. Not a spark of shame or reticence in the entire installation. It's the chance of your career.'

'D'you say you've brought their voting props along—those papers and ballot-box things?'

'No, confound you! I'm not a luggage-lifter. Apply direct to the Mayor of Chicago. He'll forward you everything. Well?'

'Wait a minute. Did Chicago want to kill 'em? That 'ud look well on the Communicators.'

'Yes! They were only rescued with difficulty from a howling mob—if you know what that is.'

'But I don't,' answered the Great Vincent simply.

'Well then, they'll tell you themselves. They can make speeches hours long.'

'How many are there?'

'By the time we ship 'em all over they'll be perhaps a hundred, counting children. An old world in miniature. Can't you see it?'

'M-yes; but I've got to pay for it if it's a blow-out, dear man.'

'They can sing the old war songs in the streets. They can get word-drunk, and make crowds, and invade privacy in the genuine old-fashioned way, and they'll do the voting trick as often as you ask 'em a question.'

'Too good!' said Vincent.

'You unbelieving Jew! I've got a dozen head aboard here. I'll put you through direct. Sample 'em yourself.'

He lifted the switch and we listened. Our passengers on the lower deck at once, but not less than five at a time, explained themselves to Vincent. They had been taken from the bosom of their families, stripped of their possessions, given food without finger-bowls, and cast into captivity in a noisome dungeon.

'But look here,' said Arnott aghast; 'they're saying what isn't true. My lower deck isn't noisome, and I saw to the finger-bowls myself.'

'My people talk like that sometimes in Little Russia,' said Dragomiroff. 'We reason with them. We never kill. No!'

'But it's not true,' Arnott insisted. 'What can you do with people who don't tell facts? They're mad!'

'Hsh!' said Pirolo, his hand to his ear. 'It is such a little time since all the Planet told lies.'

We heard Vincent silkily sympathetic. Would they, he asked, repeat their assertions in public—before a vast public? Only let Vincent give them a chance, and the Planet, they vowed, should ring with their wrongs. Their aim in life—two women and a man explained it together—was to reform the world. Oddly enough, this also had been Vincent's life-dream. He offered them an arena in which to explain, and by their living example to raise the Planet to loftier levels. He was eloquent on the moral uplift of a simple, old-world life presented in its entirety to a deboshed civilization.

Could they—would they—for three months certain, devote themselves under his auspices, as missionaries, to the elevation of mankind at a place called Earl's Court, which he said, with some truth, was one of the intellectual centres of the Planet? They thanked him, and demanded (we could hear his chuckle of delight) time to discuss and to vote on the matter. The vote, solemnly managed by counting heads—one head, one vote—was favourable. His offer, therefore, was accepted, and they moved a vote of thanks to him in two speeches—one by what they called the 'proposer' and the other by the 'seconder'.

Vincent threw over to us, his voice shaking with gratitude:

'I've got 'em! Did you hear those speeches? That's Nature, dear men. Art can't teach *that*. And they voted as easily as lying. I've never had a troupe of natural liars before. Bless you, dear men! Remember, you're on my free lists for ever, anywhere—all of you. Oh, Gerolstein will be sick—sick!'

'Then you think they'll do?' said De Forest.

'Do? The Little Village'll go crazy! I'll knock up a series of old-world plays for 'em. Their voices will make you laugh and cry. My God, dear men, where *do* you suppose they picked up all their misery from, on this sweet earth? I'll have a pageant of the world's beginnings, and Mosenthal shall do the music. I'll—'

'Go and knock up a village for 'em by tonight. We'll meet you at No. 15 West Landing Tower,' said De Forest. 'Remember the rest will be coming along tomorrow.'

'Let 'em all come!' said Vincent. 'You don't know how hard it is nowadays even for me, to find something that really gets under the public's damned iridium-plated hide. But I've got it at last. Good-bye!'

'Well,' said De Forest when we had finished laughing,

'if any one understood corruption in London I might have played off Vincent against Gerolstein, and sold my captives at enormous prices. As it is, I shall have to be their legal adviser tonight when the contracts are signed. And they won't exactly press any commission on me, either.'

'Meantime,' said Takahira, 'we cannot, of course, confine members of Leopold Vincent's last-engaged company. Chairs for the ladies, please, Arnott.'

'Then I go to bed,' said De Forest. 'I can't face any more women!' And he vanished.

When our passengers were released and given another meal (finger-bowls came first this time) they told us what they thought of us and the Board; and, like Vincent, we all marvelled how they had contrived to extract and secrete so much bitter posion and unrest out of the good life God gives us. They raged, they stormed, they palpitated, flushed and exhausted their poor, torn nerves, panted themselves into silence, and renewed the senseless, shameless attacks.

'But can't you understand,' said Pirolo pathetically to a shrieking woman, 'that if we'd left you in Chicago you'd have been killed?'

'No, we shouldn't. You were bound to save us from being murdered.'

'Then we should have had to kill a lot of other people.'

'That doesn't matter. We were preaching the Truth. You can't stop us. We shall go on preaching in London; and *then* you'll see!'

'You can see now,' said Pirolo, and opened a lower shutter.

We were closing on the Little Village, with her three million people spread out at ease inside her ring of girdling Main-Traffic lights—those eight fixed beams at Chatham, Tonbridge, Redhill, Dorking, Woking, St Albans, Chipping Ongar, and Southend.

Leopold Vincent's new company looked, with small

pale faces, at the silence, the size, and the separated houses.

Then some began to weep aloud, shamelessly—always without shame.

1912

Late Stories

~~~~~~

MRS. BATHURST

The day that I chose to visit H.M.S. *Peridot* in Simon's
Bay was the day that the Admiral had chosen to send her
up the coast. She was just steaming out to sea as my train
came in, and since the rest of the Fleet were either coaling
or busy at the rifle-ranges a thousand feet up the hill, I
found myself stranded, lunchless, on the sea-front with no
hope of return to Cape Town before five P.M. At this crisis
I had the luck to come across my friend Inspector Hooper,
Cape Government Railways, in command of an engine
and a brake-van chalked for repair.

'If you get something to eat,' he said, 'I'll run you down
to Glengariff siding till the goods comes along. It's cooler
there than here, you see.'

I got food and drink from the Greeks who sell all things
at a price, and the engine trotted us a couple of miles up
the line to a bay of drifted sand and a plank-platform half
buried in sand not a hundred yards from the edge of the
surf. Moulded dunes, whiter than any snow, rolled far inland up a brown and purple valley of splintered rocks and
dry scrub. A crowd of Malays hauled at a net beside two
blue-and-green boats on the beach; a picnic party danced
and shouted barefoot where a tiny river trickled across the
flat, and a circle of dry hills, whose feet were set in sands
of silver, locked us in against a seven-coloured sea. At

either horn of the bay the railway line cut just above high-water mark, ran round a shoulder of piled rocks, and disappeared.

'You see there's always a breeze here,' said Hooper, opening the door as the engine left us in the siding on the sand, and the strong south-easter buffeting under Elsie's Peak dusted sand into our tickey beer. Presently he sat down to a file full of spiked documents. He had returned from a long trip up-country, where he had been reporting on damaged rolling-stock, as far away as Rhodesia. The weight of the bland wind on my eyelids; the song of it under the car roof, and high up among the rocks; the drift of fine grains chasing each other musically ashore; the tramp of the surf; the voices of the picnickers; the rustle of Hooper's file, and the presence of the assured sun, joined with the beer to cast me into magical slumber. The hills of False Bay were just dissolving into those of fairyland when I heard footsteps on the sand outside, and the clink of our couplings.

'Stop that!' snapped Hooper, without raising his head from his work. 'It's those dirty little Malay boys, you see: they're always playing with the trucks. . . .'

'Don't be hard on 'em. The railway's a general refuge in Africa,' I replied.

' 'Tis—up-country at any rate. That reminds me,' he felt in his waistcoat-pocket, 'I've got a curiosity for you from Wankies—beyond Buluwayo. It's more of a souvenir perhaps than——'

'The old hotel's inhabited,' cried a voice. 'White men from the language. Marines to the front! Come on, Pritch. Here's your Belmont. Wha—i—i!'

The last word dragged like a rope as Mr. Pyecroft ran round to the open door, and stood looking up into my face. Behind him an enormous Sergeant of Marines trailed a stalk of dried seaweed, and dusted the sand nervously from his fingers.

'What are you doing here?' I asked. 'I thought the *Hierophant* was down the coast?'

'We came in last Tuesday—from Tristan D'Acunha— for overhaul, and we shall be in dockyard 'ands for two months, with boiler-seatings.'

'Come and sit down.' Hooper put away the file.

'This is Mr. Hooper of the Railway,' I exclaimed, as Pyecroft turned to haul up the black-moustached sergeant.

'This is Sergeant Pritchard, of the *Agaric*, an old ship-mate,' said he. 'We were strollin' on the beach.' The monster blushed and nodded. He filled up one side of the van when he sat down.

'And this is my friend, Mr. Pyecroft,' I added to Hooper, already busy with the extra beer which my prophetic soul had bought from the Greeks.

'*Moi aussi*,' quoth Pyecroft, and drew out beneath his coat a labelled quart bottle.

'Why, it's Bass,' cried Hooper.

'It was Pritchard,' said Pyecroft. 'They can't resist him.'

'That's not so,' said Pritchard mildly.

'Not *verbatim* per'aps, but the look in the eye came to the same thing.'

'Where was it?' I demanded.

'Just on beyond here—at Kalk Bay. She was slappin' a rug in a back verandah. Pritch 'adn't more than brought his batteries to bear, before she stepped indoors an' sent it flyin' over the wall.'

Pyecroft patted the warm bottle.

'It was all a mistake,' said Pritchard. 'I shouldn't wonder if she mistook me for Maclean. We're about of a size.'

I had heard householders of Muizenburg, St. James's, and Kalk Bay complain of the difficulty of keeping beer or good servants at the seaside, and I began to see the reason. None the less, it was excellent Bass, and I too drank to the health of that large-minded maid.

'It's the uniform that fetches 'em, an' they fetch it,' said Pyecroft. 'My simple navy blue is respectable, but not fascinatin'. Now Pritch in 'is Number One rig is always "purr Mary, on the terrace"—*ex officio* as you might say.'

'She took me for Maclean, I tell you,' Pritchard insisted. 'Why—why—to listen to him you wouldn't think that only yesterday——'

'Pritch,' said Pyecroft, 'be warned in time. If we begin tellin' what we know about each other we'll be turned out of the pub. Not to mention aggravated desertion on several occasions——'

'Never anything more than absence without leaf—I defy you to prove it,' said the Sergeant hotly. 'An' if it comes to that how about Vancouver in '87?'

'How about it? Who pulled bow in the gig going ashore? Who told Boy Nivin . . . ?'

'Surely you were court-martialled for that?' I said. The story of Boy Niven who lured seven or eight able-bodied seamen and marines into the woods of British Columbia used to be a legend of the Fleet.

'Yes, we were court-martialled to rights,' said Pritchard, 'but we should have been tried for murder if Boy Niven 'adn't been unusually tough. He told us he had an uncle 'oo'd give us land to farm. 'E said he was born at the back o' Vancouver Island, and *all* the time the beggar was a balmy Barnado Orphan!'

'*But* we believed him,' said Pyecroft. 'I did—you did—Patterson did—an' 'oo was the Marine that married the cocoanut-woman afterwards—him with the mouth?'

'Oh, Jones, Spit-Kid Jones. I 'aven't thought of 'im in years,' said Pritchard. 'Yes, Spit-Kid believed it, an' George Anstey and Moon. We were very young an' very curious.'

'*But* lovin' an' trustful to a degree,' said Pyecroft.

' 'Remember when 'e told us to walk in single file for fear o' bears? 'Remember, Pye, when 'e 'opped about in that bog full o' ferns an' sniffed an' said 'e could smell the smoke of 'is uncle's farm? An' *all* the time it was a dirty little outlyin' uninhabited island. We walked round it in a day, an' come back to our boat lyin' on the beach. A whole day Boy Niven kept us walkin' in circles lookin' for 'is uncle's farm! He said his uncle was compelled by the law of the land to give us a farm!'

'Don't get hot, Pritch. We believed,' said Pyecroft.

'He'd been readin' books. He only did it to get a run ashore an' have himself talked of. A day an' a night—eight of us—followin' Boy Niven round an uninhabited island in the Vancouver archipelago! Then the picket came for us an' a nice pack o' idiots we looked!'

'What did you get for it?' Hooper asked.

'Heavy thunder with continuous lightning for two hours. Thereafter sleet-squalls, a confused sea, and cold, unfriendly weather till conclusion o' cruise,' said Pyecroft. 'It was only what we expected, but what we felt, an' I assure you, Mr. Hooper, even a sailor-man has a heart to break, was bein' told that we able seamen an' promisin' marines 'ad misled Boy Niven. Yes, we poor back-to-the-landers was supposed to 'ave misled him! He rounded on us, o' course, an' got off easy.'

'Excep' for what we gave him in the steerin'-flat when we came out o' cells. 'Eard anything of 'im lately, Pye?'

'Signal Boatswain in the Channel Fleet, I believe—Mr. L. L. Niven is.'

'An' Anstey died o' fever in Benin,' Pritchard mused. 'What come to Moon? Spit-Kid we know about.'

'Moon—Moon! Now where did I last . . . ? Oh yes, when I was in the *Palladium!* I met Quigley at Buncrana Station. He told me Moon 'ad run when the *Astrild* sloop was cruising among the South Seas three years back. He always showed signs o' bein' a Mormonastic beggar. Yes, he slipped off quietly an' they 'adn't time to chase 'im round the islands even if the navigatin' officer 'ad been equal to the job.'

'Wasn't he?' said Hooper.

'Not so. Accordin' to Quigley the *Astrild* spent half her commission rompin' up the beach like a she-turtle, an' the other half hatching turtles' eggs on the top o' numerous reefs. When she was docked at Sydney her copper looked like Aunt Maria's washing on the line—an' her 'midship frames was sprung. The commander swore the dockyard 'ad done it haulin' the pore thing on to the slips. They *do* do strange things at sea, Mr Hooper.'

'Ah! I'm not a tax-payer,' said Hooper, and opened a fresh bottle. The Sergeant seemed to be one who had a difficulty in dropping subjects.

'How it all comes back, don't it?' he said. 'Why, Moon must 'ave 'ad sixteen years' service before he ran.'

'It takes 'em at all ages. Look at—you know,' said Pyecroft.

'Who?' I asked.

'A service man within eighteen months of his pension, is the party you're thinkin' of,' said Pritchard. 'A warrant 'oose name begins with a V, isn't it?'

'But, in a way o' puttin' it, we can't say that he actually did desert,' Pyecroft suggested.

'Oh no,' said Pritchard. 'It was only permanent absence up-country without leaf. That was all.'

'Up-country?' said Hooper. 'Did they circulate his description?'

'What for?' said Pritchard, most impolitely.

'Because deserters are like columns in the war. They don't move away from the line, you see. I've known a chap caught at Salisbury that way tryin' to get to Nyassa. They tell me, but o' course I don't know, that they don't ask questions on the Nyassa Lake Flotilla up there. I've heard of a P. and O. quartermaster in full command of an armed launch there.'

'Do you think Click 'ud ha' gone up that way?' Pritchard asked.

'There's no saying. He was sent up to Bloemfontein to

take over some Navy ammunition left in the fort. We know he took it over and saw it into the trucks. Then there was no more Click—then or thereafter. Four months ago it transpired, and thus the *casus belli* stands at present,' said Pyecroft.

'What were his marks?' said Hooper again.

'Does the Railway get a reward for returnin' 'em, then?' said Pritchard.

'If I did d'you suppose I'd talk about it?' Hooper retorted angrily.

'You seemed so very interested,' said Pritchard with equal crispness.

'Why was he called Click?' I asked, to tide over an uneasy little break in the conversation. The two men were staring at each other very fixedly.

'Because of an ammunition hoist carryin' away,' said Pyecroft. 'And it carried away four of 'is teeth—on the lower port side, wasn't it, Pritch? The substitutes which he bought weren't screwed home in a manner o' sayin'. When he talked fast they used to lift a little on the bed plate. 'Ence, "Click." They called 'im a superior man, which is what we'd call a long, black-'aired, genteely speakin', 'alf-bred beggar on the lower deck.'

'Four false teeth on the lower left jaw,' said Hooper, his hand in his waistcoat-pocket. 'What tattoo marks?'

'Look here,' began Pritchard, half rising. 'I'm sure we're very grateful to you as a gentleman for your 'orspitality, but per'aps we may 'ave made an error in——'

I looked at Pyecroft for aid. Hooper was crimsoning rapidly.

'If the fat marine now occupying the foc'sle will kindly bring his *status quo* to an anchor yet once more, we may be able to talk like gentlemen—not to say friends,' said Pyecroft. 'He regards you, Mr. Hooper, as a emissary of the Law.'

'I only wish to observe that when a gentleman exhibits

such a peculiar, or I should rather say, such a *bloomin'* curiosity in identification marks as our friend here——'

'Mr. Pritchard,' I interposed, 'I'll take all the responsibility for Mr. Hooper.'

'An' *you*'ll apologise all round,' said Pyecroft. 'You're a
rude little man, Pritch.'

'But how was I——' he began, wavering.

'I don't know an' I don't care. Apologise!'

The giant looked round bewildered and took our little
hands into his vast grip, one by one.

'I was wrong,' he said meekly as a sheep. 'My suspicions
was unfounded. Mr. Hooper, I apologise.'

'You did quite right to look out for your own end o' the
line,' said Hooper. 'I'd ha' done the same with a gentleman
I didn't know, you see. If you don't mind I'd like to hear a
little more o' your Mr. Vickery. It's safe with me, you
see.'

'Why did Vickery run,' I began, but Pyecroft's smile
made me turn my question to 'Who was she?'

'She kep' a little hotel at Hauraki—near Auckland,' said
Pyecroft.

'By Gawd!' roared Pritchard, slapping his hand on his
leg. 'Not Mrs. Bathurst!'

Pyecroft nodded slowly, and the Sergeant called all the
powers of darkness to witness his bewilderment.

'So far as I could get at it Mrs. B. was the lady in question.'

'But Click was married,' cried Pritchard.

'An' 'ad a fifteen year old daughter. 'E's shown me her
photograph. Settin' that aside, so to say, 'ave you ever
found these little things make much difference? Because I
haven't.'

'Good Lord Alive an' Watchin'! . . . Mrs. Bathurst. . . .'
Then with another roar: 'You can say what you please,
Pye, but you don't make me believe it was any of 'er fault.
She wasn't *that!*'

'If I was going to say what I please, I'd begin by callin'

you a silly ox an' work up to the higher pressures at leisure. I'm trying to say solely what transpired. M'rover, for once you're right. It wasn't her fault.'

'You couldn't 'ave made me believe it if it 'ad been,' was the answer.

Such faith in a Sergeant of Marines interested me greatly. 'Never mind about that,' I cried. 'Tell me what she was like.'

'She was a widow,' said Pyecroft. 'Left so very young and never re-spliced. She kep' a little hotel for warrants and non-coms close to Auckland, an' she always wore black silk, and 'er neck——'

'You ask what she was like,' Pritchard broke in. 'Let me give you an instance. I was at Auckland first in '97, at the end o' the *Marroquin's* commission, an' as I'd been promoted I went up with the others. She used to look after us all, an' she never lost by it—not a penny! "Pay me now," she'd say, "or settle later. I know you won't let me suffer. Send the money from home if you like." Why, gentlemen all, I tell you I've seen that lady take her own gold watch an' chain off her neck in the bar an' pass it to a bosun 'oo'd come ashore without 'is ticker an' 'ad to catch the last boat. "I don't know your name," she said, "but when you've done with it, you'll find plenty that know me on the front. Send it back by one o' them." And it was worth thirty pounds if it was worth 'arf a crown. The little gold watch, Pye, with the blue monogram at the back. But, as I was sayin', in those days she kep' a beer that agreed with me—Slits it was called. One way an' another I must 'ave punished a good few bottles of it while we was in the bay —comin' ashore every night or so. Chaffin' across the bar like, once when we were alone, "Mrs. B.," I said, "when next I call I want you to remember that this is my particular—just as you're my particular?" (She'd let you go *that* far!) "Just as you're my particular," I said. "Oh, thank you, Sergeant Pritchard," she says, an' put 'er hand up to the curl be'ind 'er ear. Remember that way she had, Pye?'

'I think so,' said the sailor.

'Yes, "Thank you, Sergeant Pritchard," she says. "The least I can do is to mark it for you in case you change your mind. There's no great demand for it in the Fleet," she says, "but to make sure I'll put it at the back o' the shelf," an' she snipped off a piece of her hair ribbon with that old dolphin cigar cutter on the bar—remember it, Pye?—an' she tied a bow round what was left—just four bottles. That was '97—no, '96. In '98 I was in the *Resiliant*— China station—full commission. In Nineteen One, mark you, I was in the *Carthusian*, back in Auckland Bay again. Of course I went up to Mrs. B.'s with the rest of us to see how things were goin'. They were the same as ever. (Remember the big tree on the pavement by the side-bar, Pye?) I never said anythin' in special (there was too many of us talkin' to her), but she saw me at once.'

'That wasn't difficult?' I ventured.

'Ah, but wait. I was comin' up to the bar, when, "Ada," she says to her niece, "get me Sergeant Pritchard's particular," and, gentlemen all, I tell you, before I could shake 'ands with the lady, there were those four bottles o' Slits, with 'er 'air ribbon in a bow round each o' their necks, set down in front o' me, an' as she drew the cork she looked at me under her eyebrows in that blindish way she had o' lookin', an', "Sergeant Pritchard," she says, "I do 'ope you 'aven't changed your mind about your particulars." That's the kind o' woman she was—after five years!'

'I don't *see* her yet somehow,' said Hooper, but with sympathy.

'She—she never scrupled to feed a lame duck or set 'er foot on a scorpion at any time of 'er life,' Pritchard added valiantly.

'That don't help me either. My mother's like that for one.'

The giant heaved inside his uniform and rolled his eyes at the car-roof. Said Pyecroft suddenly:

'How many women have you been intimate with all over the world, Pritch?'

Pritchard blushed plum colour to the short hairs of his seventeen-inch neck.

' 'Undreds,' said Pyecroft. 'So've I. How many of 'em can you remember in your own mind, settin' aside the first—an' per'aps the last—*and one more?*'

'Few, wonderful few, now I tax myself,' said Sergeant Pritchard, relievedly.

'An' how many times might you 'ave been at Auckland?'

'One—two,' he began. 'Why, I can't make it more than three times in ten years. But I can remember every time that I ever saw Mrs. B.'

'So can I—an' I've only been to Auckland twice—how she stood an' what she was sayin' an' what she looked like. That's the secret. 'Tisn't beauty, so to speak, nor good talk necessarily. It's just It. Some women'll stay in a man's memory if they once walk down a street, but most of 'em you can live with a month on end, an' next commission you'd be put to it to certify whether they talked in their sleep or not, as one might say.'

'Ah,' said Hooper. 'That's more the idea. I've known just two women of that nature.'

'An' it was no fault o' theirs?' asked Pritchard.

'None whatever. I know that!'

'An' if a man gets struck with that kind o' woman, Mr. Hooper?' Pritchard went on.

'He goes crazy—or just saves himself,' was the slow answer.

'You've hit it,' said the Sergeant. 'You've seen an' known somethin' in the course o' your life, Mr. Hooper. I'm lookin' at you!' He set down his bottle.

'And how often had Vickery seen her?' I asked.

'That's the dark an' bloody mystery,' Pyecroft answered. 'I'd never come across him till I come out in the

Hierophant just now, an' there wasn't any one in the ship who knew much about him. You see, he was what you call a superior man. 'E spoke to me once or twice about Auckland and Mrs. B. on the voyage out. I called that to mind subsequently. There must 'ave been a good deal between 'em, to my way o' thinkin'. Mind you, I'm only giving you my *résumé* of it all, because all I know is second-hand so to speak, or rather I should say more than second-'and.'

'How?' said Hooper peremptorily. 'You must have seen it or heard it.'

'Ye-es,' said Pyecroft. 'I used to think seein' and hearin' was the only regulation aids to ascertainin' facts, but as we get older we get more accommodatin'. The cylinders work easier, I suppose. . . . Were you in Cape Town last December when Phyllis's Circus came?'

'No—up-country,' said Hooper, a little nettled at the change of venue.

'I ask because they had a new turn of a scientific nature called "Home and Friends for a Tickey." '

'Oh, you mean the cinematograph—the pictures of prize-fights and steamers. I've seen 'em up-country.'

'Biograph or cinematograph was what I was alludin' to. London Bridge with the omnibuses—a troopship goin' to the war—marines on parade at Portsmouth an' the Plymouth Express arrivin' at Paddin'ton.'

'Seen 'em all. Seen 'em all,' said Hooper impatiently.

'We *Hierophants* came in just before Christmas week an' leaf was easy.'

'I think a man gets fed up with Cape Town quicker than anywhere else on the station. Why, even Durban's more like Nature. We was there for Christmas,' Pritchard put in.

'Not bein' a devotee of Indian *peeris*, as our Doctor said to the Pusser, I can't exactly say. Phyllis's was good enough after musketry practice at Mozambique. I couldn't get off the first two or three nights on account of what you might call an imbroglio with our Torpedo Lieutenant in the submerged flat, where some pride of the West country had sugared up a gyroscope; but I remember Vickery went ashore with our Carpenter Rigdon—old Crocus we called him. As a general rule Crocus never left 'is ship unless an' until he was 'oisted out with a winch, but *when* 'e went 'e would return noddin' like a lily gemmed with dew. We smothered him down below that night, but the things 'e said about Vickery as a fittin' playmate for a Warrant Officer of 'is cubic capacity, before we got him quiet, was what I should call pointed.'

'I've been with Crocus—in the *Redoubtable*,' said the Sergeant. 'He's a character if there is one.'

'Next night I went into Cape Town with Dawson and Pratt; but just at the door of the Circus I came across Vickery. "Oh!" he says, "you're the man I'm looking for. Come and sit next me. This way to the shillin' places!" I went astern at once, protestin' because tickey seats better suited my so-called finances. "Come on," says Vickery, "I'm payin'." Naturally I abandoned Pratt and Dawson in anticipation o' drinks to match the seats. "No," he says, when this was 'inted—"not now. Not now. As many as you please afterwards, but I want you sober for the occasion." I caught 'is face under a lamp just then, an' the appearance of it quite cured me of my thirsts. Don't mistake. It didn't frighten me. It made me anxious. I can't tell you what it was like, but that was the effect which it 'ad on me. If you want to know, it reminded me of those things in bottles in those herbalistic shops at Plymouth—preserved in spirits of wine. White an' crumply things—previous to birth as you might say.'

'You 'ave a beastial mind, Pye,' said the Sergeant, relighting his pipe.

'Perhaps. We were in the front row, an' "Home an' Friends" came on early. Vickery touched me on the knee when the number went up. "If you see anything that strikes you," he says, "drop me a hint"; then he went on clicking. We saw London Bridge an' so forth an' so on, an' it was most interestin'. I'd never seen it before. You 'eard a little dynamo like buzzin', but the pictures were the real thing—alive an' movin'.'

'I've seen 'em,' said Hooper. 'Of course they are taken from the very thing itself—you see.'

'Then the Western Mail came in to Paddin'ton on the big magic lantern sheet. First we saw the platform empty an' the porters standin' by. Then the engine come in, head on, an' the women in the front row jumped: she headed so straight. Then the doors opened and the passengers came out and the porters got the luggage—just like life. Only— only when any one came down too far towards us that was watchin', they walked right out o' the picture, so to speak. I was 'ighly interested, I can tell you. So were all of us. I watched an old man with a rug 'oo'd dropped a book an' was tryin' to pick it up, when quite slowly, from be'ind two porters—carryin' a little reticule an' lookin' from side to side—comes out Mrs. Bathurst. There was no mistakin' the walk in a hundred thousand. She come forward—right forward—she looked out straight at us with that blindish look which Pritch alluded to. She walked on and on till she melted out of the picture—like—like a shadow jump-in' over a candle, an' as she went I 'eard Dawson in the tickey seats be'ind sing out: "Christ! There's Mrs. B!" '

Hooper swallowed his spittle and leaned forward intently.

'Vickery touched me on the knee again. He was clickin' his four false teeth with his jaw down like an enteric at the last kick. "Are you sure?" says he. "Sure," I says; "didn't you 'ear Dawson give tongue? Why, it's the woman herself." "I was sure before," he says, "but I brought you to make sure. Will you come again with me to-morrow?"

' "Willingly," I says; "it's like meetin' old friends."

' "Yes," he says, openin' his watch, "very like. It will be four-and-twenty hours less four minutes before I see her again. Come and have a drink," he says. "It may amuse you, but it's no sort of earthly use to me." He went out shaking his head an' stumblin' over people's feet as if he was drunk already. I anticipated a swift drink an' a speedy return, because I wanted to see the performin' elephants. Instead o' which Vickery began to navigate the town at the rate o' knots, lookin' in at a bar every three minutes approximate Greenwich time. I'm not a drinkin' man, though there are those present'—he cocked his unforgettable eye at me—'who may have seen me more or less imbued with the fragrant spirit. None the less when I drink I like to do it at anchor an' not at an average speed of eighteen knots on the measured mile. There's a tank as you might say at the back o' that big hotel up the hill—what do they call it?'

'The Molteno Reservoir,' I suggested, and Hooper nodded.

'That was his limit o' drift. We walked there an' we come down through the Gardens—there was a South-Easter blowin'—an' we finished up by the Docks. Then we bore up the road to Salt River, and wherever there was a pub Vickery put in sweatin'. He didn't look at what he drunk—he didn't look at the change. He walked an' he drunk an' he perspired in rivers. I understood why old Crocus 'ad come back in the condition 'e did, because Vickery an' I 'ad two an' a hàlf hours o' this gipsy manoeuvre an' when we got back to the station there wasn't a dry atom on or in me.'

'Did he say anything?' Pritchard asked.

'The sum total of 'is conversation from 7:45 P.M. till 11:15 P.M. was "Let's have another." Thus the mornin' an' the evenin' were the first day, as Scripture says. . . . To abbreviate a lengthy narrative, I went into Cape Town for five consecutive nights with Master Vickery, and in that time I must 'ave logged about fifty knots over the ground an' taken in two gallon o' all the worst spirits south the Equator. The evolution never varied. Two shilling seats for us two; five minutes o' the pictures, an' perhaps forty-five seconds o' Mrs. B. walking down towards us with that blindish look in her eyes an' the reticule in her hand. Then our walk—and drink till train time.'

'What did you think?' said Hooper, his hand fingering his waistcoat-pocket.

" 'Several things,' said Pyecroft. 'To tell you the truth, I aren't quite done thinkin' about it yet. Mad? The man was a dumb lunatic—must 'ave been for months—years p'r'aps. I know somethin' o' maniacs, as every man in the Service must. I've been shipmates with a mad skipper—an' a lunatic Number One, but never both together I thank 'Eaven. I could give you the names o' three captains now 'oo ought to be in an asylum, but you don't find me interferin' with the mentally afflicted till they begin to lay about 'em with rammers an' winch-handles. Only once I crept up a little into the wind towards Master Vickery. "I wonder what she's doin' in England," I says. "Don't it seem to you she's lookin' for somebody?" That was in the Gardens again, with the South-Easter blowin' as we were makin' our desperate round. "She's lookin' for me," he says, stoppin' dead under a lamp an' clickin'. When he wasn't drinkin', in which case all 'is teeth clicked on the glass, 'e was clickin' 'is four false teeth like a Marconi ticker. "Yes! lookin' for me," he said, an' he went on very softly an' as you might say affectionately. "*But,*" he went on, "in future, Mr. Pyecroft, I should take it kindly of you if you'd confine your remarks to the drinks set before you. Otherwise," he says, "with the best will in the world to-wards you, I may find myself guilty of murder! Do you understand?" he says. "Perfectly," I says, "but would it at all soothe you to know that in such a case the chances o' your being killed are precisely equivalent to the chances o' me being outed?" "Why, no," he says, "I'm almost afraid that 'ud be a temptation." Then I said—we was right under the lamp by that arch at the end o' the Gardens where the trams come round—"Assumin' murder was done—or attempted murder—I put it to you that you would still be left so badly crippled, as one might say, that your subsequent capture by the police—to 'oom you would 'ave to explain—would be largely inevitable." "That's better," 'e says, passin' 'is hands over his forehead. "That's much better, because," he says, "do you know, as I am now, Pye, I'm not so sure if I could explain anything much." Those were the only particular words I had with 'im in our walks as I remember.'

'What walks!' said Hooper. 'Oh, my soul, what walks!'

'They were chronic,' said Pyecroft gravely, 'but I didn't anticipate any danger till the Circus left. Then I anticipated that, bein' deprived of 'is stimulant, he might react on me, so to say, with a hatchet. Consequently, after the final performance an' the ensuin' wet walk, I kep' myself aloof from my superior officer on board in the execution of 'is duty as you might put it. Consequently, I was interested when the sentry informs me while I was passin' on my lawful occasions that Click had asked to see the captain. As a general rule warrant officers don't dissipate much of the owner's time, but Click put in an hour and more be'ind that door. My duties kep' me within eyeshot of it. Vickery came out first, an' 'e actually nodded at me an' smiled. This knocked me out o' the boat, because, havin' seen 'is face for five consecutive nights, I didn't anticipate any change there more than a condenser in hell, so to speak. The owner emerged later. His face didn't read off at all, so I fell back on his cox, 'oo'd been eight years with him and knew him better than boat signals. Lamson—that was the cox's name—crossed 'is bows once or twice at low speeds an' dropped down to me visibly concerned. "He's shipped 'is court-martial face," says Lamson. "Some one's goin' to be 'ung. I've never seen that look but once before when they chucked the gun-sights overboard in the *Fantastic.*" Throwin' gun-sights overboard, Mr. Hooper, is the equivalent for mutiny in these degenerate days. It's done to attract the notice of the authorities an' the *Western Mornin' News*—generally by a stoker. Naturally, word went round the lower deck an' we had a private over'aul of our little consciences. But, barrin' a shirt which a second-class stoker said 'ad walked into 'is bag from the marines flat by itself, nothin' vital transpired. The owner went about flyin' the signal for "attend public execution," so to say, but there was no corpse at the yard-arm. 'E lunched on the beach an' 'e returned with 'is regu-lation harbour-routine face about 3 P.M. Thus Lamson lost prestige for raising false alarms. The only person 'oo might 'ave connected the epicycloidal gears correctly was one Pyecroft, when he was told that Mr. Vickery would go up-country that same evening to take over certain naval ammunition left after the war in Bloemfontein Fort. No details was ordered to accompany Master Vickery. He was told off first person singular—as a unit—by himself.'

The marine whistled penetratingly.

'That's what I thought,' said Pyecroft. 'I went ashore with him in the cutter an' 'e asked me to walk through the station. He was clickin' audibly, but otherwise seemed happy-ish.'

' "You might like to know," he says, stoppin' just oppo-site the Admiral's front gate, "that Phyllis's Circus will be performin' at Worcester to-morrow night. So I shall see 'er yet once again. You've been very patient with me," he says.

' "Look here, Vickery," I said, "this thing's come to be just as much as I can stand. Consume your own smoke. I don't want to know any more."

' "You!" he said. "What have you got to complain of?— you've only 'ad to watch. I'm *it*," he says, "but that's nei-ther here nor there," he says. "I've one thing to say before shakin' 'ands. Remember," 'e says—we were just by the Admiral's garden-gate then—"remember, that I am *not* a murderer, because my lawful wife died in childbed six weeks after I came out. That much at least I am clear of," 'e says.

' "Then what have you done that signifies?" I said. "What's the rest of it?"

' "The rest," 'e says, "is silence," an' he shook 'ands and went clickin' into Simons Town station." '

'Did he stop to see Mrs. Bathurst at Worcester?' I asked.

'It's not known. He reported at Bloemfontein, saw the ammunition into the trucks, and then 'e disappeared. Went out—deserted, if you care to put it so—within eighteen months of his pension, an' if what 'e said about 'is wife was true he was a free man as 'e then stood. How do you read it off?'

'Poor devil!' said Hooper. 'To see her that way every night! I wonder what it was.'

'I've made my 'ead ache in that direction many a long night.'

'But I'll swear Mrs. B. 'ad no 'and in it,' said the Sergeant, unshaken.

'No. Whatever the wrong or deceit was, he did it, I'm sure o' that. I 'ad to look at 'is face for five consecutive nights. I'm not so fond o' navigatin' about Cape Town with a South-Easter blowin' these days. I can hear those teeth click, so to say.'

'Ah, those teeth,' said Hooper, and his hand went to his waistcoat-pocket once more. 'Permanent things false teeth are. You read about 'em in all the murder trials.'

'What d'you suppose the captain knew—or did?' I asked.

'I've never turned my searchlight that way,' Pyecroft answered unblushingly.

We all reflected together, and drummed on empty beer bottles as the picnic-party, sunburned, wet, and sandy, passed our door singing 'The Honeysuckle and the Bee.'

'Pretty girl under that kapje,' said Pyecroft.

'They never circulated his description?' said Pritchard.

'I was askin' you before these gentlemen came,' said Hooper to me, 'whether you knew Wankies—on the way to the Zambesi—beyond Buluwayo?'

'Would he pass there—tryin' to get to that Lake what's 'is name?' said Pritchard.

Hooper shook his head and went on: 'There's a curious bit o' line there, you see. It runs through solid teak forest—a sort o' mahogany really—seventy-two miles without a curve. I've had a train derailed there twenty-three times in forty miles. I was up there a month ago relievin' a sick inspector, you see. He told me to look out for a couple of tramps in the teak.'

'Two?' Pyecroft said. 'I don't envy that other man if——'

'We get heaps of tramps up there since the war. The inspector told me I'd find 'em at M'Bindwe siding waiting to go North. He'd give 'em some grub and quinine, you see. I went up on a construction train. I looked out for 'em. I saw them miles ahead along the straight, waiting in the teak. One of 'em was standin' up by the dead-end of the siding an' the other was squattin' down lookin' up at 'im, you see.'

'What did you do for 'em?' said Pritchard.

'There wasn't much I could do, except bury 'em. There'd been a bit of a thunderstorm in the teak, you see, and they were both stone dead and as black as charcoal. That's what they really were, you see—charcoal. They fell to bits when we tried to shift 'em. The man who was standin' up had the false teeth. I saw 'em shinin' against the black. Fell to bits he did too, like his mate squatting down an' watchin' him, both of 'em all wet in the rain. Both burned to charcoal, you see. And—that's what made me ask about marks just now—the false-toother was tattooed on the arms and chest—a crown and foul anchor with M. V. above.'

'I've seen that,' said Pyecroft quickly. 'It was so.'

'But if he was all charcoal-like?' said Pritchard, shuddering.

'You know how writing shows up white on a burned letter? Well, it was like that, you see. We buried 'em in the teak and I kept . . . But he was a friend of you two gentlemen, you see.'

Mr. Hooper brought his hand away from his waistcoat-pocket—empty.

Pritchard covered his face with his hands for a moment, like a child shutting out an ugliness.

'And to think of her at Hauraki!' he murmured—'with 'er 'air ribbon on my beer. "Ada," she said to her niece . . . Oh, my Gawd!' . . .

'On a summer afternoon, when the honeysuckle blooms,
  And all Nature seems at rest,
Underneath the bower, 'mid the perfume of the flower,
  Sat a maiden with the one she loves the best——'

sang the picnic-party waiting for their train at Glengariff.

'Well, I don't know how you feel about it,' said Pye-croft, 'but 'avin' seen 'is face for five consecutive nights on end, I'm inclined to finish what's left of the beer an' thank Gawd he's dead!'

1904

FRIENDLY BROOK

~~~~~~

The valley was so choked with fog that one could scarcely
see a cow's length across a field. Every blade, twig,
bracken-frond, and hoof-print carried water, and the air
was filled with the noise of rushing ditches and field-
drains, all delivering to the Brook below. A week's November rain on water-logged land had gorged her to full
flood, and she proclaimed it aloud.

Two men in sackcloth aprons were considering an untrimmed hedge that ran down the hillside and disappeared
into mist beside those roarings. They stood back and took
stock of the neglected growth, tapped an elbow of hedge-
oak here, a mossed beech-stub there, swayed a stooled ash
back and forth, and looked at each other.

'I reckon she's about two rod thick,' said Jabez the
younger, 'an' she hasn't felt iron since—when has she
Jesse?'

'Call it twenty-five year, Jabez, an' you won't be far
out.'

'Umm!' Jabez rubbed his wet handbill on his wetter
coat-sleeve. 'She ain't a hedge. She's all manner o' trees.
We'll just about have to—' He paused, as professional eti-
quette required.

'Just about have to side her up an' see what she'll bear.
But hadn't we best—?' Jesse paused in his turn, both men
being artists and equals.

'Get some kind o' line to go by.' Jabez ranged up and
down till he found a thinner place, and with clean snicks
of the handbill revealed the original face of the fence. Jesse

took over the dripping stuff as it fell forward, and, with a grasp and a kick, made it to lie orderly on the bank till it should be faggoted.

By noon a length of unclean jungle had turned itself into a cattle-proof barrier, tufted here and there with little plumes of the sacred holly which no woodman touches without orders.

'Now we've a witness-board to go by!' said Jesse at last.

'She won't be as easy as this all along,' Jabez answered. 'She'll need plenty stakes and binders when we come to the Brook.'

'Well, ain't we plenty?' Jesse pointed to the ragged perspective ahead of them that plunged downhill into the fog. 'I lay there's a cord an' a half o' firewood, let alone faggots, 'fore we get anywheres anigh the Brook.'

'The Brook's got up a piece since morning,' said Jabez. 'Sounds like's if she was over Wickenden's door-stones.'

Jesse listened, too. There was a growl in the Brook's roar as though she worried something hard.

'Yes. She's over Wickenden's door-stones,' he replied. 'Now she'll flood acrost Alder Bay an' that'll ease her.'

'She won't ease Jim Wickenden's hay none if she do,' Jabez grunted. 'I told Jim he'd set that liddle hay-stack o' his too low down in the medder. I *told* him so when he was drawin' the bottom for it.'

'I told him so, too,' said Jesse. 'I told him 'fore ever you did. I told him when the County Council tarred the roads up along.' He pointed up-hill, where unseen automobiles and road-engines droned past continually. 'A tarred road, she shoots every drop o' water into a valley same's a slate roof. 'Tisn't as 'twas in the old days, when the waters soaked in and soaked out in the way o' nature. It rooshes off they tarred roads all of a lump, and naturally every drop is bound to descend into the valley. And there's tar roads both two sides this valley for ten mile. That's what I told Jim Wickenden when they tarred the roads last year.

But he's a valley-man. He don't hardly ever journey up-hill.'

'What did he say when you told him that?' Jabez demanded, with a little change of voice.

'Why? What did he say to you when *you* told him?' was the answer.

'What he said to you, I reckon, Jesse.'

'Then, you don't need me to say it over again, Jabez.'

'Well, let be how 'twill, what was he gettin' *after* when he said what he said to me?' Jabez insisted.

'*I* dunno; unless you tell me what manner o' words he said to *you*.'

Jabez drew back from the hedge—all hedges are nests of treachery and eavesdropping—and moved to an open cattle-lodge in the centre of the field.

'No need to go ferretin' around,' said Jesse. 'None can't see us here 'fore we see them.'

'What was Jim Wickenden gettin' at when I said he'd set his stack too near anigh the Brook?' Jabez dropped his voice. 'He was in his mind.'

'He ain't never been out of it yet to my knowledge,' Jesse drawled, and uncorked his tea-bottle.

'But then Jim says: "I ain't goin' to shift my stack a yard," he says. "The Brook's been good friends to me, and if she be minded," he says, "to take a snatch at my hay, *I* ain't settin' out to withstand her." That's what Jim Wickenden says to me last—last June-end 'twas,' said Jabez.

'Nor he hasn't shifted his stack, neither,' Jesse replied. 'An' if there's more rain, the Brook she'll shift it for him.'

'No need tell *me!* But I want to know what Jim was gettin' *at?*'

Jabez opened his clasp-knife very deliberately; Jesse as carefully opened his. They unfolded the newspapers that wrapped their dinners, coiled away and pocketed the string that bound the packages, and sat down on the edge of the lodge manger. The rain began to fall again through the fog, and the Brook's voice rose.

* * *

'But I always allowed Mary was his lawful child, like,' said Jabez, after Jesse had spoken for a while.

''Tain't so.... Jim Wickenden's woman she never made nothing. She come out o' Lewes with her stockin's round her heels, an' she never made nor mended aught till she died. *He* had to light fire an' get breakfast every mornin' except Sundays, while she sowed it abed. Then she took an' died, sixteen, seventeen, year back; but she never had no childern.'

'They was valley-folk,' said Jabez apologetically. 'I'd no call to go in among 'em, but I always allowed Mary—'

'No. Mary come out o' one o' those Lunnon Childern Societies. After his woman died, Jim got his mother back from his sister over to Peasmarsh, which she'd gone to house with when Jim married. His mother kept house for Jim after his woman died. They do say 'twas his mother led him on toward adoptin' of Mary—to furnish out the house with a child, like, and to keep him off of gettin' a noo woman. He mostly done what his mother contrived. 'Cardenly, twixt 'em, they asked for a child from one o' those Lunnon societies—same as it might ha' been these Barnardo children—an' Mary was sent down to 'em, in a candle-box, I've heard.'

'Then Mary is chance-born. I never knowed that,' said Jabez. 'Yet I must ha' heard it some time or other ...'

'No. She ain't. 'Twould ha' been better for some folk if she had been. She come to Jim in a candle-box with all the proper papers—lawful child o' some couple in Lunnon somewheres—mother dead, father drinkin'. *And* there was that Lunnon society's five shillin's a week for her. Jim's mother she wouldn't despise week-end money, but I never heard Jim was much of a muck-grubber. Let be how 'twill, they two mothered up Mary no bounds, till it looked at last like they'd forgot she wasn't their own flesh an' blood. Yes, I reckon they forgot Mary wasn't their'n by rights.'

'That's no new thing,' said Jabez. 'There's more'n one or two in this parish wouldn't surrender back their Bernarders. You ask Mark Copley an' his woman an' that Bernarder cripple-babe o' theirs.'

'Maybe they need the five shillin',' Jesse suggested.

'It's handy,' said Jabez. 'But the child's more. "Dada" he says, an' "Mumma" he says, with his great rollin' head-piece all hurdled up in that iron collar. *He* won't live long—his backbone's rotten, like. But they Copleys do just about set store by him—five bob or no five bob.'

'Same way with Jim an' his mother,' Jesse went on. 'There was talk betwixt 'em after a few years o' not takin' any more week-end money for Mary; but let alone *she* never passed a farden in the mire 'thout longin's, Jim didn't care, like, to push himself forward into the Society's remembrance. So naun came of it. The week-end money would ha' made no odds to Jim—not after his uncle willed him they four cottages at Eastbourne *an'* money in the bank.'

'That was true, too, then? I heard something in a scadderin' word-o'-mouth way,' said Jabez.

'I'll answer for the house property, because Jim he requested my signed name at the foot o' some papers concernin' it. Regardin' the money in the bank, he nature-ally wouldn't like such things talked about all round the parish, so he took strangers for witnesses.'

'Then 'twill make Mary worth seekin' after?'

'She'll need it. Her Maker ain't done much for her outside nor yet in.'

'That ain't no odds.' Jabez shook his head till the water showered off his hat-brim. 'If Mary has money, she'll be wed before any likely pore maid. She's cause to be grateful to Jim.'

'She hides it middlin' close, then,' said Jesse. 'It don't sometimes look to me as if Mary has her natural rightful feelin's. She don't put on an apron o' Mondays 'thout being druv to it—in the kitchen *or* the hen-house. She's studyin' to be a school-teacher. She'll make a beauty! I never knowed her show any sort o' kindness to nobody— not even when Jim's mother was took dumb. No! 'Twadn't no stroke. It stifled the old lady in the throat here. First she couldn't shape her words no shape; then she clucked, like, an' lastly she couldn't more than suck down spoon-meat an' hold her peace. Jim took her to Doctor Harding, an' Harding he bundled her off to Brighton Hospital on a ticket, but they couldn't make no stay to her afflictions there; and she was bundled off to Lunnon, an' they lit a great old lamp inside her, and Jim told me they couldn't make out nothing in no sort there; and, along o' one thing an' another, an' all their spyin's and pryin's, she come back a hem sight worse than when she started. Jim said he'd have no more hospitalizin', so he give her a slate, which she tied to her waist-string, and what she was minded to say she writ on it.'

'Now, I never knowed that! But they're valley-folk,' Jabez repeated.

' 'Twadn't particular noticeable, for she wasn't a talkin' woman any time o' her days. Mary had all three's tongue. . . . Well, then, two years this summer, come what I'm tellin' you, Mary's Lunnon father, which they'd put clean out o' their minds, arrived down from Lunnon with the law on his side, sayin' he'd take his daughter back to Lunnon, after all. I was working for Mus' Dockett at Pounds Farm that summer, but I was obligin' Jim that evenin' muckin' out his pig-pen. I seed a stranger come traipsin' over the bridge agin' Wickenden's door-stones. 'Twadn't the new County Council bridge with the hand-rail. They hadn't given it in for a public right o' way then. 'Twas just a bit o' lathy old plank which Jim had throwed acrost the brook for his own conveniences. The man wasn't drunk—only a little concerned in liquor, like—an' his back was a mask where he'd slipped in the muck comin' along. He went up the bricks past Jim's mother, which was feedin' the ducks, an' set himself down at the table inside—Jim was just changin' his socks—an' the man let Jim know all his rights and aims regardin' Mary. Then there just about *was* a hurly-bulloo! Jim's fust mind was to pitch him forth, but he'd done that once in his young days, and got six months up to Lewes jail along o' the man fallin' on his head. So he swallowed his spittle an' let him talk. The law about Mary *was* on the man's side from fust to last, for he showed us all the papers. Then Mary come downstairs—she'd been studyin' for an examination—an' the man tells her who he was, an' she says he had ought to have took proper care of his own flesh and blood while he had it by him, an' not to think he could ree-claim it when it suited. He says somethin' or other, but she looks him up an' down, front an' backwent, an' she just tongues him scadderin' out o' doors, and he went away stuffin' all the papers back into his hat, talkin' most abusefully. Then she come back an' freed her mind against Jim an' his mother for not havin' warned her of her upbringin's, which it come out she hadn't ever been told. They didn't say naun to her. They never did. *I*'d ha' packed her off with any man that would ha' took her—an' God's pity on him!'

'Umm!' said Jabez, and sucked his pipe.

'So then, that was the beginnin'. The man come back again next week or so, an' he catched Jim alone, 'thout his mother this time, an' he fair beazled him with his papers an' his talk—for the law *was* on his side—till Jim went down into his money-purse an' give him ten shillings hush-money—he told me—to withdraw away for a bit an' leave Mary with 'em.'

'But that's no way to get rid o' man or woman,' Jabez said.

'No more 'tis. I told Jim so. "What can I do?" Jim says. "The law's *with* the man. I walk about daytimes thinkin' o' it till I sweats my underclothes wringin', an' I lie abed nights thinkin' o' it till I sweats my sheets all of a sop. 'Tisn't as if I was a young man," he says, "nor yet as if I was a pore man. Maybe he'll drink hisself to death." I e'en

a'most told him outright what foolishness he was enterin'
into, but he knowed it—he knowed it—because he said
next time the man come 'twould be fifteen shillin's. An'
next time 'twas. Just fifteen shillin's!'

'An' *was* the man her father?' asked Jabez.

'He had the proofs an' the papers. Jim showed me what
that Lunnon Childern's Society had answered when Mary
writ up to 'em an' taxed 'em with it. I lay she hadn't been
proper polite in her letters to 'em, for they answered
middlin' short. They said the matter was out o' their
hands, but—let's see if I remember—oh, yes,—they ree-
gretted there had been an oversight. I reckon they had
sent Mary out in the candle-box as a orphan instead o'
havin' a father. Terrible awkward! Then, when he'd
drinked up the money, the man come again—in his
usuals—an' he kept hammerin' on and hammerin' on
about his duty to his pore dear wife, an' what he'd do for
his dear daughter in Lunnon, till the tears runned down
his two dirty cheeks an' he come away with more money.
Jim used to slip it into his hand behind the door; but his
mother she heard the chink. She didn't hold with hush-
money. She'd write out all her feelin's on the slate, an' Jim
'ud be settin' up half the night answerin' back an' showing
that the man had the law with him.'

'Hadn't that man no trade nor business, then?'

'He told me he was a printer. I reckon, though, he lived
on the rates like the rest of 'em up there in Lunnon.'

'An' how did Mary take it?'

'She said she'd sooner go into service than go with the
man. I reckon a mistress 'ud be middlin' put to it for a
maid 'fore she put Mary into cap an' gown. She was
studyin' to be a schoo-ool-teacher. A beauty she'll
make! . . . Well, that was how things went that fall. Mary's
Lunnon father kep' comin' an' comin' 'carden as he'd
drinked out the money Jim gave him; an' each time
he'd put up his price for not takin' Mary away. Jim's
mother, she didn't like partin' with no money, an' bein'

obliged to write her feelin's on the slate instead o' givin'
'em vent by mouth, she was just about mad. Just about
she *was* mad!

'Come November, I lodged with Jim in the outside
room over 'gainst his hen-house. I paid *her* my rent. I was
workin' for Dockett at Pounds—gettin' chestnut-bats out
o' Perry Shaw. Just such weather as this be—rain atop o'
rain after a wet October. (An' I remember it ended in dry
frostes right away up to Christmas.) Dockett he'd sent up
to Perry Shaw for me—no, he comes puffin' up to me
himself—because a big corner-piece o' the bank had
slipped into the Brook where she makes that elber at the
bottom o' the Seventeen Acre, an' all the rubbishy alders
an' sallies which he ought to have cut out when he took
the farm, they'd slipped with the slip, an' the Brook was
comin' rooshin' down atop of 'em, an' they'd just about
back an' spill the waters over his winter wheat. The water
was lyin' in the flats already. "Gor a-mighty, Jesse!" he
bellers out at me, "get that rubbish away all manners you
can. Don't stop for no fagottin' but give the Brook play or
my wheat's past salvation. I can't lend you no help," he
says, "but work an' I'll pay ye." '

'You had him there,' Jabez chuckled.

'Yes. I reckon I had ought to have drove my bargain,
but the Brook was backin' up on good bread-corn. So
'cardenly, I laid into the mess of it, workin' off the bank
where the trees was drownin' themselves head-down in
the roosh—just such weather as this—an' the Brook creepin' up on me all the time. 'Long toward noon, Jim comes
mowchin' along with his toppin' axe over his shoulder.

' "Be you minded for an extra hand at your job?" he
says.

' "Be you minded to turn to?" I ses, an'—no more talk
to it—Jim laid in alongside o' me. He's no bunger with a
toppin' axe.'

'Maybe, but I've seed him at a job o' throwin' in the
woods, an' he didn't seem to make out no shape,' said

Jabez. 'He haven't got the shoulders, nor yet the judgment—*my* opinion—when he's dealin' with full-girt timber. He don't rightly make up his mind where he's goin' to throw her.'

'We wasn't throwin' nothin'. We was cuttin' out they soft alders, an' haulin' 'em up the bank 'fore they could back the waters on the wheat. Jim didn't say much, 'less it was that he'd had a postcard from Mary's Lunnon father, night before, sayin' he was comin' down that mornin'. Jim, he'd sweated all night, an' he didn't reckon hisself equal to the talkin' an' the swearin' an' the cryin', an' his mother blamin' him afterwards on the slate. "It spiled my day to think of it," he ses, when we was eatin' our pieces. "So I've fair cried dunghill an' run. Mother'll have to tackle him by herself. I lay *she* won't give him no hush-money," he ses. "I lay he'll be surprised by the time he's done with *her*," he ses. An' that was e'en a'most all the talk we had concernin' it. But he's no bunger with the toppin' axe.

'The Brook she'd crep' up an' up on us, an' she kep' creepin' upon us till we was workin' knee-deep in the shallers, cuttin' an' pookin' an' pullin' what we could get to o' the rubbish. There was a middlin' lot comin' downstream, too—cattle-bars an' hop-poles and odds-ends bats, all poltin' down together; but they rooshed round the elber good shape by the time we'd backed out they drowned trees. Come four o'clock we reckoned we'd done a proper day's work, an' she'd take no harm if we left her. We couldn't puddle about there in the dark an' wet to no more advantage. Jim he was pourin' the water out of his boots—no, I was doin' that. Jim was kneelin' to unlace his'n. "Damn it all, Jesse," he ses, standin' up; "the flood must be over my doorsteps at home, for here comes my old white-top bee-skep!" '

'Yes. I allus heard he paints his bee-skeps,' Jabez put in. 'I dunno paint don't tarrify bees more'n it keeps 'em dry.'

'"I'll have a pook at it," he ses, an' he pooks at it as it

comes round the elber. The roosh nigh jerked the pooker out of his hand-grips, an' he calls to me, an' I come runnin' barefoot. Then we pulled on the pooker, an' it reared up on eend in the roosh, an' we guessed what 'twas. 'Cardenly we pulled it in into a shaller, an' it rolled a piece, an' a great old stiff man's arm nigh hit me in the face. Then we was sure. " 'Tis a man," ses Jim. But the face was all a mask. "I reckon it's Mary's Lunnon father," he ses presently. "Lend me a match and I'll make sure." He never used baccy. We lit three matches one by another, well's we could in the rain, an' he cleaned off some o' the slob with a tussick o' grass. "Yes," he ses. "It's Mary's Lunnon father. He won't tarrify us no more. D'you want him, Jesse?" he ses.

' "No," I ses. "If this was Eastbourne beach like, he'd be half-a-crown apiece to us 'fore the coroner; but now we'd only lose a day havin' to 'tend the inquest. I lay he fell into the Brook."

' "I lay he did," ses Jim. "I wonder if he saw mother." He turns him over, an' opens his coat and puts his fingers in the waistcoat pocket an' starts laughin'. "He's seen mother, right enough," he ses. "An' he's got the best of her, too. *She* won't be able to crow no more over *me* 'bout givin' him money. *I* never give him more than a sovereign. She's give him two!" an' he trousers 'em, laughin' all the time. "An' now we'll pook him back again, for I've done with him," he ses.

'So we pooked him back into the middle of the Brook, an' we saw he went round the elber 'thout balkin', an' we walked quite a piece beside of him to set him on his ways. When we couldn't see no more, we went home by the high road, because we knowed the Brook 'u'd be out acrost the meddlers, an' we wasn't goin' to hunt for Jim's little rotten old bridge in that dark—an' rainin' Heavens' hard, too. I was middlin' pleased to see light an' vittles again when we got home. Jim he pressed me to come insides for a drink. He don't drink in a generality, but he was rid of all his troubles that evenin', d'ye see? "Mother," he ses so soon as the door ope'd, "have you seen him?" She whips out her slate an' writes down—"No." "Oh, no," ses Jim. "You don't get out of it that way, mother. I lay you *have* seen him, an' I lay he's bested you for all your talk, same as he bested me. Make a clean breast of it, mother," he ses. "He got round you too." She was goin' for the slate again, but he stops her. "It's all right, mother," he ses. "I've seen him sense you have, an' he won't trouble us no more." The old lady looks up quick as a robin, an' she writes, "Did he say so?" "No," ses Jim laughin'. "He didn't say so. That's how I know. But he bested *you*, mother. You can't have it in at *me* for bein' soft-hearted. You're twice as tender-hearted as what I be. Look!" he ses, an' he shows her the two sovereigns. "Put 'em away where they belong," he ses. "He won't never come for no more; an' now we'll have our drink," he ses, "for we've earned it."

'Nature-ally they weren't goin' to let me see where they kep'' their monies. She went upstairs with it—for the whisky.'

'I never knowed Jim was a drinkin' man—in his own house, like,' said Jabez.

'No more he isn't; but what he takes he likes good. He won't tech no publican's hogwash acrost the bar. Four shillin's he paid for that bottle o' whisky. I know, because when the old lady brought it down there wasn't more'n jest a liddle few dreenin's an' dregs in it. Nothin' to set before neighbours, I do assure you.'

' "Why, 'twas half full last week, mother," he ses. "You don't mean," he ses, "you've given him all that as well? It's two shillin's worth," he ses. (That's how I knowed he paid four.) "Well, well, mother, you be too tender-'earted to live. But I don't grudge it to him," he ses. "I don't grudge him nothin' he can keep." So, 'cardenly, we drinked up what little sup was left.'

'An' what come to Mary's Lunnon father?' said Jabez, after a full minute's silence.

'I be too tired to go readin' papers of evenin's; but
Dockett he told me, that very week, I think, that they'd
inquested on a man down at Robertsbridge which had
polted and polted up agin' so many bridges an' banks, like,
they couldn't make naun out of him.'

'An' what did Mary say to all these doin's?'

'The old lady bundled her off to the village 'fore her
Lunnon father come, to buy week-end stuff (an' she forgot the half o' it). When we come in she was upstairs
studyin' to be a school-teacher. None told her naun about
it. 'Twadn't girls' affairs.'

' 'Reckon *she* knowed?' Jabez went on.

'She? She must have guessed it middlin' close when she
saw her money come back. But she never mentioned it in
writing so far's I know. She were more worritted that
night on account of two-three her chickens bein' drowned,
for the flood had skewed their old hen-house round on her
postes. I cobbled her up next mornin' when the Brook
shrinked.'

'An' where did you find the bridge? Some fur down-
stream, didn't ye?'

'Just where she allus was. She hadn't shifted but very
little. The Brook had gulled out the bank a piece under
one eend o' the plank, so's she was liable to tilt ye side-
ways if you wasn't careful. But I pooked three-four bricks
under her, an' she was all plumb again.'

'Well, I dunno how it *looks* like, but let be how 'twill,'
said Jabez, 'he hadn't no business to come down from
Lunnon tarrifyin' people, an' threatenin' to take away
children which they'd hobbed up for their lawful own—
even if 'twas Mary Wickenden.'

'He had the business right enough, an' he had the law
with him—no gettin' over that,' said Jesse. 'But he had the
drink with him, too, an' that was where he failed, like.'

'Well, well! Let be how 'twill, the Brook was a good
friend to Jim. I see it now. I allus *did* wonder what he was
gettin' at when he said that, when I talked to him about

shiftin' the stack. "You dunno everythin'," he ses. "The Brook's been a good friend to me," he ses, "an' if she's minded to have a snatch at my hay, *I* ain't settin' out to withstand her." '

'I reckon she's about shifted it, too, by now,' Jesse chuckled. 'Hark! That ain't any slip off the bank which she's got hold of.'

The Brook had changed her note again. It sounded as though she were mumbling something soft.

1914

THE WISH HOUSE

The new Church Visitor had just left after a twenty minutes' call. During that time, Mrs. Ashcroft had used such English as an elderly, experienced, and pensioned cook should, who had seen life in London. She was the readier, therefore, to slip back into easy, ancient Sussex ('t's softening to 'd's as one warmed) when the 'bus brought Mrs. Fettley from thirty miles away for a visit, that pleasant March Saturday. The two had been friends since childhood; but, of late, destiny had separated their meetings by long intervals.

Much was to be said, and many ends, loose since last time, to be ravelled up on both sides, before Mrs. Fettley, with her bag of quilt-patches, took the couch beneath the window commanding the garden, and the football-ground in the valley below.

'Most folk got out at Bush Tye for the match there,' she explained, 'so there weren't no one for me to cushion agin, the last five mile. An' she *do* just-about bounce ye.'

'You've took no hurt,' said her hostess. 'You don't brittle by agein', Liz.'

Mrs. Fettley chuckled and made to match a couple of patches to her liking. 'No, or I'd ha' broke twenty year back. You can't ever mind when I was so's to be called round, can ye?'

Mrs. Ashcroft shook her head slowly—she never hurried—and went on stitching a sack-cloth lining into a list-bound rush tool-basket. Mrs. Fettley laid out more patches in the Spring light through the geraniums on the window-sill, and they were silent awhile.

'What like's this new Visitor o' yourn?' Mrs. Fettley inquired with a nod towards the door. Being very short-sighted, she had, on her entrance, almost bumped into the lady.

Mrs. Ashcroft suspended the big packing-needle judicially on high, ere she stabbed home. 'Settin' aside she don't bring much news with her yet, I dunno as I've anythin' special agin her.'

'Ourn, at Keyneslade,' said Mrs. Fettley, 'she's full o' words an' pity, but she don't stay for answers. Ye can get on with your thoughts while she clacks.'

'This 'un don't clack. She's aimin' to be one o' those High Church nuns, like.'

'Ourn's married, but, by what they say, she've made no great gains of it . . .' Mrs. Fettley threw up her sharp chin. 'Lord! How they dam' cherubim do shake the very bones o' the place!'

The tile-sided cottage trembled at the passage of two specially chartered forty-seat charabancs on their way to the Bush Tye match; a regular Saturday 'shopping' 'bus, for the county's capital, fumed behind them; while, from one of the crowded inns, a fourth car backed out to join the procession, and held up the stream of through pleasure-traffic.

'You're as free-tongued as ever, Liz,' Mrs. Ashcroft observed.

'Only when I'm with you. Otherwhiles, I'm Granny—three times over. I lay that basket's for one o' your gran'chiller—ain't it?'

' 'Tis for Arthur—my Jane's eldest.'

'But he ain't workin' nowheres, is he?'

'No. 'Tis a picnic-basket.'

'You're let off light. My Willie, he's allus at me for money for them aireated wash-poles folk puts up in their gardens to draw the music from Lunnon, like. An' I give it 'im—pore fool me!'

'An' he forgets to give you the promise-kiss after, don't

he?' Mrs. Ashcroft's heavy smile seemed to strike inwards.

'He do. 'No odds 'twixt boys now an' forty year back. 'Take all an' give naught—an' we to put up with it! Pore fool we! Three shillin' at a time Willie'll ask me for!'

'They don't make nothin' o' money these days,' Mrs. Ashcroft said.

'An' on'y last week,' the other went on, 'me daughter, she ordered a quarter pound suet at the butchers's; an' she sent it back to 'um to be chopped. She said she couldn't bother with choppin' it.'

'I lay he charged her, then.'

'I lay he did. She told me there was a whisk-drive that afternoon at the Institute, an' she couldn't bother to do the choppin'.'

'Tck!'

Mrs. Ashcroft put the last firm touches to the basket-lining. She had scarcely finished when her sixteen-year-old grandson, a maiden of the moment in attendance, hurried up the garden-path shouting to know if the thing were ready, snatched it, and made off without acknowledgment. Mrs. Fettley peered at him closely.

'They're goin' picnickin' somewheres,' Mrs. Ashcroft explained.

'Ah,' said the other, with narrowed eyes. 'I lay *he* won't show much mercy to any he comes across, either. Now 'oo the dooce do he remind me of, all of a sudden?'

'They must look arter theirselves—'same as we did.' Mrs. Ashcroft began to set out the tea.

'No denyin' *you* could, Gracie,' said Mrs. Fettley.

'What's in your head now?'

'Dunno . . . But it come over me, sudden-like—about dat woman from Rye—I've slipped the name—Barnsley, wadn't it?'

'Batten—Polly Batten, you're thinkin' of.'

'That's it—Polly Batten. That day she had it in for you with a hay-fork—'time we was all hayin' at Smalldene—for stealin' her man.'

'But you heered me tell her she had my leave to keep him?' Mrs. Ashcroft's voice and smile were smoother than ever.

'I did—an' we was all looking that she'd prod the fork spang through your breastes when you said it.'

'No-oo. She'd never go beyond bounds—Polly. She shruck too much for reel doin's.'

'Allus seem to *me*,' Mrs. Fettley said after a pause, 'that a man 'twixt two fightin' women is the foolishest thing on earth. 'Like a dog bein' called two ways.'

'Mebbe. But what set ye off on those times, Liz?'

'That boy's fashion o' carryin' his head an' arms. I haven't rightly lookcd at him since he's growed. Your Jane never showed it, but—*him!* Why, 'tis Jim Batten and his tricks come to life again! . . . Eh?'

'Mebbe. There's some that would ha' made it out so— bein' barren-like, themselves.'

'Oho! Ah well! Dearie, dearie me, now! . . . An' Jim Batten's been dead this——'

'Seven and twenty years,' Mrs. Ashcroft answered briefly. 'Won't ye draw up, Liz?'

Mrs. Fettley drew up to buttered toast, currant bread, stewed tea, bitter as leather, some home-preserved pcars, and a cold boiled pig's tail to help down the muffins. She paid all the proper compliments.

'Yes. I dunno as I've ever owed me belly much,' said Mrs. Ashcroft thoughtfully. 'We only go through this world once.'

'But don't it lay heavy on ye, sometimes?' her guest suggested.

'Nurse says I'm a sight liker to die o' me indigestion than me leg.' For Mrs. Ashcroft had a long-standing ulcer on her shin, which needed regular care from the Village Nurse, who boasted (or others did, for her) that she had dressed it one hundred and three times already during her term of office.

'An' you that *was* so able, too! It's all come on ye before your full time, like. *I*'ve watched ye goin'.' Mrs. Fettley spoke with real affection.

'Somethin's bound to find ye sometime. I've me 'eart left me still,' Mrs. Ashcroft returned.

'You was always big-hearted enough for three. That's somethin' to look back on at the day's eend.'

'I reckon you've *your* back-lookin's, too,' was Mrs. Ashcroft's answer.

'You know it. But I don't think much regardin' such matters excep' when I'm along with you, Gra'. 'Takes two sticks to make a fire.'

Mrs. Fettley stared, with jaw half-dropped, at the grocer's bright calendar on the wall. The cottage shook again to the roar of the motor-traffic, and the crowded football-ground below the garden roared almost as loudly; for the village was well set to its Saturday leisure.

Mrs. Fettley had spoken very precisely for some time without interruption, before she wiped her eyes. 'And,' she concluded, 'they read 'is death-notice to me, out o' the paper last month. O' course it wadn't any o' *my* becomin' concerns—let be I 'adn't set eyes on him for so long. O' course *I* couldn't say nor show nothin'. Nor I've no rightful call to go to Eastbourne to see 'is grave, either. I've been schemin' to slip over there by the 'bus some day; but they'd ask questions at 'ome past endurance. So I 'aven't even *that* to stay me.'

'But you've 'ad your satisfaction?'

'Godd! Yess! Those four years 'e was workin' on the rail near us. An' the other drivers they gave him a brave funeral, too.'

'Then you've naught to cast-up about. 'Nother cup o' tea?'

The light and air had changed a little with the sun's descent, and the two elderly ladies closed the kitchen-door against chill. A couple of jays squealed and skirmished through the undraped apple-trees in the garden. This time, the word was with Mrs. Ashcroft, her elbows on the tea-table, and her sick leg propped on a stool. . . .

'Well I never! But what did your 'usband say to that?' Mrs. Fettley asked, when the deep-toned recital halted.

' 'E said I might go where I pleased for all of 'im. But seein' 'e was bedrid, I said I'd 'tend 'im out. 'E knowed I wouldn't take no advantage of 'im in that state. 'E lasted eight or nine weeks. Then he was took with a seizure-like; an' laid stone-still for days. Then 'e propped 'imself up abed an' says: "You pray no man'll ever deal with you like you've dealed with some." "An' you?" I says, for *you* know, Liz, what a rover 'e was. "It cuts both ways," says 'e, "but *I'*m death-wise, an' I can see what's comin' to you." He died a-Sunday an' was buried a-Thursday . . . An' yet I'd set a heap by him—one time or—did I ever?'

'You never told me that before,' Mrs. Fettley ventured.

'I'm payin' ye for what ye told me just now. Him bein' dead, I wrote up, sayin' I was free for good, to that Mrs. Marshall in Lunnon—which gave me my first place as kitchen-maid—Lord, how long ago! She was well pleased, for they two was both gettin' on, an' I knowed their ways. You remember, Liz, I used to go to 'em in service between whiles, for years—when we wanted money, or—or my 'usband was away—on occasion.'

' 'E *did* get that six months at Chichester, didn't 'e?' Mrs. Fettley whispered. 'We never rightly won to the bottom of it.'

' 'E'd ha' got more, but the man didn't die.'

' 'None o' your doin's, was it, Gra'?'

'No! 'Twas the woman's husband this time. An' so, my man bein' dead, I went back to them Marshalls, as cook, to get me legs under a gentleman's table again, and be called with a handle to me name. That was the year you shifted to Portsmouth.'

'Cosham,' Mrs. Fettley corrected. 'There was a middlin'

lot o' new buildin' bein' done there. My man went first, an' got the room, an' I follered.'

'Well, then, I was a year-abouts in Lunnon, all at a breath, like, four meals a day an' livin' easy. Then, 'long towards autumn, they two went travellin', like, to France; keepin' me on, for they couldn't do without me. I put the house to rights for the caretaker, an' then I slipped down 'ere to me sister Bessie—me wages in me pockets, an' all 'ands glad to be'old of me.'

'That would be when I was at Cosham,' said Mrs. Fettley.

'*You* know, Liz, there wasn't no cheap-dog pride to folk, those days, no more than there was cinemas nor whisk-drives. Man or woman 'ud lay hold o' any job that promised a shillin' to the backside of it, didn't they? I was all peaked up after Lunnon, an' I thought the fresh airs 'ud serve me. So I took on at Smalldene, obligin' with a hand at the early potato-liftin', stubbin' hens, an' such-like. They'd ha' mocked me sore in my kitchen in Lunnon, to see me in men's boots, an' me petticoats all shorted.'

'Did it bring ye any good?' Mrs. Fettley asked.

' 'Twadn't for that I went. You know, 's'well's me, that na'un happens to ye till it *as* 'appened. Your mind don't warn ye before'and of the road ye've took, till you're at the far eend of it. We've only a backwent view of our proceedin's.'

' 'Oo was it?'

' 'Arry Mockler.' Mrs. Ashcroft's face puckered to the pain of her sick leg.

Mrs. Fettley gasped. ' 'Arry? Bert Mockler's son! An' *I* never guessed!'

Mrs. Ashcroft nodded. 'An' I told myself—*an'* I beleft it—that I wanted field-work.'

'What did ye get out of it?'

'The usuals. Everythin' at first—worse than naught after. I had signs an' warnings a-plenty, but I took no heed of 'em. For we was burnin' rubbish one day, just when we'd come to know how 'twas with—with both of us. 'Twas early in the year for burnin', an' I said so. "No!" says he. "The sooner dat old stuff's off an' done with," 'e says, "the better." 'Is face was harder'n rocks when he spoke. Then it come over me that I'd found me master, which I 'adn't ever before. I'd allus owned 'em, like.'

'Yes! Yes! They're yourn or you're theirn,' the other sighed. 'I like the right way best.'

'I didn't. But 'Arry did . . . 'Long then, it come time for me to go back to Lunnon. I couldn't. I clean couldn't! So, I took an' tipped a dollop o' scaldin' water out o' the copper one Monday mornin' over me left 'and and arm. Dat stayed me where I was for another fortnight.'

'Was it worth it?' said Mrs. Fettley, looking at the silvery scar on the wrinkled fore-arm.

Mrs. Ashcroft nodded. 'An' after that, we two made it up 'twixt us so's 'e could come to Lunnon for a job in a liv'ry-stable not far from me. 'E got it. *I* 'tended to that. There wadn't no talk nowhere. His own mother never suspicioned how 'twas. He just slipped up to Lunnon, an' there we abode that winter, not 'alf a mile 'tother from each.'

'Ye paid 'is fare an' all, though'; Mrs. Fettley spoke convincedly.

Again Mrs. Ashcroft nodded. 'Dere wadn't much I didn't do for him. 'E was me master, an'—O God, help us!—we'd laugh over it walkin' together after dark in them paved streets, an' me corns fair wrenchin' in me boots! I'd never been like that before. Ner he! Ner he!'

Mrs. Fettley clucked sympathetically.

'An' when did ye come to the eend?' she asked.

'When 'e paid it all back again, every penny. Then I knowed, but I wouldn't *suffer* meself to know. "You've been mortal kind to me," he says. "Kind!" I said. "'Twixt *us?*" But 'e kep' all on tellin' me 'ow kind I'd been an' 'e'd never forget it all his days. I held it from off o' me for three evenin's, because I would *not* believe. Then e' talked about not bein' satisfied with 'is job in the stables, an' the men there puttin' tricks on 'im, an' all they lies which a man tells when 'e's leavin' ye. I heard 'im out, neither 'elpin' nor 'inderin'. At the last, I took off a liddle brooch which he'd give me an' I says: "Dat'll do. *I* ain't askin' na'un." An' I turned me round an' walked off to me own sufferin's. 'E didn't make 'em worse. 'E didn't come nor write after that. 'E slipped off 'ere back 'ome to 'is mother again.'

'An' 'ow often did ye look for 'en to come back?' Mrs. Fettley demanded mercilessly.

'More'n once—more'n once! Goin' over the streets we'd used, I thought de very pave-stones 'ud shruck out under me feet.'

'Yes,' said Mrs. Fettley. 'I dunno but dat don't 'urt as much as aught else. An' dat was all ye got?'

'No. 'Twadn't. That's the curious part, if you'll believe it, Liz.'

'I do. I lay you're further off lyin' now than in all your life, Gra'.'

'I am ... An' I suffered, like I'd not wish my most arrantest enemies to. God's Own Name! I went through the hoop that spring! One part of it was headaches which I'd never known all me days before. Think o' *me* with an 'ed-dick! But I come to be grateful for 'em. They kep' me from thinkin' ...'

' 'Tis like a tooth,' Mrs. Fettley commented. 'It must rage an' rugg till it tortures itself quiet on ye; an' then—then there's na'un left.'

'*I* got enough lef' to last me all *my* days on earth. It come about through our charwoman's liddle girl—Sophy Ellis was 'er name—all eyes an' elbers an' hunger. I used to give 'er vittles. Otherwhiles, I took no special notice of 'er, an' a sight less, o' course, when me trouble about 'Arry was on me. But—you know how liddle maids first feel it sometimes—she come to be crazy-fond o' me, pawin' an' cuddlin' all whiles; an' I 'adn't the 'eart to beat 'er off . . . One afternoon, early in spring 'twas, 'er mother 'ad sent 'er round to scutchel up what vittles she could off of us. I was settin' by the fire, me apern over me head, half-mad with the 'eddick, when she slips in. I reckon I was middlin' short with 'er. "Lor'!" she says. "Is *that* all? I'll take it off you in two-twos!" I told her not to lay a finger on me, for I thought she'd want to stroke my forehead; an'—I ain't that make. "*I* won't tech ye," she says, an' slips out again. She 'adn't been gone ten minutes 'fore me old 'eddick took off quick as bein' kicked. So I went about my work. Prasin'ly, Sophy comes back, an' creeps into my chair quiet as a mouse. 'Er eyes was deep in 'er 'ead an' 'er face all drawed. I asked 'cr what 'ad 'appened. "Nothin'," she says. "On'y *I*'ve got it now." "Got what?" I says. "Your 'eddick," she says, all hoarse an' sticky-lipped. "I've took it on me." "Nonsense," I says, "it went of itself when you was out. Lay still an' I'll make ye a cup o' tea." " 'Twon't do no good," she says, " 'til your time's up. 'Ow long do *your* 'eddicks last?" "Don't talk silly," I says, "or I'll send for the Doctor." It looked to me like she might be hatchin' de measles. "Oh, Mrs. Ashcroft," she says, stretchin' out 'cr liddle thin arms. "I *do* love ye." There wasn't any holdin' agin that. I took 'er into me lap an' made much of 'er. "Is it truly gone?" she says. "Yes," I says, "an' if 'twas you took it away, I'm truly grateful." " 'Twas me," she says, layin' 'er cheek to mine. "No one but me knows how." An' then she said she'd changed me 'eddick for me at a Wish 'Ouse.'

'Whatt?' Mrs. Fettley spoke sharply.

'A Wish House. No! *I* 'adn't 'eard o' such things, either. I couldn't get it straight at first, but, puttin' all together, I made out that a Wish 'Ouse 'ad to be a house which 'ad stood unlet an' empty long enough for Some One, like, to come an' in'abit there. She said, a liddle girl that she'd played with in the livery-stables where 'Arry worked 'ad told 'er so. She said the girl 'ad belonged in a caravan that laid up, o' winters, in Lunnon. Gipsy, I judge.'

'Ooh! There's no sayin' what Gippos know, but *I*'ve never 'eard of a Wish 'Ouse, an' I know—some things,' said Mrs. Fettley.

'Sophy said there was a Wish 'Ouse in Wadloes Road—just a few streets off, on the way to our green-grocer's. All you 'ad to do, she said, was to ring the bell an' wish your wish through the slit o' the letter-box. I asked 'er if the fairies give it 'er? "Don't ye know," she says, "there's no fairies in a Wish 'Ouse? There's only a Token." '

'Goo' Lord A'mighty! Where did she come by *that* word?' cried Mrs. Fettley; for a Token is a wraith of the dead or, worse still, of the living.

'The caravan-girl 'ad told 'er, she said. Well, Liz, it troubled me to 'ear 'er, an' lyin' in me arms she must ha' felt it. "That's very kind o' you," I says, holdin' 'er tight, "to wish me 'eddick away. But why didn't ye ask somethin' nice for yourself?" "You can't do that," she says. "All you'll get at a Wish 'Ouse is leave to take some one else's trouble. I've took Ma's 'eadaches, when she's been kind to me; but this is the first time I've been able to do aught for you. Oh, Mrs. Ashcroft, I *do* just-about love you." An' she goes on all like that. Liz, I tell you my 'air e'en a'most stood on end to 'ear 'er. I asked 'er what like a Token was. "I dunno," she says, "but after you've ringed the bell, you'll 'ear it run up from the basement, to the front door. Then say your wish," she says, "an' go away." "The Token don't open de door to ye, then?" I says. "Oh, no," she says. "You on'y 'ear gigglin', like, be'ind the front door. Then you say you'll take the trouble off of 'oo ever 'tis you've chose for your love; an' ye'll get it," she says. I didn't ask no more—she was too 'ot an' fevered. I made much of 'er till it come time to light de gas, an' a liddle after that, 'er 'eddick—mine, I suppose—took off, an' she got down an' played with the cat.'

'Well, I never!' said Mrs. Fettley. 'Did—did ye foller it up, anyways?'

'She askt me to, but I wouldn't 'ave no such dealin's with a child.'

'What *did* ye do, then?'

' 'Sat in me own room 'stid o' the kitchen when me 'ed-dicks come on. But it lay at de back o' me mind.'

' 'Twould. Did she tell ye more, ever?'

'No. Besides what the Gippo girl 'ad told 'er, she knew naught, 'cept that the charm worked. An', next after that—in May 'twas—I suffered the summer out in Lunnon. 'Twas hot an' windy for weeks, an' the streets stinkin' o' dried 'orse-dung blowin' from side to side an' lyin' level with the kerb. We don't get that nowadays. I 'ad my 'ol'day just before hoppin',[1] an' come down 'ere to stay with Bessie again. She noticed I'd lost flesh, an' was all poochy under the eyes.'

'Did ye see 'Arry?'

Mrs. Ashcroft nodded. 'The fourth—no, the fifth day. Wednesday 'twas. I knowed 'e was workin' at Smalldene again. I asked 'is mother in the street, bold as brass. She 'adn't room to say much, for Bessie—you know 'er tongue—was talkin' full-clack. But that Wednesday, I was walkin' with one o' Bessie's chillern hangin' on me skirts, at de back o' Chanter's Tot. Prasin'ly, I felt 'e was be'ind me on the footpath, an' I knowed by 'is tread 'e'd changed 'is nature. I slowed, an' I heard 'im slow. Then I fussed a piece with the child, to force him past me, like. So 'e *ad* to come past. 'E just says "Good-evenin'," and goes on, tryin' to pull 'isself together.'

'Drunk, was he?' Mrs. Fettley asked.

'Never! S'runk an' wizen; 'is clothes 'angin' on 'im like bags, an' the back of 'is neck whiter'n chalk. 'Twas all I could do not to oppen my arms an' cry after him. But I swallered me spittle till I was back 'ome again an' the chillern abed. Then I says to Bessie, after supper, "What in de world's come to 'Arry Mockler?" Bessie told me 'e'd

---

[1] Hop-picking.

been a-Hospital for two months, 'long o' cuttin' 'is foot wid a spade, muckin' out the old pond at Smalldene. There was poison in de dirt, an' it rooshed up 'is leg, like, an' come out all over him. 'E 'adn't been back to 'is job— carterin' at Smalldene—more'n a fortnight. She told me the Doctor said he'd go off, likely, with the November frostes; an' 'is mother 'ad told 'er that 'e didn't rightly eat nor sleep, an' sweated 'imself into pools, no odds 'ow chill 'e lay. An' spit terrible o' mornin's. "Dearie me," I says. "But, mebbe hoppin' 'll set 'im right again," an' I licked me thread-point an' I fetched me needle's eye up to it an' I threads me needle under de lamp, steady as rocks. An' dat night (me bed was in de wash-house) I cried an' I cried. An' *you* know, Liz—for you've been with me in my throes—it takes summat to make me cry.'

'Yes; but chile-bearin' is on'y just pain,' said Mrs. Fettley.

'I come round by cock-crow, an' dabbed cold tea on me eyes to take away the signs. Long towards nex' evenin'—I was settin' out to lay some flowers on me 'usband's grave, for the look o' the thing—I met 'Arry over against where the War Memorial is now. 'E was comin' back from 'is 'orses, so 'e couldn't *not* see me. I looked 'im all over, an' " 'Arry," I says twix' me teeth, "come back an' rest-up in Lunnon." "I won't take it," he says, "for I can give ye naught." "I don't ask it," I says. "By God's Own Name, I don't ask na'un! On'y come up an' see a Lunnon doctor." 'E lifts 'is two 'eavy eyes at me: " 'Tis past that, Gra'," 'e says. "I've but a few months left." " 'Arry!" I says. "*My* man!" I says. I couldn't say no more. 'Twas all up in me throat. "Thank ye kindly, Gra'," 'e says (but 'e never says "my woman"), an' 'e went on up-street an' 'is mother— Oh, damn 'er!—she was watchin' for 'im, an' she shut de door be'ind 'im.'

Mrs. Fettley stretched an arm across the table, and made to finger Mrs. Ashcroft's sleeve at the wrist, but the other moved it out of reach.

'So I went on to the churchyard with my flowers, an' I remembered my 'usband's warnin' that night he spoke. 'E *was* death-wise, an' it *'ad* 'appened as 'e said. But as I was settin' down de jam-pot on the grave-mound, it come over me there was one thing I *could* do for 'Arry. Doctor or no Doctor, I thought I'd make a trial of it. So I did. Nex' mornin', a bill came down from our Lunnon green-grocer. Mrs. Marshall, she'd lef' me petty cash for such-like—o' course—but I tole Bess 'twas for me to come an' open the 'ouse. So I went up, afternoon train.'

'An'—but I know you 'adn't—'adn't you no fear?'

'What for? There was nothin' front o' me but my own shame an' God's croolty. I couldn't ever get 'Arry—'ow *could* I? I knowed it must go on burnin' till it burned me out.'

'Aie!' said Mrs. Fettley, reaching for the wrist again, and this time Mrs. Ashcroft permitted it.

'Yit 'twas a comfort to know I could try *this* for 'im. So I went an' I paid the green-grocer's bill, an' put 'is receipt in me hand-bag, an' then I stepped round to Mrs. Ellis—our char—an' got the 'ouse-keys an' opened the 'ouse. First, I made me bed to come back to (God's Own Name! Me bed to lie upon!). Nex' I made me a cup o' tea an' sat down in the kitchen thinkin', till 'long towards dusk. Terrible close, 'twas. Then I dressed me an' went out with the receipt in me 'and-bag, feignin' to study it for an address, like. Fourteen, Wadloes Road, was the place—a liddle basement-kitchen 'ouse, in a row of twenty-thirty such, an' tiddy strips o' walled garden in front—the paint off the front doors, an' na'un done to na'un since ever so long. There wasn't 'ardly no one in the streets 'cept the cats. *'Twas* 'ot, too! I turned into the gate bold as brass; up de steps I went an' I ringed the front-door bell. She pealed loud, like it do in an empty house. When she'd all ceased, I 'eard a cheer, like, pushed back on de floor o' the kitchen. Then I 'eard feet on de kitchen-stairs, like it might ha' been a heavy woman in slippers. They come up to de

stairhead, acrost the hall—I 'eard the bare boards creak
under 'em—an' at de front door dey stopped. I stooped me
to the letter-box slit, an' I says: "Let me take everythin'
bad that's in store for my man, 'Arry Mockler, for love's
sake." Then, whatever it was t'other side de door let its
breath out, like, as if it 'ad been holdin' it for to 'ear better.'

'Nothin' was *said* to ye?' Mrs. Fettley demanded.

'Na'un. She just breathed out—a sort of *A-ah*, like.
Then the steps went back an' down-stairs to the
kitchen—all draggy—an' I heard the cheer drawed up
again.'

'An' you abode on de doorstep, throughout all, Gra'?'
Mrs. Ashcroft nodded.

'Then I went away, an' a man passin' says to me:
"Didn't you know that house was empty?" "No," I says.
"I must ha' been give the wrong number." An' I went
back to our 'ouse, an' I went to bed; for I was fair flogged
out. 'Twas too 'ot to sleep more'n snatches, so I walked me
about, lyin' down betweens, till crack o' dawn. Then I
went to the kitchen to make me a cup o' tea, an' I hitted
meself just above the ankle on an old roastin'-jack o' mine
that Mrs. Ellis had moved out from the corner, her last
cleanin'. An' so—nex' after that—I waited till the Marshalls come back o' their holiday.'

'Alone there? I'd ha' thought you'd 'ad enough of
empty houses,' said Mrs. Fettley, horrified.

'Oh, Mrs. Ellis an' Sophy was runnin' in an' out soon's I
was back, an' 'twixt us we cleaned de house again top-to-
bottom. There's allus a hand's turn more to do in every
house. An' that's 'ow 'twas with me that autumn an' winter, in Lunnon.'

'Then na'un hap—overtook ye for your doin's?'

Mrs. Ashcroft smiled. 'No. Not then. 'Long in November I sent Bessie ten shillin's.'

'You was allus free-'anded,' Mrs. Fettley interrupted.

'An' I got what I paid for, with the rest o' the news. She said the hoppin' 'ad set 'im up wonderful. 'E'd 'ad six weeks of it, and now 'e was back again carterin' at Small-dene. No odds to me *'ow* it 'ad 'appened—'slong's it *'ad.* But I dunno as my ten shillin's eased me much. 'Arry bein' *dead*, like, 'e'd ha' been mine, till Judgment. 'Arry bein' alive, 'e'd like as not pick up with some woman middlin' quick. I raged over that. Come spring, I 'ad somethin' else to rage for. I'd growed a nasty little weepin' boil, like, on me shin, just above the boot-top, that wouldn't heal no shape. It made me sick to look at it, for I'm clean-fleshed by nature. Chop me all over with a spade, an' I'd heal like turf. Then Mrs. Marshall she set 'er own doctor at me. 'E said I ought to ha' come to him at first go-off, 'stead o' drawin' all manner o' dyed stockin's over it for months. 'E said I'd stood up too much to me work, for it was settin' very close atop of a big swelled vein, like, behither the small o' me ankle. "Slow come, slow go," 'e says. "Lay your leg up on high an' rest it," he says, "an' 'twill ease off. Don't let it close up too soon. You've got a very fine leg, Mrs. Ashcroft," 'e says. An' he put wet dressin's on it.'

' 'E done right.' Mrs. Fettley spoke firmly. 'Wet dress-in's to wet wounds. They draw de humours, same's a lamp-wick draws de oil.'

'That's true. An' Mrs. Marshall was allus at me to make me set down more, an' dat nigh healed it up. An' then after a while they packed me off down to Bessie's to finish the cure; for I ain't the sort to sit down when I ought to stand up. You was back in the village then, Liz.'

'I was. I was, but—never did I guess!'

'I didn't desire ye to.' Mrs. Ashcroft smiled. 'I saw 'Arry once or twice in de street, wonnerful fleshed up an' restored back. Then, one day I didn't see 'im, an' 'is mother told me one of 'is 'orses 'ad lashed out an' caught 'im on the 'ip. So 'e was abed an' middlin' painful. An'

Bessie, she says to his mother, 'twas a pity 'Arry 'adn't a woman of 'is own to take the nursin' off 'er. And the old lady *was* mad! She told us that 'Arry 'ad never looked after any woman in 'is born days, an' as long as she was atop the mowlds, she'd contrive for 'im till 'er two 'ands dropped off. So I knowed she'd do watch-dog for me, 'thout askin' for bones.'

Mrs. Fettley rocked with small laughter.

'That day,' Mrs. Ashcroft went on, 'I'd stood on me feet nigh all the time, watchin' the doctor go in an' out; for they thought it might be 'is ribs, too. That made my boil break again, issuin' an' weepin'. But it turned out 'twadn't ribs at all, an' 'Arry 'ad a good night. When I heard that, nex' mornin', I says to meself, "I won't lay two an' two together *yit*. I'll keep me leg down a week, an' see what comes of it." It didn't hurt me that day, to speak of— 'seemed more to draw the strength out o' me like—an' 'Arry 'ad another good night. That made me persevere; but I didn't dare lay two an' two together till the week-end, an' then, 'Arry come forth e'en a'most 'imself again—na'un hurt outside ner in of him. I nigh fell on me knees in de wash-house when Bessie was up-street. "I've got ye now, my man," I says, "You'll take your good from me 'thout knowin' it till my life's end. O God send me long to live for 'Arry's sake!" I says. An' I dunno that didn't still me ragin's.'

'For good?' Mrs. Fettley asked.

'They come back, plenty times, but, let be how 'twould, I knowed I was doin' for 'im. I *knowed* it. I took an' worked me pains on an' off, like regulatin' my own range, till I learned to 'ave 'em at my commandments. An' that was funny, too. There was times, Liz, when my trouble 'ud all s'rink an' dry up, like. First, I used to try an' fetch it on again; bein' fearful to leave 'Arry alone too long for anythin' to lay 'old of. Prasin'ly I come to see that was a sign he'd do all right awhile, an' so I saved myself.'

' 'Ow long for?' Mrs. Fettley asked, with deepest interest.

'I've gone de better part of a year onct or twice with na'un more to show than the liddle weepin' core of it, like. *All* s'rinked up an' dried off. Then he'd inflame up—for a warnin'—an' I'd suffer it. When I couldn't no more—an' I *'ad* to keep on goin' with my Lunnon work—I'd lay me leg high on a cheer till it eased. Not too quick. I knowed by the feel of it, those times, dat 'Arry was in need. Then I'd send another five shillin's to Bess, or somethin' for the chillern, to find out if, mebbe, 'e'd took any hurt through my neglects. 'Twas *so!* Year in, year out, I worked it dat way, Liz, an' 'e got 'is good from me 'thout knowin'—for years and years.'

'But what did *you* get out of it. Gra'?' Mrs. Fettley almost wailed. 'Did ye see 'im reg'lar?'

'Times—when I was 'ere on me 'ol'days. An' more, now that I'm 'ere for good. But 'e's never looked at me, ner any other woman 'cept 'is mother. 'Ow I used to watch an' listen! So did she.'

'Years an' years!' Mrs. Fettley repeated. 'An' where's 'e workin' at now?'

'Oh, 'e's give up carterin' quite a while. He's workin' for one o' them big tractorisin' firms—ploughin' sometimes, an' sometimes off with lorries—fur as Wales, I've 'eard. He comes 'ome to 'is mother 'tween whiles; but I don't set eyes on him now, fer weeks on end. No odds! 'Is job keeps 'im from continuin' in one stay anywheres.'

'But—just for de sake o' sayin' somethin'—s'pose 'Arry *did* get married?' said Mrs. Fettley.

Mrs. Ashcroft drew her breath sharply between her still even and natural teeth. '*Dat* ain't been required of me,' she answered. 'I reckon my pains 'ull be counted agin that. Don't *you*, Liz?'

'It ought to be, dearie. It ought to be.'

'It *do* 'urt sometimes. You shall see it when Nurse

comes. She thinks I don't know it's turned.'

Mrs. Fettley understood. Human nature seldom walks up to the word 'cancer.'

'Be ye certain sure, Gra'?' she asked.

'I was sure of it when old Mr. Marshall 'ad me up to 'is study an' spoke a long piece about my faithful service. I've obliged 'em on an' off for a goodish time, but not enough for a pension. But they give me a weekly 'lowance for life. I knew what *that* sinnified—as long as three years ago.'

'Dat don't *prove* it, Gra'.'

'To give fifteen bob a week to a woman 'oo'd live twenty year in the course o' nature? It *do!*'

'You're mistook! You're mistook!' Mrs. Fettley insisted.

'Liz, there's *no* mistakin' when the edges are all heaped up, like—same as a collar. You'll see it. An' I laid out Dora Wickwood, too. *She* 'ad it under the arm-pit, like.'

Mrs. Fettley considered awhile, and bowed her head in finality.

' 'Ow long d'you reckon 'twill allow ye, countin' from now, dearie?'

'Slow come, slow go. But if I don't set eyes on ye 'fore next hoppin', this'll be good-bye, Liz.'

'Dunno as I'll be able to manage by then—not 'thout I have a liddle dog to lead me. For de chillern, dey won't be troubled, an'—O Gra'!—I'm blindin' up—I'm blindin' up!'

'Oh, *dat* was why you didn't more'n finger with your quilt-patches all this while! I was wonderin' ... But the pain *do* count, don't ye think, Liz? The pain *do* count to keep 'Arry—where I want 'im. Say it can't be wasted, like.'

'I'm sure of it—sure of it, dearie. You'll 'ave your reward.'

'I don't want no more'n this—*if* de pain is taken into de reckonin'.'

' 'Twill be—'twill be, Gra'.'

There was a knock on the door.

'That's Nurse. She's before 'er time,' said Mrs. Ashcroft. 'Open to 'er.'

The young lady entered briskly, all the bottles in her bag clicking. 'Evenin', Mrs. Ashcroft,' she began. 'I've come raound a little earlier than usual because of the Institute dance to-na-ite. You won't ma-ind, will you?'

'Oh, no. Me dancin' days are over.' Mrs. Ashcroft was the self-contained domestic at once. 'My old friend, Mrs. Fettley 'ere, has been settin' talkin' with me a while.'

'I hope she 'asn't been fatiguing you?' said the Nurse a little frostily.

'Quite the contrary. It 'as been a pleasure. Only— only—just at the end I felt a bit—a bit flogged out, like.'

'Yes, yes.' The Nurse was on her knees already, with the washes to hand. 'When old ladies get together they talk a deal too much, I've noticed.'

'Mebbe we do,' said Mrs. Fettley, rising. 'So, now, I'll make myself scarce.'

'Look at it first, though,' said Mrs. Ashcroft feebly. 'I'd like ye to look at it.'

Mrs. Fettley looked, and shivered. Then she leaned over, and kissed Mrs. Ashcroft once on the waxy yellow forehead, and again on the faded grey eyes.

'It *do* count, don't it—de pain?' The lips that still kept trace of their original moulding hardly more than breathed the words.

Mrs. Fettley kissed them and moved towards the door.

1924

MARY POSTGATE

Of Miss Mary Postgate, Lady McCausland wrote that she was 'thoroughly conscientious, tidy, companionable, and ladylike. I am very sorry to part with her, and shall always be interested in her welfare.'

Miss Fowler engaged her on this recommendation, and to her surprise, for she had had experience of companions, found that it was true. Miss Fowler was nearer sixty than fifty at the time, but though she needed care she did not exhaust her attendant's vitality. On the contrary, she gave out, stimulatingly and with reminiscences. Her father had been a minor Court official in the days when the Great Exhibition of 1851 had just set its seal on Civilisation made perfect. Some of Miss Fowler's tales, none the less, were not always for the young. Mary was not young, and though her speech was as colourless as her eyes or her hair, she was never shocked. She listened unflinchingly to every one; said at the end, 'How interesting!' or 'How shocking!' as the case might be, and never again referred to it, for she prided herself on a trained mind, which 'did not dwell on these things.' She was, too, a treasure at domestic accounts, for which the village tradesmen, with their weekly books, loved her not. Otherwise she had no enemies; provoked no jealousy even among the plainest; neither gossip nor slander had ever been traced to her; she supplied the odd place at the Rector's or the Doctor's table at half an hour's notice; she was a sort of public aunt to very many small children of the village street, whose parents, while accepting everything, would have been swift to resent what they called 'patronage'; she served on the Village Nursing Committee as Miss Fowler's nominee when Miss Fowler was crippled by rheumatoid arthritis, and came out of six months' fortnightly meetings equally respected by all the cliques.

And when Fate threw Miss Fowler's nephew, an unlovely orphan of eleven, on Miss Fowler's hands, Mary Postgate stood to her share of the business of education as practised in private and public schools. She checked printed clothes-lists, and unitemised bills of extras; wrote to Head and House masters, matrons, nurses and doctors, and grieved or rejoiced over half-term reports. Young Wyndham Fowler repaid her in his holidays by calling her 'Gatepost,' 'Postey,' or 'Packthread,' by thumping her between her narrow shoulders, or by chasing her bleating, round the garden, her large mouth open, her large nose high in air, at a stiff-necked shamble very like a camel's. Later on he filled the house with clamour, argument, and harangues as to his personal needs, likes and dislikes, and the limitations of 'you women,' reducing Mary to tears of physical fatigue, or, when he chose to be humorous, of helpless laughter. At crises, which multiplied as he grew older, she was his ambassadress and his interpretress to Miss Fowler, who had no large sympathy with the young; a vote in his interest at the councils on his future; his sewing-woman, strictly accountable for mislaid boots and garments; always his butt and his slave.

And when he decided to become a solicitor, and had entered an office in London; when his greeting had changed from 'Hullo, Postey, you old beast,' to 'Mornin', Packthread,' there came a war which, unlike all wars that Mary could remember, did not stay decently outside England and in the newspapers, but intruded on the lives of people whom she knew. As she said to Miss Fowler, it was 'most vexatious.' It took the Rector's son who was going into business with his elder brother; it took the Colonel's nephew on the eve of fruit-farming in Canada; it took Mrs. Grant's son who, his mother said, was devoted to the ministry; and, very early indeed, it took Wynn Fowler, who announced on a postcard that he had joined the Flying Corps and wanted a cardigan waistcoat.

'He must go, and he must have the waistcoat,' said Miss Fowler. So Mary got the proper-sized needles and wool, while Miss Fowler told the men of her establishment— two gardeners and an odd man, aged sixty—that those who could join the Army had better do so. The gardeners left. Cheape, the odd man, stayed on, and was promoted to the gardener's cottage. The cook, scorning to be limited in luxuries, also left, after a spirited scene with Miss Fowler, and took the housemaid with her. Miss Fowler gazetted Nellie, Cheape's seventeen-year-old daughter, to the vacant post; Mrs. Cheape to the rank of cook, with occasional cleaning bouts; and the reduced establishment moved forward smoothly.

Wynn demanded an increase in his allowance. Miss Fowler, who always looked facts in the face, said, 'He must have it. The chances are he won't live long to draw it, and if three hundred makes him happy—'

Wynn was grateful, and came over, in his tight-buttoned uniform, to say so. His training centre was not thirty miles away, and his talk was so technical that it had to be explained by charts of the various types of machines. He gave Mary such a chart.

'And you'd better study it, Postey,' he said. 'You'll be seeing a lot of 'em soon.' So Mary studied the chart, but when Wynn next arrived to swell and exalt himself before his womenfolk, she failed badly in cross-examination, and he rated her as in the old days.

'You *look* more or less like a human being,' he said in his new Service voice. 'You *must* have had a brain at some time in your past. What have you done with it? Where d'you keep it? A sheep would know more than you do, Postey. You're lamentable. You are less use than an empty tin can, you dowey old cassowary.'

'I suppose that's how your superior officer talks to *you?*' said Miss Fowler from her chair.

'But Postey doesn't mind,' Wynn replied. 'Do you, Packthread?'

'Why? Was Wynn saying anything? I shall get this right next time you come,' she muttered, and knitted her pale brows again over the diagrams of Taubes, Farmans, and Zeppelins.

In a few weeks the mere land and sea battles which she read to Miss Fowler after breakfast passed her like idle breath. Her heart and her interest were high in the air with Wynn, who had finished 'rolling' (whatever that might be) and had gone on from a 'taxi' to a machine more or less his own. One morning it circled over their very chimneys, alighted on Vegg's Heath, almost outside the garden gate, and Wynn came in, blue with cold, shouting for food. He and she drew Miss Fowler's bath-chair, as they had often done, along the Heath foot-path to look at the biplane. Mary observed that 'it smelt very badly.'

'Postey, I believe you think with your nose,' said Wynn. 'I know you don't with your mind. Now what type's that?'

'I'll go and get the chart,' said Mary.

'You're hopeless! You haven't the mental capacity of a white mouse,' he cried, and explained the dials and the sockets for bomb-dropping till it was time to mount and ride the wet clouds once more.

'Ah!' said Mary, as the stinking thing flared upward. 'Wait till our Flying Corps gets to work! Wynn says it's much safer than in the trenches.'

'I wonder,' said Miss Fowler. 'Tell Cheape to come and tow me home again.'

'It's all downhill. I can do it,' said Mary, 'if you put the brake on.' She laid her lean self against the pushing-bar and home they trundled.

'Now, be careful you aren't heated and catch a chill,' said overdressed Miss Fowler.

'Nothing makes me perspire,' said Mary. As she bumped the chair under the porch she straightened her long back. The exertion had given her a colour, and the wind had loosened a wisp of hair across her forehead. Miss Fowler glanced at her.

'What do you ever think of, Mary?' she demanded suddenly.

'Oh, Wynn says he wants another three pairs of stockings—as thick as we can make them.'

'Yes. But I mean the things that women think about. Here you are, more than forty—'

'Forty-four,' said truthful Mary.

'Well?'

'Well?' Mary offered Miss Fowler her shoulder as usual.

'And you've been with me ten years now.'

'Let's see,' said Mary. 'Wynn was eleven when he came. He's twenty now, and I came two years before that. It must be eleven.'

'Eleven! And you've never told me anything that matters in all that while. Looking back, it seems to me that *I*'ve done all the talking.'

'I'm afraid I'm not much of a conversationalist. As Wynn says, I haven't the mind. Let me take your hat.'

Miss Fowler, moving stiffly from the hip, stamped her rubber-tipped stick on the tiled hall floor. 'Mary, aren't you *anything* except a companion? Would you *ever* have been anything except a companion?'

Mary hung up the garden hat on its proper peg. 'No,' she said after consideration. 'I don't imagine I ever should. But I've no imagination, I'm afraid.'

She fetched Miss Fowler her eleven-o'clock glass of Contrexéville.

That was the wet December when it rained six inches to the month, and the women went abroad as little as might be. Wynn's flying chariot visited them several times, and for two mornings (he had warned her by postcard) Mary heard the thresh of his propellers at dawn.

The second time she ran to the window, and stared at the whitening sky. A little blur passed overhead. She lifted her lean arms towards it.

That evening at six o'clock there came an announcement in an official envelope that Second Lieutenant W. Fowler had been killed during a trial flight. Death was instantaneous. She read it and carried it to Miss Fowler.

'I never expected anything else,' said Miss Fowler; 'but I'm sorry it happened before he had done anything.'

The room was whirling round Mary Postgate, but she found herself quite steady in the midst of it.

'Yes,' she said. 'It's a great pity he didn't die in action after he had killed somebody.'

'He was killed instantly. That's one comfort,' Miss Fowler went on.

'But Wynn says the shock of a fall kills a man at once—whatever happens to the tanks,' quoted Mary.

The room was coming to rest now. She heard Miss Fowler say impatiently, 'But why can't we cry, Mary?' and herself replying, 'There's nothing to cry for. He has done his duty as much as Mrs. Grant's son did.'

'And when he died, *she* came and cried all the morning,' said Miss Fowler. 'This only makes me feel tired—terribly tired. Will you help me to bed, please, Mary?—And I think I'd like the hot-water bottle.'

So Mary helped her and sat beside, talking of Wynn in his riotous youth.

'I believe,' said Miss Fowler suddenly, 'that old people and young people slip from under a stroke like this. The middle-aged feel it most.'

'I expect that's true,' said Mary, rising. 'I'm going to put away the things in his room now. Shall we wear mourning?'

'Certainly not,' said Miss Fowler. 'Except, of course, at the funeral. I can't go. You will. I want you to arrange about his being buried here. What a blessing it didn't happen at Salisbury!'

Every one, from the Authorities of the Flying Corps to the Rector, was most kind and sympathetic. Mary found herself for the moment in a world where bodies were in the habit of being despatched by all sorts of conveyances to all sorts of places. And at the funeral two young men in buttoned-up uniforms stood beside the grave and spoke to her afterwards.

'You're Miss Postgate, aren't you?' said one. 'Fowler told me about you. He was a good chap—a first-class fellow—a great loss.'

'Great loss!' growled his companion. 'We're all awfully sorry.'

'How high did he fall from?' Mary whispered.

'Pretty nearly four thousand feet, I should think, didn't he? You were up that day, Monkey?'

'All of that,' the other child replied. 'My bar made three thousand, and I wasn't as high as him by a lot.'

'Then *that's* all right,' said Mary. 'Thank you very much.'

They moved away as Mrs. Grant flung herself weeping on Mary's flat chest, under the lych-gate, and cried, '*I* know how it feels! *I* know how it feels!'

'But both his parents are dead,' Mary returned, as she fended her off. 'Perhaps they've all met by now,' she added vaguely as she escaped towards the coach.

'I've thought of that too,' wailed Mrs. Grant; 'but then he'll be practically a stranger to them. Quite embarrassing!'

Mary faithfully reported every detail of the ceremony to Miss Fowler, who, when she described Mrs. Grant's outburst, laughed aloud.

'Oh, how Wynn would have enjoyed it! He was always utterly unreliable at funerals. D'you remember—' And they talked of him again, each piecing out the other's gaps. 'And now,' said Miss Fowler, 'we'll pull up the blinds and we'll have a general tidy. That always does us good. Have you seen to Wynn's things?'

'Everything—since he first came,' said Mary. 'He was never destructive—even with his toys.'

They faced that neat room.

'It can't be natural not to cry,' Mary said at last. 'I'm *so* afraid you'll have a reaction.'

'As I told you, we old people slip from under the stroke. It's you I'm afraid for. Have you cried yet?'

'I can't. It only makes me angry with the Germans.'

'That's sheer waste of vitality,' said Miss Fowler. 'We must live till the war's finished.' She opened a full wardrobe. 'Now, I've been thinking things over. This is my plan. All his civilian clothes can be given away—Belgian refugees, and so on.'

Mary nodded. 'Boots, collars, and gloves?'

'Yes. We don't need to keep anything except his cap and belt.'

'They came back yesterday with his Flying Corps clothes'—Mary pointed to a roll on the little iron bed.

'Ah, but keep his Service things. Some one may be glad of them later. Do you remember his sizes?'

'Five feet eight and a half; thirty-six inches round the chest. But he told me he's just put on an inch and a half. I'll mark it on a label and tie it on his sleeping-bag.'

'So that disposes of *that*,' said Miss Fowler, tapping the palm of one hand with the ringed third finger of the other. 'What waste it all is! We'll get his old school trunk to-morrow and pack his civilian clothes.'

'And the rest?' said Mary. 'His books and pictures and the games and the toys—and—and the rest?'

'My plan is to burn every single thing,' said Miss Fowler. 'Then we shall know where they are and no one can handle them afterwards. What do you think?'

'I think that would be much the best,' said Mary. 'But there's such a lot of them.'

'We'll burn them in the destructor,' said Miss Fowler.

This was an open-air furnace for the consumption of refuse; a little circular four-foot tower of pierced brick over an iron grating. Miss Fowler had noticed the design in a gardening journal years ago, and had had it built at the bottom of the garden. It suited her tidy soul, for it saved unsightly rubbish-heaps, and the ashes lightened the stiff clay soil.

Mary considered for a moment, saw her way clear, and nodded again. They spent the evening putting away well-remembered civilian suits, underclothes that Mary had marked, and the regiments of very gaudy socks and ties. A second trunk was needed, and, after that, a little packing-case, and it was late next day when Cheape and the local carrier lifted them to the cart. The Rector luckily knew of a friend's son, about five feet eight and a half inches high, to whom a complete Flying Corps outfit would be most acceptable, and sent his gardener's son down with a barrow to take delivery of it. The cap was hung up in Miss Fowler's bedroom, the belt in Miss Postgate's; for, as Miss Fowler said, they had no desire to make tea-party talk of them.

'That disposes of *that*,' said Miss Fowler. 'I'll leave the rest to you, Mary. I can't run up and down the garden. You'd better take the big clothes-basket and get Nellie to help you.'

'I shall take the wheel-barrow and do it myself,' said Mary, and for once in her life closed her mouth.

Miss Fowler, in moments of irritation, had called Mary deadly methodical. She put on her oldest waterproof and gardening-hat and her ever-slipping goloshes, for the weather was on the edge of more rain. She gathered fire-lighters from the kitchen, a half-scuttle of coals, and a fag-got of brushwood. These she wheeled in the barrow down the mossed paths to the dank little laurel shrubbery where the destructor stood under the drip of three oaks. She climbed the wire fence into the Rector's glebe just behind, and from his tenant's rick pulled two large armfuls of good hay, which she spread neatly on the fire-bars. Next, jour-ney by journey, passing Miss Fowler's white face at the morning-room window each time, she brought down in the towel-covered clothes-basket, on the wheelbarrow, thumbed and used Hentys, Marryats, Levers, Stevensons, Baroness Orczy's, Garvices, schoolbooks, and atlases, unrelated piles of the *Motor Cyclist*, the *Light Car*, and catalogues of Olympia Exhibitions; the remnants of a fleet of sailing-ships from ninepenny cutters to a three-guinea yacht; a prep.-school dressing-gown; bats from three-and-sixpence to twenty-four shillings; cricket and tennis balls; disintegrated steam and clockwork locomotives with their twisted rails; a grey and red tin model of a submarine; a dumb gramophone and cracked records; golf-clubs that had to be broken across the knee, like his walking-sticks, and an assegai; photographs of private and public school cricket and football elevens, and his O.T.C. on the line of march; kodaks, and film-rolls; some pewters, and one real silver cup, for boxing competitions and Junior Hurdles; sheaves of school photographs; Miss Fowler's photograph; her own which he had borne off in fun and (good care she took not to ask!) had never returned; a playbox with a secret drawer; a load of flannels, belts, and jerseys, and a pair of spiked shoes unearthed in the attic; a packet of all the letters that Miss Fowler and she had ever written to him, kept for some absurd reason through all these years; a five-day attempt at a diary; framed pictures of racing motors in full Brooklands career, and load upon load of undistinguishable wreckage of tool-boxes, rabbit-hutches, electric batteries, tin soldiers, fret-saw outfits, and jig-saw puzzles.

Miss Fowler at the window watched her come and go, and said to herself, 'Mary's an old woman. I never realised it before.'

After lunch she recommended her to rest.

'I'm not in the least tired,' said Mary. 'I've got it all arranged. I'm going to the village at two o'clock for some paraffin. Nellie hasn't enough, and the walk will do me good.'

She made one last quest round the house before she started, and found that she had overlooked nothing. It began to mist as soon as she had skirted Vegg's Heath, where Wynn used to descend—it seemed to her that she could almost hear the beat of his propellers overhead, but there was nothing to see. She hoisted her umbrella and lunged into the blind wet till she had reached the shelter of the empty village. As she came out of Mr. Kidd's shop with a bottle full of paraffin in her string shopping-bag, she met Nurse Eden, the village nurse, and fell into talk with her, as usual, about the village children. They were just parting opposite the 'Royal Oak,' when a gun, they fancied, was fired immediately behind the house. It was followed by a child's shriek dying into a wail.

'Accident!' said Nurse Eden promptly, and dashed through the empty bar, followed by Mary. They found Mrs. Gerritt, the publican's wife, who could only gasp and point to the yard, where a little cart-lodge was sliding sideways amid a clatter of tiles. Nurse Eden snatched up a sheet drying before the fire, ran out, lifted something from the ground, and flung the sheet round it. The sheet turned scarlet and half her uniform too, as she bore the load into the kitchen. It was little Edna Gerritt, aged nine, whom Mary had known since her perambulator days.

'Am I hurted bad?' Edna asked, and died between Nurse Eden's dripping hands. The sheet fell aside and for an instant, before she could shut her eyes, Mary saw the ripped and shredded body.

'It's a wonder she spoke at all,' said Nurse Eden. 'What in God's name was it?'

'A bomb,' said Mary.

'One o' the Zeppelins?'

'No. An aeroplane. I thought I heard it on the Heath, but I fancied it was one of ours. It must have shut off its engines as it came down. That's why we didn't notice it.'

'The filthy pigs!' said Nurse Eden, all white and shaken. 'See the pickle I'm in! Go and tell Dr. Hennis, Miss Postgate.' Nurse looked at the mother, who had dropped face down on the floor. 'She's only in a fit. Turn her over.'

Mary heaved Mrs. Gerritt right side up, and hurried off for the doctor. When she told her tale, he asked her to sit down in the surgery till he got her something.

'But I don't need it, I assure you,' said she. 'I don't think it would be wise to tell Miss Fowler about it, do you? Her heart is so irritable in this weather.'

Dr. Hennis looked at her admiringly as he packed up his bag.

'No. Don't tell anybody till we're sure,' he said, and hastened to the 'Royal Oak,' while Mary went on with the paraffin. The village behind her was as quiet as usual, for the news had not yet spread. She frowned a little to herself, her large nostrils expanded uglily, and from time to time she muttered a phrase which Wynn, who never restrained himself before his womenfolk, had applied to the enemy. 'Bloody pagans! They *are* bloody pagans. But,' she continued, falling back on the teaching that had made her what she was, 'one mustn't let one's mind dwell on these things.'

Before she reached the house Dr. Hennis, who was also a special constable, overtook her in his car.

'Oh, Miss Postgate,' he said, 'I wanted to tell you that that accident at the "Royal Oak" was due to Gerritt's stable tumbling down. It's been dangerous for a long time. It ought to have been condemned.'

'I thought I heard an explosion, too,' said Mary.

'You might have been misled by the beams snapping. I've been looking at 'em. They were dry-rotted through and through. Of course, as they broke, they would make a noise just like a gun.'

'Yes?' said Mary politely.

'Poor little Edna was playing underneath it,' he went on, still holding her with his eyes, 'and that and the tiles cut her to pieces, you see?'

'I saw it,' said Mary, shaking her head. 'I heard it too.'

'Well, we cannot be sure.' Dr. Hennis changed his tone completely. 'I know both you and Nurse Eden (I've been speaking to her) are perfectly trustworthy, and I can rely on you not to say anything—yet at least. It is no good to stir up people unless—'

'Oh, I never do—anyhow,' said Mary, and Dr. Hennis went on to the county town.

After all, she told herself, it might, just possibly, have been the collapse of the old stable that had done all those things to poor little Edna. She was sorry she had even hinted at other things, but Nurse Eden was discretion itself. By the time she reached home the affair seemed increasingly remote by its very monstrosity. As she came in, Miss Fowler told her that a couple of aeroplanes had passed half an hour ago.

'I thought I heard them,' she replied. 'I'm going down to the garden now. I've got the paraffin.'

'Yes, but—what *have* you got on your boots? They're soaking wet. Change them at once.'

Not only did Mary obey but she wrapped the boots in a newspaper, and put them into the string bag with the bottle. So, armed with the longest kitchen poker, she left.

'It's raining again,' was Miss Fowler's last word, 'but—I know you won't be happy till that's disposed of.'

'It won't take long. I've got everything down there, and I've put the lid on the destructor to keep the wet out.'

The shrubbery was filling with twilight by the time she had completed her arrangemments and sprinkled the sacrificial oil. As she lit the match that would burn her heart to ashes, she heard a groan or a grunt behind the dense Portugal laurels.

'Cheape?' she called impatiently, but Cheape, with his ancient lumbago, in his comfortable cottage would be the last man to profane the sanctuary. 'Sheep,' she concluded, and threw in the fusee. The pyre went up in a roar, and the immediate flame hastened night around her.

'How Wynn would have loved this!' she thought, step-ping back from the blaze.

By its light she saw, half hidden behind a laurel not five paces away, a bareheaded man sitting very stiffly at the foot of one of the oaks. A broken branch lay across his lap—one booted leg protruding from beneath it. His head moved ceaselessly from side to side, but his body was as still as the tree's trunk. He was dressed—she moved side-ways to look more closely—in a uniform something like Wynn's, with a flap buttoned across the chest. For an in-stant, she had some idea that it might be one of the young flying men she had met at the funeral. But their heads were dark and glossy. This man's was as pale as a baby's, and so closely cropped that she could see the disgusting pinky skin beneath. His lips moved.

'What do you say?' Mary moved towards him and stooped.

'Laty! Laty! Laty!' he muttered, while his hands picked at the dead wet leaves. There was no doubt as to his na-tionality. It made her so angry that she strode back to the destructor, though it was still too hot to use the poker there. Wynn's books seemed to be catching well. She looked up at the oak behind the man; several of the light upper and two or three rotten lower branches had broken and scattered their rubbish on the shrubbery path. On the lowest fork a helmet with dependent strings, showed like a bird's-nest in the light of a long-tongued flame. Evidently this person had fallen through the tree. Wynn had told her that it was quite possible for people to fall out of aero-planes. Wynn told her too, that trees were useful things to break an aviator's fall, but in this case the aviator must have been broken or he would have moved from his queer position. He seemed helpless except for his horrible roll-ing head. On the other hand, she could see a pistol case at his belt—and Mary loathed pistols. Months ago, after reading certain Belgian reports together, she and Miss

Fowler had had dealings with one—a huge revolver with flat-nosed bullets, which latter, Wynn said, were forbidden by the rules of war to be used against civilised enemies. 'They're good enough for us,' Miss Fowler had replied. 'Show Mary how it works.' And Wynn, laughing at the mere possibility of any such need, had led the craven winking Mary into the Rector's disused quarry, and had shown her how to fire the terrible machine. It lay now in the top-left-hand drawer of her toilet-table—a memento not included in the burning. Wynn would be pleased to see how she was not afraid.

She slipped up to the house to get it. When she came through the rain, the eyes in the head were alive with expectation. The mouth even tried to smile. But at sight of the revolver its corners went down just like Edna Gerritt's. A tear trickled from one eye, and the head rolled from shoulder to shoulder as though trying to point out something.

'Cassée. Tout cassée,' it whimpered.

'What do you say?' said Mary disgustedly, keeping well to one side, though only the head moved.

'Cassée,' it repeated. 'Che me rends. Le médecin! Toctor!'

'Nein!' said she, bringing all her small German to bear with the big pistol. 'Ich haben der todt Kinder gesehn.'

The head was still. Mary's hand dropped. She had been careful to keep her finger off the trigger for fear of accidents. After a few moments' waiting, she returned to the destructor, where the flames were falling, and churned up Wynn's charring books with the poker. Again the head groaned for the doctor.

'Stop that!' said Mary, and stamped her foot. 'Stop that, you bloody pagan!'

The words came quite smoothly and naturally. They were Wynn's own words, and Wynn was a gentleman who for no consideration on earth would have torn little Edna into those vividly coloured strips and strings. But

this thing hunched under the oak-tree had done that thing.
It was no question of reading horrors out of newspapers to
Miss Fowler. Mary had seen it with her own eyes on the
'Royal Oak' kitchen table. She must not allow her mind to
dwell upon it. Now Wynn was dead, and everything connected with him was lumping and rustling and tinkling
under her busy poker into red black dust and grey leaves
of ash. The thing beneath the oak would die too. Mary had
seen death more than once. She came of a family that had a
knack of dying under, as she told Miss Fowler, 'most distressing circumstances.' She would stay where she was till
she was entirely satisfied that It was dead—dead as dear
papa in the late 'eighties; aunt Mary in 'eighty-nine,
mamma in 'ninety-one; cousin Dick in 'ninety-five; Lady
McCausland's housemaid in 'ninety-nine; Lady McCausland's sister in nineteen hundred and one; Wynn buried
five days ago; and Edna Gerritt still waiting for decent
earth to hide her. As she thought—her underlip caught up
by one faded canine, brows knit and nostrils wide—she
wielded the poker with lunges that jarred the grating at
the bottom, and careful scrapes round the brick-work
above. She looked at her wrist-watch. It was getting on to
half-past four, and the rain was coming down in earnest
Tea would be at five. If It did not die before that time, she
would be soaked and would have to change. Meantime,
and this occupied her, Wynn's things were burning well
in spite of the hissing wet, though now and again a book-
back with a quite distinguishable title would be heaved up
out of the mass. The exercise of stoking had given her a
glow which seemed to reach to the marrow of her bones.
She hummed—Mary never had a voice—to herself. She
had never believed in all those advanced views—though
Miss Fowler herself leaned a little that way—of woman's
work in the world; but now she saw there was much to be
said for them. This, for instance, was *her* work—work
which no man, least of all Dr. Hennis, would ever have
done. A man, at such a crisis, would be what Wynn called

a 'sportsman'; would leave everything to fetch help, and would certainly bring It into the house. Now a woman's business was to make a happy home for—for a husband and children. Failing these—it was not a thing one should allow one's mind to dwell upon—but—

'Stop it!' Mary cried once more across the shadows. 'Nein, I tell you! Ich haben der todt Kinder gesehn.'

But it was a fact. A woman who had missed these things could still be useful—more useful than a man in certain respects. She thumped like a pavior through the settling ashes at the secret thrill of it. The rain was damping the fire, but she could feel—it was too dark to see—that her work was done. There was a dull red glow at the bottom of the destructor, not enough to char the wooden lid if she slipped it half over against the driving wet. This arranged, she leaned on the poker and waited, while an increasing rapture laid hold on her. She ceased to think. She gave herself up to feel. Her long pleasure was broken by a sound that she had waited for in agony several times in her life. She leaned forward and listened, smiling. There could be no mistake. She closed her eyes and drank it in. Once it ceased abruptly.

'Go on,' she murmured, half aloud. 'That isn't the end.'

Then the end came very distinctly in a lull between two rain-gusts. Mary Postgate drew her breath short between her teeth and shivered from head to foot. '*That's* all right,' said she contentedly, and went up to the house, where she scandalised the whole routine by taking a luxurious hot bath before tea, and came down looking, as Miss Fowler said when she saw her lying all relaxed on the other sofa, 'quite handsome!'

1915

THE GARDENER

One grave to me was given
   One watch till Judgment Day;
And God looked down from Heaven
   And rolled the stone away.

One day in all the years,
   One hour in that one day,
His Angel saw my tears,
   And rolled the stone away!

Every one in the village knew that Helen Turrell did her duty by all her world, and by none more honourably than by her only brother's unfortunate child. The village knew, too, that George Turrell had tried his family severely since early youth, and were not surprised to be told that, after many fresh starts given and thrown away, he, an Inspector of Indian Police, had entangled himself with the daughter of a retired non-commissioned officer, and had died of a fall from a horse a few weeks before his child was born. Mercifully, George's father and mother were both dead, and though Helen, thirty-five and independent, might well have washed her hands of the whole disgraceful affair, she most nobly took charge, though she was, at the time, under threat of lung trouble which had driven her to the South of France. She arranged for the passage of the child and a nurse from Bombay, met them at Marseilles, nursed the baby through an attack of infantile dysentery due to the carelessness of the nurse, whom she had had to dismiss, and at last, thin and worn but triumphant, brought the boy late in the autumn, wholly restored, to her Hampshire home.

All these details were public property, for Helen was as open as the day, and held that scandals are only increased by hushing them up. She admitted that George had always been rather a black sheep, but things might have been much worse if the mother had insisted on her right to keep the boy. Luckily, it seemed that people of that class would do almost anything for money, and, as George had always turned to her in his scrapes, she felt herself justified—her friends agreed with her—in cutting the whole non-commissioned officer connection, and giving the child every advantage. A christening, by the Rector, under the name of Michael, was the first step. So far as she knew herself, she was not, she said, a child-lover, but, for all his faults, she had been very fond of George, and she pointed out that little Michael had his father's mouth to a line; which made something to build upon.

As a matter of fact, it was the Turrell forehead, broad, low, and well-shaped, with the widely-spaced eyes beneath it, that Michael had most faithfully reproduced. His mouth was somewhat better cut than the family type. But Helen, who would concede nothing good to his mother's side, vowed he was a Turrell all over, and, there being no one to contradict, the likeness was established.

In a few years Michael took his place, as accepted as Helen had always been—fearless, philosophical, and fairly good-looking. At six, he wished to know why he could not call her 'Mummy,' as other boys called their mothers. She explained that she was only his auntie, and that aunties were not quite the same as mummies, but that, if it gave him pleasure, he might call her 'Mummy' at bedtime, for a pet-name between themselves.

Michael kept his secret most loyally, but Helen, as usual, explained the fact to her friends; which when Michael heard, he raged.

'Why did you tell? *Why* did you tell?' came at the end of the storm.

'Because it's always best to tell the truth,' Helen answered, her arm round him as he shook in his cot.

'All right, but when the troof's ugly I don't think it's nice.'

'Don't you, dear?'

'No, I don't, and'—she felt the small body stiffen—'now you've told, I won't call you "Mummy" any more—not even at bedtimes.'

'But isn't that rather unkind?' said Helen, softly.

'I don't care! I don't care! You've hurted me in my insides and I'll hurt you back. I'll hurt you as long as I live!'

'Don't, oh, don't talk like that, dear! You don't know what——'

'I will! And when I'm dead I'll hurt you worse!'

'Thank goodness, I shall be dead long before you, darling.'

'Huh! Emma says, " 'Never know your luck." ' (Michael had been talking to Helen's elderly, flat-faced maid.) 'Lots of little boys die quite soon. So'll I. *Then* you'll see!'

Helen caught her breath and moved towards the door, but the wail of 'Mummy! Mummy!' drew her back again, and the two wept together.

At ten years old, after two terms at a prep. school, something or somebody gave him the idea that his civil status was not quite regular. He attacked Helen on the subject, breaking down her stammered defences with the family directness.

' 'Don't believe a word of it,' he said, cheerily, at the end. 'People wouldn't have talked like they did if my people had been married. But don't you bother, Auntie. I've found out all about my sort in English Hist'ry and the Shakespeare bits. There was William the Conqueror to begin with, and—oh, heaps more, and they all got on first-rate. 'Twon't make any difference to you, my being *that*—will it?'

'As if anything could——' she began.

'All right. We won't talk about it any more if it makes you cry.' He never mentioned the thing again of his own will, but when, two years later, he skilfully managed to have measles in the holidays, as his temperature went up to the appointed one hundred and four he muttered of nothing else, till Helen's voice, piercing at last his delirium, reached him with assurance that nothing on earth or beyond could make any difference between them.

The terms at his public school and the wonderful Christmas, Easter and Summer holidays followed each other, variegated and glorious as jewels on a string; and as jewels Helen treasured them. In due time Michael developed his own interests, which ran their courses and gave way to others; but his interest in Helen was constant and increasing throughout. She repaid it with all that she had of affection or could command of counsel and money; and since Michael was no fool, the War took him just before what was like to have been a most promising career.

He was to have gone up to Oxford, with a scholarship, in October. At the end of August he was on the edge of joining the first holocaust of public-school boys who threw themselves into the Line; but the captain of his O.T.C., where he had been sergeant for nearly a year, headed him off and steered him directly to a commission in a battalion so new that half of it still wore the old Army red, and the other half was breeding meningitis through living overcrowdedly in damp tents. Helen had been shocked at the idea of direct enlistment.

'But it's in the family,' Michael laughed.

'You don't mean to tell me that you believed that old story all this time?' said Helen. (Emma, her maid, had been dead now several years.) 'I gave you my word of honour—and I give it again—that—that it's all right. It is indeed.'

'Oh, *that* doesn't worry me. It never did,' he replied valiantly. 'What I meant was, I should have got into the show earlier if I'd enlisted—like my grandfather.'

'Don't talk like that! Are you afraid of it's ending so soon, then?'

'No such luck. You know what K. says.'

'Yes. But my banker told me last Monday it couldn't *possibly* last beyond Christmas—for financial reasons.'

' 'Hope he's right, but our Colonel—and he's a Regular—says it's going to be a long job.'

Michael's battalion was fortunate in that, by some chance which meant several 'leaves,' it was used for coast-defence among shallow trenches on the Norfolk coast; thence sent north to watch the mouth of a Scotch estuary, and, lastly, held for weeks on a baseless rumour of distant service. But, the very day that Michael was to have met Helen for four whole hours at a railway-junction up the line, it was hurled out, to help make good the wastage of Loos, and he had only just time to send her a wire of farewell.

In France luck again helped the battalion. It was put down near the Salient, where it led a meritorious and un-exacting life, while the Somme was being manufactured; and enjoyed the peace of the Armentières and Laventie sectors when that battle began. Finding that it had sound views on protecting its own flanks and could dig, a prudent Commander stole it out of its own Division, under pretence of helping to lay telegraphs, and used it round Ypres at large.

A month later, and just after Michael had written Helen that there was nothing special doing and therefore no need to worry, a shell-splinter dropping out of a wet dawn killed him at once. The next shell uprooted and laid down over the body what had been the foundation of a barn wall, so neatly that none but an expert would have guessed that anything unpleasant had happened.

* * *

By this time the village was old in experience of war, and, English fashion, had evolved a ritual to meet it. When the postmistress handed her seven-year-old daughter the official telegram to take to Miss Turrell, she observed to the Rector's gardener: 'It's Miss Helen's turn now.' He replied, thinking of his own son: 'Well, he's lasted longer than some.' The child herself came to the front-door weeping aloud, because Master Michael had often given her sweets. Helen, presently, found herself pulling down the house-blinds one after one with great care, and saying earnestly to each: 'Missing *always* means dead.' Then she took her place in the dreary procession that was impelled to go through an inevitable series of unprofitable emotions. The Rector, of course, preached hope and prophesied word, very soon, from a prison camp. Several friends, too, told her perfectly truthful tales, but always about other women, to whom, after months and months of silence, their missing had been miraculously restored. Other people urged her to communicate with infallible Secretaries of organisations who could communicate with benevolent neutrals, who could extract accurate information from the most secretive of Hun prison commandants. Helen did and wrote and signed everything that was suggested or put before her.

Once, on one of Michael's leaves, he had taken her over a munition factory, where she saw the progress of a shell from blank-iron to the all but finished article. It struck her at the time that the wretched thing was never left alone for a single second; and 'I'm being manufactured into a bereaved next-of-kin,' she told herself, as she prepared her documents.

In due course, when all the organisations had deeply or sincerely regretted their inability to trace, etc., something gave way within her and all sensation—save of thankfulness for the release—came to an end in blessed passivity. Michael had died and her world had stood still and she had been one with the full shock of that arrest. Now she was standing still and the world was going forward, but it did not concern her—in no way or relation did it touch her. She knew this by the ease with which she could slip Michael's name into talk and incline her head to the proper angle, at the proper murmur of sympathy.

In the blessed realisation of that relief, the Armistice with all its bells broke over her and passed unheeded. At the end of another year she had overcome her physical loathing of the living and returned young, so that she could take them by the hand and almost sincerely wish them well. She had no interest in any aftermath, national or personal, of the War, but, moving at an immense distance, she sat on various relief committees and held strong views—she heard herself delivering them—about the site of the proposed village War Memorial.

Then there came to her, as next-of-kin, an official intimation, backed by a page of a letter to her in indelible pencil, a silver identity-disc, and a watch, to the effect that the body of Lieutenant Michael Turrell had been found, identified, and re-interred in Hagenzeele Third Military Cemetery—the letter of the row and the grave's number in that row duly given.

So Helen found herself moved on to another process of the manufacture—to a world full of exultant or broken relatives, now strong in the certainty that there was an altar upon earth where they might lay their love. These soon told her, and by means of time-tables made clear, how easy it was and how little it interfered with life's affairs to go and see one's grave.

'So different,' as the Rector's wife said, 'if he'd been killed in Mesopotamia, or even Gallipoli.'

The agony of being waked up to some sort of second life drove Helen across the Channel, where, in a new world of abbreviated titles, she learnt that Hagenzeele Third could be comfortably reached by an afternoon train which fitted in with the morning boat, and that there was a comfortable little hotel not three kilometres from Hagenzeele itself, where one could spend quite a comfortable night and see one's grave next morning. All this she had from a Central Authority who lived in a board and tar-paper shed on the skirts of a razed city full of whirling lime-dust and blown papers.

'By the way,' said he, 'you know your grave, of course?'

'Yes, thank you,' said Helen, and showed its row and number typed on Michael's own little typewriter. The officer would have checked it, out of one of his many books; but a large Lancashire woman thrust between them and bade him tell her where she might find her son, who had been corporal in the A.S.C. His proper name, she sobbed, was Anderson, but, coming of respectable folk, he had of course enlisted under the name of Smith; and had been killed at Dickiebush, in early 'Fifteen. She had not his number nor did she know which of his two Christian names he might have used with his alias; but her Cook's tourist ticket expired at the end of Easter week, and if by then she could not find her child she should go mad. Whereupon she fell forward on Helen's breast; but the officer's wife came out quickly from a little bedroom behind the office, and the three of them lifted the woman on to the cot.

'They are often like this,' said the officer's wife, loosening the tight bonnet-strings. 'Yesterday she said he'd been killed at Hooge. Are you sure you know your grave? It makes such a difference.'

'Yes, thank you,' said Helen, and hurried out before the woman on the bed should begin to lament again.

Tea in a crowded mauve and blue striped wooden structure, with a false front, carried her still further into the nightmare. She paid her bill beside a stolid, plain-featured Englishwoman, who, hearing her inquire about the train to Hagenzeele, volunteered to come with her.

'I'm going to Hagenzeele myself,' she explained. 'Not to

Hagenzeele Third; mine is Sugar Factory, but they call it La Rosière now. It's just south of Hagenzeele Three. Have you got your room at the hotel there?'

'Oh yes, thank you. I've wired.'

'That's better. Sometimes the place is quite full, and at others there's hardly a soul. But they've put bathrooms into the old Lion d'Or—that's the hotel on the west side of Sugar Factory—and it draws off a lot of people, luckily.'

'It's all new to me. This is the first time I've been over.'

'Indeed! This is my ninth time since the Armistice. Not on my own account. *I* haven't lost any one, thank God— but, like every one else, I've a lot of friends at home who have. Coming over as often as I do, I find it helps them to have some one just look at the—the place and tell them about it afterwards. And one can take photos for them, too. I get quite a list of commissions to execute.' She laughed nervously and tapped her slung Kodak. 'There are two or three to see at Sugar Factory this time, and plenty of others in the cemeteries all about. My system is to save them up, and arrange them, you know. And when I've got enough commissions for one area to make it worth while, I pop over and execute them. It *does* comfort people.'

'I suppose so,' Helen answered, shivering as they entered the little train.

'Of course it does. (Isn't it lucky we've got window-seats?) It must do or they wouldn't ask one to do it, would they? I've a list of quite twelve or fifteen commissions here'—she tapped the Kodak again—'I must sort them out to-night. Oh, I forgot to ask you. What's yours?'

'My nephew,' said Helen. 'But I was very fond of him.'

'Ah yes! I sometimes wonder whether *they* know after death? What do you think?'

'Oh, I don't—I haven't dared to think much about that sort of thing,' said Helen, almost lifting her hands to keep her off.

'Perhaps that's better,' the woman answered. 'The sense

of loss must be enough, I expect. Well, I won't worry you any more.'

Helen was grateful, but when they reached the hotel Mrs. Scarsworth (they had exchanged names) insisted on dining at the same table with her, and after the meal, in the little, hideous salon full of low-voiced relatives, took Helen through her 'commissions' with biographies of the dead, where she happened to know them, and sketches of their next-of-kin. Helen endured till nearly half-past nine, ere she fled to her room.

Almost at once there was a knock at her door and Mrs. Scarsworth entered; her hands, holding the dreadful list, clasped before her.

'Yes—yes—*I* know,' she began. 'You're sick of me, but I want to tell you something. You—you aren't married are you? Then perhaps you won't. . . . But it doesn't matter. I've *got* to tell some one. I can't go on any longer like this.'

'But please——' Mrs. Scarsworth had backed against the shut door, and her mouth worked dryly.

'In a minute,' she said. 'You—you know about these graves of mine I was telling you about downstairs, just now? They really *are* commissions. At least several of them are.' Her eye wandered round the room. 'What extraordinary wall-papers they have in Belgium, don't you think? . . . Yes. I swear they are commissions. But there's *one*, d'you see, and—and he was more to me than anything else in the world. Do you understand?'

Helen nodded.

'More than any one else. And, of course, he oughtn't to have been. He ought to have been nothing to me. But he *was*. He *is*. That's why I do the commissions, you see. That's all.'

'But why do you tell me?' Helen asked desperately.

'Because I'm *so* tired of lying. Tired of lying—always lying—year in and year out. When I don't tell lies I've got to act 'em and I've got to think 'em, always. *You* don't know what that means. He was everything to me that he oughtn't to have been—the one real thing—the only thing that ever happened to me in all my life; and I've had to pretend he wasn't. I've had to watch every word I said, and think out what lie I'd tell next, for years and years!'

'How many years?' Helen asked.

'Six years and four months before, and two and three-quarters after. I've gone to him eight times, since. To-morrow'll make the ninth, and—and I can't—I *can't* go to him again with nobody in the world knowing. I want to be honest with some one before I go. Do you understand? It doesn't matter about *me*. I was never truthful, even as a girl. But it isn't worthy of *him*. So—so I—I had to tell you. I can't keep it up any longer. Oh, I can't!'

She lifted her joined hands almost to the level of her mouth, and brought them down sharply, still joined, to full arm's length below her waist. Helen reached forward, caught them, bowed her head over them, and murmured: 'Oh, my dear! My dear!' Mrs. Scarsworth stepped back, her face all mottled.

'My God!' said she. 'Is *that* how you take it?'

Helen could not speak, the woman went out; but it was a long while before Helen was able to sleep.

Next morning Mrs. Scarsworth left early on her round of commissions, and Helen walked alone to Hagenzeele Third. The place was still in the making, and stood some five or six feet above the metalled road, which it flanked for hundreds of yards. Culverts across a deep ditch served for entrances through the unfinished boundary wall. She climbed a few wooden-faced earthen steps and then met the entire crowded level of the thing in one held breath. She did not know that Hagenzeele Third counted twenty-one thousand dead already. All she saw was a merciless sea of black crosses, bearing little strips of stamped tin at all angles across their faces. She could distinguish no order or arrangement in their mass; nothing but a waist-high wilderness as of weeds stricken dead, rushing at her. She went forward, moved to the left and the right hopelessly, wondering by what guidance she should ever come to her own. A great distance away there was a line of whiteness. It proved to be a block of some two or three hundred graves whose headstones had already been set, whose flowers were planted out, and whose new-sown grass showed green. Here she could see clear-cut letters at the ends of the rows, and, referring to her slip, realised that it was not here she must look.

A man knelt behind a line of headstones—evidently a gardener, for he was firming a young plant in the soft earth. She went towards him, her paper in her hand. He rose at her approach and without prelude or salutation asked: 'Who are you looking for?'

'Lieutenant Michael Turrell—my nephew,' said Helen slowly and word for word, as she had many thousands of times in her life.

The man lifted his eyes and looked at her with infinite compassion before he turned from the fresh-sown grass towards the naked black crosses.

'Come with me,' he said, 'and I will show you where your son lies.'

When Helen left the Cemetery she turned for a last look. In the distance she saw the man bending over his young plants; and she went away, supposing him to be the gardener.

                                                              1925

DAYSPRING MISHANDLED

C'est moi, c'est moi, c'est moi!
   Je suis la Mandragore!
La fille des beaux jours qui s'éveille à l'aurore—
   Et qui chante pour toi!

                                                    C. Nodier

In the days beyond compare and before the Judgments, a
genius called Graydon foresaw that the advance of education and the standard of living would submerge all mind-
marks in one mudrush of standardised reading-matter,
and so created the Fictional Supply Syndicate to meet the
demand.

Since a few days' work for him brought them more
money than a week's elsewhere, he drew many young
men—some now eminent—into his employ. He bade
them keep their eyes on the Sixpenny Dream Book, the
Army and Navy Stores Catalogue (this for backgrounds
and furniture as they changed), and *The Hearthstone
Friend*, a weekly publication which specialised unrival-
ledly in the domestic emotions. Yet, even so, youth would
not be denied, and some of the collaborated love-talk in
'Passion Hath Peril,' and 'Ena's Lost Lovers,' and the account of the murder of the Earl in 'The Wickwire Trage-
dies'—to name but a few masterpieces now never
mentioned for fear of blackmail—was as good as anything
to which their authors signed their real names in more
distinguished years.

Among the young ravens driven to roost awhile on
Graydon's ark was James Andrew Manallace—a darkish,
slow northerner of the type that does not ignite, but must

be detonated. Given written or verbal outlines of a plot, he was useless; but, with a half-dozen pictures round which to write his tale, he could astonish.

And he adored that woman who afterwards became the mother of Vidal Benzaquen,[1] and who suffered and died because she loved one unworthy. There was, also, among the company a mannered, bellied person called Alured Castorley, who talked and wrote about 'Bohemia,' but was always afraid of being 'compromised' by the weekly suppers at Neminaka's Café in Hestern Square, where the Syndicate work was apportioned, and where everyone looked out for himself. He, too, for a time, had loved Vidal's mother, in his own way.

Now, one Saturday at Neminaka's, Graydon, who had given Manallace a sheaf of prints—torn from an extinct children's book called *Philippa's Queen*—on which to improve, asked for results. Manallace went down into his ulsterpocket, hesitated a moment, and said the stuff had turned into poetry on his hands.

'Bosh!'

'That's what it isn't,' the boy returned. 'It's rather good.'

'Then it's no use to us.' Graydon laughed. 'Have you brought back the cuts?'

Manallace handed them over. There was a castle in the series; a knight or so in armour; an old lady in a horned head-dress; a young ditto; a very obvious Hebrew; a clerk, with pen and inkhorn, checking wine-barrels on a wharf; and a Crusader. On the back of one of the prints was a note, 'If he doesn't want to go, why can't he be captured and held to ransom?' Graydon asked what it all meant.

'I don't know yet. A comic opera, perhaps,' said Manallace.

---

[1] 'The Village That Voted the Earth Was Flat.' *A Diversity of Creatures.*

Graydon, who seldom wasted time, passed the cuts on to someone else, and advanced Manallace a couple of sovereigns to carry on with, as usual; at which Castorley was angry and would have said something unpleasant but was suppressed. Half-way through supper, Castorley told the company that a relative had died and left him an independence; and that he now withdrew from 'hackwork' to follow 'Literature.' Generally, the Syndicate rejoiced in a comrade's good fortune, but Castorley had gifts of waking dislike. So the news was received with a vote of thanks, and he went out before the end, and, it was said, proposed to 'Dal Benzaquen's mother, who refused him. He did not come back. Manallace, who had arrived a little exalted, got so drunk before midnight that a man had to stay and see him home. But liquor never touched him above the belt, and when he had slept awhile, he recited to the gas-chandelier the poetry he had made out of the pictures; said that, on second thoughts, he would convert it into comic opera; deplored the Upas-tree influence of Gilbert and Sullivan; sang somewhat to illustrate his point; and—after words, by the way, with a negress in yellow satin—was steered to his rooms.

In the course of a few years, Graydon's foresight and genius were rewarded. The public began to read and reason upon higher planes, and the Syndicate grew rich. Later still, people demanded of their printed matter what they expected in their clothing and furniture. So, precisely as the three guinea hand-bag is followed in three weeks by its thirteen and sevenpence ha'penny, indistinguishable sister, they enjoyed perfect synthetic substitutes for Plot, Sentiment, and Emotion. Graydon died before the Cinema-caption school came in, but he left his widow twenty-seven thousand pounds.

Manallace made a reputation, and, more important, money for Vidal's mother when her husband ran away and the first symptoms of her paralysis showed. His line was the jocundly-sentimental Wardour Street brand of adventure, told in a style that exactly met, but never exceeded, every expectation.

As he once said when urged to 'write a real book': 'I've got my label, and I'm not going to chew it off. If you save people thinking, you can do anything with 'em.' His output apart, he was genuinely a man of letters. He rented a small cottage in the country and economised on everything, except the care and charges of Vidal's mother.

Castorley flew higher. When his legacy freed him from 'hackwork,' he became first a critic—in which calling he loyally scalped all his old associates as they came up—and then looked for some speciality. Having found it (Chaucer was the prey), he consolidated his position before he occupied it, by his careful speech, his cultivated bearing, and the whispered words of his friends whom he, too, had saved the trouble of thinking. It followed that, when he published his first serious articles on Chaucer, all the world which is interested in Chaucer said: 'This is an authority.' But he was no impostor. He learned and knew his poet and his age; and in a month-long dog-fight in an austere literary weekly, met and mangled a recognised Chaucer expert of the day. He also, 'for old sake's sake,' as he wrote to a friend, went out of his way to review one of Manallace's books with an intimacy of unclean deduction (this was before the days of Freud) which long stood as a record. Some member of the extinct Syndicate took occasion to ask him if he would—for old sake's sake—help Vidal's mother to a new treatment. He answered that he had 'known the lady very slightly and the calls on his purse were so heavy that,' etc. The writer showed the letter to Manallace, who said he was glad Castorley hadn't interfered. Vidal's mother was then wholly paralysed. Only her eyes could move, and those always looked for the husband who had left her. She died thus in Manallace's arms in April of the first year of the War.

During the War he and Castorley worked as some sort of departmental dishwashers in the Office of Co-ordinated Supervisals. Here Manallace came to know Castorley again. Castorley, having a sweet tooth, cadged lumps of sugar for his tea from a typist, and when she took to giving them to a younger man, arranged that she should be reported for smoking in unauthorised apartments. Manallace possessed himself of every detail of the affair, as compensation for the review of his book. Then there came a night when, waiting for a big air-raid, the two men had talked humanly, and Manallace spoke of Vidal's mother. Castorley said something in reply, and from that hour—as was learned several years later—Manallace's real life-work and interests began.

The War over, Castorley set about to make himself Supreme Pontiff on Chaucer by methods not far removed from the employment of poison-gas. The English Pope was silent, through private griefs, and influenza had carried off the learned Hun who claimed continental allegiance. Thus Castorley crowed unchallenged from Upsala to Seville, while Manallace went back to his cottage with the photo of Vidal's mother over the mantelpiece. She seemed to have emptied out his life, and left him only fleeting interests in trifles. His private diversions were experiments of uncertain outcome, which, he said, rested him after a day's gadzooking and vitalstapping. I found him, for instance, one week-end, in his toolshed-scullery, boiling a brew of slimy barks which were, if mixed with oak-galls, vitriol and wine, to become an ink-powder. We boiled it till the Monday, and it turned into an adhesive stronger than birdlime, and entangled us both.

At other times, he would carry me off, once in a few weeks, to sit at Castorley's feet, and hear him talk about Chaucer. Castorley's voice, bad enough in youth, when it could be shouted down, had, with culture and tact, grown almost insupportable. His mannerisms, too, had multiplied and set. He minced and mouthed, postured and chewed his words throughout those terrible evenings; and poisoned not only Chaucer, but every shred of English literature which he used to embellish him. He was shameless, too, as regarded self-advertisement and 'recognition'—weaving elaborate intrigues; forming petty friendships and confederacies, to be dissolved next week in favour of more promising alliances; fawning, snubbing, lecturing, organising and lying as unrestingly as a politician, in chase of the Knighthood due not to him (he always called on his Maker to forbid such a thought) but as tribute to Chaucer. Yet, sometimes, he could break from his obsession and prove how a man's work will try to save the soul of him. He would tell us charmingly of copyists of the fifteenth century in England and the Low Countries, who had multiplied the Chaucer MSS., of which there remained—he gave us the exact number—and how each scribe could by him (and, he implied, by him alone) be distinguished from every other by some peculiarity of letter-formation, spacing or like trick of pen-work; and how he could fix the dates of their work within five years. Sometimes he would give us an hour of really interesting stuff and then return to his overdue 'recognition.' The changes sickened me, but Manallace defended him, as a master in his own line who had revealed Chaucer to at least one grateful soul.

This, as far as I remembered, was the autumn when Manallace holidayed in the Shetlands or the Faroes, and came back with a stone 'quern'—a hand corn-grinder. He said it interested him from the ethnological standpoint. His whim lasted till next harvest, and was followed by a religious spasm which, naturally, translated itself into literature. He showed me a battered and mutilated Vulgate of 1485, patched up the back with bits of legal parchments, which he had bought for thirty-five shillings. Some monk's attempt to rubricate chapter-initials had caught, it seemed, his forlorn fancy, and he dabbled in shells of gold and silver paint for weeks.

That also faded out, and he went to the Continent to get local colour for a love-story, about Alva and the Dutch, and the next year I saw practically nothing of him. This released me from seeing much of Castorley, but, at intervals, I would go there to dine with him, when his wife—an unappetising, ash-coloured woman—made no secret that his friends wearied her almost as much as he did. But at a later meeting, not long after Manallace had finished his Low Countries' novel, I found Castorley charged to bursting-point with triumph and high information hardly withheld. He confided to me that a time was at hand when great matters would be made plain, and 'recognition' would be inevitable. I assumed, naturally, that there was fresh scandal or heresy afoot in Chaucer circles, and kept my curiosity within bounds.

In time, New York cabled that a fragment of a hitherto unknown Canterbury Tale lay safe in the steel-walled vaults of the seven-million-dollar Sunnapia Collection. It was news on an international scale—the New World exultant—the Old deploring the 'burden of British taxation which drove such treasures, etc.,' and the lighter-minded journals disporting themselves according to their publics; for 'our Dan,' as one earnest Sunday editor observed, 'lies closer to the national heart than we wot of.' Common decency made me call on Castorley, who, to my surprise, had not yet descended into the arena. I found him, made young again by joy, deep in just-passed proofs.

Yes, he said, it was all true. He had, of course, been in it from the first. There had been found one hundred and seven new lines of Chaucer tacked on to an abridged end of *The Persone's Tale*, the whole the work of Abraham Mentzius, better known as Mentzel of Antwerp (1388–1438/9)—I might remember he had talked about him—whose distinguishing peculiarities were a certain Byzantine formation of his *g*'s, the use of a 'sickle-slanted' reed-pen, which cut into the vellum at certain letters; and, above all, a tendency to spell English words on Dutch lines, whereof the manuscript carried one convincing proof. For instance (he wrote it out for me), a girl praying against an undesired marriage, says:—

> 'Ah Jesu-Moder, pitie my oe peyne.
> Daiespringe mishandeelt cometh nat agayne.'

Would I, please, note the spelling of 'mishandeelt'? Stark Dutch and Mentzel's besetting sin! But in *his* position one took nothing for granted. The page had been part of the stiffening of the side of an old Bible, bought in a parcel by Dredd, the big dealer, because it had some rubricated chapter-initials, and by Dredd shipped, with a consignment of similar odds and ends, to the Sunnapia Collection, where they were making a glass-cased exhibit of the whole history of illumination and did not care how many books they gutted for that purpose. There, someone who noticed a crack in the back of the volume had unearthed it. He went on: 'They didn't know what to make of the thing at first. But they knew about *me!* They kept quiet till I'd been consulted. You might have noticed I was out of England for three months.

'I was over there, of course. It was what is called a "spoil"—a page Mentzel had spoiled with his Dutch spelling—I expect he had had the English dictated to him—then had evidently used the vellum for trying out his reeds; and then, I suppose, had put it away. The "spoil" had been doubled, pasted together, and slipped in as stiffening to the old book-cover. I had it steamed open, and analysed the wash. It gave the flour-grains in the paste—coarse, because of the old millstone—and there were traces of the grit itself. What? Oh, possibly a hand-mill of Mentzel's own time. He may have doubled the spoilt page and used it for part of a pad to steady wood-cuts on. It may have knocked about his workshop for years. That, indeed, is practically certain because a beginner from the Low Countries has tried his reed on a few lines of some monkish hymn—not a bad lilt tho'—which must have been common form. Oh yes, the page may have been used in other books before it was used for the Vulgate. That doesn't matter, but *this* does. Listen! I took a wash, for analysis, from a blot in one corner—that would be after Mentzel had given up trying to make a possible page of it, and had grown careless—and I got the actual *ink* of the period! It's a practically eternal stuff compounded on—I've forgotten his name for the minute—the scribe at Bury St. Edmunds, of course—hawthorn bark and wine. Anyhow, on *his* formula. *That* wouldn't interest you either, but, taken with all the other testimony, it clinches the thing. (You'll see it all in my Statement to the Press on Monday.) Overwhelming, isn't it?'

'Overwhelming,' I said, with sincerity. 'Tell me what the tale was about, though. That's more in my line.'

'I know it; but *I* have to be equipped on all sides. The verses are relatively easy for one to pronounce on. The freshness, the fun, the humanity, the fragrance of it all, cries—no, shouts—itself as Dan's work. Why "Daiespringe mishandled" alone stamps it from Dan's mint. Plangent as doom, my dear boy—plangent as doom! It's all in my Statement. Well, substantially, the fragment deals with a girl whose parents wish her to marry an elderly suitor. The mother isn't so keen on it, but the father, an old Knight, is. The girl, of course, is in love with a younger and a poorer man. Common form? Granted. Then the father, who doesn't in the least want to, is ordered off to a Crusade and, by way of passing on the kick, as we used to say during the War, orders the girl to be kept in duresse till his return or her consent to the old suitor. Common form, again? Quite so. That's too much for her mother. She reminds the old Knight of his age and infirmities, and the discomforts of Crusading. Are you sure I'm not boring you?'

'Not at all,' I said, though time had begun to whirl backward through my brain to a red-velvet, pomatum-

scented side-room at Neminaka's and Manallace's set face
intoning to the gas.

'You'll read it all in my Statement next week. The sum
is that the old lady tell him of a certain Knight-adventurer
on the French coast, who, for a consideration, waylays
Knights who don't relish crusading and holds them to impossible ransoms till the trooping-season is over, or they
are returned sick. He keeps a ship in the Channel to pick
'em up and transfers his birds to his castle ashore, where
he has a reputation for doing 'em well. As the old lady
points out:

> "And if perchance thou fall into his honde
>   By God how canstow ride to Holilonde?"

'You see? Modern in essence as Gilbert and Sullivan,
but handled as only Dan could! And she reminds him that
"Honour and olde bones" parted company long ago. He
makes one splendid appeal for the spirit of chivalry:

> "Lat all men change as Fortune may send,
>   But Knighthood beareth service to the end,"

and *then*, of course, he gives in:

> "For what his woman willeth to be don
>   Her manne must or wauken Hell anon."

'Then she hints that the daughter's young lover, who is
in the Bordeaux wine-trade, could open negotiations for a
kidnapping without compromising him. And *then* that
careless brute Mentzel spoils his page and chucks it! But
there's enough to show what's going to happen. You'll see
it all in my Statement. Was there ever anything in literary
finds to hold a candle to it? ... And they give grocers
Knighthoods for selling cheese!'

I went away before he could get into his stride on that

course. I wanted to think, and to see Manallace. But I waited till Castorley's Statement came out. He had left himself no loophole. And when, a little later, his (nominally the Sunnapia people's) 'scientific' account of their analyses and tests appeared, criticism ceased, and some journals began to demand 'public recognition.' Mannallace wrote me on this subject, and I went down to his cottage, where he at once asked me to sign a Memorial on Castorley's behalf. With luck, he said, we might get him a K.B.E. in the next Honours List. Had I read the Statement?

'I have,' I replied. 'But I want to ask you something first. Do you remember the night you got drunk at Neminaka's, and I stayed behind to look after you?'

'Oh, *that* time,' said he, pondering. 'Wait a minute! I remember Graydon advancing me two quid. He was a generous paymaster. And I remember—now, who the devil rolled me under the sofa—and what for?'

'We all did,' I replied. 'You wanted to read us what you'd written to those Chaucer cuts.'

'I don't remember that. No! I don't remember anything after the sofa-episode. . . . *You* always said that you took me home—didn't you?'

'I did, and you told Kentucky Kate outside the old Empire that you had been faithful, Cynera, in your fashion.'

'Did I?' said he. 'My God! Well, I suppose I have.' He stared into the fire. 'What else?'

'Before we left Neminaka's you recited me what you had made out of the cuts—the whole tale! So—you see?'

'Ye-es.' He nodded. 'What are you going to do about it?'

'What are *you*?'

'I'm going to help him get his Knighthood—first.'

'Why?'

'I'll tell you what he said about 'Dal's mother—the night there was that air-raid on the offices.'

He told it.

'That's why,' he said. 'Am I justified?'

He seemed to me entirely so.

'But after he gets his Knighthood?' I went on.

'That depends. There are several things I can think of. It interests me.'

'Good Heavens! I've always imagined you a man without interests.'

'So I was. I owe my interests to Castorley. He gave me every one of 'em except the tale itself.'

'How did *that* come?'

'Something in those ghastly cuts touched off something in me—a sort of possession, I suppose. I was in love too. No wonder I got drunk that night. I'd *been* Chaucer for a week! Then I thought the notion might make a comic opera. But Gilbert and Sullivan were too strong.'

'So I remember you told me at the time.'

'I kept it by me, and it made me interested in Chaucer—philologically and so on. I worked on it on those lines for years. There wasn't a flaw in the wording even in '14. I hardly had to touch it after that.'

'Did you ever tell it to anyone except me?'

'No, only 'Dal's mother—when she could listen to anything—to put her to sleep. But when Castorley said—what he did about her, I thought I might use it. 'Twasn't difficult. *He* taught me. D'you remember my birdlime experiments, and the stuff on our hands? I'd been trying to get that ink for more than a year. Castorley told me where I'd find the formula. And your falling over the quern, too?'

'That accounted for the stone-dust under the microscope?'

'Yes. I grew the wheat in the garden here, and ground it myself. Castorley gave me Mentzel complete. He put me on to an MS. in the British Museum which he said was the finest sample of his work. I copied his "Byzantine *g*'s" for months.'

'And what's a "sickle-slanted" pen?' I asked.

'You nick one edge of your reed till it drags and

scratches on the curves of the letters. Castorley told me about Mentzel's spacing and margining. I only had to get the hang of his script.'

'How long did that take you?'

'On and off—some years. I was too ambitious at first—I wanted to give the whole poem. That would have been risky. Then Castorley told me about spoiled pages and I took the hint. I spelt "Dayspring mishandeelt" Mentzel's way—to make sure of him. It's not a bad couplet in itself. Did you see how he admires the "plangency" of it?'

'Never mind him. Go on!' I said.

He did. Castorley had been his unfailing guide throughout, specifying in minutest detail every trap to be set later for his own feet. The actual vellum was an Antwerp find, and its introduction into the cover of the Vulgate was begun after a long course of amateur bookbinding. At last, he bedded it under pieces of an old deed, and a printed page (1686) of Horace's *Odes*, legitimately used for repairs by different owners in the seventeenth and eighteenth centuries; and at the last moment, to meet Castorley's theory that spoiled pages were used in workshops by beginners, he had written a few Latin words in fifteenth century script—the Statement gave the exact date—across an open part of the fragment. The thing ran: '*Illa alma Mater ecca, secum afferens me acceptum. Nicolaus Atrib.*' The disposal of the thing was easiest of all. He had merely hung about Dredd's dark bookshop of fifteen rooms, where he was well known, occasionally buying but generally browsing, till, one day, Dredd Senior showed him a case of cheap black-letter stuff, English and Continental—being packed for the Sunnapia people—into which Manallace tucked his contribution, taking care to wrench the back enough to give a lead to an earnest seeker.

'And then?' I demanded.

'After six months or so Castorley sent for me. Sunnapia had found it, and as Dredd had missed it, and there was no money-motive sticking out, they were half convinced it was genuine from the start. But they invited him over. He conferred with their experts, and suggested the scientific tests. *I* put that into his head, before he sailed. That's all. And now, will you sign our Memorial?'

I signed. Before we had finished hawking it round there was a host of influential names to help us, as well as the impetus of all the literary discussion which arose over every detail of the glorious trove. The upshot was a K.B.E.[1] for Castorley in the next Honours List; and Lady Castorley, her cards duly printed, called on friends that same afternoon.

Manallace invited me to come with him, a day or so later, to convey our pleasure and satisfaction to them both. We were rewarded by the sight of a man relaxed and un-girt—not to say wallowing naked—on the crest of Success. He assured us that 'The Title' should not make any difference to our future relations, seeing it was in no sense personal, but, as he had often said, a tribute to Chaucer; 'and, after all,' he pointed out, with a glance at the mirror over the mantelpiece, 'Chaucer was the prototype of the "veray parfit gentil Knight" of the British Empire so far as that then existed.'

On the way back, Manallace told me he was considering either an unheralded revelation in the baser Press which should bring Castorley's reputation about his own ears some breakfast-time, or a private conversation, when he would make clear to Castorley that he must now back the forgery as long as he lived, under threat of Manallace's betraying it if he flinched.

He favoured the second plan. 'If I pull the string of the shower-bath in the papers,' he said, 'Castorley might go off his veray parfit gentil nut. I want to keep his intellect.'

---

[1] Officially it was on account of his good work in the Office of Co-or-dinated Supervisals, but all true lovers of literature knew the real reason, and told the papers so.

'What about your own position? The forgery doesn't matter so much. But if you tell this you'll kill him,' I said.

'I intend that. Oh—my position? I've been dead since—April, Fourteen, it was. But there's no hurry. What was it *she* was saying to you just as we left?'

'She told me how much your sympathy and understanding had meant to him. She said she thought that even Sir Alured did not realise the full extent of his obligations to you.'

'She's right, but I don't like her putting it that way.'

'It's only common form—as Castorley's always saying.'

'Not with *her*. She can hear a man think.'

'She never struck me in that light.'

'*You* aren't playing against her.'

' 'Guilty conscience, Manallace?'

'H'm! I wonder. Mine or hers? I *wish* she hadn't said that. "More even than *he* realises it." I won't call again for awhile.'

He kept away till we read that Sir Alured, owing to slight indisposition, had been unable to attend a dinner given in his honour.

Inquiries brought word that it was but natural reaction, after strain, which, for the moment, took the form of nervous dyspepsia, and he would be glad to see Manallace at any time. Manallace reported him as rather pulled and drawn, but full of his new life and position, and proud that his efforts should have martyred him so much. He was going to collect, collate, and expand all his pronouncements and inferences into one authoritative volume.

'I must make an effort of my own,' said Manallace. 'I've collected nearly all his stuff about the Find that has appeared in the papers, and he's promised me everything that's missing. I'm going to help him. It will be a new interest.'

'How will you treat it?' I asked.

'I expect I shall quote his deductions on the evidence, and parallel 'em with my experiments—the ink and the paste and the rest of it. It ought to be rather interesting.'

'But even then there will only be your word. It's hard to catch up with an established lie,' I said. 'Especially when you've started it yourself.'

He laughed. 'I've arranged for *that*—in case anything happens to me. Do you remember the "Monkish Hymn"?'

'Oh yes! There's quite a literature about it already.'

'Well, you write those ten words above each other, and read down the first and second letters of 'em; and see what you get.'[1] My Bank has the formula.'

He wrapped himself lovingly and leisurely round his new task, and Castorley was good as his word in giving him help. The two practically collaborated, for Manallace suggested that all Castorley's strictly scientific evidence should be in one place, with his deductions and dithyrambs as appendices. He assured him that the public would prefer this arrangement, and, after grave consideration, Castorley agreed.

'That's better,' said Manallace to me. 'Now I sha'n't have so many hiatuses in my extracts. Dots always give the reader the idea you aren't dealing fairly with your man. I shall merely quote him solid, and rip him up, proof for proof, and date for date, in parallel columns. His book's taking more out of him than I like, though. He's been doubled up twice with tummy attacks since I've worked with him. And he's just the sort of flatulent beast who may go down with appendicitis.'

We learned before long that the attacks were due to gall-stones, which would necessitate an operation. Castorley bore the blow very well. He had full confidence in his surgeon, an old friend of theirs; great faith in his own constitution; a strong conviction that nothing would happen to him till the book was finished and, above all, the Will to Live.

---

[1] *Illa alma Mater ecca secum afferens me acceptum Nicolaus Atrib.*

He dwelt on these assets with a voice at times a little out of pitch and eyes brighter than usual beside a slightly-sharpening nose.

I had only met Gleeag, the surgeon, once or twice at Castorley's house, but had always heard him spoken of as a most capable man. He told Castorley that his trouble was the price exacted, in some shape or other, from all who had served their country; and that, measured in units of strain, Castorley had practically been at the front through those three years he had served in the Office of Co-ordinated Supervisals. However, the thing had been taken betimes, and in a few weeks he would worry no more about it.

'But suppose he dies?' I suggested to Manallace.

'He won't. I've been talking to Gleeag. He says he's all right.'

'Wouldn't Gleeag's talk be common form?'

'I *wish* you hadn't said that. But, surely, Gleeag wouldn't have the face to play with me—or her.'

'Why not? I expect it's been done before.'

But Manallace insisted that, in this case, it would be impossible.

The operation was a success and, some weeks later, Castorley began to recast the arrangement and most of the material of his book. 'Let me have my way,' he said, when Manallace protested. 'They are making too much of a baby of me. I really don't need Gleeag looking in every day now.' But Lady Castorley told us that he required careful watching. His heart had felt the strain, and fret or disappointment of any kind must be avoided. 'Even,' she turned to Manallace, 'though you know ever so much better how his book should be arranged than he does himself.'

'But really,' Manallace began. 'I'm very careful not to fuss——'

She shook her finger at him playfully. 'You don't think you do; but, remember, he tells me everything that you tell him, just the same as he told me everything that he used to tell *you*. Oh, I don't mean the things that men talk about. I mean about his Chaucer.'

'I didn't realise that,' said Manallace, weakly.

'I thought you didn't. He never spares me anything; but *I* don't mind,' she replied with a laugh, and went off to Gleeag, who was paying his daily visit. Gleeag said he had no objection to Manallace working with Castorley on the book for a given time—say, twice a week—but supported Lady Castorley's demand that he should not be over-taxed in what she called 'the sacred hours.' The man grew more and more difficult to work with, and the little check he had heretofore set on his self-praise went altogether.

'He says there has never been anything in the History of Letters to compare with it,' Manallace groaned. 'He wants now to inscribe—he never dedicates, you know—inscribe it to me, as his "most valued assistant." The devil of it is that *she* backs him up in getting it out soon. Why? How much do you think she knows?'

'Why should she know anything at all?'

'You heard her say he had told her everything that he had told me about Chaucer? (I *wish* she hadn't said that!) If she puts two and two together, she can't help seeing that every one of his notions and theories has been played up to. But then—but then . . . Why is she trying to hurry publication? She talks about me fretting him. *She's* at him, all the time, to be quick.'

Castorley must have over-worked, for, after a couple of months, he complained of a stitch in his right side, which Gleeag said was a slight sequel, a little incident of the operation. It threw him back awhile, but he returned to his work undefeated.

The book was due in the autumn. Summer was passing, and his publisher urgent, and—he said to me, when after a longish interval I called—Manallace had chosen this time, of all, to take a holiday. He was not pleased with Manallace, once his indefatigable *aide*, but now dilatory, and full of time-wasting objections. Lady Castorley had noticed it, too.

Meantime, with Lady Castorley's help, he himself was doing the best he could to expedite the book; but Manallace had mislaid (did I think through jealousy?) some essential stuff which had been dictated to him. And Lady Castorley wrote Manallace, who had been delayed by a slight motor accident abroad, that the fret of waiting was prejudicial to her husband's health. Manallace, on his return from the Continent, showed me that letter.

'He has fretted a little, I believe,' I said.

Manallace shuddered. 'If I stay abroad, I'm helping to kill him. If I help him to hurry up the book, I'm expected to kill him. *She* knows,' he said.

'You're mad. You've got this thing on the brain.'

'I have not! Look here! You remember that Gleeag gave me from four to six, twice a week, to work with him. She called them the "sacred hours." You heard her? Well, they *are!* They are Gleeag's and hers. But she's so infernally plain, and I'm such a fool, it took me weeks to find it out.'

'That's their affair,' I answered. 'It doesn't prove she knows anything about the Chaucer.'

'She *does!* He told her everything that he had told me when I was pumping him, all those years. She put two and two together when the thing came out. She saw exactly how I had set my traps. I know it! She's been trying to make me admit it.'

'What did you do?'

' 'Didn't understand what she was driving at, of course. And then she asked Gleeag, before me, if he didn't think the delay over the book was fretting Sir Alured. He didn't think so. He said getting it out might deprive him of an interest. He had that much decency. *She's* the devil!'

'What do you suppose is her game, then?'

'If Castorley knows he's been had, it'll kill him. She's at me all the time, indirectly, to let it out. I've told you she wants to make it a sort of joke between us. Gleeag's willing to wait. He knows Castorley's a dead man. It slips out when they talk. They say "He was," not "He is." Both of 'em know it. But *she* wants him finished sooner.'

'I don't believe it. What are you going to do?'

'What can I? I'm not going to have him killed, though.'

Manlike, he invented compromises whereby Castorley might be lured up by-paths of interest, to delay publication. This was not a success. As autumn advanced Castorley fretted more, and suffered from returns of his distressing colics. At last, Gleeag told him that he thought they might be due to an overlooked gall-stone working down. A second comparatively trivial operation would eliminate the bother once and for all. If Castorley cared for another opinion, Gleeag named a surgeon of eminence. 'And then,' said he, cheerily, 'the two of us can talk you over.' Castorley did not want to be talked over. He was oppressed by pains in his side, which, at first, had yielded to the liver-tonics Gleeag prescribed; but now they stayed—like a toothache—behind everything. He felt most at ease in his bedroom-study, with his proofs round him. If he had more pain than he could stand, he would consider the second operation. Meantime Manallace—'the meticulous Manallace,' he called him—agreed with him in thinking that the Mentzel page-facsimile, done by the Sunnapia Library, was not quite good enough for the great book, and the Sunnapia people were, very decently, having it re-processed. This would hold things back till early spring, which had its advantages, for he could run a fresh eye over all in the interval.

One gathered these news in the course of stray visits as the days shortened. He insisted on Manallace keeping to the 'sacred hours,' and Manallace insisted on my accompanying him when possible. On these occasions he and Castorley would confer apart for half an hour or so, while I listened to an unendurable clock in the drawing-room. Then I would join them and help wear out the rest of the time, while Castorley rambled. His speech, now, was often clouded and uncertain—the result of the 'liver-tonics'; and his face came to look like old vellum.

It was a few days after Christmas—the operation had been postponed till the following Friday—that we called together. She met us with word that Sir Alured had picked up an irritating little winter cough, due to a cold wave, but we were not, therefore, to abridge our visit. We found him in steam perfumed with Friar's Balsam. He waved the old Sunnapia facsimile at us. We agreed that it ought to have been more worthy. He took a dose of his mixture, lay back and asked us to lock the door. There was, he whispered, something wrong somewhere. He could not lay his finger on it, but it was in the air. He felt he was being played with. He did not like it. There was something wrong all round him. Had we noticed it? Manallace and I severally and slowly denied that we had noticed anything of the sort.

With no longer break than a light fit of coughing, he fell into the hideous, helpless panic of the sick—those worse than captives who lie at the judgment and mercy of the hale for every office and hope. He wanted to go away. Would we help him to pack his Gladstone? Or, if that would attract too much attention in certain quarters, help him to dress and go out? There was an urgent matter to be set right, and now that he had The Title and knew his own mind it would all end happily and he would be well again. *Please* would we let him go out, just to speak to—he named her; he named her by her 'little' name out of the old Neminaka days? Manallace quite agreed, and recommended a pull at the 'liver-tonic' to brace him after so long in the house. He took it, and Manallace suggested that it would be better if, after his walk, he came down to the cottage for a week-end and brought the revise with him. They could then re-touch the last chapter. He answered to that drug and to some praise of his work, and presently simpered drowsily. Yes, it *was* good—though he said it who should not. He praised himself awhile till, with a puzzled forehead and shut eyes, he told us that *she* had been saying lately that it was too good—the whole thing, if we understood, was *too* good. He wished us to get the exact shade of her meaning. She had suggested, or rather implied, this doubt. She had said—he would let us draw our own inferences—that the Chaucer find had 'anticipated the wants of humanity.' Johnson, of course. No need to tell *him* that. But what the hell was her implication? Oh God! Life had always been one long innuendo! *And* she had said that a man could do anything with anyone if he saved him the trouble of thinking. What did she mean by that? *He* had never shirked thought. He had thought sustainedly all his life. It *wasn't* too good, was it? Manallace didn't think it was too good—did he? But this pick-pick-picking at a man's brain and work was too bad, wasn't it? *What* did she mean? Why did she always bring in Manallace, who was only a friend—no scholar, but a lover of the game—Eh?—Manallace could confirm this if he were here, instead of loafing on the Continent just when he was most needed.

'I've come back,' Manallace interrupted, unsteadily. 'I can confirm every word you've said. You've nothing to worry about. It's *your* find—*your* credit—*your* glory and—all the rest of it.'

'Swear you'll tell her so then,' said Castorley. 'She doesn't believe a word I say. She told me she never has since before we were married. Promise!'

Manallace promised, and Castorley added that he had named him his literary executor, the proceeds of the book to go to his wife. 'All profits without deduction,' he gasped. 'Big sales if it's properly handled. *You* don't need money. . . . Graydon'll trust *you* to any extent. It 'ud be a long . . .'

He coughed, and, as he caught breath, his pain broke through all the drugs, and the outcry filled the room. Manallace rose to fetch Gleeag, when a full, high, affected voice, unheard for a generation, accompanied, as it seemed, the clamour of a beast in àgony, saying: 'I wish to God someone would stop that old swine howling down there! *I* can't . . . I was going to tell you fellows that it would be a dam' long time before Graydon advanced *me* two quid.'

We escaped together, and found Gleeag waiting, with Lady Castorley, on the landing. He telephoned me, next morning, that Castorley had died of bronchitis, which his weak state made it impossible for him to throw off. 'Perhaps it's just as well,' he added, in reply to the condolences I asked him to convey to the widow. 'We might have come across something we couldn't have coped with.'

Distance from that house made me bold.

'You knew all along, I suppose? What was it, really?'

'Malignant kidney-trouble—generalised at the end. 'No use worrying him about it. We let him through as easily as possible. Yes! A happy release. . . . What? . . . Oh! Cremation. Friday, at eleven.'

There, then, Manallace and I met. He told me that she had asked him whether the book need now be published; and he had told her this was more than ever necessary, in her interests as well as Castorley's.

'She is going to be known as his widow—for a while, at any rate. Did I perjure myself much with him?'

'Not explicitly,' I anwered.

'Well, I have now—with *her*—explicitly,' said he, and took out his black gloves. . . .

As, on the appointed words, the coffin crawled sideways through the noiselessly-closing doorflaps, I saw Lady Castorley's eyes turn towards Gleeag.

1928

Poems

L'ENVOI

The smoke upon your Altar dies,
  The flowers decay,
The Goddess of your sacrifice
  Has flown away.
What profit then to sing or slay
The sacrifice from day to day?

'We know the Shrine is void,' they said,
  'The Goddess flown—
'Yet wreaths are on the altar laid—
  'The Altar-Stone
'Is black with fumes of sacrifice,
'Albeit She has fled our eyes.

'For, it may be, if still we sing
  'And tend the Shrine,
'Some Deity on wandering wing
  'May there incline;
'And, finding all in order meet,
'Stay while we worship at Her feet.'

1890

THE BROKEN MEN

For things we never mention,
  For Art misunderstood—
For excellent intention
  That did not turn to good;
From ancient tales' renewing,
  From clouds we would not clear—
Beyond the Law's pursuing
  We fled, and settled here.

We took no tearful leaving,
  We bade no long good-byes.
Men talked of crime and thieving,
  Men wrote of fraud and lies.
To save our injured feelings
  'Twas time and time to go—
Behind was dock and Dartmoor,
  Ahead lay Callao!

The widow and the orphan
  That pray for ten per cent,
They clapped their trailers on us
  To spy the road we went.
They watched the foreign sailings
  (They scan the shipping still),
And that's your Christian people
  Returning good for ill!

God bless the thoughtful islands
  Where never warrants come;
God bless the just Republics
  That give a man a home,
That ask no foolish questions,
  But set him on his feet;
And save his wife and daughters
  From the workhouse and the street.

On church and square and market
  The noonday silence falls;
You'll hear the drowsy mutter
  Of the fountain in our halls.
Asleep amid the yuccas
  The city takes her ease—
Till twilight brings the land-wind
  To the clicking jalousies.

Day long the diamond weather,
  The high, unaltered blue—

The smell of goats and incense
  And the mule-bells tinkling through.
Day long the warder ocean
  That keeps us from our kin,
And once a month our levée
  When the English mail comes in.

You'll find us up and waiting
  To treat you at the bar;
You'll find us less exclusive
  Than the average English are.
We'll meet you with a carriage,
  Too glad to show you round,
But—we do not lunch on steamers,
  For they are English ground.

We sail o' nights to England
  And join our smiling Boards—
Our wives go in with Viscounts
  And our daughters dance with Lords,
But behind our princely doings,
  And behind each coup we make.
We feel there's Something Waiting,
  And—we meet It when we wake.

Ah, God! One sniff of England—
  To greet our flesh and blood—
To hear the traffic slurring
  Once more through London mud!
Our towns of wasted honour—
  Our streets of lost delight!
How stands the old Lord Warden?
  Are Dover's cliffs still white?

                                        1903

McANDREW'S HYMN

Lord, Thou has made this world below the shadow of a
    dream,
An', taught by time, I tak' it so—exceptin' always Steam.
From coupler-flange to spindle-guide I see Thy Hand, O
    God—
Predestination in the stride o' yon connectin'-rod.
John Calvin might ha' forged the same—enorrmous, cer-
    tain, slow—
Ay, wrought it in the furnace-flame—*my* 'Institutio.'
I cannot get my sleep to-night; *old bones are hard to
    please;*
I'll stand the middle watch up here—alone wi' God an'
    these
My engines, after ninety days o' race an' rack an' strain
Through all the seas of all Thy world, slam-bangin' home
    again.
Slam-bang too much—they knock a wee—the crosshead-
    gibs are loose,
But thirty thousand mile o' sea has gied them fair ex-
    cuse. . . .
Fine, clear an' dark—a full-draught breeze, wi' Ushant out
    o' sight,
An' Ferguson relievin' Hay. Old girl, ye'll walk to-night!
His wife's at Plymouth. . . . Seventy—One—Two—
    Three since he began—
Three turns for Mistress Ferguson . . . and who's to blame
    the man?
There's none at any port for me, by drivin' fast or slow,
Since Elsie Campbell went to Thee, Lord, thirty years ago
(The year the *Sarah Sands* was burned. Oh, roads we
    used to tread,
Fra' Maryhill to Pollokshaws—fra' Govan to Parkhead!)

Not but they're ceevil on the Board. Ye'll hear Sir Ken-
  neth say:
'Good morrn, McAndrew! Back again? An' how's your
  bilge to-day?'
Miscallin' technicalities but handin' me my chair
To drink Madeira wi' three Earls—the auld Fleet Engi-
  neer
That started as a boiler-whelp—when steam and he were
  low.
I mind the time we used to serve a broken pipe wi' tow!
Ten pound was all the pressure then—Eh! Eh!—a man
  wad drive;
An' here, our working' gauges give one hunder sixty-five!
We're creepin' on wi' each new rig—less weight an' larger
  power;
There'll be the loco-boiler next an' thirty mile an hour!
Thirty an' more. What I ha' seen since ocean-steam began
Leaves me na doot for the machine: but what about the
  man?
The man that counts, wi' all his runs, one million mile o'
  sea:
Four time the span from earth to moon. . . . How far, O
  Lord, from Thee
That wast beside him night an' day? Ye mind my first ty-
  phoon?
It scoughed the skipper on his way to jock wi' the saloon.
Three feet were on the stokehold-floor—just slappin' to
  an' fro—
An' cast me on a furnace-door. I have the marks to show.
Marks! I ha' marks o' more than burns—deep in my soul
  an' black,
An' times like this, when things go smooth, my wickud-
  ness comes back.
The sins o' four an' forty years, all up an' down the seas,
Clack an' repeat like valves half-fed. . . . Forgie 's our tres-
  passes!

Nights when I'd come on deck to mark, wi' envy in my
    gaze,
The couples kittlin' in the dark between the funnel-stays;
Years when I raked the Ports wi' pride to fill my cup o'
    wrong—
Judge not, O Lord, my steps aside at Gay Street in Hong-
    Kong!
Blot out the wastrel hours of mine in sin when I abode—
Jane Harrigan's an' Number Nine, The Reddick an'
    Grant Road!
An' waur than all—my crownin' sin—rank blasphemy an'
    wild.
I was not four and twenty then—Ye wadna judge a
    child?
I'd seen the Tropics first that run—new fruit, new smells,
    new air—
How could I tell—blind-fou wi' sun—the Deil was lurk-
    in' there?
By day like playhouse-scenes the shore slid past our
    sleepy eyes;
By night those soft, lasceevious stars leered from those
    velvet skies,
In port (we used no cargo-steam) I'd daunder down the
    streets—
An ijjit grinnin' in a dream—for shells an' parrakeets,
An' walkin'-sticks o' carved bamboo an' blowfish stuffed
    an' dried—
Fillin' my bunk wi' rubbishry the Chief put overside.
Till, off Sambawa Head, Ye mind, I heard a land-breeze
    ca',
Milk-warm wi' breath o' spice an' bloom: 'McAndrew,
    come awa'!'
Firm, clear an' low—no haste, no hate—the ghostly whis-
    per went,
Just statin' eevidential facts beyon' all argument:
'Your mither's God's a graspin' deil, the shadow o' your-
    sel',

'Got out o' books by meenisters clean daft on Heaven an'
    Hell.

'They mak' him in the Broomielaw, o' Glasgie cold an'
    dirt,

'A jealous, pridefu' fetich, lad, that's only strong to hurt.

'Ye'll not go back to Him again an' kiss His red-hot rod,

'But come wi' Us' (Now, who were *They?*) 'an' know the
    Leevin' God,

'That does not kipper souls for sport or break a life in jest,

'But swells the ripenin' cocoanuts an' ripes the woman's
    breast.'

An' there it stopped—cut off—no more—that quiet, cer-
    tain voice—

For me, six months o' twenty-four, to leave or take at
    choice.

'Twas on me like a thunderclap—it racked me through an'
    through—

Temptation past the show o' speech, unnameable an'
    new—

The Sin against the Holy Ghost? . . . An' under all, our
    screw.

That storm blew by but left behind her anchor-shiftin'
    swell.

Thou knowest all my heart an' mind, Thou knowest,
    Lord, I fell—

Third on the *Mary Gloster* then, and first that night in
    Hell!

Yet was Thy Hand beneath my head, about my feet Thy
    Care—

Fra' Deli clear to Torres Strait, the trial o' despair,

But when we touched the Barrier Reef Thy answer to my
    prayer! . . .

We dared na run that sea by night but lay an' held our
    fire,

An' I was drowsin' on the hatch—sick—sick wi' doubt an'
    tire:

'*Better the sight of eyes that see than wanderin' o' desire!*'
Ye mind that word? Clear as our gongs—again, an' once
 again,
When rippin' down through coral-trash ran out our
 moorin'-chain:
An', by Thy Grace, I had the Light to see my duty plain.
Light on the engine-room—no more—bright as our car-
 bons burn.
I've lost it since a thousand times, but never past return!

Obsairve! Per annum we'll have here two thousand souls
 aboard—
Think not I dare to justify myself before the Lord,
But—average fifteen hunder souls safe-borne fra' port to
 port—
I *am* o' service to my kind. Ye wadna blame the thought?
Maybe they steam from Grace to Wrath—to sin by folly
 led—
It isna mine to judge their path—their lives are on my
 head.
Mine at the last—when all is done it all comes back to me,
The fault that leaves six thousand ton a log upon the sea.
We'll tak' one stretch—three weeks an' odd by ony road
 ye steer—
Fra' Cape Town east to Wellington—ye need an engineer.
Fail there—ye've time to weld your shaft—ay, eat it, ere
 ye're spoke;
Or made Kerguelen under sail—three jiggers burned wi'
 smoke!
An' home again—the Rio run: it's no child's play to go
Steamin' to bell for fourteen days o' snow an' floe an'
 blow.
The bergs like kelpies overside that girn an' turn an' shift
Whaur, grindin' like the Mills o' God, goes by the big
 South drift.
(Hail, Snow and Ice that praise the Lord. I've met them at
 their work,

An' wished we had anither route or they anither kirk.)

Yon's strain, hard strain, o' head an' hand, for though Thy
  Power brings

All skill to naught, Ye'll understand a man must think o'
  things.

Then, at the last, we'll get to port an' hoist their baggage
  clear—

The passengers, wi' gloves an' canes—an' this is what I'll
  hear:

'Well, thank ye for a pleasant voyage. The tender's comin'
  now.'

While I go testin' follower-bolts an' watch the skipper
  bow.

They've words for every one but me—shake hands wi'
  half the crew,

Except the dour Scots engineer, the man they never
  knew.

An' yet I like the wark for all we've dam'-few pickin's
  here—

No pension, an' the most we'll earn's four hunder pound a
  year.

Better myself abroad? Maybe. *I'd* sooner starve than sail

Wi' such as call a snifter-rod *ross* . . . French for nightin-
  gale.

Commeesion on my stores? Some do; but I cannot afford

To lie like stewards wi' patty-pans. I'm older than the
  Board.

A bonus on the coal I save? Ou ay, the Scots are close,

But when I grudge the strength Ye gave I'll grudge their
  food to *those*.

(There's bricks that I might recommend—an' clink the
  firebars cruel.

No! Welsh—Wangarti at the worst—an' damn all patent
  fuel!)

Inventions? Ye must stay in port to mak' a patent pay.

My Deeferential Valve-Gear taught me how that business
  lay.

I blame no chaps wi' clearer heads for aught they make or
    sell.

I found that I could not invent an' look to these as
    well.

So, wrestled wi' Apollyon—Nah!—fretted like a bairn—

But burned the workin'-plans last run, wi' all I hoped to
    earn.

Ye know how hard an Idol dies, an' what that meant to
    me—

E'en tak' it for a sacrifice acceptable to Thee. . . .

Below there! Oiler! What's your wark? Ye find it runnin'
*   hard?*

Ye needn't swill the cup wi' oil—this isn't the Cunard!

Ye thought? Ye are not paid to think. Go, sweat that off
*   again!*

Tck! Tck! It's deeficult to sweer nor tak' The Name in
    vain!

Men, ay, an' women, call me stern. Wi' these to oversee

Ye'll note I've little time to burn on social repartee.

The bairns see what their elders miss; they'll hunt me to
    an' fro,

Till for the sake of—well, a kiss—I tak' 'em down below.

That minds me of our Viscount loon—Sir Kenneth's
    kin—the chap

Wi' Russia-leather tennis-shoon an' spar-decked yachtin'-
    cap.

I showed him round last week, o'er all—an' at the last says
    he:

'Mister McAndrew, don't you think steam spoils romance
    at sea?'

Damned ijjit! I'd been doon that morn to see what ailed
    the throws,

Manholin', on my back—the cranks three inches off my
    nose.

Romance! Those first-class passengers they like it very
    well,

Printed an' bound in little books; but why don't poets tell?

I'm sick of all their quirks an' turns—the loves an' doves
    they dream—

Lord, send a man like Robbie Burns to sing the Song o'
    Steam!

To match wi' Scotia's noblest speech you orchestra sub-
    lime

Whaurto—uplifted like the Just—the tail-rods mark the
    time.

The crank-throws give the double-bass, the feed-pump
    sobs an' heaves,

An' now the main eccentrics start their quarrel on the
    sheaves:

Her time, her own appointed time, the rocking link-head
    bides,

Till—hear that note?—the rod's return whings glim-
    merin' through the guides.

They're all awa'! True beat, full power, the clangin' cho-
    rus goes

Clear to the tunnel where they sit, my purrin' dynamoes.

Interdependence absolute, foreseen, ordained, decreed,

To work, Ye'll note, at ony tilt an' every rate o' speed.

Fra' skylight-lift to furnace-bars, backed, bolted, braced
    an' stayed,

An' singin' like the Mornin' Stars for joy that they are
    made;

While, out o' touch o' vanity, the sweatin' thrust-block
    says:

'Not unto us the praise, or man—not unto us the praise!'

Now, a' together, hear them lift their lesson—theirs an'
    mine:

'Law, Orrder, Duty an' Restraint, Obedience, Discipline!'

Mill, forge an' try-pit taught them that when roarin' they
    arose,

An' whiles I wonder if a soul was gied them wi' the blows.

Oh for a man to weld it then, in one trip-hammer strain,

Till even first-class passengers could tell the meanin'
    plain!

But no one cares except mysel' that serve an' understand
My seven thousand horse-power here. Eh, Lord! They're
    grand—they're grand!
Uplift am I? When first in store the new-made beasties
    stood,
Were Ye cast down that breathed the Word declarin' all
    things good?
Not so! O' that warld-liftin' joy no after-fall culd vex,
Ye've left a glimmer still to cheer the Man—the Arrtifex!
That holds, in spite o' knock and scale, o' friction, waste
    an' slip,
An' by that light—now, mark my word—we'll build the
    Perfect Ship.
I'll never last to judge her lines or take her curve—not I.
But I ha' lived an' I ha' worked. Be thanks to Thee, Most
    High!
An' I ha' done what I ha' done—judge Thou if ill or
    well—
Always Thy Grace preventin' me. . . .
                    Losh! Yon's the 'Stand-by' bell.
Pilot so soon? His flare it is. The mornin'-watch is set.
Well, God be thanked, as I was sayin', I'm no Pelagian
    yet.
Now I'll tak' on. . . .
    'Morrn, Ferguson. Man, have ye ever thought
What your good leddy costs in coal? . . . I'll burn 'em
    down to port.

                               1894

THE 'MARY GLOSTER'

I've paid for your sickest fancies; I've humoured your
    crackedest whim—
Dick, it's your daddy, dying; you've got to listen to him!
Good for a fortnight, am I? The doctor told you? He lied.

I shall go under by morning, and—— Put that nurse out-
    side.

'Never seen death yet, Dickie? Well, now is your time to
    learn,

And you'll wish you held my record before it comes to
    your turn.

Not counting the Line and the Foundry, the Yards and
    the village, too,

I've made myself and a million; but I'm damned if I made
    you.

Master at two-and-twenty, and married at twenty-three—

Ten thousand men on the pay-roll, and forty freighters at
    sea!

Fifty years between 'em, and every year of it fight,

And now I'm Sir Anthony Gloster, dying, a baronite:

For I lunched with his Royal 'Ighness—what was it the
    papers had?

'Not least of our merchant-princes.' Dickie, that's me,
    your dad!

I didn't begin with askings. *I* took my job and I stuck;

I took the chances they wouldn't, an' now they're calling
    it luck.

Lord, what boats I've handled—rotten and leaky and
    old—

Ran 'em, or—opened the bilge-cock, precisely as I was
    told.

Grub that 'ud bind you crazy, and crews that 'ud turn you
    grey,

And a big fat lump of insurance to cover the risk on the
    way.

The others they dursn't do it; they said they valued their
    life

(They've served me since as skippers). *I* went, and I took
    my wife.

Over the world I drove 'em, married at twenty-three,

And your mother saving the money and making a man of
    me.

I was content to be master, but she said there was better
 behind;
She took the chances I wouldn't, and I followed your
 mother blind.
She egged me to borrow the money, an' she helped me to
 clear the loan,
When we bought half-shares in a cheap 'un and hoisted a
 flag of our own.
Patching and coaling on credit, and living the Lord knew
 how,
We started the Red Ox freighters—we've eight-and-thirty
 now.
And those were the days of clippers, and the freights were
 clipper-freights,
And we knew we were making our fortune, but she died
 in Macassar Straits—
By the Little Paternosters, as you come to the Union
 Bank—
And we dropped her in fourteen fathom: I pricked it off
 where she sank.
Owners we were, full owners, and the boat was christened
 for her,
And she died in the *Mary Gloster*. My heart, how young
 we were!
So I went on a spree round Java and wellnigh ran her
 ashore,
But your mother came and warned me and I wouldn't liq-
 uor no more:
Strict I stuck to my business, afraid to stop or I'd think,
Saving the money (she warned me), and letting the other
 men drink.
And I met M'Cullough in London (I'd saved five 'undred
 then),
And 'tween us we started the Foundry—three forges and
 twenty men.
Cheap repairs for the cheap 'uns. It paid, and the business
 grew;

For I bought me a steam-lathe patent, and that was a gold
    mine too.

'Cheaper to build 'em than buy 'em,' *I* said, but M'Cul-
    lough he shied,

And we wasted a year in talking before we moved to the
    Clyde.

And the Lines were all beginning, and we all of us started
    fair,

Building our engines like houses and staying the boilers
    square.

But M'Cullough 'e wanted cabins with marble and maple
    and all,

And Brussels an' Utrecht velvet, and baths and a Social
    Hall,

And pipes for closets all over, and cutting the frames too
    light,

But M'Cullough he died in the Sixties, and—— Well, I'm
    dying to-night. . . .

I knew—*I* knew what was coming, when we bid on the
    Byfleet's keel—

They piddled and piffled with iron. I'd given my orders
    for steel!

Steel and the first expansions. It paid, I tell you, it paid,

When we came with our nine-knot freighters and collared
    the long-run trade!

And they asked me how I did it, and I gave 'em the Scrip-
    ture text,

'You keep your light so shining a little in front o' the
    next!'

They copied all they could follow, but they couldn't copy
    my mind,

And I left 'em sweating and stealing a year and a half be-
    hind.

Then came the armour-contracts, but that was M'Cul-
    lough's side;

He was always best in the Foundry, but better, perhaps,
    he died.

I went through his private papers; the notes was plainer
   than print;
And I'm no fool to finish if a man'll give me a hint.
(I remember his widow was angry.) So I saw what his
   drawings meant.
And I started the six-inch rollers, and it paid me sixty per
   cent.
Sixty per cent *with* failures, and more than twice we could
   do,
And a quarter-million to credit, and I saved it all for
   you!
I thought—it doesn't matter—you seemed to favour your
   ma,
But you're nearer forty than thirty, and I know the kind
   you are.
Harrer an' Trinity College! I ought to ha' sent you to
   sea—
But I stood you an education, an' what have you done for
   me?
The things I knew was proper you wouldn't thank me to
   give,
And the things I knew was rotten you said was the way to
   live.
For you muddled with books and pictures, an' china an'
   etchin's an' fans,
And your rooms at college was beastly—more like a
   whore's than a man's;
Till you married that thin-flanked woman, as white and as
   stale as a bone,
An' she gave you your social nonsense; but where's that
   kid o' your own?
I've seen your carriages blocking the half o' the Cromwell
   Road,
But never the doctor's brougham to help the missus un-
   load.
(So there isn't even a grandchild, an' the Gloster family's
   done.)

Not like your mother, she isn't. *She* carried her freight
each run.

But they died, the pore little beggars! At sea she had
'em—they died.

Only you, an' you stood it. You haven't stood much beside.

Weak, a liar, and idle, and mean as a collier's whelp

Nosing for scraps in the galley. No help—my son was no
help!

So he gets three 'undred thousand, in trust and the interest paid.

I wouldn't give it you, Dickie—you see, I made it in trade.

You're saved from soiling your fingers, and if you have no
child,

It all comes back to the business. 'Gad, won't your wife be
wild!

'Calls and calls in her carriage, her 'andkerchief up to 'er
eye:

'Daddy! dear daddy's dyin'!' and doing her best to cry.

Grateful? Oh, yes, I'm grateful, but keep her away from
here.

Your mother 'ud never ha' stood 'er, and, anyhow, women
are queer. . . .

There's women will say I've married a second time. Not
quite!

But give pore Aggie a hundred, and tell her your lawyers'll fight.

She was the best o' the boiling—you'll meet her before it
ends.

I'm in for a row with the mother—I'll leave you settle my
friends.

For a man he must go with a woman, which women don't
understand—

Or the sort that say they can see it they aren't the marrying brand.

But I wanted to speak o' your mother that's Lady Gloster
still;

I'm going to up and see her, without its hurting the will.

Here! Take your hand off the bell-pull. Five thousand's waiting for you,

If you'll only listen a minute, and do as I bid you do.

They'll try to prove me crazy, and, if you bungle, they can;

And I've only you to trust to! (O God, why ain't it a man?)

There's some waste money on marbles, the same as M'Cullough tried—

Marbles and mausoleums—but I call that sinful pride.

There's some ship bodies for burial—we've carried 'em, soldered and packed;

Down in their wills they wrote it, and nobody called *them* cracked.

But me—I've too much money, and people might . . . All my fault:

It come o' hoping for grandsons and buying that Wokin' vault. . . .

I'm sick o' the 'ole dam' business. I'm going back where I came.

Dick, you're the son o' my body, and you'll take charge o' the same!

I want to lie by your mother, ten thousand mile away,

And they'll want to send me to Woking; and that's where you'll earn your pay.

I've thought it out on the quiet, the same as it ought to be done—

Quiet, and decent, and proper—an' here's your orders, my son.

You know the Line? You don't, though. You write to the Board, and tell

Your father's death has upset you an' you're goin' to cruise for a spell,

An' you'd like the *Mary Gloster*—I've held her ready for this—

They'll put her in working order and you'll take her out as
  she is.

Yes, it was money idle when I patched her and laid her
  aside

(Thank God, I can pay for my fancies!)—the boat where
  your mother died,

By the Little Paternosters, as you come to the Union
  Bank,

We dropped her—I think I told you—and I pricked it off
  where she sank.

['Tiny she looked on the grating—that oily, treacly sea—]

'Hundred and Eighteen East, remember, and South just
  Three.

Easy bearings to carry—Three South—Three to the dot;

But I gave McAndrew a copy in case of dying—or not.

And so you'll write to McAndrew, he's Chief of the Maori
  Line;

They'll give him leave, if you ask 'em and say it's business
  o' mine.

I built three boats for the Maoris, an' very well pleased
  they were,

An' I've known Mac since the Fifties, and Mac knew
  me—and her.

After the first stroke warned me I sent him the money to
  keep

Against the time you'd claim it, committin' your dad to
  the deep;

For you are the son o' my body, and Mac was my oldest
  friend,

I've never asked 'im to dinner, but he'll see it out to the
  end.

Stiff-necked Glasgow beggar! I've heard he's prayed for
  my soul.

But he couldn't lie if you paid him, and he'd starve before
  he stole.

He'll take the *Mary* in ballast—you'll find her a lively
  ship;

And you'll take Sir Anthony Gloster, that goes on 'is
    wedding-trip,
Lashed in our old deck-cabin with all three port-holes
    wide,
The kick o' the screw beneath him and the round blue seas
    outside!
Sir Anthony Gloster's carriage—our 'ouse-flag flyin'
    free—
Ten thousand men on the pay-roll and forty freighters at
    sea!
He made himself and a million, but this world is a fleetin'
    show,
And he'll go to the wife of 'is bosom the same as he ought
    to go—
By the heel of the Paternosters—there isn't a chance to
    mistake—
And Mac'll pay you the money as soon as the bubbles
    break!
Five thousand for six weeks' cruising, the staunchest
    freighter afloat,
And Mac he'll give you your bonus the minute I'm out o'
    the boat!
He'll take you round to Macassar, and you'll come back
    alone;
He knows what I want o' the *Mary.* . . . I'll do what I
    please with my own.
Your mother 'ud call it wasteful, but I've seven-and-thirty
    more;
I'll come in my private carriage and bid it wait at the
    door. . . .
For my son 'e was never a credit: 'e muddled with books
    and art,
And 'e lived on Sir Anthony's money and 'e broke Sir
    Anthony's heart.
There isn't even a grandchild, and the Gloster family's
    done—
The only one you left me—O mother, the only one!

Harrer and Trinity College—me slavin' early an' late—
An' he thinks I'm dying crazy, and you're in Macassar
Strait!
Flesh o' my flesh, my dearie, for ever an' ever amen,
That first stroke come for a warning. I ought to ha' gone to
you then.
But—cheap repairs for a cheap 'un—the doctors said I'd
do.
Mary, why didn't *you* warn me? I've allus heeded to you,
Excep'—I know—about women; but you are a spirit now;
An', wife, they was only women, and I was a man. That's
how.
An' a man 'e must go with a woman, as you *could* not un-
derstand;
But I never talked 'em secrets. I paid 'em out o' hand.
Thank Gawd, I can pay for my fancies! Now what's five
thousand to me,
For a berth off the Paternosters in the haven where I
would be?
I believe in the Resurrection, if I read my Bible plain,
But I wouldn't trust 'em at Wokin'; we're safer at sea
again.
For the heart it shall go with the treasure—go down to the
sea in ships.
I'm sick of the hired women. I'll kiss my girl on her
lips!
I'll be content with my fountain. I'll drink from my own
well,
And the wife of my youth shall charm me—an' the rest
can go to Hell!
(Dickie, *he* will, that's certain.) I'll lie in our standin'-bed,
An' Mac'll take her in ballast—an' she trims best by the
head. . . .
Down by the head an' sinkin', her fires are drawn and
cold,
And the water's splashin' hollow on the skin of the empty
hold—

Churning an' choking and chuckling, quiet and scummy
    and dark—
Full to her lower hatches and risin' steady. Hark!
That was the after-bulkhead. . . . She's flooded from stem
    to stern. . . .
'Never seen death yet, Dickie? . . . Well, now is your time
    to learn!

1894

THE LAST CHANTEY

'And there was no more sea.'

Thus said the Lord in the Vault above the Cherubim,
    Calling to the Angels and the Souls in their degree:
        'Lo! Earth has passed away
        On the smoke of Judgment Day.
That Our word may be established shall We gather up the
    sea?'

Loud sang the souls of the jolly, jolly mariners:
    'Plague upon the hurricane that made us furl and flee!
        But the war is done between us,
        In the deep the Lord hath seen us—
Our bones we'll leave the barracout', and God may sink
    the sea!'

Then said the soul of Judas that betrayèd Him:
    'Lord, hast Thou forgotten Thy covenant with me?
        How once a year I go
        To cool me on the floe?
And Ye take my day of mercy if Ye take away the sea.'

Then said the soul of the Angel of the Off-shore Wind:
    (He that bits the thunder when the bull-mouthed
    breakers flee):

'I have watch and ward to keep
 O'er Thy wonders on the deep,
And Ye take mine honour from me if Ye take away the
  sea!'

Loud sang the souls of the jolly, jolly mariners:
 'Nay, but we were angry, and a hasty folk are we.
  If we worked the ship together
  Till she foundered in foul weather,
 Are we babes that we should clamour for a vengeance
  on the sea?'

Then said the souls of the slaves that men threw
  overboard:
 'Kennelled in the picaroon a weary band were we;
  But Thy arm was strong to save,
  And it touched us on the wave,
 And we drowsed the long tides idle till Thy Trumpets
  tore the sea.'

Then cried the soul of the stout Apostle Paul to God:
 'Once we frapped a ship, and she laboured woundily.
  There were fourteen score of these,
  And they blessed Thee on their knees,
 When they learned Thy Grace and Glory under Malta
  by the sea!'

Loud sang the souls of the jolly, jolly mariners,
 Plucking at their harps, and they plucked unhandily:
  'Our thumbs are rough and tarred,
  And the tune is something hard—
 May we lift a Deepsea Chantey such as seamen use at
  sea?'

Then said the souls of the gentlemen-adventurers—
 Fettered wrist to bar all for red iniquity:
  'Ho, we revel in our chains
  O'er the sorrow that was Spain's!

Heave or sink it, leave or drink it, we were masters of
        the sea!'

Up spake the soul of a grey Gothavn 'speckshioner—
    (He that led the flenching in the fleets of fair Dundee)
        'Oh, the ice-blink white and near,
        And the bowhead breaching clear!
    Will Ye whelm them all for wantonness that wallow in
        the sea?'

Loud sang the souls of the jolly, jolly mariners,
    Crying: 'Under heaven, here is neither lead nor lee!
        Must we sing for evermore
        On the windless, glassy floor?
    Take back your golden fiddles and we'll beat to open
        sea!'

Then stooped the Lord, and He called the good sea up to
        Him,
    And 'stablishèd its borders unto all eternity,
        That such as have no pleasure
        For to praise the Lord by measure,
    They may enter into galleons and serve Him on the sea.

Sun, Wind, and Cloud shall fail not from the face of it,
    Stinging, ringing spindrift, nor the fulmar flying free;
        And the ships shall go abroad
        To the Glory of the Lord
    Who heard the silly sailor-folk and gave them back
        their sea!

                                                    1893

THE LONG TRAIL

There's a whisper down the field where the year has shot
        her yield,
    And the ricks stand grey to the sun,

Singing: 'Over then, come over, for the bee has quit the
    clover,
  'And your English summer's done.'
      You have heard the beat of the off-shore wind,
      And the thresh of the deep-sea rain;
      You have heard the song—how long? how long?
      Pull out on the trail again!
    Ha' done with the Tents of Shem, dear lass,
    We've seen the seasons through,
    And it's time to turn on the old trail, our own trail,
      the out trail,
    Pull out, pull out, on the Long Trail—the trail that is
      always new!

It's North you may run to the rime-ringed sun
  Or South to the blind Horn's hate;
Or East all the way into Mississippi Bay,
  Or West to the Golden Gate—
      Where the blindest bluffs hold gold, dear lass,
      And the wildest tales are true,
      And the men bulk big on the old trail, our own
      trail, the out trail,
      And life runs large on the Long Trail—the trail
      that is always new.

The days are sick and cold, and the skies are grey and old
  And the twice-breathed airs blow damp;
And I'd sell my tired soul for the bucking beam-sea roll
  Of a black Bilbao tramp,
      With her load-line over her hatch, dear lass,
      And a drunken Dago crew,
      And her nose held down on the old trail, our own
      trail, the out trail
      From Cadiz south on the Long Trail—the trail that
      is always new.

There be triple ways to take, of the eagle or the snake,
  Or the way of a man with a maid;

But the sweetest way to me is a ship's upon the sea
  In the heel of the North-East Trade.
      Can you hear the crash on her bows, dear lass,
      And the drum of the racing screw,
      As she ships it green on the old trail, our own trail,
        the out trail,
      As she lifts and 'scends on the Long Trail—the
        trail that is always new?

See the shaking funnels roar, with the Peter at the fore,
  And the fenders grind and heave,
And the derricks clack and grate, as the tackle hooks the
        crate,
  And the fall-rope whines through the sheave;
      It's 'Gang-plank up and in,' dear lass,
      It's 'Hawsers warp her through!'
      And it's 'All clear aft' on the old trail, our own
        trail, the out trail,
      We're backing down on the Long Trail—the trail
        that is always new.

O the mutter overside, when the port-fog holds us tied,
  And the sirens hoot their dread,
When foot by foot we creep o'er the hueless, viewless
        deep
  To the sob of the questing lead!
      It's down by the Lower Hope, dear lass,
      With the Gunfleet Sands in view,
      Till the Mouse swings green on the old trail, our
        own trail, the out trail,
      And the Gull Light lifts on the Long Trail—the
        trail that is always new.

O the blazing tropic night, when the wake's a welt of light
  That holds the hot sky tame,
And the steady fore-foot snores through the planet pow-
        dered floors

Where the sacred whale flukes in flame!
    Her plates are flaked by the sun, dear lass,
    And her ropes are taut with the dew,
    For we're booming down on the old trail, our own
        trail, the out trail,
    We're sagging south on the Long Trail—the trail
        that is always new.

Then home, get her home, where the drunken rollers
        comb,
    And the shouting seas drive by,
And the engines stamp and ring, and the wet bows reel
        and swing,
    And the Southern Cross rides high!
        Yes, the old lost stars wheel back, dear lass,
        That blaze in the velvet blue.
        They're all old friends on the old trail, our own
            trail, the out trail,
        They're God's own guides on the Long Trail—the
            trail that is always new.

Fly forward, O my heart, from the Foreland to the Start—
    We're steaming all too slow,
And it's twenty thousand mile to our little lazy isle
    Where the trumpet-orchids blow!
        You have heard the call of the off-shore wind
        And the voice of the deep-sea rain;
        You have heard the song—how long?—how long?
        Pull out on the trail again!

The Lord knows what we may find, dear lass,
And The Deuce knows what we may do—
But we're back once more on the old trail, our own trail,
        the out trail,
We're down, hull-down, on the Long Trail—the trail that
        is always new!

                                                    1891

THE GIPSY TRAIL

The white moth to the closing bine,
   The bee to the opened clover,
And the gipsy blood to the gipsy blood
   Ever the wide world over.

Ever the wide world over, lass,
   Ever the trail held true,
Over the world and under the world,
   And back at the last to you.

Out of the dark of the gorgio camp,
   Out of the grime and the gray
(Morning waits at the end of the world),
   Gipsy, come away!

The wild boar to the sun-dried swamp,
   The red crane to her reed,
And the Romany lass to the Romany lad
   By the tie of a roving breed.

The pied snake to the rifted rock,
   The buck to the stony plain,
And the Romany lass to the Romany lad,
   And both to the road again.

Both to the road again, again!
   Out on a clean sea-track—
Follow the cross of the gipsy trail
   Over the world and back!

Follow the Romany patteran
   North where the blue bergs sail,
And the bows are gray with the frozen spray,
   And the masts are shod with mail.

Follow the Romany patteran
   Sheer to the Austral Light,

Where the besom of God is the wild South wind,
  Sweeping the sea-floors white.

Follow the Romany patteran
  West to the sinking sun,
Till the junk-sails lift through the houseless drift,
  And the east and the west are one.

Follow the Romany patteran
  East where the silence broods
By a purple wave on an opal beach
  In the hush of the Mahim woods.

'The wild hawk to the wind-swept sky,
  The deer to the wholesome wold,
And the heart of a man to the heart of a maid,
  As it was in the days of old.'

The heart of a man to the heart of a maid—
  Light of my tents, be fleet.
Morning waits at the end of the world,
  And the world is all at our feet!

                                        1904

THE LAST OF THE LIGHT BRIGADE

There were thirty million English who talked of
  England's might,
There were twenty broken troopers who lacked a bed for
  the night.
They had neither food nor money, they had neither ser-
  vice nor trade;
They were only shiftless soldiers, the last of the Light
  Brigade.

They felt that life was fleeting; they knew not that art was
  long,
That though they were dying of famine, they lived in
  deathless song.

They asked for a little money to keep the wolf from the
  door;
And the thirty million English sent twenty pounds and
  four!

They laid their heads together that were scarred and lined
  and grey;
Keen were the Russian sabres, but want was keener than
  they;
And an old Troop-Sergeant muttered, 'Let us go to the
  man who writes
The things on Balaclava the kiddies at school recites.'

They went without bands or colours, a regiment ten-file
  strong,
To look for the Master-singer who had crowned them all
  in his song;
And, waiting his servant's order, by the garden gate they
  stayed,
A desolate little cluster, the last of the Light Brigade.

They stove to stand to attention, to straighten the toil-
  bowed back;
They drilled on an empty stomach, the loose-knit files fell
  slack;
With stooping of weary shoulders, in garments tattered
  and frayed,
They shambled into his presence, the last of the Light
  Brigade.

The old Troop-Sergeant was spokesman, and 'Beggin'
  your pardon,' he said,
'You wrote o' the Light Brigade, sir. Here's all that isn't
  dead.
An' it's all come true what you wrote, sir, regardin' the
  mouth of hell;
For we're all of us nigh to the workhouse, an' we thought
  we'd call an' tell.

No, thank you, we don't want food, sir; but couldn't you
    take an' write
A sort of "to be continued" and "see next page" o' the
    fight?
We think that someone has blundered, an' couldn't you
    tell 'em how?
You wrote we were heroes once, sir. Please, write we are
    starving now.'

The poor little army departed, limping and lean and for-
    lorn.
And the heart of the Master-singer grew hot with 'the
    scorn of scorn.'
And he wrote for them wonderful verses that swept the
    land like flame,
Till the fatted souls of the English were scourged with the
    thing called Shame.

O thirty million English that babble of England's
    might,
Behold there are twenty heroes who lack their food to-
    night;
Our children's children are lisping to 'honour the charge
    they made—'
And we leave to the streets and the workhouse the charge
    of the Light Brigade!

                           1890

THE SETTLER

(South African War ended, May 1902)

    Here, where my fresh-turned furrows run,
       And the deep soil glistens red,
  I will repair the wrong that was done
       To the living and the dead.

Here, where the senseless bullet fell,
    And the barren shrapnel burst,
I will plant a tree, I will dig a well,
    Against the heat and the thirst.

Here, in a large and a sunlit land,
    Where no wrong bites to the bone,
I will lay my hand in my neighbour's hand,
    And together we will atone
For the set folly and the red breach
    And the black waste of it all;
Giving and taking counsel each
    Over the cattle-kraal.

Here will we join against our foes—
    The hailstroke and the storm,
And the red and rustling cloud that blows
    The locust's mile-deep swarm.
Frost and murrain and flood let loose
    Shall launch us side by side
In the holy wars that have no truce
    'Twixt seed and harvest-tide.

Earth, where we rode to slay or be slain,
    Our love shall redeem unto life.
We will gather and lead to her lips again
    The waters of ancient strife,
From the far and the fiercely guarded streams
    And the pools where we lay in wait,
Till the corn cover our evil dreams
    And the young corn our hate

And when we bring old fights to mind,
    We will not remember the sin—
If there be blood on his head of my kind,
    Or blood on my head of his kin—
For the ungrazed upland, the untilled lea
    Cry, and the fields forlorn:
'The dead must bury their dead, but ye—
    Ye serve an host unborn.'

Bless then, Our God, the new-yoked plough
   And the good beasts that draw,
And the bread we eat in the sweat of our brow
   According to Thy Law.
After us cometh a multitude—
   Prosper the work of our hands,
That we may feed with our land's food
   The folk of all our lands!

Here, in the waves and the troughs of the plains
   Where the healing stillness lies,
And the vast, benignant sky restrains
   And the long days make wise—
Bless to our use the rain and the sun
   And the blind seed in its bed,
That we may repair the wrong that was done
   To the living and the dead!

1903

MY BOY JACK

(1914–18)

'Have you news of my boy Jack?'
   Not this tide.
'When d'you think that he'll come back?'
   Not with this wind blowing, and this tide.

'Has any one else had word of him?'
   Not this tide.
For what is sunk will hardly swim,
   Not with this wind blowing, and this tide.

'Oh, dear, what comfort can I find?'
   None this tide,
   Nor any tide,
Except he did not shame his kind—
   Not even with that wind blowing, and that tide.

Then hold your head up all the more,
  This tide,
  And every tide;
Because he was the son you bore,
  And gave to that wind blowing and that tide!

1916

THE VAMPIRE

A fool there was and he made his prayer
  (Even as you and I!)
To a rag and a bone and a hank of hair
(We called her the woman who did not care)
But the fool he called her his lady fair—
(Even as you and I!)

Oh, the years we waste and the tears we waste
And the work of our head and hand
Belong to the woman who did not know
(And now we know that she never could know)
And did not understand!

A fool there was and his goods he spent
(Even as you and I!)
Honour and faith and a sure intent
(And it wasn't the least what the lady meant)
But a fool must follow his natural bent
(Even as you and I!)

Oh, the toil we lost and the spoil we lost
And the excellent things we planned
Belong to the woman who didn't know why
(And now we know that she never knew why)
And did not understand!

The fool was stripped to his foolish hide
(Even as you and I!)
Which she might have seen when she threw him aside—
(But it isn't on record the lady tried)
So some of him lived but the most of him died—
(Even as you and I!)

And it isn't the shame and it isn't the blame
That stings like a white-hot brand—
It's coming to know that she never knew why
(Seeing, at last, she could never know why)
And never could understand!

1897

WHEN EARTH'S LAST PICTURE IS PAINTED

(L'Envoi to 'The Seven Seas')

When Earth's last picture is painted and the tubes are
      twisted and dried,
When the oldest colours have faded, and the youngest
      critic has died
We shall rest, and, faith, we shall need it—lie down for an
      æon or two,
Till the Master of All Good Workmen shall put us to work
      anew.

And those that were good shall be happy: they shall sit in
      a golden chair;
They shall splash at a ten-league canvas with brushes of
      comets' hair.
They shall find real saints to draw from—Magdalene,
      Peter, and Paul;
They shall work for an age at a sitting and never be tired
      at all!

And only The Master shall praise us, and only The Mas-
    ter shall blame;
And no one shall work for money, and no one shall work
    for fame,
But each for the joy of the working, and each, in his sepa-
    rate star,
Shall draw the Thing as he sees It for the God of Things
    as They are!

                                                    1892

THE HOLY WAR

For here lay the excellent wisdom of him that built
Mansoul, that the walls could never be broken down
nor hurt by the most mighty adverse potentate unless
the townsmen gave consent thereto.

                                    Bunyan's *Holy War*

A tinker out of Bedford,
    A vagrant oft in quod,
A private under Fairfax,
    A minister of God—
Two hundred years and thirty
    Ere Armageddon came
His single hand portrayed it,
    And Bunyan was his name

He mapped for those who follow,
    The world in which we are—
'This famous town of Mansoul'
    That takes the Holy War.
Her true and traitor people,
    The Gates along her wall,
From Eye Gate unto Feel Gate,
    John Bunyan showed them all.

All enemy divisions,
  Recruits of every class,
And highly screened positions
  For flame or poison-gas;
The craft that we call modern,
  The crimes that we call new,
John Bunyan had 'em typed and filed
  In Sixteen Eighty-two.

Likewise the Lords of Looseness
  That hamper faith and works,
The Perseverance-Doubters,
  And Present-Comfort shirks,
With brittle intellectuals
  Who crack beneath a strain—
John Bunyan met that helpful set
  In Charles the Second's reign

Emmanuel's vanguard dying
  For right and not for rights,
My Lord Apollyon lying
  To the State-kept Stockholmites,
The Pope, the swithering Neutrals,
  The Kaiser and his Gott—
Their rôles, their goals, their naked souls—
  He knew and drew the lot.

Now he hath left his quarters,
  In Bunhill Fields to lie,
The wisdom that he taught us
  Is proven prophecy—
One watchword through our Armies,
  One answer from our Lands:—
'No dealings with Diabolus
  As long as Mansoul stands!'

A pedlar from a hovel,
  The lowest of the low—

The Father of the Novel,
    Salvation's first Defoe—
Eight blinded generations
    Ere Armageddon came,
He showed us how to meet it,
    And Bunyan was his name!
                                    1917

FRANCE

Broke to every known mischance, lifted over all
By the light sane joy of life, the buckler of the Gaul;
Furious in luxury, merciless in toil,
Terrible with strength that draws from her tireless soil;
Strictest judge of her own worth, gentlest of man's mind,
First to follow Truth and last to leave old Truths be-
    hind—
France, beloved of every soul that loves its fellow-kind!

Ere our birth (rememberest thou?) side by side we lay
Fretting in the womb of Rome to begin our fray.
Ere men knew our tongues apart, our one task was
    known—
Each to mould the other's fate as he wrought his own.

To this end we stirred mankind till all Earth was ours,
Till our world-end strifes begat wayside Thrones and
    Powers—
Puppets that we made or broke to bar the other's path—
Necessary, outpost-folk, hirelings of our wrath.
To this end we stormed the seas, tack for tack, and burst
Through the doorways of new worlds, doubtful which
    was first,
Hand on hilt (rememberest thou?) ready for the blow—
Sure, whatever else we met, we should meet our foe.
Spurred or balked at every stride by the other's strength,
So we rode the ages down and every ocean's length!

Where did you refrain from us or we refrain from you?
Ask the wave that has not watched war between us two!
Others held us for a while, but with weaker charms,
These we quitted at the call for each other's arms.

Eager toward the known delight, equally we strove—
Each the other's mystery, terror, need, and love.
To each other's open court with our proofs we came.
Where could we find honour else, or men to test our
claim?
From each other's throat we wrenched—valour's last re-
ward—
That extorted word of praise gasped 'twixt lunge and
guard.
In each other's cup we poured mingled blood and tears,
Brutal joys, unmeasured hopes, intolerable fears—
All that soiled or salted life for a thousand years.
Proved beyond the need of proof, matched in every clime,
O Companion, we have lived greatly through all time!

Yoked in knowledge and remorse, now we come to rest,
Laughing at old villainies that Time has turned to jest;
Pardoning old necessities no pardon can efface—
That undying sin we shared in Rouen market-place.

Now we watch the new years shape, wondering if they
hold
Fiercer lightnings in their heart than we launched of old.
Now we hear new voices rise, question, boast or gird,
As we raged (rememberest thou?) when our crowds were
stirred.
Now we count new keels afloat, and new hosts on land,
Massed like ours (rememberest thou?) when our strokes
were planned.
We were schooled for dear life's sake, to know each other's
blade.
What can Blood and Iron make more than we have made?
We have learned by keenest use to know each other's
mind.

What shall Blood and Iron loose that we cannot bind?
We who swept each other's coast, sacked each other's
    home,
Since the sword of Brennus clashed on the scales at Rome,
Listen, count and close again, wheeling girth to girth,
In the linked and steadfast guard set for peace on earth!

Broke to every known mischance, lifted over all
By the light sane joy of life, the buckler of the Gaul;
Furious in luxury, merciless in toil,
Terrible with strength renewed from a tireless soil;
Strictest judge of her own worth, gentlest of man's mind,
First to face the Truth and last to leave old Truths be-
    hind—
France, beloved of every soul that loves or serves its kind!
                                                    1913

MESOPOTAMIA

They shall not return to us, the resolute, the young,
    The eager and whole-hearted whom we gave:
But the men who left them thriftily to die in their own
    dung,
    Shall they come with years and honour to the grave?

They shall not return to us, the strong men coldly slain
    In sight of help denied from day to day:
But the men who edged their agonies and chid them in
    their pain,
    Are they too strong and wise to put away?

Our dead shall not return to us while Day and Night di-
    vide—
    Never while the bars of sunset hold.
But the idle-minded overlings who quibbled while they
    died,
    Shall they thrust for high employments as of old?

Shall we only threaten and be angry for an hour?
    When the storm is ended shall we find
How softly but how swiftly they have sidled back to
        power
    By the favour and contrivance of their kind?

Even while they soothe us, while they promise large
        amends,
    Even while they make a show of fear,
Do they call upon their debtors, and take counsel with
        their friends,
    To confirm and re-establish each career?

Their lives cannot repay us—their death could not
        undo—
    The shame that they have laid upon our race.
But the slothfulness that wasted and the arrogance that
        slew,
    Shall we leave it unabated in its place?

                                                    1917

THE VETERANS

(*Written for the gathering of survivors of the Indian
Mutiny, Albert Hall*, 1907)

        To-day, across our fathers' graves,
            The astonished years reveal
        The remnants of that deperate host
            Which cleansed our East with steel.

        Hail and farewell! We greet you here,
            With tears that none will scorn—
        O Keepers of the House of old,
            Or ever we were born!

        One service more we dare to ask—
            Pray for us, heroes, pray,

That when Fate lays on us our task
   We do not shame the Day!

                    1907

THE WHITE MAN'S BURDEN

(*The United States and the Philippine Islands*)

Take up the White Man's burden—
   Send forth the best ye breed—
Go bind your sons to exile
   To serve your captives' need;
To wait in heavy harness
   On fluttered folk and wild—
Your new-caught, sullen peoples,
   Half devil and half child.

Take up the White Man's burden—
   In patience to abide,
To veil the threat of terror
   And check the show of pride;
By open speech and simple,
   An hundred times made plain,
To seek another's profit,
   And work another's gain.

Take up the White Man's burden—
   The savage wars of peace—
Fill full the mouth of Famine
   And bid the sickness cease;
And when your goal is nearest
   The end for others sought,
Watch Sloth and heathen Folly
   Bring all your hope to nought.

Take up the White Man's burden—
  No tawdry rule of kings,
But toil of serf and sweeper—
  The tale of common things.
The ports ye shall not enter,
  The roads ye shall not tread,
Go make them with your living,
  And mark them with your dead!

Take up the White Man's burden—
  And reap his old reward:
The blame of those ye better,
  The hate of those ye guard—
The cry of hosts ye humour
  (Ah, slowly) toward the light:—
'Why brought ye us from bondage,
  'Our loved Egyptian night?'

Take up the White Man's burden—
  Ye dare not stoop to less—
Nor call too loud on Freedom
  To cloak your weariness;
By all ye cry or whisper,
  By all ye leave or do,
The silent, sullen peoples
  Shall weigh your Gods and you.

Take up the White Man's burden—
  Have done with childish days—
The lightly proffered laurel,
  The easy, ungrudged praise.
Comes now, to search your manhood
  Through all the thankless years,
Cold-edged with dear-bought wisdom,
  The judgment of your peers!

1899

RECESSIONAL

God of our fathers, known of old,
   Lord of our far-flung battle-line,
Beneath whose awful Hand we hold
   Dominion over palm and pine—
Lord God of Hosts, be with us yet,
Lest we forget—lest we forget!

The tumult and the shouting dies;
   The Captains and the Kings depart:
Still stands Thine ancient sacrifice,
   An humble and a contrite heart.
Lord God of Hosts, be with us yet,
Lest we forget—lest we forget!

Far-called, our navies melt away;
   On dune and headland sinks the fire:
Lo, all our pomp of yesterday
   Is one with Nineveh and Tyre!
Judge of the Nations, spare us yet,
Lest we forget—lest we forget!

If, drunk with sight of power, we loose
   Wild tongues that have not Thee in awe,
Such boastings as the Gentiles use,
   Or lesser breeds without the Law—
Lord God of Hosts, be with us yet,
Lest we forget—lest we forget!

For heathen heart that puts her trust
   In reeking tube and iron shard,
All valiant dust that builds on dust,
   And guarding, calls not Thee to guard.
For frantic boast and foolish word—-
Thy mercy on Thy People, Lord!

                1897

'FOR ALL WE HAVE AND ARE'

For all we have and are,
For all our children's fate,
Stand up and take the war.
The Hun is at the gate!
Our world has passed away,
In wantonness o'erthrown.
There is nothing left to-day
But steel and fire and stone!
　　Though all we knew depart,
　　The old Commandments stand:—
　　'In courage keep your heart,
　　In strength lift up your hand.'

Once more we hear the word
That sickened earth of old:—
'No law except the Sword
Unsheathed and uncontrolled.'
Once more it knits mankind,
Once more the nations go
To meet and break and bind
A crazed and driven foe.

Comfort, content, delight,
The ages' slow-bought gain,
They shrivelled in a night.
Only ourselves remain
To face the naked days
In silent fortitude,
Through perils and dismays
Renewed and re-renewed.
　　Though all we made depart,
　　The old Commandments stand:—
　　'In patience keep your heart,
　　In strength lift up your hand.'

No easy hope or lies
　Shall bring us to our goal,
But iron sacrifice
　Of body, will, and soul.
There is but one task for all—
　One life for each to give.
What stands if Freedom fall?
　Who dies if England live?

　　　　　　　　　　1914

THE BENEFACTORS

Ah! What avails the classic bent
　And what the cultured word,
Against the undoctored incident
　That actually occurred?

And what is Art whereto we press
　Through paint and prose and rhyme—
When Nature in her nakedness
　Defeats us every time?

It is not learning, grace nor gear,
　Nor easy meat and drink,
But bitter pinch of pain and fear
　That makes creation think.

When in this world's unpleasing youth
　Our godlike race began,
The longest arm, the sharpest tooth,
　Gave man control of man;

Till, bruised and bitten to the bone
　And taught by pain and fear,
He learned to deal the far-off stone,
　And poke the long, safe spear.

So tooth and nail were obsolete
  As means against a foe,
Till, bored by uniform defeat,
  Some genius built the bow.

Then stone and javelin proved as vain
  As old-time tooth and nail;
Till, spurred anew by fear and pain,
  Man fashioned coats of mail.

Then was there safety for the rich
  And danger for the poor,
Till someone mixed a powder which
  Redressed the scale once more.

Helmet and armour disappeared
  With sword and bow and pike,
And, when the smoke of battle cleared,
  All men were armed alike. . . .

And when ten million such were slain
  To please one crazy king,
Man, schooled in bulk by fear and pain,
  Grew weary of the thing;

And at the very hour designed
  To enslave him past recall,
His tooth-stone-arrow-gun-shy mind
  Turned and abolished all.

All Power, each Tyrant, every Mob
  Whose head has grown too large,
Ends by destroying its own job
  And works its own discharge;

And Man, whose mere necessities
  Move all things from his path,
Trembles meanwhile at their decrees,
  And deprecates their wrath!

1919

THE CRAFTSMAN

Once, after long-drawn revel at The Mermaid,
He to the overbearing Boanerges
Jonson, uttered (if half of it were liquor,
        Blessed be the vintage!)

Saying how, at an alehouse under Cotswold,
He had made sure of his very Cleopatra
Drunk with enormous, salvation-contemning
        Love for a tinker.

How, while he hid from Sir Thomas's keepers,
Crouched in a ditch and drenched by the midnight
Dews, he had listened to gipsy Juliet
        Rail at the dawning.

How at Bankside, a boy drowning kittens
Winced at the business; whereupon his sister—
Lady Macbeth aged seven—thrust 'em under,
        Sombrely scornful.

How on a Sabbath, hushed and compassionate—
She being known since her birth to the townsfolk—
Stratford dredged and delivered from Avon
        Dripping Ophelia.

So, with a thin third finger marrying
Drop to wine-drop domed on the table,
Shakespeare opened his heart till the sunrise
        Entered to hear him.

London waked and he, imperturbable,
Passed from waking to hurry after shadows . . .
Busied upon shows of no earthly importance?
        Yes, but he knew it!

                1919

'WHEN 'OMER SMOTE 'HIS BLOOMIN' LYRE'

(*Introduction to the Barrack-Room Ballads in
'The Seven Seas'*)

When 'Omer smote 'is bloomin' lyre,
    He'd 'eard men sing by land an' sea;
An' what he thought 'e might require,
    'E went an' took—the same as me!

The market-girls an' fishermen,
    The shepherds an' sailors, too,
They 'eard old songs turn up again,
    But kep' it quite—same as you!

They knew 'e stole; 'e knew they knowed.
    They didn't tell, nor make a fuss,
But winked at 'Omer down the road,
    An' 'e winked back—the same as us!

                                        1896

EPITAPHS OF THE WAR

THE WONDER
Body and Spirit I surrendered whole
To harsh Instructors—and received a soul . . .
If mortal man could change me through and through
From all I was—what may The God not do?

HINDU SEPOY IN FRANCE
This man in his own country prayed we know not to what
    Powers.
We pray Them to reward him for his bravery in ours.

THE COWARD
I could not look on Death, which being known,
Men led me to him, blindfold and alone.

SHOCK

My name, my speech, my self I had forgot.
My wife and children came—I knew them not.
I died. My Mother followed. At her call
And on her bosom I remembered all.

A GRAVE NEAR CAIRO

Gods of the Nile, should this stout fellow here
Get out—get out! He knows not shame nor fear.

PELICANS IN THE WILDERNESS
A Grave near Halfa

The blown sand heaps on me, that none may learn
  Where I am laid for whom my children grieve....
O wings that beat at dawning, ye return
  Out of the desert to your young at eve!

THE FAVOUR

Death favoured me from the first, well knowing I could
    not endure
To wait on him day by day. He quitted my betters and
    came
Whistling over the fields, and, when he had made all sure,
  'Thy line is at end,' he said, 'but at least I have saved its
    name.'

THE BEGINNER

On the first hour of my first day
  In the front trench I fell.
(Children in boxes at play
  Stand up to watch it well.)

A DEAD STATESMAN

I could not dig: I dared not rob:
There I lied to please the mob.
Now all my lies are proved untrue
And I must face the men I slew.
What tale shall serve me here among
Mine angry and defrauded young?

CONVOY ESCORT

I was a shepherd to fools
  Causelessly bold or afraid.
They would not abide by my rules.
  Yet they escaped. For I stayed.

UNKNOWN FEMALE CORPSE

Headless, lacking foot and hand,
Horrible I come to land.
I beseech all women's sons
Know I was a mother once.

RAPED AND REVENGED

One used and butchered me: another spied
Me broken—for which thing an hundred died.
So it was learned among the heathen hosts
How much a freeborn woman's favour costs.

SALONIKAN GRAVE

I have watched a thousand days
Push out and crawl into night
Slowly as tortoises.
Now I, too, follow these.
It is fever, and not the fight—
Time, not battle,—that slays.

THE BRIDEGROOM

Call me not false, beloved,
  If, from thy scarce-known breast
So little time removed,
  In other arms I rest.

For this more ancient bride,
  Whom coldly I embrace,
Was constant at my side
  Before I saw thy face.

Our marriage, often set—
  By miracle delayed—
At last is consummate,
  And cannot be unmade.

Live, then, whom Life shall cure,
    Almost, of Memory,
And leave us to endure
    Its immortality.

                                        1919

DANNY DEEVER

'What are the bugles blowin' for?' said Files-on-Parade.
'To turn you out, to turn you out,' the Colour-Sergeant
        said.
'What makes you look so white, so white?' said Files-on-
        Parade.
'I'm dreadin' what I've got to watch,' the Colour-Sergeant
        said.
    For they're hangin' Danny Deever, you can hear the
        Dead March play,
    The Regiment's in 'ollow square—they're hangin' him
        to-day;
    They've taken of his buttons off an' cut his stripes
        away,
    An' they're hangin' Danny Deever in the mornin'.

'What makes the rear-rank breathe so 'ard?' said Files-on-
        Parade.
'It's bitter cold, it's bitter cold,' the Colour-Sergeant said.
'What makes that front-rank man fall down?' said Files-
        on-Parade.
'A touch o' sun, a touch o' sun,' the Colour-Sergeant said.
    They are hangin' Danny Deever, they are marchin' of
        'im round,
    They 'ave 'alted Danny Deever by 'is coffin on the
        ground;
    An' 'e'll swing in 'arf a minute for a sneakin' shootin'
        hound—
    O they're hangin' Danny Deever in the mornin'!

' 'Is cot was right-'and cot to mine,' said Files-on-Parade.
' 'E's sleepin' out an' far to-night,' the Colour-Sergeant
said.
'I've drunk 'is beer a score o' times,' said Files-on-Parade.
' 'E's drinkin' bitter beer alone,' the Colour-Sergeant said.
  They are hangin' Danny Deever, you must mark 'im to
    'is place,
  For 'e shot a comrade sleepin'—you must look 'im in
    the face;
  Nine 'undred of 'is county an' the Regiment's disgrace,
  While they're hanging' Danny Deever in the mornin'.

'What's that so black agin the sun?' said Files-on-Parade.
'It's Danny fightin' 'ard for life,' the Colour-Sergeant said.
'What's that that whimpers over'ead?' said Files-on-
Parade.
'It's Danny's soul that's passin' now,' the Colour-Sergeant
said.
  For they're done with Danny Deever, you can 'ear the
    quickstep play,
  The Regiment's in column, an' they're marchin' us
    away;
  Ho! the young recruits are shakin', an' they'll want their
    beer to-day,
  After hangin' Danny Deever in the mornin'!

                                                    1890

                        TOMMY

I went into a public-'ouse to get a pint o' beer,
The publican 'e up an' sez, 'We serve no red-coats here.'
The girls be'ind the bar they laughed an' giggled fit to die,
I outs into the street again an' to myself sez I:
  O it's Tommy this, an' Tommy that, an' 'Tommy, go
    away';
  But it's 'Thank you, Mister Atkins,' when the band
    begins to play—

The band begins to play, my boys, the band begins to
   play,
O it's 'Thank you, Mister Atkins,' when the band
   begins to play.

I went into a theatre as sober as could be,
They gave a drunk civilian room, but 'adn't none for me;
They sent me to the gallery or round the music-'alls,
But when it comes to fightin', Lord! they'll shove me in
   the stalls!
   For it's Tommy this, an' Tommy that, an' 'Tommy,
      wait outside';
   But it's 'Special train for Atkins' when the trooper's on
      the tide—
   The troopship's on the tide, my boys, the troopship's on
      the tide,
   O it's 'Special train for Atkins' when the trooper's on
      the tide.

Yes, makin' mock o' uniforms that guard you while you
   sleep
Is cheaper than them uniforms, an' they're starvation
   cheap;
An' hustlin' drunken soldiers when they're goin' large a
   bit
Is five times better business than paradin' in full kit.
   Then it's Tommy this, an' Tommy that, an' 'Tommy,
      'ow's yer soul?'
   But it's 'Thin red line of 'eroes' when the drums begin
      to roll—
   The drums begin to roll, my boys, the drums begin to
      roll,
   O it's 'Thin red line of 'eroes' when the drums begin to
      roll.

We aren't no thin red 'eroes, nor we aren't no blackguards
   too,
But single men in barricks, most remarkable like you;

An' if sometimes our conduck isn't all your fancy paints,
Why, single men in barricks don't grow into plaster saints;
  While it's Tommy this, an' Tommy that, an' 'Tommy,
    fall be'ind,'
  But it's 'Please to walk in front, sir,' when there's trou-
    ble in the wind—
  There's trouble in the wind, my boys, there's trouble in
    the wind,
  O it's 'Please to walk in front, sir,' when there's trouble
    in the wind.

You talk o' better food for us, an' schools, an' fires, an' all:
We'll wait for extry rations if you treat us rational.
Don't mess about the cook-room slops, but prove it to our
    face
The Widow's Uniform is not the soldier-man's disgrace.
  For it's Tommy this, an' Tommy that, an' 'Chuck him
    out, the brute!'
  But it's 'Saviour of 'is country' when the guns begin to
    shoot;
  An' it's Tommy this, an' Tommy that, an' anything
    you please;
  An' Tommy ain't a bloomin' fool—you bet that
    Tommy sees!

                                1890

GUNGA DIN

  You may talk o' gin and beer
  When you're quartered safe out 'ere,
  An' you're sent to penny-fights an' Aldershot it;
  But when it comes to slaughter
  You will do your work on water,
  An' you'll lick the bloomin' boots of 'im that's got it.
  Now in Injia's sunny clime,
  Where I used to spend my time
  A-servin' of 'Er Majesty the Queen.

Of all them blackfaced crew
The finest man I knew
Was our regimental bhisti, Gunga Din,
      He was 'Din! Din! Din!
  'You limpin' lump o' brick-dust, Gunga Din!
      'Hi! Slippy *hitherao!*
      'Water, get it! *Panee lao,*[1]
  'You squidgy-nosed old idol, Gunga Din.'

The uniform 'e wore
Was nothin' much before,
An' rather less than 'arf o' that be'ind,
For a piece o' twisty rag
An' a goatskin water-bag
Was all the field-equipment 'e could find.
When the sweatin' troop-train lay
In a sidin' through the day,
Where the 'eat would make your bloomin' eyebrows
      crawl,
We shouted 'Harry By!'[2]
Till our throats were bricky-dry,
Then we wopped 'im 'cause 'e couldn't serve us all.
      It was 'Din! Din! Din!
  'You 'eathen, where the mischief 'ave you been?
      'You put some *juldee*[3] in it
      'Or I'll *marrow*[4] you this minute
  'If you don't fill up my helmet, Gunga Din!'

'E would dot an' carry one
Till the longest day was done;
An' 'e didn't seem to know the use o' fear.
If we charged or broke or cut,
You could bet your bloomin' nut,

---

[1] Bring water swiftly.
[2] O brother.
[3] Be quick.
[4] Hit you.

'E'd be waitin' fifty paces right flank rear.
With 'is mussick[1] on 'is back,
'E would skip with our attack,
An' watch us till the bugles made 'Retire,'
An' for all 'is dirty 'ide
'E was white, clear white, inside
When 'e went to tend the wounded under fire!
    It was 'Din! Din! Din!'
  With the bullets kickin' dust-spots on the green.
    When the cartridges ran out,
    You could hear the front-ranks shout,
  'Hi! ammunition-mules an' Gunga Din!'

I shan't forgit the night
When I dropped be'ind the fight
With a bullet where my belt-plate should 'a' been.
I was chokin' mad with thirst,
An' the man that spied me first
Was our good old grinnin', gruntin' Gunga Din.
'E lifted up my 'ead,
An' he plugged me where I bled,
An' 'e guv me 'arf-a-pint o' water green.
It was crawlin' and it stunk.
But of all the drinks I've drunk,
I'm gratefullest to one from Gunga Din.
    It was 'Din! Din! Din!
  ' 'Ere's a beggar with a bullet through 'is spleen;
    ' 'E's chawin' up the ground,
    'An' 'e's kickin' all around:
  'For Gawd's sake git the water, Gunga Din!'

'E carried me away
To where a dooli lay,
An' a bullet come an' drilled the beggar clean.
'E put me safe inside,

---

[1] Water-skin.

An' just before 'e died,
'I 'ope you like your drink,' sez Gunga Din.
So I'll meet 'im later on
At the place where 'e is gone—
Where it's always double drill and no canteen.
'E'll be squattin' on the coals
Givin' drink to poor damned souls,
An' I'll get a swig in hell from Gunga Din!
    Yes, Din! Din! Din!
  You Lazarushian-leather Gunga Din!
    Though I've belted you and flayed you,
    By the livin' Gawd that made you,
  You're a better man than I am, Gunga Din!
                    1890

THE WIDOW AT WINDSOR

Ave you 'eard o' the Widow at Windsor
  With a hairy gold crown on 'er 'ead?
She 'as ships on the foam—she 'as millions at 'ome
  An' she pays us poor beggars in red.
    (Ow, poor beggars in red!)
There's 'er nick on the cavalry 'orses,
  There's 'er mark on the medical stores—
An' 'er troopers you'll find with a fair wind be'ind
  That takes us to various wars.
    (Poor beggars!—barbarious wars!)
      Then 'ere's to the Widow at Windsor,
        An' 'ere's to the stores an' the guns,
      The men an' the 'orses what makes up the forces
        O' Missis Victorier's sons.
      (Poor beggars! Victorier's sons!)

Walk wide o' the Widow at Windsor,
  For 'alf o' Creation she owns:

We 'ave bought 'er the same with the sword an' the flame,
   An' we've salted it down with our bones.
      (Poor beggars!—it's blue with our bones!)
Hands off o' the sons o' the Widow,
  Hands off o' the goods in 'er shop,
For the Kings must come down an' the Emperors frown
   When the Widow at Windsor says 'Stop!'
      (Poor beggars!—we're sent to say 'Stop!')
        Then 'ere's to the Lodge o' the Widow,
          From the Pole to the Tropics it runs—
        To the Lodge that we tile with the rank an' the
          file,
          An' open in form with the guns.
      (Poor beggars!—it's always they guns!)

We 'ave 'eard o' the Widow at Windsor,
  It's safest to leave 'er alone:
For 'er sentries we stand by the sea an' the land
  Wherever the bugles are blown.
      (Poor beggars!—an' don't we get blown!)
Take 'old o' the Wings o' the Mornin',
  An' flop round the earth till you're dead;
But you won't get away from the tune that they play
  To the bloomin' old rag over'ead.
      (Poor beggars!—it's 'ot over'ead!)
        Then 'ere's to the Sons o' the Widow,
          Wherever, 'owever they roam.
        'Ere's all they desire, an' if they require
          A speedy return to their 'ome.
      (Poor beggars!—they'll never see 'ome!)

                              1890

MANDALAY

By the old Moulmein Pagoda, lookin' lazy at the sea,
There's a Burma girl a-settin', and I know she thinks o'
  me;

For the wind is in the palm-trees, and the temple-bells
    they say:
'Come you back, you British soldier; come you back to
    Mandalay!'
      Come you back to Mandalay,
      Where the old Flotilla lay:
      Can't you 'ear their paddles chunkin' from Ran-
        goon to Mandalay?
      On the road to Mandalay,
      Where the flyin'-fishes play,
      An' the dawn comes up like thunder outer China
        'crost the Bay!

'Er petticoat was yaller an' 'er little cap was green,
An' 'er name was Supi-yaw-lat—jes' the same as Thee-
    baw's Queen,
An' I seed her first a-smokin' of a whackin' white cheroot,
An' a-wastin' Christian kisses on an 'eathen idol's foot:
      Bloomin' idol made o' mud—
      Wot they called the Great Gawd Budd—
      Plucky lot she cared for idols when I kissed 'er
        where she stud!
      On the road to Mandalay ...

When the mist was on the rice-fields an' the sun was
    droppin' slow,
She'd git 'er little banjo an' she'd sing '*Kulla-lo-lo!*'
With 'er arm upon my shoulder an' 'er cheek agin my
    cheek
We useter watch the steamers an' the *hathis* pilin' teak.
      Elephints a-pilin' teak
      In the sludgy, squdgy creek,
      Where the silence 'ung that 'eavy you was 'arf
        afraid to speak!
      On the road to Mandalay . .

But that's all shove be'ind me—long ago an' fur away,
An' there ain't no 'buses runnin' from the Bank to Man-
    dalay;

An' I'm learnin' 'ere in London what the ten-year soldier tells:

'If you've 'eard the East a-callin', you won't never 'eed naught else.'

 No! you won't 'eed nothin' else

 But them spicy garlic smells,

 An' the sunshine an' the palm-trees an' the tinkly temple-bells;

 On the road to Mandalay . . .

I am sick o' wastin' leather on these gritty pavin'-stones,

An' the blasted English drizzle wakes the fever in my bones;

Tho' I walks with fifty 'ousemaids outer Chelsea to the Strand,

An' they talks a lot o' lovin', but wot do they understand?

 Beefy face an' grubby 'and—

 Law! wot do they understand?

 I've a neater, sweeter maiden in a cleaner, greener land!

 On the road to Mandalay . . .

Ship me somewheres east of Suez, where the best is like the worst,

Where there aren't no Ten Commandments an' a man can raise a thirst;

For the temple-bells are callin', an' it's there that I would be—

By the old Moulmein Pagoda, looking lazy at the sea;

 On the road to Mandalay.

 Where the old Flotilla lay,

 With our sick beneath the awnings when we went to Mandalay!

 On the road to Mandalay,

 Where the flyin'-fishes play,

 An' the dawn comes up like thunder outer China 'crost the Bay!

          1890

PRIVATE ORTHERIS'S SONG

(From 'The Courting of Dinah Shadd')

My girl she give me the go onest,
   When I was a London lad;
An' I went on the drink for a fortnight,
   An' then I went to the bad.
The Queen she give me a shillin'
   To fight for 'er over the seas;
But Guv'ment built me a fever-trap,
   An' Injia give me disease.
(*Chorus*) Ho! don't you 'eed what a girl says,
         An' don't you go for the beer;
         But I was an ass when I was at grass,
         An' that is why I'm 'ere.

I fired a shot at a Afghan,
   The beggar 'e fired again,
An' I lay on my bed with a 'ole in my 'ed,
   An' missed the next campaign!
I up with my gun at a Burman
   Who carried a bloomin' *dah*,
But the cartridge stuck and the bay'nit bruk,
   An' all I got was the scar.
(*Chorus*) Ho! don't you aim at a Afghan,
         When you stand on the skyline clear;
         An' don't you go for a Burman
         If none o' your friends is near.

I served my time for a Corp'ral,
   An' wetted my stripes with pop,
For I went on the bend with a intimate friend,
   An' finished the night in the 'shop.'
I served my time for a Sergeant;
   The Colonel 'e sez 'No!

The most you'll see is a full C.B.'
    An' . . . very next night 'twas so!
(*Chorus*) Ho! don't you go for a Corp'ral
          Unless your 'ed is clear;
          But I was an ass when I was at grass,
          An' that is why I'm 'ere.

I've tasted the luck o' the Army
    In barrack an' camp an' clink.
An' I lost my tip through the bloomin' trip
    Along o' the women an' drink.
I'm down at the heel o' my service,
    An' when I am laid on the shelf,
My very worst friend from beginning to end
    By the blood of a mouse was myself!
(*Chorus*) Ho! don't you 'eed what a girl says,
          An' don't you go for the beer;
          But I was an ass when I was at grass,
          An' that is why I'm 'ere!

                                    1940

SHILLIN' A DAY

My name is O'Kelly, I've heard the Revelly
From Birr to Bareilly, from Leeds to Lahore,
Hong-Kong and Peshawur,
Lucknow and Etawah,
And fifty-five more all endin' in 'pore'.
Black Death and his quickness, the depth and the thick-
    ness
Of sorrow and sickness I've known on my way,
But I'm old and I'm nervis,
I'm cast from the Service,
And all I deserve is a shillin' a day.

(*Chorus*) Shillin' a day,
     Bloomin' good pay—
     Lucky to touch it, a shillin' a day!

Oh, it drives me half crazy to think of the days I
Went slap for the Ghazi, my sword at my side,
When we rode Hell-for-leather
Both squadrons together,
That didn't care whether we lived or we died.
But it's no use despairin', my wife must go charin'
An' me commissairin', the pay-bills to better,
So if me you be'old
In the wet and the cold,
By the Grand Metropold, won't you give me a letter?

(*Full chorus*) Give 'im a letter—
      'Can't do no better,
      Late Troop-Sergeant-Major an'—runs
        with a letter!
      Think what 'e's been.
      Think what 'e's seen.
      Think of his pension an'——
      GAWD SAVE THE QUEEN!

               1892

THAT DAY

It got beyond all orders an' it got beyond all 'ope;
 It got to shammin' wounded an' retirin' from the 'alt.
'Ole companies was lookin' for the nearest road to slope;
 It were just a bloomin' knock-out—an' our fault!

  Now there ain't no chorus 'ere to give,
   Nor there ain't no band to play;
  An' I wish I was dead 'fore I done what I did,
   Or seen what I seed that day!

We was sick o' bein' punished, an' we let 'em know it, too;
   An' a company-commander up an' 'it us with a sword,
An' someone shouted, ' 'Ook it!' an' it come to *sove-ki-poo*,
   An' we chucked our rifles from us—O my Gawd!

There was thirty dead an' wounded on the ground we
      wouldn't keep—
   No, there wasn't more than twenty when the front
      begun to go—
But, Christ! along the line o' flight they cut us up like
      sheep,
   An' that was all we gained by doin' so!

I 'eard the knives be'ind me, but I dursn't face my man,
   Nor I don't know where I went to, 'cause I didn't 'alt to
      see,
Till I 'eard a beggar squealin' out for quarter as 'e ran,
   An' I thought I knew the voice an'—it was me!

We was 'idin' under bedsteads more than 'arf a march
      away:
   We was lyin' up like rabbits all about the country-side;
An' the Major cursed 'is Maker 'cause 'e'd lived to see that
      day,
   An' the Colonel broke 'is sword acrost, an' cried.

We was rotten 'fore we started—we was never disci*plined*;
   We made it out a favour if an order was obeyed.
Yes, every little drummer 'ad 'is rights an' wrongs to
      mind,
   So we had to pay for teachin'—an' we paid!

The papers 'id it 'andsome, but you know the Army
      knows;
   We was put to groomin' camels till the regiments with-
      drew,
An' they gave us each a medal for subduin' England's foes,
   An' I 'ope you like my song—because it's true!

An' there ain't no chorus 'ere to give,
  Nor there ain't no band to play;
But I wish I was dead 'fore I done what I did,
  Or seen what I seed that day!

                                          1896

THE LADIES

I've taken my fun where I've found it;
  I've rogued an' I've ranged in my time
I've 'ad my pickin' o' sweethearts,
  An' four o' the lot was prime.
One was an 'arf-caste widow,
  One was a woman at Prome,
One was the wife of a *jemadar-sais*,[1]
  An' one is a girl at 'ome.

Now I aren't no 'and with the ladies,
  For, takin' 'em all along,
You never can say till you've tried 'em,
  An' then you are like to be wrong.
There's times when you'll think that you mightn't,
  There's times when you'll know that you might;
But the things you will learn from the Yellow an' Brown,
  They'll 'elp you a lot with the White!

I was a young un at 'Oogli,
  Shy as a girl to begin;
Aggie de Castrer she made me,
  An' Aggie was clever as sin;
Older than me, but my first un—
  More like a mother she were—
Showed me the way to promotion an' pay,
  An' I learned about women from 'er!

---
[1] Head-groom.

Then I was ordered to Burma,
    Actin' in charge o' Bazar,
An' I got me a tiddy live 'eathen
    Through buyin' supplies off 'er pa.
Funny an' yellow an' faithful—
    Doll in a teacup she were—
But we lived on the square, like a true-married pair,
    An' I learned about women from 'er!

Then we was shifted to Neemuch
    (Or I might ha' been keepin' 'er now),
An' I took with a shiny she-devil,
    The wife of a nigger at Mhow;
'Taught me the gipsy-folks' *bolee;*[1]
    Kind o' volcano she were,
For she knifed me one night 'cause I wished she was
        white,
    And I learned about women from 'er!

Then I come 'ome in a trooper,
    'Long of a kid o' sixteen—
'Girl from a convent at Meerut,
    The straightest I ever 'ave seen.
Love at first sight was 'er trouble,
    She didn't know what it were;
An' I wouldn't do such, 'cause I liked 'er too much,
    But—I learned about women from 'er!

I've taken my fun where I've found it,
    An' now I must pay for my fun,
For the more you 'ave known o' the others
    The less will you settle to one;
An' the end of it's sittin' and thinkin',
    An' dreamin' Hell-fires to see;
So be warned by my lot (which I know you will not),
    An' learn about women from me!

---

[1] slang.

What did the Colonel's Lady think?
  Nobody never knew.
Somebody asked the Sergeant's Wife,
  An' she told 'em true!
When you get to a man in the case,
  They're like as a row of pins—
For the Colonel's Lady an' Judy O'Grady
  Are sisters under their skins!

1895

THE SERGEANT'S WEDDIN'

'E was warned agin 'er—
  That's what made 'im look;
She was warned agin' im—
  That is why she took.
Wouldn't 'ear no reason,
  'Went an' done it blind;
We know all about 'em,
  They've got all to find!

Cheer for the Sergeant's weddin'—
  Give 'em one cheer more!
Grey gun-'orses in the lando,
  An' a rogue is married to, etc.

What's the use o' tellin'
  'Arf the lot she's been?
'E's a bloomin' robber,
  An' 'e keeps canteen.
'Ow did 'e get 'is buggy?
  Gawd, you needn't ask!
'Made 'is forty gallon
  Out of every cask!

Watch 'im, with 'is 'air cut,
  Count us filin' by—

Won't the Colonel praise 'is
    Pop—u—lar—i—ty!
We 'ave scores to settle—
    Scores for more than beer;
She's the girl to pay 'em—
    That is why we're 'ere!

See the Chaplain thinkin'?
    See the women smile?
Twig the married winkin'
    As they take the aisle?
Keep your side-arms quiet,
    Dressin' by the Band.
Ho! You 'oly beggars,
    Cough be'ind your 'and!

Now it's done an' over,
    'Ear the organ squeak,
' *'Voice that breathed o'er Eden'*—
    Ain't she got the cheek!
White an' laylock ribbons,
    'Think yourself so fine!
I'd pray Gawd to take yer
    'Fore I made yer mine!

Escort to the kerridge,
    Wish 'im luck, the brute!
Chuck the slippers after—
    (Pity 'tain't a boot!)
Bowin' like a lady,
    Blushin' like a lad—
'Oo would say to see 'em
    Both is rotten bad?

Cheer for the Sergeant's weddin'—
    Give 'em one cheer more!
Grey gun-'orses in the lando,
    An' a rogue is married to, etc.
                                    1896

CHANT-PAGAN

(*English Irregular, discharged*)

Me that 'ave been what I've been—
Me that 'ave gone where I've gone—
Me that 'ave seen what I've seen—
   'Ow can I ever take on
With awful old England again,
An' 'ouses both sides of the street,
And 'edges two sides of the lane,
And the parson an' gentry between,
An' touchin' my 'at when we meet—
   Me that 'ave been what I've been?

Me that 'ave watched 'arf a world
'Eave up all shiny with dew,
Kopje on kop to the sun,
An' as soon as the mist let 'em through
Our 'elios winkin' like fun—
Three sides of a ninety-mile square,
Over valleys as big as a shire—
'*Are ye there? Are ye there? Are ye there?*'
An' then the blind drum of our fire . .
An' I'm rollin' 'is lawns for the Squire,
                              Me!

Me that 'ave rode through the dark
Forty mile, often, on end,
Along the Ma'ollisberg Range,
With only the stars for my mark
An' only the night for my friend,
An' things runnin' off as you pass,
An' things jumpin' up in the grass,
An' the silence, the shine an' the size

Of the 'igh, unexpressible skies—
I am takin' some letters almost
As much as a mile to the post,
An' 'mind you come back with the change!'
                                   Me!

Me that saw Barberton took
When we dropped through the clouds on their 'ead,
An' they 'ove the guns over and fled—
Me that was through Di'mond 'Ill,
An' Pieters an' Springs an' Belfast—
From Dundee to Vereeniging all—
Me that stuck out to the last
(An' five bloomin' bars on my chest)—
I am doin' my Sunday-school best,
By the 'elp of the Squire and 'is wife
(Not to mention the 'ousemaid an' cook),
To come in an' 'ands up an' be still,
An' honestly work for my bread,
My livin' in that state of life
To which it shall please God to call
                                   Me!

Me that 'ave followed my trade
In the place where the Lightnin's are made;
'Twixt the Rains and the Sun and the Moon—
Me that lay down an' got up
Three years with the sky for my roof—
That 'ave ridden my 'unger an' thirst
Six thousand raw mile on the hoof,
With the Vaal and the Orange for cup,
An' the Brandwater Basin for dish,—
Oh! it's 'ard to be'ave as they wish
(Too 'ard, an' a little too soon),
I'll 'ave to think over it first—
                                   Me!

I will arise an' get 'ence—
I will trek South and make sure
If it's only my fancy or not
That the sunshine of England is pale,
And the breezes of England are stale,
An' there's somethin' gone small with the lot.
For *I* know of a sun an' a wind,
An' some plains and a mountain be'ind,
An' some graves by a barb-wire fence,
An' a Dutchman I've fought 'oo might give
Me a job were I ever inclined
To look in an' offsaddle an' live
Where there's neither a road nor a tree—
But only my Maker an' me,
And I think it will kill me or cure,
So I think I will go there an' see.
                              Me!

                                        1903

PIET

(*Regular of the Line*)

I do not love my Empire's foes,
    Nor call 'em angels; still,
What *is* the sense of 'ating those
    'Oom you are paid to kill?
So, barrin' all that foreign lot
    Which only joined for spite,
Myself, I'd just as soon as not
    Respect the man I fight.
        Ah, there, Piet!—'is trousies to 'is knees,
        'Is coat-tails lyin' level in the bullet-sprinkled breeze;
        'E does not lose 'is rifle an' 'e does not lose 'is seat.
        I've known a lot o' people ride a dam' sight worse
            than Piet.

I've 'eard 'im cryin' from the ground
    Like Abel's blood of old,
An' skirmished out to look, an' found
    The beggar nearly cold.
I've waited on till 'e was dead
    (Which couldn't 'elp 'im much),
But many grateful things 'e's said
    To me for doin' such.
        Ah, there, Piet! whose time 'as come to die,
        'Is carcase past rebellion, but 'is eyes inquirin' why.
        Though dressed in stolen uniform with badge o' rank
           complete,
        I've known a lot o' fellers go a damn' sight worse than
           Piet.

An' when there wasn't aught to do
    But camp and cattle-guards,
I've fought with 'im the 'ole day through
    At fifteen 'undred yards;
Long afternoons o' lying still,
    An' 'earin' as you lay
The bullets swish from 'ill to 'ill
    Like scythes among the 'ay.
        Ah, there, Piet!—be'ind 'is stony kop—
        With 'is Boer bread an' biltong,[1] an' 'is flask of awful
           Dop;[2]
        'Is Mauser for amusement an' 'is pony for retreat,
        I've known a lot o' fellers shoot a dam' sight worse
           than Piet.

He's shoved 'is rifle 'neath my nose
    Before I'd time to think,
An' borrowed all my Sunday clo'es
    An' sent me 'ome in pink;

---

[1] Dried meat.
[2] Cape brandy.

An' I 've crept (Lord, 'ow I've crept!)
  On 'ands an' knees I've gone,
And spoored and floored and caught and kept
  An' sent him to Ceylon![1]
    Ah, there, Piet!—you've sold me many a pup,
    When week on week alternate it was you an' me
      ' 'ands up!'
    But though I never made *you* walk man-naked in the
      'eat,
    I've known a lot of fellows stalk a dam' sight worse
    than Piet.

From Plewman's to Marabastad,
  From Ookiep to De Aar,
Me an' my trusty friend 'ave 'ad,
  As you might say, a war;
But seein' what both parties done
  Before 'e owned defeat,
I ain't more proud of 'avin' won
  Than I am pleased with Piet.
    Ah, there, Piet!—picked up be'ind the drive!
    The wonder wasn't 'ow 'e fought, but 'ow 'e kep'
      alive,
    With nothin' in 'is belly, on 'is back, or to 'is feet—
    I've known a lot o' men behave a dam' sight worse
    than Piet.

No more I'll 'ear 'is rifle crack
  Along the block'ouse fence—
The beggar's on the peaceful tack,
  Regardless of expense;
For countin' what 'e eats an' draws,
  An' gifts an' loans as well,
'E's gettin' 'alf the Earth, because
  'E didn't give us 'Ell!

---

[1] One of the camps for prisoners of this war was in Ceylon.

Ah, there, Piet! with your brand-new English plough,
Your gratis tents an' cattle, an' your most ungrateful frow,
You've made the British taxpayer rebuild your country-
      seat—
I've known some pet battalions charge a dam' sight less
     than Piet.

1903

THE RETURN

(*All Arms*)

Peace is declared, an' I return
    To 'Ackneystadt, but not the same;
Things 'ave transpired which made me learn
    The size and meanin' of the game.
I did no more than others did,
    I don't know where the change began.
I started as a average kid,
    I finished as a thinkin' man.

    If England was what England seems,
        An' not the England of our dreams,
    But only putty, brass, an' paint,
        'Ow quick we'd drop 'er! But she ain't!

Before my gappin' mouth could speak
    I 'eard it in my comrade's tone.
I saw it on my neighbour's cheek
    Before I felt it flush my own.
An' last it come to me—not pride,
    Nor yet conceit, but on the 'ole
(If such a term may be applied),
    The makin's of a bloomin' soul.

Rivers at night that cluck an' jeer,
    Plains which the moonshine turns to sea,

Mountains which never let you near,
    An' stars to all eternity;
An' the quick-breathin' dark that fills
    The 'ollows of the wilderness,
When the wind worries through the 'ills—
    These may 'ave taught me more or less.

Towns without people, ten times took,
    An' ten times left an' burned at last;
An' starving dogs that come to look
    For owners when a column passed;
An' quiet, 'omesick talks between
    Men, met by night, you never knew
Until—'is face—by shellfire seen—
    Once—an' struck off. *They* taught me too.

The day's lay-out—the mornin' sun
    Beneath your 'at-brim as you sight;
The dinner-'ush from noon till one,
    An' the full roar that lasts till night;
An' the pore dead that look so old
    An' was so young an hour ago,
An' legs tied down before they're cold—
    These are the things which make you know.

Also Time runnin' into years—
    A thousand Places left be'ind—
An' Men from both two 'emispheres
    Discussin' things of every kind;
So much more near than I 'ad known,
    So much more great than I 'ad guessed—
An' me, like all the rest, alone—
    But reachin' out to all the rest!

So 'ath it come to me—not pride,
    Nor yet conceit, but on the 'ole
(If such a term may be applied),
    The makin's of a bloomin' soul.

But now, discharged, I fall away
 To do with little things again. . . .
Gawd, 'oo knows all I cannot say,
 Look after me in Thamesfontein![1]

> *If England was what England seems,*
> *An' not the England of our dreams,*
> *But only putty, brass, an' paint,*
> *'Ow quick we'd chuck 'er! But she ain't!*
>   1899

'CITIES AND THRONES AND POWERS'

(From 'A Centurion of the Thirtieth')

Cities and Thrones and Powers
 Stand in Time's eye,
Almost as long as flowers,
 Which daily die:
But, as new buds put forth
 To glad ncw men,
Out of the spent and unconsidered Earth
 The Cities rise again.

This season's Daffodil,
 She never hears
What change, what chance, what chill,
 Cut down last year's;
But with bold countenance,
 And knowledge small,
Esteems her seven day's continuance
 To be perpetual.

So Time that is o'er-kind
 To all that be,

---

[1] London

Ordains us e'en as blind,
  As bold as she:
That in our very death,
  And burial sure,
Shadow to shadow, well persuaded, saith,
  'See how our works endure!'

1906

THE RECALL

(From 'An Habitation Enforced')

I am the land of their fathers.
In me the virtue stays.
I will bring back my children,
After certain days.

Under their feet in the grasses
My clinging magic runs.
They shall return as strangers.
They shall remain as sons.

Over their heads in the branches
Of their new-bought, ancient trees,
I weave an incantation
And draw them to my knees.

Scent of smoke in the evening,
Smell of rain in the night—
The hours, the days and the seasons,
Order their souls aright,

Till I make plain the meaning
Of all my thousand years—
Till I fill their hearts with knowledge,
While I fill their eyes with tears.

1909

THE WAY THROUGH THE WOODS

(From 'Marklake Witches')

They shut the road through the woods
Seventy years ago.
Weather and rain have undone it again,
And now you would never know
There was once a road through the woods
Before they planted the trees.
It is underneath the coppice and heath
And the thin anemones.
Only the keeper sees
That, where the ring-dove broods,
And the badgers roll at ease,
There was once a road through the woods.

Yet, if you enter the woods
Of a summer evening late,
When the night-air cools on the trout-ringed pools
Where the otter whistles his mate,
(They fear not men in the woods,
Because they see so few.)
You will hear the beat of a horse's feet,
And the swish of a skirt in the dew,
Steadily cantering through
The misty solitudes,
As though they perfectly knew
The old lost road through the woods. . . .
But there is no road through the woods.

1910

SIR RICHARD'S SONG

(A.D. 1066)
(From 'Young Men at the Manor')

I followed my Duke ere I was a lover,
  To take from England fief and fee;
But now this game is the other way over—
  But now England hath taken me!

I had my horse, my shield and banner,
  And a boy's heart, so whole and free;
But now I sing in another manner—
  But now England hath taken me!

As for my Father in his tower,
  Asking news of my ship at sea,
He will remember his own hour—
  Tell him England hath taken me!

As for my Mother in her bower,
  That rules my Father so cunningly,
She will remember a maiden's power—
  Tell her England hath taken me!

As for my Brother in Rouen City,
  A nimble and naughty page is he.
But he will come to suffer and pity—
  Tell him England hath taken me!

As for my little Sister waiting
  In the pleasant orchards of Normandie,
Tell her youth is the time for mating—
  Tell her England hath taken me!

As for my comrades in camp and highway,
  That lift their eyebrows scornfully,
Tell them their way is not my way—
  Tell them England hath taken me!

Kings and Princes and Barons famèd,
  Knights and Captains in your degree;
Hear me a little before I am blamèd—
  Seeing England hath taken me!

Howso great man's strength be reckoned,
  There are two things he cannot flee.
Love is the first, and Death is the second—
  And Love in England hath taken me!

                                              1906

A CHARM

Take of English earth as much
As either hand may rightly clutch.
In the taking of it breathe
Prayer for all who lie beneath.
Not the great nor well-bespoke,
But the mere uncounted folk
Of whose life and death is none
Report or lamentation.
  Lay that earth upon thy heart,
  And thy sickness shall depart!

It shall sweeten and make whole
Fevered breath and festered soul.
It shall mightily restrain
Over-busied hand and brain.
It shall ease thy mortal strife
'Gainst the immortal woe of life,
Till thyself, restored, shall prove
By what grace the Heavens do move.

Take of English flowers these—
Spring's full-facèd primroses,
Summer's wild wide-hearted rose,
Autumn's wall-flower of the close,

And, thy darkness of illume,
Winter's bee-thronged ivy-bloom.
Seek and serve them where they bide
From Candlemas to Christmas-tide,
    For these simples, used aright,
    Can restore a failing sight.

These shall cleanse and purify
Webbed and inward-turning eye;
These shall show thee treasure hid
Thy familiar fields amid;
And reveal (which is thy need)
Every man a King indeed!

                                    1910

COLD IRON

(From 'Cold Iron')

'Gold is for the mistress—silver for the maid—
Copper for the craftsman cunning at his trade.'
'Good!' said the Baron, sitting in his hall,
'But Iron—Cold Iron—is master of them all.'

So he made rebellion 'gainst the King his liege,
Camped before his citadel and summoned it to siege.
'Nay!' said the cannoneer on the castle wall,
'But Iron—Cold Iron—shall be master of you all!'

Woe for the Baron and his knights so strong,
When the cruel cannon-balls laid 'em all along;
He was taken prisoner, he was cast in thrall,
And Iron—Cold Iron—was master of it all!

Yet his King spake kindly (ah, how kind a Lord!)
'What if I release thee now and give thee back thy
        sword?'
'Nay!' said the Baron, 'mock not at my fall,
For Iron—Cold Iron—is master of men all.'

'Tears are for the craven, prayers are for the clown—
Halters for the silly neck that cannot keep a crown.'
'As my loss is grievous, so my hope is small,
For Iron—Cold Iron—must be master of men all!'

Yet his King made answer (few such Kings there be!)
'Here is Bread and here is Wine—sit and sup with me.
Eat and drink in Mary's Name, the whiles I do recall
How Iron—Cold Iron—can be master of men all!'

He took the Wine and blessed it. He blessed and break the
    Bread.
With His own Hands He served Them, and presently He
    said:
'See! These Hands they pierced with nails, outside My
    city wall,
Show Iron—Cold Iron—to be master of men all.

'Wounds are for the desperate, blows are for the strong.
Balm and oil for weary hearts all cut and bruised with
    wrong.
I forgive thy treason—I redeem thy fall—
For Iron—Cold Iron—must be master of men all!'

'Crowns are for the valiant—sceptres for the bold!
Thrones and powers for mighty men who dare to take
*   and hold!'*
'Nay!' said the Baron, kneeling in his hall,
'But Iron—Cold Iron—is master of men all!
Iron out of Calvary is master of men all!'

1910

THE WASTER

From the date that the doors of his prep-school close
    On the lonely little son
He is taught by precept, insult, and blows
    The Things that Are Never Done.

Year after year, without favour or fear,
    From seven to twenty-two,
His keepers insist he shall learn the list
    Of the things no fellow can do.
(They are not so strict with the average Pict
    And it isn't set to, etc.)

For this and not for the profit it brings
    Or the good of his fellow-kind
He is and suffers unspeakable things
    In body and soul and mind.
But the net result of that Primitive Cult,
    Whatever else may be won,
Is definite knowledge ere leaving College
    Of the Things that Are Never Done.
(An interdict which is strange to the Pict
    And was never revealed to, etc.)

Slack by training and slow by birth,
    Only quick to despise,
Largely assessing his neighbour's worth
    By the hue of his socks or tie,
A loafer-in-grain, his foes maintain,
    And how shall we combat their view
When, atop of his natural sloth, he holds
    There are Things no Fellow can do?
(Which is why he is licked from the first by the Pict
    And left at the post by, etc.)

                                                    1939

HARP SONG OF THE DANE WOMEN

(From 'The Knights of the Joyous Venture')

    What is a woman that you forsake her,
    And the hearth-fire and the home-acre,
    To go with the old grey Widow-maker?

She has no house to lay a guest in—
But one chill bed for all to rest in,
That the pale suns and the stray bergs nest in.

She has no strong white arms to fold you,
But the ten-times-fingering weed to hold you—
Out on the rocks where the tide has rolled you.

Yet, when the signs of summer thicken,
And the ice breaks, and the birch-buds quicken,
Yearly you turn from our side, and sicken—

Sicken again for the shouts and the slaughters.
You steal away to the lapping waters,
And look at your ship in her winter-quarters.

You forget our mirth, and talk at the tables,
The kine in the shed and the horse in the stables—
To pitch her sides and go over her cables.

Then you drive out where the storm-clouds swallow,
And the sound of your oar-blades, falling hollow,
Is all we have left through the months to follow.

Ah, what is Woman that you forsake her,
And the hearth-fire and the home-acre,
To go with the old grey Widow-maker?

1906

A ST. HELENA LULLABY

(From 'A Priest in Spite of Himself')

'How far is St. Helena from a little child at play?'
What makes you want to wander there with all the world
    between?
Oh, Mother, call your son again or else he'll run away.
(*No one thinks of winter when the grass is green!*)

'How far is St. Helena from a fight in Paris Street?'
I haven't time to answer now—the men are falling fast.
The guns begin to thunder, and the drums begin to beat.
(*If you take the first step, you will take the last!*)

'How far is St. Helena from the field of Austerlitz?'
You couldn't hear me if I told—so loud the cannon roar.
But not so far for people who are living by their wits.
(*'Gay go up' means 'Gay go down' the wide world o'er!*)

'How far is St. Helena from an Emperor of France?'
I cannot see—I cannot tell—the Crowns they dazzle so.
The Kings sit down to dinner, and the Queens stand up to
        dance.
(*After open weather you may look for snow!*)

'How far is St. Helena from the Capes of Trafalgar?'
A longish way—a longish way—with ten year more to
        run.
It's South across the water underneath a falling star.
(*What you cannot finish you must leave undone!*)

'How far is St. Helena from the Beresina ice?'
An ill way—a chill way—the ice begins to crack.
But not so far for gentlemen who never took advice.
(*When you can't go forward you must e'en come back!*)

'How far is St. Helena from the field of Waterloo?'
A near way—a clear way—the ship will take you soon
A pleasant place for gentlemen with little left to do.
(*Morning never tries you till the afternoon!*)

'How far from St. Helena to the Gate of Heaven's Grace?'
That no one knows—that no one knows—and no one ever
        will.
But fold your hands across your heart and cover up your
        face,
And after all your trapesings, child, lie still!

                                                    1910

THE FABULISTS

When all the world would keep a matter hid,
　　Since Truth is seldom friend to any crowd,
Men write in fable as old Æsop did,
　　Jesting at that which none will name aloud.
And this they needs must do, or it will fall
Unless they please they are not heard at all.

When desperate Folly daily laboureth
　　To work confusion upon all we have,
When diligent Sloth demandeth Freedom's death,
　　And banded Fear commandeth Honour's grave—
Even in that certain hour before the fall,
Unless men please they are not heard at all.

Needs must all please, yet some not all for need,
　　Needs must all toil, yet some not all for gain,
But that men taking pleasure may take heed,
　　Whom present toil shall snatch from later pain.
Thus some have toiled, but their reward was small
Since, though they pleased, they were not heard at all.

This was the lock that lay upon our lips,
　　This was the yoke that we have undergone,
Denying us all pleasant fellowships
　　As in our time and generation.
Our pleasures unpursued age past recall,
And for our pains—we are not heard at all.

What man hears aught except the groaning guns?
　　What man heeds aught save what each instant brings
When each man's life all imaged life outruns,
　　What man shall pleasure in imaginings?
So it has fallen, as it was bound to fall,
We are not, nor we were not, heard at all.

1917

A PICT SONG

(From 'The Winged Hats')

Rome never looks where she treads.
　　Always her heavy hooves fall
On our stomachs, our hearts or our heads;
　　And Rome never heeds when we bawl.
Her sentries pass on—that is all,
　　And we gather behind them in hordes,
And plot to reconquer the Wall,
　　With only our tongues for our swords.

We are the Little Folk—we!
　　Too little to love or to hate.
Leave us alone and you'll see
　　How we can drag down the State!
We are the worm in the wood!
　　We are the rot at the root!
We are the taint in the blood!
　　We are the thorn in the foot!

Mistletoe killing an oak—
　　Rats gnawing cables in two—
Moths making holes in a cloak—
　　How they must love what they do!
Yes—and we Little Folk too,
　　We are busy as they—
Working our works out of view—
　　Watch, and you'll see it some day!

No indeed! We are not strong,
　　But we know Peoples that are.
Yes, and we'll guide them along
　　To smash and destroy you in War
We shall be slaves just the same?
　　Yes, we have always been slaves,

But you—you will die of the shame,
    And then we shall dance on your graves!

    We are the Little Folk, we, etc.

                    1906

MacDONOUGH'S SONG

(From 'As Easy as A.B.C.')

Whether the State can loose and bind
    In Heaven as well as on Earth:
If it be wiser to kill mankind
    Before or after the birth—
These are matters of high concern
    Where State-kept schoolmen are;
But Holy State (we have lived to learn)
    Endeth in Holy War.

Whether The People be led by The Lord,
    Or lured by the loudest throat:
If it be quicker to die by the sword
    Or cheaper to die by vote—
These are things we have dealt with once,
    (And they will not rise from their grave)
For Holy People, however it runs,
    Endeth in wholly Slave.

Whatsoever, for any cause,
    Seeketh to take or give
Power above or beyond the Laws,
    Suffer it not to live!
Holy State or Holy King—
    Or Holy People's Will—
Have no truck with the senseless thing.
    Order the guns and kill!
        Saying—after—me:—

Once there was The People—Terror gave it birth;
Once there was The People and it made a Hell of Earth.
Earth arose and crushed it. Listen, O ye slain!
Once there was The People—it shall never be again!

1917

THE HERITAGE

Our Fathers in a wondrous age,
   Ere yet the Earth was small,
Ensured to us an heritage,
   And doubted not at all
That we, the children of their heart,
   Which then did beat so high,
In later time should play like part
   For our posterity.

A thousand years they steadfast built,
   To 'vantage us and ours,
The Walls that were a world's despair,
   The sea-constraining Towers:
Yet in their midmost pride they knew,
   And unto Kings made known,
Not all from these their strength they drew,
   Their faith from brass or stone.

Youth's passion, manhood's fierce intent.
   With age's judgment wise,
They spent, and counted not they spent,
   At daily sacrifice.
Not lambs alone nor purchased doves
   Or tithe of trader's gold—
Their lives most dear, their dearer loves,
   They offered up of old.

Refraining e'en from lawful things,
    They bowed the neck to bear
The unadornèd yoke that brings
    Stark toil and sternest care.
Wherefore through them is Freedom sure;
    Wherefore through them we stand,
From all but sloth and pride secure,
    In a delightsome land.

Then, fretful, murmur not they gave
    So great a charge to keep,
Nor dream that awestruck Time shall save
    Their labour while we sleep.
Dear-bought and clear, a thousand year,
    Our fathers' title runs.
Make we likewise their sacrifice,
    Defrauding not our sons.

                                              1905

MOWGLI'S SONG AGAINST PEOPLE

(From 'Letting in the Jungle')

I will let loose against you the fleet-footed vines—
I will call in the Jungle to stamp out your lines!
    The roofs shall fade before it,
    The house-beams shall fall;
And the *Karela*,[1] the bitter *Karela*,
    Shall cover it all!

In the gates of these your councils my people shall sing.
In the doors of these your garners the Bat-folk shall cling;
    And the snake shall be your watchman,
    By a hearthstone unswept;
For the *Karela*, the bitter *Karela*,
    Shall fruit where ye slept!

A wild melon.

Ye shall not see my strikers; ye shall hear them and guess.
By night, before the moon-rise, I will send for my cess,
    And the wolf shall be your herdsman
      By a landmark removed;
    For the *Karela*, the bitter *Karela*,
      Shall seed where ye loved!

I will reap your fields before you at the hands of a host.
Ye shall glean behind my reapers for the bread that is lost;
    And the deer shall be your oxen
      On a headland untilled;
    For the *Karela*, the bitter *Karela*,
      Shall leaf where ye build!

I have untied against you the club-footed vines—
I have sent in the Jungle to swamp out your lines!
    The trees—the trees are on you!
      The house-beams shall fall;
    And the *Karela*, the bitter *Karela*,
      Shall cover you all!

                                1895

SONG OF THE GALLEY-SLAVES

(From 'The Finest Story in the World')

We pulled for you when the wind was against us and the
    sails were low.
    Will you never let us go?
We ate bread and onions when you took towns, or ran
    aboard quickly when you were beaten back by the
    foe.
The Captains walked up and down the deck in fair
    weather singing songs, but we were below.
We fainted with our chins on the oars and you did not see
    that we were idle, for we still swung to and fro.
    Will you never let us go?

The salt made the oar-handles like shark-skin; our knees
   were cut to the bone with salt-cracks; our hair was
   stuck to our foreheads; and our lips were cut to the
   gums, and you whipped us because we could not
   row.
   Will you never let us go?
But, in a little time, we shall run out of the port-holes as
   the water runs along the oar-blade, and though you
   tell the others to row after us you will never catch us
   till you catch the oar-thresh and tie up the winds in
   the belly of the sail. Aho!
   Will you never let us go?

1893

THE ROMAN CENTURION'S SONG

(Roman Occupation of Britain, A.D. 300)

Legate, I had the news last night—my cohort ordered
   home
By ship to Portus Itius and thence by road to Rome
I've marched the companies aboard, the arms are stowed
   below:
Now let another take my sword. Command me not to go!

I've served in Britain forty years, from Vectis to the Wall.
I have none other home than this, nor any life at all.
Last night I did not understand, but, now the hour draws
   near
That calls me to my native land, I feel that land is here.

Here where men say my name was made, here where my
   work was done;
Here where my dearest dead are laid—my wife—my wife
   and son;
Here where time, custom, grief and toil, age, memory,
   service, love,
Have rooted me in British soil. Ah, how can I remove?

For me this land, that sea, these airs, those folk and fields
    suffice.
What purple Southern pomp can match our changeful
    Northern skies,
Black with December snows unshed or pearled with Au-
    gust haze—
The clanging arch of steel-grey March, or June's long-
    lighted days?

You'll follow widening Rhodanus till vine and olive lean
Aslant before the sunny breeze that sweeps Nemausus
    clean
To Arelate's triple gate; but let me linger on,
Here where our stiff-necked British oaks confront Euro-
    clydon!

You'll take the old Aurelian Road through shore-descend-
    ing pines
Where, blue as any peacock's neck, the Tyrrhene Ocean
    shines.
You'll go where laurel crowns are won, but—will you e'er
    forget.
The scent of hawthorn in the sun, or bracken in the wet?

Let me work here for Britain's sake—at any task you
    will—
A marsh to drain, a road to make or native troops to drill.
Some Western camp (I know the Pict) or granite Border
    keep,
Mid seas of heather derelict, where our old messmates
    sleep.

Legate, I come to you in tears—My cohort ordered home!
I've served in Britain forty years. What should I do in
    Rome?
Here is my heart, my soul, my mind—the only life I
    know.
I cannot leave it all behind. Command me not to go!

                                        1924

DANE-GELD

(A.D. 980–1016)

It is always a temptation to an armed and agile nation
To call upon a neighbour and to say:—
'We invaded you last night—we are quite prepared to
  fight,
  Unless you pay us cash to go away.'

And that is called asking for Dane-geld,
  And the people who ask it explain
That you've only to pay 'em the Dane-geld
  And then you'll get rid of the Dane!

It is always a temptation to a rich and lazy nation,
  To puff and look important and to say:—
'Though we know we should defeat you, we have not the
    time to meet you.
  We will therefore pay you cash to go away.'

And that is called paying the Dane-geld;
  But we've proved it again and again,
That if once you have paid him the Dane-geld
  You never get rid of the Dane.

It is wrong to put temptation in the path of any nation,
  For fear they should succumb and go astray;
So when you are requested to pay up or be molested,
  You will find it better policy to say:—

'We never pay *any*-one Dane-geld,
  No matter how trifling the cost;
For the end of that game is oppression and shame,
  And the nation that plays it is lost!'

1911

NORMAN AND SAXON

(A.D. 1100)

'My son,' said the Norman Baron, 'I am dying, and you
    will be heir
To all the broad acres in England that William gave me
    for my share
When we conquered the Saxon at Hastings, and a nice lit-
    tle handful it is.
But before you go over to rule it I want you to understand
    this:—

'The Saxon is not like us Normans. His manners are not
    so polite.
But he never means anything serious till he talks about
    justice and right.
When he stands like an ox in the furrow with his sullen set
    eyes on your own,
And grumbles, "This isn't fair dealing," my son, leave the
    Saxon alone.

'You can horsewhip your Gascony archers, or torture
    your Picardy spears;
But don't try that game on the Saxon; you'll have the
    whole brood round your ears.
From the richest old Thane in the county to the poorest
    chained serf in the field,
They'll be at you and on you like hornets, and, if you are
    wise, you will yield.

'But first you must master their language, their dialect,
    proverbs and songs.
Don't trust any clerk to interpret when they come with
    the tale of their wrongs.
Let them know that you know what they're saying; let
    them feel that you know what to say.

Yes, even when you want to go hunting, hear 'em out if it
  takes you all day.

'They'll drink every hour of the daylight and poach every
  hour of the dark.
It's the sport not the rabbits they're after (we've plenty of
  game in the park).
Don't hang them or cut off their fingers. That's wasteful
  as well as unkind,
For a hard-bitten, South-country poacher makes the best
  man-at-arms you can find.

'Appear with your wife and the children at their weddings
  and funerals and feasts.
Be polite but not friendly to Bishops; be good to all poor
  parish priests.
Say "we," "us" and "ours" when you're talking, instead
  of "you fellows" and "I."
Don't ride over seeds; keep your temper; and *never you
  tell 'em a lie!*'

1911

EDGEHILL FIGHT

(Civil Wars, 1642)

Naked and grey the Cotswolds stand
  Beneath the autumn sun,
And the stubble-fields on either hand
  Where Stour and Avon run.
There is no change in the patient land
  That has bred us every one.

She should have passed in cloud and fire
  And saved us from this sin
Of war—red war—'twixt child and sire,
  Household and kith and kin,

In the heart of a sleepy Midland shire,
    With the harvest scarcely in.

But there is no change as we meet at last
    On the brow-head or the plain,
And the raw astonished ranks stand fast
    To slay or to be slain
By the men they knew in the kindly past
    That shall never come again—

By the men they met at dance or chase,
    In the tavern or the hall,
At the justice-bench and the market-place,
    At the cudgel-play or brawl—
Of their own blood and speech and race,
    Comrades or neighbours all!

More bitter than death this day must prove
    Whichever way it go,
For the brothers of the maids we love
    Make ready to lay low
Their sisters' sweethearts, as we move
    Against our dearest foe.

Thank Heaven! At last the trumpets peal
    Before our strength gives way.
For King or for the Commonweal—
    No matter which they say,
The first dry rattle of new-drawn steel
    Changes the world to-day!

                                            1911

THE DUTCH IN THE MEDWAY

(1664–72)

If wars were won by feasting,
　　Or victory by song,
Or safety found in sleeping sound,
　　How England would be strong!
But honour and dominion
　　Are not maintainèd so.
They're only got by sword and shot,
　　And this the Dutchmen know!

The moneys that should feed us
　　You spend on your delight,
How can you then have sailor-men
　　To aid you in your fight?
Our fish and cheese are rotten,
　　Which makes the scurvy grow—
We cannot serve you if we starve,
　　And this the Dutchmen know!

Our ships in every harbour
　　Be neither whole nor sound,
And when we seek to mend a leak,
　　No oakum can be found;
Or, if it is, the caulkers,
　　And carpenters also,
For lack of pay have gone away,
　　And this the Dutchmen know!

Mere powder, guns, and bullets,
　　We scarce can get at all;
Their price was spent in merriment
　　And revel at Whitehall,
While we in tattered doublets
　　From ship to ship must row,

Beseeching friends for odds and ends—
    And this the Dutchmen know!

No King will heed our warnings,
    No Court will pay our claims—
Our King and Court for their disport
    Do sell the very Thames!
For, now De Ruyter's topsails
    Off naked Chatham show,
We dare not meet him with our fleet—
    And this the Dutchmen know!

                      1911

Essays

LITERATURE

~~~~~~

(Speech at Royal Academy Dinner, May 6, 1906)

A great, and I frankly admit, a somewhat terrifying, honour has come to me; but I think, compliments apart, that the most case-hardened worker in letters, speaking to such an assembly as this, must recognise the gulf that separates even the least of those who do things worthy to be written about from even the best of those who have written things worthy of being talked about.

There is an ancient legend which tells us that when a man first achieved a most notable deed he wished to explain to his Tribe what he had done. As soon as he began to speak, however, he was smitten with dumbness, he lacked words, and sat down. Then there arose—according to the story—a masterless man, one who had taken no part in the action of his fellow, who had no special virtues, but who was afflicted—that is the phrase—with the magic of the necessary word. He saw; he told; he described the merits of the notable deed in such a fashion, we are assured, that the words 'became alive and walked up and down in the hearts of all his hearers'. Thereupon, the Tribe seeing that the words were certainly alive, and fearing lest the man with the words would hand down untrue tales about them to their children, took and killed him. But, later, they saw that the magic was in the words, not in the man.

We have progressed in many directions since the time of this early and destructive criticism, but, so far, we do not seem to have found a sufficient substitute for the necessary word as the final record to which all achievement must look. Even to-day, when all is done, those who have done it must wait until all has been said by the masterless man with the words. It is certain that the overwhelming bulk of those words will perish in the future as they have perished in the past; but it is true that a minute fraction will continue to exist, and by the light of these words, and by that light only, will our children be able to judge of the phases of our generation. Now we desire beyond all things to stand well with our children; but when our story comes to be told we do not know who will have the telling of it. We are too close to the tellers; there are many tellers and they are all talking together; and, even if we know them, we must not kill them. But the old and terrible instinct which taught our ancestors to kill the original storyteller warns us that we shall not be far wrong if we challenge any man who shows signs of being afflicted with the magic of the necessary word. May not this be the reason why, without any special legislation on its behalf, Literature has always stood a little outside the law as the one calling that is absolutely free—free in the sense that it needs no protection? For instance, if, as occasionally happens, a Judge makes a bad law, or a surgeon a bad operation, or a manufacturer makes bad food, criticism upon their actions is by law and custom confined to comparatively narrow limits. But if a man, as occasionally happens, makes a book, there is no limit to the criticism that may be directed against it. And this is perfectly as it should be. The world recognises that little things like bad law, bad surgery, and bad food, affect only the cheapest commodity that we know about—human life. Therefore, in these circumstances, men can afford to be swayed by pity for the offender, by interest in his family, by fear, or loyalty, or respect for the organisation he represents, or even by a desire to do him justice. But when the question is of words—words that may become alive and walk up and down in the hearts of the hearers—it is then that this world of ours, which is disposed to take an interest in its future, feels instinctively that it is better that a thousand innocent people should be punished rather than that one guilty word should be preserved, carrying that which is an untrue tale of the Tribe. The chances, of course, are almost astronomically remote that any given tale will survive for so long as it takes an oak to grow to timber size. But that guiding instinct warns us not to trust to chance a matter of the supremest concern. In this durable record, if anything short of indisputable and undistilled truth be seen there, we all feel, 'How shall our achievements profit us?' The Record of the Tribe is its enduring literature.

The magic of Literature lies in the words, and not in any man. Witness, a thousand excellent, strenuous words can leave us quite cold or put us to sleep, whereas a bare half-hundred words breathed upon by some man in his agony, or in his exaltation, or in his idleness, ten generations ago, can still lead whole nations into and out of captivity, can open to us the doors of the three worlds, or stir us so intolerably that we can scarcely abide to look at our own souls. It is a miracle—one that happens very seldom. But secretly each one of the masterless men with the words has hope, or has had hope, that the miracle may be wrought again through him.

And why not? If a tinker in Bedford gaol; if a pamphleteering shopkeeper, pilloried in London; if a muzzy Scot; if a despised German Jew; or a condemned French thief, or an English Admiralty official with a taste for letters can be miraculously afflicted with the magic of the necessary word, why not any man at any time? Our world, which is only concerned in the perpetuation of the record, sanctions that hope just as kindly and just as cruelly as Nature sanctions love.

All it suggests is that the man with the Words shall wait upon the man of achievement, and step by step with him try to tell the story to the Tribe. All it demands is that the magic of every word shall be tried out to the uttermost by every means, fair or foul, that the mind of man can suggest. There is no room, and the world insists that there shall be no room, for pity, for mercy, for respect, for fear, or even for loyalty between man and his fellow-man, when the record of the Tribe comes to be written. That record must satisfy, at all costs to the word and to the man behind the word. It must satisfy alike the keenest vanity and the deepest self-knowledge of the present; it must satisfy also the most shameless curiosity of the future. When it has done this it is literature of which it will be said, in due time, that it fitly represents its age. I say in due time because ages, like individuals, do not always appreciate the merits of a record that purports to represent them. The trouble is that one always expects just a little more out of a thing than one puts into it. Whether it be an age or an individual, one is always a little pained and a little pessimistic to find that all one gets back is just one's bare deserts. This is a difficulty old as literature.

A little incident that came within my experience a while ago shows that that difficulty is always being raised by the most unexpected people all about the world. It happened in a land where the magic of words is peculiarly potent and far-reaching, that there was a Tribe that wanted rain, and the rain-doctors set about getting it. To a certain extent the rain-doctors succeeded. But the rain their magic brought was not a full driving downpour that tells of large prosperity; it was patchy, local, circumscribed, and uncertain. There were unhealthy little squalls blowing about the country and doing damage. Whole districts were flooded out by waterspouts, and other districts annoyed by trickling showers, soon dried by the sun. And so the Tribe went to the rain-doctors, being very angry, and they said, 'What is this rain that you make? You did not make rain like this in the time of our fathers. What have you been doing?' And the rain-doctors said, 'We have been making our proper magic. Supposing you tell us what you have been doing lately?' And the Tribe said, 'Oh, our head-men have been running about hunting jackals, and our little people have been running about chasing grasshoppers! What has that to do with your rain-making?' 'It has everything to do with it,' said the rain-doctors. 'Just as long as your head-men run about hunting jackals, and just as long as your little people run about chasing grasshoppers, just so long will the rain fall in this manner.'

1906

AN INTERVIEW WITH
MARK TWAIN

You are a contemptible lot, over yonder. Some of you are Commissioners, and some Lieutenant-Governors, and some have the V.C., and a few are privileged to walk about the Mall arm in arm with the Viceroy; but I have seen Mark Twain this golden morning, have shaken his hand, and smoked a cigar—no, two cigars—with him, and talked with him for more than two hours! Understand clearly that I do not despise you; indeed, I don't. I am only very sorry for you, from the Viceroy downward. To soothe your envy and to prove that I still regard you as my equals, I will tell you all about it.

They said in Buffalo that he was in Hartford, Conn.; and again they said 'perchance he is gone upon a journey to Portland'; and a big, fat drummer vowed that he knew the great man intimately, and that Mark was spending the summer in Europe—which information so upset me that I embarked upon the wrong train, and was incontinently turned out by the conductor three-quarters of a mile from the station, amid the wilderness of railway tracks. Have you ever, encumbered with great-coat and valise, tried to dodge diversely-minded locomotives when the sun was shining in your eyes? But I forgot that you have not seen Mark Twain, you people of no account!

Saved from the jaws of the cowcatcher, me wandering devious a stranger met.

'Elmira is the place. Elmira in the State of New York—

this State, not two hundred miles away'; and he added, perfectly unnecessarily, 'Slide, Kelley, slide.'

I slid on the West Shore line, I slid till midnight, and they dumped me down at the door of a frowzy hotel in Elmira. Yes, they knew all about 'that man Clemens,' but reckoned he was not in town; had gone East somewhere. I had better possess my soul in patience till the morrow, and then dig up the 'man Clemens'' brother-in-law, who was interested in coal.

The idea of chasing half a dozen relatives in addition to Mark Twain up and down a city of thirty thousand inhabitants kept me awake. Morning revealed Elmira, whose streets were desolated by railway tracks, and whose suburbs were given up to the manufacture of door-sashes and window-frames. It was surrounded by pleasant, fat little hills, rimmed with timber and topped with cultivation. The Chemung River flowed generally up and down the town, and had just finished flooding a few of the main streets.

The hotel-man and the telephone-man assured me that the much-desired brother-in-law was out of town, and no one seemed to know where 'the man Clemens' abode. Later on I discovered that he had not summered in that place for more than nineteen seasons, and so was comparatively a new arrival.

A friendly policeman volunteered the news that he had seen Twain or 'some one very like him' driving a buggy the day before. This gave me a delightful sense of nearness. Fancy living in a town where you could see the author of 'Tom Sawyer,' or 'some one very like him,' jolting over the pavements in a buggy.

'He lives out yonder at East Hill,' said the policeman; 'three miles from here.'

Then the chase began—in a hired hack, up an awful hill, where sunflowers blossomed by the roadside, and crops waved, and 'Harper's Magazine' cows stood in eligible and commanding attitudes knee-deep in clover, all ready to be transferred to photogravure. The great man must have been persecuted by outsiders aforetime, and fled up the hill for refuge.

Presently the driver stopped at a miserable, little white wood shanty, and demanded 'Mister Clemens.'

'I know he's a big bug and all that,' he explained, 'but you can never tell what sort of notions those sort of men take into their heads to live in, anyways.'

There rose up a young lady who was sketching thistle-tops and golden-rod, amid a plentiful supply of both, and set the pilgrimage on the right path.

'It's a pretty Gothic house on the left-hand side a little way further on.'

'Gothic hell!' said the driver. 'Very few of the city hacks take this drive, 'specially if they know they are coming out here,' and he glared at me savagely.

It was a very pretty house, anything but Gothic, clothed with ivy, standing in a very big compound, and fronted by a verandah full of chairs and hammocks. The roof of the verandah was a trellis-work of creepers, and the sun peeping through moved on the shining boards below.

Decidedly this remote place was an ideal one for work, if a man could work among these soft airs and the murmur of the long-eared crops.

Appeared suddenly a lady used to dealing with rampageous outsiders. 'Mr. Clemens has just walked downtown. He is at his brother-in-law's house.'

Then he was within shouting distance, after all, and the chase had not been in vain. With speed I fled, and the driver, skidding the wheel and swearing audibly, arrived at the bottom of that hill without accidents. It was in the pause that followed between ringing the brother-in-law's bell and getting an answer that it occurred to me, for the first time, Mark Twain might possibly have other engagements than the entertainment of escaped lunatics from India, be they never so full of admiration. And in another man's house—anyhow, what had I come to do or say?

Suppose the drawing-room should be full of people,—suppose a baby were sick, how was I to explain that I only wanted to shake hands with him?

Then things happened somewhat in this order. A big, darkened drawing room; a huge chair; a man with eyes, a mane of grizzled hair, a brown moustache covering a mouth as delicate as a woman's, a strong, square hand shaking mine, and the slowest, calmest, levellest voice in all the world saying:—

'Well, you think you owe me something, and you've come to tell me so. That's what I call squaring a debt handsomely.'

'Piff!' from a cob-pipe (I always said that a Missouri meerschaum was the best smoking in the world), and, behold! Mark Twain had curled himself up in the big armchair, and I was smoking reverently, as befits one in the presence of his superior.

The thing that struck me first was that he was an elderly man; yet, after a minute's thought, I perceived that it was otherwise, and in five minutes, the eyes looking at me, I saw that the grey hair was an accident of the most trivial. He was quite young. I was shaking his hand. I was smoking his cigar, and I was hearing him talk—this man I had learned to love and admire fourteen thousand miles away.

Reading his books, I had striven to get an idea of his personality, and all my preconceived notions were wrong and beneath the reality. Blessed is the man who finds no disillusion when he is brought face to face with a revered writer! That was a moment to be remembered; the landing of a twelve-pound salmon was nothing to it. I had hooked Mark Twain, and he was treating me as though under certain circumstances I might be an equal.

About this time I became aware that he was discussing the copyright question. Here, so far as I remember, is what he said. Attend to the words of the oracle through this unworthy medium transmitted. You will never be able to imagine the long, slow surge of the drawl, and the deadly gravity of the countenance, the quaint pucker of the body, one foot thrown over the arm of the chair, the yellow pipe clinched in one corner of the mouth, and the right hand casually caressing the square chin:—

'Copyright? Some men have morals, and some men have—other things. I presume a publisher is a man. He is not born. He is created—by circumstances. Some publishers have morals. Mine have. They pay me for the English productions of my books. When you hear men talking of Bret Harte's works and other works and my books being pirated, ask them to be sure of their facts. I think they'll find the books are paid for. It was ever thus.

'I remember an unprincipled and formidable publisher. Perhaps he's dead now. He used to take my short stories—I can't call it steal or pirate them. It was beyond these things altogether. He took my stories one at a time and made a book of it. If I wrote an essay on dentistry or theology or any little thing of that kind—just an essay that long (he indicated half an inch on his finger), any sort of essay—that publisher would amend and improve my essay.

'He would get another man to write some more to it, or cut it about exactly as his needs required. Then he would publish a book called "Dentistry by Mark Twain," that little essay and some other things not mine added. Theology would make another book, and so on. I do not consider that fair. It's an insult. But he's dead now, I think. I didn't kill him.

'There is a great deal of nonsense talked about international copyright. The proper way to treat a copyright is to make it exactly like real estate in every way.

'It will settle itself under these conditions. If Congress were to bring in a law that a man's life was not to extend over a hundred and sixty years, somebody would laugh. That law wouldn't concern anybody. The man would be out of the jurisdiction of the court. A term of years in copyright comes to exactly the same thing. No law can make a book live or cause it to die before the appointed time.

'Tottletown, Cal., was a new town, with a population of three thousand—banks, fire-brigade, brick buildings and all the modern improvements. It lived, it flourished, and it disappeared. To-day no man can put his foot on any remnant of Tottletown, Cal. It's dead. London continues to exist. Bill Smith, author of a book read for the next year or so, is real estate in Tottletown. William Shakespeare, whose works are extensively read, is real estate in London. Let Bill Smith, equally with Mr. Shakespeare now deceased, have as complete a control over his copyright as he would over his real estate. Let him gamble it away, drink it away, or—give it to the church. Let his heirs and assigns treat it in the same manner.

'Every now and again I go up to Washington, sitting on a board to drive that sort of view into Congress. Congress takes its arguments against international copyright delivered ready made, and—Congress isn't very strong. I put the real-estate view of the case before one of the Senators.

'He said: "Suppose a man has written a book that will live for ever?"

'I said: "Neither you nor I will ever live to see that man, but we'll assume it. What then?"

'He said: "I want to protect the world against that man's heirs and assigns, working under your theory."

'I said: "You think that all the world has no commercial sense. The book that will live for ever can't be artificially kept up at inflated prices. There will always be very expensive editions of it and cheap ones issuing side by side."

'Take the case of Sir Walter Scott's novels,' Mark Twain continued, turning to me. 'When the copyright notes protected them, I bought editions as expensive as I could afford, because I liked them. At the same time the same firm were selling editions that a cat might buy. They had their real estate, and not being fools, recognised that one portion of the plot could be worked as a gold mine, another as a vegetable garden, and another as a marble quarry. Do you see?'

What I saw with the greatest clearness was Mark Twain being forced to fight for the simple proposition that a man has as much right to the work of his brains (think of the heresy of it!) as to the labour of his hands. When the old lion roars, the young whelps growl. I growled assentingly, and the talk ran on from books in general to his own in particular.

Growing bold, and feeling that I had a few hundred thousand folk at my back, I demanded whether Tom Sawyer married Judge Thatcher's daughter and whether we were ever going to hear of Tom Sawyer as a man.

'I haven't decided,' quoth Mark Twain, getting up, filling his pipe, and walking up and down the room in his slippers. 'I have a notion of writing the sequel to "Tom Sawyer" in two ways. In one I would make him rise to great honour and go to Congress, and in the other I should hang him. Then the friends and enemies of the book could take their choice.'

Here I lost my reverence completely, and protested against any theory of the sort, because, to me at least, Tom Sawyer was real.

'Oh, he is real,' said Mark Twain. 'He's all the boy that I have known or recollect; but that would be a good way of ending the book'; then, turning round, 'because, when you come to think of it, neither religion, training, nor education avails anything against the force of circumstances that drive a man. Suppose we took the next four-and-twenty years of Tom Sawyer's life, and gave a little joggle to the circumstances that controlled him. He would, logically and according to the joggle, turn out a rip or an angel.'

'Do you believe that, then?'

'I think so. Isn't it what you call Kismet?'

'Yes, but don't give him two joggles and show the result, because he isn't your property any more. He belongs to us.'

He laughed—a large, wholesome laugh—and this began a dissertation on the rights of a man to do what he liked with his own creations, which being a matter of purely professional interest, I will mercifully omit.

Returning to the big chair, he, speaking of truth and the like in literature, said that an autobiography was the one work in which a man, against his own will and in spite of his utmost striving to the contrary, revealed himself in his true light to the world.

'A good deal of your life on the Mississippi is autobiographical, isn't it?' I asked.

'As near as it can be—when a man is writing to a book and about himself. But in genuine autobiography, I believe it is impossible for a man to tell the truth about himself or to avoid impressing the reader with the truth about himself.

'I made an experiment once. I got a friend of mine—a man painfully given to speak the truth on all occasions—a man who wouldn't dream of telling a lie—and I made him write his autobiography for his own amusement and mine. He did it. The manuscript would have made an octavo volume, but—good, honest man that he was—in every single detail of his life that I knew about he turned out, on paper, a formidable liar. He could not help himself.

'It is not in human nature to write the truth about itself. None the less the reader gets a general impression from an autobiography whether the man is a fraud or a good man. The reader can't give his reasons any more than a man can explain why a woman struck him as being lovely when he doesn't remember her hair, eyes, teeth, or figure. And the impression that the reader gets is a correct one.'

'Do you ever intend to write an autobiography?'

'If I do, it will be as other men have done—with the most earnest desire to make myself out to be the better man in every little business that has been to my discredit;

and I shall fail, like the others, to make my readers believe anything except the truth.'

This naturally led to a discussion on conscience. Then said Mark Twain, and his words are mighty and to be remembered:—

'Your conscience is a nuisance. A conscience is like a child. If you pet it and play with it and let it have everything that it wants, it becomes spoiled and intrudes on all your amusements and most of your griefs. Treat your conscience as you would treat anything else. When it is rebellious, spank it—be severe with it, argue with it, prevent it from coming to play with you at all hours, and you will secure a good conscience; that is to say, a properly trained one. A spoiled one simply destroys all the pleasure in life. I think I have reduced mine to order. At least, I haven't heard from it for some time. Perhaps I have killed it from over-severity. It's wrong to kill a child, but, in spite of all I have said, a conscience differs from a child in many ways. Perhaps it's best when it's dead.'

Here he told me a little—such things as a man may tell a stranger—of his early life and upbringing, and in what manner he had been influenced for good by the example of his parents. He spoke always through his eyes, a light under the heavy eyebrows; anon crossing the room with a step as light as a girl's, to show me some book or other; then resuming his walk up and down the room, puffing at the cob pipe. I would have given much for nerve enough to demand the gift of that pipe—value, five cents when new. I understood why certain savage tribes ardently desired the liver of brave men slain in combat. That pipe would have given me, perhaps, a hint of his keen insight into the souls of men. But he never laid it aside within stealing reach.

Once, indeed, he put his hand on my shoulder. It was an investiture of the Star of India, blue silk, trumpets, and diamond-studded jewel, all complete. If hereafter, in the changes and chances of this mortal life, I fall to cureless ruin, I will tell the superintendent of the workhouse that Mark Twain once put his hand on my shoulder; and he shall give me a room to myself and a double allowance of paupers' tobacco.

'I never read novels myself,' said he, 'except when the popular persecution forces me to—when people plague me to know what I think of the last book that every one is reading.'

'And how did the latest persecution affect you?'

'Robert?' said he, interrogatively.

I nodded.

'I read it, of course, for the workmanship. That made me think I had neglected novels too long—that there might be a good many books as graceful in style somewhere on the shelves; so I began a course of novel reading. I have dropped it now; it did not amuse me. But as regards Robert, the effect on me was exactly as though a singer of street ballads were to hear excellent music from a church organ. I didn't stop to ask whether the music was legitimate or necessary. I listened, and I liked what I heard. I am speaking of the grace and beauty of the style.

'You see,' he went on, 'every man has his private opinion about a book. But that is my private opinion. If I had lived in the beginning of things, I should have looked around the township to see what popular opinion thought of the murder of Abel before I openly condemned Cain. I should have had my private opinion, of course, but I shouldn't have expressed it until I had felt the way. You have my private opinion about that book. I don't know what my public ones are exactly. They won't upset the earth.'

He recurled himself into the chair and talked of other things.

'I spend nine months of the year at Hartford. I have long ago satisfied myself that there is no hope of doing much work during those nine months. People come in and call. They call at all hours, about everything in the world.

One day I thought I would keep a list of interruptions. It began this way:—

'A man came and would see no one but Mr. Clemens. He was an agent for photogravure reproductions of Salon pictures. I very seldom use Salon pictures in my books.

'After that man, another man, who refused to see any one but Mr. Clemens, came to make me write to Washington about something. I saw him. I saw a third man, then a fourth. By this time it was noon. I had grown tired of keeping the list. I wished to rest.

'But the fifth man was the only one of the crowd with a card of his own. He sent up his card. "Ben Koontz, Hannibal, Mo." I was raised in Hannibal. Ben was an old schoolmate of mine. Consequently I threw the house wide open and rushed with both hands out at a big, fat, heavy man, who was not the Ben I had ever known—nor anything like him.

' "But is it you, Ben?" I said. "You've altered in the last thousand years."

'The fat man said: "Well, I'm not Koontz exactly, but I met him down in Missouri, and he told me to be sure and call on you, and he gave me his card, and"—here he acted the little scene for my benefit—"if you can wait a minute till I can get out the circulars—I'm not Koontz exactly, but I'm travelling with the fullest line of rods you ever saw."

'And what happened?' I asked breathlessly.

'I shut the door. He was not Ben Koontz—exactly—not my old school-fellow, but I had shaken him by both hands in love, and . . . I had been boarded by a lightning-rod man in my own house.

'As I was saying, I do very little work in Hartford. I come here for three months every year, and I work four or five hours a day in a study down the garden of that little house on the hill. Of course, I do not object to two or three interruptions. When a man is in the full swing of his work these little things do not affect him. Eight or ten or twenty interruptions retard composition.'

I was burning to ask him all manner of impertinent questions, as to which of his works he himself preferred, and so forth; but, standing in awe of his eyes, I dared not. He spoke on, and I listened, grovelling.

It was a question of mental equipment that was on the carpet, and I am still wondering whether he meant what he said.

'Personally I never care for fiction or story-books. What I like to read about are facts and statistics of any kind. If they are only facts about the raising of radishes, they interest me. Just now, for instance, before you came in'—he pointed to an encyclopædia on the shelves—'I was reading an article about "Mathematics." Perfectly pure mathematics.

'My own knowledge of mathematics stops at "twelve times twelve," but I enjoyed that article immensely. I didn't understand a word of it; but facts, or what a man believes to be facts, are always delightful. That mathematical fellow believed in his facts. So do I. Get your facts first, and'—the voice dies away to an almost inaudible drone—'then you can distort 'em as much as you please.'

Bearing this precious advice in my bosom, I left, the great man assuring me with gentle kindness that I had not interrupted him in the least. Once outside the door, I yearned to go back and ask some questions—it was easy enough to think of them now—but his time was his own, though his books belonged to me.

I should have ample time to look back to that meeting across the graves of the days. But it was sad to think of the things he had not spoken about.

In San Francisco the men of 'The Call' told me many legends of Mark's apprenticeship in their paper five-and-twenty years ago; how he was a reporter delightfully incapable of reporting according to the needs of the day. He preferred, so they said, to coil himself into a heap and meditate until the last minute. Then he would produce copy bearing no sort of relationship to his legitimate work—copy that made the editor swear horribly, and the readers of 'The Call' ask for more.

I should like to have heard Mark's version of that, with some stories of his joyous and variegated past. He has been journeyman-printer (in those days he wandered from the banks of the Missouri even to Philadelphia), pilot-cub and full-blown pilot, soldier of the South (that was for three weeks only), private secretary to a Lieutenant-Governor of Nevada (that displeased him), miner, editor, special correspondent in the Sandwich Islands, and the Lord only knows what else. If so experienced a man could by any means be made drunk, it would be a glorious thing to fill him up with composite liquors, and, in the language of his own country, 'let him retrospect.' But these eyes will never see that orgy fit for the Gods!

1890

MY GREAT AND ONLY

Whether Macdougal or Macdoodle be his name, the principle remains the same, as Mrs. Nickleby said. The gentleman appeared to hold authority in London, and by virtue of his position preached or ordained that music-halls were vulgar, if not improper. Subsequently, I gathered that the gentleman was inciting his associates to shut up certain music-halls on the ground of the vulgarity aforesaid, and I saw with my own eyes that unhappy little managers were putting notices into the corners of their programmes begging the audience to report each and every impropriety. That was pitiful, but it excited my interest.

Now, to the upright and impartial mind—which is mine—all the diversions of Heathendom—which is the British—are of equal ethnological value. And it is true that some human beings can be more vulgar in the act of discussing etchings, editions of luxury, or their own emotions, than other human beings employed in swearing at each other across the street. Therefore, following a chain of thought which does not matter, I visited very many theatres whose licenses had never been interfered with. There I discovered men and women who lived and moved and behaved according to rules which in no sort regulate human life, by tradition dead and done with, and after the customs of the more immoral ancients and Barnum. At one place the lodging-house servant was an angel, and her mother a Madonna; at a second they sounded the loud timbrel o'er a whirl of bloody axes, mobs, and brown-paper castles, and said it was not a pantomime, but Art; at a third everybody grew fabulously rich and fabulously poor every twenty minutes, which was confusing; at a fourth they discussed the Nudities and Lewdities in false-palate voices supposed to belong to the aristocracy and that tasted copper in the mouth; at a fifth they merely climbed up walls and threw furniture at each other, which is notoriously the custom of spinsters and small parsons. Next morning the papers would write about the progress of the modern drama (that was the silver paper panto-mime), and 'graphic presentment of the realities of our highly complex civilisation.' That was the angel house-maid. By the way, when an Englishman has been doing anything more than unusually Pagan, he generally con-soles himself with 'over-civilisation.' It's the 'martyr-to-nerves-dear' note in his equipment.

I went to the music-halls—the less frequented ones—and they were almost as dull as the plays, but they intro-duced me to several elementary truths. Ladies and gentle-men in eccentric, but not altogether unsightly, costumes told me (a) that if I got drunk I should have a head next morning, and perhaps be fined by the magistrate; (b) that if I flirted promiscuously I should probably get into trou-ble; (c) that I had better tell my wife everything and be good to her, or she would be sure to find out for herself and be very bad to me; (d) that I should never lend money; or (e) fight with a stranger whose form I did not know. My friends (if I may be permitted to so call them) illustrated these facts with personal reminiscences and drove them home with kicks and prancings. At intervals circular ladies in pale pink and white would low to their audience to the effect that there was nothing half so sweet in life as 'Love's Young Dream,' and the billycock hats would look at the four-and-elevenpenny bonnets, and they saw that it was good and clasped hands on the strength of it. Then other ladies with shorter skirts would explain that when their husbands

Stagger home tight about two,
    An' can't light the candle,
    We taik the broom 'andle
An' show 'em what women can do.

Naturally, the billycocks, seeing what might befall, thought things over again, and you heard the bonnets murmuring softly under the clink of the lager-glasses: 'Not *me*, Bill. Not *me!*' Now these things are basic and basaltic truths. Anybody can understand them. They are as old as Time. Perhaps the expression was occasionally what might be called coarse, but beer is beer, and best in a pewter, though you can, if you please, drink it from Venetian glass and call it something else. The halls give wisdom and not too lively entertainment for sixpence—ticket good for four pen'orth of refreshments, chiefly inky porter—and the people who listen are respectable folk living under very grey skies who derive all the light side of their life, the food for their imagination and the crystallised expression of their views on Fate and Nemesis, from the affable ladies and gentlemen singers. They require a few green and gold maidens in short skirts to kick before them. Herein they are no better and no worse than folk who require fifty girls very much undressed, and a setting of music, or pictures that won't let themselves be seen on account of their age and varnish, or statues and coins. All animals like salt, but some prefer rocksalt, red or black in lumps. But this is a digression.

Out of my many visits to the hall—I chose one hall, you understand, and frequented it till I could tell the mood it was in before I had passed the ticket-poll—was born the Great Idea. I served it as a slave for seven days. Thought was not sufficient; experience was necessary. I patrolled Westminster, Blackfriars, Lambeth, the Old Kent Road, and many, many more miles of pitiless pavement to make sure of my subject. At even I drank my lager among the billycocks, and lost my heart to a bonnet. Goethe and

Shakespeare were my precedents. I sympathised with them acutely, but I got my Message. A chance-caught refrain of a song which I understand is protected—to its maker I convey my most grateful acknowledgments—gave me what I sought. The rest was made up of four elementary truths, some humour, and, though I say it who should leave it to the press, pathos deep and genuine. I spent a penny on a paper which introduced me to a Great and Only who 'wanted new songs.' The people desired them really. He was their ambassador, and taught me a great deal about the property-right in songs, concluding with a practical illustration, for he said my verses were just the thing and annexed them. It was long before he could hit on the step-dance which exactly elucidated the spirit of the text, and longer before he could jingle a pair of huge brass spurs as a dancing-girl jingles her anklets. That was my notion, and a good one.

The Great and Only possessed a voice like a bull, and nightly roared to the people at the heels of one who was winning triple encores with a priceless ballad beginning deep down in the bass: 'We was shopmates—boozin' shopmates.' I feared that song as Rachel feared Ristori. A greater than I had written it. It was a grim tragedy, lighted with lucid humour, wedded to music that maddened. But my 'Great and Only' had faith in me, and I—I clung to the Great Heart of the People—my people—four hundred 'when it's all full, sir.' I had not studied them for nothing. I must reserve the description of my triumph for another 'Turnover.'

There was no portent in the sky on the night of my triumph. A barrowful of onions, indeed, upset itself at the door, but that was a coincidence. The hall was crammed with billycocks waiting for 'We was shopmates.' The great heart beat healthily. I went to my beer the equal of Shakespeare and Molière at the wings in a first night. What would my public say? Could anything live after the abandon of 'We was shopmates'? What if the redcoats did

not muster in their usual strength. O my friends, never in
your songs and dramas forget the redcoat. He has sympathy and enormous boots.

I believed in the redcoat; in the great heart of the people: above all in myself. The conductor, who advertised
that he 'doctored bad songs,' had devised a pleasant little
lilting air for my needs, but it struck me as weak and thin
after the thunderous surge of the 'Shopmates.' I glanced at
the gallery—the redcoats were there. The fiddle-bows
creaked, and, with a jingle of brazen spurs, a forage-cap
over his left eye, my Great and Only began to 'chuck it off
his chest.' Thus:

> 'At the back o' the Knightsbridge Barricks,
>   When the fog was a gatherin' dim,
> The Lifeguard talked to the Undercook,
>   An' the girl she talked to 'im.'

'Twiddle-iddle-iddle-lum-tum-tum!' said the violins.

'Ling-a-ling-a-ling-a-ling-ting-ling!' said the spurs of
the Great and Only, and through the roar in my ears I
fancied I could catch a responsive hoof-beat in the gallery.
The next four lines held the house to attention. Then
came the chorus and the borrowed refrain. It took—it
went home with a crisp click. My Great and Only saw his
chance. Superbly waving his hand to embrace the whole
audience, he invited them to join him in:

> 'You may make a mistake when you're mashing a tart,
>   But you'll learn to be wise when you're older,
> And don't try for things that are out of your reach,
>   And that's what the girl told the soldier, soldier, soldier,
> And that's what the girl told the soldier.'

I thought the gallery would never let go of the long-
drawn howl on 'soldier.' They clung to it as ringers to the
kicking bell-rope. Then I envied no one—not even Shakespeare. I had my house hooked—gaffed under the gills,

netted, speared, shot behind the shoulder—anything you
please. That was pure joy! With each verse the chorus
grew louder, and when my Great and Only had bellowed
his way to the fall of the Lifeguard and the happy lot of
the Undercook, the gallery rocked again, the reserved
stalls shouted, and the pewters twinkled like the legs of
the demented ballet-girls. The conductor waved the now
frenzied orchestra to softer Lydian strains. My Great and
Only warbled piano:

> 'At the back o' Knightsbridge Barricks,
>   When the fog's a-gatherin' dim,
> The Lifeguard waits for the Undercook,
>   But she won't wait for 'im.'

'*Ta-ra-rara-rara-ra-ra-rah!*' rang a horn clear and
fresh as a sword-cut. 'Twas the apotheosis of virtue.

> 'She's married a man in the poultry line
>   That lives at 'Ighgate 'Ill,
> An' the Lifeguard walks with the 'ousemaid now,
> An' (*awful pause*) she can't foot the bill!'

Who shall tell the springs that move masses? I had
builded better than I knew. Followed yells, shrieks and
wildest applause. Then, as a wave gathers to the curl-over,
singer and sung to fill their chests and heave the chorus
through the quivering roof—alto, horns, basses drowned,
and lost in the flood - to the beach-like boom of beating
feet:

> 'Oh, think o' my song when you're gowin' it strong
>   An' your boots is too little to 'old yer;
> An' don't try for things that is out of your reach,
>   An' that's what the girl told the soldier, soldier, so-holdier!'

Ow! Hi! Yi! Wha-hup! Phew! Whew! Pwhit! Bang!
Wang! Crr-rash! There was ample time for variations as

the horns uplifted themselves and ere the held voices came
down in the foam of sound—

'That's what the girl told the soldier.'

Providence has sent me several joys, and I have helped
myself to others, but that night, as I looked across the sea
of tossing billycocks and rocking bonnets, my work, as I
heard them give tongue, not once, but four times—their
eyes sparkling, their mouths twisted with the taste of
pleasure—I felt that I had secured Perfect Felicity. I am
become greater than Shakespeare. I may even write plays
for the Lyceum, but I never can recapture that first fine
rapture that followed the Upheaval of the Anglo-Saxon
four hundred of him and her. They do not call for authors
on these occasions, but I desired no need of public recognition. I was placidly happy. The chorus bubbled up
again and again throughout the evening, and a redcoat in
the gallery insisted on singing solos about 'a swine in the
poultry line,' whereas I had written 'man,' and the pewters began to fly, and afterwards the long streets were
vocal with various versions of what the girl had really told
the soldier, and I went to bed murmuring: 'I have found
my destiny.'

But it needs a more mighty intellect to write the Songs
of the People. Some day a man will rise up from Ber-
mondsey, Battersea or Bow, and he will be coarse, but
clearsighted, hard but infinitely and tenderly humorous,
speaking the people's tongue, steeped in their lives and
telling them in swinging, urging, dinging verse what it is
that their inarticulate lips would express. He will make
them songs. Such songs! And all the little poets who pretend to sing to the people will scuttle away like rabbits, for
the girl (which, as you have seen, of course, is wisdom)
will tell that soldier (which is Hercules bowed under his
labours) all that she knows of Life and Death and Love.

And the same, they say, is a Vulgarity!

1890